BLITZ

Also by Daniel O'Malley

The Rook

Stiletto

BLITZ

A NOVEL

DANIEL O'MALLEY

LITTLE, BROWN AND COMPANY
New York • Boston • London

Copyright © 2022 by Daniel O'Malley

Little, Brown and Company
Hachette Book Group
1290 Avenue of the Americas, New York, NY 10104
littlebrown.com

First Edition: October 2022

Little, Brown and Company is a division of Hachette Book Group, Inc. The Little, Brown name and logo are trademarks of Hachette Book Group, Inc.

The publisher is not responsible for websites (or their content) that are not owned by the publisher.

The Hachette Speakers Bureau provides a wide range of authors for speaking events. To find out more, go to hachettespeakersbureau.com or call (866) 376-6591.

ISBN 9780316561556
LCCN 2022936435

Printing 1, 2022

LSC-C

Printed in the United States of America

For Tim and Sandra

When a high explosive bomb falls and explodes a number of things happen. Anything very close to the explosion is likely to be destroyed, and any house which suffers a direct hit is almost sure to collapse... Other dangers of a less spectacular kind can cause far more casualties... Blast can shatter unprotected windows at considerable distance and fragments of glass can be deadly, while bomb splinters can fly and kill at a distance of over half a mile if there is nothing to stop them.

—Ministry of Home Security, *Your Home as an Air Raid Shelter* (one of the bestsellers of 1940)

The first thing which the rescue squads and the firemen saw, as their torches poked through the gloom and the smoke and the bloody pit which had lately been the most chic cellar in London, was a frieze of other shadowy men, night-creatures who had scuttled within as soon as the echoes ceased, crouching over any dead or wounded woman, any soignée *corpse they could find, and ripping off its necklace, or earrings, or brooch: rifling its handbag, scooping up its loose change.*

—Nicholas Monsarrat, *Breaking In, Breaking Out*

Freedom is only the distance between the hunter and his prey.

—Bei Dao

BLITZ

1

The three women stood in the sky above London and waited for the Blitz to come.

It was bitterly cold, so they wore goggles and thickly padded boilersuits with many layers underneath. Each of them had, slung over her shoulder by a slender strap, a buff cardboard box holding a gas mask. Far above them, the thinnest of crescent moons shone with a faint light, and thick clouds were smeared about the sky so that the stars were almost entirely concealed.

"And here they come," said Bridget grimly. She pointed to the east, across Limehouse and Poplar. It was too dark to see the aircraft themselves, but she could hear the very faintest droning as the night winds carried the sound of the bombers toward them.

"Are we sure it's the Germans?" asked Usha. Her tone was dry, but it lacked her usual calm. Her hand was firm in Bridget's but she gave a little nervous clench as she spoke, and Bridget looked at her, startled. For the previous twenty-three nights, she, Usha, and Pamela had sat in the cellar of their mistress's house and listened to German bombs falling above them. Every thud that sent dust down from the ceiling had made Bridget want to scream, but the Indian woman never turned a hair, even when the thuds were horribly close and it seemed like the world was about to collapse on them.

Even now, Usha was able to maintain a bearing of unruffled sophistication while wearing a boilersuit and a balaclava and standing on absolutely nothing ten thousand feet above a city that was being attacked. Admittedly, it was her supernatural power that was keeping the two of them up in the air, so of course she was more at ease than Bridget, but she should have seemed at least a *little* bit discommoded. It just seemed terrifically unfair.

Next to them, Pamela hung silently in the air. Unlike the other two, she wasn't wearing a balaclava, and her face in the faint moonlight was expressionless. Her arms were crossed, and the only movement about her was her hair as the air that held her up rippled over and around her. As always, Bridget found her presence reassuring. The only full-fledged Pawn of the three of them, she was easygoing when off duty, but when she was in her professional mode, as now, she was completely focused. She was always calm, cool, and collected, whether responding to a scheduling mix-up or a mass murder.

The blacked-out city spread out beneath the three of them, and they could make out only the vaguest impressions of the buildings and streets. The winding strip of the Thames, however, was clear.

Over the past few months, as she'd gotten to know Usha and Pamela and they had begun taking her on flying jaunts, Bridget had learned it was best if she didn't think of the vista as the actual ground but rather as an elaborate picture that had nothing to do with her present situation. For her, the key to flying comfortably under someone else's power was maintaining an air of detachment. Otherwise, it was too easy to start feeling panicky, and panicking in those circumstances was never a good idea.

"Bastards," said Pamela tightly. "Bloody bastards." Bridget looked to her in surprise. The blond woman didn't even seem aware that she'd spoken, but she had shifted, and her arms were now at her sides. It was surprising, though. Pamela was normally far too disciplined to allow herself any sort of emotional outburst, even on the most terrifying missions.

Although this isn't really a mission, Bridget thought. *We're just observing. Very definitely only observing.* Lady Carmichael had been reluctant to give the three of them permission to go up into the skies during the bombing, and it had only been after repeated requests that she'd agreed. Even then, she was very firm in her restrictions.

"I don't blame you for not wanting to stay in the shelter," the Lady had said sympathetically. "I feel a bit trapped myself sometimes. So you may go out, but you must absolutely keep yourselves away from the airplanes and the bombing. *Well* away. And you don't come back to the ground until the all-clear siren has gone. I don't want even the slightest possibility of any of you getting hurt."

And so the three of them stood there just watching as balls of fire flared and spread on the ground.

Except that, from what Bridget could see in the darkness, Pamela's hands were clenched, and her lips were pressed together tightly. Normally, Pamela diverted away the worst of the winds, but now the air about them swirled and snapped, flapping their clothes.

The Nazis are bombing her city, and she hates it.

I don't blame her. I hate it too.

As they watched, there was a distant flash on the ground. A few seconds later, they heard the muffled *crump* of the bomb. Then another flash and another eventual boom. Then more. The glow of fire grew and outlined buildings.

"They're hitting Wapping tonight," said Usha. "Hard. I suppose they're targeting the docks."

"And nothing's being done," said Bridget. "Why aren't they doing *something?*" The women could see more and more explosions flaring in the darkness. "It burns me that we knew they were coming, we could hear them, and now it's all just happening." A blaring started coming up out of the city with a chorus of roaring sirens rising and falling.

"There goes moaning Minnie," said Usha.

"Yes, *finally,*" said Bridget. "They could have been sounding that alarm minutes ago if we'd just—"

"Bridget," said Usha.

"Yes?"

"Stop. Just stop."

Bridget just stopped. They were both apprentices, and Usha had been with the Checquy for only three years, but at twenty-four, the Indian woman was six years older. That combined with her natural authority made her words seem as good as an order. Bridget stared down at the ground beneath them, half expecting to see a torrent of little lights as people streamed from their houses to backyard Anderson shelters and Tube stations.

But of course that's ridiculous. She had read that people had taken to arriving early at the Underground, as early as four in the afternoon, to be certain of getting a good spot for their bedding and food. *And no one is going to risk a flashlight in their own backyard,* she thought. *Not when they say a Jerry pilot can see the light from a cigarette.* She was a trifle dubious about that claim, though.

As she mused, searchlights sliced up from the ground and swept about, and the women could hear the crack of the antiaircraft guns.

"Does the ack-ack actually hit much?" asked Bridget finally.

"I don't believe so," said Usha. "I gather that they're firing to make people feel better as much as from any belief that they'll hit a bomber. It's good to be seen doing something."

"Well, that's a depressing thought," said Bridget. She squinted into the darkness. The sound of the bombers was now lost in the noise of the attack, and she couldn't see any sign of the actual airplanes. There were supposed to be British Hurricanes flying about, fighting back, but she'd read reports that such efforts were useless, and she could see why.

How on earth could they find the enemy's planes in this darkness?

The explosions were still coming, spreading out across the city, an irregular line of flashes advancing toward them. The noise was getting louder too, and Bridget cocked her head, listening. She pulled her balaclava up over her goggles to better focus on hearing and felt the biting wind on her face.

"One of them is coming this way," she said. She looked all about her. "Ah, it's there." She pointed up and to the left. A patch of darkness was cutting through the clouds a few thousand feet above them. "It's pretty low, really."

"Probably hoping for a good shot at—oh!" exclaimed Usha. "Look over there! I think they've hit a church!" Bridget squinted, following the other woman's pointing finger. She opened her mouth to say something but was suddenly smacked in the face and chest by a violent, howling torrent of wind. Usha's hand tightened around hers as the two of them were buffeted backward.

For a single horrible moment, Usha must have lost her focus, because the two of them *dropped.* The fall was no more than a few feet, but it seemed to last for a long time, and then they were once again standing on empty, impossibly solid air like a glass floor. Their knees buckled, and the wind blew them back and sent them skidding along the surface that Usha had created. They scrabbled on the sky before managing to bring themselves to a stop, then braced themselves against the wind and stood.

Bridget let go of a breath she hadn't realized she was holding and carefully loosened her death grip on Usha's hand. She thanked the heavens that Usha had spread the gravity out rather than simply making a small platform and for the ten-foot-long leather strap that connected their wrists in case of nasty accidents. Then: *Pamela!* They looked around for their comrade, but she was gone.

"Where did she go?" shouted Bridget above the roar of the wind. Without Pamela keeping them in a bubble of comparative calm, they were exposed to all the force of the winter night. Bridget's eyes met Usha's, and her stomach twisted. They looked below, scanning the darkness for a sign of Pamela falling, tumbling down to the city, perhaps unconscious or sick or wounded. But there was nothing, no flicker of movement.

Where is she? Oh God, where is she? Has she already hit?

"There she is!" exclaimed Usha.

"Where? Where?" asked Bridget desperately, peering down into the darkness.

"Not there—up!" Bridget looked up. She could just see Pamela coursing away from them. She was clearly alive and well and directing all her will to her flight.

"But what the bloody hell is she doing?" shouted Usha. She sounded more irritated than concerned. Bridget squinted at their comrade thoughtfully. Pamela was flying away at a tremendous speed but curving up as well, and her arms were in front of her, almost clawing at the air.

"Aw, Christ," said Bridget to herself, and Usha somehow heard her through the wind.

"What?"

"She's going after that Jerry plane, the bomber!" shouted Bridget. Usha's head whipped back to stare incredulously at Pamela. Beyond their friend, they could just make out the shape of the aircraft, which did not appear to be flying in a straightforward manner. It was being tossed about, and as they watched, it abruptly dropped several dozen feet. *That has to be Pamela's doing,* thought Bridget.

"Has she gone mad?" exclaimed Usha.

Bridget could only shrug helplessly. *How high is that plane? Is there enough air for Pamela?* The air where they were standing was already bitingly cold in their throats, a sign that they were at the limits of safety. Pamela, of course, could go higher than they could. Not only was she more accustomed to it—in her lifetime of training, she had spent hours and hours at extreme altitudes—but she could also force some air to come with her. Still, even she could not go as high as a plane whose crew wore oxygen masks. *What does she mean to do? Can she bring down the plane? Does she have the strength?* There were ten thousand things that made what was happening impossible.

Plus, of course, there was the one thing that made it absolutely impossible.

"We'll have to go after her!" shouted Usha. "Try to stop her!" Bridget nodded helplessly. Their hands tightened around each other's, and then the invisible ground vanished beneath their feet. Bridget's stomach lurched as they were suddenly tearing forward and upward, like divers falling diagonally up rather than straight down. Bridget hurriedly pulled the balaclava over her face before the wind could snatch it off her head.

The wind howled around them and buffeted them about. The thin strap holding Bridget's gas-mask box snapped wildly in the gale and hit her on the back before the strap broke and the box was gone behind them, abruptly subjected to the gravity of the Earth.

Good luck, little box, thought Bridget ridiculously. She couldn't help but pity it, torn from one plunge to another. Because with Usha, it wasn't flying, it was falling. There was no air carrying them, no sheath of invisible energy wrapped around them. They were simply plummeting upward, and the source of their gravity, the point pulling them with all the mass of the Earth, was Pamela.

But what if she's going higher than we can go? thought Bridget. She could just make out the distant figure of their friend and the German bomber. The plane had turned and was now flying in a broad curve before them, clearly trying to escape London and the bizarre conditions that kept forcing it down. Every few moments, it plunged several dozen feet almost on the spot. Bridget winced at the thought of the effort Pamela must be bringing to bear. Her friend was powerful, and the plane had already been flying lower than most bombers, but dragging it down had to be incredibly difficult, especially since she was coursing after it with horrendous speed.

The speed of Usha and Bridget's upward fall was continuing to increase, and the screaming of the wind almost drowned out the sound of the bombing attack behind them. Still, despite the turbulence, Bridget realized that the air was actually helping to push them along. *We must be in Pamela's slipstream.* She knew that her friend would be drawing air from all around to keep herself aloft and rush her after her prey. *I think we're catching up to her!*

Meanwhile, even as they gained on her, Pamela was gaining on the aircraft. The beleaguered bomber had slowed considerably, and as they watched, it abruptly began to descend to a level at which the three women could breathe. Then Bridget felt the pressure of acceleration as Usha warped the rules of physics around them a little more.

Can we catch up to her? thought Bridget desperately. And if they did, then what? Would they tackle her in midair? *Perhaps we'll be able to drag her down. Or slap some sense into her.* The din from the bomber roared in their ears. It was now flying directly across their path, and they could hear the thunderous cracks of the wind striking the aircraft.

What does she mean to do? Bridget wondered. Pamela was drawing closer and closer to the bomber; she looked as if she meant to start punching it. *She's crazy!* Pamela's powers over air didn't give her any special physical strength or resistance to injury. She could call down incredible force, but she could still be hurt by the bulk of the aircraft or by . . .

The gunners! Bridget suddenly remembered, aghast. She'd read the files and knew that the Heinkel had machine guns to protect itself. There were guns at the front, at the rear, on its back, on its belly, sticking out from the sides. The five-man crew included three gunners and a bombardier, who would also act as the nose gunner.

"Pamela!" Bridget screamed at her. "You've got to stop!" It

seemed impossible that their friend could hear her, but she had to try. As they watched, Pamela closed the gap between herself and the plane. She dived down under the fuselage and kept pace below the aircraft.

There would be a gunner lying down in the enclosure that bulged out of the aircraft's belly. He would be looking ahead, but could he miss seeing her?

At Bridget's side, Usha shouted something incredulous, but the actual words were lost in the gale. For a moment, their course had altered violently, yanked down to follow Pamela's maneuvers, but then they swooped up, and Bridget could tell that Usha had shifted their focus of gravity from Pamela to the aircraft itself.

Good thinking. With the unpredictable movements of the plane and the presence of those scything propellers, something could easily go wrong—*messily* wrong—if they tried to follow her under. For all the speed she could muster, Usha possessed nothing like Pamela's agility in the open air. They plunged toward the bomber.

"Usha, go for the side!" she shouted. "There's a gunner on the back!" The Indian woman nodded tightly, and their fall curved a little.

"Get your feet ready!" shouted Usha, and she twisted in the air to reorient herself and pulled Bridget with her.

They sliced past the aircraft's tail, and as its side came under them, they paused in midair, and then, through Usha's will, the side of the plane was where down was, and they landed on top of it, just ahead of the tail.

"Brace!" exclaimed Usha. They fell to their knees, as firmly planted on the metal of the aircraft as they would be on the deck of a ship. The wind rushed past them, ready to push them back if they stood up, but they crouched against it.

My God, she's good, thought Bridget weakly. The artistry required to guide them through the air and bring them to this point was incredible. "What now?" shouted Bridget. "Can you see her?"

"No! You?"

Bridget shook her head. She scanned all around, but in the darkness, she couldn't find Pamela; she didn't know if she was still under the plane. "Then we move!" declared Usha. She pointed to the front of the plane, and Bridget nodded.

The two women crawled over the metal side of the Heinkel to where it curved down to the plane's belly. It was awkward, since they had to keep holding hands, and the aircraft still pitched about occasionally, but for them, the metal was the ground, so they didn't need to worry about falling off. The wind was nowhere near as bad as it had been. The aircraft was still descending, but far more smoothly.

They had to follow a tricky, narrow route as they moved forward. On one side, below them, a gunner's nest bulged out. Above them, a machine gun jutted out of the aircraft's side, with spy holes for that gunner to peer through.

But although Bridget scanned the area every few moments, there was no sign of their comrade in the darkness.

Then, as the two women drew near the glass dome that formed the nose of the aircraft, Bridget's eye was caught by a flicker of movement. She gasped and tugged on Usha's hand to get her attention.

As the two of them watched in disbelief, Pamela rose up out of the darkness in front of the plane. Her arms were spread wide, and her face was emotionless. She must have been flying backward, because she remained about fifteen yards ahead of the bomber.

"Oh…*crikey*," said Bridget. She was braced for the plane's front machine gun to burst into action and shred her friend, but nothing happened.

Pamela suddenly lunged toward the cockpit. They lost sight of her, but they could hear the sound of her landing on the glass and her distant raised voice. She was screaming. If there were words, Bridget could not make them out.

The plane jinked abruptly, which Bridget absolutely could not blame it for. She could only imagine what had gone through the minds of the men in the cockpit when they were suddenly confronted by a screaming face swooping out of the darkness and pressing itself against the glass in front of them twelve thousand feet up. The engine roared, and the stars above wheeled madly as the plane was flung into a tight curving turn. Bridget's stomach turned too as her eyes argued with her inner ears. Thanks to Usha's firm grip on gravity, it didn't feel as if the world had been tipped on its side, only as if a horrendous new wind was blasting them.

The two women clinging to the fuselage exchanged looks and nods, then resumed their frantic crawl toward the front. The plane kept shifting direction, twisting in the air as if trying to shake off an insect. *Keep going,* Bridget told herself grimly. *Keep...going.* Finally, they reached the front and peered up through the glass dome.

Despite the plane's wild tossings-about, Pamela remained fixed to the glass. She was still screaming, and as they watched, she hammered her fist against the windshield. *Is she trying to punch through?* thought Bridget dazedly. This was not the focused attack that she would expect from Pamela. This was wild, incoherent rage.

Bridget felt a tap on her shoulder and turned to look at Usha. *On three!* her friend mouthed at her, and Bridget nodded. She could visualize the plan without any explanation. On the count of three, Usha would switch their gravity, fixing it on Pamela, and they would fall onto her and wrestle her away from the plane and out into the night sky.

And then what do we do about the Nazis that have seen her? she thought. The entire situation had all sorts of dire implications, and she could not think them out now. *Bugger it,* she decided. *This is the best we can do.* The two of them brought themselves up to their knees. Usha held up her closed fist and unfolded a finger. *One.*

Bridget focused on Pamela, flailing madly at the glass. She could visualize the fall—just a few yards, really.

Two.

It would need to be done right; they had to tackle their friend and keep hold of her to stop her escaping and coming back to the plane. Then Usha could get them safely down to the ground. Bridget tensed in preparation.

Three gunshots rang out, bursting through the glass. Bridget could see the sparkling sprays of glass powder as the holes were punched out. She shot a look at Usha, whose eyes were wide in shock. Her hand was still, the third finger forgotten. Bridget snapped her gaze back to Pamela, who, as if in slow motion, toppled back and away from the glass. She fell down past them, into the darkness, and was swept away under the plane.

"No!" screamed Bridget. *"Oh Jesus, no!"*

The plane leveled out, presumably as the occupants came back to a world where the impossible didn't happen. The cockpit wouldn't be pleasant with holes shot in the glass, but they would be wearing oxygen masks. They could now focus on a nice normal problem, like flying an aircraft over a city whose residents would like to shoot them down. At that moment, through her grief, in the back of her mind, Bridget almost found herself envying them—that sounded so uncomplicated.

"We've got to go after her!" She hauled Usha to her feet. They were about to turn and run back along the underside of the plane when there came a massive rushing of air beneath them, and Pamela sped by, swooping back up toward the cockpit. If she had been shot, there was no sign of it, and now she was accompanied by a roaring sound, and the air about her shivered and blurred.

As they watched, Pamela landed again on the nose of the plane. There were more gunshots, but they didn't connect, glancing off the torrent of wind that she had wrapped around herself. And then there were no more shots, only the unmistakable sound of someone having run out of bullets. The whole world seemed to fall silent; even the roar of the engines faded away in the distance. Pamela was no longer screaming. Instead, there was a look of deadly intentness on her face. Usha and Bridget watched as, with dreadful slowness, their Pawn friend lifted her hand and placed it against the glass.

"Pamela!" shouted Usha. *"Pamela!"* She looked down at them and jerked her head to the side. The message was clear: *Leave.* "No! Come with us!" But Pamela had already turned her gaze back to the windshield and whatever she saw through it. Were the men inside as hypnotized as Usha and Bridget? The two women could not take their eyes off the look of grim determination on Pamela's face.

And then everything flared burning white.

Bridget fell back, sprawled on the metal of the plane, and instinctively flung her free hand over her eyes. Her other hand, though, she kept firmly clutched on Usha's.

What has she done? For a second, she thought that Pamela had somehow summoned a thunderbolt to smite the invaders. But as the light continued to burn even through her fingers, she realized what had happened. They had been pinioned by a searchlight on the ground.

Great booms thundered below them, which she blearily recognized as the antiaircraft fire. *Of course. Where there's a spotlight, there will be ack-ack.*

Are . . . are we in range of those guns?

There was an explosion of light and noise way off to the side. Deafened, Bridget and Usha flinched as a concussive wave of heat smacked into them. The aircraft juddered and tilted for a moment, and there was a rattling of metal against the fuselage. Dazed, she realized it was shrapnel. *I guess we are in range.* The crews on the ground would be working feverishly to get more shells into the air, bringing their guns to bear against this one aircraft that had come so low. As Bridget pictured it, there was another explosion, this one behind them, and the aircraft bucked again. This time she could swear that she heard the shrapnel whizzing by her.

We have to get out of here! We're going to be killed by our own guns!

And then under Bridget's back, the metal of the plane shrieked as a tremendous pulse tore through it. Screws and bolts were forced out of their places, seams and welds tore, and the skin of the aircraft buckled and warped as all the air inside was commanded into a hurricane. Pieces of metal were sent scything out and away. Bridget flung up a hand as a jagged shard spun at her, and it bounced off her palm. She could smell fuel in the air.

"Usha, we've got to—" She was cut off by a tremendous lurch beneath her. She and Usha were thrown into the air as the plane jolted, faltered, and began to twist away from above them. No longer holding hands, they fell apart.

It's all right, Bridget told herself firmly as she plummeted through the air. *It's all right. No need to panic; we've got the belt.* The leather strap that connected their wrists pulled taut. *See?* Her eyes followed it to Usha. The girl was directly above her, her arm outstretched, as it had been yanked down by the tether. She looked at Bridget dazedly, but her eyes focused and she nodded. *All we have to do is haul ourselves to each other and join hands, and then Usha will have a little word with gravity.*

We've done this before; we've practiced in the sky with the belt. The lovely, lovely belt.

Bridget's eye was caught by a sparkle on the belt, a shine that hadn't been there before. She squinted and realized that a fragment of shrapnel had speared the leather. It was lodged a few feet from her hand and had cut the strap almost in half.

Well, that's not good, but there's still no need to panic. Absolutely no need to panic at all.

But, you know, you should still probably hurry the hell up, she told herself.

She reached with her other hand and was about to pull herself up toward Usha when there was an earsplitting detonation and a burst of light below them. An antiaircraft shell had gone off, and though they were far from the fire, and no shrapnel hit them, the concussion wave swept up and struck them.

Whereupon the belt snapped.

All right, now you can panic.

Bridget screamed. The blast set her tumbling in the air, and the world spun beneath her. She caught glimpses of the plane falling, a wing lost, explosions from the ack-ack blossoming, and the beams of the searchlights sweeping back and forth. There were fires in the city and thick clouds of smoke that glowed momentarily as bombs fell. It was as if she were falling into hell.

As she flailed through the air, Bridget looked around frantically for Usha. She caught a glimpse of the plummeting bomber silhouetted against the burning city. Was it beneath her? She had lost all track of how things related to each other. Bridget hadn't caught sight of Pamela, but the trio's dark boilersuits, ideal for concealing them from outside eyes, were also ideal for concealing them from one another. *So make yourself more visible!* She tore off her balaclava and let her hair fly about—its red wasn't as visible as Pamela's blond, but it was something, even in the dark. She ripped off her gloves as well. *Maybe my hands will catch the light and she'll see me.*

"Usha! *Usha!*" she screamed. She flung out her arms and legs, trying to arrest her mad spinning, but it did no good. The wind roared in her ears, and the flash of another spotlight cut across her. She could make out the shapes of buildings beneath her. The booming of the antiaircraft guns was now thunder, blasting all around her. She could see their flashes. The rising smoke was in her mouth. The ground was coming up and up and up to her... "Oh God!" she screamed. *I'm going to die!* She closed her eyes. *Gerald.*

And then she felt a hand closing tight in her hair, and the horrible, blessed, stomach-turning sensation of coming to the peak of a jump and starting to fall back *down,* away from the Earth. Disbelieving, she opened her eyes and saw Usha above her, her face intent. *Saved!* They surged up, away from the smoke and the fire and the horrendous sound of the bombs and guns, away from the sound of the bomber crashing into the city. They soared, slowing gently until they finally stopped on solid air.

"Oh God." Bridget dropped to her knees and vomited. Usha kept her hand in Bridget's hair, holding it out of her face. Even in her stunned, trembling state, it was mildly interesting to watch the puke falling between her hands and continuing on its way down through the sky. *God help anyone it lands on,* she thought shakily. Gasping, she spat again and again, then wiped her mouth and nose on her sleeve. The freezing night air now felt much better on her face. It felt clean. She breathed it in, cold in her throat.

"Are you all right?" asked Usha.

Bridget reached up and took her friend's hand. "Thank you," she said. "Thank you so much." Usha squeezed her hand and helped her up to her feet. "Have you seen any sign of Pamela?"

Usha shook her head. "No. The last I saw, she was still on the front of the plane."

"Then she'll be dead!" Bridget gasped. "She'll have been killed when the ack-ack hit the plane."

"It wasn't ack-ack that destroyed the plane," said Usha flatly. "There was no explosion, no heat." Bridget stared at her in dazed bewilderment. "It was Pamela—she sent her powers ripping through it."

"What? No, she wouldn't..." Bridget began, but she paused in the face of Usha's certainty. *She's right. There was no explosion.* "But then she must be alive. She'd have flown off before it crashed, surely?"

"I don't think we can make any assumptions about what Pamela

would or would not do," said Usha. "Not after tonight." Bridget
stared at her. Pamela and Usha were the closest of friends, had been
since before the war. But the woman's voice was grim, as cold as
Bridget had ever heard it.

"Well, then, we'll have to go down to the plane."

"No, Bridget," said Usha. "I think that's about as bad an idea as it
is possible to have."

"What are you talking about? We *have* to go down there!"

"Down there are fires," said Usha. "There are bombs, there are
guns firing, and there are witnesses."

"But we've got to find her," said Bridget, incredulous. "We've
got to know!" It seemed like the most obvious thing in the world,
and yet Usha stood there in the darkness, regal and unmoved, like a
statue.

"And what will we find? If she is not there, then we have put ourselves in danger for nothing. If she is down there, then she is probably
dead. If she is not dead, then the wardens will come soon, and they'll
be able to help her."

"How can you say that? How can you rely on that? She's
your friend! And she's one of *us*." Absurdly, Bridget thought about
wrenching her hand out of Usha's so that she would fall, and they
would *have* to go down. Her fellow apprentice regarded her for a long
moment. Then, her expression unchanging, she lifted her chin
slightly in assent, and they began to sink. It was a slow, measured
descent, and Bridget could almost feel Usha's thoughts clamped
around them.

It was quieter than it had been. There were no bombers above
them—clearly they'd moved on to other targets, and though the
searchlights still waved back and forth, the ack-ack had stopped. The
fires continued to rage throughout the city, and the smoke billowed
up. Bridget hadn't seen where the plane went down, but apparently
Usha knew, because she directed them in a straight line to a specific spot.

As they moved through the air, Bridget had to hold her hand over
her mouth and nose because of the smoke, but they quickly cut
through the worst of the fug, and suddenly there was a landscape of

rooftops drifting beneath them. The world was filled with a haze of smoke, dust, and fog. Distant fires were partially concealed in the haze.

All in gray and black, the roofs rippled at a thousand different angles. A couple of them had holes punched in them where bombs had fallen on previous nights but failed to explode. Through the holes, Bridget caught glimpses of jagged beams and rafters and the filthy floors of garrets and attics. She felt the hair on the back of her neck stand up. They were looking into the centuries-old entrails of the city, torn open and exposed.

"Where are we?" she whispered. Usha shrugged.

"Slums," she said. "Rookeries."

They floated over a burned-out crater where a bomb had done its job. And then another. Between the roofs, the alleys and streets were pitch-black and silent. It was as if everyone in the world had died. A cat perching on the ridge of a roof looked up at them with calm incuriosity.

"There, that chimney," said Usha, and Bridget started at the sudden sound of her voice. She was pointing at a roof where a row of chimney pots clustered in the haze. "At the end, where the pots have been broken off."

"Yes, I see," whispered Bridget. They floated down and alighted softly and silently on the stones of the chimney. Something—perhaps a bomb blast, perhaps storms—had smashed several chimney pots off their bases, and though there were some jagged remains underfoot, the two women stood as easily on the top of the chimney stack as angels on the head of a pin. Around them, the rooftops spread off dimly into the darkness, some of them steep and peaked, others flatter and slanted. Bridget opened her mouth to ask why they had stopped here, but the fog and dust parted for a moment in front of them, and she saw.

Before them was a void in the city where something had cut down through houses and shops. Bridget could just see the remains of the buildings that had been smashed down. Walls leaned crazily over wreckage. The ground was a mess of bricks and timbers, and in a few spots they could see where cellars had caved in. As they stood, there was the startling sound of brickwork collapsing, and then only silence again.

"Where are the people?" she asked softly.

"In shelters, I suppose." Usha pointed to a tiny yard where the unmistakable hump of an Anderson shelter was crouched. "Or in the Underground."

"And the wardens?" asked Bridget helplessly. "The fire brigade?"

"I expect they'll come. But there are no fires. Look there." She pointed to the end of the cut, where a dark mass lay crumpled. "There it is." Bridget peered at the wreckage of the aircraft. There was no movement, no sound. No sign of Pamela.

"We'll have to go closer," said Bridget.

They jumped, almost weightless, floated through the air, and landed gently just before the wreckage. It was a mess. Already broken by Pamela, the plane had lost its other wing as it careened through the houses. Great holes had been torn in it. It had finally come to a halt when it smashed up against a building that refused to fall. The cockpit was a crumpled mass of metal, with every piece of glass crushed away. And yet it was still frightening, half shrouded in dust and fog, rearing up before them like a beast of burned metal ready to strike.

God, thought Bridget. *No one could have survived inside that. But what about Pamela?*

"Pamela," she whispered. Then: "Pamela!" Her voice echoed, bouncing off the walls of the neighboring buildings. *"Pamela!"* There was no answer. "What do you think?"

"I would have expected there to be a fire," said Usha.

"Um, I think that Pamela must have torn open the fuel tanks," said Bridget.

"Ah. And perhaps it had finished its bombing run, so it was empty."

"And Pamela?"

"I don't know," said Usha. "But we're not going to climb up onto it. Or into it." She looked around the darkness. "We can't stay here long, Bridget. People will come."

Bridget looked at her helplessly. "Can you take us up above it?"

Usha sighed heavily but nodded.

Then, as one, they turned at the sound of approaching motor vehicles. *The fire brigade*, thought Bridget. *They had to show up at some point.*

"We should go," said Usha. She held out her hand, and Bridget took it. The dust and smoke swirled around them, and they rose up and away into the darkness, still without any answers.

2

It started with the smallest of signs. So small, in fact, that it would be months before Lyn, looking back on that day, realized its significance. It happened at six thirty that morning when she rolled over in bed to paw at her mobile, which was chiming a gratingly jaunty little tune to show that it was *time to wake up, time to wake up, your three-year-old will be rousing herself soon and causing chaos.* As she struggled to open her eyes or at least randomly swipe in the correct alarm-killing pattern, Lyn felt the snap of a static electric shock.

"Ow!"

"Hmmf?" hmmfed Richard from the other side of the bed.

"Just the stupid phone," said Lyn. "Go back to sleep, my love." Her husband had gotten in from patrol only a couple of hours earlier. When he was on late shifts, it was her turn to be responsible and tend to the stock. She managed to lever herself out of bed and wander down to the kitchen, where Skeksis the whippet was waiting patiently to be let out.

Another static shock when she touched the door handle.

"Ow! Bloody hell!" *I hate the winter,* she thought foggily as she made coffee and winced at the sound of her small child failing to make it safely down the last two stairs. "I'm coming, darling." Luckily, it was just a minor stumble, not a concussion.

But the day did not improve. It was Lyn's turn to open the library, but her car had decided that it wanted to suffer from battery issues, and her mobile had joined it in a show of solidarity. By the time she got Emma to day care, she was running forty-five minutes late and nursing a throbbing headache.

Thank God I work in a place where I can legitimately tell people to shush.

To make matters worse, the headache continued throughout the day, despite aspirin, coffee, a lunchtime spent lying on a couch in a dark office, and repeated silencings of the reading public of South Shields, a town in northeast England. At the end of the day, when she picked up Emma, it was still pulsing in her brain. When they took Skeksis out for a walk, Lyn kept everyone moving fast. *If I can wear the both of them out, I can feed and water them and put Emma right to bed,* she told herself. *I'll leave food for Richard to reheat, then I can go to sleep, and hopefully I will wake up feeling better, with this shitty day behind me.* Both the whippet and the three-year-old were panting by the time they got back to the house, and the pair retired to the couch in the sitting room to watch cartoons.

"Ow! Bastard!" Another static shock, this time when she picked up a jar of pasta sauce. Even the jar was spiting her, refusing to open. She strained and twisted the top with all her might, and as it finally popped open, she saw stars floating in her vision. *Great, I've probably given myself an aneurysm from opening a jar of Bolognese.* She stood still for a few seconds and waited for the sparks to fade.

Except that they didn't. Instead, they turned red and continued to sparkle in her vision. Was it her imagination, or had one just alighted on the curtain and left a tiny burn mark?

No, she thought dizzily. *No, this isn't right.* Everything was getting fuzzy. In the next room, Skeksis began whining, a plaintive high-pitched whimpering that cut through her head. Lyn put a hand down on the counter to steady herself, and there was a crackling sound and a tingling under her palm. With an effort, she looked down and, disbelieving, saw a mass of writhing tendrils of red electricity extending out from under her hand, the ends dancing to the metal of the sink.

With a shriek, she snatched her hand away, then watched in shocked horror as, for an eye-burning moment, a wriggling thumb-thick bolt of crimson lightning coursed between her hand and a copper saucepan hanging by the stove. The saucepan burst with a loud report. Distantly, she heard the dog's whining turn into a full-throated howl, like a scream. And then she heard Emma's shocked cry, which broke down into confused crying.

"It's okay, baby," she whispered. It was automatic; it was all she could think to say, but she couldn't call to her—the breath in her body was pumping in and out, and she was gasping and wheezing. The pain in her head grew, and she felt like her skull was going to crack open. "I'm coming," she said. But she couldn't.

What is this? What is happening to me? Because it *was* her. Even through the pain in her head, Lyn could feel something surging within her, a tingling and churning rising up her spine. Her knees buckled, and she fell back against the door of the refrigerator.

The pain rushed from her head, and lightning exploded out of her. The room was filled with thunderous cracks as red electricity burst at random points from her skin. Under her horrified gaze, a bolt erupted from the back of her forearm and arced across the room to melt a door handle. Streamers of electricity rose up from her shoulders and face to shatter the light fixtures. Her wedding ring was alight with a corona of sparks. The glass in her wristwatch was powder.

And yet there was no pain, no burning, just waves and waves of a surging sensation. She clenched her fists against it, and lightning discharged crazily out of her knuckles and struck a pot of water that had been heating up on the stove. It was flung into the air by the impact, and the lightning branched into a hundred rivulets of light that smashed the water into steam. A bunch of bananas on the counter burst out of their skins.

She couldn't do anything, couldn't think. All she could do was loll back and watch blankly as electricity arced from her elbows and scrawled massive burns across the walls. At points, they flared madly, and lines charred along the plaster where wiring burned out.

And then, in the middle of the maelstrom, through the cracking of the lightning, through the torrent of sensation that threatened to overwhelm her mind, through the madness of it all, she heard a small sound. A sound that she could never ignore.

"Mummy?"

She looked over at the door to the living room, where, to her horror, Emma was standing, eyes wide, tiny hands reaching out to her for comfort. *No!* She couldn't let her baby come near her. The kitchen was a nightmare, and she was the epicenter. It took all her strength to focus through the waves of sensation that were roaring through her, but Lyn managed to scream out:

"Get away!"

Her little girl's face crumpled, and Lyn felt a pang through her heart.

"Mummy!" Emma wailed and took a step into the kitchen.

"G-go! *Go!*"

Screaming and sobbing, her daughter turned around and ran from her. Lyn caught a glimpse of her running up the stairs. The distant howls of the dog suggested that he had fled to the bedroom as well.

With a massive effort, Lyn stood. She had some vague, unformed thought of getting out of the house. She couldn't muster any idea of what might happen then, but she would be away. Her baby would be safe. She took a faltering step, and sparks crawled crazily out from under her shoe. She could not do it. The power rippled through her again and again, and she leaned forward, bone-weary, and put her hands on the wooden countertop. Sweat dripped off her face.

Unaware of the massive streamers of scarlet electricity that were now discharging from her spine and scribbling themselves across the ceiling, all Lyn could do was stare down at her hands on the counter. From under her palms, patches of charring spread out across the wood, with veins of red glowing and tracing their way like the branches of a tree. Perfect little fractal patterns.

Pretty, she thought faintly.

And then she knew no more.

Darkness hung before Lyn. She could not feel anything beyond an embracing warmth.

I died . . .

Then tiny sparks glimmered in the darkness, a sea of stars spreading away into infinity.

I'm dead . . .

Before her, above her, emerging blurrily from the darkness, was a figure. She struggled to focus and saw a pair of chocolate-brown eyes and a strong jaw. A handsome figure with broad shoulders dressed in a fireman's outfit.

I'm dead and I'm in heaven . . .

Two figures, also dressed like firemen, flanked the handsome man. They were markedly less impressive than the first one. And there was the strong smell of smoke about them. There were soot marks on their faces, and smears of sweat.

I'm not dead. These are actual firemen. Because of the fire...

"Emma!" Lyn sat bolt upright, and the three firemen moved back.

"Your daughter's fine," said the middle fireman soothingly. "She's at your neighbor's. We've checked her over, and she's fine."

"I need to see her!"

"As soon as we've made sure that you're all right. We don't want to frighten her."

"She's okay?"

"She's okay."

"You swear?"

"I promise."

"Okay. And where's my dog?" she demanded.

"The dog's also okay. We took him over to the neighbor's as well, and your husband's on the way." Lyn looked around warily. She was wrapped in a blanket; they'd laid her out on her own front lawn. The dark void peppered with stars that she had mistaken for the mysterious beauty of the afterlife had, in fact, been the night sky. "Mrs. Binns, can you tell us what happened?"

"What happened?" Lyn repeated. And it all came flooding back to her, like a dream that you remember the next morning when you're in the shower. The horrible, impossible maelstrom of electricity coming out of her skin, the complete lack of control, the destruction that had poured from her, her daughter's distraught and bewildered face. It was all real.

Oh God. Emma! What if I've damaged my baby's psyche? She wanted nothing more than to find her daughter and hold her close and forget about all this. And then she thought of what might happen while she was hugging her child, and she almost burst into tears.

Be calm, she told herself. *Deep breath. You have to be sensible.*

She glanced at the burly men and noticed for the first time that they looked frightened. "What happened?" she asked again. "I have no idea."

"So we found you in here," said the good-looking fireman, whose name was Brett.

"I see," said Lyn weakly. *Bloody hell.*

The kitchen was a disaster. It looked exactly like you'd expect it to if lightning had erupted out of someone's skin and set about flaying the walls until a bewildered fire department had arrived, carried an unconscious woman out into the garden, then liberally hosed down the smoldering walls. It stank and was sopping wet. Food, water, and charred bits of the decor had combined on the floor to make a vile sludge. Part of the counter was burned to charcoal. The appliances were blackened, and all the cutlery in the open drawer had been welded together. Even if one did not take the supernatural elements into consideration, it was still a nightmare to behold.

Ridiculously, the jar of spaghetti sauce was sitting unharmed on the unburned part of the counter.

"And you were in here when this all happened?" asked Brett.

"I don't know," said Lyn.

"Your daughter says you were in here, and you were sparking."

"I was sparking?" She put all the bewildered incredulity she felt into her response.

Lyn had been carefully checked over by the paramedics once they'd arrived, and they'd bemusedly pronounced her fine. No burns, no harm. Mild smoke inhalation, which was treated with a few minutes of oxygen from a mask. She'd spent those minutes and the brief walk from the ambulance to the house thinking very hard, very quickly.

What had happened in the kitchen had profound, terrifying implications. The sheer impossibility of the occurrence left Lyn questioning all her ideas about herself, about the world, about reality and God.

The most immediate profound and terrifying implication, however, was what would happen to anyone who told the truth. The truth was demented. The truth was insane. Anyone who stated it would be labeled crazy, and Lyn decided that she was very definitely not going to be that person. She would have quite enough to deal with in working out the ramifications of these events. Coming up with the official explanation could be someone else's problem.

The firemen were beginning to understand that it would be *their* problem, and they were looking increasingly desperate at the prospect. Lyn almost felt sorry for them, but she couldn't spare much concern for anything but her own immediate troubles.

"Well, she *said* you were sparking," said Fireman Brett, looking uncomfortable.

"Yeah, she's *three,*" said Lyn, mentally apologizing to her daughter.

"Mrs. Binns, we're just trying to understand..." The fireman's voice had taken on a pleading tone that was quite at odds with his made-for-a-calendar physique and face.

"And I told you, I have no idea what happened," said Lyn firmly.

"Mrs. Binns, there are holes burned in your clothes," said one of the other firemen.

"Yeah," agreed Lyn, plucking helpfully at her shirt, where a large hole had been singed above her left collarbone.

"But there are no marks on your skin." He said it almost accusingly.

"Yeah," agreed Lyn again. He waited expectantly, but no further response was forthcoming. Behind her, the battered range hood fell from the ceiling with an enormous clatter.

"There will have to be an investigation," said one of the firemen finally.

"Yes, I would hope so," said Lyn levelly. "I want to know what happened here as much as you do. Probably more. After all, this is my house."

One of the firemen idly reached out and picked up the miraculously intact jar of Bolognese sauce. The lid rattled loosely, and he put his hand on it to tighten it. As he did, there was a snapping sound, and red light flared. Lyn and the other firemen watched in shock as strands of crimson electricity crackled out of the metal jar lid and writhed all over him. He stood taut, his back arched, muscles frozen, unable to let go of the jar. Clenched grunting sounds came out of his mouth: *"Hng! Hng! Hng! Hng! Hng! Hng!"*

My God, thought Lyn. *It's happening again! Maybe it's not me after all. Maybe it's the kitchen! Or the jar!* Whatever the cause, though, it was clear that the fireman was having a far different experience from her own. The electricity was erupting into him rather than out of him. It was clearly agony, and no one dared touch him.

And then it was over. The sparks dissipated, and the jar fell from his hands and smashed on the sopping floor. His eyelids fluttered, and he collapsed to the ground.

"Chris!" shouted Brett. Lyn had to give the firemen credit. They might not have been able to provide an explanation for the inexplicable, but they knew how to treat a downed comrade. While she stood by uselessly, the two unharmed firemen sprang into action as smoothly as if it had all been choreographed. Within moments, they were crouched by the fallen fireman, taking his pulse (which was apparently still pulsing), checking his breathing (which was labored), and urgently calling his name (which was still Chris). He made weak moaning sounds, which the other firemen seemed to take as a good sign.

"Mate, you're going to be fine," said Fireman Brett. "We've got you, Chris."

"This place is not safe," said Fireman Not-Brett-or-Chris. "I don't know what's going on here, but we all need to get out immediately." They looked around warily, ready for another burst of electricity to flare up out of an unexpected source. A moment later, Chris was hoisted up by his comrades and hustled out of the house.

"Am I under arrest?"

"No," said the man.

"Because my husband is a cop, and I help him study for all his exams," said Lyn. "So I know the protocols for arresting somebody. And you've followed none of them."

"This is a hospital," said the woman. "People aren't brought to hospital to be arrested." Lyn opened her mouth to point out that people who were brought to hospital weren't generally placed in a hurriedly vacated doctors' lounge with no windows and several resuscitation mannequins lying about like people who had decided to take their limbs off and enjoy a good nap, but something told her that it would be better to ask questions than provide information. Providing information could be a slippery slope.

"Then why am I here? The paramedics said I was all right," said Lyn.

"The paramedics said quite a few things," said the man. "And the firemen said quite a few more. Rather frantically. Many of those things made no sense, which caught the attention of some people."

"And are you those people?" asked Lyn.

"Yes," said the woman.

Lyn sat back in her chair and regarded them carefully. They'd introduced themselves as "Jane Pumphrey and Norman Smalls from the National Emergency Services Response and Evaluation Services Office," which really told her absolutely nothing, although the double use of the word *services* had set her soulless-bureaucracy senses tingling. They hadn't offered her their cards.

To make matters even less clear, while Jane Pumphrey was dressed in an expensive suit, Norman Smalls wore a long-sleeved T-shirt, torn sweatpants, and running shoes. For different reasons, they both looked tremendously out of place in the lounge, and yet they did not seem ill at ease or uncomfortable. Rather, they had an air about them of utter calm and certainty. Lyn recognized it as the sort of poise that came from authority and power, and she wanted nothing to do with it. In fact, this quality, which screamed *government,* was stirring up an almost atavistic response in her body. Vague memories and instincts were twitching in the back of her mind, urging her to get up, bolt past these people, and flee down the corridors.

You don't need to run away, she told herself. *This is not an incomprehensible situation. Authority is not something for you to fear. You are an adult; you have control; you can understand this and address it. You're a librarian, for God's sake. You married a cop!*

"Can I leave?" she said finally.

"Of course," said Ms. Pumphrey.

"Excellent, goodbye." Lyn stood up and walked to the door.

"If you really feel safe doing so."

Lyn's hand froze on the doorknob. She looked back at the man and the woman. They had not stirred from their places on the stained furniture. Mr. Smalls was scrolling through some notes on a tablet; Ms. Pumphrey was leaning forward in her seat, staring down into a Styrofoam cup of coffee.

"What is that supposed to mean?" Lyn asked.

"Well, you know what happened in your house," said the man.

"No, actually, I don't know!" snapped Lyn. "And no one seems able to tell me."

"Lots of damage," the man continued as if she hadn't spoken. "And then later, a fireman touched an item in your kitchen and was shocked with an estimated electrical charge of…" He looked over at his colleague.

"Fifty thousand volts at twenty-six watts," she supplied without looking up from her coffee.

"Nasty," said the man. "That's about what a law-enforcement-grade stun gun will put out."

"So what are you saying?" asked Lyn. "You think there was a law-enforcement-grade stun gun lying around the house and it burned down my kitchen and then—what? Hid itself in a jar of spaghetti sauce?"

"No, everyone agreed it just came out of nowhere," said the man. "No wires, no battery. We've searched for a source and found nothing. The firemen are adamant that nothing was touched once they vacated the premises, which they did pretty damn briskly. So it's a mystery, as is the event that led to the fire department being summoned to your house in the first place."

For a few moments, the man's eyelids fluttered oddly and his eyes rolled back in his head to show the whites, then he was gazing at her again. Lyn drew back in shock.

"When they arrived, the firemen found a few little fires burning on the walls and several dozen spots smoldering on the walls and floor," he went on. "The counter was in flames. You were unconscious on the floor. They removed you and extinguished the flames, doing all the damage that one might expect with a firehose." Lyn closed her eyes at the thought of her house.

"Water and smoke damage aside, the place is in quite a state. Long lines of charred plaster on the ceiling. In some areas, the wiring had scorched along the walls. A very bizarre distribution of damage, with no apparent cause. No indication of electrical faults. The stove was untouched. No immediate signs of accelerants that might have been splashed about." He shrugged. "Of course, it's only a preliminary examination, but in my initial, albeit expert, opinion, it makes no sense."

"How can that be?" Lyn asked.

"As you said, it's your house."

"Yes?"

"You were there for both events," said the man.

"Are you saying that it was *me?*" demanded Lyn. "Are you insane?"

"Your daughter keeps saying, 'Mummy was sparking, Mummy was a storm,'" said the woman. "And then she cries."

"You talked to my daughter?" Lyn took an enraged step toward them.

"No," said the man mildly. "But she talks, and she was heard."

"She's three!"

"She was there," said the woman. "You know what she saw."

"It's late," said the man. "Your daughter should be asleep right now, but she isn't. When she finally *does* get to sleep, what do you think she's going to be dreaming about?" Lyn felt tears prickle her eyes at the thought.

"What do you think she's going to be dreaming about for the rest of her life?" asked the woman. It was that question that undid Lyn. She held her hands up to her eyes, a panicked gesture she hadn't made since she was a child.

"Oh God," she said weakly.

"Will she be safe around you? Will your husband?" asked the woman.

"You don't know *why* it happened or *how* it happened," said the man. "But Lynette, you do know *what* happened."

"It was me," she whispered.

"We know."

They had the good manners to avert their eyes while she wept.

"And what happens now?" asked Lyn once she'd calmed down. She blew her nose, and Ms. Pumphrey wordlessly provided her with a tissue.

"We can help you," said Mr. Smalls. "This is actually not a unique situation."

"What? So all over England, people are suddenly shooting lightning out of themselves?"

"Not lightning," said Mr. Smalls. "But the impossible is far more common than you'd believe."

"Oh, I don't know," said Lyn wearily. "After tonight, you wouldn't believe what I'd believe."

"She's asleep," said Ms. Pumphrey suddenly. Lyn and the man looked over at her. The woman was, once again, staring down into her cup of coffee. She picked up her phone from the table and made a call. "It's me. Please let the Lady know that the child is asleep, so she can begin. Thank you."

"Would you believe that Emma will enjoy a night free of bad dreams?" asked Mr. Smalls.

"How can you know that?" asked Lyn. She looked over at Pumphrey. "Wait—how do you know my daughter's asleep?"

Without glancing up, the woman gestured for Lyn to come over. "Look," she said.

Lyn followed the woman's gaze and peered down into the cup of coffee. Just below the surface, there were faint cloudy lines that shifted about.

"What am I supposed to be looking at?"

"Here, this will help," said the woman. Light glimmered brownly in the depths of the cup, and the lines sprang into sharp contrast. Lyn gasped as she found herself looking down at the small but unmistakable image of her daughter curled up asleep. She was in the guest bedroom of the home of their friends the Mayles. As Lyn watched, Emma moved and snuggled up against her father. Richard was sitting up next to her on the bed, staring blankly at his tablet. Skeksis was curled up between his knees.

"What is this? You're—what? You're—you're scrying my family? In a cup of *coffee?*"

"Legally, *scrying* is seeing the future," said the woman. "I'm showing the present. Of a location within a 36.876-kilometer radius. Through an aperture of up to 41.34 inches."

"Is it magic?"

The woman shrugged. "It's just something I can do."

"Okay..." said Lyn. "And in a cup of coffee. Why not? Much more discreet than a crystal ball." For the first time, Ms. Pumphrey smiled.

Lyn stared down at the tiny image of Richard in the coffee. He looked exhausted and worried, for which she could not blame him at all. He'd been dragged off shift with the news that his house had caught fire but that everyone was all right. He'd arrived home to find his daughter and dog ensconced at the neighbors', with word left that his wife was unharmed but had been taken to the hospital for observation. They'd spoken on the phone, and, still reeling from the events in the kitchen,

Lyn had told him not to come to the hospital, to stay with Emma and Skeksis. She was fine, she promised. She'd see him tomorrow.

I'm so sorry, my love.

"And you say my daughter isn't going to have any nightmares about this?"

"Well, for the next four nights, she won't," said the man. "But children are resilient, and sleep is a great healer. Four nights of untroubled sleep won't solve all your problems, but it can make a tremendous difference."

"And how is this happening? This absence of bad dreams?"

"Someone very important is willing to take time out of her busy schedule to make it so," said Ms. Pumphrey. "As a sign of good faith."

"Who are you people? I can't believe the National Service Servicing Services, or whoever you claim to work for, is staffed by employees with magic powers. Are you even with the government?"

"Absolutely," said Mr. Smalls. "We're the part of the government that deals with and is staffed by the inexplicable. Which now includes you."

"So you think you're going to deal with me?" asked Lyn, her eyes narrowed. *I've heard that before.*

"You're not a problem to be dealt with, Lynette Binns," said Ms. Pumphrey. "We think that you have tremendous potential. You can work with us to make the world safer."

"You want to offer me a job?"

"We want to offer you help," said Pumphrey. "We can help you find answers. We can teach you to control this force within you. And we'll fix your kitchen."

"And if I say no?" asked Lyn warily.

"You've already demonstrated what can happen when you don't know how to control this," said Pumphrey. "Today, your kitchen was destroyed, and a fireman was electrocuted. Who knows what could happen tomorrow? You have a child and a husband. Are you willing to risk their safety? You live in a town and work with members of the public. You have friends. At any moment of any day, you could accidentally kill everyone around you."

"And yet *you* two came in here with me," said Lyn. "Are you shockproof as well as being clairvoyant and"—she looked at Smalls uncertainly—"wearing gym clothes?"

"No, and that's why they pay us the not-big-enough bucks," said Ms. Pumphrey. "And why you're in the nearest windowless government room we could find that wasn't in a basement." She smiled a little smile. "The National Health Service is an invaluable resource for our work, but usually it's a case of alerting us to the unusual rather than providing a comparatively flameproof place to have a discussion." She eyed the mannequins dubiously.

"The government really does that sort of thing?" asked Lyn. The hair on the back of her neck was standing up.

"Take it from us," said Smalls, "it is tremendously difficult to be different. One needs every resource one can get. For instance, how would you keep your situation a secret? It happened accidentally once—why couldn't it happen again? How do you think people will regard you if they learn that you might inadvertently kill them? You have the internet. You know how reasonable the world can be."

"And there's the question of your daughter," said Pumphrey. "Quite aside from whether the government could, in good conscience, leave a child in a home that might explode at any moment— my apologies, it's a vivid image, but you have to concede that it's not inaccurate—quite aside from that, it's not unheard of for these sorts of things to be genetic. Are you willing to take the risk that, if Emma does share your gift, she'll be able to control it without support?"

"But you think your people *can* help," said Lyn. "With all of that."

"Yes." The two of them spoke in unison.

As far as Lyn could tell, she didn't really have a choice.

"Fine, I'm in." *Whatever* in *is*.

"Excellent!" exclaimed Ms. Pumphrey. "This is your first step in your new understanding of the world. You're going to see things and do things that you couldn't possibly imagine."

"Sounds amazing," said Lyn cautiously.

"It absolutely is. But first there are some forms you'll need to fill out."

As soon as Lyn agreed to sign on with this madness, Pumphrey made a call, and within half an hour, a woman in her fifties arrived wheeling two large suitcases. She introduced herself as "Mrs. Good-man, your legal adviser and chatelaine," then directed Lyn, Pumphrey, and Smalls to stack the chairs and resuscitation mannequins in a corner. Meanwhile, she set about unpacking the suitcases, which were apparently crammed full of documents. She laid the papers out in a queue that started out orderly but then branched out several times and was punctuated by thick bound booklets.

"Do I really have to do this now?" asked Lyn. "It's been an incredibly long and bizarre day."

"It's quite necessary," said Mrs. Goodman. "We need to place you under our legal protection and authority as soon as possible, and you need to make some important decisions."

"This all seems extremely complicated," said Lyn. "I didn't have to sign this many forms when I bought a house. Or had a baby."

"This is a little more involved," said Mrs. Goodman. "It's like building a house. You have to lay very strong foundations before you can move on to the next thing. For instance, I can't actually tell you the name of the organization until you've signed this nondisclosure form."

"Oh," said Lyn. She scanned the document quickly and didn't see anything alarming. "Shouldn't I have a lawyer review these?"

"I'm acting as your lawyer," said Mrs. Goodman. "And as your lawyer, I recommend that you sign that form." Lyn nodded with exhaustion and signed. Pumphrey and Smalls quickly signed as witnesses.

"So, now that you've signed," said Mrs. Goodman, "I can advise you that the organization in question is the Checquy Group. We usually just refer to it as the Checquy." She pronounced it "Sheh-kay."

"Is that French?"

"It's archaic," said Mrs. Goodman. "And possibly mispronounced. The Checquy is the department within the British government responsible for individuals and occurrences for which there is no scientific or rational explanation, the unregulated existence of which could cause damage to public safety; that, if publicized, could result in damage to public order and sanity; and that, if left unchecked, could result in damage to civilians and property and/or may lead to the catastrophic breakdown of society."

"How often do occurrences like that happen?" asked Lyn faintly.

"Often enough to justify a government department," said Mrs. Goodman.

"And I'm going to join this department?"

"You must understand that the events of today have served to redefine you in the eyes of the British legal system. As a result, under law, your rights, obligations, and privileges are now different from those of a normal citizen. This is automatic. You don't have to sign an acknowledgment of the law for it to affect you."

"Wait, so I don't have a choice?"

"No," said Mrs. Goodman.

"But, but...oh my *God!*" exclaimed Lyn. "What rights have I lost?"

"You don't need to panic," said Pumphrey soothingly. "Think of it like enlisting in the army."

"Except I didn't *enlist!*" Lyn took a deep breath. "Look, give me an example of a right I don't have anymore."

"You no longer get to vote," said Smalls. "And you can't travel overseas without authorization."

"Why not?"

"Well, the travel restriction is because you're going to become privy to a lot of classified information," said Smalls. "And also, you're a deadly weapon."

"No, I'm not!"

"You can blow up a kitchen with your skin," pointed out Pumphrey.

"Oh yeah. Okay," said Lyn. She'd actually managed to forget about that in the face of all these revelations. *Calm down,* she told herself. *This can't be as bad as it seems.* "So what happens now?"

"First, you have automatically become a ward of the Checquy," said Mrs. Goodman.

"Once again a ward of court," muttered Lyn.

"The Checquy will provide you with monitoring, accommodation, training, employment, and support services," continued Mrs. Goodman. "Initially, you'll need to stay at a secure facility while your abilities are assessed and you learn to control them." Lyn opened her mouth to object, and the lawyer shot her a stern look. "This is for your own safety and the safety of those around you."

"I can see why that would be necessary," said Lyn reluctantly. "When?"

"Immediately," said the lawyer. "You'll be transported there directly from this facility once we've finished the paperwork."

"But my husband! And Emma!" said Lyn. "I'll need to say good-bye. And explain this to them." The immensity of it all hit her. "Oh God. How am I going to explain it to Richard?"

"We'll get to that in a moment," said Mrs. Goodman. "Don't forget to initial there. And there. And there."

"How long is it going to take?" asked Lyn. "The training, I mean."

"We have no way of knowing," said Mrs. Goodman flatly. She oversaw three more signatures, and after each piece of paper received its scrawled *Lynette Binns,* she presented it to Pumphrey and Smalls for witnessing, then filed it away in one of her suitcases. "And done!" She snapped the cases shut and locked them. "Now we must discuss the impact this is going to have on your personal life."

"Pretty damn huge, I would say!"

"Absolutely," said Mrs. Goodman. "So, here's a big decision for you to make: To what extent do you wish to discard your current life?"

"I beg your pardon?" Lyn stared incredulously at the woman.

"Make no mistake, Mrs. Binns," said the lawyer, "your education, your marriage, giving birth to a child—none of these are as significant as what has happened today. Your life is going to change radically. And *you* will change radically.

"For many people, this represents too drastic and problematic a shift, so we offer the option of commencing a completely new life. You can take a new name, get a new face—we have the best plastic surgeons in the world—and walk away from your old life completely. We can facilitate a variety of scenarios."

"You're serious," said Lyn wonderingly.

"We can fake a death. We can arrange your disappearance. If you want a divorce, we can work to make it as smooth and fast as possible."

"I love my husband!" said Lyn. "And I have a child! I am not walking away from either of them."

"There's no need to get offended," said Mrs. Goodman calmly. "Many people find it very therapeutic to walk away. A completely clean break to begin a completely different life. And you could rest assured that those you left behind would be generously provided for and given a rational, plausible explanation. Previously unknown trust funds can come to light; life insurance policies that you never told anyone about can pay out; scholarships can be offered."

"Is this what you did?" Lyn asked Pumphrey. "Did you just walk away from *your* life?"

"I came in when I was five," said Pumphrey. "It was a bit different for me."

"You bring *kids* into this?"

"Mrs. Binns, please," said Mrs. Goodman. "It's late. Now, I take it you are electing not to discard your previous identity and life?"

"That's right," said Lyn firmly.

"Good, well, that means a bit less activity tonight. We won't need to fake your death. Pawn Smalls, can you let Pawn Meijer know that we shan't need a corpse speed-grown?" The man nodded and set about composing a text message on his phone, and Mrs. Goodman turned her attention back to Lyn. "But we *do* still have quite a bit to get through, so let us continue."

"Fine," said Lyn. A thought occurred to her, and she turned to Ms. Pumphrey. "Before I forget, Emma has a sleep every day after lunch, about noon." The other woman stared at her for a moment, then made a face.

"Norman, you can be the one to let Lady Farrier's office know they'll need to organize her entire schedule for the next few days around a three-year-old's nap time."

3

"Just be careful up there. Be sensible." That's what Lady Carmichael had said to them when she gave them permission to go up in the sky during the bombings. She had gazed at them over her desk, her green eyes serious. "If you really wish to go, then you must promise me this."

The warning had definitely been directed more to Usha and

Bridget than to Pamela. Usha and Pamela were both older, but Usha was an apprentice, like Bridget; Pamela was a full-fledged Pawn. Moreover, Pamela was the ideal Pawn. Utterly professional, she was a consummate operative, a decorated foot soldier in the Order of the Checquy. Without her, they would never have been allowed to go up in the night sky during a bombing attack.

Except that Pamela had not only *not* been careful or sensible, she had been as uncareful and unsensible as it was possible to be.

And now we don't know where she is. Is she alive? Is she injured? Has she gone mad?

Bridget was torn between concern for Pamela and concern for Usha and herself.

The Lady had not told them to avoid interfering in the bombing, nor had she warned them against being seen. She hadn't needed to. Such things went without saying. Admittedly, they went without saying because they had already been said many, many times.

All three of the women in the sky had been well aware of the repercussions of meddling in nonsupernatural matters. Even Usha, who had been an apprentice for only three years, knew. It was one of the first things drilled into the minds of fledgling Checquy agents:

Human minds are brittle. Human society is brittle. This world is brittle. If we interfere, we could break all three, very easily. And we do not want that.

The Checquy histories were littered with examples of Checquy operatives who had misused their powers on civilians: The man whose arm was instantly jellified when he slapped his wife in a drunken rage. The shopkeeper who was rude to a Pawn in Belfast and found himself suffering from an uncontrollable desire to swallow the contents of his cashbox. He ingested five shillings before the compulsion evaporated.

The punishment for such infractions varied. Long, complex investigations and tribunals would examine every detail of the occurrence. Some earned the culprit a slap on the wrist; some prompted far harsher punishments. But there was one type of offense for which no leniency was entertained, and that was interference in affairs of state.

In her head, Bridget ran through all the intricacies of the damnation that Pamela's actions would bring down upon them. She wanted to be sick. The Roman penalty for patricide had nothing on the

Checquy punishment for interfering in nonsupernatural affairs of state. It was grotesque, agonizing, and full of highly symbolic elements, including (but not limited to) the participation of the heraldic beasts of the monarch.

Where are they even going to get that many weasels? Bridget wondered weakly. *Let alone a lion and three leopards?*

There was no hope of mercy, no possibility of the punishment being commuted—that guarantee was one of the foundations that allowed the Checquy to function within the government. Every king, queen, minister (prime or otherwise), parliamentarian (rump or otherwise), prince, baron (robber or otherwise), lord (protector or otherwise), bishop (arch- or otherwise)—indeed, any individual with any earthly authority in the British Isles who had ever dealt with the Checquy had been of the unwavering opinion that Pawns and the Court of Checquy should not exert any influence on the work of government. They were to deal with the supernatural and the inexplicable and leave everything else alone.

As a result, powered operatives of the Checquy could not vote, could not serve in the nonsupernatural armed forces, and could not hold elected office (although, curiously, no authority figure had ever suggested that the Checquy's separation from government affairs should extend so far as its members not paying taxes).

Most important, operatives of the Checquy were absolutely forbidden to interfere with any military operations except under the direst circumstances. The possible repercussions of Checquy troops deploying in a war were too terrifying to entertain, no matter how swiftly it might end a conflict.

What have we done? Bridget brooded. *What will happen because of us?*

And what will happen to us? It was a shameful thought, but she couldn't help it. They touched down softly on the roof of Apex House. As soon as Bridget let go of Usha's hand, she felt gravity settle itself about her, and she staggered and almost fell to her knees. The madness of the night's events had left her utterly exhausted. She and Usha had not exchanged a word during the journey back from the site of the plane crash. They had seen no sign of Pamela, and Usha had taken them high above the city, as far from the fires and the smoke and the chaos as possible.

"Evenin', ladies." Bridget turned to see a guard approaching from the other end of the roof. He was a Retainer—one of the nonpowered employees of the Checquy. He was dressed in the overalls and helmet of an air-raid warden and carrying a thermos in one hand and the buff box of a gas mask loosely in the other. *I'll have to get another mask,* thought Bridget vaguely, remembering the loss of her own in that wild chase across the skies.

"Hello, Kenneth," said Bridget. It required all her strength to sound calm. "So I take it there were no bombs dropped on the house tonight?"

"Not here, miss, nah. But an incendiary landed on the office down the road, and there was a lot of running about. Alf and Roger nipped over to help where they could, so it's just me here at the moment. It's been an ugly night," said the sentry, shaking his head. "Very ugly. I'd much rather be up top like you three."

"Has Pamela returned, then?" asked Usha.

"Pawn Verrall hasn't signed in here," said Kenneth. "You all three went up together, right?"

"We got separated," Usha said.

Bridget regarded her sideways but didn't say anything. *Perhaps she's right. This isn't the person to report tonight's happenings to. We'll have to go to the duty officer. This is too big to let everyone know about.*

"If you don't mind my saying," remarked Kenneth, "you two ladies look like you could do with a rest."

"It's not been pleasant up there," said Bridget. "As you said, Kenneth, it's a bad night for London."

"And not a blessed thing that we can do about it," said the guard dolefully. "All we can do is keep calm and muddle on. Now, you two want to get downstairs and get something hot inside you."

"Good advice, Kenneth, thank you. Keep your eyes open," said Bridget.

"No fear, miss. Hitler won't get the drop on *this* house. God help him if he did!"

"Indeed," said Usha. "Good night."

"Good night," said Bridget. They went through a small metal door, clattered down a winding wooden staircase, and emerged into a darkened hallway. A small light was shining from a tiny booth built into the wall like a ticket taker's cubby. An older woman sat inside reading a battered novel. She looked up at them sourly.

"Sign in, please."

Bridget carefully entered her name, identity number, and the time—the wall clock said half past three in the morning—in the proffered ledger. A quick scan of the book confirmed that Pamela had not signed in. Usha filled in her details, and the woman counter-signed with a sniff. The two of them moved on down the corridor, their footsteps echoing on the linoleum. They passed many doors to many small offices, all of them dark and silent.

Are we honestly not going to talk about what happened? wondered Bridget. *How can she be so calm? We have just witnessed a disaster—a* deliberate *disaster—that has huge implications, and she doesn't seem at all bothered.* They came to stairs leading down into darkness and paused.

Bridget unholstered a flashlight and shone it in front of them. As they started down the stairs, she found herself chewing her lip, hard. Her hands were so sweaty that she kept having to transfer the torch so she could wipe her palms on the legs of her overalls.

"Bridget," said Usha suddenly, "I don't think we should tell anyone what Pamela did."

"*What?* Are you fucking mad?" In her shock, Bridget had forgotten her usual awe of the other woman, and Usha's eyebrows jumped up in surprise. A small part of Bridget's brain reflected that it was entirely possible no one had ever spoken to Usha like that in her whole life. The larger part of her brain did not care. "No, we absolutely have to report it!"

"Keep your voice down."

"Oh, please, there is no one else here," whispered Bridget furiously. "Everyone in the building is down in the vaults except for the guards, and they're not wandering the halls. Now, tell me what on earth you can be thinking."

"Look, perhaps Pamela came in through one of the ground-floor entrances and has already gone to the watch office or to Lady Carmichael and confessed everything," said Usha.

"You think she's alive?"

"You think she's dead?"

"I don't know *what* to think!" exclaimed Bridget. "I don't know if she's lying dead or injured on the street or flying around like a storm goddess smashing down other planes or if she's come to her senses and is currently downstairs being clapped in irons and muzzled."

"I see your point. But if she hasn't confessed, then we can't be the ones to turn her in."

"We absolutely can. We *have to.* I understand that she's your friend, but I think perhaps you don't understand the situation. You've been with the Checquy only a comparatively short time."

"It's been three years, thanks."

Yes, well, they picked me up when I was two days old, thought Bridget. "Usha, this isn't some little prank that we can keep secret, like finding a burglar and dropping him in the Serpentine or having a midnight feast on top of Big Ben or filling someone's bedroom with live baby eels."

"What? When did you do that?"

"Pamela has broken the law," continued Bridget. "She has used her powers to interfere in the war!"

"Yes, but what has she really done?" asked Usha. "In the grand scheme of things? She brought down a single plane. It does happen without our interference, you know. Not nearly enough, but it does happen."

"Do you seriously not see what this means?" Bridget said. "This is an escalation of the war. Supernatural escalation. It's opened the door to retaliation."

"From what? The vague possibility of some theoretical German version of the Checquy?" The Indian woman rolled her eyes.

"Is that so absurd?" asked Bridget incredulously.

"I realize that I have not learned everything about this world," said Usha, "but my understanding is that, as far as the Checquy are aware, there are only two other similar organizations on the planet: that American group—which, as I recall, *we* founded—"

"The Croatoan," said Bridget coldly. The Croatoan had been formed when the thirteen colonies became independent and some Checquy operatives there had elected to remain and protect their adopted homeland from supernatural threats.

"Yes," said Usha. "And those people in Iceland, the...the Yarnsmidders."

"The Járnsmiður," said Bridget.

"Yes, them. So, hundreds of years of exploration, the establishment of the British Empire, Checquy agents concealed within trading companies and missionary organizations across the world, near-total access to the intelligence resources of the British government...and yet the Checquy has only found one completely separate state-based organization."

"There was one other," said Bridget. "I suppose you haven't yet learned about the Grafters."

"I think perhaps I've heard them mentioned once or twice."

"They were Belgians, alchemists, working for the Spanish government a few centuries back. On the orders of their masters, they twisted themselves into monsters and came to invade Britain. It was hideous." Bridget took a deep breath. All the stories from her childhood were coming back to her, and she could feel her stomach knotting. "No normal army could ever stand against them. They laid waste to towns and fields. Civilians were slaughtered. The Checquy losses were horrible. We won, but only barely, and it nearly destroyed us. It shows what happens when nations send soldiers like us against soldiers like us."

"Fine," said Usha, and, perhaps sensing Bridget's agitation on the subject, she wisely elected not to pursue the topic of the Grafters. "But there is no reason to believe that any more exist."

"Except that *we* exist, Usha," said Bridget. "The Order of the Checquy. It's 1940, and, absurd as it may sound, we're a government agency of supernatural soldiers working out of Whitehall. It's *real*." She sighed. "Look, the very first lesson we are taught is the vital importance of secrecy. The Checquy spends huge amounts of money to keep this secret. People *die* to keep it. And if such an organization can exist here, a similar one can exist elsewhere—also as a well-kept secret. We can't take the chance of inadvertently causing a supernatural war."

"Bridget, do you realize that you are talking about an uneasy truce with an enemy that might not even exist? An enemy that might *never* have existed? Does that not strike you as completely absurd?"

"It strikes me as entirely the right thing to do," said Bridget.

Usha stared at her in bemusement. "I—but—you..." She closed her eyes and pinched the bridge of her nose. "All right, fine. Well, you know Pamela. She's been brought up the same way you have, in..." She paused for a moment as if carefully choosing her words. "She's utterly professional, utterly devoted to the Checquy. You know all the things she has gone through, and she has never broken her oath or strayed from her duty. She's stronger than both of us." Bridget nodded. "She would not have done what she did without a good reason."

"What reason could possibly be good enough?" asked Bridget.

"Well, if she shows up, we can ask her," said Usha.

The two women resumed their poorly lit trip down the stairs. The floors they passed got progressively nicer, carpeted rather than covered in linoleum or rubber. Portraits and landscapes were hung on the walls, and the occasional trophy head surveyed the halls, its tusks or antlers or eyeglasses catching the light of Bridget's torch.

When they finally reached the ground floor, they moved through wide office hallways with velvet settees waiting outside polished office doors and display cases that used to hold strange and beautiful curios from around the world but that were now empty. They passed through an enormous, dimly lit foyer where huge windows set high in the walls had been covered with thick blackout curtains. In another little cubby, another woman sat reading a novel. She looked up at the sound of their footsteps echoing off the stone walls and ceiling; when asked, she confirmed that Pawn Verrall had not entered through that door.

Above them, tapestries and banners hung silently. They walked through more hallways and finally came to another staircase, this one leading underground.

As they descended, the broad stairs quickly became less elegant. Marble gave way to concrete; concrete gave way to stone. The small glow of Bridget's torch was the only illumination, a bubble of dim light in the pitch-blackness. The steps dipped unevenly in the middle, worn by centuries of Checquy feet. Finally, they came to a large set of double doors that swung open easily under Usha's touch.

Light and noise flooded out, and the two women put their hands up to shield their eyes. Before them was a flurry of activity. The deep cellars of Apex House had been adapted to act as not only a shelter but the organization's watch office during the night bombings. The low barrel-vaulted ceilings had electric lights bolted onto them, their wires stapled to centuries-old masonry. People bustled about between desks. A fug of cigarette smoke hung in the air, and the smell of cabbage and beef wound its way through the room. The chambers were filled with the sounds of typewriters and people talking on bulky telephones.

A flimsy plywood wall had been erected between some massive stone pillars, and many maps had been glued up on it, tessellated to form a huge picture of the British Isles. As Bridget and Usha watched, a man in a suit hurried up and carefully inserted a pin into one map, marking a spot just outside the city of Bath.

"Miss Mangan, Miss Khorana," said a tall man stationed by the door. He jotted down their names and the time. "Welcome back to the ground. Finally. I'm certain you'll want a wash, a cup of tea, and then some sleep." The tone in his voice left no doubt that, for the good of all, the wash was the most pressing of the wants. Bridget looked down at herself and winced. Their boilersuits were coated in dust and soot, and when she gave herself a surreptitious sniff, she wanted to reel back from her own body. The clothes under the boilersuit had absorbed what smelled like a lifetime's worth of terrified stress-sweat as well as a strong odor of smoke.

"Yes, hello," said Usha. "Has Pawn Verrall come in?"

"I'm not certain," said the man, clearly taken aback by the briskness with which his comment regarding the wash had been brushed aside.

"Let's go to the duty officer first," suggested Bridget. *If Pamela has come in and confessed what she's done, then it will be painfully obvious because the floor will be littered with people having heart attacks.*

"Yes, good," said Usha, moving purposefully on into the cellars. Bridget gave the man an apologetic smile and followed. They weaved between desks, where Checquy operatives in sober clothes were busily working, despite the lateness of the hour. Heads were bowed over reports; phones were spoken into at varying volumes depending on the quality of the connection and whether the person on the other end of the line was being bombed. The war was continuing all over the world, and this had resulted in a torrent of reports of possible supernatural occurrences that the Checquy needed to scour carefully in order to identify which had to be investigated further.

A gentleman's suit full of moving verdant vines was seated at the Hong Kong desk. The mass of plants had not bothered to form a facsimile of a head, but multiple tendrils spilled out of the sleeves and between the lapels of the coat, typing, writing with pens, and flipping through papers. Bridget nodded to it and received a sort of rustling demi-bow of acknowledgment in return, but Usha kept her eyes firmly ahead.

Off to one side, a canteen had been set up. Massive urns of tea and Bovril stood brewing, and two men in camouflage were busily making sandwiches. A couple of office boys moved about distributing files and collecting documents when called. As far as Bridget could tell, the amount of activity was no greater than it had been when they'd left earlier that night.

There has definitely been no word of what Pamela did, she thought grimly. *But does that mean she hasn't told them? Or that she hasn't returned yet? Does it mean she's dead? Or hurt?* They stood aside for an old woman who came pushing a tea trolley. She smiled at them in thanks, and red light shone out of her mouth; Bridget could see that her teeth were glowing rubies. Several people were gathered near the duty officer's desk, talking anxiously.

"Oh Christ. This does not look good," Bridget murmured to Usha.

"Not necessarily" was Usha's reply. "There's no sign of Pamela."

"Maybe that's because they've already imprisoned her. Oi, Petey!" She reached out and collared one of the office boys who was trotting past.

"Ow! Miss Mangan!"

"Ah, you're fine," said Bridget. "What's going on over there?"

"Dunno," said the boy, rubbing his neck. "A few minutes ago they got called over to Pawn Kenward's desk. I suppose word came in of something big."

"Petey, you know Pawn Verrall, right?"

"The Lady's aide? Course."

"Have you seen her about? Was she part of that meeting?"

"Dunno." The boy shrugged.

"All right, ta," said Bridget. She and Usha exchanged looks. "I suppose we'd better go over." They moved warily toward the group. A semicircle of people stood around the watch desk, blocking the women's view of its occupant.

"Do you think we ought to telephone the Lord and Lady?" one woman said.

"And what would they do?" asked a man. "The bombing is still going on. They wouldn't be able to come here to do anything."

"Shall we rouse Bishop Pringle?" asked another woman. "He's asleep down in the crypt."

Oh God, they're talking about waking up the Court, thought Bridget, feeling faint. *It has to be about Pamela.* She snuck a look at Usha, who had gone very still. *We are in so much trouble.*

"We need to start mobilizing troops now," a man said.

I think I'm going to be sick.

"Before the telephone went down, the Bath office advised that there'd been no bombings there, so a team was dispatched to the site immediately," said the unseen occupant of the desk in the tone of a man who was in no mood to have his people panicking. "The Bath Barghests can be activated if necessary." Bridget flinched at the mention of the Barghests, the elite commandos of the Checquy, dedicated warriors who were trained by the best that the British Empire could produce. For them to be called out meant that things had gotten very, *very* bad.

"Plus," the unseen person continued, "they have that man who does that thing with the lava. So I think that we can all stop pissing on ourselves and each other and be satisfied with that for now. Agreed?" There was a murmur of general, if somewhat cowed, agreement. "All right, back to work, then."

They're not talking about Pamela at all! thought Bridget, so relieved that her knees almost buckled. *It's just something apocalyptic happening in Bath! Either she hasn't been here or she hasn't told them!*

Oh, shit.

That means she might really be dead... and it's up to us to tell them.

"Of course it had to happen at Bath," one woman said as the people dispersed. "That blinking city. Honestly, I'm almost astounded when a manifestation turns out *not* to be there."

"That's why they have their own team of Barghests," replied another woman. "And everyone posted there gets an extra two weeks of holidays each year."

"Ah, Miss Khorana, Miss Mangan," said the duty officer. "You have something to tell me." Pawn Kenward was a large man with spectacles, wearing the world's most carefully tailored suit to accommodate the double row of jagged blades of ice that sprouted up the length of his spine and along his shoulders.

"We have something to tell you?" repeated Bridget weakly. Pawn Kenward regarded her over his glasses, then stood up from the stool he was obliged to sit on (he would have shredded the back of any chair). The glittering, razor-sharp blades on his shoulders flexed and caught the light. A faint mist curled off the ice.

"You've been out in the London sky during the bombings, you return hours late, you look as if someone demolished a house while you were sleeping in it, and you come straight to my desk. You have something to tell me. Now report."

"Yes, sir," said Bridget automatically. She'd instinctively stood at attention but her stomach was twisting madly.

All her life, she'd been trained to keep secrets from everyone *except* the Checquy. They were her family, her army. You could hope to survive against the terrors you faced only if you knew that you could trust your comrades implicitly. Now a superior officer was calling for information—had ordered her to brief him—and against every instinct she had, she was hesitating.

Plus, there was the horror, a remnant of schoolroom days, she felt at the idea of informing on her friend. Bridget had been in Lady Carmichael's household for only a few months, but she'd grown very fond of both Pamela and Usha.

And now, because of them, I have to worry about whether to report a crime. A huge crime—possibly treason! And is it treason if I don't report it?

Usha was looking at her with wide, pleading eyes. It was the first time that Bridget could recall her seeming vulnerable.

"The bombing has been very bad, sir," she said finally. "As bad as we've seen. Major fires." Pawn Kenward's face grew bitter, and he closed his eyes. "Whitehall hasn't been hit too hard, although I expect you heard about the incendiary down the road from here?" He nodded without opening his eyes. "It seemed to be all right when we came, but the East End was a nightmare."

"Where is Pawn Verrall?" he asked.

Oh God. She stared at him.

"We were separated, sir," Usha said. "It's very rough up there."

"Thank you, ladies," he said. "I expect she'll be in soon enough. Now, go away. Get some sleep. And if you see Elaine, send her over, would you, please? I want to take off my coat, and she's the only one who can undo all the buttons on the back without cutting herself to ribbons."

"Yes, sir," said Bridget. Usha nodded and they moved away, deeper into the vaults.

"Thank you," said Usha quietly.

"I can't believe I did that," said Bridget, dizzy with horror. "It's going to be so much worse now when it all comes out. Let's find out if she's here and get some answers before I decide to go back and tell Pawn Kenward everything."

"If she's here, then whatever her state of mind, she's probably gone for a wash," Usha said. Bridget nodded, and they moved toward the shelter section of the vaults.

The shelters had been established on the orders of Lady Carmichael well before the outbreak of the war and long before other such measures were being instituted around the country. There had been some derisory snorts when they were set up, derision that had quickly evaporated once bombs actually started falling. Apex House had been built with an eye toward the very real chance of its occupants being attacked (quite possibly by the good citizens of London), and so it was far more fortified than the usual government offices, making it quite desirable for those operatives willing to spend the night at their workplace.

However, operatives could not bring their civilian families to the highly classified interior of Apex House, so there were many who used the sheltering options taken by millions of regular citizens. They slept in Anderson shelters buried in their backyards or in Morrison shelters bolted together in their dining rooms, or they took refuge in cellars, in cupboards under stairs, in public shelters, or in the Underground.

And of course, there were Pawns whose abilities afforded them different options entirely. Every night, one London secretary wove a mesh of impenetrable hardened air around the inside of her bedroom that would keep herself and her canary safe even if her lodgings received a direct hit. At bedtime, the Checquy's chief quartermaster oozed her way into the heart of a large rock in the churchyard across the street from her house. The chaplain of Apex House spent each night at the bottom of the men's bathing pond on Hampstead Heath, rising up to the surface very early each morning and then walking across the heath to his home to get ready for the day.

Until that night, Bridget, Pamela, and Usha had been sleeping (or at least *trying* to sleep) through the raids in the very nicely appointed cellar-shelter of Lady Carmichael's house. Still, they were familiar with the layout of these vaults, and they headed for the large section that had been set aside for ablutions. It was screened off and partitioned with green canvas walls and strictly divided by gender. There were different sections for apprentices, Pawns, Retainers, the Barghests, the Court, and the maintenance staff. A male and a female attendant were always present, regardless of the hour. The facilities were primitive, although it was generally believed that the sections for the maintenance staff were by far the most pleasant. No one had ever dared enter, however, and risk incurring their wrath.

"Good morning, ladies," said the female attendant. "It looks like you've had a strenuous night."

"I have not been so exhausted since the day I was born," said Bridget. "And someone else was doing all the work on that occasion."

"Well, then, it's a wash you'll need. And some fresh clothes, and then you can toddle on down to the undercroft and have a nice sleep."

"That sounds very pleasant, thank you," said Usha. "First, can you please tell me, have you seen Pawn Verrall this evening?"

"I don't believe she's come in yet," said the attendant. "But if she had, she'd be in the Pawns' section."

"Of course she would be," said Usha with a sigh. Bridget was able to muster up mild amusement at the sight of Usha dealing with the unfamiliar experience of being forbidden to enter a place she wished to go. "Well, if you see her, could you let her know that we'd like to meet with her?" The attendant said she would and led them to the female apprentices' section.

"Each of you has a little curtained-off area to have a nice cat-wash," said the attendant cheerfully. "I'll just fetch some cans of hot water."

"What's a cat-wash?" Usha asked Bridget quietly.

"A kettle of hot water in the bowl—you wash your face, then your neck and shoulders, and you move on down until you reach your ankles, then you stand in the bowl to wash your feet," explained Bridget, who had taken plenty of them in the course of her life.

"But no actual cats are involved," said Usha, looking relieved. "Don't they wash that way in India?"

"Something similar," said Usha, "although we don't call it that, at least not in my family. Besides, my father embraced British baths very early on, so we had proper tubs in the house."

"I'm sure," said Bridget.

"And then always a proper massage afterward."

"Uh-huh."

"Although maybe the servants took cat-baths," mused Usha. "But how do I wash my hair?"

"Probably not very successfully," said Bridget grimly. "I expect she'll pour water over your hair if you ask. I doubt there will be a massage, though."

"War truly is hell," said Usha. The two of them were sufficiently filthy, however, that even the cat-wash felt good, and Bridget was glad to scrub her face with a flannel and let the smell of rose-scented soap replace, or at least dilute, the stink that was wrapped around her.

"Miss Mangan?" came the voice of the attendant at the curtain.

"Hmm?"

"Pawn Verrall has just come in."

"Oh!"

Thank God she's alive.

Oh God. She's alive. What will happen now?

"Thank you!" Bridget hurriedly finished her wash and teetered for a moment on her feet. The three of them had brought overnight bags to the shelter, but despite how much she wanted to slide into her nightgown and robe, she hurriedly donned one of the smart little suits that Lady Carmichael had bought for her, along with her softest cotton gloves.

She rushed out of the bathing area, hopping as she pulled her second shoe on. She scanned the room and saw Pamela across the way, by the entrance. Usha was with her, fully dressed—she must not have lingered like Bridget, just scrubbed herself down and then waited by the entrance for her friend.

Bridget moved toward them, then stopped. Usha was talking intently to Pamela, who stood there, silent. The Pawn was covered in dust, and although she looked icy calm, there were tear trails smeared through the dirt on her face. She was nodding dully, and when she looked over at Bridget, her eyes were unreadable.

Then Pamela started walking toward the watch officer's desk. She moved slowly, painfully, as if she had just finished running several marathons. That made sense. Some supernatural powers required no exertion at all to activate, but many drew upon the wielder's own energy. Bridget had never heard of Pamela engaging in the sort of action she'd seen that night, but she could well believe it was utterly exhausting.

Bridget watched as her friend spoke to Pawn Kenward. She was braced for him to leap up in shock, for ice to erupt up out of the floor and hold Pamela captive. Instead, he nodded seriously as she spoke. Then Pamela turned and walked weakly toward the baths.

Nothing else happened. Pawn Kenward had turned his attention back to the reports.

She didn't tell him! Bridget thought. She looked over at Usha, who returned her gaze levelly. *What did Usha tell her?* Her fists clenched as she walked toward the other woman, and there were so many emotions swirling in her that she didn't know what she was going to say or do. Usha stood calmly watching her approach.

I could hit her, Bridget thought. *I could lay her out flat.* "Well?" she asked finally.

"I told her that we'd said nothing except that we'd gotten separated up in the skies," Usha said quietly.

Bridget stared at her. "What did *she* say?" asked Bridget through gritted teeth.

"She didn't say anything," Usha said.

"So what will happen?" Bridget asked. Usha shrugged. "I *need* answers. I need an explanation." Usha nodded. There were some empty desks nearby, and they sat at them, waiting for Pamela to emerge. When she finally came out, clean, her wet hair pulled up, she still moved stiffly, but the old Pamela was back behind her eyes.

"Hello," she said warily. "I expect we need to have a bit of a conversation."

"Where can we talk?" asked Usha. "There is no privacy in this place."

"The games room," said Pamela. "No one will be there at this hour."

In a fit of possibly deluded optimism on someone's part, a section of the vaults had been set aside for the purposes of recreation during the bombing raids. Early in the evenings, you might see Pawns and Retainers there, but anyone off shift at this point had long ago gone to sleep in the undercroft below, so it was as secluded a place as they were going to find.

Behind thick curtains was a lounge with a billiard table, a couple of dartboards, and several scrounged tables at which one could play a selection of board games or deal out a deck of worryingly singed playing cards. A gramophone sat in the corner by some sofas, and a half-completed Victorian-era jigsaw puzzle of a scene of somewhere along the Thames dominated one table. A chess set had been left in midgame with a note saying *Kindly do not disturb.* Bridget noted that other people had appended comments and suggested moves to the end of the note. At one point, an argument had broken out in increasingly emphatic handwriting, and additional pieces of paper had been stuck to the bottom of the note to accommodate the debate. Two duplicate boards had been set up at other tables, apparently to allow demonstrations of the proposed strategies, and additional written debates had broken out there as well.

"Well," said Bridget. "What will we play?"

Usha looked at her as if she were demented, but Pamela was nodding thoughtfully. "We'll need a cover if someone walks in."

"Dominoes," suggested Bridget. The three of them sat and laid out a careful pretense of a game.

"Now," said Usha firmly, "explain."

The Pawn did not take her eyes off the dominoes in front of her.

"Pamela?" prompted Bridget.

"Usha said that you didn't tell the watch officer," said Pamela. "Thank you."

"Thank you?" repeated Bridget. *"Thank you? Thank you* is not good enough! *Thank you* is not what you say to someone who has betrayed everything in her life to cover up *your* betrayal of everything in her life! You know what you say to that person? You give her a bloody explanation, and you make it damn good!"

"I don't have an explanation for you," said Pamela quietly.

"Oh," said Bridget, deflating slightly. She waited, but no further response appeared to be forthcoming. Pamela just stared at her dominoes. "So, what was — why did you do that?"

"I'm afraid I can't tell you," said Pamela. At this, she looked up at them, and Bridget saw a deep haunted sadness in her eyes.

"Why not? Was it a mission?" asked Bridget. At the thought, she felt a tremendous weight lift off her chest. "Did Lady Carmichael order you to do it? Because if she did, that's a different story."

"No, it wasn't a mission," said Pamela. She looked up when Bridget made a whimpering sound of pain. "Are you all right?"

"Did something heavy just drop onto my chest?"

"What? Look, Lady Carmichael doesn't know anything about it. And I'm asking you to please not tell her. Please don't tell anyone."

"Pamela!" exclaimed Usha.

"So you acted on your own," said Bridget. "You interfered in the war."

"Yes," said Pamela, her voice wavering a little. She put her hand to her eyes for a moment and looked as if she would break down in tears.

"You know what this means!" Bridget said to Pamela. She wanted to shout, to scream, but she didn't dare. "For all of us! How in God's name could you be so...so..." All the words hung unspoken in the air: *Stupid. Reckless. Dangerous. Irresponsible. Insane.* Her friend looked at her, silent.

"I'm sorry," Pamela said finally.

Bridget and Usha could only stare at her helplessly. Bridget was completely taken aback by Pamela's lack of an explanation.

"Did it make a difference?" asked Usha finally.

"No," said Pamela softly. Very deliberately, she placed a domino down on the table.

"Will you be doing it again?" asked Bridget warily.

"No, I won't do it again." She looked up at them. "I promise."

"No one needs to know," said Usha to Bridget, and Bridget could not tell if she was asking or commanding.

"How can you say that? This has massive implications!"

"No," said Usha. "There were no witnesses. Even if your worst nightmares came to pass, Bridget, and there is some sort of German Checquy that works for the Nazi Party"—her patronizing tone made Bridget want to slap her—"and they are only waiting for a justification to attack, they won't know. After all, everyone in the plane was killed. You saw the damage. No one could have survived that."

"*She* killed them!" exclaimed Bridget.

"They were enemy combatants," Usha pointed out.

"That doesn't matter! In fact, it makes it worse! We cannot involve ourselves in the war like that. And she killed them."

"You don't know that for certain," said Usha. "The crash might have killed them."

"*She* crashed the plane!"

"If people are going to take part in a war, there is a very real possibility that their plane will crash," said Usha in a reasonable tone. "They have to accept that."

"Yes, but not because a sweet young English rose lands on their windshield at twelve thousand feet and hits them with the sky!"

"Are you honestly taking the side of the Nazis bombing this city?" asked Pamela.

"No! Of course not."

"Ah, excellent!" came a hearty voice at the door. They looked around to see a distinguished-looking older man entering the lounge wearing silk pajamas and a magnificent viridian dressing gown.

"Bishop Pringle!" exclaimed Pamela. "Good even—morning." They all stood hurriedly.

"I didn't think there'd be anyone in the games lounge at this hour. Ladies, shall we make a foursome for whist?"

Bridget woke up and wished she hadn't. Her head ached with the dull pain of not enough sleep, and as the events of the night before cleared their throats in her head, she made a little whimpering sound. Bishop Pringle had kept the three women playing whist for a full hour and a half, until Bridget had fallen asleep in her seat and her head dropped onto the table with a humiliating and painful thud. When they were finally permitted to shuffle down to the undercroft, they were all so exhausted that there was no more conversation about Pamela's actions.

Did we decide we would cover for her? thought Bridget fuzzily. That was her vague understanding. Pamela had promised never to do it again and asked them to keep it secret, and they hadn't said no.

She sat up and looked around blearily. The dim undercroft stretched off into the darkness; it was filled with rows of camp beds, but she seemed to be the only person there. Everyone else had apparently roused themselves for the day, and those Checquy staff regularly on night shift had probably gone back to their own homes to sleep. Along the walls were wooden partitions that had been put up to give high-level operatives their own private rooms, and a gigantic curtain separated the men's sleeping quarters from the women's.

And yet, for all the signs of habitation, the place still felt like a centuries-old subbasement that had served, at various times, as a crypt for the corpses of the honored fallen, a granary, an unauthorized priest hole, a morgue, a nursery, a mathematician hole, a gymnasium, the office of the Checquy Ethics Committee, an amateur mushroom farm, a battleground between soldiers of the Checquy and an unexpectedly sentient and mobile mushroom crop, a prison, an armory, the residence of a particularly eccentric Lord, a chapel dedicated to the illegal worship of an unknowing clerk in the accounting section, an archive, another battleground between soldiers of the Checquy and some unexpectedly resilient (and this time rather vengeful) mushrooms, a studio for a life-drawing class, then a gymnasium again before it had been hastily modified to serve as a shelter beneath the equally hastily modified wartime headquarters. The centuries of activity had left their mark everywhere, but especially in the air, where the traces of all the previous occupants combined to form the smell of old, dead history, with a strong undertone of morels.

Floating over all of it was the more recent and unmistakable smell of unattended-to chamber pots. It was a point of some resentment amongst many of the staff that there were no actual flushing toilets in the vaults or the undercroft. Anyone spending the night in the shelter was issued a china chamber pot or, or for the latecomers, a wooden bucket. It was the responsibility of the most junior apprentices to check under the cots each morning and empty and clean any soiled containers—part of the fine British tradition of building character in those destined for power by making them do base and degrading tasks. Bridget knew that the assumption of chamber-pot duty was a frequent stake in bets among the apprentices.

A few chemical toilets were clustered in a corner behind a hanging tarpaulin in an effort to quarantine really objectionable smells. Personally, Bridget was not overly fussed by the odor—for her first fifteen years, she had lived in homes with outhouses, but indoor plumbing was an amenity that it was very easy to get accustomed to.

It's still better than the Cabinet war rooms, she reminded herself. *They only get that claustrophobic half-height cellar to sleep in.* She had visited the government command center a couple of times, attending Lady Carmichael as she met with the Prime Minister, and she had been aghast at the cramped conditions of the facility, hastily tucked in under some office building over on the Horse Guards Road.

Her wristwatch showed that it was a little past ten in the morning, definitely far too early to be awake after the night she'd had, but that meant she was significantly late for her duties. *I'm going to guess that Lady Carmichael gave orders to let all of us sleep,* she thought as she hurriedly pulled on her shoes and gloves. *Otherwise, the attendants would have turned me out of bed and onto the flagstones before the sun rose.* The problem was that both Pamela and Usha tended to be early risers, even after a late night of flight and treason, while Bridget generally had to set three alarm clocks to ensure she would wake up on time.

She'd been too sleepy to change out of her suit before flopping down on her assigned cot and was well aware of how rumpled she looked now as she walked up the steps out of the undercroft. The vaults were largely empty, with most of the work having shifted upstairs. The Checquy was a twenty-four-hour operation, but it was much bigger during the daytime, far too big to cram into the cellars. The only officers still there were packing up the canteen or updating the massive blackboards that showed the status of operations around the empire. That way, when night fell and the watch office opened, the transition could be relatively seamless.

Bridget paused to check on the problem that had broken out in Bath and saw that it had been resolved with four civilian deaths, two Checquy maimings, and the total petrification of a hectare and a half of grass, hedges, and trees, including seven large oak trees that would need to be removed before a public road could be reopened, as people would surely notice the new hundred-foot-tall statues. Abruptly realizing that she was famished, Bridget hastily grabbed a few pieces of cold toast and rushed upstairs.

The lobby of Apex House was bustling with the usual crowd. Several of them nodded to her in recognition as she hurried into the packed lift and wedged herself in amongst the taller people, who were all dressed in distinctly unrumpled suits. She could feel their eyes on her, so she elected not to keep eating her toast but to hold it in an awkwardly reverent way, as if it were highly classified, possibly supernatural toast that had been urgently requested for delivery to the executive floor.

There was only one other person in the lift when it reached the top: Pawn Gregory, a tall man in his forties who oversaw much of the internal security of the Checquy's London facilities. As the lift doors opened, he regarded with a raised eyebrow the toast that was starting to wilt in Bridget's hand.

"Miss Mangan."

"Pawn Gregory," she replied, unwilling to be cowed.

"After you."

"Thank you, sir."

By the time she reached Lady Carmichael's suite of offices, the toast had been consumed, and she'd stopped in the ladies' room to wash her face, wipe off her gloves, and despair of her hair. In the suite, Pamela was going over the day's schedule with the Lady's secretaries. The doors to the Lady's personal office were closed.

"Ah, good morning, Miss Mangan," said Pamela. Her back was straight and her hair was brushed. There was no hint in her demeanor that the previous night had been anything unusual, but there were large dark patches under her eyes.

"Good morning, Pawn Verrall." In the office, it was titles and formality. "I'm sorry I'm late."

"Not at all, it was a long night. And then we got caught by Bishop Pringle." The secretaries all made sympathetic noises. "You can go in." Bridget nodded obediently and opened the doors. She blinked at the sudden brightness. The heavy bulletproof curtains had been drawn back, and light streamed in through windows that had asterisks of tape stuck on them.

Lady Carmichael's office was large and impressive, but it always felt very empty, with barren walls and a few unoccupied niches. One of the secretaries had explained that there had been several valuable French Impressionist paintings and some lovely sculptures in the office, but they were removed and sent to the Lady's country house for safekeeping once the war began.

Behind her desk, Lady Sara Carmichael was talking on the telephone. A slim woman in her forties, she wore her black hair elegantly arranged in a chignon and had on an expensively tailored suit.

Carmichael was not actually a member of the British aristocracy; she was one of the two heads of the Checquy, and Lady was effectively her military rank. The titles of Checquy's executive hierarchy were based on chess pieces, with the two Rooks running domestic operations, the Chevaliers overseeing international operations, the Bishops providing supervision and direct administration, and the Lord and Lady holding power—equally—over the whole organization.

There were some who felt that such archaic nomenclature had no place in a modern organization, but the weight of tradition was too heavy to move. Besides, it served as an important reminder for members of the Checquy that they could be sacrificed, especially the Pawns, who were sent out into the field with every expectation of their being removed from the game permanently.

As Lady of the Order of the Checquy, Sara Carmichael wielded astounding authority and commanded hundreds of operatives around the globe, most of them possessed of supernatural abilities and the rest of them just very, very good at what they did. She managed to do all this while also maintaining her roles as a prominent member of society (she was the owner of a giant mercantile business), the mother of four, and overseer of the education and well-being of two Checquy apprentices: Bridget and Usha.

Still on the phone, she smiled at Bridget—who nodded in respectful greeting—and gestured toward the conference table at the side of the room. Usha was already there, reading over documents.

Bridget padded over to the table, where multiple files had neatly been laid out. Each morning, the Lady's office received summaries of the previous twenty-four hours' major events, both supernatural and otherwise. Bridget sat down next to Usha.

"Morning," she said.

"Good morning," said Usha tightly. The door opened and Pamela entered. She placed a few notes on the desk for the Lady's perusal, and Carmichael scanned them quickly and nodded without ending the call. Pamela joined the other two at the table. Bridget noticed that she still moved painfully.

"Are you all right?" Bridget asked the Pawn in a low tone. "Did you not sleep?"

"I slept like the dead," Pamela said quietly. "Only just managed to get into the office before the Lady. But I'm still drained from last night."

Bridget nodded. She waited, hoping that Pamela might say something more about the activities of the previous night, but the Pawn was silent. In fact, both Pamela and Usha were staring at her without speaking.

"What?" asked Bridget in a low tone. Pamela flicked her eyes toward the Lady in warning, then wordlessly slid over a purple file. It was thick, containing as it did reports on the latest supernatural occurrences from all around the empire. The section on England was first, of course, and most of that was taken up with the manifestation at Bath, but there had been a scattering of other events.

"Page four," muttered Usha. Bridget narrowed her eyes and then turned to the section on London.

Incident Report

Fatalities (human):

- Mrs. Margaret Oakley (age sixty-seven) of 32 Roper Lane, Moon Ditch, Canley

- Mr. Peter Jinks (age thirty-five) and Mrs. Edith Jinks (age thirty-three) of 34 Roper Lane, Moon Ditch, Canley

At about 6:45 a.m., Martin Herriot, an air-raid warden, observed that the back doors of two adjacent houses had been left open, revealing lights burning within. He proceeded first to no. 32 to warn the occupant(s) they were violating the blackout. Upon entry, he discovered the corpse of Mrs. Margaret Oakley on the floor of the kitchen, her body charred but her clothes undamaged.

Mr. Herriot shouted to see if there was anyone else in the house and received no answer. He left and proceeded to no. 34. He noted that the door appeared to have been forced open. He shouted, received no response, and entered. He discovered the body of Mrs. Edith Jinks in the hallway in a similar condition to that of Mrs. Oakley. Part of her face was so badly charred that it had crumbled into ash on the floor.

Mr. Herriot departed the premises and repaired to the nearest warden's post to report what he had seen. The warden on duty, who had received a standard class C Checquy briefing for dealing with unusual circumstances, alerted the authorities, and a Checquy investigation team was dispatched to the site.

The team found the charred body of Mr. Peter Jinks in an upstairs bedroom. There were signs of a struggle, and the room appeared to have been partially ransacked, with drawers pulled out and clothing rifled through.

A preliminary autopsy has revealed that the victims were burned from the inside out. *That combined with the largely undamaged condition of their clothes indicates a nonnatural factor.*

Known supernatural elements: Initial research has revealed no record, historical or recent, of a phenomenon or individual causing such an ignition pattern except for the currently active Pawn Charlotte Taylor (forty-six).

It has been confirmed that at the time of the incident, Pawn Taylor was asleep with her husband, two children, cat, and two rabbits in an Anderson shelter in the back garden of their home in Edinburgh. We have also confirmed that the evening before, she departed the Edinburgh office for home at 5:30, and she arrived back at work the next day at 8:05 a.m. This is judged to be insufficient time to travel to London, engage in seemingly motiveless murders of individuals to which she has no known connection, return to her home in Edinburgh, then commence a day at the office.

Her involvement in these deaths is deemed unlikely.

Working hypothesis: A burglar, taking advantage of the air raid to rob homes, was surprised by Mrs. Oakley, who is known to have eschewed seeking shelter during air raids in favor of falling asleep in an armchair in her kitchen. The situation may have ignited the burglar's abilities, and he killed Mrs. Oakley.

It is possible that the violence of the ignition served to unhinge the burglar mentally. He then proceeded to the Jinks residence next door and set about robbing that house. Neighbors report that during air raids, the Jinkses took shelter in a cupboard under their stairs.

It is surmised that Mr. Jinks, a stoker, emerged from shelter upon hearing the intruder, went upstairs, confronted him, and was killed. His body was burned so intensely that it was partially fused to the floor.

Mrs. Jinks was killed after her husband. It is not known whether the burglar sought her out or she confronted him.

Actions under way:
A tracking team of four has been established under Pawn Sofia Abravanel out of the Rookery.

At the time of this writing, a Checquy forensic team is examining both houses for any clues about the identity of the killer. It is not yet apparent what, if anything, was stolen from either house.

Given the similarity of the burn signature to the abilities of Pawn Taylor, some familial connection cannot be ruled out. Pawn Taylor has only two children, both of whom are under the age of twelve. The Checquy acquisition records will be examined to see if she has any blood relations living in London.

Well, all right, thought Bridget. *It's unpleasant, but it's not the worst thing I've ever read. It wouldn't even be the worst thing I've ever seen.* Looters were an ongoing problem during the Blitz, with some fools greedy enough to risk the bombs for the chance to pillage houses. *They've got a team on it; I expect they'll track this burglar down and either kill him or recruit him. So why are Pamela and Usha looking like they might throw up on the table?* She raised her eyebrows at them and shrugged slightly.

The two women exchanged glances, and Usha silently pushed over the red folder that contained the report from the War Office on the previous night's war-related attacks in the United Kingdom. Bridget opened it and scanned the details, wincing at the figures of estimated bombs dropped, buildings destroyed, fires ignited, lives lost. And then, at the end, there it was:

Crashed:

One (1) Luftwaffe Heinkel He 111 aircraft in residential area, eastern Moon Ditch in the London district of Canley.

Four houses brought down by the crash, but with no explosions, indicating that the aircraft had already dropped its entire bomb payload. Preliminary investigation shows minimal damage from ack-ack. Engineers have identified no damage that would result in the downing of the aircraft, although the condition of the wreckage makes effective examination difficult. Possible cause: mechanical difficulties.

Of special concern is the number of bodies found on the aircraft. The He 111 carries a crew of five (5), but only four (4) corpses, all strapped into their seats, were aboard. The navigator/bombardier/nose gunner — a crucial

member of the crew without whom no bombing mission could be flown —
was missing.

The local constabulary have been alerted and are on the lookout for the
missing crewman.

4

"Y ou want to send me to *boarding school?*" asked Lyn.

The signing of the legal documents had taken roughly forever. Before she commenced, she'd had to submit to an alcohol breath
test and a saliva drug test. She'd signed, she'd initialed, she'd pressed
her fingers against seals and been recorded reading parts of the documents aloud. Twice, she'd been obliged to don some sort of official
legal lipstick and close her mouth around folded paper. Three times,
she'd been obliged to pause in the reading and signing to take a
multiple-choice test to ensure she understood all the details of what
she was agreeing to.

And now, having blindly committed her life to this "Checquy
Group," she was learning about the place they would be sending her.

"In many ways, it's the best boarding school in the world," said
Mrs. Goodman.

"Putting aside the fact that I am thirty-five, is it going to connect
me to the future elite and allow me to forge invaluable personal connections that will give me advantages in business and politics?"

"I'm afraid that's not one of the ways in which it's the best boarding school in the world," conceded Mrs. Goodman. "But it is a place
where we can help you and train you in as safe an environment as
possible."

"And it's an actual boarding school? One with children?"

"Yes."

"And I have to go immediately?"

"Tonight."

"So what am I going to tell my husband?" asked Lyn.

"I have a script here," said the Checquy lawyer, drawing a folder out of a case. "In a moment, you'll call him and explain that during your examination, you were diagnosed with a serious medical condition, unconnected to the fire in your house, and you're being moved to a specialist clinic to receive intensive treatment that will be paid for entirely by the National Health Service and an established charity trust."

"What medical condition?" asked Lyn suspiciously.

The Checquy lawyer shrugged. "I never remember the name. It's obscure, something to do with bone marrow, and it can be crippling or even fatal if left untreated," she said. "And if I recall correctly, it's hereditary, so there will be a good reason to examine your daughter later."

"And I'll be at this boarding school for, what, a few weeks?"

"Well...no. I expect you'll be a while longer. But hopefully after a few weeks, you'll have enough control to meet with your husband safely. For the moment, though, do you think you can successfully lie to him over the phone?"

"Please. My ability to do so is one of the key pillars of our successful marriage."

The phone call to Richard was exactly as exhausting and stressful as one would expect, made all the more so by Mrs. Goodman's staring fixedly at her throughout. Lyn spent most of the call convincing him not to drive immediately to the hospital, then she was obliged to spell out the lengthy Latin name of her assumed disease so that he could read up on it. He offered to call the library in the morning and let them know why she wouldn't be in, but Mrs. Goodman had already advised her that one of their doctors would be delivering a letter to her employers.

"I'll call you tomorrow, my love," said Lyn. "Kiss Emma for me."

"I will, babe," said Richard. "You focus on getting well, and I'll take care of everything here. I love you." He hung up and Lyn wiped her eyes.

"Nicely done," said Mrs. Goodman. "Now I want you to put this on." She held up a bulky hooded silver coverall.

"Dare I ask?"

"It's seventy-five percent Nomex, and twenty-five percent stainless-steel thread," said the lawyer. "The steel makes the suit into a Faraday cage. It's what the workers wear when they're crawling about on power lines. In their case, it keeps the electricity flowing safely around their bodies. We're hoping that if you create electricity, it will stay in the suit."

"If I 'create electricity.'" Lyn snorted as she struggled into the thick suit. "That sounds so ridiculous."

"Tell that to your kitchen," said Mrs. Goodman. "As it is, we don't yet know exactly how your power works." She had reached into her briefcase and pulled out a pair of rubber gloves, and she was now putting them on. "But if something *does* happen, it's always better to have covered the painfully obvious. Now, give me your fitness tracker and your mobile phone."

"They're both fried," warned Lyn.

"Regardless," said the lawyer. "From now on, you're not to use any commercial device that has GPS capabilities."

"Why not?"

"We don't want you to be trackable by anyone. At some point, you'll be issued a Checquy-approved phone." She handed Lyn a receipt for the items she'd taken and stowed them away in a couple of zip-up pouches. "We'll reimburse you for the cost of these. Oh, be sure to pull down the veil."

"Tracked by whom?" asked Lyn, as she dragged a fine metal mesh over her face and gingerly snapped it onto the catches on the collar of the suit.

"Any parties that aren't us," said Mrs. Goodman, waving her hand vaguely. "Other governments, the internet, anyone. After all, you are now a government secret. You are classified."

"Yes, I feel so discreet," said Lyn, "dressed as I am like a beekeeper from space. How do you propose to get me out of here looking like this?" There was a knock at the door; it opened to reveal Pumphrey, Smalls, and a hospital gurney.

"We're taking you out to the loading dock as a corpse," said Mrs. Goodman. "A corpse that then gets a long ride in a Rolls. Hop up, and we'll put a sheet over you."

"Exactly how long a ride are we talking?" asked Lyn. "Because this suit is incredibly hot."

"Don't worry, the Nomex is fire-retardant."

But wouldn't that just keep the fire in with me? Lyn thought but did not say. She doubted the answer to that question would reassure her.

A long car was waiting for them, looking mildly appalled at being parked so near the dumpsters. Lyn fumbled her way in through the door, unwieldy in the Faraday suit, and ended up sprawled on the floor while Mrs. Goodman slid in smoothly and took up residence on the rear-facing seat. Lyn levered herself up onto the slippery leather seat and, with difficulty, fumbled the seat belt over her bulky besuited self.

"We'll be driving through the night," said Mrs. Goodman, opening a laptop and beginning to type. "You may want to get some sleep."

It was easy advice to take, even in the humid confines of the Faraday suit.

Lyn woke up sweltering and lying on a surface that was moving about. The mesh mask above her face was dripping and doing an unfairly good job of keeping her stale breath contained in the vicinity of her nostrils. She sat up and took stock of the situation. She was still in the back of the car. Mrs. Goodman was seated across from her, tapping away on a laptop computer, just as she had been when Lyn fell asleep. Behind the lawyer, though, through the window, Lyn could see early-morning light and the horizon going up and down in a very nautical manner.

"We're on a boat?" asked Lyn.

"Yes, we are steaming toward the Estate, the secret training academy of the Checquy Group," said Mrs. Goodman.

"Cool. And where exactly is that?"

"Kirrin Island...offshore."

"Really? An offshore island, you say." She looked out the window at the water passing by. "You're not going to give me any more information?"

"It's classified."

"Yeah, but so am I, apparently," said Lyn. "And I'm going to be living there for an unspecified amount of time." The lawyer shrugged and turned her attention back to the computer. Lyn sighed and shifted uncomfortably. The bulky coverall was awkward, and a surreptitious sniff confirmed that it was not only fire-retardant, it was also very effective at holding in sweat and odors. As she'd slept, she'd been marinating in her own perspiration, and her clothes had stuck to her.

Between this sauna suit and last night's fire, I smell like a chargrilled badger.

A rotund lady dressed in an academic gown was waiting for them at the dock. She stepped forward and made a slight bow, completely unfazed by Lyn's outfit.

"Lynette Binns? I am Steffi Blümen, headmistress and chief instructrix of the Estate school. You are most welcome." She spoke with a thick German accent, but her English was perfect.

"Thank you," said Lyn. "It's very nice to be here."

"Well, I don't believe that for a moment," said Blümen, "but it's very polite of you to say so. Now, from what I understand, it's been less than a day since your powers ignited?"

"Yeah, it happened last night when I was making dinner."

"Did you get to have any dinner?"

"Uh, no. It exploded."

"Breakfast?"

"We've been driving through the night," said Mrs. Goodman in a defensive tone.

"Wearing *that* the whole time?" asked the German lady, and she eyed the heavy coverall disapprovingly.

"We haven't established Lyn's exact powers yet, Frau Blümen," said the lawyer. "*Or* her level of control. And I had to share a car with her."

"Well, fine," said Blümen. "Mrs. Binns—may I call you Lynette?"

"Lyn, please."

"Excellent. Lyn, we have a reception suite waiting for you. You can shower, have a good breakfast, and then we can start your orientation." They walked to a spot where several small electric buggies were parked. Mrs. Goodman excused herself, saying she had paperwork to finish up and would see Lyn later. She settled herself heavily into one of the carts, then laid a patch of rubber on the pavement as she peeled away, tires squealing, up one of the paths.

"Would you like a brief tour first?" asked Frau Blümen.

"Sure," said Lyn. In truth, she really wanted just to be brought to a shower so she could start scouring away the stink of smoke and sweat, but the prospect of seeing an actual magical academy was too tempting to put off.

For a supernatural school hidden away on an island, the Estate itself was remarkably unremarkable. Oh, it was handsome enough, consisting of redbrick buildings with pointed roofs and several court-yards and cloisters, but it was hardly the otherworldly complex of spires and stained glass that Lyn had vaguely imagined.

"How old is this place?" she asked.

"It was founded after the Second World War," said Blümen. "Of course, the Checquy has been around for centuries, but until then, it never had a central school. Everything worked on a master-apprentice system."

They entered one of the buildings, and the atmosphere was simi-larly mundane. Classes were in session; Lyn could see the students through the windows in the doors. A casual glance in passing showed no obvious inexplicability among the student body. There was the familiar smell of schools everywhere—cleanser, whiteboard marker, teenager sweat. As Frau Blümen led her down the hallways, however, there was also the occasional whiff of something unexpected—sulfur, or basil, or rain on a hot highway. The walls were hung with class portraits and oil paintings of landscapes, and children's drawings and projects were stuck up on corkboards. Lyn stepped closer to look at some of the projects. They had all been written in copperplate hand-writing of varying quality, and all appeared to be the work of class 2R. Henry had made a poster on seeds, Madeline had done one on birds, and Maisie had made one on how to assault the Ratcliffe-on-Soar Power Station in the event of newt people taking it over.

Well, this bodes incredibly fucking weird, thought Lyn. "So, the chil-dren who live here," she said. "Are they like me? Do their families just think that they're off at hospital or boarding school?"

"There are a few like that," said Blümen. "Our approach depends on the circumstances of each student."

"The circumstances as in . . . what? Money?"

"No. For the most part, our students are removed completely from their former lives. A great deal of effort is made to ensure that the families will not expect to see their children again."

Lyn gasped. *"You steal children?* And, what, fake their deaths?"

"Calm down, do," said Blümen. "We very rarely just steal children."

"But you *have* done it?"

"You don't understand the full situation."

"I have a kid," said Lyn tightly. "I understand the situation exactly." She could imagine someone coming to her home and taking Emma out of her bed. *Is that how it works?* she wondered. *Do the children simply vanish? Surely the government doesn't just knock at parents' doors and state that they are taking their son or daughter. There would be outrage! No one would remain silent. I certainly wouldn't—I'd raise the biggest stink in the world. It would be a gigantic scandal.* Just the thought had her cheeks burning with rage. *They must do it by stealth.*

Frau Blümen stopped abruptly in the middle of the hall, and Lyn, taken by surprise, was thrown off balance.

"You need to be disabused of some notions," said Blümen flatly. "Right now. You are a grown woman, and in some ways that makes this easier and in other ways more difficult. But you must understand the situation."

"I...all right," said Lyn, wide-eyed.

"You have a normal child," said Blümen. "The children here, however, are like you—a danger to others. We have students who have enormous destructive potential, children who are poisonous, who can damage people's psyches or health, who can damage the environment by coughing or the economy by cracking the knuckles of their toes.

"There are other students whose abilities are not as harmful. Some are merely inexplicable. And yet they represent just as much of a danger to society because of the implications of their existence." She sighed sympathetically at Lyn's expression. "You see, Lyn, the supernatural casts doubt on many of the foundations of today's society— logic, reason, science. It defies the systems that people take for granted. And people respond to the inexplicable or the inhuman in various different ways, most of them unhealthy. Some feel an instinctive revulsion and terror—there have been situations in which parents have turned on their own supernatural children."

"That's horrible," said Lyn sadly. It didn't surprise her, though. She knew how cruel people could be to their children.

"If you gave birth to a cloud of ice-cold mist that screamed with the voice of a baby, would you be able to mother it once it turned back into a human?" asked Blümen. "Would you be able to care for it if it didn't? If you knew the little boy next door might accidentally age your daughter thirty years, would you allow her to play with him?"

"Well, I—" began Lyn awkwardly.

"For the security and the sanity of the world, these children must be kept separate from society. And so children are taken from their parents because we do not trust the parents to keep our secrets, and we do not trust them to raise these children the way they should be raised. When you have been here awhile, you will see why," said Blümen calmly. She started walking again. Lyn followed her through the corridors. She was uncertain now of how she felt; she was half convinced by the logic of the other woman's words, and yet she kept thinking of her own daughter being taken from her.

They rounded a corner.

"Ah, this is useful," said the headmistress. "Look there."

Lyn's first thought was that she was looking at a series of statues running the length of the hall. Then she looked more closely and felt the hairs on the back of her neck tremble.

"What on—"

"This is Andrew Chen," said Blümen. "Well, it's various moments in his past fourteen minutes and thirty-eight seconds." Lyn moved warily toward the bizarre display. It looked exactly like a ten-year-old-ish boy of Asian descent had elected to stop midstride and stand dead still, and a group of his identical friends had elected to do the same, each one a few seconds behind the boy in front of him. It was uncanny, reminding her of those photographs that showed the gait of a galloping horse or the flapping of an eagle's wings with several phases on a single image.

"Unbelievable," she muttered, peering at the nearest statue. The boy stared beyond her, focused on something else. She could see the shine in his eyes, and his mouth was open, his tongue frozen in a moment of speech. She looked at Blümen. "Is it him? Is he locked in these things?"

"No, it's just a three-dimensional image. The real Andrew moves on and leaves these things behind him."

"So, like, holograms or something?"

"We have no idea." The headmistress shrugged. "You can touch it, but your hand will go through."

"Yeah, thanks, I'll just take your word for it," said Lyn.

"He used to do it all the time," said Blümen. "Before we taught him control, every few heartbeats, one of these images would be created, duplicating Andrew's situation at that moment." She examined the image critically. "It looks like he was running late to class, which is probably why his control slipped, and he left these behind him. As I said, each image lasts for fourteen minutes and thirty-eight seconds, but no piece of equipment we possess can detect them. They don't show up on film or digital media. And no signals can pass through them."

"I beg your pardon?"

"Light, radio, radar, microwaves—nothing passes through them."

"And what does that mean?" asked Lyn.

"We're still investigating," said Blümen. "Our physicists are terrifically excited by the implications, but then, they're in a state of almost constant excitement here. We've had to schedule enforced naps for all the scientists on Kirrin Island to keep them from working until they keel over."

"And he just started doing it one day?"

"We discovered him when his mother went in for an ultrasound, and the sonographer thought she was carrying either nine boys or one boy with eighteen arms and legs and several sets of genitalia. Both scenarios interested us. Fortunately, the sonographer had been briefed to keep an eye out for any unorthodox infants, and she alerted us."

"You paid off a sonographer?" asked Lyn.

"We have a network of medical professionals throughout the country who let us know if they see anything incredibly strange. In fact, the Checquy was one of the driving forces behind the creation of the National Health Service. In olden times, the Church was the most useful source of intelligence, but now people go to their doctors with their concerns. We're also tapped very deeply into law-enforcement networks."

"Really?" asked Lyn. She'd never heard her husband mention anything like it.

"Absolutely. Anyway, can you imagine what kind of life Andrew Chen would have had if we hadn't brought him here?" Lyn was silent. It didn't bear thinking about. "And *his* abilities are not intrinsically harmful; we haven't even found an offensive application. If society knew about people like our students, there would be an outcry. At best, the government would still have to take them, but they'd go to a prison rather than a school. At worst, there would be witch hunts with people getting lynched in Hyde Park."

At that moment, a bell rang, and classroom doors banged open. Lyn flinched as a horde of students swarmed out, boys and girls of all ages and races.

She watched these potential threats to civilization with wary fascination. They each wore a school uniform consisting of a red blazer over a white shirt and gray trousers or a gray skirt or kilt, and they moved along the corridors in a reassuringly ordinary scramble on their way to their next classes. Most of them looked like normal children, but some decidedly did not. She gasped at the sight of a teenage girl who appeared to be made entirely out of crude oil and who was carefully holding her books on a wooden tray, presumably so as not to stain them.

Amongst them were the teachers, all of them wearing academic gowns over their clothes. One man was wearing camouflage fatigues under his robes; another wore pajamas and a bathrobe under his. Nobody gave Lyn in her head-to-toe space garb a second glance, but everyone acknowledged the headmistress with a "Morning, Frau" or a "Hi, Frau Blümen."

A baby goat came rushing down the hallway, bouncing from side to side, its little hooves clopping on the linoleum. It abruptly morphed into a small boy, who shamefacedly stood aside for the women. Frau Blümen affectionately ruffled his hair as they passed, and when Lyn looked behind them, the goat was prancing away, kicking its heels up joyfully.

Well, that's hardly an end-of-the-world-causing ability, thought Lyn, *but I could see how it might spur on an angry mob. Or at least a horde of journalists.* Next to her, the headmistress spoke out of the side of her mouth.

"Don't worry about what's coming down the hall, she's harmless."

"What?" asked Lyn, turning back from watching the goat to look ahead of them. "Bloody hell!" A seething wall of electric-pink flame was roaring down the hall toward them. Lyn barely had time to notice that the fire wasn't burning the pictures on the wall, wasn't burning anything, before the blaze was upon them. Despite Blümen's warning, despite her protective suit, Lyn instinctively threw up her arms to shield her face.

There was no heat; there was barely any pressure, just the feeling of a slight cool breeze through the mesh of her mask and a faint smell of deodorant, and then the fire was past them.

"Genevieve, you're late!" Blümen called after the inferno. "And school colors, please!"

There came an inhuman voice made up of the crackling of the fire. "Yes, Frau Blümen." It sighed heavily. You could practically hear the eyes rolling, although there were no eyes to roll. As Lyn watched, the pink flames deepened and became the same red as the students' blazers. Around the edge, the fire darkened to the gray of their trousers and skirts.

"Teenagers." The headmistress sighed. "You have a daughter, yes?"

"A three-year-old."

"Well, when she hits adolescence, remember, it's all about setting reasonable boundaries."

"I'm sorry, but how do you set boundaries with a student who is *fire?*"

"She's only fire when she feels like it. The most important lesson we teach here is control—control over one's abilities and control over oneself. Some of our pupils possess potentially devastating powers. Our first priority is to ensure that they won't harm themselves or others—yet another reason why they must be removed from their families. Then we work very hard to raise them to be stable. But"—she sighed heavily—"there will always be times when you have to make allowances. And so, while we don't mind if Genevieve elects to manifest herself as fire in the halls, we require her to do so in a version of the school uniform." She looked at her watch and made a face. "We should go."

The rooms that had been prepared for Lyn were in a building that was located a noticeable distance from the rest of the school, and they turned out to be surprisingly luxurious. The furniture looked expensively comfortable, a large bowl of fruit stood on a sideboard, and vases of flowers were dotted about strategically. A huge window looked out on the sea, and a television set was playing soft, gentle welcoming music. In fact, if she ignored the fact that there were no doorknobs on the inside of the doors, it was nicer than the nicest hotel she had ever stayed in.

"It's beautiful," she said. "I'm actually a little worried that I might damage it. You know, if something happens."

"Not to fret," said Frau Blümen blithely. "Everything here is replaceable, plus the windows are military-grade blast-resistant, and there's a Faraday cage built into the walls should you happen to have any little accidents."

"You had the room prepped in case I exploded?" said Lyn, trying to ignore Frau Blümen's vaguely toilet-training-esque language.

"We try to cover most eventualities when people are new to their powers," said the headmistress. "Now, there are panic buttons by the door, by your bed, and by the toilet. Also, there are cameras covering every room, including the bathroom and the sauna." She caught Lyn's horrified look even through the mesh of her mask. "This is so that we can monitor you. If something *does* happen, we must be able to come help you as quickly as possible, and it's important that we have a detailed record for analysis. I'm afraid it means, though, that you'll have very little privacy for a while." She looked at her watch. "Why don't you shower and have breakfast? There's a room-service menu on the desk there; just ring through with what you'd like. If you drop the Faraday suit on the floor, we'll bring you a fresh one later. You'll need to wear it whenever you come out of the suite. And there are clothes for you in the drawers of the bureau. They're a little plain, I'm afraid, just hospital scrubs, but it won't matter if your body incinerates them."

Lyn hesitated, then said, "All right, thank you." She looked around. "Is there a phone? I'd like to call my husband and let him know that I'm okay."

"No phone. We have some prep work to do before you speak with him again," said Frau Blümen apologetically. "But our very first priority is ensuring that you won't injure yourself or others with your powers."

"I can't help but feel a little bit like I'm being held prisoner," said Lyn.

"Absolutely not," said Frau Blümen. "Someone will be by to pick you up later." The headmistress left, closing the door behind her, and there were several heavy-sounding *clonk*s as various locks engaged. For a moment, Lyn stared at the door, fighting the impulse to pound on it and yell to be let out.

Instead, she drew in a deep breath, then exhaled slowly. *Okay, so this is all happening,* she thought. *You're at a magic school, and nothing will ever be the same again. Stay calm, let's see where this takes you.*

Stay calm.

And then, before she knew it, she was clawing very uncalmly at the metal veil covering her face, tearing it off, wrenching the hood back. Her hands were shaking as she fumbled with the zip on the horrible bulky suit, and then it was down around her ankles, and she was kicking the weight of it away, and finally she was out of it, down on her knees, gasping. She could not find it within herself to give a damn that people must be watching her through the cameras.

Okay, she thought. *Okay, okay, okay, okay.*

You're good. You're fine.

You're fine.

Deep breath. In through the nose.

You stink, but you're fine.

And then, despite herself, she had to admit that everything was *not* fine. The moment's pause and the undeniable realness of the room had done it. Lyn could not pretend to herself that this was a dream or a delicious adventure that she had been swept into. She had been torn away from her life, from her love, and from her child.

Emma! Oh, my baby!

She had seen impossible things and become an impossible thing. She had been brought to this place and could not leave. She wanted a long hot shower; she wanted to eat; she wanted to go to the toilet; she wanted to scream.

But at that moment, there was nothing she could do but cry.

⋆   ⋆   ⋆

They gave her a few hours to recover from the journey. Long enough for her to eventually pick herself up off the floor, wipe her nose on her sleeve, and peel off her horrible stinking clothes. She used the intricate Japanese toilet, warily pushing buttons that were labeled but not in English, and discovered that there were more features on Japanese toilets than were dreamed of on any commode she'd previously encountered. She then tottered into a shower that felt like it was scouring her down to her bones. Between the eighteen shower jets and the unexpectedly strategic nozzles of the toilet, she felt as if her every surface had been power-washed.

When they came to collect her, she was sealed up in a fresh Faraday suit, having first strenuously applied several layers of tactical-grade deodorant and dusted herself down with a mentholated body powder. She was escorted to a fortified-looking building, introduced to a team of people in white coats (and other clothes underneath the coats, of course, but the coats were the notable feature), and shown into an unnerving room entirely covered in shiny ceramic tiles, even the door.

A voice over an intercom instructed her to attach sensors to various points on her body, which she did, and then she spent two and a half hours utterly failing to project electricity from her skin onto a device in the middle of the room. No lightning. Not even a spark. Not even a static shock from the hospital scrubs she was wearing.

I wonder what they'll do if it never happens again, she wondered. *Would they let me go home?*

Probably not, she decided. *I've seen too much. And signed all those forms.* And truth be told, in her heart of hearts, she wasn't certain that she wanted to go back to her old life. Not completely. Oh, she missed her family, desperately. Just the thought of Emma made her tear up. Half a dozen times, she'd had to bite her lip and blink rapidly at the thought of her home.

But still.

The little she'd seen in the halls of the school had already revealed that the world was much more interesting than she had ever imagined. She emerged from the tiled room and was permitted to sit down on a sofa and suck down some water via a straw inserted gingerly through the grille of her face mesh. Meanwhile, the white-coated people were looking over readings and chattering amongst themselves.

"Now, *this* is very interesting," said one.

"Okay." Lyn yawned and slumped back in her seat.

"Annette—"

"Lynette," she interrupted. "But really, I prefer Lyn."

"Yes," said the woman, blinking at her. About Lyn's age, she'd been introduced as Dr. Allard and was the leader of the team doing the examination. She seemed to be far more interested in the powers than in the person who possessed them and in fact did not always seem to be entirely certain who Lyn was. Half the time, she forgot that Lyn was not one of her colleagues, which was a good trick, since the scientists were all in lab coats and Lyn was in a new, much-less-vile-but-still-getting-a-bit-whiffy Faraday suit. "Now, the most interesting part of the report regarding the initial manifestation has always been the secondary event."

"Pardon?" said Lyn.

"The jar shocking the guy," said one of the other scientists, whose name Lyn had forgotten but who appeared to act partially as Dr. Allard's colleague and partially as her caregiver.

"Yes!" said Dr. Allard. "The Bolognese and the emergency services worker!"

"Sounds like the world's most uninspired erotic short story," remarked Lyn. Dr. Allard stared at her blankly. "Anyway, you're more interested in that than the lightning?" she asked hastily.

"Well, electricity-casting is hardly unheard of," said the doctor. "We've seen it before. In fact, one of the graphic designers at the Rookery does it, although perhaps not on the scale of the manifestation in the subject's kitchen."

"*She's* the subject," one of the other scientists reminded her, nodding at Lyn.

"Yes..." said Dr. Allard vaguely. "Anyway, I think we are seeing something quite new. Now, look at this."

She directed Lyn's attention to one of seven huge video monitors, not the one showing the porcelain room Lyn had just emerged from but the one showing a table that appeared to be made of rubber. On it was a Faraday suit that Lyn recognized as the one that she'd worn earlier.

"The suit was carefully removed from the suite using nonconducting tongs," said Dr. Allard. "And now we are going to place a biological sample onto it."

"It's the ham from my bloody sandwich," Lyn heard one of the scientists mutter to himself. Meanwhile, under Dr. Allard's supervision, another scientist was manipulating some controls, and on the screen, a robotic arm unfolded itself from the ceiling and held a slice of ham above the suit. Lyn could see a few streaks of mustard clinging to the lunch meat.

"And...release the ham!" said Dr. Allard. The meat landed on the suit, and they all flinched away as the screen flared for a moment. By the time the monitor had regained its composure, the ham was engulfed in dancing red electricity that seemed to be boiling out of the suit.

"Oh my God!" exclaimed Lyn.

"Yes," said the doctor in satisfaction. "I posit that we are seeing electricity being, I don't know, *impregnated* in an object and remaining there until released. In fact, I think it is specifically the metal in the suit that contained the energy. Jamison, make a note. We'll need to review the footage in more detail to confirm if it's coming from the cloth too, but I expect that it is the metallic fibers that are holding on to this energy. So, whereas normally a Faraday suit would prevent electricity from getting in—or out, as we'd hoped in your case—it appears that it is actually absorbing the electricity and releasing it onto whatever subject touches it." At this, all of the scientists looked at Lyn in her metal-fibered suit and shuffled a small distance away. "My word," said Dr. Allard happily as the suit on-screen continued to flare and spark. "Just look at that meat char."

Yes, thought Lyn. *Well, I'm definitely not getting sent home now.*

Some more experimentation and several more requisitioned and subsequently carbonized sandwich fillings later, Dr. Allard had established that it *was* the metal in the suit that was storing up the electricity. Troublingly, it seemed that the amount of physical pressure required to unleash the energy varied. Sometimes it was a hard slap; sometimes all it took was the slightest touch.

"This variation is an aspect of your powers that we will need to address," said Dr. Allard. Lyn nodded, horrified at the thought that the Faraday suit had offered minimal protection to those around her and that she could have harmed anyone who'd bumped into her with the right amount of force.

The scientists had hurriedly come up with a solution to prevent Lyn from flash-frying anyone who accidentally brushed against her. There was still the worrying possibility that lightning might be launched directly out of her skin, as had happened in the kitchen, so she continued to wear the Faraday suit, but they'd had her don a suit of red nonconducting plastic *over* that to prevent anyone from coming in contact with the charged metal fibers.

Satisfied that she was unlikely to hurt anyone in the immediate future and unconcerned by the fact that she was now being poached alive as a result of her four layers of clothes, the scientists sent her off, rustling like a shopping bag, to the administration building to continue her induction into the Checquy while they had lunch and speculated excitedly.

"Now, Mrs. Binns," said the slim young administrator who'd been introduced as Pawn Blom. "I'm going to be addressing some security issues." Lyn nodded. "First, do you use social media at all?"

Lyn blinked. "Yeah," she said. "You know, I share photos, bitch about the weird people who come into the library, catch up with friends…"

"All right, well, you're not permitted to use social media when you're a part of the Checquy. We want to minimize the amount of publicly available information about you."

"So I'm just cutting my friends out of my life?" asked Lyn.

Blom bit his lower lip in a way that suggested it would make his life a lot easier if she did just that but also that he accepted it was not likely. "That might get attention," he said. "Especially since you've elected to maintain your previous life and identity. You're sure you still want to do that, right?"

"Yes!"

"Fine. We'll need to wean you off the internet. First, you'll need to log in to your accounts and post these statements I've drafted. They're about how you're going to be away from home receiving treatment for your unspecified medical condition, so you won't be posting anything online for a while. This will give you a nice excuse for several weeks of internet neglect. Then, later, you can be one of those people who announce that they're leaving social media to focus on their actual lives."

"I hate those people," remarked Lyn.

"Yes, everyone does. And I can advise you that almost none of them are doing it because they've been inducted into a secret government organization. That's why it's such a good cover."

"Is this really the most pressing priority?" asked Lyn as she typed in the status updates.

"Much of your life from now on is about disengaging from civilians," said Blom. "This is just the first step. Are you done with the social media?"

"Yes," sighed Lyn. He checked the posts, and she tried not to feel insulted.

"The next step is to address your immediate domestic situation. I understand that you have a small child. Will your husband need support in taking care of her while you're here?"

"Emma goes to day care," said Lyn. "But Richard has a full-time job, and it involves some night shifts."

"Do you think a nanny or an au pair would be helpful?"

"Well, yeah, absolutely," said Lyn, a little taken aback. "But how would I explain that to Richard? And there's the cost."

"The Checquy has created a trust to assist sufferers of Juhász-Koodiaroff-Grassigli syndrome and their families." Blom paused as Lyn looked at him blankly. "That is the disease that we're claiming you have. The trust can provide funds for domestic assistance." He made a note on his computer. "I'm just adding this to the list of things you'll need to discuss with your husband today. We can make the arrangements for a Checquy caregiver to arrive at your home tomorrow."

"Do you ever find the trust has to help people who actually *have* Juhász...Something-Something syndrome? The disease?" asked Lyn curiously. "Wait—is it real?"

"It is real," said Blom. "I gather there was some thought given to just making up a disease, but analysts did a cost-and-effort estimation and decided that latching onto an already existing disease was cheaper and simpler than making up a new one and producing all the supporting materials for it." He shook his head. "We'd have needed people writing articles for medical journals; we'd have needed fake patients. So inefficient. Plus, what if non-Checquy people decided they wanted to study our fictional disease? Or some people said they had it? So they did another major analysis and picked Juhász-Koodiaroff-Grassigli syndrome."

"How rare is it?"

"I think there's a new sufferer found in the UK about once every six years," said Blom. "And of course we help them. The situation benefits everyone. It makes the trust look more convincing, and the real patients get far more support than they ever would have otherwise. Now, there's a lot more to get through. You need a full legal briefing on your new status and its benefits and limitations, a basic orientation on the Checquy and how it works, and an explanation of the circumstances in which you can use your powers once you know how they work. There are forms for adding you to the payroll. Someone will be taking your medical and personal history, and you'll undergo security vetting. Your social adviser will sit with you to work out a plan and a schedule for, uh, disentangling you from some portions of your old life." He noted Lyn's expression. "You'll be quitting your old job," he told her, "and you'll also receive a script for explaining things to your friends and family."

He closed the massive binder from which he had been reading, lifted it with some difficulty, and passed it across the desk to her. "Here is your initial briefing package, Mrs. Binns. A schedule of appointments, a brief explanation of each one, and a map. Also, here is a brochure for the Juhász-Koodiaroff-Grassigli clinic at which you aren't actually being treated. We own that as well."

"Your dinner will be brought around in forty-five minutes," said Blom after he'd taken her back to her suite. "And someone will be in to show you how to apply the sensors that you will wear when you go to sleep. They'll record your vitals and also register if you have any incidents in the night."

"Okay, thanks," said Lyn. Blom closed the suite door, and the locks clonked in sequence behind him.

This all feels very familiar, she thought. *Back in the system, but with even less control over my life.* And yet she couldn't bring herself to feel any resentment. It meant the end of an exhausting day and an evening of relative privacy. She placed the binder on the dining table and gratefully peeled off the plastic suit and then the Faraday suit and left them lying on the floor. She eyed the silvery material thoughtfully.

So, is it now charged with electricity? she wondered. *If I tossed a piece of ham on it, would it be fried?* She sat down at the table and let out a long sigh. She scratched her hands through her sweaty hair and leaned her chair back on two legs. An actual moment to herself. An actual moment to think. She'd cried out all the pressing despair and fear and could now contemplate the situation without getting overwhelmed by emotion.

It was dizzying to realize that not even twenty-four hours earlier, she'd been hurrying Emma and the dog along on their walk because she had a headache and wanted to get home. Since then, the madness of everything she'd seen and experienced had engulfed her, and now she was here, accepting it. Perhaps it was because everyone around this place was so blasé about the extraordinary.

They all just take it for granted! she marveled. *Like that kid we passed today who turned into music. A little girl literally evaporated before my eyes and went echoing down the hallway as the violin music from that Russell Crowe movie! And no one batted an eye!*

She held up her hand and contemplated her own skin.

It doesn't look different, she mused. *Does it feel different?* She closed her eyes and tried to take stock of her own body. *Maybe a little different,* she decided. She vividly remembered the overwhelming sensation when the electricity roared out of her in the kitchen, and there was still a distant echo of that feeling, the faintest flow within her. But she couldn't sense a way to release it, to activate it.

But I'll figure it out, she resolved. *If it's a part of me, then the rest of me can learn to control it.* She held up her other hand, with her wedding ring on it, and her eyes narrowed.

Then she brought that hand down with a sharp slap on the table. Electricity flared up scarlet out of the ring, crawled over the wood, and danced over the binder.

"Oh, fuck!" She flinched away instinctively, attempting to escape

from her own hand, and managed to send herself and the chair falling backward onto the carpet. The breath was knocked out of her, and she sat up wheezing. The ring was doing nothing now. It was sitting innocently on her finger. She looked around the room, then up to the corner where she'd noted a security camera was fixed.

"Did—did you see that?" She panted at the camera. It moved up and down, a little camera nod. "Okay, I'm okay. Don't worry, I'm okay." She looked down at her ring. It didn't appear to be any the worse for its experience as a supernatural capacitor. "My ring's okay." Cautiously, she reached over and tapped it against a chair leg. Nothing. *Must be out of charge.*

She stood up and noticed that the fruit bowl on the table was different than the one that had been there that morning. Not only had the fruit selection been changed, but the bowl was now wooden instead of metal. In fact, looking around, Lyn realized that all the metal fixtures in the suite had been either removed or covered in some sort of thin rubber sheeting.

She sighed. She was exhausted, she ached, and the sauna in the bathroom seemed extremely appealing. *But if I take a sauna and then a shower, I am going to fall dead asleep immediately. And I can't do that, because I am back at school, and I already have homework.*

There was a mountain of reading to be done, but first there was the task she was simultaneously looking forward to and utterly dreading. She opened the binder to the page with the details of Juhász-Koodiaroff-Grassigli syndrome and refreshed her mind as to the symptoms of the disease and the correct pronunciation. A phone had been added to the room in her absence, and she followed the printed instructions for dialing an outside line. There was the sound of a phone ringing and then a brief pause as it was answered.

"Hello?" said the best voice in the world, and Lyn felt her eyes get hot.

Keep it together, she told herself. *If you start crying, if you lose it, who knows what you'll say.* She took a breath and made herself calm down. "Hello, my love," she said.

"You wouldn't believe how much I miss you," he said. "Me and Emma both."

"How is my baby?" asked Lyn.

"She's actually doing all right, I think," said Richard. "She woke up this morning very calm and wasn't at all worried when I explained that you had to go away for a while."

I'll bet, thought Lyn. *I expect she was given a very reassuring explanation in her dreams.*

"She misses you, of course, but she seems determined to behave. It's quite uncharacteristic, really. Wait, she wants to talk to you." Then Emma came on the phone, and it took all of Lyn's strength to remain calm and collected while her daughter chattered about her day at day care and what her bed at the neighbors' was like and how she missed her mummy.

"I miss you too, darling," said Lyn. "You be good for Daddy, and I can't wait to see you. No, I don't need to talk to Skeksis, I—all right. Hello, puppy, I've been pressed into government service because I can bleed lightning out of my skin, and now I'm at an insane magic school." She paused, and finally Richard came back on the phone. "They both sound good," she said. "How are you?"

"How are *you?*" he asked. "That's much more important. What do the doctors say?"

"I think I feel all right. It was just preliminary stuff today," she said. "Lots of tests, and doctors laying out the whole course of treatment." She hurriedly looked in the binder at the script she'd been given with its suggested lines. "Uh, once the treatment starts, I'm going to be having a lot of fatigue, needing a lot of sleep, so I won't be able to call every day. Maybe not even every other day."

"Yeah, I've been reading up on it," said Richard. "What do the doctors say about your..." He swallowed. "Do they think it will be all right?" He paused. "How bad is it?"

Lyn closed her eyes. She hated lying to him, putting him through this pain. "They said it looks promising," she said, and when he sighed with relief, she bit her lip in shame. "But they warned me that it's a long, slow process, and I need to get used to that idea."

"I suppose we do too, then," said Richard.

"It won't be easy," said Lyn. "But in the meantime, you and I have got to be organized. We need to figure out how we're going to arrange things." She led him carefully to the idea of an au pair and mentioned the fact that she wouldn't need to pay for the private treatment she was receiving. She also told him that they didn't have to worry about the cost of the fire-damage repairs.

"Where is this money coming from?" asked Richard doubtfully.

"Apparently some rich couple's kid died of Juhász-Koodiaroff-Grassigli syndrome back in the 1950s, and they sank all this money into the clinic and various support funds," said Lyn, recounting a story provided by the brochure for the clinic. "If you're going to get an obscure disease, I guess this is the one you want, at least in terms of financial perks."

"Yeah, but even the kitchen?"

"They think it's possible that I started the fire because of the disease," said Lyn, wincing at the truth of it. "Maybe had a seizure or something while I was using the stove. Anyway, they said they'll cover it. In the meantime, you and Emma and Skeksis get to stay in a dog-friendly furnished flat. And I wish I were there with you."

"How *is* the place?" he asked. "Is it nice at least?"

"It's very nice," said Lyn. "They've made it comfortable, I have a room to myself, and there's a gorgeous view of the oce—" She was cut off by a loud click. "Richard? Hello?" The only response was the humming of the dial tone. *Great. I expect the phone connection on this island is dodgy beyond belief.* She sighed in irritation and was about to put the phone down when it clicked again, and a woman's voice came on the line.

"I'm terribly sorry to have interrupted you, Mrs. Binns, but if you'll recall, the clinic to which you're claiming to have been sent is not on the coast. It's inland, in the Highlands, and not on a lake or a river. Would you like to call your husband again immediately or would you like to review the material first?"

5

Lady Carmichael, I have a coordination meeting now with the other aides of the Court," Pamela said. "I thought I might take Bridget and Usha along."

Bridget looked up, startled, from the brief that she had been failing to read for the past half hour. Her entire mind was consumed by the horrendous implications of those two reports.

"That sounds fine, Pamela," said the Lady. The three rose and left the office. They walked through the corridors of Apex House but said nothing until they came to an empty conference room.

"Are we early for the meeting?" asked Bridget.

"Yes, I thought this would be a good opportunity to talk." The two women looked at Pamela. "About the reports." They said nothing. "So, what do you think?"

"I think that *you* think that a downed German bomber pilot has Checquy-type powers," said Usha flatly. "And that he is now wandering around the East End killing people."

"Not the pilot, the bombardier," Bridget said tightly to Usha. "And we know he survived the crash. No one could have lived through it without some sort of power. And Wapping is right next to Canley. So, yes, I think that is *exactly* what the situation is. Wait a moment." A thought occurred to her, and she looked at Pamela. "Is that why you brought the plane down? Because you knew about the man with the powers?"

"No, I had no idea," said Pamela. "Of *course* I had no idea."

"There's no 'of course' about any of this," Usha said.

"This is a nightmare," said Bridget. "A Nazi with powers unleashed in London. Murdering civilians."

"Well, not to sound unfeeling, but won't this solve our problem?" asked Usha. "*All* of our problems? The Checquy will track this man down, they'll put him down, and you can both calm down."

"Unless they *don't* put him down," objected Bridget.

"He's an enemy combatant, and he's murdered people using supernatural abilities," said Usha. "I don't think they're going to give him some strudel and a bus ticket home."

"No one else knows that the man who killed those people is an enemy combatant," Bridget said. "But people will figure it out. The only reason it hasn't happened yet is that there's so much madness going on at the moment, and we knew what to look for."

"Probably," conceded Usha. "But you can relax. Even if they do figure it out, it's the Nazis who broke your 'uneasy truce with an enemy that might not even exist.' *They* sent a powered soldier over here."

"Yes, but we moved first," said Bridget. "We initiated supernatural warfare." She realized with a twist in her stomach that she'd said "we." *I suppose I've committed to being part of this.* "And because Pamela was on the front of the plane, he saw her," she continued. "In fact, he saw her without a balaclava, so he might actually be able to identify her. But even if he can't, he knows there is a flying woman who brought down a plane. If the Checquy take him alive, they'll interrogate him, he'll identify us, and we'll be imprisoned, sewn into a sack with a menagerie of animals, and dropped off a mountain into the sea.

"Now, if the police or the Home Guard get him," she continued, "he may kill a vast number of them and then be handed over to the Checquy, in which case they'll interrogate him, he'll identify us, and we'll get sewn into a sack with a menagerie of animals and dropped off a mountain into the sea. And if no one catches him and he somehow manages to get back across the Channel and share word of what happened with his superiors, then the war changes irrevocably, supernatural war starts, and the world might end."

"At least we'll have avoided the sack with the menagerie," said Pamela.

"I still think you're overestimating the likelihood of a German Checquy existing," said Usha. "And the implications."

"Are you serious?" asked Bridget. "It's *more* likely now that there's a German Checquy. Because now we *know* they have a soldier who can roast his victims."

"And as to the implications, they're horrendous," said Pamela. "Do you think that the three of us couldn't destroy society pretty well just by ourselves? Imagine two whole armies like us." Despite herself, Bridget couldn't help but feel rather chuffed at being included in the hypothetical destruction of society. Her powers weren't anywhere near as high magnitude as those of the other two.

At that moment, the door opened, and three men came in. Bridget identified them as the aides-de-camp of the two Bishops and Lord

Pease. All three looked surprised at the presence of Bridget and Usha but said nothing.

"You two had better sit back against the wall," Pamela said in a low tone. "There aren't enough seats for everyone at the table."

The meeting was then joined by Pawn Benjamin Astin, the somewhat rumpled other aide of Bishop Alrich. Since the Bishop was a vampire and not generally active during daylight hours, his office was obliged to be a round-the-clock operation, with the day crew actually the smaller of the two. The fact that Astin hadn't gone home to sleep after having handed over the reins of the Bishop's office to his daytime counterpart meant this meeting was important.

Two more men joined the throng, the aides of the Rooks. There were some greetings and hand-shakings, and then they all settled down to fill and light their pipes, unscrew their fountain pens and flip open their notebooks, or, in the case of Pawn Astin, apologize to everyone and, with a faint crackling noise, retract his five o'clock shadow back into his face.

"Late night, Astin?" asked Pawn Vallely, aide to one of the Rooks, and there was some predictable sniggering. Bridget bowed her head so that she could roll her eyes. As a result of the current roster, it was *always* a late night for Pawn Astin.

She looked around with interest. Her and Usha's invitation to the meeting might have been Pamela's gambit to talk to them in private, but it was the first time she'd been present for a gathering of the aides. She noticed that, aside from Pamela, everyone at the table was male. Dressed in suits, they ranged in age from mid-twenties (Pawn Astin) to mid-fifties. There was a general air of tobacco, Savile Row, and important busyness.

Imagine being the only woman amongst this lot every day, thought Bridget. *You'd need a wash afterward just to get rid of the stink of self-satisfaction.*

"I see you've brought a couple of little friends, Pamela," said a man Bridget didn't recognize.

"Yes, Sleator, I thought it would be useful for the Lady's apprentices to see where the real organization of the Checquy happens," Pamela said dryly. There were some chuckles, genuine ones this time. Pawn Ibsen, the aide to Lord Pease, cleared his throat.

"If we could get on, I need to be back shortly. Lord Pease is leaving for Lambeth Palace in half an hour. Pamela, would you agree that the first priority is the gathering of the Court?" Bridget frowned a little — she'd had no idea they were planning such a gathering. Responsible for supernatural security throughout the British Empire, the executives of the Checquy were all horrendously busy and had been even before the nation entered into war. As a result, they were generally called together for only the most serious issues, such as organization-level matters, internal inquests and trials, and holiday parties.

And aren't the Chevaliers out of the country? The Chevaliers, who oversaw international operations, had both been traveling madly about the globe ever since war broke out.

"Yes," said Pamela. "So, what is the situation with the Chevs?" The two relevant aides exchanged glances.

"Chevalier Flaherty and his people have not yet departed Tresco," one of them said. "Fog. His aide has advised me that they still anticipate arriving this evening."

"Please keep me abreast of any developments," Pamela said. "And Chevalier Tremethyk?"

"His ship will be docking in Liverpool later this morning, and he'll be traveling directly to Bufo Hall by motor."

Bridget frowned. Located in Oxfordshire, Bufo Hall was one of the Checquy's stately homes — each member of the Court was assigned a home for his or her private use. However, Bufo Hall was the country residence of Chevalier Flaherty, not Chevalier Tremethyk.

"So we can still assume the meeting at Bufo will start tomorrow an hour after dusk," Pamela said.

Tomorrow! thought Bridget, surprised. Tomorrow was Saturday. If the entire Court was meeting on the weekend, and the Chevaliers had been summoned from overseas to attend, it was a major event. As apprentice to the Lady, she was in the center of things, aware of all operations and significant developments in the organization, so why was this the first she was hearing of it?

"Do you know anything about this meeting?" she whispered to Usha.

"If apprentices *must* be seen, they should not be heard," said Pawn

Vallely sharply. A muscular man in his forties, he was staring at her, his lip curled. Bridget could feel her cheeks burning as all of the men regarded her disapprovingly. "I will thank you to keep any comments completely to yourself unless you wish to leave this room."

Then Pamela spoke. "It's always entertaining to watch a man commit long, slow professional suicide," she said languidly without looking up from her notes.

"What—*what* did you say?"

"You're a fool, Vallely." She raised her eyes and regarded him levelly. "She'll be giving you orders in five years." The room was silent. The Pawn, a good two decades older than Pamela, stared at her in outrage. Bridget could see his face turning red. Pamela, however, gazed at him coolly until he subsided. "Now, the schedules of the Rooks?"

The meeting continued, although now with a marked air of wariness as the men studiously avoided looking at Bridget and Usha.

"And of course, there is the Cadwallader lecture at the club this afternoon," said Pamela. Bridget made a little involuntary noise; she'd completely forgotten about it.

Pawn Mungo Cadwallader had just returned from Singapore, where he had served as the head of the Checquy colonial office for sixteen years and led a life of great derring-do. He had served as escort to trading vessels through the Strait of Malacca, protecting them from the tiny Malay pirate clan of Tan Johan, whose leader could breathe out vast clouds of horrific, razor-sharp fibers. For all other pirates, however, Cadwallader was obliged to stand aside and let the traders defend themselves.

Despite the injunction against Checquy agents operating outside the strait settlements, Cadwallader and a couple of subordinates had been known to take a launch across the Johore Strait to visit friends on the great rubber estates. From there, they would go on forays deep into the Malayan interior, and they returned with troubling reports of men made of mirrors walking in the jungles, valleys where the afternoon rainfall burned human flesh but left everything else unharmed, tigers that could become intangible, and abandoned temples that had not been built for humans to enter.

He knew everyone worth knowing and had heard everything worth hearing in that part of the world. He would sit in the Singapore Club and, over whisky sodas, engage in quiet conversation with the senior men of the settlement about the affairs of the Great Powers. He entertained the visiting planters when they came in from their remote estates to attend the races, and, in their cups, they told him about the whispered fears of their workers and mysterious deaths among the rubber trees. He walked unseen and unheard through the native districts and the kampongs and heard when a child was born with monstrous features or some other trait that might make it of interest to the Checquy.

In all, he was a figure of great romance as well as an expert on the South China Seas, and it had been arranged for him to spend an evening speaking to the students of the Checquy, a lecture to be accompanied by a magic-lantern presentation. Apprentices from all over the British Isles had jumped at the chance to come to London and listen to him. It was also an opportunity for them to gather with other apprentices, even if it meant possibly getting blown up by a passing German bomber. Until Pamela's actions of the previous night, Cadwallader's visit had been one of the two primary focuses of Bridget's thoughts for several weeks.

The other primary focus, who was probably at this moment sitting and reading in the Great Court of Trinity College, Cambridge, was far too complicated to think about just then.

"Lady Carmichael will not be attending," Pamela said.

"It's a very good opportunity for her to speak to the young people of the Checquy," said the aide to Bishop Pringle.

"She's giving a speech at a charity event to raise funds for wounded soldiers," Pamela said. "If you'd like to take it up with Rebecca Steward, I can arrange a meeting." The room fell silent at the mention of Lady Carmichael's redoubtable chatelaine. Pamela asked, "Lord Pease will attend, correct?"

"Yes, he'll say a few words to the gathered apprentices and then introduce Cadwallader," said his aide. "Are either of the Rooks going to be there?" He was informed, rather sullenly, by Pawn Vallely that they would not, and the meeting was adjourned. Pamela left the room and Bridget and Usha followed quietly.

"I'm sorry about the, um..." Bridget fumbled.

"You were completely fine," Pamela said. "You didn't disturb any-one apart from a couple of men who felt threatened by your presence because it reminded them of your existence and how much you're going to accomplish."

"Still, thank you," Bridget said. Pamela gave her a wink. "What is this meeting at Bufo Hall? If the Chevs have been summoned back, it must be pretty significant."

"That's sealed to the Court," Pamela said. "Best if you don't men-tion it in the halls, although I expect word will get out soon enough."

"So will we be attending?" asked Usha intently.

Pamela shook her head. "No apprentices," she said.

"Oh," said Bridget.

"It's not just you. There also won't be any support staff—no secre-taries or minute-takers. Just the Court and their aides."

Interesting.

They returned to the Lady's office and settled into their regular tasks. There was no time during the workday when Bridget, Usha, and Pamela could be alone together without drawing notice. Bridget could do nothing but turn the implications of the Nazi's survival over and over in her mind.

She found herself looking at Pamela. Was *she* having trouble focus-ing? It didn't seem possible that the calm, diligent Pawn working away intently on the Lady's speech for an upcoming function was the same person who had unleashed a plane-destroying windstorm in a fit of fury last night. Pamela brushed an errant strand of blond hair back behind her ear, and the intent expression on her face was a million miles from the look of overwhelming rage with which she'd con-fronted the bomber.

Bridget glanced at Usha, who was reviewing the financial records for the Checquy's St. Albans office, and wondered if she was having trouble with her work. With an effort, Bridget tried to drag her atten-tion back to her own seemingly impossible task: drafting a routine piece of correspondence for the Lady's signature. It was her third attempt; she'd begun the second draft with *Dear Nazi.*

The rest of the day was pure agony. Lady Carmichael's schedule was packed with meetings at which all three of them were expected to be present. Pamela was the only one ever called upon to speak— apprentices were too junior—but Bridget and Usha were often subjected to rigorous questioning afterward as the Lady carefully took them through what had been said and why she had made the decisions she had.

At the best of times, it was exhausting, but with the specter of the previous night's events hanging over them and the possible doom-laden revelations of today looming before them, there was no room in their minds for much coherent thought.

"All three of you are very dull today," said Lady Carmichael disapprovingly. For a moment, Bridget hoped that they might be dismissed to go sleep, but instead the Lady ordered that some of her precious hoarded supplies should be used to brew them tiny cups of Turkish coffee. It was so fiendishly intense that after drinking it, Bridget felt as if she could no longer close her eyes at all. "I know how late you got in," the Lady said, "and it is showing in your work. If this is going to be the result, then I don't want you watching the attacks from the sky. You should all go to bed early tonight."

"We have the lecture," Pamela reminded her.

"Oh, yes, of course," said Lady Carmichael. "And you're staying at the club?" They nodded. "Fine, but if you go out flying, I will know." Bridget had absolutely no doubt that she would. There were distinct advantages to being an apprentice to the Lady of the Checquy, but a disadvantage was that the entire organization kept an eye on you and advised her of any missteps you made.

The three of them were permitted to leave the office early so they could go home and change. It was one of the rare occasions when Pamela was able to leave before Lady Carmichael. Even though the Lady and Pamela lived in the same house, Pamela almost always departed work at least an hour after the Lady.

As the motorcar carried them through the streets, Pamela raised the privacy panel so they could speak without the driver hearing them.

"An actual private moment to talk, finally," said Usha. "Now, what do you think we should do about the Nazi? We can't just pray that they don't take him alive."

"No," said Bridget faintly. Her constant brooding had led her to an unavoidable conclusion. "We're going to have to hunt him down ourselves." She was aghast at what she was saying, at the prospect of digging themselves further into deceit and disobedience, but it all made horrible sense. "It's our only chance to save ourselves and prevent the Checquy from entering the war. We have to get him before the Checquy does and before he can escape."

"Absolutely," said Usha. "After all, we have so much free time. And no one is keeping an eye on us, so we can wander around the city as we please. Except that we have no free time, and Lady Carmichael keeps an eye on every move we make. Plus, at any moment, we could be dispatched across the country as her emissaries. *Or* attached to an armed assault mission as a learning opportunity. *Or* presented with a written assignment that must be finished by the end of the day on pain of an extremely patient but disappointed lecture followed by another written assignment with an even shorter time frame."

"Are you *still* sulking about that?" asked Pamela.

"No!"

"I read that paper, it was ridiculous. You proposed allowing those mantises to run wild through East Anglia for three months without any intervention."

"The farms would have recovered eventually, and with judicious investment in barley futures, we would have made an incredible profit."

"That is not what we're here for."

"*This* is not what we're here for," said Bridget in irritation. "Can we focus on the idea of tracking down this Nazi?"

"It's not the most insane idea ever," mused Pamela.

"Of course not," said Usha acidly. "The most insane idea ever was 'I shall bring down a German bomber for no apparent reason.' You may recall it. It was yours."

"I'm not going to keep apologizing for that," said Pamela. "This is the situation we're in, and we have to address it. And yes, we're all extremely busy, but we'll figure something out. Plus, we have advantages no one else has. Our position within the Checquy means that we have access to all the information, both mundane and supernatural, that comes into the government. And we'll be able to look at it through a unique lens because we're the only ones who know that the missing German airman and the supernatural murderer are the same person."

"We're the only ones for now," said Bridget. "But they will figure it out. It's what the Checquy does."

"Which is why we need to move quickly," Pamela said.

They looked at Usha, who pursed her lips. "Fine," she said. At that point, the car stopped. They'd arrived at the Lady's house. "But we'll have to start after tonight because we definitely have to go to the lecture. Lady Carmichael is already paying more attention to us than is helpful."

There was time for each of them to enjoy an actual human-style bath and get dressed in nice going-out clothes. Usha was by far the best dressed, of course, wearing one of the chic suits she had bought in Paris before the war. Even though both of Usha's maids had been evacuated to the countryside with the Carmichael children, Usha's hair looked as if it had been done by a professional. With her impeccable posture displaying her tall, full figure at its intimidating best and her straight nose making her appear even more regal, she looked as if she owned the place. Still, Bridget and Pamela were also turned out quite respectably. Lady Carmichael, knowing of the inevitable shortages that the war would bring, had had a couple of good suits and dresses made for them both.

The chauffeur drove them the few streets to Kendall Square, where the Caïssa Club sat, possibly the least discreet secret government facility in the history of covertness. Established in 1700, the club had begun as a private tavern where Checquy operatives, regardless of rank, could gather to gossip about work without fear of inadvertently driving the party at the next table into gibbering madness. It was where Pawns could enjoy a few drinks and let down their hair or uncoil their proboscises without exciting comment or mobs. The need for security and discretion meant that the place was entirely staffed by members of the Checquy.

In time, it grew from a tavern to a full-fledged club. To members of the Checquy, it became a home away from home, one equipped with an excellent library, a reading room, parlors for bridge and billiards, and sleeping accommodations. The shared dining room was sumptuous, and the smaller private dining rooms that anyone could reserve allowed for excellent dinner parties. The cocktail bar was famous in the Checquy for having created such celebratory beverages as the Beadle's Viscera, the Porthmadog Haze, and the Invocation of the Dread Fomor During the Winter Solstice on the Rocks of Carrickfergus on the rocks with a twist.

The Caïssa was the place where a country Pawn or Retainer could stay when he or she came to London to attend the theater, do some shopping, or take part in strategy meetings or tribunals. London staff might stop by for an evening cocktail or a meal on the weekend or to attend a lecture. Retired Checquy operatives came for lunch and to drowse in the armchairs in the gallery; the younger ones gathered in the ballroom for dances.

Gambling was permitted, but not for stakes beyond grains of wheat, large pots of which stood in the corners of the gaming rooms. Debts represented leverage and were therefore a weakness that the Checquy could not permit its operatives to have, not even if the debts were to each other.

The three women were dropped off at the ladies' entrance. Although the Caïssa was plainly inspired by the great gentlemen's clubs of London, its membership was not. The undeniable fact that supernatural powers occurred just as often in females as in males meant that, from its beginning, the Checquy had included women in its ranks. As some forgotten Rook had once remarked, excluding women from the troops would have been equivalent to combating the malevolent with one arm, one leg, and half of one's head removed.

Admittedly, it was not all delightful camaraderie and fairness. There was still prejudice and patronizing behavior within the Checquy, an organization that was still a part of society, with all its flaws. For one thing, the unpowered operatives—the Retainers—were primarily drawn from the military, the churches, the civil services, and academia, which meant they were mostly men, many of whom had spent their lives thinking they were the stronger sex. Newly inducted operatives were often obliged to make some hasty mental adjustments upon learning they would be working, fighting, and dying alongside—and sometimes answering to—women who could obliterate them with no more effort than it took to blink.

In the meantime, the Caïssa had a smoking room where both gentlemen and ladies could enjoy a cigar or unclench their pores without any eyebrows being raised. Women could dine alone or drink at the bar without being harassed, and they could take their turns at snooker, darts, and baccarat without any sniffs about propriety.

Given the size of the membership and the hulking presence of the building on a busy street, it was generally acknowledged that there was no point in attempting to conceal the Caïssa's existence. It was, undeniably, a private social club in the middle of London. Since no outsider knew anyone who admitted to being a member, and no information was ever released about it, the club simply sat there, largely unremarked upon, in plain sight.

That said, there were limitations to what the London public would accept, and a private club that welcomed both men and women members was simply not believable. Boodle's, White's, and Blades would have accepted a member with a seven-foot-long trifurcated barbed tongue or a coiffure made of bats before they accepted a woman. Such an institution would have drawn far too much attention, so the club consisted of two buildings connected back to back, allowing completely separate entrances for men and women. Thus the ladies entered via the Mission for the Reclamation of Reduced Females while the gentlemen all appeared to be members of the Cadgers Club.

Over the years, the Caïssa had been the site of many events that had passed into Checquy lore. There had been the time in 1866 when neighbors thought a fire had broken out on the club roof in the middle of the night and summoned the fire brigade. It turned out to be Pawn Tony Francis, who had taken to lying in the nude on the roof in order to draw his caloric intake from the stars and who, in his sleep, had begun radiating out his own *aurora Antonii*.

In 1882, the already fading custom of honor-dueling ended completely in the Checquy after what happened with Pawn Stephen Chambers and his old rival Chevalier Theresa Moutarde. He confronted her in the club's breakfast room and accused her of grotesque dishonor, and a flabbergasted crowd followed them to the club's dueling parlor and watched open-mouthed from the viewing gallery as the infamous Duel of Fire and Despair commenced. In the first five seconds, the Chevalier's right arm was burned off her body. She was still able to unleash her abilities upon her adversary, however, and, weeping uncontrollably, Pawn Chambers promptly turned his powers upon himself and incinerated his own head. The next day, the entire Court signed a formal decree prohibiting dueling (the newly left-handed Chevalier's signature was noticeably shaky). No one ever established the exact cause of the duel, but popular rumor had it that it was over Pawn Chambers's wife, who was noticeably philosophical about her abrupt widowhood and was seen to travel to and from the funeral in Chevalier Moutarde's carriage.

And just last year, there had been an enormous scandal during the spring ball when two apprentices, Irene Ploughman and Maude Culverwell, got into an actual fistfight over a boy. No powers were used, but a table got knocked over in the scuffle, and old Pawn Kearns was bumped into and spilled his drink!

Usha inevitably raised a sardonic eyebrow whenever she entered the building. Her father had always been denied access to English clubs in India, despite his phenomenal wealth and sophistication, but here, in the heart of the empire, his daughter was an automatic member of what was arguably the most exclusive club in the world, one in which membership came largely as a result of being born outside the natural order of things. Membership could not even be handed down to one's children except in rare instances when an operative had a child with supernatural abilities, something over which one had no control.

Bridget normally felt a massive swell of affection for the Caïssa Club whenever she walked down this corridor to the central atrium. Her masters had brought her there several times over the years when they'd come to town, and she'd always loved it. She'd been introduced to various Pawns and made friends with apprentices, and the staff had always greeted her by name. Whenever they spent the night there, she'd drift off happy in the knowledge that she was in the safest place in the world. Now, however, her thoughts were overshadowed by the issue of the downed German soldier.

"Oh God," said Usha, quietly horrified. Bridget looked up, startled.

"What? What is it?"

"A horde of enthusiastic youths."

The central hall was crawling with apprentices, most of them between thirteen and twenty-four, and their excited chatter filled the space. Bridget couldn't blame them. It was rare that this many Checquy young people were gathered in one place. Some might be visiting London for the first time. But it was more than that. Apprentices tended not to see many of their peers. Some might study with a few contemporaries in a district or city, but others lived in comparative isolation with their masters, dotted around the nation. In all cases, their social circles were necessarily small.

The Checquy did make an effort to keep its younger members in contact with one another. Aside from sponsoring lectures, it organized camps and training sessions around the country, and there was a pen-pal program. For some, today was a chance to reunite; for others, it was their first opportunity to meet some of their dearest friends.

For all of them, though, it was a time to relax. In their day-to-day lives, apprentices were always under pressure to remain discreet, concealing their true nature from the civilians around them. It was heady to be plunged into a situation in which everyone knew the truth of matters and there was no need to hide. In one corner, a girl was removing a broad hat with thick veils to reveal that she had the head of a fox. There was a roar of approval from the crowd, and, startled, she pricked up her ears before opening her jaws in a vulpine grin.

There were squeals and laughter when a young man tilted his head back and a cloud of sweet-smelling dragonflies flew out of his mouth and darted about the room. A boy just barely sixteen peeled off a wig to uncover constellations of tiny stars twinkling under the skin of his bald pate. Caught up in the spirit of the crowd, Bridget removed her gloves, revealing the shimmering mother-of-pearl of her palms and the undersides of her fingers. She threw her hands up in the air, and the silvery rainbow surface caught the light. From the gallery above, a few elderly Pawns and Retainers looked down with benign smiles.

"We should go to the bar," said Usha firmly. "I'm going to need a preemptive recovery beverage in the face of all this bonhomie." She moved forward purposefully, and the crowd parted in front of her almost as if that were her power. Bridget and Pamela followed in her wake.

The bar was crowded, and not even Usha could part the masses of excited apprentices at the center. The three friends had to move off to the side and wait for the flow of young people to carry them forward.

Finally, though, they were all three leaning against the famous infamous bar. As she always did, Bridget traced a reverent hand over the wood. Despite being more than two hundred years old, it was pristine, apart from some spilled beer that the harried-looking bartender had yet to mop up. Its oak had come from an early prototype of a tank that a mad genius had constructed back in the 1700s as part of his startlingly almost-successful attempt to carve out his own kingdom in Shropshire.

The mad genius in question was a rogue scholar named Alfred Henty who had left the University of Glasgow in the middle of his studies and was not heard from again until the day, fifteen years later, that he drove his homemade war vehicle out of a barn near Ludlow. Over the course of four days, Henty wreaked utter havoc across the countryside. Able to reach dizzying speeds and drive over the roughest terrain (including bogs, forests, and houses) and composed of wood that would not burn and could withstand cannonballs, the tank fired munitions that exploded with hundreds of crimson sparkles that burned through all encountered materials. No conventional forces were able to stand up to him, and soon an entire company of regular soldiers had fallen before his war machine. Henty was well on his way to leveling the seat of local government in Shrewsbury when the Checquy finally caught up to him.

The Henty tank proved capable of shrugging off supernatural attacks as easily as it did conventional assaults, so eventually, the Checquy attacked the man inside the machine. Pawn Lorna Flinders, whose abilities warped the human ability to reason, was hastily brought in to direct her power at the driver of the tank. After half an hour of her attention (during which the tank abruptly veered off its path and demolished a lonely church for no apparent reason and then spent twenty minutes moving in a very tight figure eight in a barley field), the thing stopped.

As far as anyone could tell, there were no signs of life within, but it was difficult to be certain because no one could work out how to open it. After two days of fruitless attempts to pry up one of the hatches or pierce the armor, the machine was laboriously transported to a Checquy facility in Market Drayton, where the staffers set about trying to bore their way in.

Meanwhile, another team of Pawns had followed the trail of destruction back to Henty's barn, only to find that, despite having been constructed eighty years earlier with no apparent subsequent maintenance and seeming on the verge of collapse, the entire structure was also impregnable. The battered, faded, apparently rotting wood had evidently received the same treatment as the wood of the vehicle. It could not be penetrated or torn away. The slumping thatched roof was similarly invulnerable, and close examination revealed that it, like the barn, had been coated with some sort of artillery-level varnish.

It was generally held to be a tremendous pity that Henty had refused to surrender to the authorities. Despite his diabolical intentions, he had clearly possessed a genius that could have revolutionized society.

After twelve years of grimly determined effort, the staff at Market Drayton succeeded in cutting through the tank's armor. A slim-shouldered nine-year-old apprentice was squeezed in through the hole, and he announced that the thing was filled with odd controls, an intricate brass clockwork engine, some cannonballs that were vibrating slightly in their loading racks, and the horribly decomposed corpse of the driver, still firmly strapped into his seat. They deduced from what remained of the man and the sprays of blood across the controls that Henty had torn out his own throat.

The tank itself was held in a Checquy facility in Market Drayton to this day. Bridget had visited the place and seen it. Over the centuries, it had not deteriorated at all, and parts of its design had been used when creating tanks for the Great War. It had taken nineteen years to saw a section of the machine's frame away. The Lord of the time, who had been involved in the first disastrous assault on the Henty tank, agreed that it should be placed as a trophy in the Caïssa, where its strength had allowed it to withstand centuries' worth of wear and abuse from intoxicated supernatural patrons.

The barn had never been breached and remained an impenetrable mystery in the heart of the British countryside.

"Bridget?" Usha asked.

"Hmm?" replied Bridget absently.

"Who is that man at the end of the bar?" Usha nodded to a huge redheaded man in his late thirties. As they watched, a nervous-looking boy apprentice no older than fourteen came up to him and asked him something, never daring to lift his gaze from the ground. The man patted him gently on the shoulder and led him away through the throng. Remarkably, no one stepped in to take the man's place at the bar. "That keeps happening. I've seen three people come up to him, ask him something, and then go off with him for a few minutes. Is he an apprentice?"

"Oh, no, that's Sergeant Morrison," said Bridget.

"Sergeant? So he's a Retainer, not a Pawn?" asked Usha.

"No, he's a Pawn, but he came to the Checquy only about ten years ago, and he was already a sergeant in the Border Regiment, so he's always known as Sergeant Morrison."

"But what is he doing?" Her friend sounded suspicious.

"Uh, it's a little complicated," said Bridget. "Well, actually, no, it's not complicated at all. It's just a bit sensitive. Sergeant Morrison's power, when he activates it, changes the way that people see him."

"What do you mean? Do they instinctively like him or something?" The man returned to his place at the bar. Usha eyed him warily.

"No. When it's activated, people who look at him see their mother." Usha stared at Bridget. "I know, it sounds absurd, but if he were to use his powers now, and you and I looked at him, you would see your mother and I would see my mother."

"But...forgive me, but I understand that you never knew your mother," said Usha. Bridget nodded, unconcerned. "So who would you see? Your first foster mother?"

"No, I would actually see the woman who gave birth to me. Except that she would be wearing a coat and a regimental tie." She looked over at Morrison. "And drinking a pint of stout."

"But how can that work? Is he drawing memories from your head? Memories that you didn't even know you had?"

"No, apparently I would see her as she actually is now. Unless she is dead. Then I would see her as she was when she gave birth to me." Usha looked over to Pamela, who nodded in confirmation.

"It's true. They've performed extensive tests," said the Pawn.

"So those people who are going up to him are..."

"They want to see what their mothers look like, yes," said Bridget. "Remember, an awful lot of us were taken from our families when we were very young. He goes off with them to an out-of-the-way place so they can do it in private and also because he's trying to prevent other people from seeing their mothers if they don't want to."

"Does he charge?" asked Usha.

"No!" exclaimed Bridget. "He's just a nice person. I think he views it as something of a sacred obligation, a service."

"And he's a soldier."

"A damned good one," said Pamela. "Extremely effective in battle. I understand his power is very disconcerting for the enemy. A soldier will hesitate to shoot at his mother, even if she is charging at him with a machine gun or a sword."

"Have either of you ever asked him to use his power for your mothers?" Usha said.

"No," said Pamela. Bridget shook her head.

"May I ask why not?" It was quite a personal question, but neither woman took offense.

"Well, I have memories of my mother," Pamela said. "And I treasure them. I was sad when I was parted from her." Her eyes went distant for a moment, and then she shook her head. "But the distance from her makes it easier to bear. I think that suddenly seeing her again, feeling that shock of familiarity and recognition—that would be too much."

"I just don't need to know," said Bridget. "On an intellectual level, yes, I realize that I had a father and a mother, maybe siblings, but they're just..." She waved her hand. "Theoretical. I was raised by people who made me feel loved, and if I started to brood on what might have been, it would open doors that I don't need opened." Usha nodded in understanding, but she looked a little sad. "If you went over, Usha, if you wanted to see your mother, I'm sure he wouldn't mind."

"I think it would be a bit strange," Usha said, wrinkling her nose. "But I can see why others would be curious."

"Bridget, I think that man over there is trying to get your attention," said Pamela.

"Bridget! Bridgey!"

Bridget turned around and saw a familiar figure pushing through the crowd toward her.

"Oh my God! Edwin!" They hugged, and then Bridget held the curly-haired young man at arm's length and regarded him critically. "You've gotten marginally taller!" She turned to Pamela and Usha. "This is Edwin. We were apprentices together in Derry under Pawn Connifer. Edwin, this is Usha and—"

"Pawn Verrall, of course," said Edwin, hastily improving his posture in the presence of greatness. His accent was the twin of Bridget's. "It's a pleasure to meet you both. I hope Bridget is doing us all proud. We were so thrilled when she was chosen to be apprentice to the Lady."

"She's doing very well," said Pamela, and Bridget flushed a little.

"Would you mind if I stole her away for a catch-up before the lecture?" asked Edwin. "There are a few others here who would love to see her."

"Go, go, of course," said Pamela. "We'll find each other afterward."

"I can guarantee that we'll be here at the bar," said Usha, grimly regarding the crowd of supernatural young people. "In fact, we should order all the drinks we're going to want now, in advance."

"In that case, can we take these gin and tonics?" asked Bridget.

"With my blessing," said Usha. Pamela winked at the two apprentices and turned back to her friend.

"You're moving in high circles, Bridget," said Edwin as they edged through the crowd.

"Yeah, but a lot of it involves sitting quietly and not saying much," said Bridget grimly, remembering the meeting she'd attended earlier.

"And here I was thinking you were ensuring there's a civilized Irish accent echoing in the corridors of power. Now, come on, we've got some talking to do." Armed with their beverages, they passed through the throng.

As they made their way down the hall, she said, "It is so good to see you, Edwin, you cannot believe it." The prospect of spending some time with people who had not just launched a secret and illegal plan to bypass the laws of the land in order to conceal their crimes was so delicious that she could barely stand it. They entered a quieter sitting room, all burgundy walls and leather chairs. A group of seven people were mingling there, all Edwin and Bridget's age. She recognized everyone, although some she knew better than others.

She and Ruth had spent a summer together learning Sercquiais from a Pawn who lived above a shop out on the Channel Islands. Lewis, the boy with the rings of glowing fungus around his left biceps, had been based in London and shared unarmed combat classes with Bridget until he was assigned to a new master in Kent four months ago. The others she knew only vaguely.

The atmosphere in the room was markedly different than it was in the foyer, and not just because of the strong smell of cantaloupe that Bridget happened to know was coming from the albino girl whose name was…something like Alexandra? Whereas the crowd in the hall and corridors had been excited, there was an air of seriousness here. They were all looking at Bridget expectantly and with a disconcerting hint of nervous deference.

"Hello," she said cautiously. "It's good to see all of you. Ruth, it's been, God, how long since Sark?"

"Hello, Bridget," said Ruth, looking down and biting her lip. "Is it three years?"

"Yes, I think that's right. Pawn de Carteret elected to stay, you know, even when the Germans came."

"I heard," said Ruth. She didn't look up. "I wasn't surprised."

Six months earlier, in May, the British government had suggested an evacuation of the island. France had been about to fall, and there was no reason to think that the Germans would stop at the shore of the Channel. Nevertheless, many had elected to stay, and Bridget and Ruth's teacher had stated firmly that she was there to protect anyone who lived on Sark. On July 4, a small force of German troops had taken over the Channel island. The Checquy had received no word from Pawn de Carteret since, and Bridget was privately a little worried about how her strong-willed teacher would do under the occupation.

"So, I, um, I sense that we're not just going to be sitting around gossiping about that girl in Dundee who got herself in trouble with her master, are we?" said Bridget, naming the biggest scandal to hit the Checquy in the past two months. She looked around as, behind her, Edwin shut the door.

"No, Bridget," he said shamefacedly. "We want to ask you something."

Oh, this sounds bad, thought Bridget. She lifted her glass and swallowed the rest of her gin and tonic in three quick gulps. She waved for him to continue.

"We want you to talk to Lady Carmichael," said Ruth.

"About what?" said Bridget warily.

"We want to help with the war effort."

"For God's sake," said Bridget to no one in particular. "You have got to be kidding me." *Is it catching? Is everyone around me looking to kick off a supernatural war?* She reached back, took Edwin's gin and tonic, swilled the beverage down, and looked around at the other apprentices, who were all staring at her with hopeful, shining eyes.

She couldn't help but remember the occasion a few weeks ago when she and Pamela had accompanied Lady Carmichael on an important visit.

Usha had been on assignment in Cardiff for a week, compiling a report on the Checquy office there, so only Bridget and Pamela accompanied the Lady on her visit to the New Public Offices in Whitehall. A large, white Baroque revival building, it hulked majestically above the street, and serious-looking men in suits and uniforms walked briskly in and out. The taped asterisks on the windows and the sandbags piled along the walls and the entrances and up around the statue of Clive of India made the place look as if it were growing itself a new shell for wartime.

They were met at a side door by two solemn civil servants who guided them through back corridors that had been ordered clear of personnel. All three women were dressed in Wren uniforms — uniforms to which they had no right at all but that ensured their presence in the corridors raised neither eyebrows nor questions.

Lady Carmichael and her two aides were taken past heavy utilitarian doors, down a set of stairs, and into a warren of basement corridors that was unexpectedly busy, full of people rushing about in too much of a hurry to take notice of the visitors.

The group passed an open door and saw a room dominated by a vast map of Europe. To reflect the curvature of the Earth, it was a collage of smaller maps, fanning in an arc across the wall. Bridget was reminded of the maps pinned up in the vaults of Apex House. She recognized the uniforms of the Royal Navy, the British Army, and the Royal Air Force on the men in the room, some of whom were staring up at the map while others sat working at desks that held multiple telephones. They moved along until their guide stopped them in the middle of the hall.

"Please wait here," he said. "I shall be back shortly." The three women stood against the wall to allow the denizens of the underground complex to hurry about on their important business. Next to them was a stout door with heavy metal handles and some handwritten instructions pinned to its side:

IF THIS DOOR SHOULD BE BLOCKED BY DEBRIS ON THE OUTSIDE, THE OCCUPANTS SHOULD:

1. *RELEASE THE LOCKING HANDLES*

2. *USE THESE CROWBARS TO LEVER OPEN THE DOOR BY INSERTING THE FLATTENED ENDS BETWEEN DOOR AND FRAME AT THE <u>RIGHT-HAND SIDE</u> AND THE THRESHOLD*

Bridget looked down. Sure enough, a rack below the sign held two crowbars. The matter-of-fact tone of the instructions in case of disaster made the hair on the back of her neck stand up. All too easily, Bridget could imagine being buried alive down here.

"Ladies?" Their guide was back. "He is ready for you." They took a few steps down the corridor and went through a door into a room with a large green-topped table. Another fanned collage of maps was on the wall, this one showing Europe and Asia. Next to it, a portrait of the King in military uniform stared solemnly at them.

But what drew the eye in the room was the man in his sixties seated at the table. Somehow, despite her time amongst the highest ranks of the Checquy, Bridget had never seen him in person, but she recognized him from a thousand photographs, drawings, and news-reels. The round face and receding hairline did nothing to detract from her awe. He was poring over a mass of papers, and a cigar lay smoking in an ashtray by his hand. Eventually he looked up.

"Ah, the Ivory Lady of the Order of the Checquy!" Bridget noted that Pamela's mouth twisted a little at the words.

"The Prime Minister of the United Kingdom of Great Britain and Northern Ireland," said Lady Carmichael. There was a dryness to her tone. The Lady of Checquy was always so warm and charming; the chill in her voice surprised Bridget. Meanwhile, the aforementioned Prime Minister was rising to his feet. "This is my aide, Pamela Ver-rall, and Bridget Mangan, one of my apprentices."

"Of course, of course. A pleasure." He shook their hands, and for a long, agonizing, starstruck moment, Bridget could not quite recall how to let go. "Ladies, please be seated. Thank you for coming, Mrs. Carmichael." Pamela and Bridget exchanged glances. Churchill had failed to use the title Lady. As Sara Carmichael was not a member of the nobility and had not been granted an honorary title publicly, he was justified in not doing so. However, the omission by the head of the government, himself the grandson of a duke and the son of a lord, could only be deliberate, and pointed.

"It is my pleasure, Prime Minister," said Carmichael.

Touché, Bridget thought. The Lady of the Checquy had not said *Of course* or *I am at your service*, a subtle reminder that it was not within even this man's authority to summon or command her. She would come or not, as she pleased. Judging from the pursing of the Prime Minister's lips, he understood her point, and he was not best pleased by it.

"Welcome to the Cabinet war rooms," he said finally.

"Thank you, Prime Minister, it is an interesting installation you have here."

"I fancy it is the nerve center of the British war effort," Churchill said. "A layer of concrete five feet thick protects this complex from

Hitler's Blitzkrieg. Information flows in, and decisions flow out. It is from this room that the war is directed." He did not need to say that it was he who was doing the directing. "Do you know why I have asked you to come here today?"

"I fancy that I do," said Lady Carmichael grimly.

"Every day for the past week, German aircraft have flown above London and dropped bombs on our city. Yesterday at around eleven a.m., Buckingham Palace suffered a direct hit." He paused and gazed meaningfully at the three Checquy women. "It was the third hit on the palace in the week. Their Majesties were in residence, taking tea at the time. Thankfully, they were unharmed, but four workers were injured and there was significant damage to the palace."

"I am aware of this, Prime Minister," said the Lady.

"The attacks come during the day; they come during the night. At any moment, the sirens may go off, and our citizens must scrabble for shelter. And we do not know when it will stop."

"Terrible," said Lady Carmichael, shaking her head.

"Can nothing be done?"

The Lady regarded him carefully. "I had understood that a great deal was being done."

"By *others*, yes," said Churchill. "But not by the Order of the Checquy."

"Prime Minister, you know the strictures under which the Checquy exists."

"Yes, yes. I read the briefings that your offices provided, and I have read the histories and the dossiers and my predecessors' notes." Pamela and Bridget exchanged glances at this. "I am well aware of the tremendous difference that the Checquy could make to the war effort, but I am not asking for you to wave a magic wand and kill Hitler. I do not wish for you to summon Gogmagog to swat down Heinkels over Deptford. I appreciate the need to keep the existence of the Checquy and its foes secret. But there must be some subtle ways in which your people can contribute, mitigate the harm that is being done to the populace."

"No." This was said flatly, with no hint of apology or regret. The Prime Minister was still. Bridget felt sweat gathering at the small of her back.

"No? Not even small, low-key assistance? Do you not have someone who could hear the planes coming and give us that extra few
minutes' warning? Someone who can scry a vision of Hitler's headquarters? Can you not even give your countrymen that little aid?"

"No."

"And you do not need to consult with your counterpart?" he asked
finally. "Your 'Lord'?" Bridget could practically hear the quotation
marks the Prime Minister had dropped around the title of Lord Pease,
a man who had been born to a thirteen-year-old prostitute and spent
the first fourteen years of his life in a workhouse. "You do not need to
inquire about his thoughts on this weighty matter?"

"No."

"Very well, then. That is your decision, and it is your right to
make it." He took up his cigar. "Truthfully, I continue to be uncomfortable with the idea of a group of people wielding such power and
authority in this country simply because of a freak happenstance of
birth."

"As you are a child of the aristocracy, I would expect you to understand it quite well," said Lady Carmichael evenly. "The key difference
is that *we* are expected to lay down our lives as a matter of course due
to this happenstance of birth."

"The aristocracy lay their lives down for this nation and have done
so for centuries!" the Prime Minister barked. "There are *always* sacrifices in wartime."

"I know—just look at the Dardanelles."

A heavy silence fell in the room.

"I want to like you, Sara."

"Feel free, Winston. But do not ever make the mistake of thinking
that I can be commanded or seduced or wheedled away from my duty."

"Your duty," he said. "Your duty to the people of this land."

"Yes."

"The people of this land are dying," he said. "They are being murdered by a foreign power that is all the more malevolent for its unremarkable, mundane nature. It is not the evil of the supernatural. It is
the evil of mankind, the evil that suppurates from the basest part of
us. It is an evil that you and I know to be a thousand times greater

than the evil of any foe you have faced. It is coming to conquer, and to subjugate, and to murder. It will burn books; it will burn buildings; it will burn men, women, and children.

"And you, Lady of the Checquy, are standing by and letting it happen."

Bridget and Pamela barely dared to draw breath. The Prime Minister and the Lady regarded each other, and it was almost as if heat were coming off their stares. Finally, without breaking eye contact, Lady Carmichael spoke.

"Of course I have thought about using the power of the Checquy to help in the war. Who would not? Who would not wish to be the avenging angel that could solve all problems easily and gloriously? But even if there were not innumerable laws and oaths preventing me from doing so, my own conclusions tell me that it would be too dangerous.

"These islands are not unique in being home to the supernatural," she said. "In every land that the British Empire has spread to, we have found the inexplicable waiting for us. In Africa, in the territories of the South China Seas, in India, where I was born, they continue to find new impossibilities. The American colonies had far fewer manifestations, but they were there, and from all reports, they continue to emerge." Her mouth twisted. "You're well aware of the dangers of Australia. And the Continent has already proven that it can yield up terrifying forces and entities, so it would be delusional to believe that there are no such forces in Germany or in any of the countries they have conquered."

"The Nazis are not ones to practice restraint," Churchill said. "They have already shown that there is nothing they will not countenance. If they had access to soldiers like the Checquy's, they would use them."

"There are some things that even evil blanches at," Lady Carmichael said. "You cannot rule a world if that world is destroyed. The risk of war between supernatural forces is too great. Every time it has happened in recorded history, it has been disastrous for all concerned." The Prime Minister looked skeptical. "If you doubt me, there are several acres on the Isle of Wight that will illustrate the dangers. You are talking about powers that cannot be resisted, and any risk of escalation is too great. Even a small indulgence, a tiny use of our abilities, could result in discovery." She sighed but did not look away. "In my role with the Checquy, I spend a large amount of time contemplating the possibilities and the implications of my abilities and those of the people for whom I am responsible. I see such horrible risks that sometimes it takes all my strength to make a simple decision for fear of what might happen because of the power and the authority I possess. So, Prime Minister, I understand the position you are in."

"I wonder if you do," he said gravely. "In so many ways, I envy you. Not for your authority. Not for your wealth. Not for your supernatural ability. I envy you your freedom. You are free to act as you see fit. There is no judgment for you. You do not need to provide explanations to the populace. You do not need to reassure them. Your place in history and that of your subordinates is unscrutinized."

"If not for me and the decisions I make and the sacrifices of my *subordinates,* there will be no history," said Lady Carmichael coldly. "There will be no one to remember what has come before. There will be no one to write the books or read them. Not merely in this land but in all lands, everywhere. That is the responsibility we carry. Think upon that before you criticize my actions or inactions. They are never the result of a casual or a passionate decision. Humanity cannot afford them to be."

They continued to stare unflinchingly at each other, two of the most powerful people in the nation, in the world. And then the Lady spoke again, and Bridget heard the familiar kindness in her voice.

"Surely as a writer and a politician, you have always understood the importance of *le mot juste,* Winston. The best possible word at the best possible time. The judicious application of one's ability. That is what the Checquy must be built around. If we did what you are asking, we might win the war, but we would lose everything we had fought for. Our world is much more fragile than one expects. It would be too easily broken."

"I understand," the Prime Minister said finally. "Lady Carmichael."

He understood, Bridget thought as she glanced around at the apprentices gathered in the room. *But will these kids understand? My God, look at them. They seem ready to start frying Nazis right this minute. Thank God none of them can fly or there'd be even more illegally downed bombers littering the streets of London.* Even as she thought this, she recalled that the boy in the corner, William, was unbelievably gifted with magnetism. It was well within his abilities to yank a plane out of the sky and crumple it into a cube if the mood took him. *You've got to talk to them. Calm them down, talk them out of this.*

"You cannot seriously be thinking about entering the war, just walking out on the battlefields to fight like it's 1677," Bridget said, trying to sound like the voice of authority and reason. "Have you forgotten everything we were ever taught? Think of the conflict with the Grafters!" She was pleased to see most of them flinch at the word. "We absolutely cannot use our powers to fight a war with Germany."

"What are you, daft?" said Edwin. "None of us are suggesting that we use our abilities to fight the Jerries."

"Oh," said Bridget after a pause, somewhat nonplussed.

"We know what would happen," said Ruth. "Of course we can't take any steps that would escalate this into a supernatural conflict." The apprentices were looking at Bridget as if she'd suggested that they fight the war by stomping on baby chicks.

"Yes," said Bridget woodenly. "That *would* be ridiculous."

"Not least because, as you might recall, my power is the ability to change the color of people's hair by touching it," said Ruth. "It's not exactly the most combat-applicable gift in the world."

"You can also make their hair fall out," said Lewis encouragingly.

"Yes, Hitler, beware," said Ruth sourly.

"But we want to help in some way," said Edwin. "Bridget, the Nazis want to conquer the world. They are committing atrocities wherever they go, and they will not stop at the Channel Islands. An invasion could happen any day. Everywhere we look, there are posters calling on us to support the war effort. 'Dig for Victory!' 'Make Do and Mend!' Men my age are enlisting as pilots and soldiers. They're fighting to defend this country, but I'm not allowed to—the government won't let me—and you wouldn't believe the looks I get, walking around in civilian clothes at the age of nineteen. And they're *right* to look at me like that! I keep expecting some lady in the street to hand me a white feather for cowardice."

"But you know how important the work of the Checquy is," said Bridget. "I mean, we're training to fight the fights that absolutely no one else can. And you're already doing it! Edwin, I read about you in dispatches just last week. It was you who made the breakthrough that cracked the case of the Gloucester Vivisectionist. You put together the detail that he was taking only his victims' muscles with the fact that the soil in the Forest of Dean lacked nitrogen and realized that the stolen muscle was being used as a source of protein. If not for you, they might never have figured out that the murderer was a beech tree."

"Well, yes, but that was small..." said Edwin.

"It was five people who got torn apart in the street!" exclaimed Bridget. "And we didn't even have to kill the tree to stop it. It was just a matter of spreading some really good fertilizer around the place."

"Bridget, people are dying every night because of the Germans," said Lewis. "More than die in a month from manifestations. Civilians are dying in their homes when bombs fall on them!"

"Yes, thank you, Lewis, I live in London, I know about the bombings. And the reason that more people aren't dying from manifestations is that the Checquy is there, doing its job. You're helping the country now," said Bridget. "Surely you know that."

"Not helping enough," said a dark-haired girl named Madge who hadn't spoken until then. "There is an army coming, and the Court is making us stand by and do nothing. And it will be bad. Alexandrina, tell her what you saw." The albino girl looked up, and Bridget could see a faint shimmer on the air in front of her eyes.

"I've seen what's happening in France," she said quietly.

"Oh, good *God!*" exclaimed Bridget. "Are you serious? What is wrong with you people? You *cannot* do that!"

"I didn't go physically," said Alexandrina defensively. "I set up a relay of prisms and looked through that. I've done it lots of times before." Bridget was staring at her in horror. "I couldn't take it any farther than Paris. I barely kept it cohesive at all."

"I don't care! Checquy members do not operate outside British territory without express permission from the Court. And definitely not in enemy-occupied territory. Jesus Christ!" She threw her glass onto the floor, where it failed to shatter. The others all looked down at it in bewilderment, but she didn't need to see it to know that she'd lost control of her powers.

Calm yourself.

"Paris has been occupied," said Alexandrina quietly. "On top of every French government building, there was a flag with a swastika. German soldiers were goose-stepping in the Place de la Concorde. They've reset all the *clocks* to German time!" She sounded like she was about to weep. "And there are so many German troops through-out the countryside." Her hands were clenched. "They're not going to stop at the Channel."

"I know that," said Bridget, breathing heavily. "Everyone knows that. It's why we're at war." She looked around at them. "Are you the only ones who are talking like this?"

"No," said Ruth. "There are others. You understand, we were all brought up to protect this land. But even if we weren't, there are some things that one cannot simply stand by and allow to happen."

"They will come, Bridget, and even if they leave us alive, they will smash everything we know and love," said Lewis. "We know that we can't use our powers to contribute to the war effort, we understand that, but we're still people, this is still our country." He stopped, and she saw that there were actually tears glinting in his eyes.

"Bridget, you *have* to talk to the Lady," said Ruth. "Tell her that she has to let us do this. Let me be a Land Girl, let Alexandrina go work in a factory, let Madge join the Women's Voluntary Services. The boys aren't even allowed to be messengers or join the wardens!"

"If I can't be a soldier or a pilot or in the Home Guard or do any-thing that might lead to actual fighting, fine! But let me do *some-thing*," said Edwin. He was pleading, and it cut Bridget in the heart to see her friend like this.

"We wouldn't use our powers," said Ruth. "And we could just do it part-time. You know, keep up with our studies and our training."

"Even conscientious objectors can do alternative work," said Lewis bitterly. "They can work on farms or in mines or drive ambulances.

Conchies can help protect the country against Jerry invasion, but we can't!"

"Bridget, please," said Edwin. "Please talk to her." In the background, over the distant chatter of their fellow apprentices, there was the sound of a gong being rung. They were being summoned to the ballroom. The apprentices in the room kept staring at her, eyes wide open, full of hope.

"Fine, I'll talk to her," said Bridget finally. "In the meantime, go on to the lecture." They filed out silently. Edwin was the last, and he waited uncertainly.

"Aren't you coming?" he asked.

"No, I'm going to stay in here and brood," said Bridget. She couldn't face the prospect of sitting in a crowd of people and trying to pay attention to a lecture. She needed quiet and dimness to think. And alcohol. "Have them send in a Singapore Sling," she added. *I might as well get some touch of the Far East out of the evening.* "On second thought, have them send in three."

Usha and Pamela watched the excited apprentices streaming into the Caïssa's lecture hall.

"It's a nice treat for them," Usha remarked.

"And a good chance to see their peers," Pamela said. "Growing up, I was always so delighted to meet other apprentices. I imagine it was like meeting cousins — they were obliged to be happy to see you."

"We should move into the hall," Usha said. "Get some seats before they're all taken."

"Probably."

Neither of them made a move from the bar.

"Or we could stay here and have another drink," said Pamela.

"Now, that's the kind of insight that has gotten you where you are today," said Usha. She gestured to the bartender, who obligingly brought two more gin and tonics. The exodus of the apprentices meant that there were now actually chairs and tables available, and the two women took advantage of this.

Pamela sighed and sipped her drink. "I actually argued against this." Usha looked at her questioningly. "Bringing all these kids together in

London—it seemed so risky. But everyone else thought it would be bad for morale to cancel." She regarded them as they moved into the lecture hall. "Perhaps they were right. The kids do all look happy."

"The apprentices I've come across are usually very serious," said Usha.

"You have to grow up pretty quickly in the Checquy."

"Bridget certainly seemed glad to see her friends," said Usha.

"It's a good thing, as it may be the last bright spot in her schedule for a while."

"Oh, she'll get a letter or a visit from Gerald pretty soon and be in a state of bliss," Usha said.

"She and that boy do adore each other," Pamela said, smiling.

"Do you think it will work out between them?"

"Honestly, I don't know," Pamela said. "Relationships with non-Checquy can be difficult in any case, but when they're as clever as he is?" She shrugged and made a face. "People like that realize there's something strange going on and try to figure it out. If they *do* learn, and if they don't crack, they'll turn the implications over and over—and that's not healthy for anyone."

"The Carmichaels seem to make it work," said Usha.

"Well, they've known each other since they were children. And besides, he's always been aware that it was an unequal match. I'm not sure which would be harder for a man, knowing your wife possesses inhuman powers or knowing she possesses orders of magnitude more money than you. Still, she's lucky. He seems all right with it." She took a drink. "Plus, she hasn't told him everything."

"I don't think any wife tells her husband *every*thing," said Usha dryly. "Although concealing one's devastating supernatural abilities and the true nature of one's secret government work is quite a lot to not mention." Pamela smirked, and they sat quietly until Usha said, "Perhaps we should address the elephant in the room."

"Oh God," said Pamela, putting her drink down and twisting around to scan the room. "Is Pawn Gentill drunk and doing her party trick again?"

"What? No! I'm talking about"—Usha paused and looked around before continuing in low tones—"our friend whose plane you brought down." Pamela's face grew still. "Pamela, can you not tell me what's going on? I appreciate that perhaps you can't tell Bridget—she's been brought up in this thing her whole life. She follows the rules. It nearly killed her not to report you. But I hold *you* ahead of the Checquy. Our friendship is more important, so you can tell me."

"I can't," said Pamela tightly.

"You *can*. I won't think any less of you, if that's what you're worried about. Or is someone threatening you?" Pamela closed her eyes and shook her head. "I have to know if...do *you* know why you did it?"

Pamela opened her eyes. "What? Are you asking if I'm going mad?" Usha shrugged awkwardly.

"I'm not insane, Usha. I know exactly why I did it." Her mouth twisted as if she had tasted something bitter. "And I know why it was the wrong thing to do. But telling you would only make things worse."

"How? I don't understand."

"It would make things worse for you," said Pamela. "And it would add another crime to my tally. If you don't want to help me hunt him down, I understand."

"Of course I'm going to help hunt him down," said Usha. She paused. "And if ever you decide that you *do* need to tell someone, I'm always here."

"I know," said Pamela. "There's no one else I would rather confide in." The two women were silent for a moment.

"Should we go out now?" suggested Usha. "Start tracking him tonight?"

"With two drinks sloshing around inside us?"

"There is an old saying in my country: There is no better time than the present for hunting down a fugitive Nazi who may be using inhuman powers to murder Londoners."

"Yours is a rich and beautiful culture filled with much wisdom," Pamela said. "But the tracking team will still be investigating the site. We'll get their report tomorrow, and then we'll see if there are any clues."

"And if they track him down in the meantime?"

"Then let's hope they shoot first and ask questions later," said Pamela.

"Cheers to that," Usha said, and she raised her glass. "Another drink, then?"

"Yes. I'll get this round."

In the end, Bridget went home, frustrated, after only a single Singapore Sling. Sitting alone and getting drunk seemed like the most depressing and useless way of addressing her various concerns.

Besides, the last thing she wanted was to spend the night lying on a camp bed in the club's capacious cellars surrounded by whispering and giggling apprentices. Or by Edwin and his friends staring at her again with imploring eyes. So, instead, she left a message for Pamela and Usha at reception and walked back to the Carmichael house on Belgrave Square.

Leominster, the butler, met her at the door and advised her that she was the first to arrive home. She thanked him and asked if the cook could make her a sandwich to take to her bedroom for dinner. One of Lady Carmichael's enormous Russian boarhounds insinuated himself under her hand, and she scratched him absently as she climbed the stairs and proceeded down the hall to her room. Against all the house rules, the dog stepped up onto her bed—which creaked a little in protest—and settled down with a deep sigh. Bridget kicked off her shoes, peeled off her stockings, and settled at the other end of the bed, her feet resting against his flank.

"Bloody hell, what a mess," she said to the dog. He opened an eye, regarded her, and shut it again.

I do understand how Edwin and that lot feel, though, she thought. Hadn't she said as much herself just the night before, watching the planes coming in and wishing she could warn people? *God, was it really only last night?* It seemed like weeks ago. Life had been so much simpler before the war, when all she needed to worry about was learning how to protect the nation from eldritch horrors, occasionally snatching some time to think about the boy she liked.

Still, she couldn't shake the memory of her peers staring at her with all their hopes on their faces, desperate to help with the war in some way.

Is that why Pamela did what she did? Did her hatred of the war push her to break the law?

It seemed too prosaic a reason for Pamela's actions. Pamela had been in the Checquy since she was tiny; its laws and teachings were in her blood, and she was exceptional in every way. During her apprenticeship, she had distinguished herself not only by her phenomenal supernatural abilities but by her brilliance and supreme self-discipline. When Pamela finished her apprenticeship and was promoted to the rank of Pawn, the Lady of the Checquy had personally selected her to be her aide-de-camp. And Bridget was sure she was being trained and groomed for even more tremendous things. Her career prospects aside, Pamela simply had too much self-control. Even the junior apprentices knew they could not use their powers in the war.

Then why? Why did she do it?

There was a knock on the door, and Bridget looked up, startled out of her thoughts. "Yes?" Leominster entered and pointedly did not mention the dog on the bed.

"A letter came for you in today's post, Miss Mangan."

"Thank you, Leominster." Was it her imagination or was there a hint of a smile as he brought her the envelope? She looked down at the name of the sender.

It wasn't her imagination.

Gerald Nash, the twenty-year-old son of acquaintances of Lady Carmichael's. Neither he nor his parents had anything to do with the Checquy—indeed, they had no inkling of its existence.

Bridget and Gerald had met at a large, formal, and totally agonizing dinner party. At that point, she had been a member of the Carmichael household for only three days and was still trying to settle into her situation. She moved about the house cautiously, petrified of knocking over something that was worth more than she was. The presence of servants made her nervous; she was worried about saying something inappropriate in front of the Lady's family; and Usha and Pamela were intimidating figures who took their grand surroundings completely for granted.

Hovering over it all was the awful knowledge that she was sharing a house with the commander of her organization and with the commander's family, so her whole career depended on how well she comported herself in every aspect of her life. She did not dare to leave her bedroom in the morning without checking herself three or four times in the mirror; she woke up early to study the newspaper rigorously in preparation for any breakfast-table conversation; and she tidied her room religiously so the servants would not judge her.

The dinner party was especially dreadful because the guests were almost all civilians and all extremely impressive in their own ways. Lady Carmichael had invited guests prominent in politics, the Church, the military, industry, the aristocracy, the arts, and academia. There would not be room for inane remarks, although Bridget hoped there would be room for her to shut up and get out of the way.

A maid helped Bridget into her new dress (a gift from the Lady) and did her hair, but a broken heel had nearly sent her tumbling down the staircase. By the time she'd gotten herself into a pair of heels hurriedly borrowed from Usha, the guests had all arrived and were enjoying drinks in the receiving room.

They were dressed in gowns and dinner jackets, and the room was filled with the chatter of easy conversation. In her cover role as "private secretary," Pamela had escaped attending, but Usha was there, magnificent in couture and several important-looking jewels. The Indian woman smiled and nodded at Bridget but did not break off from her conversation with the slightly worried-looking financial editor of the *Times*.

Mrs.—in this company, she was *not* Lady—Carmichael took her around and introduced her to the guests as "my ward Miss Bridget Mangan." Everyone was polite, although when Bridget spoke, she saw a few eyebrows rise at her Irish accent. And was that a curled lip under the aquiline nose of the industrialist?

You are an apprentice to the Lady of the Checquy, Bridget told herself. *Which means that she has seen promise in you. But you will have to live up to that promise. There will be tests. And this party, with these wealthy, educated, privileged people, is one of them.*

She was the youngest person in the room, although her eye was caught by a man about her age. At first glance, he was the very picture of a sophisticated student, completely at ease and deferring in conversation to his elders and betters. It was only when she looked more closely that she realized he was almost as uncomfortable as she. Both of them were awkward in their outfits, Bridget continuously smoothing down her dress, the young man periodically hooking his finger into the stiff collar of his shirt.

Gerald Nash, she remembered. *Son of Professor Phillip and Mrs. Helen Nash of Cambridge University, both of whom are currently talking to Miss Flora Ingham, the sculptress. He's studying classics at Trinity.* She'd memorized everyone on the guest list. Now she looked at him thoughtfully. Of less than average height, he was only a little bit taller than she. He had straight brown hair and wore glasses and a deliberately serious expression that kept slipping as he took in the activity around him.

She scanned the room, catching snatches of conversations. Nobody seemed particularly interested in seeking out the opinion of an eighteen-year-old girl of whom they had never previously heard. Which suited Bridget just fine, as she was happy to stand quietly and observe.

Her eyes met Gerald's just as she was very obviously shifting her weight in her uncomfortable heels and he was shrugging his shoulders in his obviously itchy dinner jacket. They smiled awkwardly, then looked away.

And then looked back.

And smiled again.

From then on, they had a silent conversation across the room. When the sculptress laughed loudly at some remark, a sound like a goose being backed over by a car, Bridget and Gerald glanced at each other, eyes wide open in incredulity. When a bishop delivered a long, meandering description of the role of the priesthood in ancient Greece and the salutary lessons that today's society could take from their example, Bridget looked questioningly at Gerald, who shook his head very slightly to indicate that His Lordship didn't know what he was talking about. Bridget rolled her eyes discreetly at a colonel's completely unrealistic assessment of London's preparations for an attack, and Gerald had to snort back a laugh. He put his finger to his collar again; she raised an eyebrow, and he hurriedly lowered his hand and grinned for a moment before stifling the expression.

When it came time to adjourn to the table, they were pleased to find that they were seated next to each other. Bridget had a moment's worry that he'd turn out to be less interesting when he actually spoke, but he turned out to be even more interesting. At first they were both overly formal, as though pretending to be grown up.

"I do beg your pardon, Mr. Nash, but how does your family know the Carmichaels?" she asked.

"My father is a don at Cambridge. He and my mother came to know the Carmichaels when they endowed a chair at his college. They turned out to enjoy one another's company."

"That's nice."

"Yes," he agreed. "This is, however, the first time I have come to one of these dinners."

"Well, you blend in very well," she assured him.

He smiled and then said quietly, "I confess I am utterly bewildered by the array of cutlery." She could hardly blame him. He had been raised with money and had dined at the high table of his father's college, but Lady Carmichael's dinner parties were serious business. Thus, before them were all the utensils for a twenty-course meal (not including the second dessert, which would be taken in a different room).

"I can help you," she said. She didn't mention that in preparation for her entrance into Lady Carmichael's household, she had received rigorous training in the most formal of table manners. The terrors of table conversation aside, she could have dined confidently in the collected company of the King, the pope, the archbishop of Canterbury, and that terrifying Checquy etiquette instructor who used a riding crop on students when they passed the port the wrong way. "That is a fish knife."

"And this?"

"A bone-marrow spoon."

"Honestly?"

"Oh, yes. Now, these are the legume tweezers, and this is your parfait trowel."

"Of course I know a parfait trowel. We're not complete savages in Cambridge."

"I do beg your pardon. Perhaps, however, you are not acquainted with the beef chisel or the cheese auger?"

And with that, they were off and running.

They talked about the war, of course—every conversation nowadays included the war. Gerald's call-up had been delayed because he'd had quite a serious illness, but he was recovering. She was surprised he had time to study at all, between military training and fire-watching duties at the university. But they discussed lots of other things as well. They talked about his classes—he told her he was reading classics at Cambridge, which she already knew—and her volunteer work, and the rest of the world.

Gerald seemed to be interested in everything, and in addition to having actual things to say, he had actual questions to ask. He wanted to know all about Bridget. She took him swiftly through her fictional life story—the mother lost in childbirth, the father who had worked for Mrs. Carmichael and died a year ago. Gerald could tell that she didn't want to talk about it, and they moved on quickly. He was interested in her thoughts on matters, and thanks to the Checquy's broad-scope policy on education, she had lots of thoughts on lots of matters.

The conversation drew them together. When they both liked something, they didn't always like it for the same reasons, and when they disagreed on something, it was exciting because then they could debate and unsuccessfully try to convince each other.

He liked Greek folk music and collected it on 78 rpm records, which had become nearly impossible to find thanks to the war. He was interested to hear that she liked American blues music (a taste she had acquired from her master during her apprenticeship in the Channel Islands). They argued, and they laughed.

To Gerald, the whole world was fascinating and full of potential. For Bridget, whose fate had been largely determined the moment her mother delivered her and her palms caught the light, such an attitude was intoxicating. The world seemed better through his eyes. And in the delight of his company, Bridget forgot to worry that she was seated across from a duke or that every move she made and bite she took was possibly being evaluated by her supreme commander.

At one point, she looked up from her conversation with Gerald to find that the whole table was listening with interest.

At the end of the evening, when all the guests except the Nashes had departed, Gerald and Bridget were still debating interpretations of the Titanomachy, and Usha had to suggest that they continue the argument the next day so that Gerald's parents could go back to their hotel and everyone else in the household could go to bed.

The next day, Lady Carmichael and the Nashes sat in the Grill Room at the Savoy and watched as both Gerald and Bridget produced written notes they had drafted of points with which to continue their debate. The lunch lasted for two hours and bled into afternoon tea. The day after that, Usha agreed to act as chaperone so Gerald could come to the house and his parents and the Carmichaels could get on with their scheduled lives.

Over the course of that weekend, Bridget and Gerald found that they enjoyed each other's company more than they enjoyed anyone else's. He was terribly clever, and although he aspired to be serious and sober, his tremendous sense of the absurd meant that he was continually amused, and he made her laugh as well.

When she was with Gerald, Bridget could taste what life might have been like if she hadn't been taken in to the Checquy. After the Nashes left (almost missing their train, because Gerald insisted on dropping off three books and a phonograph record for Bridget), the two began exchanging letters.

From then on, he always accompanied his parents when they came to visit the Carmichaels, even if it was just for tea during a day trip to the city. On several occasions, he came by himself, sometimes writing ahead to let them know he would be in London, other times stopping by unexpectedly when he and some chums came to town on a lark. Such larks became increasingly rare, however, as various chums were called up to service and as the bombings intensified and London became a less desirable destination.

Each time they met, it was wonderful. Always properly chaperoned, either by Lady Carmichael or Pamela or Usha, but just…wonderful. He was thoughtful and kind and funny, and the sight of him made her heart beat hard. Although their attachment was deeply personal to her, it was clear that the entire household was well aware and approved.

Pamela and Usha had said how nice he was and never remarked on any potential problems, but she'd seen the question in their eyes: If this continued, how was she going to address the issue of all her secrets? Quite aside from the truth about her family and her work and her situation in the Carmichael house, there was the fact of her inhuman features. Gerald had never commented on her ever-present gloves, but sometimes she imagined his reaction if he were to see her bare hands. Checquy members' relationships with normal people could be fraught even if the normal person was clever and open-minded; every apprentice knew that. There were some secrets that could never be revealed, and Bridget hated the idea of lying to Gerald forever if their relationship continued as smoothly as it had so far.

But that was something that could be pushed to the back of her mind, a problem for another day. Far more immediate and dreadful was the presence of the war and the knowledge that Gerald was a young man of conscriptable age. Guiltily, she had used the authority of Lady Carmichael's office to check his records, and she saw that he had been granted a deferment.

That meant that every moment with him was something precious to be savored with all her might.

And here was a new letter from him.

I shouldn't read it now, she thought. She needed to bend her mind to the challenge of tracking down one deadly fugitive in all of London.

But I won't be able to concentrate if I have the letter hanging in the back of my mind, she thought as she opened the envelope.

6

Usha settled in the leather chair and closed her eyes for a moment. The fire crackled in the fireplace, and outside, beyond the thick blackout drapes, the wind howled. At the Caïssa Club, she and Pamela had had one more drink, and then Pamela's ingrained sense of responsibility had kicked in, and she decided that she really ought to sit in on the rest of the lecture. Usha's ingrained sense of responsibility, however, led her to decide that she shouldn't go if she didn't feel like it—and hadn't she wanted some time to herself? So she said goodbye to Pamela, went back to the Carmichael house, asked that a fire be lit in her bedroom, and turned her attention to the papers locked in a secret drawer of her jewelry case.

Dear Daddyji and Mamaji,

Today I received your letter dated two weeks ago, and it was so good to hear from you. I am glad that everyone at home is keeping well. I miss you all very much. It really is like holding a piece of home—I can even smell Lahore in the paper. It was the first I have gotten from you in a while; the war, of course, is disrupting the mails, but you should be aware that there is also the very real possibility that our correspondence is being intercepted, and not only by business competitors.

I know that you have not received all of my messages; thank you for letting me know which ones arrived. Rest assured that you will not have missed too much important intelligence. I hope that the messages I concealed in my correspondence have been of some help to the family in weathering the war and protecting the business, but I must tell you that I have not given you the entire story. The truth is that what has happened to me over the past three years is far too complex to conceal in the body of a letter. No system of code phrases could encompass the unbelievable developments of my life.

In a way, really, it is a good thing that you are so far away when I tell you this. If I came to you and told you my story, you would immediately send for the doctor or possibly have me committed to a madhouse. If I were there with you in Lahore, I could prove the truth of this story easily. Although, depending on how you reacted to my proof, I might immediately have to send for a doctor or possibly have you committed to a madhouse. Perhaps it is just as well that I am 3,900 miles away from you; this way, there will not be any awkward medical interludes.

To give you the full story, I need to go back to when I arrived in London. The servants and I had enjoyed several weeks in Paris. (I suppose it is safe now to confess that I acquired far more new clothes than I admitted to, although presently it is looking more and more like the wisest of investments as shortages loom on the horizon.) The ferry from Calais to Dover was an easy trip, and Mrs. Carmichael was there to meet me, as she had promised in her letter. I recognized her from your description: tall and slim, with dark hair and those unmistakable solemn green-gray eyes. Of course, she stood out in the crowd not only because of her imperial bearing and expensively gorgeous clothes but because of her entourage. She was accompanied by her husband, Steven, her four children, and a seeming platoon of servants, some British and some Indian.

I did not lie to you in my previous letters about Mrs. Carmichael's hospitality. She is as kind and friendly as you remember. She welcomed me warmly, said how glad she was that I had finally accepted her invitation, introduced me to her family, greeted my servants in flawless Punjabi, and ushered me to the Golden Arrow, a famous boat-train connecting London and Dover. A woman named Rebecca Steward, who appeared to be Mrs. Carmichael's chatelaine/drill sergeant, coordinated moving the luggage. Also present was a Miss Pamela Verrall, Mrs. Carmichael's private secretary.

Although the Golden Arrow is renowned for its luxury, it was apparently not luxurious enough for the Carmichaels, who had arranged for their private carriage to be attached to the rear of the train. (Alternatively, it is possible they felt that our combined staff and all my luggage might overwhelm the capacity of a normal carriage.) As a result, we spent the ninety-eight minutes of travel time drinking tea and eating exquisite cakes in a sitting room that, apart from its narrowness and continuous slight rocking, gave every appearance of having been lifted whole from some unsuspecting stately home.

When we arrived in London, we were smoothly transferred to a convoy of Rolls-Royces and whisked through the city to the Carmichael house on Belgrave Square. My first impressions of the city were not, I am afraid, very favorable. Even though it was early afternoon, the streets were full of a thick insalubrious fog that the children advised me was a "London particular"—the city's famous mixture of mist and smoke. The fogs are apparently less common than they once were, but this one did not lack for strength. I could actually taste it, and I could only half see the buildings lining the streets; it was as if they'd been partially shaded over with pencil.

The streets were still busy, with crowds hustling about and buses looming out of the cloud. It was very different from Paris, and it might as well have been a different world from India. Honestly, after that first drive through the city, I could see why the British established their *empire. Any right-thinking person would cheerfully subjugate another nation just to get out of this city.*

Once we arrived at the Carmichael house, situated in the center of a magnificent white stuccoed terrace, I was installed in a beautiful bedroom and sitting room with a view onto the square. Amita, Shirina, and the bodyguards were given rooms in the staff quarters at the top of the house, and I understand that they are remarkably pleasant chambers, warm and well furnished. I'm told it is very important to Mrs. Carmichael that her servants be comfortable, and as a result she has their absolute loyalty. I have a feeling that even the bootboy would kill for her.

The first few weeks proceeded pleasantly. I settled into the household and became accustomed to their ways and schedules. Mr. Carmichael goes to work at his barrister's chambers, although obviously there is no financial reason for him to do so. I would have expected Mrs. Carmichael to live the hobnobbing life of a massively wealthy London lady, but she does not. Oh, she does socialize—her connections in London society are extensive—but I was advised that she spent a great deal of time involved in charity work. Indeed, quite frequently she is absent late into the night.

I'll confess I've become very fond of everyone, especially the children. The oldest, Ralph, is twelve and reminds me very much of our Arjun. Ralph's periodic departures for Eton mirror Arjun's to St. Xavier's in Lucknow. Lilian, Thomas, and Rosalind are all quite adorable, and although they try to maintain the reserve one expects from upper-class English children, they are still quite lively and intent on having adventures. On my birthday, most touchingly, they attempted to make and bring me breakfast in bed. The kitchen was eventually cleaned, but the bedclothes had to be thrown away.

The children are being rigorously educated—including the girls, which is interesting. At the moment, the three youngest are being taught at home by a cadre of tutors. Sitting in on their lessons, I was put in mind of the Ottoman sultans who, for all their power and wealth, were still required to learn a practical trade, just in case it was all suddenly lost.

In addition to the Carmichaels, their servants, and two gigantic pet Russian boarhounds named Vasily and Nestor, Miss Verrall is also resident in the house. She is my age, and she told me that she had no family left and that the Carmichaels, knowing her through old family connections, had taken her in and given her a position. She did not seem overly concerned about the loss of her relations, but I put that down to either the famous English stiff upper lip or the possibility that she had lost them a long time ago. In any case, she is serious and clever, and we very quickly became friends. Every day she went along with Mrs. Carmichael to the offices of the family business, but she and I also spent a great deal of time together, enjoying London in each other's company or taking the children out for jaunts to see the sights.

Of course, during this time I was not simply swanning around London going to museums and galleries and expanding my wardrobe (although I did all those things as well). With my bodyguards, I visited our offices here and made myself known to our representatives. Their surprise at the sudden appearance of an imperious daughter of the Khorana family was matched only by their horror when I ordered a full accounting of the books. The fact that I oversaw every step of the process and that I was flanked by the foreboding presence of Kabir and Ratanchit seems only to have increased their bewildered terror. Their relief that all the numbers added up correctly was really quite pathetic.

Of course, there was also a good deal of socializing to be done.

During my journey from India, I had experienced some occasional moments of apprehension at the prospect of navigating the shoals of this gigantic city, the capital of the empire. I wondered if the great and good would gobble me up, but they really are just people. It was almost a little disappointing, but I've found that the high society of London is like the high society of anywhere else when it comes to the variety and proportions of who is pleasant, who is interesting, who is useful, and who is none of those things.

In any case, it all proved quite easy. I had the letters of introduction from you and from the Marquess of Linlithgow, and the Carmichaels took me to many parties and gatherings.

Since I am here to support the family enterprises, not to find a wealthy or titled husband, I really saw no point in trying to enter the vaunted London season (diminished as it may be); at least, not as a competitor. Far better, I felt, to attend the balls and dinners as an exotic visitor, a curiosity, than as a damned interloper. Accordingly, whilst having afternoon tea with three of the biggest gossips in society, I made a few strategic mentions of a fictional arranged marriage waiting for me back in India, and after that I was warmly welcomed by every mama and eligible daughter in town. I made many acquaintances and connections and settled into a position that, if not really a true part of society, was comfortably overlapping.

I continue to be amazed by how much useful business intelligence one can pick up at the buffet table of a country-house party. And people in their cups at the regatta at Henley, while they do spend an awful lot of time talking about rowing, also swap a good deal of gossip about what they've heard in the corridors of the Dominion Office and how things are going for poor Cousin Billy's business interests in Bechuanaland.

Of course, part of the reason Mrs. Carmichael had repeatedly invited me to England was to train me in how a woman might run a commercial empire. What I saw was not exactly what I'd envisioned. She seemed to spend little actual time at her business offices. I had expected one of two extremes—either she would be tremendously hands-on and manage every small detail or, like so many heiresses I have met, she would let her male employees do as they pleased provided the wealth continued to pour in.

Instead, she is a master of strategic oversight. She selects excellent people and delegates power and authority to them. This is not to say that she pays no attention to the business. She reviews summaries and results and expertly identifies what needs to be addressed before it becomes a problem. This combined with unannounced, detailed, and seemingly random spot checks ensures that the fortunes of Carrisford & Crewe are not harmed by incompetence or corruption. And there are a number of fortunes. Built on her father's initial (fabulously lucrative) investment in diamond mines, the company has expanded under Mrs. Carmichael's leadership to include a variety of interests around the globe, including real estate, shipping, and manufacturing. It is far more diverse than our own import/export business and, accordingly, even more complex.

I was learning a great deal from her, but it was not the intense business apprenticeship I had expected.

And so life proceeded along very easily and quite rewardingly for a while until one night I woke up and cracked my head on the ceiling.

You read that correctly.

It had been an exhausting evening even before the impossible happened. The Carmichaels and I had come back from a party, a ball that went very late indeed. By the time we'd said our goodbyes and arrived back at the house, I was completely worn out. I barely managed to stay awake as Shirina helped me undress, and she essentially had to tip me into bed.

Despite my exhaustion, disappointingly, I did not sleep like the dead. Rather, I had strange, surreal dreams in which I had no body, and there was no light, only sensations that rippled through me. It was alien and terrifying. When I finally woke up, I flung myself upright, gasping in desperation, but I had barely lifted my shoulder blades off the mattress before my forehead smacked into the ceiling.

It hurt exactly as much as you would guess.

The thing about getting hit in the face with an unexpected ceiling is that it skews one's priorities. It hurts so much that one's only immediate concern is the possibility of having broken one's skull, not the bewildering proximity of the roof.

The room was pitch-black — the curtains drawn and the lights out — so I had absolutely no frame of reference. I spent a few moments carefully feeling the ceiling in disbelief as the bed bobbed slightly underneath me. If I hadn't just emerged from that nightmare, I would have thought it was a dream. But the pain in my forehead was enough to convince me that it was really happening.

It was at that point that, despite myself, I started to scream.

Whereupon the bed fell out from under me, crashed to the floor, and shattered with a horrendous din. I, however, remained hanging in the air, just below the ceiling, as the sheets and blanket slithered off me and landed on the wreckage below. This development did nothing to stop me from screaming in the darkness. I honestly thought that I might be going mad as I flailed in the air.

Pamela Verrall flung open my bedroom door. The light flooded in, and the image I saw will always stay with me: Pamela standing poised in her nightgown, hair swinging behind her in a braid, a pistol in one hand and a short sword in the other. It was so astounding a tableau that I stopped screaming and stared at her. It was as good as a slap across the

*face or a bucket of cold water over the head. Pamela turned on the bed-
room light and took in the situation, and although she looked startled at
the sight of my bed in splinters and me hovering up in the rafters, she
did not look nearly as flabbergasted as I felt my position warranted.*

"Usha?" she said levelly.

"Ye—yes?" I gulped.

"What kind of cakes were served at today's afternoon tea?"

"What?" I said.

*She narrowed her eyes and hefted her sword, tightening her grip.
"What kind of cakes were served at today's afternoon tea?"*

My God, *I thought.* I really am going mad. *But there was something about the way she held the pistol that made me answer.* "Um,
there was a cherry tart," *I said,* "and the children had cream buns."

"Fine," she said, relaxing a little bit. "Are you in any pain?"

"No . . ."

*Pamela looked over her shoulder. I could hear the rest of the house-
hold approaching. One of the dogs trotted in, looked up at me, and sat
down, completely unconcerned. "Don't make any noise," she told me.
She put the sword and pistol down on a low table and turned, partially
shutting the door behind her and blocking the gap with her body.*

*"Everything's fine, everybody," I heard her say. "Usha's bed col-
lapsed. Something must have given way—a peg or a slat or something."*

*Apparently this explanation (which seemed absolutely preposterous
to me) was accepted. Perhaps everyone was too sleep-raddled to question it—it was four in the morning, after all. There was a muffled
question. "No, she's all right, Amita. I'll calm her down, but perhaps,
Mrs. Carmichael, you might be able to help."*

*Amita's voice sounded very insistent, but she was eventually dis-
patched to the kitchen to make me a cup of tea. The hall must have
cleared, and Pamela and Mrs. Carmichael came into the room and
shut the door. Mrs. Carmichael's reaction was, if anything, even more
measured than Pamela's had been.*

*"Ah, it's happened. Excellent." I was amazed by her complete
lack of astonishment, but Pamela looked even more bewildered.*

*"Um, I've established personality and identity, my Lady," she said
hesitantly. I noticed but didn't remark on the "my Lady" bit, although*

I had never heard her address Mrs. Carmichael in that manner before. At the time, it seemed like the least important element of what was happening. "She knew what we had for tea today."

"Hm? Oh, yes. Thank you, Pamela." Mrs. Carmichael looked up at me. "Usha, are you feeling all right?" By this time, I'd calmed down a little and was actually beginning to feel somewhat irritated. I have always had the impression that the English will cling to restraint in the face of the Apocalypse—I expect the British Empire was built entirely on the power of understatement—but to be blasé in these circumstances seemed entirely unreasonable.

"Oh, quite well, thank you, Mrs. Carmichael," I said—a little tartly, I admit. "Why do you ask?" She favored me with a wry smile.

"Yes, point taken. Let's get you down from there and then we can address the greater issues." I waited expectantly, eager to see how she would proceed. I had some vague idea of seeing them struggle with ladders, but instead Mrs. Carmichael calmly sat down on a footstool and settled her nightgown and robe around her. "Now, Usha, it's clear that this has been a bit of an unexpected development for you."

"Yes . . ."

"Well, you needn't worry. You see, I've been anticipating something like this for quite a while."

"Then why on earth do you keep living here?" I burst out.

"I beg your pardon?"

"If you live in a haunted house, then move," I said. "Or have the place demolished and build a new one. I assume that exorcism doesn't work, because surely you can afford to have all the requisite holy men brought in. This is not safe—you have children living here. And animals!" I gestured at the boarhound, who had padded over to Mrs. Carmichael and was having his ears absently scratched. The ladies exchanged glances.

"Usha, it's not the house doing this," said Pamela gently. "It's you."

"It most certainly is not!"

"It really is," she said. "I mean, not even the sheets or the bed stayed up. It's you."

"Are you saying I'm a witch?"

"Well, no, not a witch—" began Mrs. Carmichael.

"*Perhaps it's a cursed ring or something,*" I interrupted. I really was becoming quite desperate for any explanation beyond what they were saying, even dragging out vague memories of nursery stories.

"*Are you wearing any rings?*" asked Pamela doubtfully. As it happened, I was, but one was brand-new from Boodles and one had belonged to you, Mamaji, and I really didn't believe that either one could be cursed—especially the one from Boodles. Still, I gingerly took them off and dropped them. They bounced off the mattress, but I remained firmly tethered to the ceiling.

"*Did you want to try the nightgown?*" Mrs. Carmichael asked dryly. "*It's from Harrods.*"

"I think we can agree that Harrods wouldn't sell anything that would have this sort of effect. Not without warning the client and probably charging a great deal more for it. Which means it's you who's doing this." She frowned a little. "Truthfully, I'm a trifle surprised that this is so unexpected for you. Did you really not have the slightest inkling?"

"You knew this would happen to me?" I exclaimed, for the first time focusing on what she had said earlier.

"There have been indicators for over a year now," she said mildly. "Little occurrences around you."

"I've been here for only five months," I pointed out.

"Yes, but the signs were seen in Lahore."

"By whom? My parents?" I confess, I felt a stab in my stomach at the thought that you might have kept this from me. "Did they know about this?"

"No, they have no idea. But we have people there," Mrs. Carmichael said.

"You have people in my house?"

"We have people in many places," she said. "They are trained to see. They saw, and word came to me. It was the reason I pressed so enthusiastically for you to come here. It was fortunate that this didn't happen before you arrived."

I was so shocked at her matter-of-factness that I couldn't say anything. The idea that I had been under observation and that she had reached around the Earth and manipulated circumstances to bring me here was dizzying.

"Well, anyway, it's clear that you can't get yourself down. Pamela?" Miss Verrall stepped forward and raised her hands. I tensed as I felt the air around me stir, and then I was being gently but firmly pushed down by a strange breeze. It settled itself into bands across my hips and shoulders, ruffling my nightgown, and swung me down into a standing position as the floor came slowly nearer. Miss Verrall's eyes were bright as my feet came to rest on the blankets from my shattered bed.

"You—you're the witch!" I breathed. "Why did you do this to me?"

"She brought you down," said Mrs. Carmichael calmly. "You got yourself up there. Now, Pamela, relax your touch a little. Let us see if Usha stays down." The ribbons of force on my shoulders lifted slightly, and I made a little squeak as the floor dropped away from me. Mrs. Carmichael hmmed a little and gestured for Verrall to bring me down to earth again. At that point there was a knock at the door, and Amita entered carrying a cup of tea.

"Mistress, is all well?" she asked me.

"She is quite well," said Mrs. Carmichael in her beautiful Punjabi. "But I think that it might do us good to have a little medicinal drink for all our nerves. Amita, please ask Leominster to bring us a bottle of brandy and three glasses." Amita looked at me uncertainly; I gave her the least genuine smile of my life, and she seemed mollified. She handed me the tea and scuttled off to find the Carmichaels' imposing butler.

"Usha," said Mrs. Carmichael, "you do not need to worry. As you have seen, your situation is not unique, and it is not to be feared. Really, it's a cause for celebration." I opened my mouth to say something, but she looked at me and I closed my mouth again. "But before we order a cake made, let us address the immediate concern. Obviously, we can't leave you lying on the ceiling, but I'd rather we didn't have to actually tie you down for the rest of the night."

"I appreciate that sentiment," I said, "but I'm still not convinced that—" I stopped when I noticed that they were both staring at the cup I was holding. My eyes swiveled down and then almost popped out of their sockets when I saw that the tea was slowly rising up in a wavering, hot, milky column. Almost despite myself, I moved the cup about a little, and the tentacle of liquid stretched, its surface rippling slightly. It hung in the air, billowing and spreading out in front of us in a great glistening fan. The milk separated itself from the tea and flowed on the darkened water in a tracery of white veins and channels.

I watched, utterly transfixed, as the liquid floated up and up and out and out until it was joined to the cup in my hand by the very faintest of threads.

Which then snapped.

At that point, the tea seemed to remember where and what it was, and it splashed down on the floor.

"Yes, very well," I said breathlessly. "I see your point."

"Could you feel it?" asked Pamela intently.

"Yes! Yes! I could feel the shape of it!"

"Hold that feeling in your mind," she said. "We need to explore it and adapt it to the moment." I realized that the air was still closed around me, holding me on the ground. But I was also aware of another force wrapped around me, creating a space in which down was up. "Excellent," said Pamela. "We will try a few standard techniques and see what works."

It took several hours and quite a few glasses of brandy, but eventually Pamela blinked, the currents of air that had been coursing around me dissipated, and I stayed on the ground through my own will.

It's difficult to explain, but it was as if there were an invisible cage or a field of my own thoughts, one that I could shape and extend out around myself and anything I touched and in which gravity was twisted. This field included the bed (at least for a while) and the tea, drawing them in different directions. Through my own tentative experimentation and some of Pamela's suggestions, I had found the way to make things normal.

"Well done," said Mrs. Carmichael, yawning. She was slumped on the chair in front of my dressing table and had the look of a woman who was ready to pass out on the floor. She lifted a toast of brandy dregs. "Cheers. And congratulations on your accomplishment. This is your first step into a new world."

I sighed. I had spent hours in concentration with a constant undercurrent of panic. Now I was torn between an exhilarated satisfaction at my accomplishment and a growing horror at what this all meant. Nothing would ever be the same. The rest of my life would have this in

*it, this inexplicable element that set me apart. I could foresee every-
thing being tainted by it.*

*"Are you certain it's not the house?" I said hopelessly. "Maybe it's
the place that enables me to do . . . it. After all, you said that the two of
you have had experience with this sort of thing."*

"Yes, but never at home. We know about it because of our work."

"What?"

*It was then that I learned that your old friend and business associate
is far more than what you had believed. Yes, Sara Carmichael is the
sole owner of the Carrisford & Crewe business empire, but if you can
believe me, that fabulous wealth represents only the smallest fraction of
the power she possesses. She also stands at the head of a secret organization within the British government, the Order of the Checquy.*

*This organization has a history that apparently stretches back cen-
turies, owing allegiance not to the King-Emperor or to Parliament but
rather to its mission to defend the populace against supernatural threats.
Mrs. Carmichael explained that the eruption of my new abilities was
far from a unique occurrence, that the Order of the Checquy consists of
a small army spread across the empire, with most of its soldiers possessing similarly strange, even unbelievable abilities.*

*This revelation brought me a new perspective on practically every-
thing in the household. To begin with, Pamela is not a secretary. She is
a decorated Checquy operative and aide-de-camp to Lady Carmichael
(Lady is Mrs. Carmichael's title within the organization).*

*Rebecca Steward is aware of Lady Carmichael's work, as indeed
are several of the servants. They are classified within the Checquy as
"Retainers," employees who do not possess inhuman abilities. (This
means that the scullery maids have a higher security clearance than
some government ministers.) I gather that this tradition of Retainers
began centuries ago, when all the servants in a Checquy person's
household had to be made aware of the truth. Now it is a term that
refers to all nonpowered employees, of whom there are many.*

*Mr. Carmichael is aware that his wife has secret government responsi-
bilities, but he is happily ignorant of the existence of the supernatural.
He is certainly not aware of her inhuman abilities. (I can hardly blame
her for concealing them from him—they are quite terrifying.)*

I gather that there is a great deal of variation in the extent to which family members and households of Checquy operatives are informed of the truth. Not only does it represent a highly important government secret, but it is also a revelation about the nature of the world. Many people are not able to cope with the information that walking amongst them are individuals with powers that defy explanation—individuals who could destroy them with a thought.

Still, for much of the Checquy's history, it was necessary for everyone in an entire household to be aware. When a family member had to go out to do combat in the middle of the night or take a powered apprentice into his or her home, the others in the family and any servants needed to be prepared. Their discretion was assured through a combination of oaths, laws, threats, and bribes.

In this house, however, the children remain in a blissful state of ignorance—a situation possible because Lady Carmichael takes in only adult apprentices.

I've been told that these abilities can appear at any time in a person's life. For Pamela, they came when she was a child. Bridget Mangan, who joined the household a few months ago for the final stage of her apprenticeship, was actually born with the distinguishing hallmarks of her powers plain to see. These abilities do not appear to have any rhyme or reason—there is no pattern that anyone can find. They simply occur.

Pamela, for instance, can control the air with her mind. Since that evening, I've seen her shift the winds with a gesture, punch through plate glass with a focused blast of air, and lift herself into the sky. She came into this power at about the age of five, and as soon as the Checquy learned of what she could do, they wasted no time in acquiring her.

That is what they do, you see. They claim any person with such powers for their own, taking people from their old lives and training them as their operatives. Pamela told me that she served multiple apprenticeships in preparation for her role as a soldier. The first priority, of course, was ensuring that she could control her power—the prospect of a five-year-old whose temper tantrum might level a house or kill someone could not be tolerated, not least because it would be terribly indiscreet.

There was no Checquy operative with exactly the same powers as Pamela, no one who could tutor her in the precise means by which she could control them. But I've learned that's the way for most people in our circumstances. The Checquy cannot give you a map to your solution, but they can teach you to draw your own map.

Young Pamela was moved immediately to Misselthwaite Manor, an isolated house in Yorkshire, where an extremely gentle and courageous staff took care of her and guided her through the techniques of exploration and self-control (the drastically abridged version of which I received that fateful night, although presumably young Pamela's education featured rather less brandy and swearing). I understand that it is not easy to instruct a child in the discipline of being a deadly weapon, not without removing all traces of her humanity in the process. The Checquy, however, has no interest in soulless soldiers bereft of compassion and individuality. Instead, Pamela was taken patiently through the exercises necessary to define her power again and again, always with kindness and encouragement.

"At first it consisted of a great deal of guided meditation," Pamela told me. "Just me and my instructor sitting in a roomful of tapestries as I felt my way through my powers. And if you have ever dealt with a five-year-old, I think you can appreciate the agony it was for both of us, getting me to sit still and just think. There were tears on both sides. But we made progress.

"And then there was lots of cautious experimentation out on the empty moors and gentle conversations in a beautiful walled garden, and gradually I learned control."

I gather it didn't always go smoothly or easily, but if windows were punched out accidentally or part of the roof was torn off in a fit of frustration or a teacher was temporarily suffocated, there were no punitive canings or scoldings or orders to go to bed without supper. An accidental vortex above the house was treated as an opportunity, not a failure.

After nine months, the little girl emerged, calm and in control. Her mastery was rudimentary, and her self-discipline was still forming, but both were strong enough to ensure there would be no disasters. With her basic training and orientation complete, Pamela was ready to be placed in her first apprenticeship.

"Until I was eleven, I lived with a Checquy Pawn and her husband in Oxford," Pamela told me. "They were lovely — I still write to them. They schooled me and three other girls in the basic skills of reading, writing, firearms, arithmetic, religious education, history, unarmed combat, science, sketching and watercolors, armed combat, and, of course, the core skill of any Checquy operative."

"Which is?" I asked her.

"Keeping one's abilities secret."

Always, she had to exercise her power, refining her control and developing new applications.

On her eleventh birthday, Pamela was sent from Oxford to her second apprenticeship, as part of the entourage of a Checquy commander in Newry, Northern Ireland. The Checquy had identified her potential, and the orchards of County Armagh were experiencing a manifestation (the coy term they use to describe any supernatural occurrence).

This was a particularly horrific and extensive one, though, a veritable plague. And while the manifestation had come to the attention of the Checquy only by chance, it had the potential to engulf the entire nation. I think it is worth telling you the details so that you might have an understanding of the Checquy and the scale of what it faces. Pamela recounted the story one long evening as we sat and drank Manhattans, and her casual tone as she described the horrors was hair-raising.

"It began on a cold November morning," Pamela told me, "when Checquy troops were summoned to investigate a report from Malachi Doyle, a farmer outside Portadown. He had complained to the local priest that his wife had been acting strangely for days. She didn't speak, she didn't seem to be eating, she'd stopped doing her chores, and she wouldn't meet his eyes." She took a sip of cocktail, then put on a startlingly good Irish accent: " 'Also, Father, the cow has stopped giving milk. A new cow, and no milk! What do you think of that?' "

The bemused but fortunately Checquy-trained priest knew Mrs. Doyle well enough to understand that not speaking or eating was completely out of character. If he had an opinion on the cow, history has not recorded it. He visited the Doyle farm, and the woman ignored him completely, walking around the farmyard silently for hours on end. Soon the telegraph wires were carrying the message to Belfast.

"Checquy troops from Belfast and Dublin soon arrived at the Doyle farm," Pamela said, "and when they approached Mrs. Doyle, she hurled herself fifty feet through the air and tore the head off a Pawn with her bare hands." I felt a chill run along my flesh. "Under a hail of gunfire and summoned hailstones, her skin shredded off to reveal a bubbling mass of intense pink flesh that had filled the skin perfectly. The eyes, shockingly human, stared unblinkingly.

"As the Pawns watched, the flesh deflated, turned a muddy yellow, and furled itself tightly around a gaunt torso that seemed to consist of bundles of fluted bony rods topped by a small wedge-shaped skull. The eyes drew back on stalks into the skull, and the legs split at the hips to form four multijointed appendages. Four additional arms unfolded themselves from the fasces of the torso, and cruel spikes slid out of their ends."

It was the first Checquy encounter with the race of creatures that would be labeled Furca malificarum by the Order's scientists and "Spindles" by its soldiers. The Spindles proved to be fast, deadly, and able to absorb an astounding amount of punishment before they died. The one that had taken the place of Mrs. Doyle killed two more Pawns before it was brought down.

When the surviving troops cautiously investigated the cow, no fewer than six Spindles burst out of its hide, where they had been interlocked to form the necessary bulk. By the time the Spindles were subdued, the cowshed, the farmhouse, and several outbuildings were ablaze, and seventeen apple trees and four Pawns had been cut in half. The flayed corpses of Mrs. Doyle and the cow were found in an outbuilding.

Closer examination of the Spindle corpses revealed that their flesh was extremely malleable, their muscles permitting them to take an infinite variety of shapes—this was how they had worn the skins of their prey so perfectly. Their skeletal structure was, if anything, even more dangerous. Immensely dense, their bones could hinge and telescope in a bewildering array of configurations.

The most troubling finding, however, was the Spindles' numbers. The fact that there had been several creatures suggested that this was not the mutation of one person or a single creature born with unknowable powers. And no one believed that all seven members of a brand-new species would have been content to live out their lives masquerading as a farmwife and a cow. It was likely that there were more.

Additional Checquy operatives were brought in from Dublin, Limerick, Belfast, and Liverpool. (Some were selected entirely for their ability to do a passable Irish accent.) They spread out through the region, cautiously searching for more of the creatures.

At first, the search was hampered by the fact that the Spindles could take the place of other creatures almost perfectly—even their eyes could shift in shape and color. It seemed impossible to identify them by sight, so the search focused on seeking out flayed corpses, either human or animal.

For a few days, there were no results. And then, with startling convenience, Pamela told me, a Spindle attempted to take the place of Pawn Doris Caomhánach in the village of Mountbolus.

"Well, it was convenient for the Checquy as a whole," Pamela corrected herself. "Pawn Caomhánach found it inconvenient to have a monster try to skin her in her bed, and although that Spindle's opinions were never ascertained, I expect it probably found it decidedly inconvenient to have its intended prey raise her hand and solidify the light around it into an unbreakable prison."

So the Checquy now had a live—if severely discommoded—Spindle to experiment on and observe. Scientists quickly discovered several important facts: Spindles did not need oxygen or water, they did not excrete, and they were largely fireproof.

"But their combat abilities did dip slightly when exposed to subzero temperatures," Pamela told me. "The only really heartening discovery was that the Spindles could not talk. They could make sounds, but they could not speak human languages. Identifying creatures masquerading as humans became as simple as asking them whether they were creatures masquerading as humans.

"Of course, the Pawns used alternative questions that were less likely to prompt uncomfortable responses from actual humans, and the operatives had to be prepared for answers that involved attempts to disembowel them and steal their skin, but it made things a good deal easier."

The scouring of the Emerald Isle for these creatures continued, and it represented a logistical nightmare. Not only were the Spindles' numbers and distribution unknown, but they had to be eliminated without the populace becoming aware. Their bizarre nature and scattered placement made the campaign unlike anything the Checquy had previously undertaken.

"If they had had any sort of coherent strategy, the Spindles could have colonized the island of Ireland completely," Pamela told me grimly. "If they had possessed the ability to cross water, they could probably have taken the entirety of Great Britain. But their motivations didn't appear to be conquest." She shook her head. "They were just so odd. They favored smaller, isolated communities and farms, and once they were established, they didn't reproduce. They didn't cultivate crops, they didn't build anything, they didn't travel, they didn't eat. They seemed content with doing a poor job of pretending to be human. Their motivation was, in every way, incomprehensible."

And there were other factors that limited them. They could not steal the form of any creature smaller than a ten-year-old boy, and their gregarious nature meant that even if they took on the forms of undomesticated animals, they would still cluster together. A farm in County Waterford was identified as a manifestation site when a Checquy Pawn noticed two stags and a wild boar wandering around the yard with the chickens.

And yet, despite these limitations, the Spindles proved to be horrendously dangerous. No matter what skin they took on, their physical capabilities made them deadly. If their borrowed skin was damaged, they would not hesitate to don a new one. As a result, all but one of a party of Pawns were slaughtered when they joined a camp of what they thought were colleagues by the river Suck.

The work continued, inch by laborious inch, day by grueling day, death by painful death. And even as the island was slowly cleansed, more questions arose. What were these creatures? What did they want? Why were they drawn to patches of mint? Most pressing of all was the question of their origin. Established colonies did not appear to be sending out offshoots, but they had to be coming from somewhere. Twice, Checquy scouts encountered small parties of unskinned Spindles traveling across the countryside at night.

Every encounter with a Spindle was recorded meticulously on the maps, and eventually the Checquy cartographers identified the pattern and the starting point of the Spindle outbreak. All the clues led back to the region where the first Spindles had been discovered: the orchards of County Armagh.

Winter set in, and it was at this point that Pamela was sent to Northern Ireland to serve as cupbearer, page, and apprentice to the Checquy general Rook Desmond Bax.

As the Checquy closed in on the epicenter of the Spindle outbreak, they found that some Spindles had not donned the skins of other creatures but instead had taken to roosting in trees, where, with their ability to restructure their skeletons, they were mistaken for branches until they dropped down on Checquy soldiers and eviscerated them.

Fortunately, it was an incredibly harsh winter that year, resulting in a county full of mildly weakened Spindles and citizens who were not interested in leaving their fireplaces. The battlefield consisted of a wasteland of icy-cold mud and forlorn fruit trees. It was the paranormal equivalent of the Western Front, and Pamela had a front-row seat. She sat in on high-level planning and strategy meetings and attended pitched battles as an observer.

"All of this when you were just eleven?" I asked her, incredulous.

"Not all children live beautiful lives of school and play, you know," Pamela said. "For centuries, children have had to grow up much sooner than might be ideal."

I was aware of that, of course. I'd seen children begging on the street or working like adults both here and in India. But it was difficult to reconcile the neatly turned-out woman before me, who sat easily in an armchair, wearing a silk summer dress, her hair in a tidy braid, with the image of a child in body armor with a pistol on her hip, learning how to wage a war while knee-deep in a quagmire.

"And then," Pamela said blithely, "on my twelfth birthday, it was decided that I was old enough to be deployed in battle."

I suspect she deliberately waited until my mouth was full before she told me that.

For her first mission, Pamela was set to act as bait for a war party of Spindles. The least threatening member of the Checquy forces, she sat, smeared with crushed mint, in a clearing for five hours with four Pawns buried in the mud around her, waiting.

"Weren't you afraid?" I asked.

"Of course," Pamela replied. "I knew exactly what might happen to me. One of my responsibilities had been to bring water to the injured in the hospital tents, so I'd seen the kind of wounds the Spindles could inflict."

"But you were a child."

"I was a warrior," Pamela corrected me. "I am a warrior now. We're all warriors, Usha. You too. We may do most of our work in an office, but every one of us knows that at any time we might get the call. Just as I did that morning, under the trees." She could see my incredulity and smiled. "Look, I'd always known that I'd have to fight someday. All my teachers were very clear about that. So, yes, I was frightened, but I was more frightened of not doing my job when the moment came."

Her fears were unnecessary. She acquitted herself well in the ensuing battle, spinning up a small personal cyclone that contained enough force to send several Spindles flying and shatter their exoskeletons against an oak tree. She was mentioned in dispatches and was awarded a medal once she'd had a wash.

Pamela showed me a photograph from that day. A solemn little girl in a mud-stained dress staring out at the camera with fierce eyes. There's a smear of blood on her brow and a stack of Spindle corpses behind her.

"I was responsible for four of them," Pamela told me, and I could not read her tone. Was there pride? Guilt? Sorrow at the idea of her childhood self becoming a soldier? She was calm, leaning back in her chair. "But they weren't the last ones. It took so long."

She was there for the end of the conflict, when grim, exhausted Pawns hacked and burned and bludgeoned their way through a final ring of hulking Spindle sentries. She saw the nest they had been guarding, which was nothing more than a large rabbit hole in the side of a bank. She watched as the Pawns dug down, slowly excavating the source of the Spindles, a massive conglomeration of flexing segmented limbs and bloated pulsating sacs. She observed as, over the course of weeks, troops carefully killed it.

"The thing proved incredibly resilient," Pamela remembered. "It was able to withstand massive damage, and so, methodically and *meticulously, we took it to pieces. We dug down to reveal new bits, cut them off, and destroyed them. Sometimes we were obliged to pause operations when a new Spindle was disgorged from an uncovered sac or squirmed out of the earth from down below." She sighed, and for a moment, her eyes were distant, looking back at a scene in her past. "The Pawns would kill it, sometimes suffering casualties in the process, then return to the digging."*

Finally, they reached a point when there was no more entity left to kill. No more branchings-off of ligaments, fibers, or ganglia down into the dirt. No more limbs that sometimes flailed out to impale a Pawn. No more mud-stained wombs bulging with the knobbly forms of Furca malificarum *warriors. There had been no sign of anything like a brain or a heart. Samples had been taken and spirited away to secret facilities to be studied.*

"There was no indication of any cause for the organism's existence," Pamela said blithely. "It was simply a thing that happened."

Apparently, we live in a world where such things simply happen.

By the time the operation was done, completely done, spring was approaching. And so the Checquy filled in the excavation, paid off the farmer whose property had been host to the damned creatures, and went back to their regular posts.

*D*addyji, *you will have noted in my description of the campaign that the Checquy drew troops from both Northern Ireland and Ireland and that they operated in both countries. Mamaji, I cannot conceive that you will have noted it, since your level of interest in Ireland is nonexistent, so I shall simply tell you that the island was partitioned in 1922 and is now home to the British state of Northern Ireland and the independent state of Ireland. They are very much different countries, and that separateness is, politically, very important.*

It is not, however, important to the Order of the Checquy, which has always been completely removed from politics.

As far as the Checquy is concerned, politics and governments and parliaments and national borders are incidental compared to its mission of protecting the populace of the British Isles from the ravages of the supernatural. As the empire expanded, the Checquy gingerly extended its bailiwick into the new lands. The New World, India, Africa, the Pacific, the Caribbean, the South China Seas. Offices and subsections were set up in each new colony, dominion, or protectorate. They had differing levels of presence and responsibility as dictated by circumstances and funding.

But Ireland is different. The island of Ireland, Great Britain, the Isle of Man, the Channel Islands, and the Hebrides are the core responsibility of the Checquy, woven inextricably into its mission. This is a policy that dates back to a time before there was a nation of Ireland—indeed, before there was a nation of England. The Checquy's written records stretch back centuries, and their spoken stories go back even farther.

For instance, it is told that in the year 815, reaving parties from the surprisingly warlike people of Cockaigne began striking around the different kingdoms. It is told that the force of supernatural warriors that drove away the deadly (and exceptionally rotund) raiders included soldiers sent by the kingdoms of Osraige, Cé, Mercia, Wessex, Brycheiniog, Glywysing, Bréifne, and Cat. The Order's duty has always been bound to the land, regardless of who happens to rule it.

Accordingly, years ago, when it was agreed that the Irish Free State would be established as a self-governing dominion within the British Empire, substantial, highly secret provisions were written into the Anglo-Irish Treaty of 1921. These provisions stated that the Checquy would continue to conduct operations throughout the entirety of Ireland. The Checquy would retain full rights of free and unrestricted movement, and its networks of communication within the new government and police would be unimpeded, no matter which side of the border a particular manifestation occurred in, whether on or under Irish soil, in or under Irish waters, in Irish airspace or astral space, in a collective or singular consciousness, in a collective or singular subconsciousness, in actual or metaphorical territory, or within Irish citizens.

Irish citizens who displayed supernatural abilities would fall under the authority of the Checquy. Checquy operatives who were Irish citizens would pay their taxes to the Irish government, but they could not be deployed in nonsupernatural warfare, nor could they be asked to employ their supernatural abilities at the command of the government.

I gather that some of the Irish signatories to the treaty were abso-lutely appalled at the thought of sharing a government department with the United Kingdom. The prospect of co-funding operations with the British, giving up Irish citizens to a faceless organization, and allow-ing British troops to roam about the country was not to be entertained; and they did not hesitate to express their dissatisfaction in camera. *Their objections died away abruptly, however, once they were given demonstrations of the kinds of threats that the Checquy was responsible for suppressing. Apparently, the sight of huge multi-mouthed stoats that screamed out obscene threats and whose leavings rendered the soil sterile and smoking served as a very effective debate winner.*

However, as the Irish Free State evolved from a dominion of the British Empire to the completely independent country of Ireland that exists today, changes had to be made. The attributes of the border between the two countries, the distribution of manifestations, and the near-fanatical dedication of the Checquy to the protection of all people in the land, regardless of nationality, meant that division of the organiza-tion was not practicable. The last factor in particular was the sticking point—Irish and British Pawns would have been invading back and forth across the border to come to the aid of their comrades and the popu-lace, and the possibility of active rebellion against both governments did not seem impossible. The argument against the splitting of the Checquy was made all the stronger since the Lord and Lady of the Checquy and both Rooks were Irish themselves. And so the nature of the Order of the Checquy was rewritten. It would no longer be a singular government department but rather a joint project between two nations.

Thus, the president of Ireland and the Taoiseach have the same authority over Checquy forces in their territory as the Prime Minister does in the United Kingdom. They, along with a couple of other Irish figures of authority, are on the council that selects new members of the Court of the Checquy. They also have access to Checquy bodyguards, and certain members of the Irish government are made privy to details of unimaginable secret events. Crucially, there is no automatic crossover of supernatural information between the UK and Ireland—neither government is informed of what is happening in the other's territory without permission. There are Checquy offices in several cities and towns throughout the nation, so it is as much a creature of the Irish government as of the British.

But I digress.

Talking about the Checquy tends to lead to that.

*W*ith the completion of the Spindle campaign, Rook Bax retired, so Pamela was sent to live with a Pawn in Bath. I understand that city is a particular hotbed of supernatural activity, and during her four-year placement she learned a great deal about the day-to-day business of the Checquy, both administrative and military.

From there, she was assigned to the northeast of Scotland, where an old man in a cottage in the Grampians spent seven months teaching her how to fly.

"He was foul-tempered beyond belief," Pamela told me. "The house was miles and miles from the nearest village, there was no electricity or running hot water, and it was my job to dig a new pit for the privy. Nothing to read but what I'd brought with me. No wireless. Nothing but the impossibly clear skies above the Highlands. It was the best time of my life."

After that, it was a two-year placement in Ceylon in the household of the governor, where she learned how to manage an outpost of the empire.

When Pamela returned to England, her progress was reviewed by a promotion board, and although she was not yet twenty, her accomplishments and abilities were judged sufficient for her to be made a full operative of the Checquy, a rank that brings with it the title of Pawn. It sounds rather dubious to my ears, but the Checquy members are at once warriors and civil servants. If you have some sort of inhuman ability, you receive a chess-based title; the troops are labeled Pawns, while the upper-level managers receive the less depressing designations.

"For my first independent assignment, they sent me to the village of Plymtree in Devon," Pamela remembered.

"Was it nice?" I asked.

"It was lovely. Tiny, but lovely. I was the only member of the Checquy for forty miles in any direction."

"What was your mission?"

"For a year, I was the local supernatural constable." She smiled. *"Undercover, of course."*

This assignment was meant to test her ability to handle problems on her own and to assure the Checquy that she could associate with normal people. She succeeded on both counts.

During her time among the populace, *"that young Miss Verrall staying in Rose Cottage"* became a beloved part of the community, teaching Sunday school, singing in the choir, and regularly visiting some of the old folks. She identified a local boy as a potential Checquy operative and arranged for him to be spirited away. She enlisted the local justice of the peace as a feeder to the Checquy network of information-gathering.

"I also *managed to solve a quaint rural murder,"* Pamela told me. *"Although it turned out not to be supernatural in any way."*

I gather that Pamela is something of a rising star, which is why she is now aide-de-camp to Sara Carmichael, who is Lady of the Checquy, one of the two heads of the Order. *(The titles King and Queen aren't used, for obvious reasons.)* Since Pamela and I were the same age, living in the same house, and already friends, it was decided that she would help train me and act as my support in my induction into the Order. From the moment I was brought down from the bedroom ceiling, there had been no question in her and Lady Carmichael's mind but that I would join. It seems that there are secret laws of the land, laws of the empire, that mandate that subjects who have unexplainable gifts must put them to the service of protection.

Of course, my experience has been drastically different from Pamela's. She has never known anything but the Checquy. She grew up knowing the supernatural world and her place within it. She was raised to her mission. With me, they had to be much more subtle, more seductive.

It began with the training. Once I got over the shock of discovering my abilities, I became absorbed in learning everything I could about them. Pamela and I traveled to a small house on Salisbury Plain, much to the bewilderment of my staff, who could not seem to conceive of my staying in a three-room house without someone to cook and clean for me. I was a trifle taken aback by the prospect myself, but Pamela pointed out that the isolation meant that I could experiment without *fear of being observed by any civilians — or accidentally crushing them. Plus, she felt that I should learn how to cook at least one thing by myself. Under Pamela's careful guidance, I explored the boundaries of what I could do with my powers and learned the secret of making cheese on toast.*

The training took weeks and involved much careful experimentation. It was terribly frustrating at first — an errant thought or twitch might send me bouncing and flailing across the grass and into a hedge — but slowly I learned to impose my will on the laws of gravity within the field around my body. Now, down is where I decide it is. I can cancel out the attractive force of the Earth, creating a space in which everything is weightless, or I can intensify the pull of gravity. I can tell the glass in my hand that across the room is a point where the gravity is a hundred times stronger than the Earth's, and it flings itself there at blinding speed. I can walk up the walls of Westminster Abbey and sit on the ceiling of St. Paul's.

And I can move myself through the sky.

Oh, my parents, I cannot tell you the delight of kicking off from the ground and watching the grasslands drift gently away and down, the sensation of a warm summer breeze wafting you along. And then you set a faint pull in the air so that you dive smoothly up to where you want to go, declare that gravity exists in the sky at the exact point where your feet are, and stand firmly and safely five thousand feet above the surface of the Earth. You look down and see miles and miles of empty countryside with the occasional line of a Roman road sketched into the grass or perhaps a small stand of trees. It is like the best of dreams come to life.

The only thing that makes it better is to turn and see your closest friend soaring next to you, taking delight in your accomplishments. Pamela and I spent hours in the air, and she taught me not just the craft but the art of flying. Of course, we have different strengths and limitations — she is reliant on the winds lifting her, with all the accompanying buffeting and need for space, but her years of experience and her control make her by far the more accomplished flier.

The evenings were spent eating exceedingly plain meals and talking. In truth, Pamela did most of the talking. At first, it consisted of filling in the gaps in the life story she'd told me before I entered her world. This is when I learned about her training, the Spindle campaign, and her various apprenticeships. But as she went on, there were, necessarily, details and context about the Checquy—its history and the way it is now. I learned about its mission, its work, and the dangers that come with being different from other people.

It seems that the Checquy have a thousand cautionary tales to tell, and these are all the more dreadful because they are not simple fables but actual historical anecdotes, each with a terrifying moral. For example:

If they know what you are, normal people will fear and hate you.

As they feared and hated the woman in Devonshire in 1775 whose power struck her and everyone she touched permanently deaf and blind. She was driven out of her village to die of exposure by the road.

If they know what you are, normal people will use you.

Like the girl and boy in Glasgow whom the Checquy discovered in 1889; their family had kept them locked in a room because of their powers—not to keep them safe or even to protect others, but because their breath could coat objects in a fine film of silver. They were prisoners, their gifts exploited.

If they know what you are, normal people will kill you.

Just as they killed the feathered man in Wednesbury who, in 1902, was burned at the stake by his family and neighbors before the Checquy could take him in.

Each story demonstrated a different reason for joining the Order, and while I was not so naive that I didn't recognize the purpose of these tales, they made a lot of sense. Growing up in our family, I know well the price of power and the danger that can come with it.

I was fascinated by it all. Just the few anecdotes that Pamela shared with me cast the whole world in a new light. The promise of more, of seeing the hidden face of history where unimaginable forces acted in the shadows, was too intriguing. When we returned to London, my real apprenticeship under Lady Carmichael began. I became immersed in the world of the Checquy. By that point, they did not have to persuade me.

Once I had signed all sorts of binding and terrifying contracts, I was permitted to accompany Lady Carmichael and Pamela as they went about their Checquy duties. Their routines abruptly took on new meaning. Some days are indeed spent at the corporate offices of Carrisford & Crewe, but the far greater portion of their attention is given to Apex House in Whitehall. That is the headquarters of the Checquy, the place from which the supernatural affairs of the British Empire are overseen.

At first, I was simply given tours of Checquy facilities in London. I was taken through offices that could have been any government or business department, provided that one did not look too closely at the paintings on the walls or the occasional unorthodox taxidermy that might loom in an alcove. Staff bustled about, and if some of the office girls bore heavy battle scars or an elderly mustachioed clerk abruptly effervesced into a sparkling cloud of floating gems, well, I was not so gauche as to stare when no one else did. Although I'll confess my jaw did drop when a walrus came swimming majestically through the air down the hall, followed by a small entourage of civil servants, and Pamela dropped a hasty curtsy.

After a while, I began to accompany them on trips around the country. We visited Checquy outposts so that Lady Carmichael could inspect the troops and assess conditions. Once again, the facilities appeared to be normal offices on the surface, but we were guided back, past wooden doors that proved to be armored, to corridors where secure rooms held armories and cells. Pamela took me to an archive in Workington and showed me the preserved corpse of a Spindle floating in a glass case. Even though it was over ten years dead and I was looking at it through the haze of the embalming fluid, the deadliness of its form was clear.

Pamela and I accompanied Lady Carmichael to viewings in secret morgues around the British Isles, where we saw corpses from Checquy operations. Sometimes the bodies were the monsters that had been put down; sometimes they were civilians who had been killed; sometimes they were the Checquy operatives who had died in the line of duty.

Sometimes the bodies were not entirely dead.

As long as I live, I will never forget seeing the body of a carpenter from Frome that would not stop burning, even though he had been dead for several months. His clothes had long since burned away, and his flesh was rotting, but he was not consumed by the fire. Nor could the flames be put out, even when the corpse was submerged in water or sealed in an airtight container.

Throughout these journeys, I was introduced to various Checquy personnel. God alone knows who they thought I was to be part of the Lady's retinue, but I was both fascinated by and wary of them. Pawns have inhuman abilities, and I always found myself hesitating before shaking hands with them. This was not, I hasten to say, because of their appearance.

Oh, there was the occasional heavily veiled woman whose head turned out to be a loose cage of bone wires surrounding a swirling constellation of tiny fragments of teeth or a man whose horrible burn scars were actually putty that he laboriously applied each morning to conceal the fact that he was made out of silk. But for the most part, the Pawns of the Checquy look like normal people—almost offensively normal, given how abnormal they are. There are people of every race, every body type, every age. And they seem to come from every walk of life. Many of them work in the government offices of the Order, but not all. They are scattered about the land, in different segments of the community, living normal lives until they are called upon. I gather they are all quite well paid—the Checquy has substantial funds—but they still have other positions and occupations.

My hesitation was because of the powers they possessed. You cannot make any assumptions. There is a fat old illiterate woman who works as a backstreet abortionist in Leeds who also happens to wield the power of the sun and has been known to blast assailants to their component atoms. There is a farmer in Devon who sees not with his eyes but from an invisible point some fifty feet above his own head. There is a celebrated Oxford don who can turn into a female rhinoceros whenever the occasion calls for it.

It is as you often say, Daddyji: "Never underestimate a person's potential." The fortune of our family was built on that maxim. You saw the seeds of genius in the street child scrawling numbers in the dirt, took him in, and gave him the opportunity to grow into our head of finance. You saw the opportunities that would arise if you ensured that every one of your children received the best education possible. You dismissed the presumed limitations of caste and sex and class, and our company has flourished where others have failed. But I suspect that you never conceived of the kind of potential that lies locked in some people.

What I have seen exceeds every wild belief I have ever heard of anywhere, even in India, where we are not quite so hidebound as others about what is possible and what is not. In the face of miracles such as these, one must question everything one has ever taken for granted.

I went to meetings attended by members of the highest echelons of the organization and witnessed decisions made that affected lives all over the globe. I was in the room when Prime Minister Chamberlain met with Lady Carmichael. I observed meetings of the Court of the Checquy, the eight individuals who command the forces of the Order all over the world. I was there strictly as a silent spectator, of course, but afterward Lady Carmichael and Pamela discussed what had occurred, and they began to solicit my opinion. I was encouraged to ask questions, and my understanding of the Checquy grew.

Some of what I learned was exhilarating, and some of it was distressing. Very rarely are the Checquy heads called upon to attend an actual manifestation, but they must be informed of all that occurs, and the choices they must make are sometimes horrible. I witnessed Lady Carmichael, that most elegant and gentle of ladies, give the order for an infant in Plymouth to be beheaded. I saw the Court of the Checquy command the subtle destruction of acres of crops in South Africa—a move that would ruin the livelihood of scores of innocents. I was there when they sent troops into a shipping office in Halifax with a warrant to kill all the people they found, regardless of whether or not they were perspiring brown oil from their pores.

And I saw why those decisions were the right ones to make.

The information I had access to in Lady Carmichael's office gave me tremendous insights into important events. It almost killed me not to alert you to the business opportunities. Honestly, the Checquy could make enormous fortunes every year if its abilities and connections were turned toward financial goals. But I have seen that saving hundreds of lives or enabling human civilization to continue unmolested brings a joy and satisfaction even greater than a healthy profit.

In short, I became—and I remain—convinced of the need for the Order of the Checquy. I have always known the world is not safe, that men can be wicked and that evil exists. But those threats as I knew them seem so mundane now. Mankind is given the opportunity to

commit crimes against itself only because the supernatural has not oblit-
erated or enslaved it—an end that is all too possible. The power that
exists within the Checquy manifests outside the Checquy as well. I
have seen it, and I have seen it turn vile.

I am happy to be part of the Checquy, but I am also under no illusions that I would have had any choice in the matter—I know the
secret laws that govern people like me. And since joining, I have not
been called upon to enter any haunted houses or deep, dark woods or
mysterious caverns. My powers placed me under the Order's authority,
but my real value to it has proven to be my education and experience.
It turns out that the training you gave me in running an international
house of commerce lends itself to certain elements of managing covert
supernatural military operations. My expertise in anticipating the
financial, legal, and social implications of events has made all the difference in some Checquy projects. You would be proud of me, I think.

I hope.

I am not yet a Pawn like Pamela. It is not immediately clear when I
will be promoted or what will occur once I am. I may be sent to a posting
somewhere in the British Isles, or I may remain in London in Lady
Carmichael's household. For the moment, like Bridget, I am the Lady's
apprentice, something of a chela to her guru. I will not graduate to the
rank of Pawn until I have successfully served at least three years of an
apprenticeship. Bridget, who has been in the Checquy since she was an
infant, is far more qualified than I am, but a Pawn must also be at least
twenty years old (although exceptions are made, as in Pamela's case).

And as all this has happened to me, the world has had the effron-
tery to continue on its own path; extraordinary developments in my life
have not prompted everything else to pause. I was distantly aware of
the Phony War that has now quite definitely become an Actual War.
The Evacuation from Dunkirk. The Battle of Britain. And while war
rages around the world, planes from Germany fly over London almost
every night and drop bombs. My bedroom window now has tape
starred across it in case of bomb blast, and the square my room over-
looks is being used as a tank park.

The gorgeous flower beds of the back garden were rooted out to
make way for potatoes, carrots, leeks, and cabbages. The window

boxes there now hold tomato plants. The lawns are home to several chickens and a goat, for whom I am responsible. (Mamaji, you will be pleased to know that your insistence on us children learning to look after our household animals has borne fruit. One does not forget how to milk a goat, no matter how hard one might try.)

The children have been evacuated to a house out in the country, along with their cousins on Mr. Carmichael's side. Amita and Shirina have gone with them. I felt that I could not expect them to stay in a war zone, but the journey back to India would not be safe either. Besides, the children adore them. The dogs, however, have stayed here in the city. They serve as useful alarms—often they are barking before the air-raid siren goes off.

Ratanchit and Kabir asked my permission to enlist in the armed forces. They were torn over asking, far more than I was over giving them leave to do so. I miss them, but I can now defend myself far more effectively than ever they could.

Our family house in Kensington remains unscathed for now, but if the Luftwaffe continues its current pace of bombing (and it seems to show no sign of slowing down), it may not remain standing for long. Accordingly, I have set about acquiring a home in the countryside (not too distant from the City, Daddyji) that could house the whole family if worse comes to worst in India and you are obliged to come here. Hopefully, this will not prove necessary, but as you know, I like to be prepared.

In the meantime, the furniture remains in the London house, but the really valuable art has been moved out to Lady Carmichael's country house, where, hopefully, the children are not taking it upon themselves to improve it. (In a moment of unbelievable lack of foresight, I told them how some painters used to paint new pictures over old ones. Lady Carmichael forgave us all, eventually, saying she'd never liked that landscape anyway, but I still wince whenever I think of it. At least they didn't start with one of the Monets.)

Those of us who remain in London sleep in the cellar, which Lady Carmichael has had reinforced and buttressed. An escape tunnel to the back garden has been built. It seems like the end of the world, and yet I still have to wake up each morning and deal with even bigger problems.

The final secret that I have not put into my letters to you is that it is not just the war that is keeping me here in England. The Checquy have made it clear to me that I am now theirs. Oh, I retain many freedoms but I am no longer in charge of my own life. And for all that the work is fascinating and rewarding, I chafe against the idea that I belong to an institution, and I think they see that. The Checquy is accustomed to submission, and my questions about returning home have prompted some stilted replies: "Why, in the future, when your apprenticeship is over, you may very well be posted in India. There are Checquy outposts throughout the empire, you know. In fact, there is one in Lahore!"

I am not quite convinced. I think they fear that our family wealth and my own . . . self-assurance . . . could prompt me to take my freedom, especially if I was posted far from the eyes and central authority of London. I came to them too old, you see, and with too much power of my own. Unlike Pamela and Bridget, who have never known anything other than the Checquy, I have been the mistress of my own fate, and while I believe in the work of the Order, I am not afraid to question the way things are done.

I expect that, if I were to flee, one of the Checquy's first actions would be to place their operatives near you, in case I tried to return to those I love best. Perhaps they have done this already. It seems likely.

Looking back on what I have just written, it all seems quite, quite insane. And yet it has become a routine part of my life. That's how the Checquy is. We really do fall down the rabbit hole, and, like this letter, our days twist off in different directions and digressions.

And so, my parents, I have stumbled into far greater discoveries than we could ever have anticipated when we planned my journey here. Discoveries that have led me to swear oaths of mickle might, committing myself to such levels of fealty and secrecy that this letter would be accounted as the very highest of treasons.

I hope that you can believe me. But if you cannot believe anything else in this letter, then believe in my love for you.

Your daughter,
Usha

⋆   ⋆   ⋆

Usha regarded the letter for a long moment. She'd been working on it for days, carrying it about with her, and now it was finished.

So, do you feel better for having written this? she asked herself. *This letter that you can never send? This letter that no one else can ever read?*

She regarded it for a moment more, and then she reached out and lowered her fingertip onto the center of the topmost sheet. Under her touch, the paper shivered, then crumpled itself. It rustled as it drew to a point under her finger. Then the next page followed suit, and the next, and the next. In the end, the entire long letter had become a pellet so densely compacted that it could never be unfolded. Usha rolled it under her finger, then flicked it into the fireplace, where it was consumed utterly.

The air-raid sirens went off outside, and she got up to make her way down to the cellar.

7

And this one's clean too! Congratulations, Lyn, you've done it!"
Lying on the table were thirty-two glistening pieces of, well, you probably had to call them jewelry, although they were in no way decorative. Two earrings, ten finger rings, ten toe rings, two bracelets, two armlets, two anklets, two thighlets, a necklet, and the world's plainest diadem.

Over the past two months, every night after her dinner, her glass of wine, her phone call home, her sauna (she'd swiftly become addicted), and her shower, Lyn had methodically donned all the pieces and gone to bed. Every morning, she removed them and placed them gently on a rubber cushion, upon which they were ferried away. Then, in a laboratory, she sat with the scientists, rustling and sweating in her plastic suit layered over her Faraday suit, and watched, cringing, as each piece was struck firmly with a little felted mallet to see if any electricity flashed out from it. Every flare of light had been a sign of failure.

The process of defining her abilities had involved a great deal of cautious, methodical experimentation. Lyn was quite certain that she would never have gained such a good understanding on her own, not if she'd had years to experiment. The cleverness and the focus of the scientists had been terrifically reassuring, especially their belief that her powers were not an amorphous, unknowable force but rather something that was waiting to be understood and mastered.

Most important, the scientists had never treated her like a freak or a specimen; they made her feel like she was part of the team. Even Dr. Allard, for all her clinical focus and her complete lack of social skills, was not devoid of empathy when she remembered who Lyn actually was.

Through various trials, they learned that her ability was focused in her skin. She could not activate it via her hair, her nails, or her teeth, but she could instill the power through any part of her epidermis— the nape of her neck, say, or the sole of a foot, or the inside of a nostril. Any metal touching her skin would be imbued with that red electricity; the energy would then wait, hidden and undetectable, until physical contact unleashed it. Only metal could receive and store the magic. She could touch wood, stone, cloth, plastic, glass, fruit, animals (for which she was profoundly grateful), anything nonmetal without accidentally turning it into a weapon.

Two weeks into Lyn's training, a young Belgian woman was flown to Kirrin Island on a helicopter, and she strode into the laboratory looking like she'd stepped out of a magazine. Sunglasses, a button-down shirt of the sort of deliberate simplicity that meant it was incredibly expensive, a leather skirt, and a pair of astounding elaborate cobalt boots.

"Mrs. Binns, I'm Odette Leliefeld," she'd said, offering her hand without a moment's hesitation. "I'm here to perform some exploratory surgery to test the parameters of your abilities."

"Please, call me Lyn."

"Odette."

"It's nice to meet you, although I have to say, mildly nervously, that you seem much too young to be a surgeon." *Especially one who is going to be surgeoning on me.*

"It's my superpower," said Odette dryly.

"I think you got a better one than I did," said Lyn.

"I don't know, yours is pretty cool," said the young woman. "And mine didn't come as simply. It took years and years of study and a regular series of injections into my spine and brain." She noticed that Lyn was staring at her quizzically. "I'm a Grafter."

"Right, of course," said Lyn a little cautiously. The Grafters had been explained in one of the briefing packets she'd been given: A cabal of Belgian scientists who apparently had unparalleled knowledge of the biological sciences, the Grafters were almost as recent an addition to the Checquy as she herself was. The briefing packet had used some very careful language when describing them, and Lyn, using her librarian's eye for subtext, had deduced that the Grafters' recent incorporation into the organization was something of a touchy subject. She looked at Odette, considering. The woman appeared perfectly normal, but there was something... "It's odd, but you seem very familiar for a covert supernatural surgeon."

The Belgian woman winced a little. "I'm dating—"

"Oh my God, yes!" exclaimed Lyn, snapping her fingers in realization. "You're that Belgian girl who's dating Prince Nicholas!"

"Yes," said Odette.

"Okay, then."

The press (and therefore the rest of the world) had been very interested when the third (soon to be shunted down to fourth) in line to the British throne had begun dating a new sweet young thing. Uncharacteristically for the popular prince, this new squeeze was not a sporty member of the established British upper classes. Nor was she a celebrity in any way, and she did not appear interested in becoming one. She did not give interviews, and while she was not perturbed by photographers, she did not pander to them either. She dressed fashionably, but not to an outrageous extent.

As far as diligent journalists could tell, Odette Leliefeld was not particularly rich, although apparently her family had enough money that she didn't need to be gainfully employed. She was vaguely understood to be researching a book when she wasn't accompanying the prince to parties, charity dos, or sporting events, and when he wasn't accompanying her to lectures, horse shows, or art exhibitions.

The general, slightly bewildered impression among the press (and therefore the rest of the world) was that she was a quite pretty, very calm young woman of good manners and intellect who had moved to London from the Continent, knew no one important apart from the man she was dating, and was very boring. The bookies gave it no more than an even chance of lasting through the end of the year.

There had certainly been no mention in the press of her being employed by the British government in any capacity, least of all as a worryingly young surgeon for a covert supernatural agency.

"So does he know?" asked Lyn.

"That I'm part of the Checquy?" said Odette. "Yes, that's how we met."

"And you two are allowed to date?"

"We had to get permission from his people and from the Checquy before we could go out," said Odette. "I believe it meant rather a lot of work for a few bureaucrats, getting all the clearances and so forth, but I think it was worth it." She smiled a smile that only just missed out on being a smirk.

"So they sent you here to Kirrin Island just to operate on me?" said Lyn warily.

"Yes, but I'm always happy to come up. My little brother is studying here as well, so I get to bother him and bring him a care package from London."

"Nice. I also have to say that I love your boots. They're amazing."

"Thank you, I designed them myself. Although they're actually not boots—I'm experimenting with utility hooves for three weeks."

"Oh," said Lyn. It was an indication of how far she'd come that this struck her as only mildly bizarre. "That sounds...handy."

"Yeah, they're fun," said Odette. "But," she added ruefully, "I got so caught up in the design and the intellectual challenge of it all that it was only after they were on that it occurred to me that I'd be wearing them all the time. Including the shower and in bed. And by that stage, I'd committed to the project."

"Does this mean you're going to be wearing high heels while you do surgery on me?"

"They can shift into several different forms," Odette assured her. "The muscles reset and the plates and scales realign. A few seconds' concentration, and I'm wearing sensible flat soles."

"Gross," said Lyn. "But cool."

"Plus, they have retractable talons in them."

"And they stay blue?"

"Oh no, I would never have done it if it meant they had to stay one color," said Odette.

The first surgery was to be done while Lyn was awake. There would be no anesthetic, much to her concern.

"We have to know what happens if your bodily structure is compromised while you're awake," explained Odette. "Can't send you into combat if you electrocute everyone around you when you get injured. In fact, they probably can't let you work in an office if a paper cut does the same thing."

"Will it hurt?"

Odette made a face. "You've given birth, right?"

"Yes," said Lyn warily.

"Well, then, you'll be fine," said Odette.

"What? Why? Will it hurt that much?"

"Look, we have to know how your power works. *You* have to know. I promise, I'll keep the discomfort as minimal as I can."

In the operating theater, Lyn tried to be calm as a couple of scientists set about buckling wool-lined cuffs around her wrists and ankles and broad straps across her waist and shoulders. Then more straps were spiderwebbed across her.

"Are the restraints necessary?" she asked. "I'm always all right when I give blood. I don't flinch at all."

"This is a little more than giving blood," said Odette flatly. "You should be clear on this, Lyn: I am going to be making incisions into your skin. I'm less worried about you flinching than about you instinctively punching me in the face." The Belgian girl had donned a Faraday suit that was studded with sensors, and there were rubberized booties over her hooves. She nodded to an aide to start the recording equipment going, then took up a scalpel. Lyn had turned down the offer of a screen to shield her from the sight of her surgery, and she made herself watch as the metal blade came toward her stomach.

Don't flinch, Lyn told herself.

Odette had gone very still, impossibly still, except for the smooth, almost robotic glide of her arm. Through the mesh of her veil, Lyn could see her eyes were intensely focused. Everything about her spoke of an inhuman level of self-control.

Oh my God, it really is her superpower.

The scalpel, a metal razor in a metal handle, touched Lyn lightly, and she was still. She felt a slight tingle.

"I think it's electrified now," she said.

"We expected that," said Odette, her eyes not shifting at all. "We have alternatives, obsidian or plastic or bone, but we judged that metal was a more likely weapon. Now, we need to examine further. I'm going to cut now." She moved softly, and Lyn barely felt a thing, but a line of blood followed the scalpel. "Okay, paper-cut-level does not prompt a reaction. Lyn, I'm going to have to cut deeper."

"Yep," said Lyn tersely.

Now, *that* hurt. *"Fu—"* began Lyn, but she was cut off when red electricity poured out of her body, writhed up the scalpel, and bounced around Odette's silvery Faradayed form. It crackled over Lyn's stomach but didn't hurt Odette at all. Despite the energy wreathing her, the Belgian girl did not flinch.

"Well, I think we can call that a reaction," said Odette dryly. "Anyway, good news, Lyn: your body will protect itself, but not to an unreasonably paranoid extent. That's a cut depth that would need to be deliberately inflicted. Even a slip with a kitchen knife probably wouldn't go that deep."

"That. Is. *Such.* Good. *News!"* said Lyn through gritted teeth. She was clutching the edges of the operating table.

"Hmm, all right. Now, I'm afraid we'll need to do a little more exploration. I need to check your body's reaction while you're unconscious," said Odette. She placed a mask over Lyn's face. "Breathe deep, and when you wake up—"

"It's all over." Lyn opened her eyes, completely awake. The pain in her stomach had vanished. She looked down and saw smooth, undisturbed skin.

"No stitches?" she asked. "No scar?"

"I assumed you'd prefer not to have any," said Odette, who had changed back into her civvies. Her hooves were once again boots. "It was an interesting surgery session, although I truly do wish the pain hadn't been necessary. Your body reacts in the same manner if you're unconscious, by the way. And it's not just your skin that can serve as the source of the electricity. All your tissues can produce it."

"I see," said Lyn weakly. She had a vision of her heart pumping away in her chest with sparks crawling and flickering around it. All the meat of her, a battery. "I'm sorry, what was that?"

"Your blood and bones, however, did not seem to carry the energy. And the sensors in the suit showed that the amount of electricity coming out of you was enough to shock an adult into insensibility. No arcing, though—it just attacked the source of the damage."

"Well, thank you very much," said Lyn. "I suppose." She smiled weakly.

"I'm glad to be of help, but I am sorry it had to hurt," said Odette. They shook hands. "Reach out if you have any questions or thoughts you want to share. Now I have to go see my brother. He asked me to bring him some proper Dutch *drop*." She produced a bag of licorice. "Want some?" Lyn did her best not to recoil.

"Thank you, but I'm not a fan," she said.

"I'm always glad to hear that," said Odette. "Means more for me!" And she took her leave.

After that, the Checquy gave Lyn a medical-alert bracelet made of plastic. The plate on the bracelet read:

Severely allergic to metal. Do not puncture, cut, or contact skin with metal implements. Use rubber gloves and specialized medical kit in handbag. Immediately contact personal physician.

A phone number was listed below that.

"If you ever need emergency medical attention when you're not here on the island, this will hopefully prevent any hapless civilian medical personnel from getting tased while giving you first aid," said Dr. Allard.

"Do people actually have severe allergies to metal?" asked Lyn dubiously.

"Oh, yes," said Dr. Allard. "I don't think they're generally allergic to every metal, but lots of people have reactions to nickel or copper. We anticipate that knowledge will be enough to make people believe a universal metal allergy is possible. At least this might give them pause."

They gave her the specialized medical kit: a small plastic box that contained scalpels with wooden handles and blades of obsidian, a hypodermic with a needle made of carbon fiber, and several pairs of thicker-than-normal latex gloves. They also gave her a handbag in which to carry the case. Lyn had not thought it was possible to make her protective ensemble any more outlandish, but the addition of a crimson Hermès bag made her look like a 1970s-era Dr. Who creature that had suddenly come into money.

The research continued. They found that once the corralled electricity was released, it behaved pretty much as normal electricity did, apart from its characteristic of burning a pattern into its first point of contact: a perfectly uniform circle within another circle. The scientists examined slow-motion footage of the energy being unleashed and observed the rings forming, but they could not identify why it happened.

"It's a little thing," one of the scientists, Dr. Hopkins, mused, "but there's no reason in physics why it should happen like that. We've seen electricity blast craters and trenches into something or just leave burn marks. And Lichtenberg figures—those fern patterns of burns—can form when it spreads out within an insulating material. But this thing with the circles? It's exclusive to your power, completely distinct. It happens with every substance your power touches. So it must be important."

Privately, Lyn thought that the electricity made that pattern because it *wanted* to. She'd come to think of the red energy as a living thing, coiled up cunningly in the matrix of molecules just waiting for something to release it. But once the energy had vacated the metal, it was normal, unchanged by its temporary tenant.

They advised her that they had been conducting testing on rats and pigs using some of the rods she had infused with energy. Shuddering, she refused their offer to observe the trials, but they required her to review the close-up photographs and read the reports.

"You have a weapon," said Dr. Allard severely. "You have to understand the implications and the ramifications of your abilities, have a full understanding of what you can unleash."

And despite her fears, Lyn agreed. Her memories of the firefighter who had been shocked flickered, like a flip-book of photos. And besides, he'd lived. Now, though, in the reports, she saw what happened when something was electrocuted and killed by the energy from her skin. She saw photographs from the trials with annotations highlighting the peculiar burned double ring that marked the contact point of her power with the victim's tissue. She also saw photographs showing that same double ring branded on the palm of the firefighter. And she resolved to learn how to control the spark inside her.

Gaining that control had been frustrating, embarrassing, and exhausting. The only thing Lyn could compare it to was her faint memory of being toilet-trained, but she had to assume this was much worse, because back then there hadn't been a team of twelve people watching the results every day, and no one had started writing his or her doctoral dissertation on how long it took her to use the potty successfully.

Over the course of weeks, she learned to isolate the part of her that felt the energy and then worked out how to clench it shut and modulate it. Now she could adjust the amount of electricity she poured into an item. There were limits, however, to how much energy an object could receive, determined mainly by its size.

As a rule of thumb, anything up to the size of a coin could give a nasty shock. A carving knife could hold enough charge to zap someone unconscious. And from there on up, depending on the time and focus she brought to bear on the object, Lyn learned that she could instill enough electricity to stop someone's heart. The upper limit had not yet been established—the scientists were disinclined to have metal objects holding potentially catastrophic amounts of electricity sitting around the laboratory. Besides, it took a long time to charge a large item. Lyn could charge up a coin with a moment of thought, but from there the process slowed.

And yet, apart from the time requirement, there did not appear to be an end point to how much energy she could call upon. It was like there was an inexhaustible wellspring within her. Alone in her suite, where she didn't have to wear the suits, Lyn would sometimes stare down at her bare, normal hands, trying to believe that she was now a deadly weapon.

Extensive tests of her body revealed no root source of the energy. Indeed, as far as modern technology could tell, there was no unusual energy within her at all. Examination of skin cells and biopsies showed nothing, no sparks cavorting about in her DNA. They injected her with dyes, scanned her with PETs, MRIs, a Geiger-Müller counter, and various other devices whose names she could not recall, but to no avail. A Sri Lankan lady came in and stared at her fixedly for several moments before shrugging. No magically glowing organs whatsoever. Wherever the energy came from, it was not biological.

"It is almost like you are a conduit," mused Dr. Allard over afternoon tea (each day, the examinations were paused at three; a trolley was wheeled in, and they all sat down to eat exquisite little cakes and drink very good tea). "Or a gateway to somewhere else."

"Where?" asked Lyn nervously.

"Who knows?" The doctor shrugged. She had once mentioned that she'd worked with a boy whose mouth could act as a portal to a spot on Hungerford Common; unanswerable impossibilities did not bother her. "We shall turn that over to the philosophers, theologians, and theoretical physicists. They will go nuts for it. Fancy another scone?"

Every morning, Lyn would touch five small ingots of metal and fill them with the electricity. A complex schedule had been worked out for when each would eventually be tapped to see how long the energy would remain dormant. It was possible, explained one of the scientists, that it might dissipate on its own over time. So far, all of them had remained active over the course of days and even weeks.

To her relief, there were no more outbreaks like the kitchen incident, where lightning had poured out of her uncontrollably, but she'd also never figured out how to voluntarily shoot it out from herself and launch it across the room. The only way she had yet learned to send the power from her body was directly into metal.

The remaining challenge, and the most difficult, had been reining in her powers while she slept. It wasn't a matter of willfully holding the power in but of training her body and mind to do it automatically. Thus the jewelry, which would suck up any nocturnal energy spillage. The tests each morning revealed if she'd lost control during the night.

Several times, she'd been woken when a nighttime twitch had unleashed the electricity stored in a bracelet or a toe ring, and the room had flared up red. They'd placed a fire extinguisher next to her bed, just in case, although she'd never done worse than scorch the sheets. She scratched herself on the rings in her sleep; the bracelets had left grooves in her cheeks (she was a front-sleeper, resting her face on her crossed forearms), and her forehead had broken out in little pimples under the metal of the diadem. Over the weeks, she'd learned to hate those pieces of jewelry. But to her immense satisfaction, she'd also learned not to infuse them with energy.

Now, finally, she had gone five entire nights without any accidents. She looked up with a big grin at the scientists gathered around her. She couldn't help laughing with delight as they applauded. There was a pop as Dr. Allard, still with no visible expression on her face, opened a bottle of champagne.

"Congratulations, Mrs. Binns," she said flatly. "You can take off the suits."

"Thank God!" exclaimed Lyn, undoing zips and shucking off her layers. In hopeful preparation for the results, she'd worn her scrubs underneath. She happily accepted a bubbling flute; all the scientists shook her bare hand with no sign of hesitation.

"We also got you a celebration cake," said Dr. Allard. "Hopkins, fetch the cake. Meanwhile, we will make a toast. Cheers."

"Cheers!" said everyone, and the doctor nodded approvingly.

"Your level of control, although it is still very rudimentary, means that you will no longer need to be sequestered, and the Checquy will not have to put you down."

Lyn choked on her champagne. "That—that was a possibility?" she said, aghast.

"Of course not! She was joking," one of the scientists replied, a little too quickly for Lyn's comfort. She looked warily at Dr. Allard, who was busily using a protractor to ensure that the cake was sliced evenly.

"Anyway, I want to thank you all so much," said Lyn, "for your patience, your kindness, and for making me feel that this wasn't the end of the world and that there was hope for me."

"We all enjoy working with you, Lyn," said Hopkins. "And we're looking forward to continuing the work."

"Oh?"

"Absolutely. There's so much left for us to discover. We need to establish how you react to different conditions, what effect different factors might have." Lyn nodded reluctantly. They'd paid a great deal of disconcerting attention to her menstrual cycle in the beginning. Apparently, it sometimes had a notable effect on one's powers, although it hadn't on hers.

"For instance, do different foods provoke a response?" continued Hopkins. "We'll need to try every type of alcoholic beverage. That's always an amusing set of tests. At least two of the team will drink with you...for control purposes. What else? Oh, various medications, just to make sure that an aspirin won't make you explode. And of course, there's always the question of how you react to different stimuli. Temperature, humidity, fear, exhaustion, hunger, sexual stimulation...don't worry, we let you take care of that one yourself!" he said hurriedly, having caught Lyn's horrified look. "But we *will* need to monitor the process. Ignorance is dangerous. And besides, you can't have sex until we've signed off that it will be safe."

After the celebration cake was devoured down to the crumbs, Lyn was told she had an appointment with Pawn Blom. She hadn't seen him once in the two months since she had begun her assessment and training. Evidently, the Checquy wanted her to focus on the vital task at hand. Now that she had passed her tests, however, it was apparently time for the next stage in her education.

"Dr. Allard and her team have given you clearance to become a fully enrolled student here at the Estate," said Pawn Blom.

"What was I before?" asked Lyn suspiciously.

"Legally, you were just a ward of the Checquy," said the Pawn.

"I was getting paid that much just to be a ward?" Her paycheck was pretty damn extraordinary.

"Yes. But now you will be formally enrolled in the school, which brings a commensurate change in status, additional pay, and new responsibilities."

"Like what?"

"You can now be summoned to active Checquy duty immediately, working under the Official Secrets Act, the Unofficial Secrets Act, the Secret Officials Act, and the Official Acting Unofficial Secret Officials Act."

"So I could get the call right now to go do...what? Fight monsters?"

"Yes, theoretically," said Blom. "Although that's unlikely at this stage, especially given your combat skills." He sniffed. "Early evaluation has stated that you are fighting at a beginner level. Your physical trainer is designing a regimen for you suited to your temperament and abilities, but we've already enrolled you in the basic kindergarten-level martial arts class."

"I'm learning how to fight kindergarteners?"

"You'll be learning, with kindergarteners, how to fight," corrected Blom meticulously. "Although I believe there *is* a specialized course in how to fight very short people. Your academic adviser will work with you to plan a course of study beyond the core curriculum. Your career adviser will sit you down to talk about possible paths within the Checquy." He continued down his list.

"I expect that since you're coming from civilian life, you won't need a sociability coach to prepare you for interactions with normal people. Your financial planner will assist you with money-management strategies. Your therapist will have a consultation with you. The chaplain will have tea with you. Oh, and someone will give you a tour of the Estate and show you where your peg is and where the toilets are."

"So I can move about unsupervised?" asked Lyn eagerly.

"Absolutely," said Pawn Blom.

"Outstanding."

So far, her view of the Estate had consisted of her suite, a generally deserted guest gym, the testing building, and the paths between them. She'd heard and seen the other students about, but her schedule and movements had been so curtailed by the need to learn control that she'd really had nothing to do with them. At times, seeing a little girl in the distance suddenly increase the length of her shins to go striding across a playing field like a stilt walker or a teenage boy becoming a dodecahedron of ebony tumbling along a lawn, Lyn had felt a bit embarrassed at the idea of all these children knowing how to control their powers when she couldn't. The prospect of getting a bit more freedom was very exciting.

"You'll be moving out of the guest quarters into a dormitory today, and I'll take you to meet your dorm parent. Then you'll be introduced to your roommate."

"Oh, a roommate! Okay…there are other adult students here?" Lyn said eagerly. She was definitely looking forward to meeting people who weren't scientists.

"No, not at the moment," said Blom. "I believe your assigned roommate is fifteen years old."

"What?"

"We don't say 'What,' we say 'Pardon,'" said Blom primly.

"Saying 'Pardon' implies that I'm at fault," retorted Lyn. "A fifteen-year-old?"

"Only seniors get rooms to themselves, and Georgina was the oldest girl who didn't have a roommate," said Blom.

"I'm not a senior? Really?"

"No, you only just started. Now, first we need to get you kitted out."

"Excellent—you would not believe how much I am looking forward to clothes that are not hospital scrubs."

"Here's your school tie," said the quartermaster, a large Scottish man with a shaved head and military bearing. "And, finally, here are your garters," he said, passing over two strips of elastic tipped with Velcro at either end. "You can get a detention if you're wearing socks and they're not pulled up."

"Right," said Lyn dryly. "Thanks."

"Uniform is to be worn every weekday until five o'clock or if you're doing sports or combat activity. And for chapel on Sundays."

I can't believe this is happening. The image of herself in a school uniform had been the most demented thing she'd seen since that one consulting scientist had abruptly departed a meeting by swallowing himself.

"That's your on-campus uniform taken care of. Normally we'd set you up with a public one as well." He gestured at a mannequin in a corner that was wearing the most astonishingly ugly outfit, an eye-burning ensemble of purple and orange stripes. Lyn recoiled. "But because of your age, we'll have to find you something else. If you went out in public wearing that, it'd get more questions than we want. And now let's pull together your go-kit."

"And what's that?"

"It's a bag you take with you if you're called out on a mission." He placed a large duffel on the counter. "Core equipment to serve you for four days out in the field. First, you'll need five pairs of socks and five pairs of knickers." He produced what she could only assume were official government-issue underpants. They were spectacularly uninteresting. "Madam Smiling over there will get you fitted for some combat bras, although you can also wear whatever suits you best."

Lyn watched as he added intimidatingly chunky combat boots, placing them next to her polished leather school shoes. Then there were two sets of dark waterproof coveralls, five sets of beige disposable coveralls, five T-shirts, two pairs of sturdy trousers, a baseball hat, a wide-brimmed sun hat, some disposable booties, two head nets to protect against mosquitoes and midges, a chain-mail head net for other things, a flat box of latex gloves, and a pair of thick leather gloves. Also sunscreen. Insect repellent. Chemical mace (which was, ill advisedly in her opinion, in a package that looked identical to the insect repellent). Safety glasses and a box of disposable respiratory masks. A long oilskin coat with a curious short cape over the shoulders.

"What if something takes more than four days?" she asked curiously.

"If the Checquy is unable to provide you with fresh supplies within four days, then you've got worse things to worry about than dirty undies," he said gravely. He added a toiletries bag containing various articles, including an official Checquy toothbrush (unmarked but with a pointed handle apparently sufficiently hardened to act as a weapon if necessary). He inquired flatly about her preferences regarding menstrual products, then placed a box of tampons in the bag.

"Now, weaponry." He put a startlingly large machete into the bag and added another that appeared to be made entirely out of wood.

"Why wood?" asked Lyn.

"Sometimes there's things that can't be harmed by metal," said the Scotsman darkly. "Always best to have options."

"No weapons made of glass?" asked Lyn jokingly.

"We've actually got some glass daggers and swords in storage," he said conversationally. "There was a Pawn back in the early twentieth century who could render glass unbreakable, but it gets a bit tricky if one of the weapons gets lost. We're supposed to be concealing the impossible, not scattering it about. So we hand them out only if we know we need them specifically."

"Yeah, right," said Lyn. She raised her eyebrows when he produced what she recognized as an expandable baton. "My husband has one of these." She picked it up, startled by its weight.

"Oh, aye? Is he a copper or just, like, a violence freak?"

"No, he's a policeman," said Lyn. "And he had to undergo all sorts of training before he was allowed to have one."

"Yeah." The quartermaster nodded knowledgeably. "They can do some ugly damage."

"Yes. So shouldn't *I* get some sort of training before you give me this?"

"Well, you'll be getting training eventually, but you know, you're not going to be subduing football hooligans who will sue you for police brutality. If ever you need to use this, you'll be hitting something with it as hard as you bloody well can. It's not complicated. So it's a standard part of the kit we give out to everyone here."

"Everyone? You're giving weapons to the children?"

"Only those over twelve." He caught her expression. "Let's face it, for a lot of these kids, a baton's a bit of a stepdown in the offensive-capability department. And they know exactly how much trouble they'd get in if they used it for unauthorized purposes.

"These are not your standard children," he continued. "They're trained to be professional, honorable, and self-disciplined. Like warriors. So you don't see a lot of the usual kid behavior. For instance, there's rarely any bullying. Partly because they all have powers, and partly because they know they'll be relying on one another in a few years. The person you're pushing around today may be the person you'll someday need to pull your arse out of the maw of a giant rat.

They understand that, 'cause it's drilled into them from day one. Anyway, here." He handed her a thick packet of money. "Count this, and sign for it."

Lyn counted it, twice, and looked up in amazement. "Two thousand pounds!"

"Yeah, and we've got the serial numbers listed, so don't get any amusing ideas about dipping into it for coffee money when you leave the island. They do a random check at least once a year."

"This is for my go-kit? Why would I need this when I'm out in the field?"

"You realize that when we say 'out in the field,' it's not necessarily an actual field? You get deployed everywhere—little towns, big cities, forests, fens. Money can be an important tool—it'll solve almost as many problems as a machete and with a lot less mess. Just make sure you get a receipt for everything."

"What are these playing cards for?" Lyn asked. The quartermaster had placed a small shrink-wrapped deck on the top of the bag. "Tarot?"

"Nah. It can get dull, even at manifestations. There can be a lot of downtime between the fountains of bats and the clouds of bile."

"Georgina, this is Mrs. Lynette Binns, your new roommate."

"Please, call me Lyn."

"It's very nice to meet you, Lyn. Welcome."

"Thank you."

Georgina Rackham was the most professional-looking fifteen-year-old Lyn had ever seen. Her posture was ramrod straight, and she was immaculately turned out. Her school uniform was ironed to within an inch of its life. Her red blazer gave no sign of ever having been worn before that day, and her gray skirt hung as straight as if little lead weights had been sewn into the hem. It was like a schoolgirl outfit that a marine drill sergeant might prepare for going into a highly unorthodox war zone. Her chestnut hair was braided with mathematical precision. Her shoes were polished to a mirror shine. She was actually standing at attention. She had the kind of poise that one got from either growing up with money or knowing exactly how to kill everyone in the room.

Hell, it could be both, thought Lyn. The kid had probably been making more money every year since she was born than Lyn or her husband made annually in their grown-up jobs. *And, God, what's her power? Is it considered rude to ask? Am I going to be sharing a room with a girl who might turn me into a pangolin if she gets irritated?*

"Well, I shall leave you two to get to know each other while Lyn unpacks," said the dorm parent, a slim lady who was a couple of years younger than Lyn. "Georgina, you'll take her to the dining hall at dinnertime, yes?"

"Of course, Mrs. Chu."

Mrs. Chu nodded approvingly and shut the door. Lyn and Georgina stared at each other.

"Well, this is unbelievably weird," said Lyn.

Georgina shrugged a reassuringly teenager-ish shrug. "I assumed that I would be getting a roommate at some point. I just didn't think that it would be someone who was—how old are you?"

"Thirty-five," said Lyn.

"Yes, I did not expect that. Anyway, that's your bed, I made it up for you."

"Thank you, that was very kind of you." The bed had been made military-style, which was not something one normally saw done with a plump flowered duvet, but Georgina had somehow managed to force it into hospital corners.

"That's your desk, and that's your wardrobe. We share a bathroom, but it's just the two of us."

"Thank God," said Lyn, who had endured communal bathrooms for a sizable portion of her youth and had sworn never to do so again, an oath she took just as seriously as her marriage vows. Plus, the prospect of daily showering with a bunch of teenage girls was just too hideous for words.

The room itself was cozier than she had anticipated, with none of the antiseptic institutional features she had dreaded. Rather than easily moppable linoleum, the floor was covered in a plush dark red carpet. The walls were freshly painted, and the handsome furniture looked as if it hadn't weathered the depredations of too many generations of students. There were curtains at the windows, and those windows were unbarred and could actually be opened, so a sweet sea breeze was coming in.

All in all, it was very cozy, although nowhere near the hotel-like luxury of the suite she'd been occupying for the past two months. It was clear that Georgina had hurriedly cleared half the room of her possessions—there were still marks on the walls where posters had been taken down, and some piles of books on Georgina's bookshelf weren't quite as orderly as the others.

Lyn looked curiously at the girl's side of the room. The desk was very tidy, with no computer, and paper notebooks were stacked on one side. (Lyn had been advised that the Estate placed a heavy emphasis on writing by hand.) One of the notebooks was open, and she noticed that Georgina had that day attended a lecture on the poet Keats and taken exquisite, meticulous notes.

Above the bed was the sort of taped-up collage of photos, posters, prints, and postcards that seems to grow across the wall like a ruffled coral reef. There were pictures of Georgina with other girls in Checquy uniforms, one of her running in some sort of school track event, and a couple of her in a formal dress and a fancy hairstyle on the arm of a nervous-looking and very skinny boy in a tuxedo. These were interspersed with pictures of actors Lyn recognized and musicians whose music she supposed she might vaguely know but whose faces she could not have picked out of a lineup. A battered-looking teddy bear sat on the bed, leaning against the pillow. On the bookshelves was a mix of textbooks, novels, and some magazines.

"How do you get possessions?" asked Lyn. "Do we get to go shopping?"

"Sometimes we do field trips off the island," said Georgina. "But we get pocket money every week, and we can ask Mrs. Chu to order us things. We have access to the internet in the computer lab, but it's read-only. We can't post things or e-mail people or anything. Not till we graduate. And even then it's very restricted under the various Secrets Acts."

"Students, before dinner, I would like you all to meet Mrs. Lynette Binns. Mrs. Binns, if you would stand up, please?" Lyn felt her face flushing as she stood. The dining hall was large, with a high vaulted ceiling of white plaster crisscrossed by dark wooden beams, and filled with many round tables at which were seated the members of the student body of the Estate school, aged seven to nineteen. All of them, along with the faculty sitting along a table on a dais at the end of the room, were now staring at her.

Oh God, I hope my powers don't activate under tremendous embarrassment. They haven't tested that one yet.

She put on a smile that felt massively unconvincing and that probably showed too many teeth and looked around. A sea of faces stared back at her curiously. There were no walls of flames at any of the tables, but there were some distinctly odd-looking individuals, including what appeared to be a bear seated on its haunches on the floor so that its eyes were at the level of its dining companions.

"Mrs. Binns is a new student here," said Frau Blümen, "and she is still learning about the Checquy, so I expect you will all make her feel welcome." The ensuing deathly silence did not feel particularly welcoming, but Lyn told herself it was because they were all obediently remaining silent. "She will be attending a variety of different classes with different years, so no matter your age, she may be your classmate. Mrs. Binns, would you like to say anything?"

"Oh, yes, thank you, Frau Blümen."

You don't have to be afraid of them. You don't even know if you feel nervous because they have superpowers or because you're in front of a crowd of a few hundred people.

"First, you don't have to call me Mrs. Binns, you can just call me Lyn. It's, um, it's extremely weird to be back at school." There were some smiles at that, especially from the younger children. "I expect I'll get lost a lot, so I'll probably end up asking some of you for directions to class. What else? Oh, before I came here, I was a librarian in South Shields. I have a husband, Richard, who is a policeman, and I have a daughter, Emma, who is three years old, and she would think you are all amazing. So I'm glad to be here, and I look forward to meeting you and studying with you here, and I guess we'll eventually be working together out in the world, so, yeah, thank you very much."

There was some very kind applause, and she smiled weakly and sat down. Then everyone's head snapped down as a brief grace was said, and soon plates of food were ferried out of the kitchens by the students whose turn it was to act as waitstaff.

Georgina had explained that the seating arrangements were different every evening. Mondays, Wednesdays, and Fridays, you sat with people from your age group—unless you were Lyn, in which case you sat with the fifteen-year-olds. (Lyn desperately hoped this was so that she would bond with her roommate, not because the Estate thought she would be attending for another four years.) Tuesdays, Thursdays, and Saturdays, you ate with your tutor group—a little prepackaged family of people from all age groups with whom you would also meet twice a week. Sundays was far more free-form; there was a standing hot and cold buffet, and people could simply wander in when they wanted and eat where they wanted.

The dining hall filled with the sound of young people eating and chattering away, but there was a bubble of pointed silence at her table. The rest of her companions were eyeing her warily.

"Look, you can relax," said Lyn. "I'm not a teacher, I'm not a member of staff, I'm never going to repeat anything you say here or judge you. Well, I mean, I won't *say* anything judgmental. And I'm not going to get you in trouble. You can talk—I don't care." The girls exchanged looks.

"So, is your husband hot?" asked one of the girls whose name Lyn had not managed to remember. The other girls giggled, except for Georgina, who looked mortified.

Remember, they're fifteen.

"Yes," said Lyn calmly. "That was one of the reasons I married him. I'd show you a picture, but I don't have one." *I should look into that, though.* There had been mention that, once she'd established control over her power, the Estate could arrange for her to meet her family at the clinic. *Surely I can get some of my possessions sent here.*

"How did you two meet?" asked another girl. All the girls were listening intently. *I guess it makes sense,* she thought. *They want to know about how life works outside the island. I mean, who knows how long they've been here? All of their lives?*

"We met through friends," she said. "My best friend, Jenny, was going out with his cousin, and we met at a barbecue they were having. He got up to do something, and I took his seat, and when he came back, he just sat on me, on my lap, and he wouldn't get up until he finished his food." The girls were all hanging on the story like it was *Pride and Prejudice 2: Pray, Let Us Go A-Barbecuing.* "And then he asked for my number, and he called me up and we went for a drink." The girls all nodded solemnly.

And then proceeded to interrogate her as to every single detail of their first date, including what she wore, what he wore, what they talked about, whether they'd kissed, how had the kiss been, and had she known at that very moment that they were going to get married?

"They seem nice," said Lyn. She was lying on her bed, her eyes shut, as Georgina bustled about getting ready for bed. "The girls at dinner."

"Yeah," said Georgina.

"I suppose you've known them a long time."

"Hm, all my life, except for Sophie. She came when we were seven."

"Did she take coming here all right?" asked Lyn drowsily.

"I think she cried a lot at first," said Georgina vaguely. "But she got over it." There was a curious gagging sound, and Lyn opened her eyes to see that the girl had both index fingers deep in her mouth and seemed to be fiddling about with a thoughtful expression.

What is this? I am not here to be her big sister, but if she turns out to be bulimic, won't I have to do something about it?

"I hate to interrupt you," said Lyn, "but I really do have to ask what you're doing." Her roommate took her fingers out of her mouth.

"I'm far-tasted," said Georgina.

Lyn blinked. "I need more details before I decide whether or not to freak out."

The girl rolled her eyes. "It's one of my abilities."

"So, far-tasted as in you...taste things at a distance?" asked Lyn warily.

"Yes."

"Like, without using your tongue?"

"I use my tongue," said Georgina as if it were painfully obvious. "It just doesn't have to touch things in order for me to taste them."

"Okay." Lyn hesitated. "Have you tasted me?"

"Uh, *no*."

"You don't need to look at me like that. It's not an unreasonable question. I don't know how it works, and you've already looked at me and listened to me from a distance."

"I prefer not to taste people. It's why I wear this." She put her fingers back in her mouth and, after a couple of moments, with only a small choking sound, peeled a transparent film off the length of her tongue.

"Dare I ask?"

"It's like a contact lens, but for my taste buds," explained Georgina. "It helps keep my taste focused inside my head." She laid the film out in a shallow plastic tray, proceeded to soak it with an alarming-looking red liquid from a squeeze bottle, then closed a lid on it.

"Can you still taste through it?" asked Lyn. "Or do you take that out for meals?"

"I can taste through people and walls," said Georgina heavily. "This thing doesn't stand a chance. It's not there to block. It's like a focusing lens, but for taste."

"Okay, well, as long as this is all supposed to happen," said Lyn, closing her eyes in exhaustion.

8

The front door closed. Although the mysterious meeting of the Court would not begin until dusk, the Lady and Pamela had just departed for Bufo Hall to ensure that preparations were going smoothly. Usha and Bridget exchanged looks, but they didn't speak until they had made their way to the library and told Leominster that they did not wish to be disturbed.

The library was one of Bridget's favorite things about the Carmichael house. A long room done all in white, it always felt full of light, even on the cloudiest of days. The books, bound in brightly colored leather, glistened like jewels on the shelves, and a profusion of potted plants filled the air with perfume. By sitting on the sofa at the window end of the room, a couple of tables and clusters of armchairs between them and the room's only entrance, Usha and Bridget could be assured that their conversation would remain private even if some maid happened to open the door.

"You left the club last night without attending the lecture," said Usha. "How were your friends?"

Bridget explained that they'd told her they wanted to take a greater part in the war effort. The Indian girl stared at her for a moment, then the two of them burst out laughing.

"My God, it must be catching," Usha said finally, wiping her eyes. "So they want to follow Pamela's lead?"

"No, they want me to talk to Lady Carmichael about letting them volunteer for the various services."

"Oh no, that sounds far too sane," remarked Usha. "They'll never make it to management if that's the way they approach things. So will you talk to the Lady about it?"

"I have to," said Bridget, grimacing. "If I don't, there's a chance they'll rebel in some patriotic way. Also, I have to take into account the responsibilities of my position."

"As apprentice?"

"As apprentice to the Lady of the Checquy," said Bridget. "You may not realize it, but we have a great deal of authority and influence, more than many full-fledged operatives. I can't just shrug my shoulders and say that I'm a student. And, really, it's not an unreasonable idea. You know, the Checquy *are* part of the world, part of society. They *should* want to do something."

"And when she says no?"

"Well, she might not." Bridget shrugged. "But if she does, then at least I've tried. And, frankly, compared to our other issue, this is not something I am going to worry about too much right now."

"Yes, before Lady Carmichael gets back, let's talk about that," said Usha. "I worry that the trail is getting cold. We wasted all of yesterday and last night."

"We had work and an event to attend," pointed out Bridget.

"Except that neither of us attended it. I had too many drinks, and we both went home," Usha said. "Lost opportunities. We have to seize every moment we have. Pamela has already arranged for the Lady's office to receive any updates from the team tracking whoever killed those people in their homes and from the regular police searching for a fugitive from a German bomber crew. So far, none of them appear to have realized they're the same person."

"God, let's hope the Lady never learns we used her name without authorization," Bridget said worriedly.

"Quite. But since you, Pamela, or I review almost everything that comes in, we can intercept the material."

"So if the German pilot is captured and reveals us, we'll be the first to know that we're going to prison."

"Precisely," Usha said, unruffled. "It's always best to get news before anyone else."

"Well," Bridget ventured, "unless we want to just sit around and wait for something to happen, we need to try to predict where he might go. I've worked up some thoughts." Her friend nodded intently, listening.

"I don't think he knew about his powers before all this happened," Bridget began. "If he had, he would've been using them directly for the glory of the Reich or keeping himself quiet and away from the fray. Certainly he wouldn't be serving as a bombardier in the Luftwaffe. There's a lot of precedent for people's powers igniting in moments of terrific stress, and I don't expect it gets much more stressful than being on a plane as it crashes into a city."

"To say nothing of being confronted by Pamela in all her wrath at however many thousand feet," remarked Usha.

"Indeed. Now picture it: You're a bombardier, you're in the ruins of your plane—which, as far as you can tell, has just been brought down by an English witch—and, for reasons that are unclear, you're still alive. Maybe your powers have ignited with some impressive effect to keep you that way, or maybe it's just chance. So what do you do?"

"Go insane?"

"Well, it's certainly an option," allowed Bridget. "We won't rule it out. But insanity is too complex to factor in right now. So he's down in the heart of enemy territory, the authorities will be coming, and the bombing is still going on. He needs to get out of the plane and find shelter.

"So he gets out, hauls his arse a few streets away, picks a house at random, and breaks in. He figures that if there are people at home, they'll be in the cellar or out in the backyard in a shelter. But he doesn't count on finding an old woman drowsing in her kitchen and not giving a damn about the bombs. She sees a man burst in, tries to raise the alarm or at least an objection, and he kills her with his new powers. I don't know if he meant to, but he did it."

"But why kill the couple next door?" asked Usha. "He's got shelter, he's got privacy, he's got access to some gin."

"True. And maybe he does take the time to sit, calm down, and have a glass of something fortifying. But then he takes stock of the situation, and he knows he can't stay there. He's still quite near the crash site, and once it is determined that there was a survivor, there will be a search. He has to keep moving, and he's got to act fast because of his clothes.

"Remember," continued Bridget, "his uniform or flight suit will be pretty identifiable as German military. And the old woman's a widow. There are probably no clothes in the house that he can wear."

"So he just tries the next house along?" asked Usha skeptically.

"It's what I would have done. If he didn't find what he needed in house number two, I suppose he would have gone on to house number three. But in house number two, he finds men's clothes and, unfortunately, the man who owns them. He has to kill Mr. Jinks, then Mrs. Jinks. I'm willing to bet that he made off with at least one set of clothes, more if he had any sense. Plus some money and food."

"But where does he go from there?"

"I don't know," said Bridget. "But I don't expect he knew either."

"So where do *we* go from there?" asked Usha. Bridget opened her mouth, but at that moment someone knocked on the library door. "Come," called Usha, and Leominster entered.

"Miss Mangan," said Leominster.

"Yes?" replied Bridget, unable to keep a bit of irritation out of her voice. They *had* asked not to be disturbed, after all.

"Mr. Gerald Nash has come to call."

"Oh!" said Bridget, brightening immediately. "Really?"

"Yes, miss."

"That's wonderful! Please bring him in."

"He is in the drawing room with Mr. Carmichael."

"Then we shall join them in the drawing room."

"And, Leominster, could we please have some tea brought?" said Usha.

"Yes, miss."

"Bridget, shall we go?" asked Usha.

"Yes…" said Bridget. "Do I look all right?" She was staring grimly at her clothes. They were perfectly proper, of course, a skirt and blouse appropriate for going out into the town, but she'd picked them for their ability not to draw notice. An air of bland, slightly prim respectability was not what she would have chosen to present to Gerald. For a moment, she entertained the possibility of running up to her bedroom and changing, but it would take too long. She smoothed her uninteresting skirt and patted her hair anxiously. *Why don't they have any mirrors in this library?*

"I take it you didn't know he was coming?" said Usha.

"No, I didn't. He didn't write or telephone. There was a letter from him just yesterday, but it didn't say anything about visiting."

"Well, you look fine," said Usha. "Now, let's go see your Gerald."

Bridget did not answer, because the thought of him being "her" Gerald was too pleasant.

When they entered the drawing room, the Gerald in question was sitting on the sofa, talking intently to Mr. Carmichael, who was nodding seriously.

Bridget heard Mr. Carmichael say, "You'll have our full support," before he and Gerald looked up.

Full support on what? Bridget wondered as the gentlemen stood.

"Ladies," said Mr. Carmichael, "look who's come to visit! Although I don't think he's come to see me. I know my cue to depart. Gerald, lad, please pass on my best to your parents."

"And mine to Mrs. Carmichael, please, sir."

"She'll be sorry to have missed you. Ladies, I shall leave you to your conversation with our visitor." The two men shook hands, and Mr. Carmichael clapped Gerald on the back and moved toward the door. As he passed Bridget, he gave her an uncharacteristic pat on the shoulder, then he stepped out and closed the door behind him. *What is going on? What were they talking about?*

As she and Usha approached, Bridget could see that Gerald was trying to be grave, but a quick grin had flashed across his face at the sight of her. She felt her heart starting to beat more rapidly in her chest, and she had to press her lips together so as not to grin back at him.

We need to be respectable, she told herself. "Gerald, this is a nice surprise," she said. "We didn't know you were coming, did we?"

"No, you didn't," Gerald said, shaking their hands. "It's very good to see you. Both of you," he added hastily, in deference to Usha's presence. Usha smiled with quiet amusement. "I am sorry to just appear without any warning."

"Between you and the raids, we've gotten rather used to unexpected visitors," said Bridget. "You're a much more welcome one, though."

"They are very bad, aren't they?"

"It's not pleasant."

"I'm actually surprised the Carmichaels haven't sent you out to the countryside," he said, "to join the children at that absurd folly of a house."

"We've gone out to the Moat House a few times, but my volunteer work here in the city is important." As far as Gerald knew, Bridget donated her time to a variety of causes, including providing first aid at an emergency post, assisting with the fire watch, and helping to place refugees in homes.

"I know, and I think it's very good of you. You're making a real difference, a contribution. Still, I do worry about you, rather," said Gerald, and Bridget flushed with pleasure. "How are you doing, Usha?" he said without taking his eyes off Bridget.

"Very well, thank you, Gerald," Usha said, settling herself on a divan. "What brings you to London on this gray and smoky morning?"

"Oh, something very important," he replied. His eyes, which were usually dancing with good humor, were looking very serious as he gazed at Bridget. There was a diffident knock at the door, and a maid brought in a trolley with tea things on it.

"Ah, tea!" said Usha. "Excellent. Put it there, please, Alice. I'll pour." She gestured strategically to the far end of the room, and Bridget shot her a grateful look. The rules of the Lady's house dictated that she and Gerald should not be left alone, but Usha could give them a tiny bit of privacy. The two of them settled down on the sofa as Usha went across to the tea.

"So, did you come to town with friends? A spur-of-the-moment decision?" asked Bridget. "You didn't ring or write or anything. I got a letter from you just yesterday."

"No, it's something I've been turning over and over in my head for quite a while now," said Gerald. Suddenly, to her surprise and delight, he took her hands in his. From the beginning, he'd accepted her explanation for her ever-present gloves—that she'd suffered burns as a child—and he'd never flinched away. It was one of the many things that made him so good. "Something very important. I've made a decision."

"Oh?" said Bridget.

"Yes, and it was something I had to say to you in person." He swallowed nervously. "I don't think telephoning would have been at all appropriate."

"Oh," said Bridget faintly. *Oh my God.* Suddenly things were falling into place.

An important decision that he'd made.

To say something to me in person.

Which brought him here without any warning.

And then we walk in on Mr. Carmichael giving his approval. Of course he'd have asked Mr. Carmichael for permission—as far as Gerald knows, he's the closest thing I have to a father!

My God, he's going to propose.

My God, I'm going to be marrying the best person in the whole world.

My God.

Her hands were shaking in his.

He looked deep into her eyes.

"Bridget," he said tenderly.

"Yes?" she breathed.

"I'm enlisting."

Several years of silence later, Usha came over with the tea. Bridget and Gerald had been staring at each other, holding hands tightly. "Gerald, you take it with milk, yes? I'm afraid there are no cakes, though. The cook has become increasingly protective of the sugar."

"Oh, I quite understand," said Gerald. "If my mother knew I'd made you dip into the household's ration, she'd have the chemists at the university render me down to my basic fluids to get it back and then send it to you with an apologetic note."

"That's a disconcerting scenario to contemplate. So, you two have been uncharacteristically quiet over here. What's the latest news?" asked Usha.

"I'm enlisting in the Royal Air Force," said Gerald.

"But he can't," said Bridget, and to her horror, her voice broke. Usha looked at her, wide-eyed.

"I have to," said Gerald.

"No, you can't go. You won't be safe."

It was grotesque. It was a sickening joke that the entire world had decided to play on her. Although she had never said it or written it, Bridget loved Gerald, and she believed that he loved her. She loved him for his brilliance, and his humor, and his joy. She had found someone wonderful, someone outside the madness of the Checquy. He was so young and so full of life, and she couldn't picture him in a uniform tearing after German planes, shooting at them and being shot at, and possibly getting...she flinched from the thought.

Most bitter of all was the knowledge that she would fare better, far better, in a war zone than he would. She was the one who had trained all her life to be a fighter, to survive violence and conflict. She was the one who had faced death a dozen times before she was fifteen, the one who had fought monsters. And yet her beautiful scholar was the one going away to war.

"Nobody's safe now, Bridget. And war is terrible, I know, but I have to join. I have to do what I can to help."

"You're too young," she said weakly.

"I've already waited too long."

"But—but what about your studies?" asked Bridget, flailing about for a way—any way!—to stop this nightmare.

"I expect the ancient Greeks and Romans will still be there after the war. Slightly more ancient, but ready to be studied." He looked into her eyes.

"I'll still be here too after the war," she said. "You know that, don't you?"

"I couldn't ask you to wait for me. We have no way of knowing how long this will go on or what will happen. What could happen to either of us. I've thought a great deal about it, and I won't gamble with your happiness. You have to live your life, and I don't want you to miss out on anything that might make it richer."

"Can you really believe that I would meet someone else?" asked Bridget. "I thought you were clever enough to know what you mean to me."

He looked away, blinking rapidly. She felt his hands tighten about hers as he struggled to control his feelings. She could tell he was trying not to cry because she was doing exactly the same thing.

"Will you write to me?" he asked.

"Yes. Of *course,* yes." She closed her eyes against the tears. "When do you go?"

"In a few days."

"Have you told your parents?"

"I had to tell you first," he said, and this time she was the one to look away. "I have to go now. I have to catch the train shortly."

"But you'll come back to London?" she asked. "Before you go?" *I'll see you again?*

"Yes."

"Leominster, we're going to need some liquor."

"Miss Khorana, it's not half past ten in the morning, and I hardly think that Mrs. Carmichael would approve."

"Gerald Nash has just informed Miss Mangan that he is going away to war."

The butler took a look at the stricken Bridget on the sofa. His expression did not change.

"I shall fetch the Royal Brackla."

Usha sat down carefully next to Bridget. She had the good sense not to ask her if she was all right. "I'm so sorry," she said finally. "I actually thought he was going to propose."

"I never really dared to think that was possible," said Bridget dully. *Not until just before he told me.*

"What are you talking about? He adores you! You adore him."

"Hmm, well, you may not be aware of this, Usha, but there's a fair few people who don't care for the idea of the Irish in general, let alone the idea of introducing an Irish element into the family tree. I'm not certain that his parents would want their brilliant only son to marry some girl from Galway with no background and no family whatsoever."

"They've met you. They like you," objected Usha.

"They're nice to the girl who is the ward of their friend," corrected Bridget. "Their friend who is extremely wealthy and influential."

"You're not without means," said Usha. "The Checquy's apprentice wages are very respectable." Bridget did her best not to roll her eyes. Her savings were nothing like the stupendous fortunes that Usha's and Lady Carmichael's families possessed. "And Lady Carmichael and the Checquy between them could run up a suitable background for you."

"It's beside the point now anyway," said Bridget, and she started to cry. "Because he's going away, and he might—he might never come back!" Usha put her arm awkwardly around her, and Bridget turned into it, weeping against the other woman's shoulder. "Oh God. Oh God," she whispered brokenly. She did not hear the door open, she did not hear Leominster come and go, and she automatically accepted the glass that Usha put into her hand. The liquid burned in her mouth and throat, but she finally took a long breath.

"You should go to bed," Usha said.

"No, if I go to bed, all I'll do is lie there and want to die," said Bridget. "I need to do something."

"So what do you want to do?"

*   *   *

They took the Underground to Canley because one of the drivers had taken Lady Carmichael and Pamela to their meeting, and Mr. Carmichael would be going out shortly and would require the other car. The journey helped distract Bridget from her feelings—it was always tremendous fun to watch Usha on public transport.

Usha knew enough to dress down, but although she had traded her Paris designs for a plain gray dress and was holding a battered gas-mask box by its string, she was never going to blend in on a Tube ride to the East End. The fact that she was Indian would have gotten her some notice, but even apart from that, she was simply incapable of fading into the background. Her beauty was captivating, her bearing intimidating. As a result, the carriage was deathly silent, and all eyes were fixed on her. Several jaws dropped.

She must be the least subtle covert operative in the history of the government, thought Bridget fondly. *Even less subtle than Pawn Twombley, and his hair is constantly making that sound like dozens of parrots screaming.*

Usha seemed supremely unconcerned at being the object of everyone's attention. She looked around the carriage, and under her calm gaze, every person either looked down or straightened up. It was like traveling in the entourage of the King, if the King had taken it into his head to put on a ratty cardigan borrowed from a Checquy charwoman and ride the District line to the site of a murder.

"Who is that lady, Mummy?" a little girl asked.

"Thinks she's the Queen of Sheba," sniffed the mother. "Standing there with her nose in the air." The train stopped and the woman pulled her still-staring child along to the door. "Better than us, I *don't* think. They shouldn't be let on at all."

"Are you all right?" Bridget asked Usha in a low tone. She felt her cheeks flushing with anger. "I can't believe she said that."

"Hmm?" Usha was admiring a baby in a perambulator.

"That woman! The one with the little girl. Did you hear her?"

"I did." Usha shrugged.

"You don't seem to mind."

"I'm not pleased," said her friend. Then she lowered her voice. "But Bridget, keep in mind, these people are peasants." Bridget stared at her, shocked. "They may live in the capital of the empire and work in factories," Usha went on, "but they're still peasants. Urban peasants. And not only can this 'Queen of Sheba' speak English a lot better than they do, she could also buy and sell them using only the money from her weekly hat budget. Her *wartime* weekly hat budget."

"I—well, as long as you're all right." *She has a weekly hat budget?*

"You have to be realistic about people, Bridget. You need to be able to evaluate them for what they actually are and what their true value is. Their worth. Especially if you are going to be working at a management level. Now, I believe this next station is the one that we want."

It took them time to exit the station, partially because of the crowds and partially because they felt obliged to help the baby's mother, who was juggling shopping along with the perambulator, which seemed the size of the Carmichaels' private railcar. Bridget ended up hauling the baby's gas helmet, which came in a large, bulky cardboard box the size and shape of a tea chest.

"I ask you," the woman said as they all made their way up the stairs, "how am I supposed to lug this helmet thing around *with* a baby *and* a pram *and* shopping *and* my own mask? And you know what they say we're to do when there is a gas attack? Put our masks on first, then put baby into the helmet and keep pumping the handle or she'll suffocate! God help us! What's that? You're looking for Roper Lane? That way, ducks. Second left."

As they exited the station, the first thing that struck Bridget was the smell. The fire teams had extinguished the blazes from the previous night's bombing, but the stink of wet burned wood filled the streets. Soot and ash still drifted in the air and settled on people's hair and shoulders. The pavement was littered with broken glass that cracked and tinkled underfoot, blown out of windows the night before, and the night before *that*.

It was difficult to say whether Canley by daylight looked better or worse than Canley being bombed at night. At least at night, the smoke and the darkness had concealed the shabbiness of the place. The people had clearly had difficult lives even before the German military command decided to smash the East End. Usha and Bridget passed several sites where buildings had been destroyed by bombs, and gigantic gaps had been punched into the long rows of tenements. At one point, they saw a family grimly sifting through the wreckage of their home for any possessions they could salvage.

They arrived at the residence of the murdered Jinkses, and Bridget eyed the house thoughtfully. They had moved into an area that had some single-family homes huddled against each other.

Well, it will afford us a little bit of privacy while we investigate, she thought. She'd spent a year of her apprenticeship in a tenement in Glasgow and well recalled the interest the residents took in one another's lives. *If there'd been a murder there, Mrs. McGhie and Mrs. McGee from upstairs would have been elbowing the detectives aside, criticizing the furniture, and exchanging observations on how the corpse had really let herself go even before the beheading.*

"The police turned the house over to the Checquy team," she told Usha. "Of course, they thought they were turning it over to a special police investigative team out of Scotland Yard. I checked, and today the team is currently researching known local burglars who might have developed the power to burn people from the inside out. So we have the houses to ourselves for a little while."

"I still don't quite understand what you think we might find in these houses," said Usha. "If both the police and the Checquy have gone over them, won't they have already identified any relevant clues?"

"Maybe," said Bridget. "And we'll get details of what they find in the reports. But they don't know what we know. So we'll be looking at everything through a different lens. A better-informed lens."

"Fine," said Usha in an indulgent tone. "How are we going to get in?"

"Skeleton key," said Bridget, and she held it up. "Much less work and less conspicuous than picking the lock." Usha glanced around— there *were* a couple of women in the street looking at them. "If anyone asks us, I'm Mrs. Jinks's cousin, and we've come to set the house in order."

The latch opened easily to the Checquy-issued skeleton key, and the two women stepped in hurriedly. When the door closed, the sounds of the street were completely cut off, and the silence of an empty house wrapped around them. Bridget felt the hair on the back of her neck rise.

The police or the Checquy team had taken down the blackout curtains, because there was some light coming in the windows, but the place was still dim. There were no signs of violence, which gave the impression that the Jinkses had just stepped out.

"This feels very wrong," whispered Usha. "It's like we've broken in and they could come home at any moment."

"We *have* broken in," replied Bridget quietly. "But they're not coming home." *Because he killed them here.* Still, she agreed with Usha. It was an eerie feeling, walking quietly in someone else's house. "Let's look quickly and get out of here."

"I agree. What are we looking for?"

"Anything that's out of place or obviously missing," said Bridget. "Put yourself in his shoes. What would he need?"

"Money and, like you said, clothes," said Usha. "Maybe food?"

"Yes, good," said Bridget. "Let's start with the kitchen, then. It'll be at the back." She led the other woman down the hallway, then stopped dead. There was a stain on the floor by the cupboard under the stairs.

"Is that blood?" whispered Usha.

"Yes," said Bridget softly. "That's where he killed her. The police and the Checquy will have cleaned up some, but someone's going to have to scrub that down." She stepped carefully over the stain and pretended not to hear the distressed sound Usha made as she followed. As they entered the kitchen, she saw a flicker of movement in the corner of the room, low down. "Oh God!"

"What? What is it?" asked Usha frantically.

"It was a rat," said Bridget, embarrassed. "It's gone now."

"Oh," said Usha. "I'm surprised. This place seems very clean, apart from the bloodstain in the hallway, and I don't think it's fair to judge the homeowner for *that.*"

"It just took me by surprise. Let's see what's been left here to tempt the rats out into the open." They briskly set about checking the cupboards but found no obvious gaps. "If there's food missing here, then our fugitive Nazi is far more selective than he has any right to be," sniffed Bridget. "Does he not know there's a war on?"

"I expect he has a clue."

"But look, he left bread. He left *sugar!* That's like leaving money, and he would know that. We should take this back to Belgrave Square."

"We are not taking murder sugar," said Usha sternly.

"You're only saying that because you don't take sugar in your tea," said Bridget. "You don't realize how tight the cook is with it. Frankly, I think that most of my ration is going to the children out at the country house."

"We can't interfere with a manifestation site," said Usha. "The tracking team will be coming back at some point, and we need to leave them with an accurate situation."

"Of course," said Bridget, somewhat abashed. She really should have known better. "Still, I expect they'll be as confused as we are. Even a looter reeling from his spontaneous burning powers would have known to take the sugar. Let's check the upstairs." They headed back down the hallway, stepping carefully over the bloodstain.

"Perhaps he took food from the old lady next door," suggested Usha.

"Maybe," said Bridget dubiously. "We'll have to check. But surely he'd want as much as possible."

"I'm not sure the food question is terribly important. Even if he has a couple of days' worth of supplies, what can he do in London? Where can he go? He'll find no help, no allies. Would he even speak English, do you think?"

"As navigator and bombardier, he'll be an officer, probably a lieutenant," said Bridget. "So I wouldn't be surprised if he spoke *some* English, but I don't anticipate he'd be fluent."

"He'd have an accent, though."

"Absolutely. Which means he won't have an easy time of it here. The government already interned most Germans who were living in Britain before the war broke out. Anyone with a German accent is going to get dirty looks at best and be beaten or imprisoned at worst. Actually, getting stabbed is probably the worst," she amended. "And in the East End? The *bombed-out* East End? If he opens his mouth around here, it will quickly be filled with half a brick."

The bedroom upstairs was simple and only about a third the size of Bridget's room in Lady Carmichael's house. While Usha checked the wardrobe, Bridget examined the dresser. There was a formal photograph of the Jinkses on top, taken on their wedding day. They stared out with fixed smiles on their faces, her arm linked through his.

I am so sorry, Bridget thought as though addressing them. *This shouldn't have happened to you. I'll do everything I can to prevent it from happening to anyone else.* She sighed and began looking through the drawers. *But what are we going to do with the German if we do find him?* she wondered. She didn't exactly want to broach the subject with Pamela and Usha. She suspected that she wouldn't like the answer because turning him in was absolutely not an option.

"Anything?" called Usha from the other side of the room.

"I really can't tell," said Bridget wearily. She had found which drawers belonged to the husband and which to the wife, but it was impossible to know if clothes had been taken or if it was laundry day or if Mr. Jinks simply did not own many shirts. "There are no obvious gaps, but I don't know what it looks like normally." *Maybe this was a stupid idea.*

"Well, there are some empty hangers," said Usha. "And I don't see any sign of a man's winter coat. We'll have to remember to check downstairs. Do you want to look in the house next door?"

"Maybe..." said Bridget absently. *Where would he go from here?* "You know what he really needs?" she mused. "Clothes and food are important, but what would be his most immediate need?"

"A ticket back to Germany?"

"Shelter. No one knows better than he that the bombings will continue."

"So he waited here that first night, then he left. Maybe we should start looking at local shelters, staking out the Underground stations."

"Yes," said Bridget. "Although...that's risky, at least at first. He won't know how it all works, and he won't have an identity card." For almost a year, ever since the war had begun in earnest, every man, woman, and child was required to carry an identity card. She and

Usha each had several cards with different identities. "He'll need somewhere to rest, a place he can reconnoiter from, figure out how things work. Somewhere secure."

"Such as?" asked Usha impatiently.

Bridget looked around. "This seems pretty secure."

"You can't be serious! The police came here, and they turned it upside down. They'll have searched the place thoroughly, including the cellar and the attic and every cupboard."

"Yes, of course," said Bridget. "But he had to know that would happen. Well, he probably wouldn't have anticipated the Checquy team, but he knew people would come. But think about it. It's daytime, so he goes out first thing, presumably wearing clothes belonging to Mr. Jinks. Maybe he keeps an eye on the place from down the street. He sees the police come and go. He sees the Checquy team come and go. He keeps track of how many go in and how many come out. He's got the keys—he'll have found them after he killed the occupants. So he can come back any time he wants. No one lives here anymore, there's plenty of food, there's a lavatory and bath. And it provides some shelter from the bombs."

"And then we arrive," said Usha. "And we find no sign of him."

"We were hardly stealthy," said Bridget. "If he heard us coming in the front door, all he'd have to do is nip out the back." She paused as she thought it through, trying to place herself in the circumstances of the Nazi. "Or, if he was upstairs here, he'd hide in a place where we wouldn't look. Where we'd have no reason to look." She glanced up, and Usha followed her gaze to the ceiling.

"Really?" she asked.

"There's a hatch in the hallway," said Bridget softly. The two women paused, thoughtful.

"What, do you think he's up there right now?" Usha whispered.

"No?" Bridget breathed her answer uncertainly. *We should have checked to see if the back door was unlocked.*

Usha was looking decidedly unhappy. They were both suddenly unwilling to speak. *What can we do?* thought Bridget. *We can't call the authorities. If they come and capture him, he'll fall into the hands of the Checquy, and the truth about Pamela will come out, and the three of us are doomed.*

For a single demented moment, she actually thought about setting the house on fire, just in case he really was there, tucked away in the crawl space like a maggot in an apple.

The two women stared at the white plaster of the ceiling for several silent, unmoving moments.

Then there was the faintest sound from above, the slightest scuffle.

"Argh!" shrieked Bridget. The two women clutched at each other, then burst out laughing.

"Another rat!" Usha gasped. "Oh God!"

"It's a good thing I'm trained in combat! Thank God for my nerves of steel!" Bridget choked out. She was trying to breathe, but the nervous hilarity was too much. "Oh my God!"

"Evil and rats, beware!" exclaimed Usha, and the two of them dissolved into laughter.

"Don't! Don't! Oh Christ, I think I wet myself," Bridget said, wiping tears from her eyes.

And then he burst down through the ceiling.

9

L yn?"
     "Hmm?"

"Do you have parents?"

Lyn opened her eyes. There was no light in the room except for the glow from the alarm clock, which advised her she'd been dozing in the dark for twenty minutes. She resisted the urge to turn on her bedside light; she sensed this was a conversation that might be easier to have without eye contact. There was a certain tone in Georgina's voice, a note of yearning that suggested she was having a lot of feelings at that moment and they could only come out in the darkness.

In the five weeks that they'd been sharing a room, they'd become friends in an odd sort of way. Georgina was quite a reserved person, with the self-assurance of someone who's been raised to power and the insecurities of a girl who's fifteen years old. From the beginning, Lyn had decided that it was not her place to be a big sister. Still, there were times when the girl asked for advice, and she felt that she had to give it.

This, however, was a new type of conversation.

Lyn did not point out snottily that *everyone* had parents, partially because it would have been *really* snotty and partially because, given the nature of the student body, she couldn't be certain that was the case.

"Um, well," said Lyn, "my maiden name is Dwyer, but the Dwyers weren't my birth parents. They adopted me when I was eleven. They were lovely, but they've both passed away." Now *she* was grateful for the darkness. "Before that, it was foster homes and institutions."

"And your birth parents?" asked Georgina's voice.

"I don't know," said Lyn. "I don't remember them at all."

"Do you know anything about them, though?"

"No," said Lyn. "And neither does anyone else."

"But do you think about them?" persisted Georgina. "Your birth parents? Who they might have been?"

"When I was about your age, it became the most important thing in the world," said Lyn. "My adoptive parents didn't want to give me the details until I was eighteen, but I wore them down, and they let me read the information they had. It wasn't pleasant.

"Someone had found me when I was about three years old, maybe an undernourished four, sitting in the gutter in just a grubby T-shirt in a *very* rough area in Birmingham. I guess I'd toddled away from home. No one ever claimed me. No one had any idea who I was or to whom I belonged. Apparently it happens," she said ruefully. "In some places, babies are born off the books. Not the best places."

"Oh." Georgina sounded subdued, and Lyn didn't blame her. It was hardly a basket in the bulrushes.

"Yeah. I understand it's generally because the conditions are so bad that any baby born in that situation will automatically be taken into custody by the state. So it's likely that I was born at home, in secret, to someone who would not have been considered a fit mother."

"And does that bother you?" Georgina asked with the complete lack of tact that only a fifteen-year-old could exhibit.

"It did for a while," said Lyn. "But my very earliest memories are of yelling, and dim smoky light, and a carpet under my hands that was rough and gritty. I remember getting hit—you know, slapped in the face. So I don't think it was a nice place at all. And the fact that no one came looking for me or tried to claim me, well, that tells me everything I need to know. So it doesn't bother me anymore. I focus on becoming the person I want to be, not the person I might have been."

She didn't tell Georgina about what kind of child she had been. When the authorities found her, she'd been practically feral. She'd bitten, hit, and screamed and had a deep suspicion of human beings. She had scars whose origin she did not know. Her language skills had not been at age level, and the authorities were *pretty* sure that she said her name was Lynette but not absolutely sure. Still, she'd answer to it (often with screams and biting), so that was the name they put on her file.

Lyn had promptly been absorbed into an overcrowded, under-funded, largely disillusioned local system. A screaming, violent child who did not accept affection was not easy to place, especially one with a history of running away. She had bolted from the police station as soon as the responsible adult's back had turned, and they found her an hour later grimly trudging along a road. They brought her back. She was placed in a series of group homes, each of which she ran away from again and again. Never with any clear destination in mind, as far as anyone could tell. Just an angry determination.

The group homes were followed by some less-than-ideal foster families from which she also frequently ran away. The local police knew her, but not with a fondness built of friendliness. It hadn't been a case of her casually greeting the constables by name and asking after their families. Instead, she would sit silently sullen in the rear of the police car as she was hauled back to wherever she had been placed. She could easily have ended up on a very dark path. It had only been the incredible patience, kindness, and, eventually, love of Kylie and Anthony Dwyer that had saved her.

Lyn and Georgina were quiet in the darkness for a while.

"What about you?" Lyn asked finally. "How old were you when you came here?"

"I don't remember any place except the Estate," said Georgina. "I don't know anything about my parents or if I have any brothers or sisters or family." Lyn bit her lip. During her time at the Estate, she'd gained a greater appreciation of why the Checquy took children away from their families, but it still grated. She kept thinking about how she would feel if someone had come and taken Emma away. Naturally, that idea upset her much more than the fact that someone had come and taken Lyn herself away.

"Do you think they think about me?" asked Georgina. "Do you think they miss me?"

Lyn hesitated. This was moving into dangerous territory. She remembered her own volatility at that age and how essential everything had seemed. If she gave her instinctive answer and told the girl that *of course* her family thought about her and mourned her loss— well, who knew what that might prompt? She could all too easily imagine Georgina taking off to find her family. Lifelong training and discipline were all very well, but no power on earth could stop a teenager from feeling dangerously passionate about something.

This can't be the first time this sort of thing has happened here, she thought. *The Estate must have some procedure.* "You should talk to your counselor about this," said Lyn carefully.

"I'm not going to run away, Lyn. I know I can't ever see them. I just—if someone took your little girl away, you wouldn't just forget her, would you?"

"No," said Lyn heavily. "Never."

"I suppose that's enough," said Georgina sadly.

"Ugh! *What?*" Lyn had been dragged out of sleep by a grating noise and an unpleasant pressing sensation on her cheek. She brushed away whatever it was and was jolted fully awake by the sensation of squirming wetness against her hand. *"The hell?"* She slapped on her bedside lamp, then shrank back, holding her hand over her mouth in horror.

The room was filled with scores of thin clear tendrils that hung in the air and writhed about. They twisted over and around each other, brushing their tips against every surface. As she watched, the one she had pushed away reached down and began running itself over her blanket. It glistened slickly. Lyn pulled the blanket up to her chin.

"Georgie!" she whispered. "Georgina!" She peered through the mass of movement but could barely make out her roommate. Then the strands parted briefly, and she caught a glimpse of her. Georgina was asleep lying flat on her back, and to Lyn's horror, it appeared as if the things were pouring into her open mouth. Another of those grating sounds came rumbling out of Georgina's mouth, and her face twisted as if in pain. *"Georgina!"*

The tendrils all shivered, and the girl sat up, looking confused but nowhere near as upset as Lyn would have been if she'd awoken to find a cloud of filaments emerging from her mouth and floating about her like so much demonic pasta. Georgina looked over at her blearily, blinked, and the entire mass dived down into her mouth, making the most disgusting sound Lyn had ever heard.

"Oh my God, Georgina!" She leapt out of bed and rushed over. "How do you feel?"

"How do I feel?" asked Georgina blearily.

"Jesus, that stuff!"

"What are you talking about?"

"That stuff!" exclaimed Lyn. "The cellophane-noodle-looking things that crawled into your mouth. Did you—wait a minute. Have they possessed you?" She reached out and closed her hand around the bedside lamp, ready to charge it up and shock her poor ensorcelled roommate.

"What? No, that was my tongue!"

"Your tongue?" Lyn sat down on the bed.

"Uh, *yeah,* it's one of my abilities!" She smacked her lips and made a face like she'd just tasted something bitter. "My taste buds can extrude strands. It enables for more effective and broad-range tasting."

"But isn't it incredibly unhygienic to just be licking things?" asked Lyn. *And really disgusting.*

"We all make sacrifices for the security of the populace," said Georgina dismissively. "For me, it's usually having to lick people and banisters." Lyn gagged a little. "I don't know why I did that while I was asleep, though. *That's* never happened before." She wrinkled her face. "I do taste something weird."

"It's probably the ceiling," Lyn muttered to herself. "Or my face." She was wondering grimly if the whole room would need to be wiped down with some sort of cleanser. She certainly felt like *she* could do with being wiped down.

"I know what the ceiling tastes like," said Georgina testily. "And faces."

Gross. "Wait—*my* face?" Lyn asked, but she got no answer. The girl was sitting up with her eyes closed wearing an intent expression. She turned her head back and forth thoughtfully. "What are you doing?"

"There is something very strange here," said Georgina.

Lyn said nothing, showing what she thought was astounding restraint.

"I was dreaming about something," continued Georgina, "and I could taste it. And then when I woke up, I could still taste it."

"That's a very compelling anecdote," said Lyn, yawning. "But it's"—she looked at the alarm clock—"four in the morning, and I have fencing class first thing, so I need my sleep. Write it all down in your journal and try to keep your taste buds reeled into your mouth for the rest of the night."

"Lyn, I've never tasted anything like this."

"Do you want to call someone? Let security know?"

"No," said Georgina uncertainly. "If it's nothing, word will get out. Everyone on the Estate will know that I raised a fuss." There was clearly no worse fate.

Lyn sighed. "Do you want to go take a look around?"

"Could we?"

Come seven thirty, I am going to get my exhausted arse kicked in fencing by a nine-year-old, thought Lyn wearily. *Even more than usual.* "Fine." The look of gratitude on Georgina's face in no way made it all worthwhile.

The Estate did not believe in keeping the heat on during the night, so the two pulled dressing gowns over their pajamas and donned slippers. Lyn sat yawning on her bed while Georgina ducked into the bathroom and quickly applied her tongue-lens.

The dormitory hallways were dark, with periodic lamps shining dimly on half-moon tables. The floors were polished wood scattered with rugs. Portraits, photographs, and paintings from various decades were hung up on the walls in no particular order. It wasn't really the most sensible decor for a space that would be crossed hundreds of times a day by hurrying children and adolescents, not at all the kind of hard-wearing institutional setup that could be grimly mopped each night, but it was homey and comforting. *And this* is *their home,* Lyn reminded herself. It wasn't the kind of boarding school where the students would go home at the end of each term.

They walked along quietly, and Georgina kept turning her head back and forth with a vague expression on her face.

"Are you tasting? Your mouth isn't open," Lyn said.

"My sense of taste can penetrate through my skin," said Georgina distractedly. "Thank God. This way, I don't have to walk around looking like a slack-jawed idiot."

"And do you taste anything?"

"I can taste everything," said Georgina.

"Right," said Lyn, rolling her eyes. "I've been meaning to ask, but is that not supremely unpleasant? I mean, I try not to taste anything that is not food or drink. You're tasting—what? The walls? The floor?"

"Taste is like smelling," said Georgina. "You smell things that aren't food."

"But things don't necessarily taste the way they smell," said Lyn. "I like smelling perfume; I don't like tasting it."

"I suppose you get used to it." Georgina shrugged. "Anyway, how do you know that things taste the same for you as they do for me? Or that they taste the same for you as they do for everyone else? Maybe that's why different people have different favorite foods. Maybe we all like the same taste the best, but for some people it comes from apples and for some it comes from hamburgers."

"I realize you're a teenager, and that sounds awfully profound to you, but I'm not going to have this conversation," said Lyn. "I'm prepared just to accept that you don't mind tasting doorknobs. And meanwhile, can you taste what you tasted before?"

"Faintly," said Georgina. "But not with any certainty about where it's coming from. I can't even tell the direction."

"So it's pointless and I can go back to bed?"

"Wait, there's something I can try." The girl sat down cross-legged on the floor and arranged her dressing gown around her. She reached back into her mouth and peeled off the lens.

"I thought that helped you focus," objected Lyn.

"It does, but if I have it in, I can't do *this*." She stretched her head back and opened her mouth, and Lyn flinched as those tendrils once again began to grow up out of her tongue. They didn't become as long as they had before, but they spread out around her head, pointing in all directions. With the translucent strands billowing about, it looked almost like a sea anemone was emerging from the girl's mouth. "Does it feel weird?" she asked.

"Hchack!"

"Sorry, I shouldn't have asked. I'll just wait until you're done."

"Shclacksh."

"Whatever."

Finally, after several long minutes, during which Lyn kept looking around warily, the fibers slowly drew themselves back into Georgina's mouth. She panted a few times and then carefully replaced the lens.

"It's that way," she said confidently, and pointed down the corridor. "Over toward the central hall."

"What does it taste like?" asked Lyn.

"Um, complex sugars, bitterness, and salt?" said Georgina. "And, like, a strong undertone of cottage cheese."

"That doesn't sound like something we need to be investigating. That sounds like someone is making an extremely bad lasagna."

"It's not food!"

"Well, then, what is it?"

The girl shrugged.

"You think it's something evil? Like a flatulent ghost?"

"There was also the faintest hint of copper," Georgina ventured. "That could be blood."

"Like a dead body?"

"No, I know what a dead body tastes like."

Lyn winced and rubbed her eyes. "But you taste blood."

"It might not be blood," Georgina said hastily. "It was so muted, I couldn't really tell."

"Is it . . . alive?" The girl shrugged again, which made Lyn want to say something sharp and adult-like, but she didn't. "What else could it be? Don't shrug!"

"I don't know, but it's weird."

"So I guess we should check it out." Lyn sighed. "Lead the way." They moved through the hallways, and every time a floorboard squeaked, Lyn tensed. She kept waiting for a guard or a night watchman to appear and either shoot them or berate them, but there was no sign of anyone. "Why isn't there any security?"

"Why would there be security? This is a *school*. On an *island*. No one's going to break in," said Georgina in an annoyingly reasonable tone. "I think they check the beds at about two, but after that, why would they bother? If you wake up and feel sick, you can go to the san. If a little kid has a nightmare or something, there are night matrons in their dorms."

Lyn didn't say anything. There was something incredibly annoying about a teenager speaking to you as though you were a moron. As they moved out of their dormitory area, she couldn't help but feel a bit antsy, as if they were trespassing.

"We're heading toward the dining hall," she whispered. "Maybe it's someone having a midnight feast. Or a member of the staff who wanted a snack."

"It's not food, I told you," whispered Georgina back. "But we're getting closer. *Much* closer. I'm surprised *you* can't taste it." Actually, Lyn *could* smell something, but she couldn't have described it effectively. There was a deep, sour smell, although she wasn't certain that she'd have identified it as cottage cheese. Then, from around the corner up ahead, there came a sound. It was not a little sound; more like something heavy moving.

That does not sound like a student sneaking out of bed, she thought.

Without saying anything, the two of them reached out and took each other's hands. The glances they exchanged contained several entire dialogues. A series of raised eyebrows and head jerks constituted a debate about whether they should go on or not, and a back-and-forth of slumped shoulders signaled agreement that they really ought to investigate.

As they moved forward, inch by increasingly tense inch, more sounds came clattering around the corner. Floorboards creaked painfully under a heavy weight, and something scraped loud and long against the wall.

I am so looking forward to learning that the maintenance staff is taking the opportunity to move some furniture in the middle of the night, thought Lyn tensely. She knew that she was in no way convincing herself. In fact, her brain was coming up with all sorts of reasons to worry.

There was a crash, and the dim light around the corner flickered crazily. Georgina and Lyn paused, holding their breath.

And then the two of them moved forward again, slowly, silent step by silent step, barely breathing. Lyn could feel her heart pumping hard. With every thump and rasp that came down the hallway toward them, her stomach tightened another painful ratchet. She wondered vaguely if Georgina could taste her fear. The girl's hand was wet in hers. She didn't dare blink. Both of them stared into the space ahead.

Something caught her eye, and she tightened her hand around Georgina's, their skin slick with sweat. The girl turned to look at her questioningly. Her eyes were wide, and her mouth was twisted as if she was tasting something horrible. Which she was. Lyn nodded silently down at the floor, where there was a scar in the floorboards.

It started out narrow but widened and deepened, gouging deep into the wood. There was another scar ahead of it, then another. There were broad scrape marks on the walls at intervals. Georgina's eyes took in the damage, and she looked up at Lyn in horror. They stared at each other.

This cannot be happening. This cannot be my life.

Lyn turned and looked back down the corridor. There were no signs of damage. It was as if the something had simply manifested where they were standing and had then proceeded down the hallway.

A clatter from up ahead startled them out of their shared stare, and as one, they began to move forward again. They had to go on, despite themselves. It was as if the sheer impossibility of what they were seeing, the trail of damage, compelled them. Nothing could be as bad as not knowing.

There were periodic thuds vibrating through the floor. They could hear the rugs tearing and the wood splintering. There was a strange wuffling sound and occasionally a whoosh. And there was a scrabbling noise, like giant fingernails going back and forth over the surface of a wooden desk.

They came to the turn. Slowly, very carefully, they leaned forward, just enough to see around the corner.

The hall was wide, with high curving ceilings. A long strip of skylight ran the length of it, and moonlight poured in so that the little lamps dotted here and there were barely needed. It was a grand space, one of those spaces designed to evoke a school's history and tradition, even if the school hadn't actually been around that long. Trophy cases lined the walls, filled with gleaming cups and shields, and between them hung portraits of past teachers, class photos, and paintings of battles. The occasional potted palm stood guard over a bust or a piece of sculpture. It was the kind of place that a graduate would remember nostalgically.

It held something else as well.

Lyn's eyes and brain fought for a moment, unable to reconcile what they were seeing, unable to reconcile the *scale* of it. It didn't belong in the hallway. It didn't belong in the *world*.

Standing in the middle of the corridor, side-on to them, was a monstrous, gigantic insect.

Its body was roughly the size of a VW minibus, and it had a grayish-white carapace, almost translucent, with a red-brown core. Two smooth eyes, solid black, stared out from beneath stubby antennae. As Lyn and Georgina watched, red-tipped quills wetly sheathed and unsheathed themselves in and out of its tubelike mouth. Below the head was the thorax, as the librarian part of Lyn's brain helpfully noted. From it sprouted six segmented limbs, each tipped with a strong red claw and a smaller pincer-type claw. Below that was a massive elongated abdomen-tail, almost as long as the rest of it put together.

As though not registering their presence, the thing dragged itself over to the wall, its massive claws digging into the floor and leaving the gouges they'd seen earlier. It leaned forward, sweeping its antennae back and forth across the wall. This was the source of the scrabbling sound they'd heard.

Insects use their antennae for smelling, Lyn recalled faintly. *Or is it touch?*

Its smell was ripe and sour, and now that they knew what it was coming from, it suddenly seemed so much worse. *And Georgina tasted it!* thought Lyn, appalled. Just the thought made her want to retch.

It moved awkwardly. Its stubby legs tipped with large claws were clearly not designed for moving along any flat surface, let alone on a polished wooden floor. As they watched, one of its legs slid out from under it, and it scrabbled frantically to right itself. It put out another leg to steady itself and effortlessly smashed a trophy case.

The two of them withdrew very, very slowly and leaned against the wall, side by side, silently letting out their painfully held breath.

"Okay," breathed Lyn. "Okay." She looked at Georgina, who was staring straight ahead. *And now I have to be the adult.* "Do you know who that is?" she asked softly.

The girl shot her an outraged look. "That's not a student!" she squeaked, then clapped her hands over her mouth. The noise from around the corner had halted. They could imagine the creature pausing, listening. They braced themselves for the sound of it turning and clawing its massive way toward them, thundering down the hall.

A long silence.

And then the renewed sound of its shuffling and exploring.

Lyn took a breath. She brought her mouth close to Georgina's ear. "Are you sure?" she said so faintly she could barely hear it herself. The girl looked up at her and nodded.

"I would know if someone in the school did this," she whispered. "If someone became *that.*"

"There's that kid who turns into a bear. I've seen her, or him, at meals."

"That's Louise. She doesn't turn into a bear—she *is* a bear."

Lyn looked at her. "What?"

"She was *born* a bear."

Despite the nightmarish situation at hand, Lyn stared at the girl for several long seconds as she processed this revelation, then shook her head. *If I live, I'll follow up on that.* "We have to go and get help." Georgina nodded vigorously. "Quietly."

They turned, and Georgina's foot caught in one of the gouges on the floor, then hooked into a torn loop of rug. She stumbled and the rug tore further, tripping her and sending her falling forward as all the sound in the world went away.

Oh.

Lyn lunged for her, but she was too late and too far away. She could see the girl drawing in her breath, pressing her lips hard together, determined not to make a sound. Trying to catch herself, Georgina managed to soften the landing a little with her arms, but her chest hit the floor hard and forced her caught breath out of her mouth.

"Buh!"

Oh.

Fuck.

From around the corner came another horrible silence, then the sound of massive claws hauling a monster their way.

"Run!"

Lyn dragged Georgina to her feet. The girl feverishly kicked away the loop of torn carpet, and then they were running, their dressing gowns flapping, as, behind them, the insect rounded the corner.

"Help!" screamed Georgina. *"Help!"* Lyn shot her a startled glance. After their torturous silence, the girl's scream was shocking, but of course it made perfect sense.

Absolutely, let's make this someone else's problem!

"Help!" Lyn screamed. She dared a look behind them. The insect seemed to almost fill the corridor. Its dark eyes were fixed on them, and those horrible spikes at its mouth were jutting forward. As it scrabbled along, it slammed back and forth against the walls. And yet, for all its clumsiness, the thing was *fast,* and the racket of those huge limbs punching down onto the floor was deafening. It smashed the lamps as it came, so it seemed to be drawing the darkness with it.

Why is no one coming? Lyn wondered.

Wait—we're leading it to the dormitories! Lyn stumbled to a halt, and Georgina hesitated. "Keep going!" Lyn shouted. "Get help! I'll...I'll do something!" The teenager stared at her incredulously. "Go! *Go!*" Georgina nodded, then looked beyond Lyn to the thing bearing down on them. She pivoted and bolted down the corridor, still screaming for help.

Lyn turned.

I am going to die, she thought grimly. But she couldn't just let it tear its way into the dormitory. She reached into the pocket of her dressing gown and drew out the baton she'd taken from her go-kit. She'd grabbed it, a paranoid afterthought, while Georgina was in the bathroom putting in her tongue-lens. Lyn shrugged off her robe, and with a now-practiced snap of her arm, she extended the baton out to its full merciless length. The Checquy armorers had modified it, so now it was as long as a sword. She tightened her grip on it and unclenched her powers.

The insect came on; the racket of its approach was earsplitting, and it took all of Lyn's will to stand there, unmoving. Every moment that passed, she could feel more energy coursing out of her hand and into the telescoping metal segments of the baton.

Just a little more... It came on, churning and impossible, like a vision from a fever dream.

Just a little more... To her shock, the insect shrieked, a sound that tore through the air. It bore down on her, only meters away.

Now!

She struck out to the side with the baton, and when the metal touched the wall, the imprisoned electricity burst out, shockingly bright. Streamers of crimson energy flared into the corridor and traced charred lines along the wall, floor, and ceiling. The insect reared back, and its feet scrabbled beneath it.

"See what I can do?" Lyn screamed at it. She poured more power into the baton, and while the insect regarded her, she swung out and smashed the weapon to the other side. It flared again, less bright this time, but still dazzling in the dimness. It faded, but the double-ring signature of her power glowed a few moments longer, scorched into the wall. "Now back off or this is what you'll get!"

The insect did not move back. She had hoped that it might be frightened off, but all it did was stand staring at her. Its sharp mouthparts sucked in and out slowly.

I am going to die here, Lyn thought again grimly. *I am going to be eaten by a giant bug in the hallway of a magical boarding school, and my family will never know. I wonder what my daughter will think happened to me. I wonder what they will tell her.*

Lyn and the bug stared at each other, and she could actually see the moment the insect came to a decision. It seemed to set all six of its shoulders in determination.

"Yeah, you and me both," she said, and she tightened her grip on the baton. Her eye was caught by a spot of bright color off to the side, and she reached out and pulled the fire alarm that was mounted on the wall. *We should have done that sooner,* she thought absently. There was little danger of any fire-fleeing students rushing into this hall—it was in an administrative area, quite a way from the dormitories. The insect cocked its head as the siren began to scream, then it screamed in reply. It drew itself up, dug its claws into the floor, and rushed forward.

In the back of her mind, Lyn could hear a conversation she'd had with her combat instructor several weeks earlier.

"In some ways, Lynette, you're quite lucky."

"Yes! I! Feel! Lucky!"

"Don't talk—focus on your movement. You must be *explosive.* And *lunge!* Now, as I was saying, you are quite lucky, by which I mean in your abilities. In a combat application, that is." Lyn did not reply, but she did roll her eyes a little, even as she tried to ignore her screaming muscles. Pawn Fenton was one of the Estate's combat instructors, and he did like to pontificate, especially when his students were collapsing from exhaustion. She held her position, the heavy training rod in her hand held at the prescribed angle.

"As in life, you are luckier than most, not as lucky as some. And *lunge!* I appreciate that this may not be what you want to hear. And *lunge!* I want to see you really pushing off from your left leg. You will find a role in the Checquy that suits your skills and your inclinations, but the destructive nature of your abilities makes it more likely that your presence will be requested in a combat situation." He paused. "I can see why you might feel this to be a disadvantage.

"But the nature of your abilities also gives you certain advantages. You do not affect an opponent directly. Unlike many of my other students, you need not touch your enemies in order to use your powers on them. I had to develop a customized martial art for Elspeth Fowler that enabled her to rub her armpits on people." Lyn paused and looked at him, startled. "She turns her opponent's skin to glass. It's very effective, but very specific, and it makes for possibly the most undignified fighting style in history, but we have to tailor these things because touch is so often a factor. For instance, a few moments of flesh-to-flesh contact allows Pawn Levy to tap into a person's senses — 'bugging' his very person, if you will.

"Why, even Rook Thomas was forced to stand in this room as a shy little girl and learn to grapple, to pin, to choke, and to activate her abilities as she did so. She was always very cautious in her approach to combat. Although," he mused, almost to himself, "there are rumors that she's moved beyond her previous limitations." He shook his head wryly. "The quiet ones can often surprise you.

"You, however, enjoy the luxury of at least a little distance from your foes. And *lunge!* And as a result, I feel that the baton offers you an ideal tool. It is concealable, it can intimidate, and if you do not wish to use your powers on someone, you can still use it to give them a damn good thrashing. You will be trained in kendo, escrima, tahtib, bataireacht, krabi-krabong, calinda. At some point, we will look at other, longer weapons to train you in for specific deployments. A spear or the three-sectional staff, perhaps. I'm sure we could work out some sort of metal-laced whip that might channel your power and really extend your reach.

"In the meantime, you are fortunate that there is an entire martial art based almost entirely on the concept of poking someone from a distance.

"And *lunge!*"

★   ★   ★

Now Lyn burst forward as explosively as Pawn Fenton could ever have wanted, thrusting the baton out before her. One leg kicked forward, and the other straightened to push her toward her enemy. She dropped down, twisted around the insect's darting head, and stabbed the end of the baton against its thorax.

Will it work? she thought. *Is there enough power?* She'd had only a little time to charge it up again. And did insects even suffer from electricity? She dimly remembered something about ants conducting it without any ill effect... *My corpse is going to look so stup*—Crimson electricity erupted out of the metal with an earsplitting crack and wrapped like a cage around the insect. The creature shrieked and flung itself back. She could see the ring-within-a-ring pattern burned into its chitin. It shook its head, but it did not fall. Instead, with a wet punching sound, its teeth and quills unsheathed themselves forcefully.

"You want more?" Lyn screamed at it, pouring her energy into the baton. *"You want more?"*

Apparently, the creature *did* want more, or else it felt that fleeing was not an option, because it lashed out at her with a clawed limb. Hours of practice jump-started her instincts, and she twisted down to avoid it, then came up close to smash her baton onto the creature's carapace and unleash another flood of electricity. It fell back and convulsed madly on the floor. She retreated a couple of steps, panting, waiting to see what would happen.

"Well done, Lynette," said someone behind her. Lyn didn't dare take her eyes off the monster, but she recognized the voice as belonging to Pawn Yerushalmi, the elderly lady who lectured every Tuesday and Thursday on the legal strictures of the Checquy. "*Very* well done. Now, would you like to take a step back, perhaps?"

"I can take it!" insisted Lyn, her heart pumping. Sparks were still flickering about the monster's carapace, but they were fading, and it seemed to be preparing itself again.

"Oh, I've no doubt," said Pawn Yerushalmi. "You've already acquitted yourself marvelously. But this is such a valuable learning opportunity, I'm sure you wouldn't begrudge some of your fellow students a chance."

Despite herself, Lyn looked over her shoulder. Improbably, Pawn Yerushalmi was dressed in an exquisitely cut business suit and was flanked by two large men who held machine guns pointed at the insect. Behind them were five students of different ages, all of them in nightwear and dressing gowns. Her incredulous eye was caught by a little Pacific Islander boy in red pajamas and a tartan dressing gown. He couldn't have been more than six, but he didn't seem perturbed by the monster down the hallway as it righted itself.

"I guess that's fine," she said uncertainly. She stepped back against the wall.

"Jolly good! Now, Ludo, perhaps you should go first?" The little boy nodded seriously and came forward. The Pawn crouched down next to him, speaking softly in his ear. The final traceries of electricity had fizzled off the insect; it had regained control of its limbs, and it apparently decided it had waited long enough. It began to move toward them.

"Everyone, you'll want to shield your eyes and hold your nose for this. And try to clench your buttocks as tightly as you can."

"Now, Lyn, would you like a hot chocolate or a brandy?" asked Frau Blümen. "Or some kirsch? Or all of them? Perhaps in the same mug? Or if you're hungry, we could do a raclette. I have a grill in one of the cupboards."

"I think I'm fine, thank you," said Lyn. She looked down at her hands and was pleased to see that they weren't shaking. After all five of the students had taken their turns unleashing their powers on the creature, it had been Lyn who delivered the coup de grâce. All the power that the baton could hold had been released in a single devastating strike that made the students cover their ears. That had been ten minutes ago. Now she was seated in the headmistress's office, wrapped in a blanket.

"Frau Blümen, what was that thing? Where did it come from?"

"Not entirely certain yet," said the headmistress. "It's why we're on lockdown, and we're still doing a head count."

"Do you think it might have eaten someone?" asked Lyn, aghast.

"It might have *been* someone," said Blümen seriously.

"Georgina said it wasn't a student. She said there was no one who turned into a giant insect."

"Not as far as we know," said Blümen. "But people's powers can be very unpredictable. They can change or evolve. We had a girl who, overnight, began instilling an overpowering fear of carpets in everyone around her. Before that, her only ability had been to alter the ambient temperature by about ten degrees. So you never can tell. Thank God that carpet-fear thing lasted only as long as she was in one's immediate area," she said. "But the odds of an unrelated manifestation occurring here randomly are fairly small. The insect would almost *have* to be connected to one of our students or staff in some way."

"But if that thing was once a person..." *Then I killed someone!* Lyn began to feel ill. At that moment, the headmistress's phone rang.

"*Ja?*...Oh? That's excellent news, thank you." She hung up. "Well, the head count is finished. Everyone is accounted for. No one is missing."

"Oh, thank God," said Lyn. She felt limp with relief.

A knock came at the door, and a member of the staff hurried in and gave the headmistress a note. She scanned it and brushed her hand over her eyes in frustration. "My God. All right, thank you. We'll need to keep the entire island on high alert. The situation has *not* been contained. These things consume human blood, and where there's one, there is very likely to be more. Everyone will need to be checked, with armed or powered guards present." The aide nodded and left hurriedly.

"Frau Blümen, what's the—" Lyn began, but the headmistress had a finger in the air.

"Lyn, give me one moment, please." She picked up her telephone and dialed while, in the background, a siren began to wail. The headmistress's fingers drummed fretfully on her desk.

Why is she so stressed? I mean, the thing was terrifying, but that little kid was able to knock it back on its arse. Of course, he was laid out unconscious afterward, but I'm sure they have others who can do something similar. Unless...how many more monsters might there be?

"Good morning, Miffy, it is Steffi here. I am sorry to bother you at this hour. We have a situation at the Estate...no, no deaths, not as far as we know, but I am afraid we are going to need some heavy-duty combat support. My office will be calling the watch office with the details, but you can cut through the red tape and get immediate action. May I formally request the immediate dispatch of at least two units of troops?" She paused to listen to the answer, her head cocked.

"Yes, I think a team of Barghests would not be out of place. Can you also ask the Rookery to alert the coast guard and the navy? We will need to establish a quarantine area. I would also like a bomber circling overhead...yes. Explosives and napalm." Lyn's jaw dropped. "Thank you, *Liebchen.* It is all very inconvenient, but I hope we can contain it. Yes, call me back, please." She hung up and sighed.

"God, what is it?" asked Lyn.

"They've identified the creature. *Pediculus humanus capitis.*"

"What's that?" asked Lyn in a hushed tone. It sounded positively demonic.

"Head lice."

"Ugh!" Lyn automatically put her hand to her head.

"Hmm, lice are inconvenient in a school even when they're normal, especially in a boarding school with little children. But the nature of this one represents a major problem."

"No kidding."

"My suspicion is that the louse fed on a student's blood and was altered, growing to the giant size you encountered." Lyn remembered the damage to the hall, the way it seemed to begin suddenly out of nowhere. She could picture a louse dropping off some student's head as weird blood coursed through its system. *But it would have needed hours to pass after the bite,* she thought. *Since Georgina didn't taste it until four in the morning, and it hadn't gone very far from the place where it got big.* Maybe it had lain on the floor twitching for hours before suddenly erupting up into the huge monster she'd fought.

And there might be more of them! She remembered checking Emma's head after an outbreak at her nursery school and finding a few of the little insects. Who knew how many more might be scattered around the halls, ready to become abruptly gigantic.

Or they could be on someone's head, a child in the evacuated crowd. She imagined a child suddenly crushed as the lice on her head abruptly grew to more than a hundred times their normal size. The idea of those creatures manifesting in the middle of a crowd of students left her ill with fear.

"You should get them to spread out," Lyn said urgently. "The students. In case one of the bugs is still on the kid who caused this. Or they can jump from head to head, right?"

"No, that is a myth."

"Are you sure?" said Lyn dubiously. "I remember reading it in *Hating Alison Ashley.* It's always stuck with me."

"No, they don't do that."

"Wait—whose was it, though?" Lyn asked. "Whose blood?"

"No idea," said Blümen. "Hold on." She took a walkie-talkie out of her desk drawer and issued a series of instructions, ordering security to spread the staff and students out in the school's various playing fields.

"As we were saying…I don't know whose blood would have caused this. No one with the power to make insects grow has been identified, but then it's not something you automatically test for. We'll have the creature autopsied, of course. Hopefully, we can find some of the blood it consumed and do a DNA test. Otherwise, the scientists will have to check the effects of everyone's blood on head lice."

"Everyone at the Estate?"

"And anyone who has recently visited," said Frau Blümen grimly. "I know, it would take forever." She spoke again into the radio. "Miss Teoh, please break out armor for everyone. I don't think we have enough infant-size armor, so be sure to sequester them in the middle of the chapel oval, well away from the rest of the school. They and their caregivers should be the first ones checked for head lice. We will also need the combs, the shampoo, and the chain saws out of storage." She paused and looked at Lyn.

"What?"

"You just scratched your head."

"It's all this talk of head lice!" exclaimed Lyn. "It's put the thought in my mind. I don't have them!"

"Let me just check," said Steffi. "We'll all have to get screened anyway." She opened her desk drawer and took out a magnifying glass and a large pistol.

"What are you doing? Are you going to kill me if I turn out to have nits? Are you going to shoot the lice off my head?"

"No, of course not," said Steffi. "But if there is a chance that a monster is suddenly going to grow in this room, I want to have a weapon handy. Why are you staring at me like that?"

"You just scratched *your* head."

The headmistress guiltily put her hand down. "*Oh mein Gott!* All right, fine. You check me, then I will check you."

A few minutes of intensive and extremely wary scrutiny of their respective scalps revealed no eggs and no bugs.

"And thank God for that," said Blümen. "We'd better go down and see how things are going." She donned a shoulder holster over her academic gown, slid the pistol into it, and unlocked a cupboard in the corner. As Lyn watched incredulously, the plump headmistress took out a large weapon that seemed to consist mainly of tubes and began checking it.

"What is that?" asked Lyn warily.

"Flamethrower. If you're going to go wandering through halls that may contain giant bloodsucking creatures, you want to have a flamethrower on you. First thing a prospective teacher ought to learn."

"What are you going to do about the Estate buildings?" asked Lyn. "Are you seriously just going to bomb the place?"

"Not if I can help it. Once the troops arrive, they will accompany the cleaners as they vacuum every hallway and room. Then the vacuums will need to be incinerated. And all the bedding and hats on campus too, probably." She sighed.

"Lice aren't normally transmitted through sheets or headwear," Lyn observed helpfully.

"Yes, well, I don't like relying on 'normally' in this job, especially when there may be huge monsters wandering around the school. Unless we can identify the source of the blood, there will be a lot of things burning." She grimaced. "It's going to be another one of those

nights when everyone gets shampooed and hosed down on the playing fields with armed guards standing watch. And my budget is blown
for another year." Lyn got up and followed her out of the office.

"Now, if we survive, I'm going to set you some homework on this
night's occurrence," said Blümen.

"Homework?"

10

U sha's and Bridget's laughter cut off into screams as they fell back
in shock. Plaster and dust cascaded down, spreading out into
the bedroom and covering the man who had just burst out of the
ceiling.

He's real! It's really real! thought Bridget dazedly. Up until that
moment, the German soldier had seemed almost hypothetical, a concept to be dreaded distantly, like smallpox or the big bad wolf or a tax
audit. Now he was undeniable and all the more shocking for having
seemingly come out of nowhere. She squinted at him through the
dust. Despite her consternation, her training automatically came to
the fore, and she began analyzing the situation.

The man had landed easily on his feet in a crouch, as if the Germans had given the Luftwaffe special training in how to burst abruptly
through ceilings. Ridiculously, she'd always imagined him in a crisp
Nazi uniform, but he was wearing civilian clothes that did not fit terribly well. *He must have lifted them from Mr. Jinks's closet.*

Under the dust, he had close-cropped sandy hair and high cheek-
bones with a scabbed-over cut across his forehead. He was fit and
strong with broad shoulders, and when he looked up at them, his deep
blue eyes were fixed and intent. There was no doubt in those eyes, no
panic. This was a man who knew exactly what he needed to do. He
straightened up, and she noticed that he stood a full head taller than
her and had a pistol in his hand.

A lifetime of training kicked in, and she kicked out. Her foot snapped forward with as beautiful a strike as her savate instructor could have hoped for and sent the gun flying across the room. The Nazi stepped back, startled, but quickly drew a knife from a sheath at his belt.

Bridget shot a look at Usha, who was still coughing from the dust and trying to come to terms with what had just happened.

"Usha, go!" barked Bridget. For all Usha's power and the rudimentary combat training she'd received, she was no combatant and had never been in a real fight before. If she were to touch the man, she could probably crush him down to a nugget, but he would likely kill her before she could do so. Bridget far outstripped her in actual fighting skill, and they both knew it.

Bridget reached inside her coat and pulled out her own weapon: a vicious switchblade. The blade flicked open. It was a cruel weapon, modified by Checquy armorers specifically for fighting, but it felt very small compared to her opponent's dagger, which was clearly not something that had been stolen from the kitchen of either of his victims—it was an actual combat knife.

She took a breath and prepared herself to kill a man.

He stepped forward, his dagger held low, and Usha leapt back in a long shallow glide that took her to the door of the bedroom. The Nazi tracked her impossible movement thoughtfully, then looked back to Bridget. She watched him for any sign that he might be unleashing his powers. He had burned those people in their houses. Could he do the same to her? *Does he need to touch me?* she thought. *Can he do it just by looking at me?* She braced herself for a conflagration to erupt inside her, but all she could feel was the pounding of her heart. *Maybe he doesn't yet know how to control it.* Her thoughts were broken off as he burst toward her, holding his knife.

She spun aside and cut at his eyes, forcing him to flinch back. *He's had training,* she acknowledged grimly. His blade had come close to gutting her. *He's bigger and stronger, and he has a knife that's twice as big.* She didn't dare look behind her to see if Usha had left.

He'll be worrying about her, she thought. *He'll think that she might go for help. He needs to move fast.*

He knew it. He rushed forward and stabbed out. Her knife was too small to effectively parry his blade, but she dodged out of the way again. The two stepped back, light on their feet, constantly shifting position. They held their knives ready to stab out or cut back as they adapted to each other's stances. It was a tight, intricate, awkward dance — the Jinkses' bedroom, while larger than Bridget had anticipated, was still not the ideal place for a knife fight.

You've trained for worse, she told herself. Quite aside from hours and hours of standard combat training, the Checquy had put her and her fellow students into unorthodox scenarios to prepare them for unusual circumstances: Fighting with bricks on your belly in a hypocaust. Fighting with quarterstaves while hip-deep in a bog. Fighting with tridents while hip-deep *upside down* in a bog. Fighting with truncheons while teetering on the ceiling beams of a church.

Still, none of those meticulously designed situations had included the occasional errant slipper that skidded under her foot or the projecting knobs on the foot of the bed that caught at her opponent's arm when he swiped out at her. The two of them moved back and forth with short careful steps, always wary of losing their balance or giving the other person an advantage.

Something nagged at Bridget's thoughts — the way he was fighting was peculiar. He'd clearly been schooled in how to use a knife, but he attacked in an oddly stilted way.

He's not using his size or his strength, she realized. *He's so focused on the knife that he's forgotten his other advantages. And remember, he doesn't know* your *advantage, so use it.*

She allowed a look of frightened uncertainty to cross her face and took a hesitant half step back. The Nazi, clearly thinking this was an opportunity, lunged forward, and this time she moved toward his attack. Startled, he stabbed down awkwardly at her face and then actually gasped as she brought her free hand up and *caught* the blade. Her knees buckled a little under the force of his blow, and they could both hear the knife tearing through her glove. Despite herself, despite her determination, she screamed at the pain.

For a moment he looked utterly triumphant. Then, when she failed to yield or let go of the blade, an expression of shock came across his face. He twisted the knife, and the sound as it scraped across the impenetrable nacreous coating of her palm set Bridget's teeth on edge. It hurt horribly, but she knew it wasn't actually doing any damage to the surface of her skin. She closed her fingers tightly, twisted the blade out of his grip, and flung it back behind her.

"*Was?*" he exclaimed.

"You wouldn't believe what you've gotten yourself into," she told him.

As he gaped at her in stupefaction, she brought up her own knife, aiming to stab up under his ribs. Despite his shock, he had the presence of mind to push away from her. She felt the blade rip through his clothes, but it skittered over his ribs.

Not a kill, she noted clinically. He gasped in pain and clapped one hand to his sternum, where a line of red was bleeding through his shirt. He scrambled back and stooped quickly to pick up his pistol, which Bridget had shamefully forgotten about in the excitement of possibly getting knifed or burned to death.

Oh, right. Fuck.

The man did not hesitate; he flicked off the safety and chambered a round. Even as he was bringing the pistol up, Bridget stepped forward, reached out, and closed her hand around the end of the barrel. The man shoved her arm away briskly and sent her stumbling to her knees.

Did I do it? Was there enough time?

His eyes were fixed on her, unwavering. With an effort, she broke away from that gaze and looked down at the barrel of the gun that was pointed directly at her face. *A Luger,* she acknowledged weakly. Nothing drew the attention like a gun, especially when it was aimed directly at one's face. And there was a lustrous white shine at the end of it.

She looked back up at him and raised an eyebrow.

He seemed startled, but then his eyes narrowed, and she closed her eyes as he pulled the trigger.

The sound of the gunshot was deafening, and Bridget dropped her knife to clap her hands over her ears. It was only after a moment that she realized she had ears to clap her hands over, and a head that they were still attached to.

It worked! she thought dazedly.

The iridescent nacre that covered her palms and the underside of her fingers was able to resist cuts and burns, but it could do more.

When she felt the occasion warranted it, a clear liquid would seep out of her skin and harden into an incredibly strong pearl-like substance. While the liquid set almost instantly, it took a moment of focus to produce—a moment that Bridget had not been certain she'd had.

She became distantly aware, beyond the ringing in her ears, of the unmistakable sound of a man cursing. She opened her eyes. The gun was lying on the floor in front of her. Its barrel had ruptured on one side, and the breach block at the rear of the gun appeared to have blown out. The seal of pearl that she'd locked around the end of the barrel had held. *Thank God,* she thought. Even though she'd seen the shine before he fired, there had been a distinct possibility that she hadn't made it thick enough.

The German was clutching his hand to his stomach. He'd obviously been injured when the gun misfired. She had a confused idea of gases and components bursting out the back of the pistol.

All right, she thought tiredly. *Time for me to finish this.*

Bridget's knife was on the floor by her knees, and she reached out to pick it up. As she wearily got to her feet, the man's gaze focused on her. The look in his eyes was enraged, panicked. He saw the knife in her hand and came to a decision. Before she could react, he bolted, charging past her to the hallway.

Well, I didn't expect that. She shook her head. *Christ, I can't let him get away!*

"Usha!" she shouted. She had no idea if her friend was still nearby. *Did she go for help? Is she waiting for him at the bottom of the stairs?* "He's coming!" She took a few tottering steps toward the door, then stepped back in surprise as Usha rushed past the doorway, shoving a large chest of drawers in front of her like a battering ram.

What in the hell? Bridget wondered. Then she recalled that there was more than one bedroom on this floor, and while a dresser was a complete beast to maneuver, rendering it completely weightless would make the task a good deal easier. Bridget hurried to the door and saw Usha charging down the hallway, screaming as she went. Beyond her, the German was at the top of the stairs. He was looking back in astonishment at the bureau bearing down on him like the wrath of the god of bedroom furniture. In a move that Bridget could hardly blame him for, he turned and fled.

Usha did not pause but continued on her inexorable progress down the hall. When she reached the head of the stairs, she shoved the hurtling chest of drawers down and leapt onto the back of it.

She's going to ride it down like a damn bobsleigh! thought Bridget incredulously. The racket was unbelievable as the bureau bashed its way down the steps. *What on earth will happen to her at the bottom?* She hurried down the hall but paused as she saw her friend rising weightlessly back up through the air.

The Indian woman was inverted with one leg kicked forward and her body arched back like a dancer photographed in a moment of mid-acrobatics. Her hair floated behind her as if she were underwater. Even in the chaos, when the smashing of the chest of drawers into the wall resounded, it was a moment of unearthly grace. Usha rose up in the stairwell and twisted in the air, slowly and in perfect control. She landed smoothly back at the top of the stairs, and her hair again settled onto her shoulders as she released her power.

Bridget let out a breath she hadn't realized she'd been holding

"Missed him!" Usha spat. "The bureau almost smashed him at the bottom but he got away just at the last minute." She turned and looked at Bridget. "Are you all right?"

"Yeah, I think so."

"Well, come on!" Usha exclaimed. "We've got to get after him!"

"No, wait!" Bridget ran back to the bedroom. "Can't leave these behind!" She held up the German's combat knife and the ruined pistol with its incriminating blockage of pearl on the end. "Can't leave a sign that it was you and me here."

"You think that the civilians aren't going to be able to describe us after we come running out into the street?" Usha asked skeptically, and Bridget paused. It was a good point. She tucked the ruined gun away inside her coat.

"I've got an idea," she said finally.

When the two of them emerged from the house, there were already several people gathered cautiously near the door. They were mostly housewives looking anxious, but several men were there too. Two women were helping up an old man who had clearly been knocked over onto the pavement, and he was pointing in outrage down the street. There were angry mutterings and lots of commiseration over people today and how standards were falling, even in wartime. However, the sight of Usha and Bridget covered in plaster and wheezing in their gas masks diverted all attention from the fallen man and prompted shrieks of terror.

"Gas! Gas attack!"

"Oh, blimey! We're done for!"

The crowd scattered, all of them fumbling at their gas-mask boxes. Several women began weeping, and one frantically tried to get her little boy to agree to put on his brightly colored Donald Duck gas mask.

"This is dreadful!" exclaimed Bridget. "We've started a panic!"

"They'll figure out soon enough that there's no gas," replied Usha, her voice muffled through the rubber of her mask. "Someone will look at a postbox and then there will be outrage." She was referring to the tops of the city postboxes, which had been coated with a special paint that would show the presence of gas. She looked up when she heard the distant sound of a warning rattle. Clearly, someone had informed the local air warden. "Well, that's torn it, there's going to be a *lot* of outrage. But by that time, we'll be long gone. Now, which way?"

"That way," said Bridget firmly, and she indicated the direction that the old man had been pointing. The two women set off running down the street. All around them, people had donned their gas masks in fear. "This could actually help us—he'll be the only one in the crowd without a gas mask."

"Plus, he's leaving us a trail," said Usha. "Look." She pointed to several drops of blood glistening in the road. "How badly did you cut him?" she asked curiously.

"Not fatally," said Bridget, "but hopefully enough to slow him down. And the hand that was holding the gun is in bad shape too." They rounded a corner and peeled off their gas masks. Bridget gratefully gasped in the air and wiped her face. Even those few minutes wearing the mask, laboriously sucking the air in through the filter, had left her out of breath. The street was busy, and the sound of the rattles was spreading. Everywhere, people were looking up in fear. She scanned the crowds for the man. "Any sign of him?"

"There!" said Usha, standing on her tiptoes. She pointed ahead. "Hurry!" They began to push past people, but the panic was growing and the two women were jostled roughly as the crowds around them desperately tried to escape from the nonexistent gas. Children wept, and a couple of babies screamed as their mothers feverishly put the massive gas helmets on them.

"Hell, we'd better put the masks back on," said Bridget. "Otherwise we'll just get attention."

"No one here is paying attention to anything but themselves," said Usha, but she still held her gas mask up in front of her face, her thumbs inside the straps, and Bridget hastily copied her. As one, they thrust their chins forward into the masks and pulled them tightly over their heads.

Then, however, there was the problem of trying to scan the crowds through small mica eyepieces that steamed up almost immediately. It was almost impossible to get a clear view, and with everyone running around, they couldn't make any meaningful progress anyway. Within minutes, the street was practically deserted except for three mothers who were slowly pushing perambulators while awkwardly pumping the bellows for their babies' gas helmets. Finally, the two apprentices stood alone. The pavement was littered with discarded boxes for gas masks and there were several dropped bags of shopping. Bridget winced at all the chaos.

"We are in so much trouble," she said grimly. And it was all for nothing—there was no sign of the fleeing German. He had completely vanished in the panicking crowd.

"Maybe we try to follow the blood trail?" suggested Usha. But they could find nothing. He'd stopped bleeding or he'd bound up his wounds or they were looking in the wrong places. They regarded each other dispiritedly.

"What now?" asked Bridget.

"Do we go back to the house?" said Usha. "Maybe he'll have left some clues behind."

"The police will be there by now," said Bridget. "Or, even worse, the Checquy. They'll be questioning any locals they can lure out. I'm already worried we might have been seen going into the house. Let's just go back home."

★   ★   ★

"That madness was *you?*" asked Pamela incredulously. "The entire Court got pulled out of the meeting when we heard there'd been a gas attack over in the East End. Well, except for Bishop Alrich, of course. Everybody in the building was putting on their gas masks! Rook McGillicuddy had to coil up his proboscis extra tightly to ensure it fit into his mask. Do you have any idea how much trouble that whole alarm caused? And it was nothing? You faked it?"

"It made sense at the time," said Bridget defensively. She and Usha had limped home, looking like absolute hell. After a brisk wash, they met up in the lounge, which was where they were now, drinking (not nearly enough) gin and (far too much) tonics. Pamela had returned from the Court meeting looking extremely tired only to be met with the revelations about her friends' activities in Canley.

"And you actually saw him? The German?"

"Better than that," said Usha. "Bridget sliced him up."

"My God," said Pamela.

"Not fatally, though," said Bridget. "I don't think."

"Did he use any powers?"

"Not that we could tell," said Bridget.

"No one burned to death," said Usha. "And he certainly seemed to bleed like a normal person."

"We'll scan the police reports for any knife-wounded corpses, then," said Pamela. "Maybe we'll get lucky and he'll bleed to death in a park."

"That would make things a lot easier," said Bridget.

"Yes, I'll mention it in my prayers tonight," said Usha.

"Let's take stock of our situation, then," said Pamela.

"We've definitely left him worse than we found him," said Usha. "He's down a combat knife, a gun, a shelter that had food in it."

"Plus he's bleeding from his chest and may have a pretty badly mangled right hand," said Bridget. The damaged gun was locked away in the bottom drawer of her desk upstairs.

"This will make him all the more desperate, though," said Pamela. "We already know that he'll kill to get what he needs."

"And we know what he looks like."

"He knows what *we* look like," said Usha. "All three of us now. We absolutely cannot allow the Checquy to capture him."

"So where do we go from here?" wondered Bridget. "We're back where we started, with no leads."

"We'll need to do what you did before," said Pamela. "Put ourselves in his head. What will he need? What would a man like this seek out?"

"Treatment for his injuries," suggested Bridget. "Although I expect it's a bit late for us to check the hospitals now."

"Shelter," said Pamela, who had begun writing a list.

"Food," said Bridget.

"Weapons," said Pamela.

"Sex," said Usha archly.

"I don't expect he'll be in a position to ask any young ladies out to a tea dance," said Bridget.

"All right, well, everyone have a think about where to go from here," said Pamela. She scanned the list. "You say he didn't use his powers," she remarked thoughtfully.

"No," said Bridget. "He had a gun, but when he lost that, he came at us with the knife."

"So perhaps he doesn't know how to use his powers," mused Pamela. "Maybe they come out under specific circumstances. After all, the Jinkses and the old woman were killed when he was under tremendous stress."

"Well, we've just put him under a hell of a lot more," said Bridget grimly.

The next morning, Bridget sat at the big table in the Lady's office at Apex House and anxiously scanned the newspapers for anything about the fake gas attack in Canley. There was very little beyond the fact that it had most definitely been a fake and was absolutely no cause for concern. At all.

Bridget suspected that the government censors had been torn between the opportunity to lecture the populace on being calm and responsible and the fear of letting the enemy know that anything untoward had happened. Well aware that the Germans scrutinized all newspapers, the censors were paranoid about releasing any information that might aid or encourage the enemy or damage British morale.

The police reports noted that there had been some minor injuries in the crowd, but there was no mention of the initial source of the panic. She hoped the authorities were too busy to investigate any further. If some future update mentioned two women who had emerged from the murder scene wearing gas masks, she didn't know what they would do. Some local was going to remember seeing them go into that house, and Usha was sufficiently striking that someone in the Checquy could easily put two and two together. *Especially since the house is part of a Checquy investigation.* She stared down at the reports, so lost in depressing thoughts that she was only distantly aware of someone entering the Lady's office.

"Good morning, ladies! Good morning, my Lady! Good *morning,* Bridget!"

"Oh, blinking hell," muttered Bridget to herself, deliberately not looking up. The plummy voice belonged to her least favorite person in the Checquy, a man who seemed to take her pointedly brief answers as a sign that she was shyly enamored of him. Of course, as far as he could see, *all* women were enamored of him, and she'd once heard him say that the shy ones were always worth the pursuit. Presumably this was why he usually made a special attempt to flirt with her.

Maybe I should be friendlier to him. It might actually serve to put him off a bit, she mused before deciding that it would simply take too much strength this morning. *Besides, he might take it as a sign of progress.*

"Good morning, Pawn Wattleman," said Lady Carmichael, sounding amused.

"Henry," Pamela said, nodding. Usha said nothing, merely looking at him with disdainful acknowledgment, which did nothing at all to dampen his confidence. It was a matter of some debate among the female staff of Apex House as to whether his gargantuan ego was actually supernatural or simply built on the fact that he was extremely good-looking. Tall, with thick dark hair that fell over his right eyebrow, defying the inevitable sculpted Brylcreem. A light scar slashing across his right cheek added an intriguing air of danger, and his amused smile promised a good time.

Pawn Henry Wattleman was the same age as Pamela, who had known him all her life and, much to her mortification, enjoyed the dubious honor of being his first kiss. (They'd both been fifteen, attending a dance for young Checquy operatives held at a country house. Both of them had been fairly intoxicated on filched wine. Pamela always made it very clear that it had gone no further than kissing, partly because he was so obnoxious and partly because he'd then promptly vomited all over her dress, stumbled out into the garden, knocked over some statuary, staggered through a wall, and passed out in a hedge.)

"He's always been like that," Pamela had said of Wattleman. "Absolutely convinced that he's God's gift to women and absolutely certain that everything is going to work out for him. And the irritating thing is that it so often does."

Any female member of the Checquy was a viable target for his attentions. The rumor mill around Apex House could not agree on who had succumbed to his advances and who had not, but speculation was rife. In any normal government organization, his lothario-esque conduct would have been looked at askance, but as the agency tasked with addressing supernatural affairs, the Order of the Checquy was obliged to take a sensible, measured, and rational approach to the surreal, the impossible, and the ridiculous.

And nothing was quite as ridiculous as the vagaries of human sexuality.

The Checquy recognized that sex was one of the driving impulses of the human psyche and physiology, and as such, it represented a distinct vulnerability. Accordingly, operatives were given a thorough grounding in the dangers they might face.

The most attention-grabbing dangers, of course, came from the paranormal. There were, inevitably, supernatural creatures that used sex as a weapon. Pawns and Retainers were trained to recognize and resist the captivating temptations of the Hungarian *lidérc,* whether it manifested in the form of a fiery satanic lover or a featherless chicken. They knew never to take a hat-wearing South American man to bed without first checking to see if the chapeau concealed a blowhole, marking him as a *boto,* a river dolphin in disguise. Most male

Checquy operatives were able to resist the lure of a Venus mantrap's vulvar blossoms and could master themselves sufficiently to flee to a safe distance and alert the authorities. (Teams of heterosexual female operatives would be hastily assembled to cut free any entranced and subsequently mortified men who *had* been ensnared, and then they would root the whole thing out of the ground.)

Despite their training and knowledge, though, the soldiers of the Checquy could still be susceptible to the amorous lure of the supernatural. There were some threats that, though well known, still claimed their share of victims. Over the centuries, many Pawns had fallen prey to the seductive charms of succubi, incubi, and, in several memorable and bewildering instances, incunabula.

Certain events had passed into organizational legend. In 1860, for instance, while on a picnic, Pawn Gawain was enslaved by the sexual wiles of a dryad that stepped out of a pistachio tree in Kew Gardens. Under her direction, he committed a series of plant-related crimes in a state of apparent (and priapic) ecstasy. When his comrades finally put him down, an autopsy revealed vines twined throughout his body and thorns caged around his heart. It proved necessary to hold a closed-casket funeral, since the morticians had been unable to tone down either the gigantic grin that covered his face or the other significant hallmark of the dryad's influence.

In 1889, Major Sid Winton, a Retainer who'd been recruited into the Checquy from the Royal Northumberland Fusiliers, was obliged to confess to his superior that, after a moment of weakness with a smooth-skinned woman with thick, dark brown hair and striking violet eyes who'd been hanging around the cordon of a manifestation site in Limehouse, he appeared to have gotten pregnant.

The awkwardness of that conversation was surpassed only by the awkwardness of the discussion Winton had to have with his wife, a Pawn who outranked him.

As a Retainer, Winton was not believed to possess any inhuman capabilities. His wife was a Pawn, so there was the momentary thought that she might have been the impregnator, but her only known supernatural gift affected hydrogen molecules, and besides, she'd been away on assignment on Prince Edward Island for five months. Winton's symptoms, his weight gain, and the *placement* of that weight gain were all consistent with those of a three months' pregnant woman, which tallied exactly with his ill-advised tumble with the girl whose name he'd never learned.

A cautious exploratory surgery revealed that Winton did not possess any unexpected, previously latent female bits tucked away inside. There was no womb, no uterus—he was a bog-standard man. But lodged within his body was a smokily glowing scarlet orb that could not be removed or breached. Close examination through the haze within revealed what appeared to be a human fetus.

Pawn Winton, who had not risen to her high position by not being supremely practical, decided after some reflection that she would eventually forgive her husband for his unfaithfulness and that she would need to make preparations now for that forgiveness whenever it occurred, which would probably be after the baby was born (if her husband survived). She hurriedly announced to all her non-Checquy friends that she was expecting. The three other Winton children (who had been borne by the female Winton, thank you very much) were quickly sent to visit with relatives until their father's confinement was over, and Mr. and Pawn Winton went off to the country together. The plan was that they would return after the pregnancy came to term. If the baby was human, they would claim it had arrived via the traditional route. If it was not passably human or not safe, then the Checquy would take care of it, and the Wintons would quietly let people know that they had suffered a tragedy.

It was assumed within the organization that Winton himself was the supernatural element, that an ability had suddenly manifested within him, and that he'd managed the unprecedented feat of going from Winton the Retainer to Winton the Pawn.

But then the other pregnancies emerged.

The first was a seventeen-year-old boy who hung himself in a Stepney graveyard. His oddly swollen belly prompted an autopsy, which revealed a dull red orb nestled within him. Inevitably, the body came to the Checquy, whose scientists couldn't penetrate that sphere either. The generally accepted theory was that the young man had been driven mad by the inexplicable circumstances and had

committed suicide out of shame and horror. The lack of light ema-
nating from the orb suggested that the infant inside had also perished.
A friend, when questioned, remembered that he'd enjoyed "a shag
with a fine-lookin' bint he'd chatted up on a street corner. Stunning
eyes, she 'ad. Almost purple, weren't they, Mick?"

Whoever or whatever that violet-eyed girl was, she'd certainly
been sociable. Two other men were eventually discovered to have
gotten pregnant by her. Inevitably, the Checquy labeled her "the
Impregnatrix."

The next victim to come to light was Joe Peck, a grizzled dock-
hand in his late forties. He'd been quietly surprised when a sweet-
faced girl young enough to be his daughter, with striking eyes and
gorgeous dark hair, had invited him into the alley behind the pub for
a few minutes of intense pleasure. He'd been even more surprised
when she didn't charge him. Later, when he put on weight and kept
falling asleep at work, when his ankles swelled up and he noticed a
faint glow coming from his growing belly, he'd broken the custom of
a lifetime and actually gone to the district nurse.

Fortunately, the local GP had the right sort of connections. After
the Stepney suicide was found, the Checquy had briefed local medical
practitioners so they would be on the lookout for similar symptoms.
Peck's doctor reached out to the contact he'd been provided, and the
Checquy came right away.

Peck took the impossible news that he was pregnant with the same
calm with which he'd accepted an existence consisting almost entirely
of hard knocks. His unflappability had seen him through the death of
his wife years ago and had kept him going through the growing difficulty of life as an aging and illiterate laborer. He nodded once, then
knocked out the ashes of his pipe.

"Can't be havin' no more of that, then," he said and stowed the
pipe away in an inner pocket. "Nor no rum nor porter, I s'pose."

The Checquy liaison was somewhat nonplussed by Peck's distinct
lack of flabbergastedness, but eventually she collected herself and
offered him the help of a private charity. They could provide the support he would need in his unique situation. The dockworker considered it for a moment before nodding a silent acceptance. He was

swiftly taken off to a large house in the Warwickshire countryside, where he was introduced to Major Winton, who'd also been brought there for his confinement.

They were joined shortly afterward by Christopher Mulgrew, a recent graduate of the Brompton Academy in London. He and some friends had ventured forth on a lads' night out to explore the big bad city. He'd thought that he'd gotten lucky when, in fact, he'd been spectacularly unlucky. When his symptoms emerged, his monied family sent him to one of the best doctors in Harley Street, who had promptly punted him along to the Checquy.

As best the Checquy could tell, all the men had been gotten with child on the same day and in roughly the same neighborhood. The fathers-to-be provided consistent descriptions of their lover's appearance (with varying degrees of bitterness), and it was clear that a single person (or entity) was responsible. There was a great deal of relief all around—the prospect of multiple Impregnatrices wandering about had had everyone sweating. Portraits were hastily drawn and distributed to Checquy investigative teams, who spread out into Stepney, Limehouse, Mile End, and Poplar looking for her. The trail was months cold, but there was the unnerving possibility that she was still sauntering around fecundating unsuspecting men.

Meanwhile, preparations were being made for the three men to give birth. A team of doctors and scientists had been installed at the manor, led by Gammer Shandy, an elderly country midwife whose understanding of childbirth was held to be unparalleled, despite her lack of formal schooling.

"Never seen a man in pig before," she remarked, "let alone three of 'em. But I expect I'll be able to cope with any surprises."

The pregnancies proceeded normally. The men complained of tender nipples, nausea, heartburn, constipation, and the increasing discomfort from the stretching of their bellies. Gammer Shandy treated them accordingly, brewing them relentlessly foul teas from weeds of the fields and applying odoriferous poultices to their bellies and perinea with stern injunctions to let them seep into the skin for several hours.

Peck and Winton spent a great deal of time sitting in the garden.

Despite their different backgrounds, the two men got on famously. Winton would read aloud from the newspaper, and Peck would knit baby clothes—a skill he'd learned from a Norwegian sailor. Young Christopher Mulgrew, however, sulked inside, avoiding people as much as he could. The sight of his own body filled him with humiliated loathing, and the daily doctors' examinations were agonies of shame for him.

Despite their continued nausea, the men did periodically become ravenously hungry and were prey to sudden, intense cravings. Peck and Mulgrew were continuously requesting oranges and cooked barley, while Winton was discovered one afternoon shamefacedly gnawing on the arm of a mahogany chair. Gammer Shandy ordered that he should be allowed to continue.

"That's t' babby saying what it wants," she advised. This proclamation prompted some excited speculation among the gathered scientists about the possible nature of the babies, but she cut them off. "It's all normal. I've seen women swallowing coal and seeking out seaweed."

Special birthing suites were prepared in the manor. As far as the doctors could tell from the exploratory surgery, the fetus in Major Winton looked normal, but no one could be certain what would happen when the babies were born. They might transform or possess unexpected powers, so the suites were fortified against a variety of eventualities. Buckets of sand and water were placed strategically in case of emergency, and armed troops stood ready in designated spots.

At night, the faint red light could be seen spreading downward within the men's bodies. The rather nervous hypothesis of the scientists was that the orbs were preparing for their occupants' exits. The men complained of dull aches as their internal organs were nudged about. Much to their relief, there was no sprouting of breasts, but feelings were mixed about the lack of changes to their genitals. The first question anyone had, after all, was how the babies were going to come out.

Given that the orbs within Winton and the boy who had committed suicide had been unbreakable and unremovable, cesareans were impossible. Various alarming scenarios were sketched out. The walls of the birthing suites were hastily repainted with an easy-to-wash veneer.

At last, all three men went into labor on the same day, each exactly nine months after the conception, down to the hour. They were hurried to their assigned birth suites, and Gammer Shandy hobbled from room to room, attended by her entourage of white-coated scientists and doctors.

The men's labors were said to have been spectacularly painful and spectacularly undignified, although specific details were never released, much to the frustration of the entire Checquy. *All three were brought to bed of fine boys* was all Gammer Shandy wrote in her official report. The old midwife judged that the privacy of the birthing bed extended even to men, and none dared gainsay her decades of experience and wisdom. Not even the foot soldiers who were present dared go against her orders. Those outside the rooms, however, reported bloodcurdling screams unlike anything they'd ever heard.

And in the end, there were simply three normal baby boys. No inhuman features, no unholy manifestations. The skies did not turn red, the plants around the house did not die, the earth remained still. Local clergymen did not bleed, animals did not howl, and no one even felt any chills, although everyone who witnessed the births needed several stiff drinks afterward.

The babies themselves behaved as normal, healthy babies did. They didn't even look particularly alike, each taking more after his father than his mother. The small army that had been encircling the house was stood down, the trenches were filled in, the fences were dismantled, the artillery was wheeled away, and the wet nurses were brought in.

Once his ordeal was over, Christopher Mulgrew wanted nothing more to do with any of it. He gladly took the money offered, left the child in the custody of the Checquy, and went off to university, determined to forget the experience as soon as possible.

Joe Peck, on the other hand, had no such intentions.

"If anyone tries to take my little lad from me," he said grimly, enjoying his first pipe in months, "they'll find themselves regrettin' it."

The Checquy, somewhat taken aback, believed him, and after casting about for options, they finally offered him a place in the organization as a Retainer. He was quite different from their usual recruits, who were drawn from the best that the Church, academia, the military, and the civil service had to offer, but he brought a solid, unflappable practicality to the role and faced down horrors that sent more experienced operatives fleeing in terror. Over the years, he became a beloved and highly decorated colleague, working closely with Major Winton.

Christopher Mulgrew's child was placed with the Winton family, and the constant congratulations that Pawn Winton received on her twins pushed back her forgiveness of her husband an additional two months. Joe Peck and his little lad were placed in the row house next door. Over the weeks and months that followed, the Checquy thoroughly examined all three babies and confirmed that they were perfectly human. The boys would grow up together. It all seemed a most satisfactory ending.

And yet there were concerns. The circumstances of the boys' conception, gestation, and delivery were disquieting to everyone who heard about them, especially the men (women who heard about it tended to find the whole thing hilarious—disquieting, but hilarious). And it was not just members of the Checquy who knew of the events. Reports had to be made to the powers of the land, and this story was too juicy not to spread a little, even if it was a state secret.

A couple of weeks later, after some concerned private conversations in various offices, drawing rooms, and the peers' dining room at the Palace of Westminster, the Lord of the Checquy was invited to spend a Saturday to Monday at Hatfield House in Hertfordshire. Hatfield House was the country seat of the Marquess of Salisbury, who also happened to be the Prime Minister. Also attending were several concerned civil service mandarins, a couple of MPs, a viscount, and an earl. The days passed pleasantly with a very satisfying shoot, much playing of whist, and many excellent meals. And then Sunday afternoon, while the wives were doing whatever wifely things they did, the gentlemen gathered in the billiard room. Very quietly, over a game of snooker, the possibility of sterilizing the babies was mooted.

"I mean to say, old boy, who knows what odd traits are curdling away in those boys' blood?"

"Hmm, quite. Possibly waiting to infect future generations. You know, what if they had daughters, eh? Daughters who could go around getting men up the duff?"

"Ugly thought, what?"

"Nasty."

"So what do you think, Lorridaile?"

All eyes turned to Sir Hugh Lorridaile, the doughty Lord of the Checquy. Born to a fine old family, he'd come to his powers late in life and maintained his connections to the greatest houses of the kingdom. The men in the billiard room knew him, they thought. He was one of them.

Still, as the Lord considered the question, there was a stillness about him that made them a little nervous. He took up a cue and surveyed the distribution of the balls on the table. "It seems a dangerous precedent to set," he remarked finally as he lined up his cue. "I don't like to think how my troops would react if we started neutering people for being different. They might wonder what could happen to them. A bit of a thin end of the wedge, hmm?" He didn't take his eyes off the table. "And besides"—he paused as he launched his shot, and there was silence in the room except for the repeated clacking as the cue ball ricocheted about the table. The gathered great and good silently watched the white ball move without any loss of momentum as it knocked the balls into pockets in order: red, yellow, red, green, red, brown, red, pink, red, black. It stopped abruptly in the middle of the table—"one never knows what might turn out to be useful," he finished.

A thoughtful and intimidated silence ensued, broken finally by the Prime Minister, who had been sitting, unspeaking, by the fireplace.

"Quite so," he said heavily. This pronouncement was followed by a frantic flurry of agreement.

"Hm, yes! Good thinking!"

"Sound man, that."

"Won't be our problem anyway, leave it to those who come after us."

And so the little boys went ungelded. But all three of them were placed on a Checquy watch list for regular observation, and it was decreed that all of their descendants for the next three generations would be under similar surveillance.

No explanation was ever produced for who or what the Impregnatrix was, where she'd gone, or what her plan had been. She'd come out of nowhere, briskly knocked up four men, then vanished without a trace (except, of course, her three sons, a tragic suicide, some rather hurt feelings, and some extremely hurt genitals). But the whole affair served as a salutary lesson for generations of Checquy apprentices as to why they needed to be cautious when it came to matters of the loins.

Male students, in particular, tended to take the story to heart.

Of course, the greatest supernatural danger when jousting on the lists of love and lust was the Checquy itself. Simply by virtue of what they were, the operatives of the Checquy could bring a new and terrifying element to any normal sexual occurrence. Every child born to a Pawn parent was welcomed under strict, fortified conditions in case the event duplicated the unfortunate birth of Pawn Lewis's daughter in 1362, which had resulted in Saint Marcellus's flood or the Grote Mandrenke (the Great Drowning of Men)—a massive Atlantic gale that wiped out the port of Ravenser Odd in East Yorkshire and the harbor of Dunwich.

Thankfully, most births were fairly mundane. It was the other dangers of an active love life that more frequently yielded disastrous results. The Chevalier Caroline Penhaligon was the most famous example of what could happen when the supernatural met the venereal. She'd contracted something nasty after an ill-advised dalliance with a strapping young apprentice to the local blacksmith. The disease's unfortunate interaction with her abilities brought new meaning to the complaint "It burns when I piss" after the east wing of Bufo Hall was consumed by purple flames.

Aside from the predations of the supernatural, though, the Checquy took a practical approach to sexual relationships. It was pointless to deny that people's lusts and impulses could be used to manipulate them. And even the lowest-ranked Pawn—the most junior clerk or tea lady—was entrusted with secrets that affected the nation's security. Any weakness that might be used against them had to be addressed. To the Checquy, ignorance was a weakness that could not be permitted. Forewarned was forearmed.

From the appropriate age, the young of the Checquy were given a frank and fearless explanation of the basics. All the children spent at least two seasons on a farm, where they developed the clear-eyed matter-of-factness about the mechanics of it all that every country child possesses.

Later, as they grew, they were brought in single-sex groups to a private lecture hall in St. Fiacre's College at Cambridge for classes on attraction, ardor, and how the human body works (the classes were theoretical only—there were no practical sessions). Thus, even in the infamously prudish Victorian period, no Checquy woman went to her wedding bed ignorant of what was going to happen (although several of the women's new spouses were taken aback by the forthright and well-informed approach their blushing brides brought to pleasure and intimacy).

The classes also acknowledged that different forms of lust and attraction existed. The Checquy studiously withheld judgment. After centuries of being confronted with the profoundly abnormal, the Order had developed a big-picture perspective. Compared to little badgers that burrowed into people's eyes and controlled their minds, what two (or more) consenting adults did together tended to pale as a matter of concern. So, unless they endangered the organization's secrecy, Checquy operatives were allowed to get up to whatever they wished to in the bedchamber.

In such a (comparatively) permissive culture, it took real effort to shock, but Wattleman had gained notoriety from his intense and seemingly indiscriminate pursuit of absolutely everything that wore a skirt. To make matters infinitely more irritating, he was an extremely competent operative, and his star was continually on the rise.

He'd first made his name as a result of a particularly daring operation in which he had single-handedly infiltrated a ring of conspirators who threatened to subvert the entire nation.

A group of bright young artists had formed a web of connections through the use of a peculiar abstract sculpture. The item, whose origin could never be established, linked the minds of those who touched it, amplifying their intellect and their creativity even as it twisted their morality. It also instilled a fanatical loyalty to the ever-growing cabal. When they were not throwing infamous parties, experimenting with cocaine and polyamory, or writing extremely witty poems and novels, the group was plotting how to lure key figures of national power into their coterie.

By the time the Checquy uncovered the scheme, the conspirators had drawn in and suborned several influential members of the aristocracy, the heiress to a publishing empire, an MP, and the permanent secretary for the Department of Administrative Affairs, who—to the horror of the Checquy Court—also happened to be the husband of an extremely high-ranking Pawn. The Pawn in question swore that she had told him nothing about the Checquy, but there was the dangerous possibility that he knew *something,* and what he knew, the cabal would know.

The Lord and Lady of the time decided that before they destroyed the statue and took care of the cabal, they needed to know exactly how far the rot had spread. Someone had to insinuate his or her way into the group and determine the state of affairs—someone comely enough to catch a conspirator's eye, confident enough to venture in without any support, and lethal enough to handle the situation if things turned ugly. The Court turned to the promising and newly promoted young Pawn Wattleman.

Upon receiving the assignment, Wattleman immediately made the acquaintance of a member of the group, a lovely playwright whose recent works had received rave reviews. The two of them drank and flirted, and once she became aware that he had important contacts in British intelligence, she invited him to a decadent weekend party at the country manor where the sculpture was kept.

Bridget had read Wattleman's official report on the affair. After "settling in," he had departed the room he was sharing with the playwright and explored the house and grounds, identifying several luminary guests in the process. He eluded a couple of armed guards and broke into the manor's study, where he found a wealth of incriminating information, including an organizational chart that showed who had already come under the influence of the sculpture (all of whom were present that weekend) and who was to be added. His own name featured on the latter list along with two others. The Pawn whose husband was a member of the cabal had not been invited to attend the weekend, which strongly suggested that the cabal had no idea about the existence of the Checquy.

Wattleman also discovered a meticulous schedule for the rest of the weekend; that evening's activities included a cocktail hour, dinner, dancing, an orgy, ablutions, and an ominous-sounding "coalescence" in the sculpture gallery.

The conspiracy and every member of the cabal died that night when the manor mysteriously collapsed in on itself. Wattleman walked out of the wreckage smoking a cigarette and remarking that the playwright always did love to bring the house down. The uncharitable among the Checquy acidly noted that the building had been destroyed before the appointed hour for everyone to lay hands on the sculpture but *after* the appointed hour for the orgy.

After that, Wattleman's successful assignments included recovering a stolen gem that turned gold into lead (part of a convoluted plot to increase the value of the thief's own holdings), assassinating a Sheffield industrialist who was sacrificing children on a pagan altar in an (unsuccessful) attempt to live forever, and foiling a plot by Scottish nationalists to animate the trees in a Perthshire forest and use them as an army.

It had been noted that practically every mission he undertook somehow called for him to enter into a tryst with at least one beautiful woman. It was also whispered that he had, on occasion, been loaned to high-ranking non-Checquy officials to carry out private missions, although such a thing would have been illegal.

The combination of accomplishment and scandal had made Wattleman something of a legendary figure within the Checquy. Upon becoming Lady Carmichael's apprentice, Bridget was granted access to some of the Court files and she knew that Wattleman's successes had put him near the top of the list for assignments needing special discretion. As a result, it was not unusual for him to be summoned by members of the Court. Although he was attached to no particular team or office, his dapper figure was often seen roaming the hallways of Apex House.

Even in wartime, he somehow managed to be smartly put together. Today, he was wearing an impossibly new suit. Bridget noted with a sniff that his trousers featured cuffs that definitely violated the spirit of being frugal for the war effort. Cloth hadn't actually been rationed, not yet, but that was considered inevitable.

"My Lady, I was summoned, I have come."

"Sit down, please, Henry. Tea?"

"Thank you, no." To Bridget's relief, neither she nor Usha was called over to attend the conversation. Nevertheless, she kept her ears open.

"Now, what do you know about the black market?" asked Lady Carmichael.

"Why would I know anything about the black market?" he asked innocently. The Lady eyed him up and down, taking in every detail of his clothes, including the incriminating cuffs. To Bridget's delight, Wattleman actually colored a little.

"Ah, well, let's see." He sat back and steepled his fingers thoughtfully. "Since the onset of the war there have been shortages of many items, including some common household goods. It's only a matter of time before we see food and clothing rationing for the general public. As a result, the black market has assumed a far greater presence in the lives of regular civilians. That is in addition to the preexisting market for illegal goods.

"As far as I'm aware," he continued, "there's no single power behind it, although there are several significant networks. It encompasses everything from the local butcher with a bit of extra bacon under the counter for special customers to goods smuggled in from other countries."

"And spivs?" asked the Lady. The word sounded odd coming out of her mouth.

"The salesmen for the black market? You'll find them dotted about the streets," said Wattleman promptly. "Usually dressed rather flashily." Despite herself, Bridget snorted a little. The Pawn's own suit was deliberately tailored to catch the eye. "They're often the connection between the regular members of the public and the black market."

"There is a spiv that I want you to investigate."

"Surely that's not our role," said Wattleman, startled. "I mean, my Lady, these are difficult times. People want what they want, and if they can't get it from the shops because of shortages, well, they'll go where they *can* get it. It's a pity, but if a girl wants stockings or a young man wants some chocolate with which to go a-wooing, well, it's not so terrible a crime, is it?"

"This particular spiv appears to be trafficking in goods that relate very definitely to our role," said Lady Carmichael. "There have been three recent manifestations in London, all very different, two of them ending in single-person fatalities. I am concerned because all three have involved civilian women who were found to be in possession of supernatural items."

Wattleman tsked, shaking his head in disapproval.

"To make matters worse, one of the items was a femur that we believe is that of Pawn Santosuosso, who died in 1910."

"Do you think they were involved in grave-robbing?" asked Wattleman in surprise.

"Pawn Santosuosso's bones have been held in our custody since he passed away," said Lady Carmichael severely. "They were part of an armory that was removed from London as part of Operation Egg Basket."

"Oh, dear," said Wattleman gravely.

Operation Egg Basket had been the largest Checquy undertaking in decades. In the lead-up to the declaration of war, the Checquy had grimly recognized the likelihood that the capital would be bombed, if not invaded. The prospect of their staff being killed and their facilities destroyed was bad enough, but it also put the Order in a peculiarly vulnerable situation. They were the custodians of a large number of supernatural artifacts and prisoners that had been acquired over the centuries. Additionally, they were responsible for several massive archives of documents, any one of which would have shaken society to its core if released. All of these represented not only invaluable assets but also horrendous vulnerabilities.

For instance, no one could be certain how a hibernating kelpie might react were an incendiary bomb to fall upon it, but there was the alarming possibility that it might be roused from its chemically induced coma to run wild in the streets of London and drown thousands while looking for sheep to herd. And the shock wave from an explosion might shatter the fragile glass-and-amber prison that had held the Farriner fireflies since 1666.

Aside from imprisoned monsters, there were several other objects with significant abilities in the Checquy collections. If they were to fall into the hands of an invader who had no compunctions about using them, the balance of power in the war—indeed, in the *world*—would shift completely.

Until then, it had always made sense to bring dangerous objects and individuals to the most secure facilities for storage and study. The most secure facilities tended to be in large cities, as that was where large numbers of Pawns could protect them or destroy them should it prove necessary. Indeed, many of the objects had been stored under Apex House itself. Those large cities around the country, however, now formed the most delectable of targets for German bombing attacks. In the event of an invasion, they would be the primary focus. The possibility that the contents of Checquy repositories would be discovered and seized was simply unacceptable.

Accordingly, like the administrators of the nation's galleries and museums, Checquy officials began to engage in a massive relocation scheme. Pawns and Retainers were drawn from all over the British Isles and the empire to audit, catalog, and oversee the transport of strategic items and individuals.

The archives of historical documents were a comparatively simple matter—they needed merely to be shipped to a facility in the Orkney archipelago, along with the scholars who could not bear to be parted from them. Supernatural items, however, posed a far greater challenge.

The Checquy possessed facilities across the nation, but these collections called for a combination of security, remoteness, and secrecy. With museums and galleries scrabbling about for storage and government departments clamoring for their own wartime accommodations, the competition for viable abandoned mines and suitable stately homes was intense. The Checquy managed to acquire a few locations for their own exclusive use, but in some cases, they were obliged to share. Thus, works by such luminaries as Turner, Botticelli, and

Rembrandt were stored in a slate mine in Wales next to the most profane, dangerous, and inhumanly creative items ever discovered. Museum officials were, of course, kept ignorant of this.

In some cases, the Checquy had taken the horrendous risk of transporting artifacts overseas to their counterparts in the New World. The American Croatoan had initially balked at the prospect of providing any support to a war their country was not part of, but they were sensible of the dangerous consequences should the Nazis gain control of the red-winged throne or the broken toy horse. Those objects had been secretly sent by submarine to Alaska and carried to fortified warehouses deep in the interior of the country. The American government had been very deliberately *not* informed of the favor it was doing the British government (which, similarly, was not informed of the favor it was being done).

Other artifacts presented unique challenges when being moved. A battered silver saltcellar required the continuous presence of the archbishop of Canterbury as it was removed from its usual resting place in the bowels of Westminster Abbey and moved to a private chapel in Stockton-on-Tees. In order to transport nine otter skulls, a boxcar had been filled with distilled water, and a fireproof Pawn stood ready with one hand on the detonator of a ton of dynamite while with the other hand she gingerly decanted in the skulls for their journey to the bottom of a well on the island of Mull.

Some problems had been insurmountable. The frozen explosion in the cellars of the Palace of Westminster, for instance, could not be moved, for obvious reasons. Everyone had agreed that, if it *were* abruptly let loose in the course of bombing or invasion, they would simply blame it on the Germans. The roots of the demonic Roman mosaic in Manchester went too far into the ground to be excavated, so the Checquy had had to content themselves with pouring several new layers of concrete over it and hoping that there wouldn't be too much rainfall during the course of the war.

Finally, in addition to artifacts and documents, the Checquy was responsible for the sequestration of supernatural individuals and creatures. A committee had decided that the Checquy's primary prison, the Scottish castle of Gallows Keep, was sufficiently remote and secure that all its inmates could remain there. A couple of prisoners, however, were housed elsewhere, and their circumstances precluded any attempt to transfer them to the keep. Thus, a monstrous foreign monarch remained chained and entombed in the sewers under Charing Cross, while Professor Oswald Dickinson stayed under house arrest in his bungalow in Hounslow and continued to receive his regular deliveries of academic journals and cat meat.

The entire project was massively complex, took months of organization, and consumed vast resources, but until now, it had been considered a resounding success. The most dangerous items had been removed, although there were still scores of lesser items waiting to be taken to new homes. The emergence among the populace of powered artifacts that were supposed to be in Checquy custody, like Pawn Santosuosso's femur, made for some very alarming possibilities.

"One of the other items, a seashell, has also been confirmed as having come from a Checquy collection," said Lady Carmichael grimly. "We are still checking the provenance of the third item, a brooch of some sort. But given that the other two came from our holdings, I can only conclude that someone has taken advantage of the movement of Checquy materials and is stealing items and selling them."

Bloody hell, thought Bridget. Quite aside from the alarming prospects of a potential traitor selling classified government material and a weakness in the Checquy's operations, this meant that supernatural materials were being moved onto the street and seeding manifestations.

"If this is an inside job," the Lady said, "then we cannot take the risk of alerting the culprit. And if word gets out about this, it could make our position within the government very awkward. There are always some who do not think we should be enjoying our current level of autonomy." She sighed. "It has only gotten worse now that Britain is at war. These parties could use this breach in our internal security as a pretext to exert much more direct control over the Checquy." Everyone in the room was silent at the thought of this.

"Now, I have consulted with Lord Pease, and we have agreed that we need to know exactly how widespread a problem this is without ordering a gigantic and embarrassing audit that would only serve to warn any traitors. That is where you come into play, Henry.

Investigate, discreetly. If it's localized, I trust you to gather all the relevant information and eliminate the source. If it's bigger than four or five people, then let me know, and we'll escalate appropriately."

"Absolutely, my Lady," said Wattleman. "You can trust me."

"I have no doubt of that. Once we know how this is happening, I hope we will be able to find out how many artifacts have been lifted and where they are. We can then turn our attention to retrieving them. Here is the file. I do not want it to leave this room, so sit over at the conference table and take any notes you need."

"Yes, my Lady." Predictably, he sat down next to Bridget. She sighed and did not acknowledge him as he jotted down in his notebook some key details in the Checquy's esoteric shorthand. Despite herself, she noticed that his cologne was very nice. Still, she jerked her leg away when his thigh brushed against hers.

Finally, he stood up. "I believe I have all I need, my Lady. I'll move immediately." He paused thoughtfully for a moment. "I *could* do with some assistance on this one, though. If this supernatural spiv is selling mainly to women, well, a woman would come in handy."

Oh God, no, thought Bridget. She kept her eyes fixed on her papers. *Please don't, please don't . . .*

"Bridget," said the Lady.

"Hmm?" She looked up, eyes wide, as if she hadn't heard a word of the conversation. Lady Carmichael looked at her skeptically, and she felt herself flush.

"Will you be all right to assist Pawn Wattleman on this assignment?"

Bridget looked down at her hands. Upon arriving at the office that morning, Lady Carmichael had pulled her aside to talk about Gerald's decision to enlist in the war. Both of them had been nearly in tears, but Bridget had assured the Lady that she could continue in her duties and did not need to take any time off.

What about the Nazi? she thought. *I won't be able to help the other two if I'm attached to this mission for Wattleman.* She wavered but couldn't think of a good excuse. "Yes," she said finally. "I'm fine."

"Good. I do not anticipate it taking more than a few days, and it will be a valuable learning experience."

Bridget looked from the Lady to the grinning Pawn. "Yes, my Lady," she said reluctantly.

"Good. Pamela, you can go and advise Lord Pease that we've set this in motion. Let the Bishops know that Pawn Wattleman is not available for any operations, but they do not need the exact details. It is enough for them to know that he is on assignment for the Lord and me. Tell them directly, please, without their staff present."

"Yes, my Lady," said Pamela. She did not take any notes.

"Everyone, I want this kept quiet for the moment," said Lady Carmichael. Her tone was forbidding. "*Very* quiet. The fact that at least one of those manifestations was rooted in a Checquy artifact has some very serious implications. I have ordered a very discreet check of the other recovered item to see if it also came from our holdings. But this must be kept a close secret. It would not do at all for word to leak out beyond this office."

"Yes, my Lady," everyone said in intimidated unison.

"Good. Now, you two, go." Bridget nodded, got up, and joined Wattleman at the door. "Oh, Bridget," called Lady Carmichael, "if you're not going to be home tonight, please send word to the house and let Leominster know."

"My Lady, I can advise you now that she will not be returning home this evening," Wattleman said with a smirk; he shut the door before Bridget could say anything.

11

"Wake up, Lyn, it's Christmas!" Georgina was shaking her. "Shouldn't you be sullenly sleeping in?" asked Lyn, her eyes bleary. "Isn't that what teenagers do?"

"Not on Christmas! Wake up!" Georgina swept back the curtains on the window, and light flooded into the room. The morning sun was blinding off the snow outside. Lyn recoiled like a hungover vampire.

"What time is it?" Lyn's bedside clock advised her that it was seven. Beyond it was a framed photo of her with Richard and Emma and another of Skeksis looking quizzical in a knit hat. Richard had sent them to the clinic where he believed she was staying, and the staff had forwarded them to the Estate. She sighed and touched the picture of her family lightly before turning her attention to the matter at hand. There was a brightly colored stocking bulging with small wrapped gifts at the foot of her bed. Outside the door, there were sounds of giggling and people moving about.

"Come on, put on your dressing gown. We have to go to our common room for presents!"

"And coffee," said Lyn firmly. She picked up her Christmas stocking and followed Georgina out the door. There were students of all ages rushing about the corridors in their pajamas and nighties and robes, laughing and talking. Some of the smaller ones had clearly been unable to resist the urge to open some gifts from their stockings, and they had plastic toys and chocolate bars in hand.

Over the past few weeks, Lyn had come to realize that Christmas was a very big deal at the Estate. As winter set in, Kirrin Island experienced several heavy snowfalls, and the winds coming in off the sea turned bitterly cold. Much to Lyn's dismay, this had not been accepted as sufficient reason to suspend the mandatory outdoor runs. Instead, it was viewed as an excellent opportunity to work on arctic maneuvering capabilities. There had also been several gargantuan snowball fights.

As the nights became longer, students decorated the hallways with holly, ivy, tinsel, and lengths of laboriously stapled paper chains. Holiday music constantly played in the common areas, and each tutor group had been assigned one of the many common rooms to decorate and gather in for opening presents on the day.

"That way, there is a good spread of ages brought together in easily managed little celebrations," Frau Blümen explained to Lyn one evening as the two of them enjoyed a glass of wine and some trashy television in the headmistress's apartment. Since the affair with the head lice, Lyn and Blümen—or Steffi, as Lyn was now allowed to call her in private—had become quite good friends. Steffi's husband, an equally plump man named Gerhardt, bustled about in the background preparing dinner. "If we have everyone gathered in the dining hall for the presents, the occasion loses its intimate charms and very swiftly becomes chaos."

"Isn't this rather a lot of attention going into a religious holiday?" asked Lyn. "Are there any problems with everyone celebrating a Christian occasion?"

"We are a state school," said Steffi. "Although, officially, I believe we are classified as a state weapons emplacement. But when the Estate was established after the war, it was nominally Anglican. Of course, no religion really addresses our students with a constructive or appropriate attitude. They could be considered miraculous or infernal..." She trailed off. "It is not good for children to regard themselves as either divine agents or candidates for stoning. Both scenarios promote unhealthy esteem situations and a disinclination to do homework," she said disapprovingly.

"So you raise them to be atheists?"

"We encourage a reverence for the universe and a gratitude that it exists," said Steffi vaguely. "We teach them to value human life and the dignity of all living things and to accept that some things cannot be explained. We have to, really, because they themselves cannot be explained. For those who come to us already adhering to a specific religion, we maintain facilities and support them, but we do not encourage a particularly religious atmosphere."

"Then why the Christmas madness?"

"Children like to receive presents," Steffi said with a shrug. "And the winters here are so dire that we have to have something to look forward to. Plus, if we tried to cancel it, there would be riots."

Lyn and her group were allocated one of the smaller rooms. Furnished with squashy dark leather furniture and red rugs, it was normally reserved for quiet reading. There was a working fireplace, and the windows looked out onto the forest side of the Estate. A tree that brushed the ceiling had been set up on a stand, and they'd spent several hours decorating it—an endeavor characterized by vigorous debate and mild to moderate threats. Each child at the Estate received one Christmas tree ornament every year, so the placement of each treasured item was a matter of supreme importance.

In the weeks leading up to Christmas, after dinner, the group gathered in the cozy warmth of their assigned common room to watch films, play games, or read stories aloud. While the wind howled off the dark sea outside or the snow fell, they toasted marshmallows and roasted chestnuts at the fireplace or over the soles of Isaac's feet. Even the older students seemed to love it; there were none of the scoffings and eye-rollings that Lyn would have expected.

Lyn would sit wrapped in a blanket on one of the sofas, two small children nestled on either side of her, listening to Georgina read *The Church Mice at Christmas.* It was especially hard then not to think of her own small child. Richard and Emma would soon be taking Skeksis to Richard's parents' house to spend the holidays with his enormous family. Sometimes, her real life seemed impossibly distant, but whenever one of the littlest children came to her for a hug, she would feel his weight in her arms or smell her hair and feel a snatch of sorrow.

In the week before Christmas, each age group went on a special holiday trip, traveling to different cities. Lyn accompanied the nine-year-olds to Edinburgh — a city where she knew no one, so there was little chance of meeting an acquaintance. Mercifully, she was not obliged to wear the hideous purple-orange-and-lime-green-striped uniform and was passed off as a chaperone. They saw a pantomime of *Aladdin,* toured the city, and visited the Checquy offices, where the staff made much of the children and took Lyn out to the pub for some much-needed grown-up conversation. It was a good time, and when they returned to Kirrin Island, Lyn felt a sense of coming home.

On Christmas Eve, just before lunch, Father Christmas and four burly-looking elves parachuted down to the island from a gigantic Royal Air Force bomber to rapturous applause from the gathered student body. Lyn was a trifle surprised that they hadn't made a more mystical appearance but then remembered the target audience. These were children who, if confronted with a flying reindeer, would probably gather in a protective formation and evaluate what kind of threat it posed and its vulnerabilities. A really big plane, however, was inherently cool. Children under the age of twelve were each given one present to open to tide them over until morning.

The entire school was then at a fever pitch, subdued only slightly by an immense Christmas Eve dinner. Afterward, Lyn was barely able to keep her eyes open, but the students maintained their energy. The choir sang, and there was a memorable Christmas pageant featuring Louise the bear as the Virgin Mary. Then for all students over four-teen, there was a disco in the assembly hall that sounded incredibly raucous. Lyn gave in to the pleadings of some of the students and danced for a while, but she felt too ridiculous and decamped to a lounge, where she sat comfortably digesting and watching television with some of the staff and their spouses. When she finally rolled into bed, Georgina was still at the disco, all regular curfews apparently suspended for the night.

So why isn't she exhausted? Lyn wondered now as her roommate scampered ahead of her. *Please God, let it be some supernatural thing linked to her mouth, because if this is just youthful energy, then I feel far too old.*

The two of them were met with cries of delight as they entered the common room. Most of the tutor group had already arrived and were barely managing to wait for the required presence of everyone before any presents could be opened. A fire crackled in the fireplace, and Christmas music played on a stereo. In a corner of the room, the tree stood glittering. Lyn noticed that some of the ornaments had been strategically shifted about since the night before, part of the ongoing war for prominence. The gifts under the tree had been speculatively squeezed and rattled as soon as they began to appear a few days earlier, and they'd been obsessively cataloged and gloated over by the younger ones.

In addition to the stockings, which were filled with a variety of small gifts and treats, every student at the Estate received a gift from Steffi, a gift from the dorm parent, a gift from Father Christmas (regardless of the child's age), a gift selected by a randomly assigned student at the Estate, and a gift from each child's godparents—Chec-quy operatives who wrote letters and sent postcards throughout the year and sent the children gifts on their birthdays and at Christmas. Lyn's own godparents were a financial manager named Colette in the Checquy's Penzance office and a man named Marijn who had a very long Dutch job title.

"You have a Grafter godparent," said one of the children enviously. "They give *really* good presents." This one certainly sent unorthodox presents. Colette had sent her a bottle of very good champagne; Marijn's gift was a cubical fishbowl filled with exceptionally rigid gelatin. Nestled in the center of the transparent mass were two brightly colored tropical fish. The handwritten note from Marijn wished her a *vrolijk kerstfeest* and advised her that when the bowl was put in direct sunlight, the gelatin would melt into water and the fish would come out of stasis. They would require no feeding ever but should receive a couple of hours of direct sunlight every day. The faint smell of pineapple that they would emit was quite normal, and he hoped that she would enjoy them.

"And you've got a box from your family!" squealed one of the littler children.

"Yes indeed!" said Lyn carefully. She was always a little tentative about mentioning her family around the other students, unsure how they would feel about the idea. After all, they'd been taken from their families. There were only a couple of children on the Estate who had actual blood siblings attending the school. She'd mentioned this concern to Steffi, who had encouraged her to be open about it.

"All of these children are well aware of their circumstances," the plump headmistress said. "They grow up here knowing that they are different from other children but also knowing that they are loved. However, when they go out in the world, many of them will marry normal people. I think it is probably a good idea for them to see you and understand how others live."

"Open it!" the children gathering around her now squealed. There were several boxes inside—clearly Richard had gotten a few friends to contribute to her care package. The tutor group was fascinated by the earrings from Richard, the homemade cookies from her mother-in-law (which were promptly shared around), and the framed painting by Emma. Her friends had sent along small treats appropriate for someone who was supposed to be tucked away in a private hospital room.

"And my friend Jenny has sent me..." Lyn opened it carefully. "A fireman calendar!" There were appreciative *ooh*s from around the room. *A sexy fireman calendar. Thanks, Jen.*

"Can I see?" asked a little boy named Rupert. "You know, I want to be a fireman!" Lyn hastily scanned the back of the calendar. The firemen in the pictures weren't wearing much in the way of upper-body protection, but they were all wearing pants.

"Here you go!" She handed it to him. *That's definitely not getting put up in the bedroom,* she told herself. She felt a responsibility to be a good example for Georgina, and a series of muscular firemen portraits did not match the tone she wanted to set. Especially the picture with the suggestive placement of the hose. *I'll hang it up in my workroom.*

Once she'd reached a certain level of skill, Lyn had been assigned a room for her own private studies and experimentation. Rather than a quiet little carrel in the library, however, it turned out to be a battered white room with one glass wall and a sprung floor, located in a thick-walled building some distance from the rest of the school. The furniture consisted of a scarred desk and chair and a decades-old armchair. It put her in mind of the studios that art students at her university had been assigned, although this one had much greater insulation. When the Estate students were at work, the corridors of the building echoed with the sound of controlled explosions, the screeching of spectral parrots, and the sloshing of whatever lurid fluids José was producing out of his skin that day.

She had spent hours and hours in that room with only the music and news from an elderly battered radio for company. She'd sat with her fingers placed on metal plates hooked up to sensors, carefully feeling out the finer nuances of her abilities. It hadn't always been successful—crimson electricity had burned trails along the walls, and she'd exploded three hapless stereos during her experiments. But gradually she'd refined her control.

The Checquy had been indulgent and provided her with most of the materials that she requested as she explored the possibilities of her powers. Some careful exploration with mercury revealed that she could pour energy into a few drops of the liquid metal, add them to a much larger bottle of the stuff, and all of it would be electrified, even when it was divided into smaller and smaller portions. She could energize a handful of finely ground metal powder and fling it into the air, where it would hang for a few minutes, waiting for any disruption that would spark a small storm of electricity. Out of idle curiosity, she'd found that she could electrify a knife with a kiss or a plastic-handled fork while it was in her mouth.

Most satisfying of all, she had finally, *finally* figured out how to regulate the nature of the energy, so now it was her choice as to how much force would unleash it from the metal. It could be the most delicate touch or the equivalent of a good slap.

It had been exhausting but satisfying, and she felt she had earned a break.

After all the presents had been duly opened and squealed over, the younger children started playing a board game, and the older ones read instructions for new possessions or paged through books or watched a film on the television that had been brought in. A buffet of pastries had been set up and ravaged. "All right, I'm going to go make a call," Lyn said finally. "I need to see if my in-laws have had their big Christmas argument yet."

"They argue?" asked one of the girls, fascinated.

"It's a beautiful tradition," said Lyn, winking.

"You'll be back in time for the King'f Chriftmas broadcaft, won't you?" asked Jasper, a small boy with adorably tiny walrus-type tusks made of gold.

"Absolutely, mate," said Lyn. She made her way to the apartment of Amanda Chu, the dorm parent. The two of them had an awkward relationship. Though it was unlikely that Lyn would ever go to her with an emotional problem, as the other students sometimes did, Mrs. Chu was responsible for handling Lyn's communications with the outside world. She delivered all e-mails from Richard or Lyn's friends, meticulously printed out and placed into envelopes. She then went over Lyn's typed and printed responses before handing them over to a clearance clerk, who would in turn review them, transcribe them into Lyn's e-mail account, and send them off. It was sometimes difficult not to feel that Mrs. Chu was her jailor. The fact that Mrs. Chu was a couple of years younger than Lyn made it doubly weird.

They'd settled into an easy routine for telephone calls, though. Mrs. Chu greeted her warmly and led her through the apartment, past Mr. Chu and their dog, and into the study. Mrs. Chu punched a code into the telephone, then handed it to Lyn, who asked the operator to connect her to Richard's number.

"Hello, my love," she said. "Merry Christmas."

"Merry Christmas! How are you doing there?"

"It's very nice," said Lyn. "The staff go to a lot of effort to make it festive."

Richard and Emma had come to see her at the clinic in the Highlands twice over the past few months. The preparations for the visits had been extremely complicated, with Lyn having to fly in the day before to meet the staff in the special Checquy wing of the facility and get briefed on how she should behave.

An astoundingly brilliant makeup artist named Lucy had made her look drawn and pale, covering up the fact that after all her Checquy training, she was the fittest she'd ever been. Lucy had even applied little latex prosthetic scars to the insides of Lyn's elbows to suggest repeated sessions with intravenous drips. A hairdresser had meticulously thinned and lanked her hair. It had taken hours, and she didn't like to think what the entire thing had cost, but it had been completely worth it when Richard hesitantly walked into the room with Emma in his arms. At the astounding realness of holding her daughter, the sound of her voice, and the feeling of Richard's arms tight around them both, Lyn had been unable to stop herself from crying.

"How is the greater Binns clan?" she asked now.

"Everyone's asked after you," said Richard. "My brother and my mum are arguing about the turkey, Lauren and Julia are arguing about the ham, my dad and Uncle Roger are arguing about the fish."

"I'm sorry I can't be there," said Lyn truthfully. "Did Emma like her gifts?"

"She did! She's running around with her cousins. They're all wearing their dinosaur costumes, and she's already knocked over three plants with her tail. Shall I put her on?"

"In a second," said Lyn. "Did you like the books I ordered you?"

"Very much," said Richard warmly. "They look great. Thank God I married a librarian—you always give the best gifts."

"And yet even though I married a cop, I still got my pocket picked on that trip to Rome," mused Lyn wryly.

"I call the *carabinieri* every week, they are still working that case," Richard joked in response.

"I'm sure they'll crack it soon—it's only been seven years," Lyn teased. "Anyway, I'm glad you like the books, but I've got something even better for you."

"Oh?"

"I'm coming home."

"We can give you five months of leave with your family," said Mrs. Goodman. "Then you'll need to do a minimum of six months with the Notifications and Reporting section at Apex House in London."

"Why? Why there?" asked Lyn.

"Everyone has to do it, no exceptions. It serves as an orientation to the Checquy. It's like working in the mail room of a business. You'll become acquainted with the entire structure of the organization and get an in-depth understanding of our operations, the type of manifestations that can arise, and how we react. Your time here, Lynette, has very much been focused on the practical elements of your role as an operative." She looked down at her notes. "You've gained an admirable level of control over your abilities and a firm basic grounding in various forms of combat, and your fitness has improved substantially. Your psychologist says that you've dealt with your immersion in the student body and your encounter with the insect manifestation effectively and that you're emotionally and mentally stable. In short, you've gotten a good foundation as a warrior. But now it is time to begin your professional immersion in the world of the Checquy."

"I've read the assigned textbooks," said Lyn. "I know a lot of the history now, and I've read the case files for the major incidents of the past forty years."

"That's wonderful, but the knowledge you've gained is all theoretical."

"I fought a giant head louse!"

"Which got you a merit certificate at the school assembly and a very nice letter of commendation from the headmistress," said Mrs. Goodman. "But now you have to go out into the world, and this placement is part of doing that."

"Right," said Lyn. "And how do I explain this to my husband?"

"In between the hugs and the tears of reunion, you'll mention that your experience in fighting your disease has changed your outlook, and you want to do something different with your life."

"Okay..." said Lyn dubiously.

"You'll tell him that you want to apply for different jobs. And then you'll learn that you've been offered a position with the government, something very confidential. We'll hammer out the details later, depending on your progress."

"Am I ever going to be able to tell him the entire truth? About the Checquy? About *me?*"

"Maybe in a few years," said Mrs. Goodman. "If he passes his background checks and you stay together."

"Thanks," said Lyn flatly. "And after the six months at the job?"

"Well, that will depend on you and what kind of work you want to do with the Checquy. There are some roles that we can tailor for you if you don't wish to move from South Shields, but that will limit your professional options. There are lots of opportunities in the Checquy, and your ability to take them will depend on your flexibility."

"I see," said Lyn grimly.

"It's the same sort of situation that faces people in the military or the foreign service," said Mrs. Goodman reasonably.

"But Richard didn't marry someone who was going into the military or the foreign service!" exclaimed Lyn. "He married someone who was happy to be a librarian wherever his work took them."

"And are you *still* happy to be a librarian wherever his work takes you?" Mrs. Goodman asked shrewdly. Lyn opened her mouth to reply and abruptly found that she did not know what to say.

The truth was that her view of the world, her view of *herself,* had been radically altered since that evening in the kitchen. Despite herself, Lyn was not sure that she could go back to her old life, not completely. There was nothing that she wanted more than to be with Richard and Emma. That was true. She'd gone to sleep every night thinking about tucking her daughter in and falling asleep in her husband's arms. She missed her friends. But her old job, her old concerns? Knowing what she did now, going back to what she'd been before seemed impossibly limited.

But not going back felt like the worst kind of betrayal.

"It's hard becoming a different person," said Mrs. Goodman sympathetically. Lyn looked up at her helplessly.

"You'll need to talk it over, naturally," said Mrs. Goodman. "You don't need to decide right now. And of course, the Checquy can help you to cope with this challenge. For instance, if your husband is happy to move, the Checquy can find new opportunities for him."

"Within the organization?" asked Lyn. The woman shrugged.

"Possibly," she said, sounding a little dubious. "It's no little thing, though, to be brought in. And quite aside from security screening, there's the question of accepting all the revelations. As you well know, it entirely changes the way you see the world. That can be very difficult, for individuals and for relationships. But if you were to be posted in a different city or country, say, then we could pull strings to find him a position with a local organization. The fact that he works in law enforcement could make it easier. We have lots of important connections in that field." She looked at the stricken Lyn. "You've got a bit of time."

That bit of time passed very swiftly, mused Lyn five months later as she stood at the gates of Apex House in London. It was her first day of orientation, and she was struggling to come to terms with yet another drastic change in her life.

Leaving the Estate had been harder than she'd anticipated. Her teachers and the tutor group had been sorry to see her go, and they threw a little tea party for her. Georgina kept dissolving in tears, which spurred Lyn into crying as well, though not nearly as much.

"Will you write to me?" her roommate asked pitifully.

"All the time," Lyn assured her.

"I'm going to miss you." Georgina was about ready to start crying again.

"Oh, Georgie, we'll probably end up working together," said Lyn, hugging her. "I'll definitely come back for your graduation." The whole Estate had applauded her at assembly when her departure was announced, and scores of people took the opportunity to come up to her and tell her that they'd miss her.

Then, coming back home had been an adjustment. Richard and Emma had met her at Newcastle airport and they'd fallen into one another's arms. In the days that followed, Lyn had told several dozen lies about her time in the clinic. That part had been hard. She'd had to make up various people she'd met and couldn't even use names from the Estate—those were classified.

The Checquy-provided au pair, Eviyanti, was a charming matron of Indonesian descent who stayed for two more weeks, cunningly disengaging Emma's affections from her plump, cheerful self and reattaching them to Lyn with a wink. She'd been invaluable, Richard confided, but she had always maintained a brisk distance, which was just what Lyn had wanted.

The house seemed smaller than before and very quiet after the hubbub of the Estate. Richard, in typical husband-who-doesn't-cook fashion, had asked for the ruined kitchen to be replaced like-for-like, so it looked exactly the same, as if that whole madness had never happened. And for the next few months, that was almost how it felt.

Almost.

Lyn could not help but be aware of the changes of the past months. Some of them were small, simple things. Emma was undeniably taller, for instance, and a little bit more of a person. When they played together, she evinced new passions for ponies and sailboats. Little things, but Lyn couldn't help mourning the lost time with her baby— time she could never get back. And when she met up with her own friends, they were pleasant, but she felt a little disconnected from them, and it made her sad. They were unchanged and very sympathetic about her sickness (which only made her feel worse about lying to them), but she always felt stymied by the impossibility of telling them the truth. The only exception was her best friend, Jenny. Of course, she didn't tell Jenny anything about the Checquy, but their connection was so strong, built on humor and shared experiences, that it didn't make a difference.

The Checquy's fund for sufferers of Juhász-Koodiaroff-Grassigli syndrome provided a six-month recovery stipend, so Lyn had an excellent excuse for not immediately going back to work. The library administrators had unquestioningly given her leave, especially once they were informed that it could be unpaid. Richard did not raise many questions—he was just thrilled to have her back. And so they'd settled into a routine. Three times a week, when Richard was at work and Emma was at day care, Lyn took the train to Newcastle, signed in at the Checquy field office, and, in their in-house gymnasium, went through her various conditioning exercises, kata, and fencing techniques with the office's merciless trainer. This would keep her sharp. ("If at all possible," remarked the trainer, "sharper.") She then spent an hour or two in the office's Faraday cage, refining her control of her abilities, before hurrying home to pick up Emma and prepare dinner. Richard, of course, believed that she was recuperating, undergoing some sort of highly specialized physical therapy, and applying for jobs.

A few days after her return, after she'd put Emma to bed, Lyn had settled down on the couch with Richard, Skeksis lying between them. She carefully delivered the extremely tactful Checquy-supplied script about wanting to look for a different kind of job. He'd been startled, although not as startled as she had expected. She secretly suspected that Eviyanti had been doing some groundwork there.

"What kind of work were you thinking of?" Richard asked.

"There was a woman at the clinic, a patient, who had worked for the government," said Lyn. "She, um, did intelligence work and told me all about it. I think it's something I might be good at."

"I think you'd be very good at it," he said thoughtfully.

"Yeah?"

"Yeah." He nodded. He sat back on the couch and looked up at the ceiling for a few moments. Lyn stared at him, petrified despite herself. If he was really against it, well, she wasn't sure what would happen. Her conversation with Mrs. Goodman had left her with the impression that working at Apex House was nonnegotiable. "I say go for it, pet," he said finally. "If this is what you want to do, well, your disease has shown us that we should take opportunities when we can."

"I mean, there's no guarantee that I'd find anything or be hired," lied Lyn, limp with relief. "And it might mean some changes for us if I did."

"We can figure it out, Lyn. And our situation here is nice, but we're here because this is where we got jobs, not because it's our ancestral homeland or anything. I'm a cop, but I could be a cop somewhere else."

"Are you sure?" asked Lyn weakly.

"I am absolutely sure."

"Okay, then." She slid closer to him on the couch, disrupting the dog, and rested her head on his chest. "I love you, you know."

"I love you," he said, closing his arms around her. "I missed you so much, you wouldn't believe it."

"Yeah?" She looked up at him. "How did you miss me?"

"In all sorts of ways," he replied, bowing his head down to kiss her neck.

"Oh, really?" She laughed.

Now, Lyn smiled at the memory. All that awkward and undignified testing at the Estate was totally worth it to get that certificate to have sex safely. She looked around, conscious that she was wearing a brand-new suit, standing outside her new organization's headquarters, and grinning lustily.

"All right, time to go to work," she said to herself.

Apex House, the headquarters for the Checquy Group, was located in a quieter part of Whitehall, but it was still Whitehall, with the attendant hordes of civil servants bustling about on their way to work. It was impossible to tell which people were supernatural and which ones weren't—they were all in a hurry and all seemed to be carrying cups of coffee. Lyn eased herself into the current of people streaming to Apex House and let it carry her up the steps and through the large front doors to a lobby where people who knew exactly what they were doing swiped their passes easily over pads and passed smoothly through turnstiles.

There were two security desks and alert guards eyeing everyone who entered. Lyn approached the one on the left, a little nervous.

"Hi, I'm Lynette Binns. I'm here for my first day of work with Notifications and Reporting." The guard typed busily on his computer, then looked up at Lyn, comparing her face with whatever had appeared on the screen. It might have been Lyn's imagination or the reflection of the computer, but his eyes seemed to flare white for a second. Finally, he nodded, dialed an extension, and spoke into the phone in a hushed tone.

"You can take a seat, Ms. Binns. Someone will be down for you shortly."

Lyn thanked him and sat nervously on the world's least comfortable bench. She entertained herself by watching people enter the lobby and trying to identify those who had inhuman abilities. Her lessons at the Estate had informed her that most Checquy employees were nonpowered Retainers rather than supernatural Pawns. The majority of them looked perfectly normal, but there were a few possible candidates. Her skin had tingled for a moment when a tall woman bustled by, and she felt a surging sense of exhilaration when an older man in tweeds stopped at the security desk. She was trying to decide if the cobalt hair of the Indian girl was genuinely supernatural or just dyed when a toothy gentleman in a charcoal suit approached her.

"Lynette? I'm Pawn Ed Moncrieff, head of Notifications and Reporting."

"Hi!" said Lyn, scrambling to her feet. "It's good to meet you." They shook hands.

"Welcome to Apex House. We'll get you a temporary pass, then set about getting you all oriented." The security guard scanned Lyn's driver's license, asked her to sign a book, and gave her a lanyard holding a battered-looking blue plastic card labeled T. "Okay, and just swipe yourself through the turnstile."

Once through, she and Moncrieff took the lift up to the security office, chatting in the awkward *Please call me Ed, Please call me Lyn* way of people who are going to be working together. "Lyn, are you any relation to Geoff Binns, in our foreign section? Excellent chap."

"I don't think so," said Lyn.

"I would have been surprised, honestly," said Moncrieff cheerfully. "We don't get a lot of recurrence of abilities in families, as I expect you know."

"The Checquy were very interested in my history," said Lyn. "I think they were quite disappointed that I was adopted, and no one really seems to know where I came from. I couldn't tell them much about my family."

"Well, a lot of us are in that sort of situation," said Moncrieff. "Not exactly the same, but if you grow up at the Estate, you don't know that much about your family—especially if you go there very young. I got picked up when I was five months old, so I have not even the vaguest of memories of my parents." He did not seem overly concerned by this.

"Do people from the Estate ever try to seek out their biological families?" asked Lyn curiously, remembering her late-night talk with Georgina. She'd never tried it herself; it seemed like it would be a bad idea in every way. Besides the fact that the authorities had no idea about her birth family, her vague memories of her first years suggested that finding them would probably result in more disappointment than not finding them. Still, she knew that some adopted children did it.

"Hardly ever," said Moncrieff easily. "Their very existence seems so distant. I understand that adopted children can often get notions about their blood families, make them into romantic figures. But let's face it, if you've gone to the Estate, if you're a part of the Checquy, well, nothing's going to be more extraordinary than *that*." He shrugged. "Most likely, my family are just perfectly normal people, perfectly dull, with whom I have little in common. And I could never explain to them what happened. We're all so aware of the oaths and requirements of the Checquy, the secrecy. No." He shook his head firmly. "Actually, when I was courting my wife, I got the Checquy to make sure we weren't related and that there weren't any significant connections between my family and hers. Damned awkward if they were to show up at the wedding, you know. And of course, there are certain cities I'm never posted to and shouldn't visit, just in case I were to run into a close family member."

"But you didn't change your name?" asked Lyn.

"No. Well, I'd already been christened, hadn't I? But we're all unlisted in directories, and there are big no-nos on social media, so it'd be difficult for families to track us down, if they even think we're still alive." His blithe unconcern took Lyn's breath away a little, but she just nodded sagely. "And of course, things are different if you come to the Checquy later in life."

At the security office, Lyn signed a few forms, was briskly photographed, and received a bulky security pass that consisted of a plastic lozenge as thick as four credit cards. It had her photograph printed on it and a number to call if someone found it. Other than that, there were no identifying details at all—no name, no government crest, no serial number.

"This is not a valid government ID, so do not attempt to use it as such," intoned the security officer. "In addition to entry to your assigned building and workspaces, it will provide you with basic access to almost all Checquy facilities around the world, with the exception of Gallows Keep in Scotland and a couple of storage locations."

"What does basic access consist of?" asked Lyn.

"Through the main doors and the lobby turnstiles into the protected common areas," said the security officer. "The idea is that if you need to seek sanctuary from an angry mob, the Checquy can provide it, but you're not able to go wherever you want in the building. It will also not provide you with access to any parking garage. You'll need to arrange guest parking separately with whatever office you're visiting."

Lyn looked at Moncrieff. "We don't get parking?" He shook his head. *Great.* She didn't have a car in London, but she'd gotten used to the Checquy taking care of everything. When she was preparing to move here, they'd offered her a shared accommodation with a couple of other recent graduates, but she'd opted to find her own, much smaller (though still ludicrously expensive) little flat. The prospect of some time to herself was too tempting.

The security officer also gave her a laminated card with various phone numbers printed on it for IT support, security support, medical support, psychological support, and possible-accidental-electrocution-of-civilians support.

"Great," said Moncrieff. He looked at his watch. "Now we'll just trot you up to the executive offices for you to take your oath before the Lord and Lady."

"I, Lynette Binns, do hereby pledge my body, my mind, and all the gifts instilled within my frame to the service of the Checquy Group and to its mission to safeguard the land and the populace of the British Isles from those threats that must be kept secret wheresoever the writ of these lands carries authority.

"I pledge my obedience to the Lady and the Lord, and their Bishops, Chevaliers, and Rooks, as the commanders of the Checquy empowered by the will of the ruling monarch, by the legislatures of the land, and by ancient tradition. I shall direct my skills, my will, and my intellect to those tasks set me to the best of my ability.

"I pledge my silence, understanding that the greatest force at my command is not my rank nor the gifts that I possess by virtue of fate but the secrets with which I have been entrusted. I shall not reveal those secrets to any without the permission of those above me.

"I take this oath knowing that, should I break any aspect of my solemn vow, on that day the awful justice of the Checquy and of their bonded allies the Wetenschappelijk Broederschap van Natuurkundigen shall fall upon me and upon those I love and I shall become enemy, prey, vermin to be scoured from the soil. And until the day I am inevitably brought down, may my nights be filled with the horrors of Orcus, and my days the sure knowledge that my onetime brothers and sisters are coming to put me down without mercy or hesitation.

"And may I thank them when they do so.

"I vow that such a day will never come."

Lyn bowed her head. The oath was centuries old, but it had been continuously updated over the years to acknowledge changes in circumstances. That bit about the Broederschap, for instance, was apparently quite new. She'd stumbled over the Dutch pronunciation, despite the handy phonetic guide included in her oathing pack.

It had taken her ages to memorize it but even longer to overcome the knowledge that it wasn't just archaic rhetoric, that they all really meant it. Well, except for the bit about Orcus. She'd looked him up and found that he was a god of the underworld in Roman myth, specially detailed to punish oath breakers. Clearly, some Checquy oathwriter at some point had been a bit of a classicist.

But the rest of it was serious, deathly serious. The script for the oath (which had been provided to her in a lockable box) had been accompanied by an informative booklet giving details of the few people who had tried to betray, defy, or flee the Checquy and the dire punishments that had befallen them. It had made for some stomach-turning reading.

The leaders of the Checquy each laid a hand on her bowed head.

"Your oath is heard," said Lady Farrier, an impressive-looking woman with steely eyes. "Your oath is accepted."

"We take you into the service of the Checquy," said Sir Henry Wattleman. "You will be a tool and a weapon, and we pledge that your might will be used only in the cause of right. If we must call for your sacrifice, it will never be done lightly or for personal gain, only for the good of these lands and the people." They lifted their hands from her head.

"Stand, Pawn Lynette Binns," said Lady Farrier. "You are now one of us." Lyn carefully got up from the padded stool on which she had been kneeling.

"Well done," said Sir Henry. "Congratulations, Pawn Binns."

"Yes, welcome to the Checquy," said Lady Farrier. She shook Lyn's hand firmly. "We'll be following your career with great interest." It was a nice sentiment, although it didn't seem terribly sincere, since the Lord and Lady immediately turned away to discuss something else, and Pawn Moncrieff hurriedly ushered Lyn out of the room. Looking back, she caught a glimpse of the two executives squirting on some hand sanitizer and tried not to feel too offended.

"Nicely done," said Pawn Moncrieff. "Now we'll toddle on down to the Notifications area, where you can meet the team. We've gotten a little welcoming cake for you."

The Notifications and Reporting section of the Checquy was housed in a large room with no cubicles or partitions. Each of the forty-odd people had a desk with a phone and a computer. The walls were covered with framed large-scale maps of the British Isles and several street maps of major cities. The staff ran the gamut in terms of age. There were several recent graduates from the Estate who were serving their six-month assignments, including two girls and three boys Lyn recognized. But there were also a great many people who had been in the section for years. Two of them were in their seventies. Everyone seemed terribly nice, all of them gathering about the conference table in the middle of the room to partake of the welcoming cake and introduce themselves.

"And this is Pawn Liam Seager," said Pawn Moncrieff. "He'll be your mentor in the section, teach you how everything works in the office."

"Hi," said Lyn uncertainly. Pawn Seager did not look like an office worker. He looked like a man who had begun fighting supernatural threats as soon as he emerged from the womb and who'd only just won each time by the skin of his teeth. He had several scars slashed across his face and a discolored stain on his left cheek that might have been a birthmark but also looked exactly like someone had splashed his face with a liquid—there were even drops and drips dappled across his forehead. There appeared to be a sizable section missing from one of his cauliflowered ears. In fact, his whole head looked rather cauliflowered. In short, he was the roughest-looking man she had ever seen in her life. Before she'd joined the Checquy, if she had seen him walking toward her on the street, she would have crossed to the other side.

"Ah, the Delouser," said Pawn Seager. His voice was deep, and he spoke with a Liverpool accent.

"I beg your pardon?"

"We all heard about your adventure in the corridors of the Estate," he said. "You fought a giant head louse, so now you're the Delouser."

"*That's* my code name?" asked Lyn, incredulous.

"Well, we don't have code names. It's more like your nickname."

"And who uses this nickname?" asked Lyn, narrowing her eyes.

"Yeah, probably the whole organization. You're a teeny bit famous."

"The Delouser."

"Yeah."

Lyn sighed. "Okay."

"Notifications and Reporting is the clearinghouse for all the information that comes into the Checquy," began Seager. "Every day, we get dozens of calls from all over the country and the world."

"And who calls you?" asked Lyn. She was sitting next to him at his desk.

"A variety of sources. We run training programs for officials at every level of government. Local law enforcement and emergency

services are crucial, of course. Medical professionals are very useful—
if you've got little crabs bubbling up out of your toenails and wandering around your kitchen, you're going to go see a doctor pretty
quick-smart, aren't you? And the various churches are useful too, for
the more extreme incidents. We've got good connections with all the
major religious institutions throughout the British Isles."

"So every priest, rabbi, imam, and civil servant knows about the
Checquy?" asked Lyn. "My husband's a cop, and he doesn't know
about it." *He'd better not,* she thought, *or we've been wandering around living a farce this whole time.*

"No, hardly any of them do," said Seager. "And we're very strategic about who we give briefings too. It works this way: If someone is
aware of something weird going on, they call us. They don't exactly
know who we are. As far as they're concerned, we're a government
office that puts the experts onto it."

"And we hang around here every day, waiting for a phone call?"

"Or a text or an e-mail," said Seager comfortably.

"I thought we didn't use computers that were externally linked,"
said Lyn. Pawn Blom had explained that this was one of the reasons
she couldn't work from home.

"We receive external communications on those computers over
there," said Seager, pointing to a small clump of terminals along a
wall. "Everything is printed out, then scanned or transcribed into our
system."

"That sounds really inefficient," said Lyn critically. "You can't just
transfer the files across?"

"That would defeat the point of not linking to outside networks."

"All right, so we just print out all the reports people send us and
read them?"

"Not just that, no. We also scan the media and review all sorts of
documents we receive just as a standard process. Look here." He
handed her the top document from the out tray on his desk. "This is
the daily report from University Hospital in Limerick. I've already
gone through it, but now it's your turn. You should review it for anything strange."

"Like what?"

"Anything that catches your eye as potentially Checquy-related."

"But why would I be able to see something that an experienced hospital administrator or a doctor missed?" asked Lyn.

"Sometimes they do see something," agreed Seager. "That's hopefully when they'll call us or tell someone who calls us. But lots of times they won't, because they're not looking for the same sort of things you are. You know there are weird things happening in the world, so you're better placed to spot them."

"So we read reports from all the hospitals?" asked Lyn.

"Nah, just from the big hospitals in the big cities. Plus a random selection from the little ones. And then there are police reports and those from other government departments, including the intelligence agencies."

"And what if I miss something?"

"It'll either go away by itself or escalate until someone notices it." Seager shrugged.

"You don't seem awfully concerned."

"It's good if we catch something before it eats a person," said the Pawn, "but it's pretty hard to do. We've also got statisticians who identify trends and patterns, but everything needs to be scrutinized at a smaller scale as well."

"All right," said Lyn with a sigh as she opened the report.

The rest of the day passed fairly quickly. Lyn didn't find anything peculiar in the hospital report from Limerick, the report from the Ministry of Agriculture, Fisheries, and Food on the expected sugar-beet crop, or the Exchequer's daily report on currency fluctuations. Seager agreed with her, which made her simultaneously relieved that she hadn't missed anything and disappointed that she'd spent three and a half hours on nothing actually supernatural. At lunchtime she went out for a walk by herself, and the afternoon was spent being shown around the building by Moncrieff. At the end of the day, Tegan and Anne, the two girls she knew from the Estate, invited her to come out for a drink with them at a local pub, and she agreed.

"I can't believe they gave you Pawn *Seager* as a mentor," exclaimed Tegan once they were seated in an isolated corner.

"Yeah, what's his deal?" asked Lyn.

"You don't know about Liam Seager?" Anne asked incredulously.

"I do not," said Lyn. She wearily sensed that, yet again, she was going to be traumatized.

"Okay, well, first," said Anne, "he spent a lot of years in the Barghests."

"Well, *them* I know about," said Lyn. The Barghest commandos were the Checquy's elite soldiers. They were sent in when things went as badly as they possibly could. The rest of the Checquy regarded them with awe, and Lyn had heard lots of dramatic stories about them from the students during her time at the Estate.

To hear Tegan and Anne tell it, Seager had been a particularly noteworthy Barghest, which was to say he did a *lot* of fighting and killing. In his time, he had been personally responsible for the elimination of a cadre of cleaver-wielding human-flensers, a serial killer (who embarrassingly turned out not to be in any way supernatural but *did* have a black belt in jujitsu, a flamethrower, access to explosives and acid, and an intense dislike of baristas), a cloud of malevolent pollen, and the minister for transport in the British Parliament. He had also driven a school bus over a gorgon.

"There's supposed to be a set of steer's horns mounted on his living room wall," said Tegan ominously.

"Okay . . ." said Lyn, waiting for the shoe to drop.

"They say it actually came from a Minotaur," said Tegan, her eyes wide.

"Yeah," said Anne. "Or, like, a cow that was really evil in some way."

"Right," said Lyn.

"In Aberdeen, he and his team were sent to take down this gangster named Ben McNevis. He had rocklike skin and could telekinetically move rock. McNevis entombed Seager and his whole team in granite," said Anne. "Seager broke out and then smashed McNevis to powder."

"And then he snorted him," said Tegan.

After ten years characterized by stunning bouts of merciless violence (in the name of justice and order), Pawn Seager had then transferred, to much general confusion, to a secretarial position in the

Checquy's medical wing. For seven and a half years he sat in an office filing, entering data, and helping with the morning teas (in the name of justice and order). His hulking body perched on an ergonomic stool, he used two fingers to laboriously type out medical records and doctors' notes.

"Everyone thought maybe he burned out," said Anne. "After all, there was a lot of blood on his hands. A lot. Even the very hardest of men could come to question himself at that point and, you know, despair."

But Pawn Seager showed no sign of questioning himself or despairing. He did not sit for long periods staring at the wall. He did not hide, weeping, in stairwells or lavatories. He did not drink any more than he had before, and he did not rage at the heavens and curse the universe and its creator—except once, when his computer crashed, taking four hours' worth of work with it. Soon, other, darker rumors wound their way through the Checquy.

"'Cause he was reading all the medical reports," said Tegan uneasily. "All of them."

"Gosh," said Lyn, not understanding the point at all. The two girls exchanged glances and proceeded to explain.

Checquy operatives were obliged to undergo physical examinations every six months, more frequently if they were engaged in combat work or teaching. This was partly because they worked in high-stress situations under a shroud of secrecy. Confronting the unknown on a regular basis took it out of you. Protecting the populace from the monstrous was a heavy responsibility. Not being able to talk about it made it all worse. Operatives couldn't even bitch about their coworkers to their spouses in case they inadvertently breached the Official Secrets Act. As a result, vacations and therapy were mandatory lest the staff all age at the same rate as American presidents. But there was another reason for the examinations.

The Pawns themselves were all unknowns. There was no explanation for their powers, and while there were precedents for many of them, there were no guarantees how they might evolve. The example everyone remembered best was Pawn Meredith Broad, who had been active up until about five years ago. A vivacious, generous girl, she was born with the ability to rot cloth rapidly. Well, cloth made from cotton, wool, and silk. Synthetic materials were largely immune. In most cases, however, with just a thought, Meredith could cause the shirt on your back and the pants round your arse to decay into slime and dust in a few seconds.

It was a useful ability, and one that, for some reason, cropped up fairly regularly. In 1774, a Pawn with that ability had reduced a troop of rogue redcoats to a gaggle of shrieking, pasty men clutching their privates. In 1886, a Pawn and a Chevalier (father and daughter, actually) had destroyed a tapestry that would periodically unravel lone museum patrons and weave their remains into itself.

It was, in short, a power that was well documented, and during her training Meredith mastered all the applications that had been developed over the centuries. She specialized in siege situations, where the besiegers would suddenly find themselves stark naked as large men and women kicked in the doors and the walls and screamed at them to "lie down! Now! Chins and cocks to the floor!"

The tactic was extremely effective at disorienting victims and didn't have the inconvenience to Checquy troops of tear gas or setting the building on fire. Meredith liked it because she could make a genuine contribution to battle without having to put out her cigarette.

Then, about nine years into her career, something changed. Meredith, after a long day of dissolving people's clothing and filling out paperwork, put her feet up, drank a mug of Horlicks, and went to bed. That night, while she slept, all domesticated dogs within a 1,114-meter radius of her turned on their owners and mauled them to death. The dogs tore out their masters' throats and savaged their faces, then they themselves promptly expired. The next morning, Meredith awoke refreshed, completely unaware of what had happened.

The police and the Checquy were baffled by the overnight deaths of nine Putney dog owners, but no one connected them to Pawn Broad. Two more deaths occurred over the next week, people who had walked their dogs into the zone of Meredith's unknowing influence. Still, the pattern was not identified until she went on a walking vacation through the Malvern Hills and inadvertently left a trail of carnage behind her. It took only seven more deaths (three human, four canine) before the Checquy figured it out and broke the news to her.

Meredith, who was a dog lover, was aghast at the revelation. Her new power was certainly not a conscious action on her part; she hadn't been aware of it and had no idea how to stop it. She was immediately ordered to the Comb, the Checquy's key research facility. There, tucked away in Cambridgeshire, the scientists embarked on their usual rigorous examinations and experiments — with some reluctance, since they were all dog lovers, and besides, Meredith's cloth-rotting ability tended to be activated whenever she was chemically sedated.

They assembled a selection of animals, including a wolf, a coyote, a feral dog, a Tasmanian devil, a wary-looking cat, and an elderly cocker spaniel named Floyd. Floyd belonged to Pawn Mary Upton and was not doing at all well. He was having significant problems with his kidneys and was due to be put to sleep. Pawn Upton reluctantly agreed to let him take part in the experiment on the understanding that he would be given a swift and merciful release no matter what happened.

In one of the Comb's observation rooms, Meredith was given a sleeping pill and a bed in a reinforced glass booth. The animals were placed in very small reinforced glass booths around the room. Pawn Upton sat in her own reinforced glass booth, also in the room. The scientists assembled in their reinforced glass booth.

Meredith eventually fell asleep.

Several things happened then.

Every scrap of nonsynthetic cloth within 40.4 meters of Meredith immediately rotted away. Pawn Upton and most of the scientists were unconcerned by this, since they had planned ahead and were wearing polyester, but one doctor had failed to read his briefing memos, and he had to abruptly excuse himself from the booth.

All the animals remained calm except for the Tasmanian devil, which had never really taken to being placed in a reinforced glass booth, and Floyd, who went absolutely berserk. Before everyone's horrified (but not really surprised) gaze, Floyd, who had been sitting calmly, panting slightly, and staring lovingly at his owner, suddenly flung himself at the reinforced glass separating them. His lips were peeled back from his teeth, and he was *screaming,* a long, snarling scream that made even the Tasmanian devil pause. Again and again he battered himself against the glass, trying to get to Pawn Upton and maul her to death.

This went on for a few agonizing seconds, until one of the doctors gestured, and all the electrical energy in the dog's brain was snatched away. He fell to the floor, utterly still, and all the observers agreed that they needed a stiff drink.

The subsequent examinations of Meredith and of Floyd's remains revealed nothing. Both their brains appeared to be perfectly normal, and the scientists had detected no pheromones or energy waves coming from the Pawn when she slept. They promised to keep working on it, but in the meantime, arrangements were made for Meredith to move to a house outside London that had no dog owners within the deadly radius. For a few months, it worked, and she commuted every day into the city.

And then there were more attacks, miles away from Meredith's bed. It seemed that over the months, her inadvertent sphere of influence had been growing, rippling out from her mind and driving dogs to insanity and murder. When Rook Flaherty gently broke the news to her, Meredith wept for a long time.

Various possible solutions were put forward, all of them feeble. Most of them involved moving Meredith ever-increasing distances from other people or at least from dog owners. One scientist proposed doing away with sleep altogether, introducing her to meditation and using drugs to induce such light trances that her abilities would not be activated. Another bright spark proposed assembling a list of enemies of the Checquy (or the UK) who owned dogs and whose mysterious deaths would be useful. But in truth, there was only ever one solution.

It was not only the horrible nature of her new power but the fact that she could not control it. For a Pawn of the Checquy, responsibility, self-discipline, duty formed the central pillars, so the possibility of becoming a threat, a danger...a monster was the worst nightmare.

And so one morning, Meredith's body was found in her bathtub, her wrists slashed and a look of utter peace on her face.

The Checquy mourned her, because she had been charming and kind and a good soldier, but there was also a certain level of approval and relief. It was generally felt that Meredith had done the honorable thing.

And then whispers began spreading. There was no question that Meredith would have chosen to remove herself from an increasingly awful equation. She had been a Checquy Pawn to her core, and the well-being of her country was what she cared about. But was that really the way she would have done it?

"Meredith didn't like blood," said her friends. "She didn't even like needles. And she didn't like mess." She wouldn't have taken her own life that way, they argued. Pills, perhaps, or hanging. But not lying in her bath, soaking in her own blood. No one asked any questions, not officially, but they felt uneasy. Her death made people wonder, *What would the Checquy do if one couldn't or wouldn't remove oneself as a threat?* It was not a comfortable thought.

"What are you saying?" said Lyn with a sinking feeling. "Are you saying the Checquy killed her? Their own soldier?" Tegan and Anne exchanged looks again.

Apparently, Pawn Broad's death was the most well known but by no means the only one that prompted questions. Nor was hers the first. And there were other, darker rumors: Of babies and children whose powers were so destructive or dangerous that the Checquy could not wait for them to master their abilities. Of elderly Pawns whose wits had eroded, leaving them like absentminded gods who might smite someone for playing music too loud or lacking respect. Of addictions given into, and impulses unresisted. None of these could be permitted.

The fact was that, for all their awesome power and rigid discipline, the Pawns of the Checquy were human (sort of) and subject to human frailties. Every one of those weaknesses, when combined with supernatural powers, represented a potential threat, both to the Checquy and to humanity. For whatever reason, however, they tended not to happen.

Naturally, in an organization built around secrecy and paranoia, there were theories. The most popular theory was that there were mercy killings carried out by trained killers. Admittedly, *everyone* in the Checquy was a trained killer, but that was not the point. And the Pawns who thought about it usually found themselves torn as to what they thought about it. No one wanted to be put down like a rabid dog, but if one were to find oneself becoming a monster, unable or unwilling to control oneself, well, it was a little reassuring to think that the Checquy might be there in one's darkest hour with a needle or a pillow or a truckload of quick-drying cement.

Of course, no one had ever met one of these trained executioners, no one had ever announced that he or she was a trained executioner, and no one had ever dared ask the high-ranking executives of the Checquy whether these rumors were true. So the Pawns were never entirely clear whether there actually were secret warriors among them, ready to shuffle them off this mortal coil.

But if it *was* true, then Pawn Liam Seager would have been an ideal candidate for the post. As a result, since he had shifted to the Notifications and Reporting section, there had been far fewer sick days taken by any of the team, lest any sniffle be viewed as a sign that the sniffler need to be killed for the good of society.

"Okay," said Lyn dazedly. "Good to know. Thanks for that." She sat back, her mind whirling with all the new information. She remembered an offhand remark that Dr. Allard had made at one point about not having to put her down. The Checquy, it seemed, would help you not only from cradle to grave but also into the grave if they thought that best for you.

I guess it's a good thing that they won't let me be a danger, she thought weakly. *But I'm not sure how much I like being mentored by the guy who'd probably kill me.* She looked up at the two girls. "Um, I'll get the next round."

12

Y ou are a pig, Wattleman!" exclaimed Bridget. "You are a caddish *pig!*" She would have slapped him, except she knew it wouldn't do any harm to him and would probably hurt her.

"What?" he said, amused and unconcerned by being denounced in the outer office where the Lady's staff and any passersby could witness. Bridget, meanwhile, was too enraged to care.

"'My Lady, I can advise you now that she will not be returning home this evening,'" said Bridget, doing an unflattering imitation of Wattleman's refined tones.

"I was *merely* advising her that our mission would keep us out all night," protested the Pawn. "Because this will call for undercover work, and we shall need to establish a clear break from our regular lives with no visits home."

"You were *implying*," said Bridget dangerously.

"Implying what?" he asked in a tone of wounded innocence. He looked at her slyly. "I think you're hearing what you want to hear."

"Let me make this painfully clear to you: I will not be sleeping with you, Pawn Wattleman. Not tonight. Not ever."

"Is this because of that young scholar whom the office is gossiping about?" he asked.

"He is enlisting," said Bridget coldly, "so you show some respect."

"Absolutely," said Wattleman. "It's very important to respect young men who go off to face danger in the name of King and country." Bridget flushed a little, then looked around. She realized that the Lady's secretaries were staring at them in stupefaction.

"Oh, for God's sake, let's just go," she said.

"Yes indeed," said Wattleman, retrieving his hat from the stand onto which he'd no doubt languidly tossed it from across the room. He touched his brow to the onlookers. "Ladies."

"Gent," said one of the secretaries dryly, and he actually wilted a little in the face of her disdain. By the time they reached the lift, however, a few ladies had giggled in response to his sallies, and he'd recovered his vim.

"All right, Wattleman, it's your mission. I'm just the helpful woman," said Bridget. "How shall we do this?"

"Well, Mangan, first off, we'll need to stop by wardrobe. I consider it a sad indictment of society, but nonetheless, I rather think I'll stand out if I venture into the streets dressed as smartly as this."

"There is a war on, you know."

"Yes, I'm aware," he said carelessly. "You'll need to change as well."

"And what's my character?" she asked warily.

"You'll be our buyer," he said. "You read the file?"

"I read the file."

"So how do you see your character?"

"Judging by the other women, the only remarkable thing about me is that I'm a believer. I'm a civilian, no powers of my own, but I believe in magic, and I want it in my life."

"You think they knew what they were buying, then?" asked Wattleman.

"You don't buy a human thighbone because you think it will look good on the mantelpiece," Bridget said. "And you don't steal materials from the Checquy if you're just going to hawk them as bric-a-brac. I think these people know that they're buying something supernatural, but they have no idea what they're doing."

"You don't sound very impressed with them."

"Two of them managed to kill themselves," said Bridget. "The one with the stolen femur burned her house down. The one who bought the cameo brooch was poisoned and half eaten by the mist it produced, which screamed in the voice of a child. And the one who survived— the woman who bought a cockleshell—is not in good shape either."

"Other common characteristics?" asked Wattleman intently.

"The femur woman was unmarried; the other two had husbands, both away at war. They were all comfortable, had their own houses, had money to spare on mystical artifacts."

"I saw that the survivor was able to name the price she'd paid down to the shilling," said Wattleman. "Very steep, I'd say. Several months' wages for many workingmen."

"So, I'm a believer with money," said Bridget.

"Yes, but don't go mad with the wardrobe," cautioned Wattleman. "None of the women were really rich, and there *is* a war on, you know."

Bridget shot him a look, and he grinned in response.

This is going to be unbearable.

⋆   ⋆   ⋆

In the end, under the careful guidance of the Checquy's quartermaster/costumier, Bridget settled on a skirt and coat that would have been quite snappy when they were bought several years ago but were now definitely showing their age at the edges. It was an outfit that said: *Before the war came, I could buy very nice clothes, and I still have that money, but clothes are in short supply at the moment. I don't know if you've heard, but there's a war on.*

She'd refused the offer of an operational corset that would provide support for any strenuous activities. Instead, she'd opted for the old Checquy trick of a brassiere that was a size too small. It didn't provide the same level of protection, but it had the advantage of not needing to have anyone else cinch her into it.

The best part was seeing Wattleman trade his natty suit and hat for an ensemble that suggested he was the type of man who could put his hands on some smutty French postcards at a very reasonable price if that was what you were looking for.

"We'll need clothes for a few days," Wattleman said. "We'll be staying in a hotel or a boardinghouse."

"Why?"

"We don't know how late we'll be out and we can't rely on transport being available when we need it," he replied. "And we're seeking out criminals, which means we'll be interacting with dangerous people. Can't take the risk of being followed home at the end of each day. Plus, it's always best to have a comfortable bed to repair to, don't you think?"

Bridget curled her lip at him, but he had more experience with this kind of operation than she, so they were each provided with several different sets of clothes in a small suitcase as well as several new identity cards appropriate to different circumstances. The most cringeworthy were the ones that proclaimed them to be Mr. Edgar and Mrs. Clementine Polivy. When they'd been handed their fake wedding rings, Bridget had very carefully not looked in Wattleman's direction, but his wide grin shone in her peripheral vision.

They sat together at the back of an uncrowded bus and discussed the situation a little more. At one point, Wattleman casually put his hand on her knee, and she casually threatened to break his fingers.

"Regarding our assignment," Bridget said, "if this spiv is charging a high price for the goods, then I'm actually a little reassured. It means the women aren't trading themselves. That would be too depressing for words. But if he's making so much money, why is he still working a corner in Portobello Road?"

"He can't open a shop," said Wattleman, "and I'm willing to bet that he still prizes his mobility. I expect that arcane items aren't his primary business. He needs to be able to leg it down an alley if the peelers appear."

"The *peelers*? You're really getting into character, aren't you?" she remarked. "Anyway, this all seems a little ridiculous. Pawn Santo-suosso's leg bone is capable of doing tremendous damage. It's a major weapon, and this man apparently sold it to a housewife in the street."

"Obviously he doesn't really understand what he's got," said Wattleman.

"Or he doesn't have the connections to put it in front of the right people," mused Bridget.

The question as to who exactly the right people were was a complicated one. As far as the Checquy knew, there was no one secret network of supernatural crime in the British Isles or the British Empire. Certainly there appeared to be nothing on the scale of the Checquy itself. The underworld (the criminal one, not the paranormal one) was characterized by extreme paranoia when it came to anything that smacked of the unnatural. Although, to be fair, you couldn't really call it paranoia, since there actually *was* a secret government organization whose mission was to hunt down and deal with the supernatural.

Periodically, individuals who developed inexplicable powers took it as an obvious sign that they should found a criminal empire. Such individuals were usually identified and dealt with quite easily. To avoid gaining the attention of the Checquy, one needed to be incredibly discreet, and building a criminal empire was about as indiscreet as one could get short of trying to build an actual empire.

And, of course, there were individuals who, upon learning of the supernatural world, wanted to become part of it. One way to do so was to acquire pieces of it. Such pieces tended to be quite rare, which meant that they were quite expensive. Thus, there were very few collectors and correspondingly few sellers. This was one of the reasons that Lady Carmichael was so keen to have this investigated quietly—the whole thing represented a drastic departure from the way such illegal trade normally occurred.

"Anyway," said Bridget, "I'm disappointed that the surviving woman couldn't give us the seller's name."

"I expect she never knew it. But she described him and told us where he was."

"Won't he have moved on? I mean, if two of his customers died as a result of his wares?"

"I don't think this is the kind of business where they provide follow-up customer service to see how satisfied you are," said Wattleman. "And it's all word of mouth. If people know only that you can be found at a certain corner, that's where you need to be. Especially for the esoteric stuff. You can hawk watches out of a suitcase anywhere, but you can't just ask random passersby if they'd like a forbidden winter-solstice mirror from the Tang Dynasty."

"Fair enough," agreed Bridget. "So what's our strategy?"

"Well, we know where we're looking and vaguely who we're looking for."

The sole surviving woman, Dorothy Hadgraft, had been left in a pitiable condition by her purchase. The most notable effect, aside from all her hair liquefying, was that she'd lost all control of the right side of her body. It made questioning her difficult; both her memory and her speech had been affected. The interview process was ongoing, but they'd managed to identify the source of the incident (a small cockleshell that she'd activated by submerging it in a bowlful of seawater) and learn where she'd gotten it. The Checquy had linked it to the other two incidents by the details that one woman had written down in her appointment book (*Seller, crnr. of Portobello Rd. and Elgin Cres.! At last!*) and the fact that the seashell and Pawn Santosuosso's femur had been part of the same shipment sent out to a disused tin mine in Cornwall.

Mrs. Hadgraft didn't know the name of the man who'd sold her the shell, but she was able to give a vague description. Most of the details were unhelpful—spivs seemed almost to have an official uniform: a light suit, garish tie, trilby, and pencil mustache—but this one had red hair, which might help them a little.

"We'll wander by, separately, and see if we can spot him. If he's not there, we'll repair to the local alehouse for a local ale or the local chophouse for a local chop, then try again in a bit. If we haven't seen him by the end of the day, you can ask about. If he *is* there—"

"I'll approach him and try to strike up a conversation."

"There'll be no *try* about it." Wattleman snorted. "His business is to strike up a conversation with you. But you'll need to guide him toward the esoteric."

"I've got a couple of ideas about how to do that."

"Good."

"I'll make a purchase if I can," she said. The Checquy finance office (known affectionately as "the Exchecquyer," much to the despair of its staff) had supplied her with a handy stack of banknotes in keeping with the amount Mrs. Hadgraft had paid for her seashell. "It may very well be that he's not so daft as to carry the items around with him and will ask me to return."

"If we get confirmation, we'll follow him," said Wattleman. "Can't very well interrogate him on the street."

"Fine," said Bridget. She lifted his hand off her knee, where it had mysteriously settled again. He smiled innocently.

The Portobello Road market had become an odd place in wartime. Bridget could remember visiting it before the war, when it had been bustling and cheerful, but today it was subdued, and people hurried about with their heads down. The drabness combined with the descent of a thick gray fog gave it a menacing air.

Stalls loomed out of the haze, vague shapes that became only slightly sharper as you approached, and the stallholders who cried their wares did so in almost hushed tones, as if they were afraid of bringing down the bombs. The rationing system had apparently had an effect on the offerings. Even the color of the fruits and vegetables seemed muted. Rag-and-bone men were scattered about the place, with bric-a-brac displayed on their barrows. A few book and antiques stalls had been set up on the pavements. The buildings on either side seemed to lean over the street as if huddling away from the sky. The canvases and tarpaulins of the stalls spread out into the street, creating a sporadic tunnel, and in the gaps between the material, the fog and smoke oozed in.

There was no redheaded spiv at the corner of Portobello and Elgin when they walked by, though there were a couple of other gentlemen of dubious commerce standing about, one of them selling alarm clocks from out of a suitcase. Bridget and Wattleman walked a few streets away to a teashop and had a bun and a cup of tea each. When they returned, there was still no sign of him.

"You're looking for Mr. Simony, love," said one of the spivs knowledgeably when Bridget put on a Yorkshire accent and falteringly asked for a redheaded salesman. "He never appears until the afternoon. Bit of a night owl, he is. He'll be here, but come back after lunch. I'll let him know you're looking for him." Bridget thanked him and consented to buy a pair of silk stockings, which she hastily tucked away in her pocket. She felt a little guilty, but the man had been helpful, and it might be useful to be known as a woman with money to spend illegally. Besides, stockings were harder and harder to get nowadays.

"So your young man is off to war," said Wattleman. They'd taken a bus well away from the area and found a pub that was serving a late lunch based heavily on the theme of cabbages. The room was humid, and steam coated the windows, but the chatter of the patrons meant that no one could hear what they were saying.

"Yes," said Bridget coldly.

"And he's asked you to wait for him."

"He asked me not to, actually."

"Indeed?" he said, raising an eyebrow. "Sounds like a startlingly sensible young man."

"Thanks," said Bridget flatly. She gave a moment's thought to flinging her cabbage soup in his face but decided against it. It wouldn't accomplish anything beyond wasting soup and attracting attention, and she'd already gotten a few looks for eating with her gloves on.

"It's wartime, after all," he continued. "We never know what's going to happen from one day to the next. Don't know if we'll be here tomorrow to do the things we put off today. Pleasure deferred is pleasure deterred, I always say."

"Ugh. I'm sure you do," said Bridget. "And does that little aphorism ever work?"

"It does, because it's the truth." She rolled her eyes. "Mangan, every day you have just as much chance of dying horribly as that poor young man. A greater chance, probably, given our work for the Order. We all talk so much about our service and what we owe the nation. But we can't give up our lives as human beings. Duty does not mean giving up the pleasures of living. If we do that, we're just tools, weapons. We owe ourselves various things, and one of those things is connection with other people. Life is for living. We have to *live* life, not just work so that others can enjoy themselves."

Bridget stared down at her horrible soup and brooded. "You make a good point, Henry," she said softly, and his eyes brightened.

"*Well,* now."

"But whatever connection I'll be making, it won't be with *you.*"

The rest of the meal passed in thoughtful silence. It began to drizzle outside, and they had a few minutes of concern that Mr. Simony might be put off by the rain, but it had stopped by the time they'd each had a drink. When they returned to the market, Wattleman idled several yards behind her, close enough to step in and provide support if it proved to be needed. The man who'd sold Bridget the stockings saw her and nodded. He jerked his thumb at a redheaded man who was crouched over a suitcase.

"Excuse me?" she asked. He was dressed like all the other gathered spivs, but when he looked up at her, she saw that he was younger than them, barely out of his teens. He still sported the requisite pencil-thin mustache, however.

"I 'ear yer've been lookin' for me," he said. His eyes raked her up and down, expertly putting a value on every item of clothing and probably, she suspected, what was inside it. He had that kind of gaze, as if everything were for sale.

"Yes, well, I think so. I didn't know your name to ask for you. Your, um, colleague told me your last name. What should I call you?" *Give me your Christian name.*

"You don't need to call me anything," he said flatly. "You've found me—now what was yer interested in?"

"My friend said that you were good at finding, um, *unusual* antiques."

"Oh yeah?"

"Yes, Dorothy Hadgraft." He stared at her blankly. "You sold her a special seashell."

He sucked his teeth and nodded. "Ho, yes, I remember her. And you was lookin' for somefing similar, then," he said. "Yet anuvver one wantin' to make a difference, eh?"

Interesting, Bridget thought, mentally filing away the comment for later contemplation. "Can you help me?" she said.

"I expect I can find somefing in the nature hof what you are lookin' for, yes. Course, that sort of material don't come cheap."

"Dorothy told me what she paid," said Bridget.

"Yeah, but these thing ain't all the same, are they? There's not a factory stampin' 'em out. Each one's unique, an' they're not easy to come by. You gets what you gets, and if one 'antique' is bigger'n another, then it's going to cost more." He looked at her expectantly.

"And what do you have?" she asked.

"Well, nuffink 'ere. I don't stand about wif special bloody antiques tucked down me trews."

"Of course not," agreed Bridget. "When and where should we meet, then?"

"Tomorrer," he said. "We'll meet in that pub"—he nodded across the street—"at three. And we'll go from there."

"All right, then," she said uncertainly. "Thank you. I look forward to it."

"Didja want to buy some stockings till then?"

"Your colleague over there already sold me some, thank you."

"Nicely done, Mangan." Despite herself, Bridget felt a little surge of pleasure at Wattleman's praise. For all his boorishness, the man was an expert at what he did. "And what do you think our next step should be?"

"Now that we've established that he's our man, we need to question him."

"I agree. Track him, see where he lives. That may be where he's keeping the items."

"I don't think so," said Bridget. "If that was the case, why wait until tomorrow? And so late?"

"You may be right, but we're pressed for time, remember? The Lady doesn't expect this to take more than a day or two. So we'll need to question him tonight."

"Tailing someone by yourself is risky. But I can't do it—he'll know me," Bridget pointed out. "And we can't call in backup."

"No indeed," he agreed. "Which is why we'll need to find some lodgings. I have a pretty nearly foolproof way of tracking him without being seen, but I'll need a bit of privacy." Bridget stared at him a moment before she realized what he was talking about.

"*God.* Really?"

He smiled.

"Fine, but we're getting two rooms."

"Oh no, I don't think our budget will stretch to two rooms."

Piggish cad!

"Do you really have to be naked for this to work?"

"Yes," said Wattleman from behind a changing screen.

"I honestly think we could have gotten two rooms," said Bridget. She was sitting in a chair in the corner, trying to ignore the sounds of him disrobing.

"It would have broken our cover as a married couple."

"We didn't have to use *that* cover," objected Bridget. They had several different identities, after all.

"Plus, we might need the extra money," he continued, ignoring her entirely reasonable observation. "If it comes down to it, we may actually have to buy an artifact."

She wasn't certain that this hotel room didn't cost more than two very dingy rooms in a boardinghouse would have, but she was not prepared to get into an argument over the comparative prices. And although she hated to admit it, it was a very nice room, with a fire-place and a private bathroom. The hotel itself—the Brentley—was more posh than she would have chosen, but while Wattleman's rather dingy garb had raised some eyebrows when they checked in, he hadn't been concerned, so neither would she.

"Never occurred to me," said Wattleman. There was the sound of a zipper, and she cringed.

He is taking his clothes off right here in the room with me, she thought despondently. The fact that it was for professional, covert-surveillance-related reasons made it little better. The fact that he was going to have to go out naked into the cold outdoors, though, made it a lot better.

"And what will you be doing in my absence?" he asked.

"While you're out freezing your favorite bits off?" she asked. "I shall order a cocktail and take a hot bath, I think." *If I'm not on Chec-quy property, I can take a proper full bath. It's part of my cover identity.*

"You're very cruel," he said.

I'll also be sitting here brooding about Gerald. "Seriously, will you be all right?" she asked. The weather outside the window looked bitterly cold, and a wind was blowing noisily.

"I'll feel the cold, but it won't actually harm me," he assured her. She flinched—his voice hadn't come from behind the screen but the middle of the room. "And I've got a fair bit of experience at making my way about like this."

Wattleman had several different supernatural powers, but one of the oddest was his ability not to be seen. He didn't literally become invisible (exhaustive photograph and film experiments had verified that), but people did not see him if he did not wish them to. The only flaw, however, was that the effect worked only on his actual body. Thus the necessity of being nude—people would notice a set of clothing walking about by itself. He also could not carry any weapons or money. Given his other capabilities, the lack of weapons was not a serious challenge, but the lack of money was one of the reasons he'd insisted on a hotel within easy walking distance of Portobello Road. If he needed to alert Bridget to something, he was going to have to leg it back and tell her.

All of this meant, however, that there was a naked man standing in the room with her. She sighed. Like so much of her experience in the Checquy, she did not acknowledge the sheer bizarreness of the situation. *Although if I feel even the slightest brush of naked skin,* she resolved, *I will break his jaw, mission or no mission.*

Then, despite herself, she wondered what it would be like to be with a man who was invisible, to lie in a room full of sunshine with one's eyes wide open and only feel the sensations of making love. Bridget's own virginity was a matter of vague policy (her own, not the Checquy's): she would not have sex until it felt like something she definitely wanted to do with someone she definitely wanted to do it with. So far, those circumstances had not aligned. Still, she had an imagination.

It would be, she decided, incredibly one-sided. As if her partner were simultaneously not there and as there as it was possible to be.

Of course, the key would be that he could not talk, she thought. *Otherwise, you would have to admit that it was Henry Wattleman and then you would have to despise yourself for the rest of your life.*

"Mangan?"

"Hmm? Yes! I'll also call back to the office and see if they have anything on our Mr. Simony," said Bridget hurriedly.

"Jolly good. Well, out into the cold unfeeling world I go," said Wattleman's voice. "I'll knock when I come back." The door to the room opened by itself, then shut, and Bridget shuddered. She sat for a moment, considering the world.

"Will you miss me?" asked Wattleman's voice from the middle of the room.

"Jaysus! Get out!" screamed Bridget. The door opened again and closed on the sound of chuckling.

A few minutes after Wattleman left, Bridget went down to the lobby to use the telephone. The receptionist directed her to an exquisite wood and glass booth where she could make her call in private. She navigated through a series of unlisted lines, secret exchanges, and operators to reach the Lady's office and was eventually connected with Pamela.

"How are things with Henry?"

"Predictably loathsome," Bridget said. "We're following leads, and he's currently trailing someone while starkers."

"Of course he is," Pamela said. "Just count yourself lucky you've never been to a party he's attending. He's got various moves he thinks are hilarious."

"I'll keep my guard up," Bridget said sourly. "Can you have research run a very quick search for records of a Mr. Simony? Late teens, early twenties. Red hair. Accent puts him as a Cockney."

"First name?"

"Don't know, I'm afraid."

"Hold on." Bridget could hear her telling someone, "And as quick as you can, please." She came back on the line. "Hopefully they'll have us some results in a couple of minutes."

"I'll wait, then. Any developments on our man?" asked Bridget, meaning the Nazi.

"Yes, and none good. There have been three more killings."

"*What?*" exclaimed Bridget. Even through the glass, she must have been heard, because the receptionist looked over at her in surprise. With an effort, she calmed herself. "Where?" she asked in a tone she might have used at a garden party. "How?"

"Same as the others. Charred corpses, clothes unburned. In the street." Pamela's voice shook a little as she said it.

Is she blaming herself? thought Bridget. *She brought the plane down. She put this man into the city.* "Together?" she asked weakly.

"No, different streets, different times."

Christ, Wattleman and I are hunting down people who have seeded manifestations in the city, and Pamela has done the same damn thing. This is a nightmare. "Do you know who they were?"

"Not yet. It's difficult to identify charred corpses if you've no context."

"They didn't have identity cards?" Bridget asked.

"If they did, they were taken," said Pamela.

"Maybe he's building up different identities," mused Bridget. The buff-colored cards were universal—every man, woman, and child had to have one and carry it at all times. Bridget had heard that some

mothers had initially not registered their sons for the cards, for fear of
them being called up for service. They had changed their tune when
they learned one would need a card if rationing was introduced. The
problem, though, was that the cards did not feature photographs.

"As I said, we just don't know."

"Any progress from the tracking team?" Bridget asked nervously.

"Not as much as I would expect," Pamela said. "It's very odd. We
think he may be new to his powers with no practice in concealing
them, and yet they have no leads."

"We don't always catch everything right away," Bridget said. "It
took months to track down the Brighton Eructationer. And we *never*
found out what caused that flaring of the aurora borealis in Grimsby
last summer."

"This is a man with no money, no home, no support network. We
don't even know if he speaks the language. He is the most vulnerable
sort of fugitive."

"The Checquy team doesn't know that, though," said Bridget.

"I expect they'll shortly be putting two and two together on that
score," Pamela said grimly. "They've been sending reports up to this
office, and I'm seeing hints of a developing theory."

"What will happen then?"

"If the Checquy knows a Nazi is running around killing people by
supernatural means," said Pamela, her voice tight, "a lot more people
will be added to the team. It will improve their chances dramatically."

"I can't do much to help," said Bridget. "I have to stay ready for
Wattleman to return. Do you and Usha have any ideas?"

"No, and I have to accompany Lady Carmichael to a Court
meeting."

"Another one?"

"There's going to be a lot of them," said Pamela. "Ah, hold on, the
research has come back."

"That was fast."

"A request from the Lady's office gets you speed, especially when" —
Bridget heard the sound of papers being flipped through — "it appears
there isn't anything to find."

"Nothing?" asked Bridget.

"Nothing with that spelling in our records. I'll get them to check variations and see if the police have anything, but that'll take time." Pamela hesitated. "But if anything occurs to *you* about our problem, please let us know."

"Of course," said Bridget. Her mind was whirling.

When the knock finally came, Bridget was looking pensively out the window, watching the light fade and the streets fill up with people hurrying home. The sound was soft but insistent, like someone patting the door repeatedly. She opened it fast, carrying a robe that she'd kept warming by the fire. She felt something solid brush past her, and the robe was plucked from her hand. It swirled about in the air, then Wattleman was there in the robe, holding it closed in front of him and hurrying toward the fireplace. His back to her, he opened the front of the robe, let the heat of the flames pour onto him, and let out a long trembling sigh. She awkwardly looked away.

"I've got tea and brandy waiting for you," she said, looking very deliberately at a picture on the wall and gesturing at a tray that held a pot in a tea cozy and a glass of golden liquid.

"Bless you," he said. She nodded. The brandy had been madly expensive, paid for discreetly with folded banknotes to the hotel's concierge, and she'd had to order a fresh pot of tea every hour to ensure it was warm when he arrived. The hotel probably thought she was either mad or suffering from a very particular kidney condition. "God, but it's horrible out there."

She looked over cautiously. He was still standing in front of the fire with his robe held open. It would have looked obscene, like he was flashing the fireplace, except that he was shivering, and she could see that his hair was wet. She thought she could hear his teeth chattering.

"Would you like me to draw you a bath?" she asked. The choice of hotel, with its private bathrooms, was making more and more sense. Earlier, she'd resolved that she would take the bed, and he would have to sleep on the sofa, but seeing what he'd just endured, that seemed churlish.

"No time," he said, regret in his voice. "Let me warm up a little bit and then we'll go."

"So you found his place?"

"Yes. Had to wait for hours, dancing about behind him to try and keep warm." She noticed that his feet were wet and absolutely filthy. "He just hung about, chatting to his colleagues about who's better, Betty Grable or Gypsy Rose Lee."

"So, nothing useful?"

"Please." He snorted. "They all agreed on Betty Grable. It took all my strength not to step in and correct them."

"Right," said Bridget dryly. "And no sales?"

"He sold some stuff to a few punters."

"No artifacts, though, that you could see?"

"Not unless he's stumbled upon several diabolical wristwatches or some demonic packets of cigarettes," said Wattleman. "I mean, I know you can't ever take anything for granted in this job, but they were all sold to men, so I think we're safe.

"When he finally left, I almost lost him. The little weasel really can move, and he kept wriggling through crowds—which is something I'm not going to try while stark-bollock naked."

"But you kept up with him?"

"Obviously. He lives in a little basement flat about twenty minutes' walk from the market. I don't know if he's going to stay there during the inevitable nightly raid or head for a shelter, so we'll want to be quick. Anyway, once I saw him go in and lock the door, I dashed back here, dodging all the blinking people in the street heading home."

"Anyone else in the place?" He shrugged. "Okay, well, we'll keep the possibility in mind when we go in. Also, Henry, we can't be certain that he won't have some supernatural item there that he might try to use."

"Yeah, so we'll have to be flexible. Can't really plan ahead too much." He sighed, closed the robe, and tied it shut around his waist before turning around. "All right, I'll have a quick cup of tea and a snort of that brandy, then I'll get dressed and we'll head out." She nodded and poured him a cup. It steamed reassuringly—the latest delivery of tea had been only about five minutes before he returned.

"Did they have anything on Simony at Apex House?" he asked.

Bridget shook her head. "Never heard of him," she said. "Nothing about any Simony in any of the Checquy records, and you know they're fiends for cross-tabulation. Every name ever encountered gets put on an index card somewhere in the bowels of the Apex." He nodded knowingly. "Anyway, Pamela's put feelers out to the police to see if they've got anything."

"Well, we can't wait," said Wattleman firmly. He threw the tea down his throat and took a swig of brandy. "I'll get my togs on and we'll go."

"Is it strange, walking about naked in front of people?" she asked curiously as he went behind the screen to dress.

"I only found I had the ability when I was fifteen," he said. "You don't get used to it." He sniffed. "Especially when it's raining, and there's rubbish in the streets." He looked down at his feet. "You'll forget about it for a moment, then remember with a start. It's exactly like those dreams where you realize you're naked in front of a large audience. And it's a bit worse because you know exactly how you've come to be in that position."

"But you know they can't see you."

"Hm, but there's always the thought that it might stop or you'll flex the wrong way somehow and suddenly be standing bare-arsed in the middle of Covent Garden with everyone staring at you, you know?"

Bridget didn't. Her hands had always been as they were. The nearest she could imagine was if her palms stopped producing pearl on command. But she'd never thought of that before. It was like worrying about all of a sudden no longer being able to pee.

Although powers abruptly stopping is all I'm going to be thinking about when next I go up with Pamela or Usha, she thought. Flying was bad enough without worrying that it might suddenly cease.

They walked briskly through the streets, which were getting darker and darker. Blackout curtains were being put up in windows, so every few moments, another homey glow was blotted out. It made the world seem much colder and grimmer. Fewer people were about now, and they all seemed to be hurrying, chins hunched down in their collars to avoid the cold wind.

Wattleman must have had an excellent sense of direction or

memory, because even without the streetlights, he seemed to know exactly where they were going, never taking a wrong turn or hesitating. They passed bombed-out sites where the ruined walls of houses teetered crookedly. Eventually, they came to a small, dingy tenement, and he led her down the steps to the door of the flat.

"Ready?" he asked. She nodded and knocked on the door.

"Who's there?" came Simony's voice.

"Mr. Simony?" Bridget called with her real accent. On the walk there, she and Wattleman agreed that he was far more likely to open the door to a woman's voice. Simony opened it a suspicious crack, and his eye focused on her.

"You?"

"Hello." She smiled. And then Wattleman stepped up and kicked the door open, hitting Simony's face. Bridget shoved forward past him, grabbed the semi-stunned man's hair, dragged him up from the floor, and marched him backward. She would give him no chance to activate any abilities he might possess or snatch any artifacts lying around the place.

Meanwhile, Wattleman had stepped in and pushed the door shut behind them. He scanned the room for other people.

"Clear here!" he called.

Bridget thrust Simony into a kitchen chair and wrenched his head back by the hair before he could scream. By the time he had managed to come to even a vague understanding of the situation, Bridget's switchblade was open in her other hand and resting on the soft spot where his neck met his jaw.

"Don't make a sound," she said. "Not a squeak, not a squeal, and certainly no bloody yelling." Simony's nod was awkward, given that Bridget was clutching his hair and had a knife at his throat. "If you move your hands at all or try anything strange, you're getting a second mouth." Her knife pricked him very gently. "Now, anyone else in the flat?" Wide-eyed, Simony shook his head as much as he dared with the blade at his throat. "I don't believe you. John, check the rest of the place!"

She resisted the urge to roll her eyes. Wattleman had insisted that they needed cover names, so they were Mary and John.

"John? Are we clear?"

"Yes, Mary, there's nobody hiding in the cupboards." To her irritation, he sounded a little amused. She took her eyes off Simony and looked around. The flat was actually one room, tiny, with a bed in one corner and a sort of kitchenette in another. In the center stood a little table with two chairs (one of which was now occupied by Mr. Simony), and that was it. She assumed the communal bathroom and lavatory was upstairs. There was nowhere to hide, unless someone had crammed himself into one of the many boxes stacked against the walls or under the flat's only armchair.

"Uh . . . right. Very good. Do you want to come here, then?"

He nodded, took off his hat, and placed it carefully on the armchair. He came behind Simony, snapped open a switchblade like hers, and laid its length along the other side of the man's throat. Bridget drew her knife back and released her grip on Simony's hair, then absently wiped her gloved hand on her skirt. "Now, Mr. Simony, let us have a conversation." She went around to the other side of the table and sat; Wattleman prompted Simony to turn on his chair and face her.

"Hands flat on the table," said Wattleman. "Good."

"I don't have anyfink here!" said Simony.

Bridget looked around at the boxes against the wall, then looked back at him.

"Well, yeah, but nuffink like what you're looking for. So help me, I swear it!"

"And what exactly *are* we looking for?" she asked.

"What? Your bloody special antiques!"

"And what makes them special?"

"They got summink about 'em, don't they?" He was staring at her in confusion. Bridget stared back at him, trying to conceal her own confusion.

Does he not know?

"They've got, like, magic, don't they?" he said finally. He shrugged. "They do fings they shouldn't do. I seen 'em spark, or I get a funny feeling. People want 'em, I sell 'em along. Nuffink to do wif me."

She stared at him in fascination. What kind of person would see an actual, logic-defying miraculous object and view it as simply something to be sold? Such a profound lack of curiosity was completely alien to her.

"How many people did you sell these items to?" she asked finally.

"Fifteen," he said.

Fifteen! Bridget and Wattleman exchanged glances.

"Who were they?" she asked.

"How should I know? Fifteen bloody stupid women who paid for 'em, that's who!"

"Did you keep any records?" asked Bridget.

"Wot? Of who I sell my goods to? A nice little record for the rozzers to find? Don't be daft!"

"What was sold, exactly?"

"Bloody hell! I dunno." The spiv squeaked when Wattleman shifted his grip on the knife, pressing the blade a little against his jugular. "Um, lemme think!" He closed his eyes. "A couple of bones, that shell, a fork..."

"Like a trident? A pitchfork?" asked Bridget.

"No, a dinner fork. Old, I fink it was silver. Had a crest on it, a nobby family crest. What else? There was a mask, like a 'eathen mask wiv beads and hair on it. Oh, and a wireless set."

"Seriously?" asked Bridget, startled.

"Yeah, I know, not what you'd expect. Lovely little piece too. Bakelite. And then a burnt bit of wood about the size of me 'and, and there was a little carved portrait of a woman in a wig, what do you call them?"

"Cameos," said Wattleman heavily.

"Yeah, one of them," agreed Simony. He seemed to have relaxed a little with the discussion of wares and sales. "In ivory, I fink. Charged a lot for that one—worth a lot just as an antique, let alone whatever she was finking it could do for her."

"And they were all satisfied with what you sold them?"

"Well, they never came back to complain, did they? And I've got my regular spot. Plus, if word gets around that I'm selling dud goods, where's that gonna leave me? Gotta be built on trust."

"You were going to sell me something," said Bridget. "What? Where is it?"

"I dunno what you were going to get. I don't keep those fings 'ere in me 'ouse, do I?"

"If they're not here, then where do you get them from?" she asked. A new spark of terror rose up in his eyes at the question. She'd touched on something here that *did* matter to him.

"I ain't telling you nuffink!"

Bridget raised an eyebrow. "Suddenly you're feeling shy? You *do* feel the knife at your throat, don't you?"

"That's nuffink to what they'll do to me if I grass on 'em!" There was something about the way he said it that made Bridget believe him. She looked at Wattleman, who shrugged a little. *What now?* she wondered. Would Wattleman torture him? Could he? She'd never received any training in that sort of thing and wasn't at all sure that she could go through with it. It was one thing to fight and kill; it was quite another to cause deliberate agony.

All right, Bridget decided. *Time to take this to another level.* She held up her hand in front of Simony and slowly peeled the leather glove off. His eyes grew huge as he saw the shimmering iridescence of her palm.

"What?" he breathed.

"There's all kinds of special in this world," she said softly. She laid her palm down flat on the wood of his tiny table, then lifted it up, leaving a perfect handprint of pearl sealed to the surface. It shone under the light, smooth and beautiful and impossible. She looked up slowly at Simony and thought his eyes were going to pop out of their sockets. She put a finger to her lips and, with the flourish of a stage magician, lifted a butter knife from the table. His eyes followed as she raised it, closed both hands around the handle, and brought it down on the handprint with all her strength, like a priestess making a pagan sacrifice. He flinched away with a little cry, and Wattleman tightened his grip on the man's hair.

The handprint was unbroken, unscarred. The knife was now bent a little at the tip, and Bridget's hands ached from the force of the strike, although she was careful not to show it.

"Lovely, isn't it?" she said without looking for an answer. "And practically unbreakable." She laid down the knife and put her hand back on the table. As Simony watched, transfixed, she slid her hand along it, leaving a shining trail of pearl. When her hand came to the discarded knife, she slid over it, locking the knife to the wood with the lustrous white strip.

Bridget silently took off her other glove, showing the nacreous coating of that palm as well. She hovered her hands over Simony's, which lay flat on the table. He eyed her hands nervously.

"If you don't tell us where you got those materials from," she said calmly, "I will encase your hands in this table. To begin with. You can imagine what comes next." She actually didn't have any idea what would come next, but apparently Mr. Simony had some pretty horrible ideas, because he looked like he was going to be ill. His hands were trembling, but he didn't seem able to lift them, as if they were already entombed.

"Oh Gawd, the Murcutts!" he blurted out, and then the rest came out quickly, as if he couldn't stop. "Bobby and Johnny Murcutt and that sister of theirs! They're the ones who give me the stuff, the special things. They put my name out as the one wif the stuff!"

"And where do I find the Murcutts? Bobby and Johnny and that sister of theirs?" asked Bridget.

"You can't tell 'em I told you!" he said frantically. "You can't!"

"We won't," said Bridget.

"They won't do anything to you," said Wattleman. "You'll be safe from them."

"You swear?"

"I swear to God," said Bridget. She turned her hands over, and the light from the bulb overhead made her palms shine brilliantly. The sight of it seemed to reassure him, as if she'd invoked a holy presence.

"I...all right," he said. He gave an address for a pub in Soho called the Moor's Head, and Bridget committed it to memory.

"And when will they be there?" asked Bridget.

"They're always there," said Simony brokenly. "It's their place." His shoulders slumped.

"Well, then," said Wattleman. He met Bridget's eyes and nodded. "Very good." She leaned back, relaxing for a moment. Simony must have sensed the change in the tension of the room, because, rat-fast, he was pushing Wattleman's hand away and coming up with a pistol from under the table.

Whereupon Wattleman's dreadful strength came into play; he pushed back and briskly cut Simony's throat.

"Jesus, Mary, and Joseph!" shouted Bridget. Blood sprayed onto the table. She hurriedly pushed her chair back and sprang up as the crimson washed over the wood and the pearl.

Wattleman shoved the spiv's head forward, and more blood poured down onto his shirt. The Pawn then very deliberately placed the point of the knife at the base of the man's skull and forced the knife in and up, twisting it easily. Simony went limp, slumping down in the chair. Wattleman briskly wiped his knife on the spiv's shoulder and closed it.

"Henry, what in the hell?" exclaimed Bridget, having gotten over her horrified astonishment.

"Oh, did I get any on you?" He looked at her carefully. "Sorry."

"What? No, I don't think so." She looked down at her clothes. They seemed blood-free. "You just killed him!"

"Well, I didn't plan to do it exactly this way, but it was going to happen eventually," said the Pawn.

"It *was?*"

"What did you think we were going to do with him?"

"Not that!"

"What did you think we were sent to do?"

"I . . . not that!"

"Mangan, this is an off-the-books operation for the Lord and Lady tracing treachery within the Checquy. No one can know about it. Simony couldn't have been taken into custody in case he talked. And you'll be reassured to know that the Checquy doesn't have a jail for keeping secrets from itself."

"He was not a supernatural threat!"

"He was knowingly trafficking in supernatural items that killed people," said Wattleman in an infuriatingly reasonable tone. "The actions of this man"—he looked down contemptuously at the slumped corpse—"resulted in one woman dying in an unquenchable fire and another in a poisonous acidic screaming mist."

"He didn't *know* the items killed people."

"He was selling human bones. This was not a man whose inherent wholesomeness gave him any reason to expect a long, secure life. And the Lady sent us to take care of the situation quietly." He looked at her curiously. "This can't be your first corpse, surely?"

"No," said Bridget. "But it is the first time someone's been killed while I was looking into his eyes and having a conversation."

"I would have killed him much more tidily, but he pulled that gun. Must have had it taped under the table. The knife was at his throat, so that seemed like the best way to stop him. But it takes a while for them to die like that, and the blood keeps coming, and if you do the brain, the heart stops pumping." He shrugged. "Saves on cleanup. That said, we'll still need to mop up the mess." There were some dirty shirts piled on the end of the bed. "Good," he said as he took them up and placed them in Simony's lap to catch the drips.

"We couldn't have taken him into custody?" asked Bridget.

"For what purpose?"

"In case we needed more information from him."

"He'd told us what we needed to know, and we've got limited time," said Wattleman. "Now we need to tidy up and get out."

"What if he lied about his source?"

"He didn't," said Wattleman with certainty. "He was too shaken to lie that coherently. Besides, everything he told us was easy to check. All his normal wares are here, as far as I can tell. Speaking of which, it might be useful to have a look through those boxes."

"You think he might really have some artifacts in there?"

"No, I believed him on that. But let's see what he was selling. And we should lift some things so as to provide a story."

"What do you mean?" asked Bridget.

"At some point, someone is going to come looking for him. If it's not these Murcutts, it will be someone else. Even a piece of shit like this may have family or friends who will notice they haven't seen him for a while. At the very least, a landlord will show up looking for rent.

"We want as few questions asked as possible, and we want to make sure that the answers take them away from us. If it's the Murcutts, we don't want to tip them off that there's an investigation into supernatural goods. If it's someone else, well, the police could be called in, and that would lead to its own very awkward consequences.

"So, whoever it is, that person finds that he's gone. That leaves a few possibilities. It could be as innocent as he's off dead drunk in a gutter or visiting his sick aunt in St. Ives. Or perhaps he died in a raid. Or his absence could be related to his business. So, whoever's asking the questions, we need an explanation other than a secret division of the government executed him for illegally selling magical goods. We'll leave the place with a jumble of things to think about—a black marketeer missing, some of his more valuable wares gone. Whoever shows up here can try to work it out."

"You keep saying that he's missing, gone," said Bridget. "We're not...you're not saying that we take him with us?"

"Not very far," he assured her. "We'll put him somewhere he won't be found immediately. Maybe never."

"What about the blood?" Bridget asked. She gestured at the slumped Simony. Most of the blood had gone down his front, but there was still a goodly amount on the table, glistening red on the pearl. She looked under the table and noticed some there too.

"I'll clean up the gore," offered Wattleman. "I spilled it, after all. But thanks to your—ha!—handiwork, it's a fairly incriminating supernatural tableau." He gestured at the pearl handprint and the broad smears of white sealed to the wood. "Can you break that stuff down or are we going to have to take the table with us? Unless you wanted to burn it?"

"It doesn't burn, but yes, I can dissolve it with my touch. Although it takes a while," said Bridget. "Much longer than it takes to generate it." She regarded the table unhappily.

"No one said this job would be easy," said Wattleman. "Or tidy. But while I mop up, you go see what there is here for us to take. In addition to the late Mr. Simony."

"Fine," said Bridget. "Hey, do you think there might be some sugar in there?"

"One can only hope. But keep an eye out for small, easily portable items. We're also going to be hauling our friend here."

There turned out to be no sugar among the boxes. As Bridget

searched the room, she found nothing that gave any impression of possible supernaturalness, but she took a few pairs of stockings. She reluctantly admitted to herself that the tins of jam would be too heavy, but she did grab a couple of bars of chocolate and put them in her handbag.

"How's it going?" she asked over her shoulder.

"'Who would have thought the old man to have had so much blood in him?'" quoted Wattleman as he dumped another gore-soaked shirt in a dark-colored canvas sack. "But I'm nearly done. Just a quick scrub-down, then it's your turn."

"Right," sighed Bridget, coming to the table. Wattleman had done a good job. The varnished surface had cleaned up well, although the sack of bloody cloth by her feet was pretty frightening to behold.

"It's got to be done," said Wattleman. "You didn't think we could leave the table this way, did you?"

"Honestly, I didn't even think that far ahead," she said. *I'm too accustomed to having the Checquy clean up these things,* she thought ruefully. "I was just looking to intimidate him."

"Well, it worked a treat," said Wattleman. "I was very surprised at how quickly he spilled his guts."

"I read a treatise on the effects of confronting people with the supernatural. The impact varies, but it's especially forceful if it happens in their own homes to something they know well and intimately. The familiar made impossible. I figured the table was something he knew pretty well, took for granted. Seeing it changed left him vulnerable."

"Indeed. I'll have to keep that in mind for the future. Do you need anything?"

"I'll need something to sop up a liquid."

"Lucky for us, Simony had quite a few shirts," said Wattleman. "Use these, then put them into the sack with the others."

Bridget put her hands down on the table, cringing a little at its warm tackiness. She closed her eyes and set about the difficult process of dissolving the pearl she'd generated.

"Lucky you can do that," remarked Wattleman from somewhere behind her.

"Yes," agreed Bridget without opening her eyes. "Otherwise, I'd still have bits of pearl stuff welded to me from when I was little."

Mastering how to dissolve the stuff—a Checquy scientist had once referred to it as "denaturing"—had been one of her earliest lessons, and the Checquy had only known she could do it because she'd done it inadvertently as a baby. She could distantly remember a few little smears of the material that she'd accidentally expressed onto herself as a child—stiff little patches on her skin with an occasional jag that caught at her clothes or scratched her. They'd been there for a few weeks and she'd felt massive satisfaction when she finally managed to peel them off. There had also been a disastrous haircut at the age of five after she'd managed to weld her hair into a massive clump of pearl during her sleep.

"So only you can dissolve it?" asked Wattleman curiously.

"There are some acids that can eat into it patchily," said Bridget. "Nothing you'd want to get on your skin. I ruined a lot of gloves while I was learning control."

"We all go through it," he said.

While the experience of generating the pearl was a warm, thrumming feeling, dissolving it brought a seeping sensation that turned her stomach a little. Bridget felt the material liquefying under her touch. She wrinkled her nose—the smell was bitterly chemical as the minerals softened and broke down.

It took her a good twenty minutes to unmake what had taken her only a few seconds to create, then she had to clean off the unrecognizable residue of the material formerly known as pearl, but eventually the table was left looking like it had suffered nothing worse than the normal depredations of a table belonging to a single man with poor housekeeping inclinations. "Finished."

Wattleman looked at it carefully. "Nicely done," he said, nodding. "A veritable tabula rasa."

Bridget rolled her eyes. "A classical education is a dangerous thing in the wrong hands." She was grateful that the flat had running water, although it did not have nearly enough soap.

Wattleman, meanwhile, had gone through the remaining boxes and taken almost all the wristwatches and jewelry (leaving a few pieces to show any investigators what Simony had been peddling) and all the money he found.

"So what are we doing with him?" Bridget asked nervously, nodding at the slumped corpse.

"I'll wrap him in the blanket from his bed. We'll take him down the street to that bombed-out house I noticed, and I'll pull some rubble down on him."

"That's . . . not a bad idea," said Bridget.

"This isn't my first corpse either," he said.

They exited the flat cautiously, surveying the street for any possible witnesses. It turned out to be the ideal circumstances for disposing of evidence. The sky above was cloudy, so no stars or moon could be seen, and with the blackout in effect, the streetlights were out and every curtain was shut tight. The city was as dark as if they'd closed their eyes. There were a few people walking cautiously through the streets, navigating the darkness in different ways. They passed a man wearing a prominent luminous badge on his lapel, and a few individuals carried flashlights whose beams were muted and diffused by tissue paper. Such measures were practically useless and only helped the Pawns to identify when someone was approaching. Whenever someone came near, they pressed themselves back into an alcove or alleyway, but they barely needed to.

Everyone here could be carrying a corpse, and we'd be none the wiser, Bridget thought. Wattleman carried the late Mr. Simony effortlessly over one shoulder, and she carried the sack containing the clothes used to clean up blood and pearl residue.

By the time they reached the bomb site that was their destination, their eyes had adapted a little, enough to make out the vague shapes of collapsed walls and jutting foundation remains. They took a few careful steps; loose rubble on the ground shifted underfoot. Bridget gratefully obeyed Wattleman's instructions to stay on the edge and act as lookout. The thump of his dropping the body made her wince, but not nearly as much as the deafening sound as he shoved a wall down on top of it. She was still coughing when he emerged from the cloud of dust.

"Do you think anyone will have heard that?" she asked dryly.

"Maybe." He shrugged. "But it's not unexpected for wreckage to shift and collapse. And the place has already been emptied, so why would anyone bother to excavate it?"

They stopped a few streets away to dump the canvas sack in a rubbish bin. It was eerie, walking through the darkness with her arm looped through Wattleman's as he guided the way.

Then, abruptly, the terrifying rising and falling sound of the airraid siren blared around them. She felt Wattleman tense, and despite herself, she drew nearer to him. There was the potential for panic curdling in her stomach, and her first instinct was to reach out to an Usha who wasn't there so they could claw themselves up into the sky, away from a ground that had suddenly become unimaginably dangerous.

"Crikey," muttered Wattleman. "Jerry's bloody early tonight. We need to hurry."

"'Ere!" came a shout right by them, and Bridget nearly leapt out of her skin. They turned to see an irate ARP warden dashing across the street toward them.

"Play petrified," said Wattleman out of the corner of his mouth.

"Done," said Bridget with feeling. *Thank God we ditched that sack already,* she thought. *Those would have looked far too suspicious.* Still, she was very aware of the stolen items that they had thrust into her handbag.

"Bloody idiots, what are you doing out? There's a bleedin' raid on!" The warden was a beefy older man; he looked like a butcher, perhaps, but wrapped in all the authority of his helmet and blue overalls.

"Yes, sir. We got turned around," said Wattleman. "We're just on our way to our lodgings." He named the hotel, but the warden shook his head.

"Too far," he said. "You'll need to come wiv me to the nearest shelter!"

"But sir—" began Wattleman in his most reasonable tone.

"No arguments, I am auforised to compel you if I see fit, and I *do,* so! Now, come wiv me!" Bridget and Wattleman exchanged looks but it would have been foolish to try to argue or flee. Beyond the wail of moaning Minnie, Bridget thought she could hear the distant drone of aircraft.

She could tell that the warden knew the darkened streets perfectly. He hustled them around corners and down alleys, taking the shortest possible route to the shelter. Then searchlights burst into the air above them, and the three of them froze for a moment. Giant beams, stark and defined, like the pointing fingers of God. And distant crumps as the bombs started to fall. The sky lightened with an orange glow again and again.

The bombs, she thought numbly. *They look different when you're on the ground.* Then the spell was broken, and they were rushing on, fear bitter in their mouths and the sound of the bombs growing louder and louder, the warden hoarsely urging them on. Finally, they rounded a corner, and the warden pointed across the street to an archway.

"There, down the steps to the Tube! Go, go!"

They hurried past the ticket office and followed the sign TO THE TRAINS. After skittering down a short, grubby flight of stairs, they turned and went down another to a larger hall. The sound of the attack outside was blessedly quieter, though they could still hear the explosions. Before them were the wooden escalators, now stationary, with men sitting on them, all looking up to the ceiling.

Bridget and Wattleman paused, gasping for air. She saw that her gloved hands were shaking, and she clenched them shut.

"Getting in a bit late, aren't we?" said the man sitting on the top step of one of the escalators. "Not to worry, safe and sound now. Go on down, missus." He shuffled to one side, and they saw men doing so all the way down the escalator, making a path for them.

"Thank you," said Bridget, and Wattleman nodded in thanks.

"You came at the right time," the man remarked cheerfully. "A couple of more hours, and we'd all have been asleep. There'd have been no shifting us then." By way of illustration, he nodded at a man sleeping on the metal between the handrails of the two escalators, seemingly unconcerned by the knowledge that a few inches beyond his head, the surface sloped down like a ski run. Even the sound of the bombs hadn't woken him. The two Checquy operatives picked their way carefully down the stairs, passing all the people who had staked out their two or three steps to sleep on, and stopped.

From there on, the station was full. Beneath advertisements for Fry's Chocolate and Andrews Liver Salt, people sat or lay on the floor, leaving a careful path down the middle for latecomers to negotiate their way farther into the station. It was startling to see normal Londoners treating this common, utilitarian space as if it were their sitting room. And yet Bridget found it charming, the cozy way that they'd all settled in, taking it for granted and going about the business of their evening.

There were old married couples who'd staked out their spots with a blanket and a couple of pillows and were chatting quietly. There were mothers surrounded by their babies and children knitting together. Schoolboys in shorts and caps sat back to back and read their comics, absorbed in the adventures of Tiger Tim and Pecos Bill. Girls with their hair in ribbons or curling papers read or played little games of tiddlywinks or nursed their dolls. Men in ties smoked and read their papers or talked or snoozed against the walls. Between a machine for weighing oneself and a presumably empty chocolate vending machine, two young women Bridget's age pored over a shared movie-star magazine. She looked at them and felt unimaginably old.

She and Wattleman stopped at a little stand where two women with their hair in kerchiefs were selling buns and tea and bought one of each. The women poured their tea into china cups, and they drank it on the spot, then passed along through the tunnels with their buns, looking for a place to settle down. It was clear that some people had gotten there well in advance to bag their spots. Corners and benches appeared to be prime territory and had apparently been claimed very early on. In fact, from the way that a few people had laid out their little encampments of blankets and pillows, Bridget could believe that some couples and families maintained a permanent presence throughout the day to hold on to a particularly plum spot.

They surveyed one of the platforms, which had a patchwork of blankets on which people sat or lay. A train stood with its doors open, and men and women were settled in there too, sleeping on the seats and the floors. Clearly, this was a favored location—deepest into the tunnel and farthest away from the chaos aboveground.

Finally, the two Checquy agents found a space in a corridor. It was a little gap between two couples who, with only minimal grumbles, squeezed up to let them lean against the wall. Wattleman settled down first after laying his coat on the ground. He held his arm open for Bridget to settle next to him. She paused.

"Darling, we're married," he said. "Besides, there's not much room, and it's better to have someone to lean on."

"Fine," said Bridget and sat down. She sighed as he put his arm around her shoulders. "Just don't get any ideas."

"Why, Mary," he said in a low tone, "I appreciate your self-confidence, but this is the last place I would think of trying anything exciting." Bridget looked around. He had a point. They were sandwiched between two elderly couples, and across the corridor from them, a family with five children was stretched out, all snoring in different keys, except for the oldest, a boy of about nine, who was awake and staring at them fixedly.

"As long as we understand each other, then," she said and snuggled down. She rested her head against his chest.

"He's a nice one, your husband," said the old lady next to her.

"No," said Bridget flatly. "He's awful. But he does have a comfortable chest." The lady laughed in delight.

"Oh, ducky!" said the lady. "That's enough for the moment." Bridget winked at her, then closed her eyes. Even if it was Wattleman, it was still nice to be held. It wasn't something that happened to her a great deal.

All around them was the noise of people settling down to sleep: The rustle of a newspaper being folded; a faint laugh. A baby fussed and was held more closely. Many people breathing—the sound of Londoners together, away from the storm.

She woke up to find Wattleman's arms closed around her, his head resting on hers. His breath was warm on her hair, but not unpleasantly so. She realized that at some point in her sleep, she had turned and closed her arms around him too. She huddled up against his warmth and slowly let herself come to full wakefulness.

Later, when they were both fully awake, she would double-check

with Wattleman to confirm her recollection of the key details—the
objects Simony had sold, the names and address of his suppliers. She'd
always been good at keeping lists in her head, and the Checquy training had only honed that with endless iterations during her youth of
Kim's game and Stalky's game (which was like Kim's game but with
dead cats). Something was tickling the back of her mind, though. A
detail, but she could not remember what.

When she opened her eyes again, she saw that the hallway was less
crowded than it had been. *The all-clear must have sounded,* she thought.
The couples on either side of them were still there, but the family
across from them had left, presumably to enjoy at least a little time in
their own beds. Her arm was cramping, and she shifted, which woke
Wattleman, who closed his arms around her more tightly for a
moment. As he came awake more fully, he loosened them but did not
let go. She did not mind; it was a little cocoon of warmth against the
chill of the corridor, and his hands were not anywhere strategic.

"What time is it?" he asked softly.

"A little after six," she whispered, nodding down the hallway to a
clock on the wall.

"We should move." And she agreed. They released each other and
stood up. Bridget discovered that the arm cramp was in fact a mere
foreshadowing of the agonizing stiffness she'd gotten from sleeping
curled up against the wall. *Still, think of the agony of sleeping on the escalator,* she reminded herself. She stretched and felt terrible—grimy
from sleeping on the floor, and worse. She wanted to scrub her hands,
knowing that there would still be traces of the late Mr. Simony's
blood on them. *I'll have to throw these gloves away,* she decided. Of
course, she'd packed several pairs, but still.

They emerged from the station to find that it was still dark out but
bright enough to find their way back to the hotel. The streets were
already full of people scurrying home from shelters or on the way to
work. They passed a space that, the night before, had been a house.
Now firemen were morosely hosing down the charred, dusty walls
and toppled stones and wood inside. The stink of burned wet books
and wood hung in the air and made Bridget want a bath even more
urgently.

As they walked, Bridget replayed her memories of Mr. Simony. She glossed over the cutting of his throat—it was not the first death she had seen, not even the first she had seen that year—and focused on something the spiv had said at the market: *Yet annuver one wantin' to make a difference, eh?* She narrowed her eyes to think. *Fifteen women,* she mused. *Fifteen women looking to buy magical items.*

"Was there anything to suggest that the three women knew each other?" she asked Wattleman. "Hadgraft and the other two?"

"Not as far as I remember," he said, frowning. "Why?"

"What were they doing with these artifacts? Why did they want them?"

"They thought they were buying magic powers," said Wattleman.

"For what, though?" Wattleman looked at her as if she were asking why people bothered using lavatories when there were perfectly good gutters everywhere. To him, one wanted supernatural power because it was supernatural power. She didn't say anything else but continued to brood as they arrived at the hotel.

"Welcome back, Mr. Polivy, Mrs. Polivy," said the man behind the desk. "We knocked at your door when the air-raid siren went off, then entered, but you were not there."

"We got caught out," said Wattleman easily. "Had to spend the night in a shelter." He gestured at their rumpled and soiled clothes.

"Of course, sir. Mrs. Polivy, there was a telephone call for you yesterday evening. Here is your message." Bridget received the slip and scanned it. She recognized the name given as one of Usha's aliases. The message was vague but contained the word *pressing,* which was code to call immediately, regardless of the hour.

Christ, what now? she thought. "Darling," she said to Wattleman, who preened, "I'm going to return this call. Why don't you go up and get clean?" He agreed, and she stepped over to the phone booth. The message directed her to call them at home, so she did. The phone at Belgrave Square was answered, of course, by Leominster, whose voice gave no impression of being ruffled by the earliness of the hour. There was a wait as he fetched Usha.

"Bridget," said Usha's voice, "you need to come back to the house today."

"Why?" asked Bridget, bewildered. "I'm in the middle of a mission, and I don't think that I could—"

"Gerald telephoned," Usha interrupted. "He's coming to call on you before he leaves to join the RAF. This will be your last chance to see him."

13

Lyn woke up in a pool of sunshine and was happy. Three months into her placement with the Notifications and Reporting section at Apex House, and she'd settled into a pleasant rhythm. She knew how things worked, she was getting to know London better, and she was making friends at the office. She'd found a good local Thai restaurant. She smiled and rolled over in bed to press her cheek against her husband's sleeping back.

There's that too, she thought. So far, Richard and Emma had made four trips to London to visit her for a few days in her small but mind-bogglingly expensive flat in South Kensington, weekend trips that had worked out nicely. Richard liked London; Emma loved it; Skeksis did not seem overly concerned by the presence of new and unfamiliar trees to sniff.

All right, time to get up. She kissed her husband's hair, and he made an affectionate, semiconscious noise before lapsing back into sleep. Emma was sleeping on the couch in the flat's living room, and she didn't even stir when Lyn kissed her goodbye. Skeksis, also on the couch, opened one eye and sleepily licked her hand. They'd all be gone by the time she got home that evening, having caught the train to Newcastle and from there to South Shields. She'd have a video chat with them, though, before Emma went to bed. That had been another important change from her time at the Estate—regaining access to phones and the internet—although she'd found the worldwide web curiously bland when she'd clicked back onto it.

"Once you've seen the viscera of the world, it's hard to place too much importance on the surface stuff." That had been the opinion of Suning, one of her colleagues in Notifications and Reporting, when Lyn had brought up the subject of internet disinterest at an office morning tea. As another recent recruit to the Checquy, Suning was definitely in a position to comment on that subject, although she had no supernatural powers at all. A third-generation Englishwoman of Chinese descent, she had worked in MI6 for four years and was snapped up by the Checquy after witnessing a fellow agent get murdered under mysterious circumstances in China. She'd recounted the details of the whole thing to an enthralled Lyn and three other newbies in the section. Lyn had found that newcomers to the Checquy tended to want to share their incredible experiences as confirmation that it was all actually happening and they weren't insane.

"Alex and I were posted in Nan'an in Fujian Province, observing, uh, cultural shifts," said Suning. It was clear that she was still keeping the secrets of her old organization. "It was a good gig, living in deep cover. One night we were coming back from dinner pretty late," she said. "The street was empty, and then this guy comes walking toward us. Normal guy, normal clothes, talking on his phone. We're passing each other under a streetlight, and the guy just reaches out, grabs Alex by the front of his shirt, swings him around, and throws him to the ground. I'm trying to pull him off Alex, yelling for help, but the guy is pressing Alex down on the road, really pushing on his shoulders, and as I watch, Alex starts sinking down into the tarmac like it's water. And the road pours into his nose and mouth, and he's thrashing, he's drowning."

In a move that seemed entirely reasonable to Lyn, Suning had lost it at that point and, screaming, bolted. A few streets away, she'd made a desperate, babbling call to her MI6 superiors describing what had happened, then continued running. The local constabulary had picked her up half a mile away and made calming noises while they tested her blood alcohol level to find her entirely sober. Regaining her senses, she pleaded with them to take her back to the place where the attack had happened, but when they did, they found only a perfectly smooth road surface with no sign of Alex or his assailant.

Upon being released by the courteous but somewhat amused

Nan'an police, Suning had advised her superiors that she needed to leave the country immediately. She spent the flight back to Britain calming herself down and analyzing the situation. Deciding that telling the truth about what she'd witnessed would certainly cost her her job and possibly her freedom of movement outside the secure wards of a mental hospital, she came up with an alternative story about Alex being murdered via the far more believable method of stabbing. If asked about her original message, she would claim to have been confused and upset at the sight of her colleague's murder. You know, the one that was definitely done with knives.

Through their various twisty channels, however, the Checquy had heard that first, frantically incoherent phone call and been mightily interested.

When Suning arrived at Heathrow, one of her superiors met her at the gate. He drove her straight to MI6 headquarters, where a man and a woman from an unidentified agency were waiting for her. She'd been expecting a debriefing, but before asking her any questions, they played her a recording of that terrified phone call. The interview room echoed with the sound of Suning gasping and weeping as she told about a man doing the impossible. When it ended, Suning was staring down at her hands, unable to make eye contact.

"I think I must have been confused..." began Suning.

"We believe your story completely," said the man. "Not the one about being confused. The one about the man with the road."

"You do?" asked Suning warily. This sounded like a trap.

"Ironically, your road story is much more plausible. Plus, there's precedent for this sort of thing," said the woman.

"You know this sort of thing is going on in China?" she asked carefully.

"Not just China," said the man. As she watched, his thick black hair turned pale, then effervesced into glistening bubbles that floated up and away from his now-bald scalp and popped against the ceiling.

"My God," said Suning softly. "Magic." She smiled. "Real magic."

"I'm glad you feel that way," said the man. As she watched, his hair regrew, darkening across his skull. His eyebrows and eyelashes had also been included in the little display, and replacements were inching their way out of his skin. "It's a handy little party trick."

They spent several hours going over every detail of the event and what might have prompted it. "We never could establish if the manifestation in Nan'an was the work of some sort of Chinese Checquy or a single lone actor," she told Lyn. "Alex was known to go off the reservation sometimes. There were many ways he could have pissed someone off."

It had been exhausting, and Suning was taken aback when they offered her a position with them.

"We're impressed with the way you've handled this situation," said the woman.

"I ran away screaming!" exclaimed Suning incredulously.

"Yes, that was the most sensible way to react," said the man approvingly. "And we're very taken with the swiftness with which you've recovered and composed yourself and with your ability to recall the details. It suggests the sort of resilience that we are always on the lookout for. If you're interested, we could train you so that next time, you won't run away screaming."

So Suning had joined the Checquy Group, undergoing a few months' training, orientation, and psychological evaluation before starting at Notifications and Reporting. She was about two months ahead of Lyn in the timeline of acclimatizing to the Checquy work environment and was often able to provide good advice and perspective on the periodic jolts of incredulity and strangeness that characterized their new place of employment. They'd become good friends, and it was nice to have someone who could agree with her that, yes, this was completely insane.

As a bonus, she was an incredibly good cook, and they'd had a few little newbie dinner parties together. The two of them often offered guidance to the young Pawns who were still getting used to being off Kirrin Island and out in the real world.

It's all working out quite well, really, Lyn thought now as she closed the apartment door behind her. She caught one more glimpse of Emma and Skeksis together on the couch. *I think it's all going to be good.*

Her commute on the Underground was fast. At her station, she was swept up in the flood of civil servants pouring off the train; she allowed it to carry her up the escalators and along the road to Apex House, where she expertly diverted herself out of the flow.

She did not use the imposing main doors but preferred a quiet side entrance. After greeting the security guards by name, she handed in her mobile phone and swiped through the gates easily. When she arrived at the Notifications and Reporting section, it was empty except for Pawn Liam Seager, who was typing away laboriously with two fingers.

"Morning, Liam."

"Good morning, Lynette. Is your family going back today?"

"Yep," said Lyn breezily. "So it's back to macaroni and cheese dinners for me."

Lyn had never come to a firm decision on how she felt about Pawn Seager. He'd been a perfectly pleasant mentor, always very patient about explaining procedures and answering questions. He'd taken her out for lunch on her first Friday and had her over to dinner twice. His wife was pleasant (and completely unaware of what he did), and his house was normal (she *had* glimpsed a set of steer's horns on the wall of his study but hadn't dared ask about them). In short, he was a very nice colleague.

Still, always in the back of her mind were the stories the younger Pawns had told her about him. The idea that the man sitting in the desk facing her was a onetime slayer of Checquy agents who had been found, in some way, unacceptable always left her feeling uneasy.

"Anything interesting so far?" she asked.

"Here's a submission that will be right up your alley," he said, leaning across their desks to hand her a folder.

"Christ, it's not nits, is it?" She was still periodically hailed around the office as "the Delouser," especially when she did something well.

"No, it's criminals and electricity."

She nodded in rueful acceptance.

If a case came up related, even tangentially, to one's abilities, one got assigned to it. It made sense, sort of. Lyn now knew more about electricity and lightning than she'd ever conceived of learning. She'd studied it on Kirrin Island in order to understand how her power worked and aid in developing new applications for it.

At least you didn't have to endure what Georgina did, she told herself, *with her endless taste flash cards.* There had been great stacks of them in Georgina's desk drawers, little pieces of cardboard, each impregnated with a different taste, for her to test herself on.

Lyn was now the section's go-to person for all things electrical, whether it was blackouts across the Midlands or the mysterious case of fourteen toasters across Dunstable all catching fire on the same morning (which, it had turned out, was *not* the result of supernatural malevolence but rather of a dodgy man selling dodgy toasters out of the back of his dodgy van).

Because her husband was a cop, everyone assumed that Lyn was also expert in crime and criminals. She knew a bit more than the average person, admittedly, but that was mainly the result of listening to Richard and his colleagues bitch drunkenly at barbecues. Still, during her time with Notifications and Reporting, she'd learned a great deal more about the British criminal underworld in a very short time.

She opened the folder, which was emblazoned with the crest of the Metropolitan Police Service. The two rather festive lions on it always looked to Lyn as if they were yelling and dancing with beverages in their paws. There were also, in large red letters, various official and alarming warnings about who was authorized to read the contents within and a list of the various acts under which a violator could be prosecuted, extraordinarily renditioned, unbelievably renditioned, dismissed, disappeared, disapparated, dispatched, dispelled, dispersed, disenfranchised, and/or disabled.

She was also warned that readers might become distressed by the contents and that if they felt panic, shortness of breath, or an onset of despair or ennui, they should advise their manager immediately. The terrifying words had long since ceased to mean much to Lyn, who automatically counted the number of pages the file contained, checked the tally against the description on the back of the folder, signed the receipt box on the front, and passed it to Pawn Seager to initial as a witness of her receipt.

"Ta." She stowed her handbag in a drawer and turned on all three of her desktop computers. One allowed her to access the digitized records of the Checquy, one granted her access to various government databases, and the third provided abominably slow access to the normal internet. Each had its own keyboard, which she'd had to label with little sticky notes so she'd remember which was which. It was an intricate little setup, designed to ensure that there was no crossover of information. Each computer's ports were sealed over, none were connected to a printer, and none of them possessed wireless capability. Layers of fiendish little programs prevented her from sending e-mails or saving notes, except on the Checquy computer, which could transmit text only to other Checquy computers.

"Coffee, Liam?" she asked.

"Please."

"White and four, right?" He nodded, and she shuddered a little.

"I'll have you know that white and four kept me going on night watch when I was in Afghanistan," said Seager. "Up until the night it felt like I was going to burst out of my skin."

"I'm not surprised. So why didn't you cut down?"

"That was the night I became Checquy-viable."

"And they're sure it wasn't the coffee?" she said, and he snorted. "Back in a tick."

The kitchenette was equipped with an extremely fancy and intricate coffee machine, but Lyn and Seager shared a little bond in preferring to drink instant coffee while their colleagues looked on in effete horror. As she fetched the milk out of the fridge, she saw that someone had stuck a sign on the door.

To whoever has been taking food out of my blue Tupperware container: <u>KINDLY STOP</u>. It contains tungsten supplements that I need in order to survive. You may want to check with your doctor to confirm that it will not have any effect on you.

She walked back into the office with both cups and nodded a greeting to the Pawns and Retainers who had arrived in the meantime. A quick check of e-mail revealed nothing of interest beyond a picture of a colleague's new puppy, and she turned her attention to the file Seager had given her.

It appeared to be a collection of documents, and she'd caught a glimpse of photos as she thumbed through it. On the top, though, was a little introduction précis, thoughtfully written up by a Metropolitan Police officer, someone senior enough to know that the material would be going off to an unnamed government agency that dealt with the unusual.

Metropolitan Police Service Submission AO-775-PS32

Over the past four weeks, five murders within the Greater London area have caught my attention as potentially being relevant to your office. Originally, given the criminal histories of all the victims, we thought they might be some grotesque, attention-grabbing form of gangland execution — perhaps a move by a new player. In-depth examination of the characteristics and the circumstances, however, have raised questions that cannot be answered. Accordingly, I have forwarded the enclosed notes to your office for your attention and review.

Summary Elements:

Victims: All five victims were male, ages twenty to fifty-five. Each had a criminal history and held a significant position within a gang or criminal organization. (See individual bios for specific affiliations.)

Location: The bodies were found in a variety of different locations, ranging from one victim's own home to a back alley. (Note: City of London Police advise that there have been no similar murders within the square mile of their jurisdiction; see pg. 19.)

Timing: Coroner placed time of death for all victims between ten p.m. and five a.m.

Witnesses: There were no witnesses to any of the murders.

DNA: Only trace DNA recovered. No DNA recovered matched anything on file.

Means of death: Coroner found that all victims were killed by electrocution with no less than one billion volts of electricity.

That's a lot, mused Lyn, taking a sip of coffee. *Like, the equivalent of getting struck by lightning— 1.21 gigawatts.* Given time, she herself could generate that, she absently acknowledged with a small sense of satisfaction, although she'd need a suitably large object to receive the energy. Not a coin or a pen. Her baton, tucked away in her go-kit in the cupboard next to her, could probably hold it.

Distinguishing marks: All of the bodies showed classic signs of death by electrocution (see enclosed reports). Three of the victims possessed burn patterns known as Lichtenberg figures.

Lyn nodded sagely at this. Her studies had taught her all about Lichtenberg figures, also known as "lightning flowers." They were the branching, fernlike marks that could come from electrical discharge. She remembered that when her powers had erupted in her kitchen, she'd watched Lichtenberg figures etching their way into the counter surface from her fingers. They were a useful indication of lightning strike.

Well, that's definitely weird, she thought. *Looking more and more like a Checquy case.*

All are also characterized by the presence of a unique, almost stylized burn mark at the point of electrocution, which we had originally taken to be some form of calling card or trademark of the killer. In criminal circles, such symbols can be used to "sign" a strategic murder so as to send a message. Our sources, however, are unaware of any individual or organization using this symbol, and our research has identified no tool or device that produces such a shape: a double circle — a ring within a ring.

Wait.

Wait, no.

Lyn stared at the words for a moment. *That—that can't be right.*

It can't *be right.*

She looked around at her colleagues, hoping that perhaps it was some sort of grotesque practical joke that she could laugh weakly at. But they were all working away, heads bent over reports. Nobody was looking at her mischievously from the corner of his or her eye. Next to her, Suning was laboriously highlighting passages in a report from the Foreign and Commonwealth Office. Nobody was paying attention to her at all.

This is impossible.

Then her hands were mechanically turning the pages in the dossier until they came to photos from an autopsy. She ignored the feathered burn marks in the flesh, her eyes drawn to the shape that had been seared into the chest of the late Barry "Baztard" Cumming, an old-school villain whose gang out of Islington was notable for brutally offering businesses brutal protection from brutality in exchange for a brutal percentage of the profits. There it was, undeniable: a perfect ring within a ring. The same double circle that she'd seen in photos taken during the trials of her powers on living creatures. It had branded itself on that fireman's palm when he'd picked up the jar in her kitchen. It had charred itself into the thorax of the giant head louse. The unmistakable, unique hallmark of her own supernatural power.

It's exclusive to your power, Dr. Hopkins had said. *Completely distinct.*

Lyn stared down at the photo and felt her breath wheezing in and out of her chest. She pressed her hands to her eyes for a moment and then, with an effort, pulled them down and forced herself to sit back in her chair. Her hands were clenching and unclenching.

This is ridiculous. This is impossible.

Except that the impossible happened every day, and she was surrounded by people who policed it. People who would turn on her immediately if they realized what she had just realized. That circle-within-a-circle mark was as damning as her fingerprints on a murder weapon.

In fact, if someone else on the team had been given that file, Lyn would at that very moment probably have been utterly bewildered as she was taken into custody by armed guards. If, that is, they hadn't simply sedated her without any warning.

They'd place me in a secure facility for questioning, she thought. *If not here, then in Scotland, at Gallows Keep.*

And then what? A trial? Her legal chatelaine, Mrs. Goodman, had explained that Pawns of the Checquy occupied a unique legal area when it came to crime and punishment. For minor infractions, Pawns were subject to the same fines and penalties as everyone else—there was no getting out of a speeding charge or a parking ticket just because your ring fingers could melt through plastic. If a crime was committed that bore the potential of a jail sentence, then things got trickier. Depending on the circumstances, the Checquy Court would step in, although you might very well end up wishing they hadn't.

There was one transgression, though, that bypassed the civilian courts immediately: the misuse of one's supernatural abilities. If you were accused of using your gifts for personal gain or in the commission of a crime, you were brought before the Court, which appointed a council of five judges drawn from all levels of the Checquy. The judges were empowered to investigate and were meticulous in finding the truth. However, it was not a case of "innocent until proven guilty," but "a threat until proven innocent." Which meant that until your innocence had been fully established, you would be in a situation coyly referred to, for reasons no one was quite certain of, as "backgammon leave."

Backgammon leave meant living in a quite comfortable, charming cottage with a garden within a heavily fortified installation whose location was undisclosed but rumored to be as pleasant as it was remote. It meant you couldn't go anywhere or see anyone other than the other backgammoners and the guards. You weren't allowed to work, although you continued to receive a reduced salary, which you couldn't spend anyway. Some people had been on backgammon leave for years before proof of innocence (or guilt) was established.

And that proof had to be convincing. The science-defying abilities of powered Checquy personnel meant that "reasonable doubt" was as pointless a benchmark as slicing open a weasel and looking through its entrails for an answer.

Of course, the whole thing represented a grotesque violation of due process, but it was underpinned by the knowledge that a rogue Pawn put everyone at risk. The government was inevitably uneasy about the idea of people wandering around with inexplicable and, in some cases, world-altering abilities. There was always the possibility that one criminal Pawn would be the thin end of the wedge that brought down everyone else. All of this meant that the judges were almost never inclined to be merciful, and no one ever got the benefit of the doubt. As Star Chambers went, it was the equivalent of a supernova.

Matters were simplified because of all the rights that Pawns did not have—the rights that Lyn had briskly signed away that night at the hospital.

If she were found guilty, then Emma and Richard would be told by a sober colleague that she'd been killed in a tragic car accident. Checquy representatives would be seen to grieve at her funeral; her body would be incinerated (after the world's most in-depth autopsy); and Richard would be given an urn that did not contain her ashes but rather those of whatever John Doe the Checquy could get its hands on or, failing that, whatever corpses the Battersea Dogs and Cats Home were able to spare. Her actual ashes would be divided and scattered at different points around the British Isles. The Checquy would write up her history as a rogue Pawn who had abused her powers, and the report would be pored over by future students at the Estate. Her family would receive her pension (plus any funds from her reduced backgammon-leave wages), and her daughter would grow up without her.

This was not panicked presumption. All of these facts Lyn had learned during her months of induction at the Estate, and they now re-presented themselves for her consideration. At the same time, almost every instinct in her body and brain were screaming, *Run, you moron!*

For a moment, she was that small feral child again, trapped in an incomprehensible, unyielding, alien system, and all she wanted was to get away. If she closed her eyes, she could visualize perfectly the room in the police station, the hard bench, the bright lights, and the large people bustling about.

This is just childhood trauma resurfacing, she told herself firmly. *You will sit, you will be calm, and you will find the evidence that this was not you. The evidence that has to exist.*

She opened her handbag and, despite her determination to maintain control, found herself clawing through her personal detritus. Because mobile phones were not permitted in Apex House, she was obliged to keep a physical appointment diary. *What are the dates of those deaths? If I can show what I was doing on those dates, if Richard and Emma were down or if I was with friends, I can prove it wasn't me.* She practically tore the book in half opening it and scrabbled frantically to see what she had been doing on the date of the first murder, which had been just under four weeks ago.

It was blank.

No *R and E staying* noted down with a little heart scrawled next to it. No dinner dates with colleagues. Not even a movie. She couldn't specifically remember the day. It had presumably been just an ordinary Thursday: she'd gone to work, gone home, and chilled quietly by herself. With no witnesses.

I didn't do it. I didn't do it! she wanted to scream so that they would believe her and assure her that of course they knew she was innocent. *All I need is an alibi for one of the days,* she told herself. *Just one day.*

The second day was the same as the first—no appointments, no drinks dates, no family visits. So was the third. The fourth she'd been home sick with a cold and spent the day in bed with no visitors. The fifth was another day without an alibi.

"No," she said softly. "No, no, no."

She had the appalling, stomach-turning sensation of the entire world falling away around her, as if someone had dimmed the houselights on reality and, in a limitless void with no sound or color or motion, she was alone with the damning dossier and her appointment diary. The diary's absolute failure to provide her with an alibi seemed like the worst kind of betrayal. It sat there smugly; if it had had arms, they would have been folded, and if it had had eyes, it would have been rolling them. *What?* it seemed to say. *I didn't do anything. Why are you looking at me?*

"Lynette?" She dragged her gaze up from her Judas Iscariot of an appointment diary to see Pawn Seager looking across at her. "Is everything all right?"

"Uh...yes," she said weakly, doing her level best not to look frightened. *Can he smell the situation? Can he sense my fear? Surely he can hear my heart beating; it's throwing itself around in my chest. I think I'm going to throw it up.* She smiled a smile that felt incredibly forced. Behind her teeth, curdling in her throat, she could hear a moan building up.

They told me at the Estate that I'm the only one whose power makes that shape, she thought again. Suddenly, she was desperate for something that might disprove that claim and put a chink in the argument against her. She turned to her computer and brought up the database that contained carefully collated records of supernatural history.

A search for *electricity* brought up scores of entries dating back centuries. Too many to look through. *You need to narrow down the search,* she thought. *You're a trained librarian.*

A search for *double ring* and *electricity* brought up her own entry—a small dossier on her abilities. But nothing else.

A search for *circle* and *electricity* brought up her own entry again, and nothing else.

Again and again, she tried, looking for different combinations of terms that might yield additional results. She expanded her search beyond the past fifteen years, broadened the parameters. She reviewed the files on electrically talented people in the Checquy. She'd already met the graphic designer at the Rookery who could shoot bolts of electricity, but she hadn't been aware of the man in the mail room who was able to redirect lightning.

Frantic, she turned to electricity-related manifestations outside the Checquy. She read about a boatbuilder who had lived in the Lake District and who, in 1929, had begun to emit a crackling electrical field from the crown of his head that shocked everyone around him into insensibility. After running in a state of escalating terror up the main street of the village of Ravenglass, panicked by the continuous electrical storm that emanated from his head and the people collapsing around him, he was shot dead by the local justice of the peace (who was *not* with the Checquy, but who happened to be there and have a shotgun in his office so that he could go hunting after work).

In the 1990s, some strange presence had roamed through the wires of the British power grid, identifiable only by the sound of whalelike singing vibrating through the walls and the surges it caused—surges that had erupted out of light fixtures and power sockets to start intense electrical fires. The Checquy had been able to affect the entity only by frantically cutting power lines across the nation, a strategy that had caused chaos and prompted a great deal of displeasure from the Prime Minister. The being had eventually been cornered in a transformer in

Hartlepool that was then disconnected and transported to a Checquy facility for, as it turned out, an entirely unproductive examination.

Six years ago, the Checquy had been called in to deal with a flock of sheep in Oxfordshire who, while grazing peacefully, had been known to summon electrical storms to drive off predators. The cautious approach of a battalion of Pawns had triggered the flock's powers, and in moments, a tempest had manifested out of absolutely clear sky above the Vale of the White Horse. A deluge of rain and a series of lightning strikes had hammered the Checquy warriors while the sheep continued to graze, completely unconcerned, in a ring of clear weather. Three Pawns had been killed before the flock was reached and tranquilized. The animals were removed to the far north of Scotland, where they lived very calm lives, and their electricity-resistant wool was used to knit protective sweaters that were carefully stored in Checquy armories.

Presumably alongside the unbreakable glass knives, Lyn thought absently.

As varied as they were, none of these manifestations involved any distinguishing mark like the double ring. She closed her eyes.

There is no proof that it wasn't me and lots of evidence that it must have been me.

An ugly thought occurred to her. *Maybe it* was *me. Maybe I'm insane, and I've been going about in my sleep killing criminals like some somnambulant vigilante.*

There's no other explanation.

No. Fuck that.

She couldn't say it was impossible—the past few months had demonstrated that *nothing* was impossible—but it was so convoluted and unlikely that she found herself dismissing it. *There would have been clues that something odd was going on,* she thought. *Wouldn't I have woken up in my clothes? Or been tired from wandering around the city all night killing people?* But none of these things had happened. She felt a sense of relief as she unpacked all this in her head. *I did not do this.*

If it's not me, then it must be someone else.

But would the Checquy accept that?

I wouldn't if I were them. They would look at all the evidence that pointed toward her. They would look for evidence that it wasn't her and not find any. They would look at her past, at her psychological evaluations from the Estate. She was under no illusions about what they would see. A woman who came from a broken background, practically feral, with a deeply ingrained mistrust of "the system."

A woman whom it would be much safer to keep on backgammon leave until more evidence came to hand. *If it ever does.* She could all too easily imagine spending the rest of her life drifting away in a garden in a prison camp while the bureaucracy desultorily tried to come to a decision.

Unacceptable. You cannot rely on the system working it out right.

And if the fierce instincts from her childhood and the intellectual calculation of her present self were in agreement about the situation, it was hard to argue with them both.

So what do I do?

As a child, whenever she'd run away, be it from the police, a foster home, or a group house, it had been with no forethought, no idea of where she was headed. She had simply taken any opportunity to bolt, to get away. Now, it took all of her self-discipline to remain calm and sit in that room, plotting out what she would do, while around her the Pawns and Retainers of the Checquy went on with their day as if the bottom had not fallen out of the world—her colleagues, who had suddenly and unknowingly become her adversaries, her would-be jailers.

You'll need a place to stay. You'll need measures to evade the Checquy. You'll need leads to follow.

"What are your thoughts on that police submission?" asked Pawn Seager suddenly, and Lyn looked up at him, wide-eyed.

"It's suspicious," she said in a measured tone. "I'm just checking some context info before I pass it along." He nodded and turned back to his work. She returned to her task, memorizing as much as she could of the dossiers and slotting the details into her understanding of the London criminal scene. She brought up additional files, memorized key names, and tried desperately to think of what else she might need to know.

Are you really going to do this? she asked herself. *And what if there's another murder? Another murder that might exonerate you?*

What if there isn't? she asked back. She could not trust the Checquy. The evidence was too damning, and she suspected that the recentness of her powers' manifestation would count against her. She hadn't had the years of indoctrination that others had.

Finally, she was done. Or at least as done as she could be.

The next step will damn you, she told herself. *Nothing makes you look guiltier than fleeing.* She contemplated her desk, the neatly stacked files, her official (plain white) Checquy coffee mug, the little terrarium of ferns she'd bought at a florist near her flat. It all represented a comforting stability. She looked at the picture of Emma and Richard, and it nearly undid her.

But there are no visitors' hours at Gallows Keep or for those on backgammon leave.

No, she decided. *I won't have that.*

Deliberately and with cautious calm, she tidied up the incriminating file and put it in her out tray under several other folders that had already been processed. Then she swiveled in her chair and opened the cupboard that contained her go-kit.

"Ed? I'm sorry to bother you, but I suddenly don't feel very well." Pawn Moncrieff looked up at her from his desk, which was covered in files.

"I'm sorry to hear that, Lyn. You *do* look a bit peaky, I must say."

"I think I'm going to go home, if that's okay with you. A day or two in bed should set me right."

"Yes, go, go," he said. "We're not swamped at the moment. Get some rest, stay hydrated, keep us posted."

"Thanks." She smiled weakly. She walked out of his little office and headed directly for the exit. Out of the corner of her eye, she could see that Pawn Seager was watching her, but he didn't say anything. She tensed at the threshold. Could he see the money and the baton in her handbag?

He doesn't know you're leaving for the day, she told herself. *As far as Seager knows, you're going out for coffee or to pay a bill or to pick up the dry cleaning. He'll have no reason to look for that file.* If she were really going home sick, she would have handed custody of the file back to Seager, but for a few hours' absence, it wasn't necessary. Ed had assumed she'd taken the appropriate steps; she'd built up a reputation in the section as being conscientious and meticulous. *The mystique of the librarian,* she thought tightly. So an advantageous web of misunderstanding and assumption lay around her departure. *When Seager does realize that I've gone for the day, it should take him a little time to find the file.*

And then he'll need to read it.

And then he'll need to put two and two together.

And then I don't know what will happen. Or how long I've got.

Lyn walked briskly down the halls. Every moment, she expected a shout from behind her, at which point everyone in the building would become her enemy. *And what will I do then?* She felt the weight of her baton in her handbag. *Will I use my powers on my comrades? Will I try to fight my way out?*

No, she decided. She could run from an army, but she wouldn't try to fight one. Just by taking the baton and the money, she'd already incriminated herself, but she wouldn't break her oath to the Checquy. No matter what happened, at least *she'd* know she'd been true. But no shout came. She rode down in the lift and passed through the little side lobby that she favored, swiping her pass and waving to the security guards.

The outside air was cool on her cheeks. The world seemed impossibly big.

"Pawn Binns!" Lyn looked back and her stomach flipped over. One of the security guards had followed her out onto the path.

They saw it already! she thought in disbelief. *They found the file! I didn't even get as far as the street.* She tried to say something, but her mouth wouldn't work.

"You forgot your phone!"

"Oh! Thank you!" She gasped. "I don't know where my head was at." She laughed weakly. He smiled, and she scribbled her signature of receipt on the clipboard. "Thanks a lot." He turned to go back into the building, and she walked with forced ease out into the street, then turned toward the nearest Tube station. Without breaking stride, she dropped her phone into a rubbish bin.

★   ★   ★

"What do you know about the Grafters?" Suning had asked as she poured them another glass of wine. It had been Friday after work, and Suning had invited Lyn over for dinner—a night that, unfortunately, would prove *not* to be one on which a key member of the London criminal community was murdered. Lyn didn't stay over, but Suning would certainly have testified that they'd both drunk too much for Lyn to have gone out a-stalking later.

"I got a thumbnail sketch at the Estate," said Lyn. She was lounging on the floor of Suning's apartment, intently spreading Brie on a cracker. "Belgian scientists, right? They signed on with the Checquy recently, and they're supernaturally gifted at medicine?"

"Nothing supernatural about them," corrected Suning. "Which is actually scarier. They're pure science. Supposedly, anyone could do it, if that person had the smarts and the knowledge."

"I'm supposed to take a class on them later." Lyn shrugged. "Maybe a little more wine in the glass, thanks." It had been a bitch of a week.

"It's not just medicine either," said Suning. "They change themselves, but not through your Checquy-style magic."

"If they tried to change themselves with my style of Checquy magic, they'd end up as little charcoal briquettes," remarked Lyn.

"They work with existing biology," said Suning. "If there's a human trait—hell, if there's an animal trait—they'll have someone who's had that trait jacked up to fifty on a scale of one to five." She shook her head.

"Oh, wait!" exclaimed Lyn. "I met one of them! Lovely girl. Great boots. She sliced me open to see what my powers would do."

"I'm not sure those powers are worth it," said Suning, shaking her head. "Sometimes I just find the whole idea of powers unbelievably creepy."

"Hey, I find it creepy, and I'm one of them," said Lyn with feeling, accepting the wine.

If there's a human trait—hell, if there's an animal trait—they'll have someone who's got that trait jacked up to fifty on a scale of one to five.

The words echoed in Lyn's mind.

So how do I lose one of these ultra-trackers? she thought as she walked briskly down the street away from Apex House. Before she'd departed the office, a quick search of the Checquy database for *tracking* had yielded four London-based operatives. One of them was a Pawn who did something Lyn didn't understand with Kirlian auras, but since he'd been sent to New Zealand temporarily, she was not going to worry about him. There was a woman in the Barghest commandos who could actually see back through time to follow someone's movements, but her power had limited range. The other two, however, were Grafters who'd had their smell and taste augmented to an unbelievable extent. They could follow spoor that would have left a bloodhound shrugging its shoulders.

Visions of prison movies flickered through her head. *Cool Hand Luke. The Shawshank Redemption.* Scattering chili powder in her wake would only draw attention; she couldn't swim the Thames, and wading down a stream in London, if she could find one, would probably create more problems than it solved. *So use a different kind of river,* she thought. The Underground seemed like much the best option. It held a mass of humanity with their own scents (some of them extremely potent) to help fog hers, and the trains would provide abrupt cutoffs in the trail as they whisked her away from station to station.

Will that be enough, though? She couldn't see how the Grafter trackers could possibly trace her scent through the Underground, but she was aware of all the security cameras in London. If the Checquy tracked her to a station, then they could follow her progress via security footage. *I'll need to mix it up,* she decided. Walk between stations, move erratically—anything that might delay their progress and buy herself time. *I'll also need to change my appearance,* she thought. *Different clothes, different...what? Hair? A wig?* And all of that would take money. The cash from her go-kit, which had seemed an outrageous amount when she'd been handed it, was now looking like not nearly enough.

She stopped at the first ATM she came to and withdrew the maximum daily amount that her two cards would allow. It didn't seem like that much, and she sighed. The bank cards could definitely not be risked again. Reluctantly, she bent them back and forth in her hands until she could tear them in half. The same would go for her Oyster card as soon as it got her to Oxford Street. From there, once she'd made some strategic purchases, she'd walk among the thousands of shoppers to Tottenham Court Road station, where she'd pay cash for a day travel card.

A stop by a pharmacist yielded a large pair of sunglasses and a pair of thick-rimmed blue-light glasses that changed the look of her face. Shops on Oxford Street provided her with jeans, fresh running shoes, a T-shirt, and a hoodie, all of which she wore out of the store. Her rolled-up suit and blouse were placed in a new backpack along with her work heels and a sweater she'd bought to change into. *Give yourself as many options as possible, because you've left all your other possessions behind.* Her hair was tucked up in a knit hat she had bought from a souvenir shop.

On each of her fingers was a ring that she'd bought from a stall. They were plain and looked exactly as cheap as they were, but they'd hold a charge.

Always seek out the crowds, she decided. The most packed train cars, the busiest places. Let the smell and particulates of other people make the trail all the more difficult for the Checquy and the Grafters to track her.

From Tottenham Court Road, she took the Tube to Covent Garden and walked amongst the tourists. From there, she walked briskly to Trafalgar Square. On the way, she stepped into an alley, looked around for security cameras, then swapped the glasses for the sunglasses, donned the new sweater, and traded the knit hat for a cheap baseball cap.

Trafalgar Square was not as busy as it could have been, but a goodly number of school groups were wandering around gaping at Nelson's Column, taking photos of the gleaming copper and glass stag sculpture that was currently occupying the fourth plinth, and screaming whenever the horde of pigeons got too enthusiastic about the possibility of bread crumbs. Lyn forced herself to move through the busiest parts of crowds. She pushed between people, apologized, then did it again. A swarm of schoolchildren engulfed her, and she allowed herself to go along with it.

All the while, she feared that the Checquy were watching her, that they were standing all around her, amusedly observing her novice attempts at spy craft. They would know her strategies—they'd taught her them, for God's sake. She was constantly glancing around, trying not to be obvious about it, for anyone looking at her intently. Or maybe it would be something less mundane. Would one of the children in the crowd reach out, grab her, and twist her away through a fold in space to a holding cell in Scotland? Would a pigeon land on her shoulder and whisper in her ear that there were snipers aiming at her head and that she should sit down on a bench and wait for further instructions? Would she just fall down dead with a heart attack? The Checquy was capable of all those things, she knew.

Would they be following her to see where she'd go? Or were they just waiting until she was alone so they could seize her without inconvenient witnesses?

It would just be adding insult to injury if I thought I'd gotten away and it turned out the hat I'm wearing was actually someone from the Checquy's tech-support section. That was enough to make her want to rip off the hat and microwave it.

Or had the police already been alerted? A pair of constables were standing by the stairs to the National Gallery. They appeared to be scanning the crowd, but who knew? One of the cops, feeling her gaze, turned and looked at her suspiciously.

Marvelous. I don't need the Checquy to track me, I can just get law enforcement interested by acting really suspicious and paranoid. Lyn nodded to the cop, smiled what felt like the world's least convincing smile, and turned away. She walked across the street and down the steps to Charing Cross station. The next train was another break in her trail, and she took a circuitous route to the busiest of London's stations: Waterloo.

Thankfully, it was absolutely packed with people. Apparently there had been a train breakdown on some crucial central juncture, which resulted in lots of people wandering around making vexed noises. Lyn moved from the Underground station to the railway terminus and weaved her way carefully through the disgruntled crowds. She took a seat at the back of a packed café and ordered a sandwich and some soup.

And breathe.

She found herself slumping at the table. Her shoulders ached, and she realized that she'd been hunching them defensively for the entire duration of her escape. She kneaded the throbbing muscles and let her mind unclench a little as well. Ever since she'd walked out of Apex House, her mind had been focused solely on the task of bewildering any hypothetical Checquy trackers, of buying herself time. Everything beyond that had been nebulous. There were still lots of questions as to what exactly she intended to do, and concern about her family also hung in the back of her mind, but she didn't allow herself to dwell on that. If she started thinking about Richard and Emma, she'd break. She didn't have that luxury. Right now, it was time to deal with her most immediate needs. And foremost in her mind was the question of where she was going to sleep that night.

When she was doing her frantic research at Apex House, Lyn had been painfully aware that the Checquy would be able to see her computer history. When they realized that she'd bolted, they would review everything she'd ever done on any of her computers. That she had looked up the Checquy's trackers would clearly show that she'd expected to be hunted. Who knew what they might read into her hurried queries on organized crime in London? It might give them pause; they might wonder why she had suddenly looked up people whom she had apparently killed. Or they could see it as a message to them, a rogue Pawn gloating. Still, that research had been necessary. She could not have gotten that information anywhere else, and she needed it for her still-vague plans. But she had not dared look online for any sort of accommodation.

Even through her haste, as she'd committed information about London's criminal ecosystem to memory, there had been the question *Where can I go for a bed and a shower that won't register me in some government-accessible system?* Her budget was not large, although the cash in her backpack and her handbag felt heavy. Most hotels would require identification and a credit card, but though she had snagged her Checquy-provided fake IDs, she knew using them would be her worst possible move.

And then an idea had come to her, drawn from something she'd heard her husband and his colleagues talking about. It could be just the thing she was looking for. She'd pursue the possibility once she'd had a vitally necessary sandwich and cup of tea.

"I need your help, please." The woman in the Waterloo station information booth looked at her, startled by the urgency in her tone.

"What is it, love? Where are you going?"

"I'm not catching a train. I need directions to a women's refuge."

14

"Henry? *Henry! Wattleman!*" Bridget pounded on the bathroom door. It opened and, of course, Wattleman was wearing only a towel. To her relief, he was not wet.

"What is it?" he asked. "What's happened?"

"Nothing, I need to take the first bath, please." She could see the tension ooze away from his face, replaced by his usual smug amusement.

"Oh? Suddenly in a hurry?"

"Yes."

"Only I've already drawn the bath and gotten undressed." He leaned back against the doorjamb, his body blocking the door.

"Yes, I see that. But I need to meet someone downstairs very shortly, and I want to wash off the rind of the Underground." *And of you.*

"So soon? It might be quicker if you joined me." He smiled languidly.

Oh, for God's sake. "Forget it," she snapped. "I'll go down like this."

"Oh, come now, we could wash each other's backs, and then you could go down to the lobby smelling sweet and not looking like someone who spent the night sleeping in the Underground."

"It is perfectly respectable to spend the night sleeping in the Underground," said Bridget. "*Far* more respectable than taking a bath with you would be."

"And you're worried about what people would think?"

"No, I'm worried about what *I* would think. And about the very likely possibility that I'd throw up in the bath," said Bridget.

"From self-loathing?" He smiled. "It's overrated."

"From all sorts of loathing," she said darkly.

"And who are you meeting, Mangan?" he asked. "Is this a briefing I should be present for?"

"Absolutely not," said Bridget. He didn't say anything. "It's...a gentleman friend."

"Not the one going off to war?"

"The very same," she said.

"But we are on a covert, off-the-books mission," Wattleman said, his eyes wide. "How does he know where to find us?"

"He knows where to find *me* because he called Lady Carmichael's house, and when he gets there, Usha will send him here. This will be my last chance to say goodbye. So, please, may I take the bathroom first?"

"Well, far be it from me to stand in the way of two young lovers," he said. "By all means, you should take the bathroom first. I'm sure your young man would prefer it if you washed. You *do* smell rather like the public." He stood aside and, with a swooping bow, gestured for her to enter. The world was merciful enough not to have his towel fall off while he did so, and she shut the door firmly behind her.

Bridget sat in the bath, held her knees, and replayed the telephone conversation she'd had with Usha. They'd agreed that when Gerald arrived at the Carmichael house, Usha would tell him that Bridget was in the city and that he should meet her in the teashop next to the Brentley Hotel.

And then the full weight of the situation had hit Bridget like a fist to the stomach.

"What am I going to do, Usha?" she had asked shakily. She felt as if she might burst into tears. "What am I going to say to him? How do I leave it between us?"

"Do you understand why he's going off to war?" asked Usha.

"Yes," said Bridget.

"Do you hate him for doing it?"

"No," said Bridget.

"Bridget?"

"Hm?"

"Do you love him?"

"I do," said Bridget, and here she broke down. "I really do." *And I'm going to lose him!* She sagged in the phone booth, her knees weak.

"Then you tell him those three things. I've never been in love, but those are the things that I would need to know in his situation. Those are the things that I would carry with me."

"And after that?" said Bridget weakly.

"He'll have things to say. Let him say them," Usha advised. "That's the best gift you can give him."

Bridget waited in the teashop and resisted the urge to call the Carmichael house to confirm that, yes, Gerald had shown up at the house and, yes, they had told him where to go. She smoothed her skirt and patted her hair, then she did it again, and she would have done it a third time if he hadn't suddenly been walking in the door in his blue RAF uniform, looking so handsome that Bridget actually gasped a little. He glanced around, saw her, and smiled.

"Hello, Gerald," she said. She stood up. "You look very dashing."

"Thank you," he said. "It doesn't feel quite like my own body. I catch a glimpse of my trousers and feel the need to salute them. Haven't worn a uniform since Harrow. I'd forgotten how they rather bully you into having better posture."

"Thank you for coming here. Shall we sit?" They settled themselves next to each other at the little table, then a waitress bustled up to take their orders, so it was a couple of minutes before they could actually talk. "I'm sorry that you've had to run around," Bridget said finally.

"Not at all. I left some books for you at the house." He hesitated. "Quite a few books, actually, and some records. So, this way you don't need to worry about hauling them home. And it was good to get the chance to see Mrs. Carmichael and Miss Khorana and Miss Verrall. They were all very kind." He paused. "Is Miss Verrall quite all right? She looked rather subdued."

She must have looked utterly exhausted, thought Bridget. "I know there's a lot going on at Mrs. Carmichael's office," she said carefully. "They're both working very long hours."

"Ah, of course," he said.

"Gerald, how long do we have before you have to go?"

He checked his watch. "About an hour, if I'm to get to the station in time for my train," he said. "And I'm afraid that I really must catch that train."

"Or there will be dire consequences for the war effort, I'm sure," she said.

"Of course, they're absolutely depending on me. I understand Hitler himself has heard that I've joined up, and he's reconsidering everything."

She smiled, and there was a long delicious moment in which they looked at each other and were comfortable being silent together. Then a voice came from behind Bridget.

"Good Lord! It's Bridget Mangan, isn't it? Bridget!"

Bridget closed her eyes for a moment. *I may have to kill him right here in the goddamn teashop,* she thought, then turned in her seat to look at Wattleman, who was grinning. He was dressed in his habitual natty clothes with—her eyes darted down for a moment—yes, with the cuffs on his trousers. His hair was brilliantined to within an inch of its life.

"Oh, heavens!" she exclaimed, getting up from her seat. Gerald also stood. "What are you doing here?" Her tone was as pleasant and surprised as she could make it, but if she'd had the power, she'd have crushed him with her gaze.

"I'm just in town for a few days on business," he said. "How wonderful to run into you."

"It's marvelous to see you." *Now piss right off.* His grin broadened.

"But I do beg your pardon, I'm interrupting." And yet he did not go away. Instead, there was an increasingly uncomfortable silence in which he clearly expected to be introduced.

"Not at all," Bridget said finally. "Gerald Nash, this is Mr., um..." She paused for a second, trying to figure out how to introduce him. If they were at Lady Carmichael's, she'd have introduced him as himself, but they were undercover and now he'd suggested that he was from out of town, so...she flailed for a few horrible moments. "Cock...ering...ham." She cringed, but apart from a slightly raised eyebrow, Wattleman did not react.

"Crosbie Cockeringham, out of Devonshire," he said, stepping forward and shaking Gerald's hand. "Pleasure to meet you."

"Good to meet you," said Gerald. Bridget regarded the two of them. Even in his uniform, Gerald looked awfully young and small next to the tall and dapper Wattleman. It seemed impossible that he was going off to war. And now he appeared uncertain as he looked up at the smirking Pawn.

"And how do you know Bridget?" asked Gerald.

"Hmm? Oh, we've known each other for years, played together as children. Practically grew up together, didn't we?"

"You're six years older than me," Bridget said flatly.

"Oh, yes, she was always running after my brothers and me," he said lightly. "Always harum-scarum in a rather grubby pinafore, trying to steal a kiss." He laughed. "And now, well, grown up into a lovely young lady." He put his hand on her shoulder, and Bridget could see Gerald's eyes on it. "Although still a little harum-scarum. Why, just last summer, she fell into the pond, and I had to go in and rescue her!" He laughed ruefully. "That was a picnic to remember, eh, Bridget?" She made some sort of weak, mildly amused noise, painfully aware that his hand was still on her shoulder. She was giving mildly serious thought to grabbing it and flipping him over her shoulder into the next table.

"And I see you're in uniform, Mr. Nash."

"Gerald has enlisted with the Royal Air Force," Bridget said.

"Yes, the blue rather gave it away," Wattleman said. "Well done, sir, I must say. How long have you been with the RAF?"

"Only the very shortest of times," Gerald said. "I'm off to commence training today."

"You're a credit to the nation." He took his hand off Bridget's shoulder. "I wish you the very best of luck. I must be off. I have several meetings. They will take up all of my morning, I should expect." He said this with a peculiar emphasis; Bridget looking at him through slitted eyes. He shook Gerald's hand. "Do take care up there, eh?"

"I shall. Thank you."

"Good to see you, uh, Crosbie," Bridget said. She was braced for him to swoop in and kiss her, but instead Wattleman stuck out his hand. She took it and felt him pass her something. He raised his eyebrows, winked, and strode out of the café. *Did he even buy anything? Or did he just come in to torture me?* She shot a look into her palm and saw that he had given her what she recognized as a standard Checquy-issue condom in its standard unmarked wrapper.

Pig!

"Your friend is very handsome," Gerald said levelly.

"What?" asked Bridget, still distracted by what she was holding. Flushing, she thrust it into her purse.

"He rescued you from a pond?"

"He's exaggerating," Bridget said.

"Ah," said Gerald. He nodded a little nod. "By how much?"

"I know how to swim. I was not in any danger of drowning."

"But you and he were together in a pond. Did he carry you out?"

"Are you jealous?" she asked, a little pleased despite herself.

"I'm curious. I've never heard this pond story."

"It's not one of my favorite anecdotes. No one sounds impressive for falling into a pond."

"It sounds adorable. With a charming rescue."

"It wasn't." She took a breath. "I really don't want to waste this time talking about a pond." *Especially since it didn't actually happen.* "Let's sit down." They did. She looked at him, and to her horror, she could feel her eyes getting a little hot and wet. She blinked furiously. "I have three things to say to you. If I don't say them right now, I'm afraid I won't say them."

"All right, and then I have three things to say to you."

"Are you making fun of me?" she asked.

"No, three happens to be the number of things I have to say as well."

"Well, let me go first, please." He nodded, and she took both his hands in hers. She'd worn silk gloves, the softest she owned.

"I understand why you're going off to the war," she said. "When we last spoke, I was upset, and I think I gave the impression that I thought you were wrong to enlist, that I didn't see why you should do it. But I really do understand, I know why it's important, and that's the first thing I have to tell you. I didn't want you thinking that I was the kind of person who wouldn't see that." He smiled and nodded.

"And the second thing I have to tell you is that I don't hate you for doing this." Their eyes were locked on each other's.

And now her eyes were streaming and he had to keep blinking. He took a deep breath and pressed his lips tightly together. "Thank you, Bridget," he said. "Thank you for that, it means everything to me."

"I'm glad, because the last thing I have to say is that I love you, Gerald." She tightened her hands on his. She'd never said it before. "I love you."

Take that with you, she thought, so glad that she'd said it. *No matter what happens, no matter what you have to face, know that you're loved.*

"*I* love *you*, Bridget. That's the first thing I had to say." He leaned forward and kissed her.

It was their first kiss, and a small part of Bridget's mind was astounded at how the rest of the world went completely away. The vast part of her mind, though, was not aware of anything but the sensation and the delight of kissing and being kissed by the man she loved. She brought her arms up around his neck and held him tightly. She thought she could feel their hearts beating together.

Eventually, reluctantly, they had to stop, mainly because the waitresses were making disapproving clucking noises.

"Whatever the two other things you have to say are, that will be difficult to surpass," she said breathlessly.

"You're actually not the first person I told it to. I spoke to my parents."

"I'm guessing you didn't tell them in exactly the same way?"

He snorted a laugh. "No indeed," he said. "But I told them how I felt about you."

"Oh," said Bridget, suddenly afraid.

"They weren't surprised."

She smiled weakly. "How did they take it?" she asked.

"They did have some concerns. They would be happy for me to 'go a-courting,' as my father rather cringe-inducingly put it. They would give us their blessing. But there's a war. And I'm going to be a pilot."

"Did they support your enlisting?"

"They actually weren't terribly surprised about that either," said Gerald. "I've been mulling it over for a while, and apparently I'm quite transparent. But it was still difficult for them to hear." He looked down at his hands for a moment. "My mother told me something I never knew, that she'd lost a fiancé in the Great War." Bridget nodded but didn't dare say anything. "I asked her if being engaged to him had made the loss of him easier or harder, and she said both.

"But that was a different kind of war. Now it's not a case of my going off to fight and you staying behind safe. This country is not safe, this city is not safe. The war is here." He clenched his hands. "I love you, Bridget, more than anything." His mouth twisted with emotion. "But I won't ask you to marry me, not as we are, not as the world is."

I would say yes! she thought in agony. *I would say yes to you!* She wanted to scream it out, but she had to let him speak his piece.

"I said it before. The world is utter madness now. A boy I went to school with was killed yesterday when a bomb fell in his back garden. On the way here, I walked past the hotel I stayed in the last time I came to see you, and it's a smoking ruin. Either one of us could die today or tomorrow. And I won't ask you to deny yourself any chance of happiness that might come your way." He reached inside his coat and took a small box from his pocket, and Bridget thought her heart would stop. He opened the box, and Bridget saw a thin gold ring set with garnets. She gasped, but not as loudly as the waitresses, who had clearly been watching.

"It was my grandmother's."

"It's beautiful," said Bridget softly.

"Take it as a gift." She took the box in trembling hands. "Don't put it on, not now. If the war ends and I come back, I'll ask you to let this ring be an engagement ring. And if I don't come back, then keep it as a reminder of my love for you." He swallowed. "And if you should meet someone who brings you happiness, then I want you to be able to be happy with him, knowing that you haven't made any promises and that I would never, ever blame you."

"I never would," said Bridget. She wiped at her eyes with the back of her wrist. The silk was soft against her face. Still holding the box tenderly, she put out her other hand, and he took it. She stood up and drew him along with her. "Come with me."

"Where?"

"I have a room in the hotel next door," she said.

"You have a room?"

"I do."

"Bridget, I don't think——"

"Come with me, love," she said. "Please."

"Are you sure?"

"I am." And she was. "The most obnoxious cad in the world said something yesterday that actually made a good deal of sense to me."

"That sounds . . . mildly ominous."

"Out of the mouths of babes and degenerates." She shrugged. "Life is for living. Especially now. Especially with the person you love."

Hand in hand, they left the teashop. They paused on the footpath.

"You should come in about five minutes after me," she said. "For appearance's sake." *Not least because the hotel staff believe I'm married to Wattleman.* He nodded a little, and she gave him the floor and the room number. "I'll see you shortly."

She tore up to the room, gently put the box with its ring on the dressing table, then cast a hurried look around. *What of Wattleman's do I need to conceal here?* She threw open the wardrobe and found that it was empty of not only his clothes but also hers.

What? Am I in the right room?

I have to be, the key worked.

Still, there were no obvious signs that either of them was staying there. The drawers of the dresser were empty, and a quick check of the bathroom revealed that his razor and both of their toothbrushes were also gone.

Have we been robbed?

And to what extent do I care?

There was a knock at the door. *I'll address the mystery of the missing possessions later,* she decided. Then her eye was caught by the edge of her suitcase, which had been placed discreetly under the bed. She dropped to her knees and found that it contained all of her things. Wattleman's bag was farther back, but it was also fully packed. She realized what had happened. Wattleman had hidden any indication that this room was anything other than a spontaneous hope for her and Gerald to be together this once. If her luggage had been seen, Gerald would have wanted to know why she wasn't staying in Lady Carmichael's house.

Oh God. It was not clear what was more disconcerting, Wattleman trying to lure her into bed or him facilitating her going to bed with someone else. *I can't decide if this is considerate on his part or just extremely awkward.* There was another knock at the door.

"Just a moment!"

She shoved the bags far back under the bed and took a frantic look in the mirror. She looked flushed and slightly rumpled. A quick clawing through her hair did nothing to improve the situation, but she shrugged and opened the door.

"Hullo," he said.

"Hullo," she said. "Would you like to—won't you please be welcome?"

He smiled. "So you took a room here," he said.

"I did."

"It's very nice," he said, not looking around at all. He had eyes only for her, and the sight of him left her weak in the knees.

And then they were kissing, and where before the kiss had been everything, now it was the beginning of something else. His arms were around her, his strength holding her close against him. She could feel the warmth of him, the heat of him, and she was undoing the buttons of his uniform coat, her hands shaking with the want of it all. She wanted to touch his skin, to touch him. She wanted all of him.

And then Gerald broke the kiss and pushed her back, gently but firmly. She felt his hands trembling a little on her shoulders.

"Bridget, no, we can't." She looked at him, wide-eyed. "I do want to. I *very much* want to, but we can't take the chance. If something were to happen, if there was a child, then, if something happened to me, you'd be left..." He trailed off, his fists clenching, and his face grew set and determined. "We can't pretend we are this foolish and this reckless."

I'd take the chance, she thought breathlessly. But he wouldn't, and that was the Gerald she loved.

"I know what you mean," she said. "But we don't have to take any chances." She turned and went to the handbag she'd dropped by the door. When she turned back, she could feel her cheeks burning. "I got us something for the weekend."

"You have French letters in your handbag?" He asked it not in a tone of incredulity or disgust but rather startled curiosity.

"Not usually," said Bridget tartly. "I asked a friend at Mrs. Carmichael's office."

"So you knew that we would..."

"No, but I thought it might happen." She bit her lip. "I hoped."

"And so you had a room here?"

"Yes." She looked up at him shyly, then reached up and touched his face.

"You can take your gloves off, my darling," Gerald said, and Bridget thrilled at hearing him say that. "I don't care about your scars. No matter what, I'll adore you."

"Thank you, love," she said. "But this"—and she gestured back and forth at the two of them—"this is already a lot. My hands would just be one more thing to make this more complicated." *Which may be the greatest understatement of my life,* she thought. "I'd feel better with them on."

"That's fine, of course." And he kissed her again. "Just remember, I love *you.* Every part of you. As you are."

Bridget flinched, and he drew back, looking at her wide-eyed, worried even, before she smiled weakly.

"Are you all right?" he asked uncertainly. "Do you—um, would you like to stop? We don't have to do this."

"No, love, I just hesitated for a moment," she assured him.

In truth, though, what he said had sent a bolt of guilt stabbing into her: *As you are.*

But he didn't really know her at all. *I have lied to him about everything I am,* she thought. *How can I be with him, how can I make a promise, even the intention of a promise, when I've kept the most important things from him? Is all this a grotesque betrayal? And if we were to marry, I might have to lie to him always.*

Most Checquy spouses did not know about their mates' real work and their powers. Those who did were entrusted with the secret only after rigorous screening and evaluation, and even then they were never made privy to the entire truth. *And what if I do tell him, and he turns against me? What if he hates me? What if my hands disgust him? What if I disgust him?* Burn scars might be unsightly, they might even be grotesque, but they were at least human.

All your life, you've known that you have to keep secrets, she told herself. *For the good of the country and for the good of anyone you might love.*

He knows the best parts of me, she finally reminded herself. *And no one knows another person entirely.*

She reached up and pulled his face down to hers.

In the end, it was not a frenzy of wild abandon. The start-stop-start of getting to this point, their moments of hesitation before they began, and the knowledge that there were other people in the building kept them in their heads. They hesitantly began to take off their shoes, and then, when they met each other's eyes, they remembered how much they adored each other and laughed at the ridiculousness of themselves. And then they were undressing each other, deliciously, with many pauses to kiss and caress and whisper.

Gerald had clearly never been with a woman before, and Bridget found that all the theoretical knowledge in the world did not make someone a confident lover. But they were young, and they were in love, and their delight in each other smoothed over any inevitable awkwardness. There were a lot of smiles, and there was some muffled laughter, and eventually there were sighs and smothered gasps of pleasure building to something as miraculous as anything Bridget had ever experienced. And then they were holding each other tightly, so tightly that it did not seem as if they could ever be parted.

She walked him through the hotel to the rear entrance, holding his hand. The place was silent, as if everyone else had tactfully departed the world. They came to the door, and he stepped through and down. He turned back and they kissed.

"Goodbye," she said.

"Goodbye."

They didn't need to say anything else. Everything had been said in the room upstairs.

She had not told Gerald that, after their lovemaking, as he lay dreamily quiet, and she moved about the room, she discovered that the condom had broken.

15

My love,

I have to go away for a while. But only for a while. When people from the office come to you, show them this card. Kiss my baby and tell her that I love her.

> *I love you.*
> *Lyn*

Lyn contemplated the text and bit her lip. She'd spent forty-five min-utes agonizing over the wording. *Has anyone in the history of the world ever written fifteen drafts of a card?* she wondered.

She absolutely had to get a message to Richard, and she didn't dare try to telephone him. E-mail was too dangerous as well—she was fairly certain the Checquy could track the origin point of an e-mail. So she'd resolved to handwrite her message to him and found that it was unbelievably difficult.

There was simply too much to say and too much she couldn't possibly say. Plus, she had no doubt that the Checquy would see it. Either Richard would show it to them or they'd intercept it, so she was writing for them as much as for him. Which meant that she had to be careful not to give away any hint of her plans.

God knows what Richard will think. She rather hoped that it would sound like she'd been sent on some supersecret assignment for King and country. Except that the bit about showing the card to her employer made it sound like she'd been accused of selling secrets to a foreign power. *It sounds like I've gone rogue—which I have, sort of—but when the Checquy read it, they'll see that I haven't revealed their existence and that I mean to come back.*

But what will they tell him? What if they tell him I'm a traitor? What if they enlist him to lure me back so they can grab me? She'd have no way of knowing, which meant that until she found an answer, she wouldn't be able to contact her family at all.

I'll have to write the Checquy a letter as well, she thought. *But that will be much longer. I need to reach out to Richard first. With this ridiculous message.* She stared at the draft some more, but she couldn't think of any words that would make the situation better. It would take several tomes and require the violation of many laws and acts to really explain.

It will have to do, she thought. She wrote it out on three separate greeting cards that she would post the next morning from three separate postboxes, appropriately disguised. One would go to the house, one would go to Richard's work, and one would go to her friend Jenny with instructions to pass it on to him.

She tossed the cards onto her narrow little bed and tried to unpack the day. That morning, she had woken up next to her husband, perfectly pleased with her life, and now she was a supernatural fugitive from the government, lying in a tiny cell-like room deep in the bowels of the Lady Cumming-Gould Memorial Refuge for Women. Not that she wasn't grateful that they'd taken her in; they'd been so kind and supportive that she'd almost wept.

The information woman at Waterloo station, whose name had

turned out to be Julie, had looked up a women's-aid number on the internet and, upon learning that Lyn had fled without her phone, actually called the hotline on her own mobile, then handed it to Lyn. A calm voice on the other end had answered and listened patiently to Lyn's situation. With a mental apology to Richard, she described a habitually violent husband whom she'd decided she had to leave.

"Are you able to travel at all?" asked the voice. "We have to be careful not to put you in the immediate area of your home. That's where you're at the most risk."

"I live in Jarrow," said Lyn, picking out the name of the first town she could think of, "but I'm in London right now. I, um, I caught the first train away. I wasn't even thinking."

"That's fine. It works well, in fact. Does your abuser have any connections in London?"

"Not really, no," said Lyn. "But he works in law enforcement, so I'm worried that he could try to track me down that way."

"I see. Well, our services and records are all kept confidential, so he will not be able to access them, regardless of his connections."

"Thank you," breathed Lyn in relief.

"Do you have any children with you?"

"No, I don't have any children." *Sorry, Emma.*

"Okay, I will check availability in the London area," said the voice. "What number can I reach you at?"

"I don't have a phone," said Lyn helplessly.

"You can use a telephone box," said the woman, "as long as it accepts incoming calls."

"You can use mine," said Julie. She gave her number to Lyn, who recited it to the hotline woman.

"I'll call you back shortly," said the woman.

"Thank you," said Lyn. "And thank *you*," she said to Julie. "You don't know what this means to me." Julie patted her gently on the hand as she accepted her phone back. "I'm just going to sit there until they call back." Lyn nodded over at a bench.

"I'll let you know when they call," said Julie. Lyn sat with her head bowed, her hair falling down around her face. She was uncomfortably aware of all the security cameras around the station. Fifteen minutes later, Julie motioned her over and gave Lyn her phone again. The voice told her that there was a place for her at the Lady Cumming-Gould Memorial Refuge for Women.

"Are you able to come to our offices?" asked the hotline woman, and she gave the address, which was within walking distance.

"Yes, that won't be a problem," said Lyn.

"From there, we'll take you to the refuge. Now, we'll be asking you to please keep the location of that refuge to yourself," said the hotline woman.

"Don't worry, I will," said Lyn with feeling.

"It's important, not just for your safety but for the safety of the other women."

"I understand. I'm very good at keeping secrets."

Upon arriving at the office of the refuge organization, she'd given a false name and, burning with shame at the lie, explained that she'd fled to London to get away from an abusive policeman husband in Jarrow. They had driven her to the refuge, a nondescript building tucked away in a backstreet of Hackney, and said that she could stay with them as long as she needed, for months, if necessary.

Months! This can't take months, and I can't take advantage of this place for more than a couple of nights, she thought. *At most.* Before accepting the spot, she'd confirmed that the shelter wasn't full. If she'd thought she was preventing an actual abused woman from getting in, she would have stayed out on the street. But a night at the refuge would give her the privacy and security she needed to plan and to come to terms with her situation. A lockable door, a small but cheerful room with a soft carpet and a bed with bright blankets, and a shower were what kept her from being a weeping, panicked mess.

Now that there was actually time to sit down and think everything through, she found that she could not visualize any way in which things could work out. *Maybe I shouldn't have run,* she thought. *Maybe the Checquy would have given me the benefit of the doubt.*

Well, it's too late now.

She turned her attention back to the pad of paper in front of her, given to her by the front office. She set about transcribing everything she could remember from her research. Names of criminals alive and dead. Gangs. Affiliations.

Addresses.

Lyn woke up and knew exactly where she was and why. It was still night out, and she'd slept badly. Every creak of a floorboard or footstep outside the door had been a Checquy soldier coming to drag her out of bed by her feet. If she'd reached out and grabbed the baton by her bed once, she'd done it seven times. She stared at the ceiling and thought she was going mad.

They'll know by now. They'll be out in the streets trying to track me. They'll have gone to my flat and torn it apart. They'll have gone to Richard and told him—what? Her message on the cards now seemed so ridiculous and pathetic that she wanted to tear them to pieces. *Is my marriage over? Am I not going to see my kid ever again?* She pressed her hands to her eyes in the darkness.

When it was finally morning, Lyn showered and came downstairs in her fear-smelling clothes and sink-washed underwear from the day before. She'd laid out an agenda for herself, and new clothes and some basic appearance-altering products were high on the list, but first things had to be first. She passed the communal room, where some women were already preparing breakfast, and went to the refuge's office. Despite the early hour, there were several women at desks, talking on phones and typing away on computers.

"Good morning, love," said the one closest the door. "Can we help you?"

"I hope so," said Lyn. "Although you've already done so much. And I'm really grateful for this place taking me in, but I can't stay here." They regarded her quietly. "I know there are women who have no other options, but I have some money—I can pay for accommodation. I can't stay here and take a place someone else might need. But I also can't risk my husband tracking me down. He's a cop, and he may have access to a lot of records. So do you have any recommendations?" The ladies in the office exchanged looks.

"I expect you'll still want to be careful with your funds," said the oldest, a plump Indian lady in her fifties. "There are some hostels around the place. They can be quite loose with the books, especially if you slip them some extra."

That sounds possible, thought Lyn. *Although it also sounds like the kind of place the Checquy might check automatically.*

"My aunt runs a bed-and-breakfast in Epping Forest," one of the support staff volunteered. She was a slim brunette whose name tag identified her as Kelly. Lyn wouldn't have put her age above twenty-seven, but she had the reassuring air of a nurse with decades of experience in the emergency department.

"Is that in London?" asked Lyn uncertainly. She'd never heard of it.

"Oh, yeah," said the woman. "Well, I mean, it's Essex, so it's out there, but it's on the Underground."

So, doable for my purposes, thought Lyn. *I don't mind a bit of a commute.*

"Let me just call her, see what's possible," said Kelly. "Are you okay with dogs?"

"I'm very okay with dogs."

"Right, excellent. It's just, there's dogs. Now, if you want to wait in the common room, maybe get some coffee, I'll come and let you know." Lyn nodded—coffee was the second thing on her to-do list.

The communal room of the women's refuge was large, but it was hardly institutional-feeling. Kitchen facilities by the entrance, then round dining tables and a lounge area with couches and comfy-looking armchairs and coffee tables. Several women were cooking, and little family groups sat at the dining area. A small, serious-looking boy was eating cereal at a table, and he gazed at her with wide eyes. She winked at him and turned her attention to the coffee. There was no expensive espresso machine, just large tins of instant, which suited her down to the ground. She was settled by a window, looking over her notes, when Kelly came over. She hurriedly turned the papers over.

"All good!" said the young woman. "She can put you up, and she's fine with doing it off the books." She named a fee that was very reasonable, even if it did mean an hour's Tube journey.

The isolation would probably be an advantage, Lyn told herself. *And at that rate, I could stay there for weeks.* "That is really wonderful, I'm so grateful," she said.

"My aunt said that she'd come and pick you up anytime from the Tube station. Now, you left your phone at home, right?"

"Yes. It was ridiculous, but I was actually worried that he might try to track it. Silly."

"Not at all," said Kelly. "If you hadn't, they'd have had you put it in a special pouch. It's called a Faraday pouch—it blocks signals."

You don't say.

"We do it for everyone. After all, there are apps for finding lost phones. But I've written down my aunt's number—her name's Mandy—and there's a pay phone at the station, so you can call her when you arrive. Before then, did you want to check your e-mail or anything?" She gestured toward a table with some elderly desktop computers.

"I—uh, I actually need to go out for a little bit. I've got to buy some toiletries and clothes. I didn't even think to pack any." *Plus I need to mail three cards from three random postboxes, preferably a good distance from here. And buy some hair dye and things.*

"We've got supplies we can give you," said Kelly. "Clothes, basics."

"Are you sure?" asked Lyn.

"It's very normal, when you leave in a hurry, to just grab whatever comes to hand. One lady came here and all she'd thought to pack was a toaster."

"Well, I'd be very grateful. I still want to stretch my legs, have a bit of a think." In truth, she didn't at all. The idea of going outside the comforting walls of the refuge was frightening; she knew about all the cameras out there in the world. But she also knew that the Checquy couldn't be watching every one of them at once. With sunglasses and a cap, she'd be just an anonymous figure on the street.

And I have to be able to go out in the world if I'm going to do this.

"Sure, go out, get some air," Kelly was saying breezily. "Just buzz the door when you want to come back in." Lyn nodded. The refuge had a reassuring security system, and the doors were much thicker than they looked, which made a depressing amount of sense.

*   *   *

"All right, babe, we are here."

Lyn opened her eyes and looked around. It was not what she had expected. For that matter, nothing had been what she expected. The words *My aunt runs a bed-and-breakfast in Epping Forest* conjured up an image of a certain type of aunt and a certain type of bed-and-breakfast. A comfy, plump, grandmotherly type, possibly in an apron, standing on the doorstep of a semidetached house and offering a plate of freshly baked scones. Possibly with a gnome or two in the garden. She'd be taking in the occasional lodger for some funds to supplement her pension and shrinking nest egg. Doilies would feature heavily in the decor. Plaster ducks would be migrating south for the winter across the walls.

That image had been dispelled when a red jeep pulled up outside the Epping Tube station blaring rock music. The aunt had turned out to be a broad-shouldered American woman in her sixties with long brown hair and a cigarette hanging from her lips. The apron had turned out to be a battered leather jacket and round sunglasses. She introduced herself as Mandy. And now the house turned out to be a large Tudor-style in its own expansive garden. Instead of gnomes, a large garden sculpture of curling steel appeared to portray nothing much in particular.

"I would not have picked this as a B and B," remarked Lyn as they pulled into the garage.

"Well, it's not really a B and B, but I do that thing where people book a room online. I like houseguests." Mandy shrugged. "Otherwise it's just me and the dogs and the fish. Kelly said you like dogs?"

"I do."

"Good, because they like people, and you won't be able to shut a door on them. At least one may want to sleep on your bed with you."

"That is entirely fine," said Lyn. Skeksis was an on-the-bed dog, and the comforting weighty presence of an animal was something she'd missed in her London flat. They entered the house and were met by two Pomeranians, an elderly golden retriever, two Portuguese water dogs, a labradoodle, and a Cavalier King Charles spaniel. Lyn crouched down to have her hands smelled, then went down on her knees to have her ears licked.

"Welcome to the house," said Mandy. "Come on through to the living room."

The living room featured several well-scratched leather couches and a few thick red rugs. Big colorful pieces of art hung on the walls, and framed photographs stood everywhere. Not a plaster duck to be seen. Lyn rather suspected that if any had dared show their beaks, Mandy would have pulled out a shotgun.

"Have a seat," said Mandy. "I just need to let the hounds out. Can I get you anything? Something to drink?"

"I'm fine, thank you," said Lyn, sitting down on what might have been the world's most comfortable couch. She was immediately flanked by a Pom and the Cav. The retriever leaned heavily against her knee, and she automatically started scratching his shoulders. The other dogs followed Mandy out. "No one else lives here?" Lyn called after her.

"No," she called back. "I married Kelly's uncle about twenty years ago, and he left about eighteen years ago, but her family liked me better than they liked him, so I kept them. There's the occasional man friend, but no actual keepers. I think my standards went up a bit."

"What brought you to England?" asked Lyn curiously.

"Oh, the love of a bad man." Mandy smiled as she came back into the room. "And an ill-advised move by a radio network to import some American on-air talent."

"Whereabouts in America are you from originally?"

"Kalamazoo, Michigan," said Mandy. "Original home of Gibson Guitars. And some other stuff, but it's the guitars that define it for me. Do you like music?"

"Is there anyone who doesn't like music?"

"They don't necessarily like me playing it loudly at night."

"Your house." Lyn shrugged. "If I can shut a door and sleep, that's all I require."

"All righty, let's go over the ground rules. I don't give out keys to guests, so if I'm not here, you're not here. I'm sure you're great, but I don't trust people that much. But I *am* here a lot of the time. We can figure out schedules, and if something happens and you need to come in and I'm not home, you can call me, and we'll work it out. Fair?"

"Absolutely," said Lyn.

"Kelly said you don't have a phone?"

"Yeah."

"A couple of the women she's sent me have been in the same situation." Mandy nodded. "I have an old spare. It's preloaded with thirty quid and it's got my number in it. Not a smartphone, but it makes calls and sends texts, and if you lose it, I don't give a shit. I'll show you around the place in a sec, but we should probably discuss time frame. I understand the situation you're in—you don't need to tell me about it unless you want to. But do you have plans, things you want to do? Or do you just need to lie low for a while and recuperate?"

"A bit of both, really," said Lyn.

"Fair enough. Well, shall we say you'll stay here a week to start with? If we get along after that, we'll play it by ear."

"That sounds great."

"Liquor cabinet's there. My only rule about that is that no one drinks alone. Me included. It's my self-discipline—keeps me from getting too rock 'n' roll. You want a cocktail?"

"Later, definitely," said Lyn.

"Great. If you're here for dinner, I'll make enough for both of us. If you're here for breakfast, the same. That's my meals policy. Let me show you your room."

The bedroom did not feel like a room made up for B and B guests. It felt like Mandy's guest room in which she stored her overflowing collections of CDs and vinyl, all meticulously shelved. Lyn carefully put her refuge-provided T-shirts, socks, and underwear in the chest of drawers and hung her balled-up work suit in the en suite. She hoped the steam might take out some of the wrinkles, but it rather looked like nothing would heal it short of dry cleaning or possibly cremation.

She badly wanted to go out immediately, catch the Tube into London, and start taking some action, but she needed just a moment to sit down and breathe. The refuge had been safe, but it had felt safe like a fortress. This felt safe like a home. She lay down on the bed and was promptly joined by Francisco, one of the Portuguese water dogs, who insinuated himself into her armpit and sighed heavily.

Let's review and prepare, she thought. There was nothing to fall back on after this. If she went about it half-assed, she'd end up dead. She didn't know how long she'd spent frantically researching the victims and their criminal networks before she left the office. It had felt like only panic-filled minutes, but it had to have been longer, given the amount of reading she'd done. Remembering the fear that had been pumping in her brain, she was surprised by what she'd managed to retain. She'd paid special attention to names and addresses but had also picked up a bigger picture of the London criminal world, slotting it comfortably into the gaps of what she'd known before. She'd written down details during her night at the women's refuge. Now she could take the time to analyze and plot.

If I am going to get my life back—my life with my family and my demented secret magic government job—then I need proof that I didn't kill those people. I have to find the person responsible.

So, who is doing this? she thought. *What can I figure out about them?*

First, they're killing criminals, not civilians, which speaks sort of well for them, I suppose.

Who kills criminals? Either vigilantes or other criminals.

And what kind of criminals are they killing?

Lyn knew that the criminal world was complex. There were the big organizations, the cartels and the mafias, with tremendous resources and international connections. They practically formed their own ecosystem, with some branches extending down to the street level and others just supplying the smaller bodies with drugs or weapons or contraband, but they were vast and faceless. Then there were the smaller groups that had their specific turf and committed more local crimes. And then there were the individual small-time criminals who answered only to themselves. There were varying levels of connection between the different types. Some had contact, some had conflict, and some stayed completely separate.

Her husband had not had to deal with any of the truly international organizations, for which she'd always been profoundly grateful. South Shields had its criminal presence, of course. Richard had been involved in breaking up a drug ring but he'd always been more heavily involved in community policing.

As far as Lyn could see, each of the men killed with electricity had been involved in small to midlevel groups with no more than ten or twenty active members each. They were local, with local bosses who called the shots and didn't take orders from anyone.

It's got to be one person doing this, she thought. *If there were multiple vigilantes, they'd be taking out more players at once. And if it were a power play by a rival criminal group, they would have taken out the leaders first, and we'd have heard of it.* The police intelligence reports she'd accessed in the office had said nothing about any bosses being killed or new players moving in.

So it was one person, vigilante or criminal, with eyes strictly on local-level crime.

Maybe this individual has been harmed by the criminals he's targeting, she mused. *Maybe he's been damaged financially.* It was probably an avenue of investigation worth pursuing, but...*But now that I'm outside the Checquy, I don't really have the resources to investigate it.*

Instead, I'll need to go dig among the local gangs of old London Town.

"Lynette! I've made chili!" Mandy's voice came through the house's intercom system.

I'll need to go dig among the local gangs of old London Town after I've had some chili.

As it turned out, she was not going to dig anywhere until the next morning, because by the time she'd eaten the chili and had a glass of wine and sat on the couch under some dogs and watched a reality show about a group of sculptors living and arguing in North Dakota, she didn't think there would be enough time to catch the Tube into the city and then back out again. Plus, she was full of chili and wine.

The next morning, Lyn came down for breakfast, but just as she was about to enter the kitchen, it suddenly occurred to her that the Checquy might have put out some sort of alert with her face and name. A police warning. Maybe there was a massive national manhunt under way. Maybe they'd accuse her of terrorism or violent mental instability—something that would warn people to keep away from her and not believe anything she said.

My picture could be on every TV in the country, she thought faintly, *just waiting for an unexpectedly cool aunt running a B and B to see it and hurriedly call the authorities.*

At that very moment, there could be an armed tactical squad waiting in the kitchen to take her down, after which they'd be treated to what Mandy had promised were the world's best scrambled eggs. Lyn noticed that her hand on the doorknob was actually trembling.

And what are you going to do? she wondered. *Turn and run? Is this how you're going to live your life?* Snorting at herself, she pushed her way through to a kitchen that had no soldiers waiting for her, just Mandy at the stove and the dogs at their bowls.

The eggs, as it turned out, were pretty damn terrific. ("The secret to really good creamy eggs is in the cooking technique," Mandy advised her. "You don't need butter, you just constantly stir them so they don't have time to set, and you take them on and off the heat as you cook them.") The coffee, however, was vile.

Afterward, she followed Mandy's directions to the Tube station and joined the crowd of people going into the City for work. She took a seat, her head bent over a newspaper. She'd done her best to alter her appearance this morning. The possibility of dyeing her hair had occurred to her, but she'd never done it before and didn't want to waste time experimenting. Instead, she'd borrowed Mandy's curling iron so that her hair hung in uncharacteristic ringlets, and she put on the blue-light glasses she'd purchased. She didn't normally wear makeup, but she'd gone quite heavy with it this morning, darkening her brows and lashes, applying a dark lipstick, and carefully applying blush to her cheeks so that she almost didn't recognize herself in the mirror.

Now, peering through her hanging hair, she scanned the train for any sign of Checquy or police who might be discreetly looking for her, though it was almost impossible to distinguish subtle observation by secret agents from the studiously polite lack of attention of London commuters. Still, she looked around warily. Paranoia was becoming her primary source of cardio.

Lyn alighted at Bank station, mingling with the commuting hordes and keeping her head bowed as she passed a couple of policemen. From there, she took a winding, circuitous train journey to the London borough of Newham. One of the murders had taken place there, and Lyn had an idea about how she could gain some information. Still, the thought of what she was going to do made her stomach knot.

Newham was home to the Rafferty firm, a group of criminals that had been operating in the area for several decades. They were an institution—local generations had grown up watching the Rafferty boys engage in various violent crimes. Members of the gang had come and gone (or been shipped off to Borstal or bedlam or prison or the grave), but it had always been led by several members of the greater Rafferty clan. Their presence on the street was strictly local, and they specialized in extracting money and goods from people through violence. They did not sell drugs or sex, although they did conduct some illegal gambling. Mostly, they provided no goods or services (unless you counted actively not harming people or robbing stores and then charging their owners for the privilege as a service).

They also ran a nice sideline business in general mayhem. Clashes with rival organizations were not uncommon and were usually characterized by gratuitous collateral damage to civilians and local architecture. Despite their capacity for startling violence, however, the Raffertys were known to run quite a profitable enterprise. The young toughs might have been the arm on the street, but the older generations oversaw it all, directing them into gainful applications of brutality.

One of the key figures in the firm was Lennie Burrowes, who'd married a Rafferty daughter thirty-odd years earlier. He'd started as street muscle, engaging in the entry-level tasks of mugging, armed robbery, and extortion. Over the years, as he'd proven his talents (he was believed to have killed three men, two of them with his bare hands), his loyalty (he'd been detained several times at Her Majesty's pleasure without ever informing on his colleagues), and his business acumen, he'd risen in the ranks. Two of his sons had joined the firm (the third had become a lawyer, representing those wayward Rafferty youths who were apprehended by the constabulary). He was part of the inner council, generally acknowledged as the most invaluable consigliere the gang possessed, and his pawnshop served as a clearing-house for the fruits of burglary, pocket-picking, armed robbery, and smashed shop windows. In short, he was now one of the grand old men of the Rafferty firm.

Or at least he had been until someone electrocuted him outside his shop as he was locking up, leaving his corpse smoking on the pavement.

His death had reportedly thrown the organization into disarray, which was exactly what Lyn was counting on. Their uncertainty might leave them vulnerable to her approach.

Or they might be so wary and paranoid that they'll shoot me as soon as I ask a question, she thought.

She stepped into the restroom of the nearest McDonald's and spent some time laboriously (and somewhat regretfully) wiping off the bulk of her makeup. She also braided her hair back in a single plait. For this, she was going to need to look like a woman focused entirely on her business, not one who was interested in beauty. Finally, she took a metal pen from her pocket and held it tightly for a moment, feeling the warmth and energy from her hand spread down into it. Then she very carefully tucked it into the inside pocket of her jacket.

The Burrowes pawnshop was wedged between a pub and a charity shop. The dossier Lyn had hurriedly read at Apex House noted that in the rear, it had a handy loading and storage area for late-night drop-offs of goods that had fallen off the backs of trucks onto the backs of other trucks. The sign on the door said OPEN, and the bell jingled as she went in. A man in his mid-twenties stood behind a counter off to the left. No one else was in the store. *You are not afraid,* Lyn told herself as she passed displays of possessions people had parted with. *You are angry, and you are in control of yourself.* She walked straight up to him, ignoring the various glass cases.

"Lennie Burrowes," she said flatly.

"Sorry to have to tell you this," said the man, "but I'm afraid he died."

"That's what I heard," said Lyn. "And I am not at all happy about that."

"And who are you, then?"

"We did business together." She eyed the man. He was tall and strong-looking, the kind of muscle that comes from going to the gym *and* doing a lot of heavy lifting. The kind of vague menace that comes from being no stranger to violence. His white button-down shirt was thin enough for her to see the vague shape of tattoos on his arms. The very image of a young tough. *If he's not involved with the Raffertys, I'll be astounded.* "And who are you, then?" she asked.

"I'm Rory, I'm his nephew. I've been running the shop since he died."

"I see. And have you taken over *all* the work he did?" She watched Rory's eyes narrow as he calculated what she was talking about.

"I've been with him for half a year," he said. "Learning the ropes, all of 'em." He looked at her. "And I don't know you. So what kind of business were you two doing?"

"We're each other's quiet out-of-town contacts," she said. "Well, we *were*."

"Oh yeah?" He leered.

"Do yourself a favor, please, and don't be a prick." To Lyn's satisfaction, her voice was unwavering, and she'd managed to insert just the right tone of confident contempt. The persona came partially from memories of bullies she'd encountered in foster care, partially from some shows she'd seen, but also from the knowledge that, thanks to her powers, she could easily destroy this man if she chose. He must have sensed it on some level, because he actually took a little step back, even though he was a head and a half taller than her. "I'm not from London. I come here for only two reasons, both of them to do with Lennie Burrowes. Sometimes I brought items here for him to buy. He'd pay top dollar. It was useful for both of us. I got anonymity, and he got exclusivity. That was the first reason.

"The second was that sometimes Lennie Burrowes would see a problem coming for him and his people, which I assume includes you. That problem would be another person. He'd call me, and I would remove that person."

"The Raffertys don't need outside help to remove people." He snorted.

"The Raffertys do a nice line in roughness," she said, and she curled her lip slightly, "but they are not what you would call subtle. They're more in the nature of a hammer, and sometimes you don't need a hammer. You need a stiletto." He looked thoughtful. "Rest assured, Lennie would call me when he needed a big problem to go away quietly. Now, if the Raffertys want the big problems to keep going away quietly, they're going to want to keep contact with me. That's one of the reasons I'm here."

"And the other reasons?" he asked.

"I heard he was murdered. I heard it was ugly. I want to know what's going on so I can decide if *I* want to keep contact with the Raffertys."

She stopped and assessed his reaction. It took all Lyn's strength and self-control not to hold her breath. His cunning little eyes darted over her, all his street instincts trying to read her. Really, she'd given him nothing, no proof at all of anything she'd just said, but she was gambling on his uncertainty and his awe for his dead uncle and maybe his desire to believe that the Raffertys were a bigger deal than he'd thought. And if he was any good at all, he'd pick up on the fact that she could be immeasurably dangerous. Not in the way she'd told him she was, but the threat was there. Was his reptilian brain twitching? Were the hairs at the back of his neck a-tremble? Did he believe her?

If he didn't buy it, if he made a move for the gun that she was certain was under the counter, then she had the next few movements mapped out in her head. She'd done them hundreds of time under the critical eye of Pawn Fenton: Left hand snapping out to grab him and jolt him through her rings, just enough to stop him for a moment. Her other hand darting into her coat pocket and producing the pen, which was loaded with enough electricity to put the conversation on hold for quite a while.

What she'd do after that, she wasn't entirely certain.

"Fancy a cuppa?" he said finally.

The sign on the door was flipped around to CLOSED. While Rory was locking the door, Lyn quickly removed the pen from her inner pocket and flicked it firmly, discharging the stored energy with a flash, a quiet pop, and a whiff of ozone. Fully charged, it felt like holding a grenade with a loose pin against her chest, and she wasn't keen on the possibility of its going off by accident. Rory looked back, startled, then shrugged a little. He led her through a door to the back space of the shop. Lyn kept one hand in her coat pocket closed around her baton, which didn't need to be charged to deliver some mayhem if necessary. She was fairly sure he'd bought her story, but she would not let her guard down.

The back room was as she might have expected, with various items of questionable provenance on benches waiting to be priced and a couple of large safes. Rory asked how she took her tea, and once the mug had been solemnly handed over, he led her through a second door and out onto the loading area. It was not the coziest of spots, consisting of a dock, a dumpster, a couple of beaten-up easy chairs, and what appeared to be several decades' worth of cigarette butts flicked into a corner. He settled into one of the chairs and looked startled when she didn't sit. She'd decided that the character she'd created, this assassin with occasional stolen goods to fence, was not someone who would ever feel at ease.

"Is it okay to talk here?" she said suspiciously. He nodded with certainty. "All right, so talk."

"What's your name?" he asked.

"Kira."

"Really?"

"No," she said flatly.

"Okay, well, I feel like I should call someone a bit higher up the tree."

"Rory, Lennie Burrowes was my point of contact," she said. "My only point of contact. Before I get to talking with someone new, I want to know the state of affairs or I'm leaving right now."

Rory appeared to have bought her story. He'd buckled to her projected authority and now was anxious to please. When she mentioned leaving, he actually sat up straight.

"It happened a week ago," said Rory hastily. "We were working here, and he let me go home early. I had a date with a bird, so I left about four. Later, one of the big men called and said that someone found Uncle Lennie dead outside the shop. We thought it was a heart attack or something. Then the filth told us he'd been electrocuted."

"And you've no idea who did it or what they wanted?"

"None, but whoever it is, they've been goin' after other people in the business," said Rory. "That old Maberly twat over in Islington, and a couple of them DiMarco boys got it too. And three of the men in the Kelton firm."

"That's more than I'd heard about," said Lyn faintly. *I wonder if any of them could have provided me with an alibi?*

"Yeah, well, people have started keeping it to themselves. The rozzers haven't managed to do anything about it, and it makes you look a bit weak to the competition, don't it, losing soldiers like that? Uncle Lennie had heard about it, we all had, and everybody's freaking out. It's bloody insane! This isn't how things are done. If you've got a problem with someone, you go after them, and you stab 'em or shoot 'em or fuckin' beat their heads in with a cricket bat, don't you? You don't take a cattle prod and zap 'em to death on the footpath. And you don't fuckin' do it for no reason. I mean, if you want to shift the borders, well, then you rough up some of the other team and send 'em scuttling back home, and everyone understands what's happening. And then, depending on how things go with that, maybe there's some fights and a killing or two or three. The main thing is you send a clear message. But this!" He shook his head. "It's mad. It's like there's a serial killer goin' after us."

"Could be. And I doubt they're done," said Lyn. "I'm going to give you a mobile number. Call me if anything new happens."

"Why would I call you?" he asked.

"I'm going to find this person, and I'm going to kill them." He looked at her, startled. She was a little startled herself.

"You? Why?"

Good question.

"I liked Lennie well enough, but it's not to avenge him. The business he brought me was profitable. This killer is causing too much disruption and getting the attention of the police. The sooner I get rid of him or her, the sooner we can go back to business as usual."

Rory looked down into his tea as if he'd find answers there. Finally, he looked up. "Uncle Lennie wasn't the only member of the family who's been killed," he said. "This fucker also killed one of the captains a couple of days ago."

"The captains?"

"Just in charge of a few lads," said Rory. "Responsible for some jobs."

"I see," said Lyn, although she didn't.

"He was smart, and the big men had their eyes on him for bigger things," said Rory. "He'd pulled some clever jobs and could handle himself in a fight. A boxer, you know. They found his body behind one of our pubs. The cops said it was electrocution, just like Uncle Lennie." His eyes bored into hers. "He was my brother."

And there it is, thought Lyn. She could almost feel the snap of her trap being set for the killer. She hadn't known about the brother, but it would lock Rory to her. She was the possibility of his revenge.

"If I hear anything," he said firmly, "I'll call you."

16

After Gerald left, Bridget went back to the room and stood there considering the situation and the state of the bedding. *Well, I can address one of those issues.* She went through Wattleman's bag to find the obligatory bottle of whisky, and strategically spilled some of it down a pillow and onto the sheets. She went down and asked for the bed to receive fresh linens, apologizing for her husband's crudity in drinking in bed, and then walked briskly out of the hotel. She'd decided she couldn't wait for Wattleman to return. Her face was set, but her mind was whirling. Too much had happened in the past couple of hours, and she was trying to figure out how she'd deal with it all.

Gerald wants to marry me.

Gerald wants to marry me, and I could be pregnant with his child.

Gerald wants to marry me, and I could be pregnant with his child, and he is gone and he might never come back.

Her time of the month had just finished a few days ago; she wouldn't know if she was pregnant for weeks. There were pregnancy tests available, but it would mean going to a Checquy doctor, explaining the situation, then having him or her inject a frog or a rabbit with her urine and evaluate the results—a test that, bewilderingly, was in no way supernatural. There hadn't been a Pawn with pregnancy-detection ability for forty-seven years, not since Pawn Barraclough passed away. Apparently he had been notoriously grumpy about constantly being bothered, but at least he'd been able to provide immediate information with a swift glance.

Although I don't know if his power worked on someone who might have become pregnant just under an hour ago.

What am I going to do if I am pregnant? she thought. *Will Gerald still want to be with me? What would his parents think? Would they still want him to marry me? What will Lady Carmichael say?*

Stop it. You need to concentrate on finding out more about these black-market dealers.

At that thought, she ducked into the nearest phone box, called the Lady's office at Apex House, and was connected to Pamela.

"You sound tense," Pamela said.

"I am unbelievably tense," said Bridget. "You sound tired." Even through the very bad connection, she could hear the exhaustion in the Pawn's voice.

"I am unbelievably tired," said Pamela. "And it's made all the worse by the latest word on our German friend. The tracking team has finally figured out that the killer and the downed Nazi pilot are probably the same person."

"Oh *Christ*."

"Hmm. So they're being given additional resources to help put this matter to bed. There were some pointed questions about a team that couldn't track down a fugitive German in the middle of wartime London, but..." She trailed off, and Bridget could practically hear her shrug. "With three times as many people working on it, I don't expect it'll be too much longer."

"I just don't see how we can hope to find him before they do," Bridget said, distressed.

"They say if you stand at Piccadilly Circus for long enough, you'll bump into every person you know," Pamela said.

"You're suggesting that we just stand about in public places and *hope?*"

"I think I was joking," said Pamela. "Although, honestly, I have no other ideas at this stage. God, I'm tired. I'm sorry. The Court has been in ongoing conference, the *entire Court,* which means Bishop Alrich, which means all night."

By including a vampire in their ranks, the Court was obliged not to commence proceedings until a good hour after sundown, allowing the Bishop a chance to wake up, drink breakfast, and review the files before having to be pleasant.

"Hopefully this thing with Wattleman will be done by tomorrow," said Bridget. "Oh! I know you'll be busy, but can you ask for any information available on Bobby and Johnny Murcutt?"

"Any odd spelling?" asked Pamela.

"No idea," said Bridget. "There's supposed to be a sister as well. Apparently they're involved in the black market out of a pub in Soho called the Moor's Head. I don't know if they own it or just work out of it."

"When do you need it?" Pamela sighed heavily before Bridget could answer. "I don't even know why I ask. In this business, it's always as soon as possible."

"Wattleman and I are going to go to the pub later today."

"All right, I'll put a priority request into the archives at the Apex and have the dossier sent over to your hotel," said Pamela. "I have to go. Lady Carmichael is waiting."

"Thanks," said Bridget.

"So what are you doing now?" Pamela asked.

"I think I'll go stand at Piccadilly Circus," Bridget said. Pamela laughed, and they hung up.

Except that Bridget really did not know what she was going to do. She did not know where Wattleman had gone, and her head was full of thoughts about herself and Gerald, so she continued on her walk and actually did come to Piccadilly Circus. Despite the war, it was a whirlwind of activity, with a mass of buses and cars honking at each other, at pedestrians, and at the injustices of the world. On the buildings were giant advertisements for Gordon's gin and Wrigley's gum "for vim and vigour." She sat for a while on a bench, drinking in the activity and watching the people go about their business. The Nazi did not happen to conveniently walk by.

Every once in a while, almost with a start, she would remember the situation with the condom and what it might mean for her.

You will not know for a while, she told herself. *There is nothing you can do until then. And you have quite enough to focus on in the meantime.*

So put it out of your head.

Now.

Eventually she roused herself and walked back to the hotel to find a package waiting for her at the desk. *The dossier from Pamela.*

When she unlocked the door to the hotel room, it was dim inside. The curtains had been drawn, and she flicked on the light to see a curled-up figure in the bed. Wattleman sat up in confusion, then vanished. Bridget sighed. There was no empty set of pajamas sitting up in confusion.

"I hope you at least have a set of bottoms on," she said flatly. There was a chuckle of amusement, then the blankets rustled themselves, and she heard the sound of footsteps going over to the suitcase. For no good reason, Bridget averted her gaze as a pair of drawers were drawn up to hug thin air, followed by trousers lifted from a nearby chair. When she looked back, Wattleman was smiling as he buttoned up his shirt.

"You startled me," he said.

"How are you feeling?" asked Bridget awkwardly. "Did you get some rest?"

"Oh, yes. I noticed there were fresh linens on the bed."

"Yes." She braced herself for some horrendous remark, but beyond a slightly knowing smile, he mercifully made no comment. "So, um, thanks," she said, blushing madly. She didn't bring up the structural failure of the condom—she couldn't believe it would have been a deliberate action on his part.

"How did you spend the rest of the day?" he asked.

"Scouting," she said, vaguely and inaccurately. "Pamela sent us a dossier." She handed it over, and he flipped through it, frowning. "It had to come from Scotland Yard. There were no records of any Murcutts in the Apex indexes." An entire team of scholars in Apex House maintained a vast and detailed catalog of supernatural history, but a note from Pamela had advised that nothing relevant had come up. "I expect she had to pull some strings to get it this quickly, though for not very much of a result."

"Have you read it?"

"I skimmed it in the lobby. The Murcutts in question are Robert, John, and Matilda. Also known as Bobby, Johnny, and Tillie. Ages thirty-one, twenty-eight, and twenty-seven, respectively. Only surviving children of George and Agnes of Soho, both deceased. George was the publican of the Moor's Head."

"How did he acquire it?" asked Wattleman.

"It doesn't say." Bridget shrugged. "Agnes was a midwife, and we have some notes that she was probably also an abortionist but she was never charged."

"Apart from that, any sniffs of criminal activity by the parents?"

"Never brought in for anything. The father died five years ago, and Robert is now the official owner of the pub. Apparently, it's quite a roaring concern, even in wartime."

"So what's the siblings' criminal record?"

"Robert's stretches back to his youth, starting with nicking fruit from Covent Garden market."

"Clearly a budding criminal mastermind."

"What, you never scrumped apples from a neighbor's orchard?" asked Bridget. She and her fellow apprentice certainly had, until the neighbor complained to their master. They'd all been forced to go over to the neighbor, beg his pardon, use their own money to pay him for permission to cut a switch each, and bring the switches back to the house for their punishment.

"Anyway," she continued, "from filched fruit, he graduated to running with some bad eggs, a bit of breaking and entering, a stay in Borstal, a robbery, and a stint inside grown-up prison. And that appears to be it. No more troubles. The system worked."

"Oh, I'm sure. And the other two?"

"Nothing," said Bridget. "Street intelligence says that Mother Agnes kept a firm hand on them both, made sure they weren't out running wild like their brother. She died three years ago."

"And then?"

"Nothing. No crimes, not even mentioned as persons of interest in any investigations."

"Are they employed?"

"The brothers run the pub. Nothing on the sister."

"Well, that's bloody useless."

"I told you, not much," said Bridget.

"Still, Simony was very convincing, and it's our only lead."

"If we're going to that pub, I suppose we should go now."

"You seem a little subdued. Are you all right?" he asked.

"I'm fine," said Bridget firmly. "Let's go do this."

Soho was not looking well, which saddened Bridget. She remembered it from before the war, when it was raffish and exciting, but now the times had made it gray and grim. There were still lots of people about, but they all had dour looks on their faces and all appeared to be in a hurry, with collars turned up and eyes fixed on the pavement. The restaurants offered severely diminished menus and did not seem to be attracting much clientele. There were gaps between buildings where bombs had fallen. A couple of prostitutes eyed Bridget and Wattleman listlessly as they passed.

The famous theaters had almost all closed because of the Blitz, with the notable exception of the Windmill Theatre, whose *Revudeville* continued to feature a variety of singers, dancers, and specialty performers, including the celebrated nude tableaux vivants. Wattleman gave a wistful little sigh as they passed it, and Bridget rolled her eyes.

"So, how do we want to do this?" she asked. "You're the expert." They were three streets away from the pub and had paused to discuss strategy.

"You'll need to go in and ask the questions," said Wattleman. "All of Simony's customers for relics were women. I'll be backup."

"So we should go in separately?"

"No, I'll come in with you."

"Oh, are we doing the husband-and-wife thing again?" asked Bridget. "Because I don't think that'll work as well."

"No, no, they won't see me."

"Why won't—oh, come on!"

"We are going into a situation we know nothing about but that may very well have supernatural elements. It would be good to have every advantage we can," he said in an infuriatingly reasonable tone.

"Fine," sighed Bridget. "So you're just going to duck into an alley and strip?"

"This *is* Soho."

"Go ahead, but I'm not carrying your clothes around."

She was, however, obliged to keep watch as Wattleman crouched behind some boxes in an alley to disrobe and disappear. His clothes were bundled up and tucked between the boxes and the wall with the vague hope that no one would find them and steal them, although since they were some of his shabby undercover garments, he didn't seem too distressed at the prospect of losing them.

To Bridget's immense satisfaction, there was a spanking breeze as they walked the last two blocks to the pub. She could only assume that Wattleman was next to her, but the other pedestrians on the pavement thankfully precluded any conversation. When they finally arrived in front of the pub, she paused and looked at it thoughtfully.

The Moor's Head was large, but it had not weathered the Blitz well. The building across the street had been bombed, and the pub's facade was peppered with scorch marks and the scars of shrapnel. That said, it did not give the impression of having been in particularly good shape to begin with. Paint was peeling, and the front step looked as if it hadn't been scrubbed in Bridget's lifetime. It was a three-story building, and someone had covered the windows with stout boards. The naive might assume it was because of the bombings, an alternative to putting stars of tape across the glass, but Bridget noted that it would also defend against any law-enforcement or criminal elements that wanted to enter unexpectedly. Regardless, the architectural decision did not add to the establishment's salubriousness. Even the hanging pub sign looked decidedly under the weather, the filth coating the letters giving the impression that the two Checquy agents were actually entering THE MOOP'S HEAD.

Bridget walked in, briefly holding the door open behind her for the invisible Wattleman to scuttle through. For all its paucity, the police report had been right on the money when it came to the brisk business the pub was doing. There were quite a few people inside, and they seemed to be enjoying themselves a bit. A man at a piano was playing a lively tune, and several patrons were carrying on a happy, slightly drunken sing-along. Despite the boarded-up windows, the space had a sort of cozy feel to it. She made her way to the bar, leaving Wattleman to come up with his own strategy.

"Half a pint of shandy, please," she said to the barman, who didn't seem to have any objection to serving a woman in the main room. Some establishments provided a parlor for women to sit in, but this did not appear to be one of them. She accepted the beverage and turned to look around.

"This is not a pub," Wattleman whispered right in her ear.

"Jaysus!" She flinched in surprise, managing to slosh half her glass down her front. She got a few looks, and the barman handed her a rag to wipe herself off with. "What was that?" she muttered between her teeth.

"This is not a pub."

"You think it's just someone's house?" she answered dryly. "Because if so, they've got a cheek. Did you see what they just charged me for a half of shandy?"

"Take a look around," said Wattleman. "Note the women in particular." Bridget carefully surveyed the room. There were a surprising number of women, all talking and laughing rather raucously. "It's a knocking shop," said his voice.

"A brothel?" said Bridget quietly, startled.

"This *is* Soho."

"Stop saying that."

"In any case, this may be bad."

"I think it's entirely appropriate," she said. "You're already naked, after all."

"A woman who comes here by herself—"

"Is a customer for supernatural artifacts," said Bridget firmly. "Which reminds me." She turned back to the bar and flagged down the barman. "Excuse me, I was looking to talk to one of the Murcutts."

"They're not in yet," he said. "At least one of them should be in soon. I'll let them know you want to chat."

"Ta."

"I'm going to have a look around the place," whispered Wattleman.

Bridget nodded. Presumably he left. Now that she knew the true nature of the business, the jollity of the establishment made sense. At least half the bonhomie was a professional facade. She eyed the men and women thoughtfully. It was an automatic reflex for her to look for supernatural elements, for any unnatural forces or physical features at play, and there were a few potential manifestations. That frizzy-haired girl in the corner, for instance. Her hand was resting firmly on the bald man's wrist, and she was gazing at him intently. Was she exerting some sort of unnatural influence? Was that why he had a sheen of perspiration across his forehead and was continually licking his lips? Or was it just that she was about eighteen, and he was about forty?

The voluptuous woman by the piano had been singing for some minutes, and the men around her were staring at her in rapt fascination. Was it her voice that exerted a hypnotic domination over them, or was it that she was practically spilling out of her low-cut dress?

Bridget came to the rueful conclusion that there were no occult forces at work in the room, just the usual forces of lust and money.

"You look a cheerful lass," said a large man who'd wandered up to the bar. "I don't think I've seen you here before. New to the Head, are you?" She looked at him in stupefaction. "No need to be shy, we know what you're here for."

"She's not one of our girls, Starkey," said the barman. "She's here to meet with the Murcutts."

"Job interview?" he said hopefully.

"Personal matter," said Bridget.

"Well, sorry, then," said Starkey.

"I quite understand," said Bridget. "An easy mistake to make, given the circumstances."

"Jimmy, give the lass a drink on me." He nodded to her and wandered back to the piano, where an impromptu knees-up was commencing.

"Another shandy?" asked the barman.

"I think I'll stick with this one," said Bridget, holding up her glass. "Maybe in a bit." He nodded and moved away, and she turned her gaze back to her drink. It seemed a pose that would discourage conversation. She became aware of a slight humming that grew closer and a little louder.

"*Hmmmm* . . . it's me," said the voice of Wattleman.

"What's with the humming?" she said to her drink.

"If you're going to be so damn jumpy, I thought a little foreplay might make initiating conversation easier."

"That was actually quite thoughtful of you," she said. "Did you find anything?"

"Well, I think I've found at least part of the reason that the police don't have intelligence on the Murcutts."

"Oh?"

"Yes. There are three bobbies upstairs in a large private room being entertained by some professional young ladies."

"You're sure they're police?"

"Quite. They were all wearing their helmets, although nothing else."

"Ugh. Anything supernatural?"

"No, not yet. Any sign of the Murcutts?" he asked. She shook her head slightly. "I'm going to take a look downstairs, see if there's anything interesting stored there. People are always putting their supernatural items in the cellar." She nodded.

Bridget sat, cautiously sipping her drink every once in a while. Behind her, the piano jangled out various cheerful tunes. Men came and went, sometimes out the front door, sometimes up the stairs with convincingly enthusiastic women. The level of cheer in the room seemed constant. The boarded-up windows gave the place a curiously timeless feel—there were no clocks anywhere, and without daylight, it was difficult to tell how much time was passing. Still, the mental clock that all Londoners had come to possess since the beginning of the Blitz was ticking away the minutes. Bridget felt uneasy, as if she should be hurrying to the nearest shelter.

"Miss?"

"Hmm?" She looked up to see the bartender addressing her.

"Miss Murcutt and Mr. John Murcutt are here. They came in through the back."

"Oh, good." She looked around. "Can I talk to them? Where should I go?"

"There's a parlor upstairs. Maudie will take you." He gestured to a heavily made-up young woman. *Where did she manage to get lipstick?* Bridget wondered absently. Cosmetics were in short supply.

"Thank you," she said. *I hope Wattleman has gotten back from the cellar.* She didn't relish the idea of going upstairs without some backup. She would even have welcomed an invisible hand on her shoulder or a tap on her wrist to let her know. The girl led her through a door marked PRIVATE and up a flight of narrow, creaking steps that probably dated back to the Conquest. Alarmingly, there were no extra creakings on the staircase behind them, which suggested that Wattleman was not present. The lights burned dimly, and she was uncomfortable. She discreetly checked her switchblade in its sheath on her forearm. There was another knife on her shin.

Then they were in a hallway lined with doors. Bridget could faintly hear noises and voices behind them, but she very deliberately focused on the swaying form of the girl, who led her to the very end of the hall and then up a flight of stairs.

That's an odd design, Bridget mused. *Stairs on opposite sides of the house from each other? It slows down the entrance.*

And it means no quick escape. She increasingly felt like a rabbit being led into a wolf's den.

"May I ask, where do you get your lipstick?" she said, if only to break her own tension. "It's lovely, and it's so difficult to get any cosmetics now."

"Oh, thanks," said Maudie. "It's from cooked beetroot."

"Ah," said Bridget.

"Yeah, and then you rub some Vaseline over it to seal it in. Works a treat, don't you think?"

"I do. I will definitely try it." *If I get out of here alive.*

"We were keeping all the ends of our lipsticks," said the girl, "and melting them down in a cup. You know, use every little bit—but then it all ran out." On the landing at the top of the second set of stairs was another door. Maudie knocked and they heard "Come." She opened it, gestured Bridget through, and then, without entering, shut it behind her.

The Murcutts' parlor did not look at all like it belonged in a brothel, and Bridget resisted the urge to remark upon this fact. It took up almost the entire third story and was brightly lit, with no coy red shades over the lamps. A plush, intricate Afghan rug covered the floor in the center of the room. There was no art on the walls, but they gleamed with white paint. A table stood off to the right with an array of decanters and bottles, a startling variety of liquors. A couple of plump overstuffed sofas were at the other side of the space, inviting one to lounge. There was no desk or chairs. It did not look like an office and certainly not like the nerve center of a black-market operation in supernatural artifacts.

There were three people in the room—a lean man standing by a side door, a large man busying himself at the table with the bottles, and, standing up from one of the sofas, a sharp-featured blond woman a couple of years older than Bridget. She was striking and drew the eye away from the men. Wearing a dress of light green silk almost shocking in its newness and delicacy, she, too, had on makeup, but it was not garishly applied like Maudie's, and it was definitely real cosmetics. She had a cocktail in one hand and a cigarette in a holder in the other.

The hair on the back of Bridget's neck prickled—the woman's bearing, her self-assurance, somehow put her in mind of Lady Carmichael. Matilda "Tillie" Murcutt held power and knew how to use it. She regarded Bridget with cool eyes, taking in every detail. Bridget could feel herself being itemized and evaluated.

"Miss Murcutt?" said Bridget. She did not step forward to shake hands.

"Yes."

"I am Miss Caswell. Thank you for seeing me." She paused, but there was no introduction to the two men, who were watching her curiously.

"And what have you come to see me about?" Tillie Murcutt asked. "I understand that you are not seeking employment?"

Bridget flushed. "No, I'm not. Your name was mentioned to me as a potential source for some unusual antiques."

"Antiques?" said Tillie, raising an eyebrow. "That's hardly our stock-in-trade, but we have connections throughout the community. We might be able to find you something appropriate. Who referred you?"

"A Mr. Simony," said Bridget carefully. This was a gamble— would Simony have pointed a customer to the Murcutts? She'd discussed it with Wattleman, and they'd agreed to try the story out. But they'd also assumed that Wattleman would be in the room to step in if things turned sour. "He didn't want to tell me at first, but he said he wouldn't be able to fetch anything for a couple of days, and I wouldn't wait. So I paid him off. I paid him a great deal."

"Simony," said Tillie musingly. "So you're interested in magic." Bridget stared at her, wide-eyed. "Don't look so innocent. That was Simony's trade, at least when it came to us, so let's not be coy. Now, please, have a seat." Bridget allowed herself to be ushered to a sofa and sat cautiously. "Can we press you to a drink?"

"Lemonade?" asked Bridget. She had no intention of drinking it.

"I expect we can get some," said Tillie. Apparently the gleaming array of bottles on the table did not include anything soft. An instruction was passed to someone outside the door while Tillie settled herself on the couch opposite Bridget. She took a long draw on her cigarette, regarding Bridget thoughtfully.

"And so you believe in magic," said Tillie. "Tell me, how did that come to happen?"

"A friend of mine had an item from Simony. She showed me."

"What item?"

"A seashell," Bridget said. That had been the only item that didn't kill its user straight out. "The things it did..." She did her best to let a look of awe come over her face. *Sell it,* she told herself. *Make her believe.* She spoke with all the passion she could muster. "It was the most amazing thing I've ever seen in my life. She wouldn't let me buy it from her, of course. No matter how much I offered." *Let this woman think that I have significant money to spend.* "But she told me where she'd gotten it. So it's not a case of believing in magic. I *know* it's real, and I want it."

The woman regarded her levelly for a few moments, then nodded.

"I've always known about magic," said Tillie. "My mother was a midwife, and *her* mother before her. They attended women in the tenements and the rookeries and the slums, and they told me about what they saw. There were all sorts of heartwarming stories about mothers and babies, but when they got in their cups, sometimes they'd tell me the other stories. The strange ones." Almost despite herself, Tillie took a long drink, finishing the cocktail. Her eyes had a faraway look.

"Sometimes they saw things that weren't normal at all. Mum remembered a baby born in an attic, a birth that thirty-odd people had crowded in to witness, singing the whole time. She said that when she cut the cord, there was a spark of light. That little babe was wrapped in a silk blanket—God knows where they got it—and carried away. Never heard any more about it, but it was damn odd.

"Gran swore she'd been at a birth where she could hear the sound of the ocean coming out of the mother, and the baby was washed out onto the mattress on a stream of seawater. Another time, there was a woman tried to pay with a little clay flower that she swore would keep you warm if you held it in your hand, even if you were naked in a winter street. And there were others.

"You see people as they really are in a birthing room. Mothers and babies and fathers. And when I say *strange,* I mean *inhuman.* Maybe even what you might call *monstrous.* Sometimes when a baby came out and my mother saw what it was, the only appropriate tool she could use was a pillow. Sometimes it was a hammer." Her eyes were distant, and Bridget found that she was holding her breath.

"They weren't flighty women, our mum and gran," said Murcutt finally. "Were they, Johnny?" She looked over at the blond man by the bottles and he shook his head. Despite his muscular build, he had the same sharp features as Tillie.

So that's John Murcutt, thought Bridget. *And who's the other man?* Thin, Mediterranean-looking, with olive skin and black hair, he didn't look like a relation.

"No," continued Tillie Murcutt. "Not the sort to make up ghost stories. They didn't have a lick of frivolity in them. I knew it was real, so when my brothers and I took up the business, I kept my eyes open. Magic sounded like an opportunity. And there's a lot more of it about than you'd expect."

Bridget started as the sound of the air-raid siren keened through the wooden shields over the windows. How much time had passed while she was waiting downstairs, lost in a reverie? And how long had she been listening to the Murcutt woman tell her stories?

"The sirens are early tonight," said Bridget. "We should go, shouldn't we? I can come back another time. Tomorrow. I have money."

"No hurry," said Tillie. She finished her cigarette and lit another. "This place hasn't been hit yet, so I don't expect it will be hit now."

What kind of demented logic is that? thought Bridget nervously.

"So, you want to buy some magic," said Tillie. "Like your friend, hmm? You want to do your bit?"

"Something like that," said Bridget vaguely. She had no idea what Tillie was talking about.

"Well, we do those sales through Simony," said Tillie. "That's been our policy. And he knows to never, ever give our names to anyone." Bridget blinked, then felt herself pinned, her limbs locked in place. She looked down in bewilderment and saw that there was no one holding her, but her clothes were furled tight about her. She tried to move but couldn't.

"What's going on?" Bridget said, her teeth gritted as she strained against her own sleeves. "What the hell is this?"

"This is Vincent," said Tillie, gesturing to the man who wasn't her brother, who'd been silent the whole time. "Known him all my life. My mum delivered him in a little place over in Seven Dials, and as soon as she cut the cord, all the bedclothes started rustling about madly. A bit unsettling. So she kept an eye on him, and it turned out that Vincent can actually control cloth with his mind. That magic you want? It's literally inside him."

Yeah, amazing, thought Bridget dryly. And then suddenly she was being forced to stand, her clothes pushing her up out of her seat. Her coat had her arms pinioned against her sides, and her gloves had forced her hands closed. Her skirt was clamped about her legs. Her heavy woolen stockings wouldn't let her bend her knees. She was trying with all her strength to push against the material, even to rip it, but the force of the grasp had her caught like a fly in amber. She teetered a little, but the clothes actually held her upright, a rigid shell enclosing her.

"When we started this business, I thought people like Vincent would be useful. I like to have aces in the hole," said Tillie. "When one is uncertain of the situation, it's best to be subtle. Especially on one's own premises. No sense in having thugs smash up the furniture when it's *your* furniture." She accepted a fresh cocktail from her brother. "Thank you, Johnny." She turned back to Bridget. "Oh, yes, he's very, very good at what he does." She lifted her glass in a toast to Vincent, then took a thoughtful drink.

"Bill Simony is the link between us and the street when it comes to magic wares. We take that very seriously, and we made sure that he would take it very seriously. Now, maybe you could pay him more than we do, but you can't put a greater fear in him than we do."

Want to bet?

"So the only way you could have gotten him to talk is through some extremely hard questioning." She pursed her lips and regarded Bridget coldly. "If we send someone around to Bill's flat, what will they find?"

A notable lack of Simony, thought Bridget. *If they look closely, they'll probably find traces of blood on the table. And some of his wares missing. But unless they start burrowing through tons of rubble nearby, they won't find him.*

"Vincent," Tillie called over her shoulder, "is she carrying any weapons?"

The slim man wrinkled his face for a moment, and Bridget felt a ripple go over her as her clothes tightened and loosened a little. It was unpleasant, intrusive, like someone briskly running his hands over her entire body.

"Knife on her right arm," he said. "And her left shin."

"I'll get those," said Johnny, the Murcutt brother. He ambled over, drink in hand, and carefully unstrapped the weapons from the furiously immobile Bridget. "Hello, got a very nasty flick knife," he said, opening her switchblade. "Not what I'd expect from a sweet young thing looking to buy antiques. Not even magic antiques." He tucked her other blade away in his coat but continued to examine the modifications to the switchblade.

"Now, we want some more information," said Tillie. "Who are you *really*? And what do you want?"

Maybe I can still work this situation, Bridget thought. "I didn't kill Simony," Bridget said truthfully. "I would never. I could never." That was much less truthful. "I just want to buy an antique. A special antique." She paused, then put a tremble in her voice. "A *magic* antique, yes. And I didn't feel safe coming to a place like this without some protection. That's why I had the knives."

"The sheath is worn," said the brother, looking up from it. "It's seen a fair bit of use." He peered closely at the switchblade. "Can't tell if this has been used recently. Don't see any blood in the join."

"You're not the kind of person who has been buying these items," said Tillie. "You need to start telling us something that makes sense unless you want things to get much more unpleasant. Do you want Vincent to start stripping off your clothes? There's men downstairs who would appreciate the show."

"There's also something on her palms," said Vincent suddenly. "I don't know what's going on there."

"Interesting," said Tillie. "Show us, please."

Against her will, Bridget's coat bent her arms up, and her gloves turned her palms up and spread her fingers. The cloth of the gloves shivered and then tore open, splitting at the center of her wrist and peeling back to the base of her middle fingers. The rainbow shimmer of her palms flared in the bright light of the room, and everyone was silent for a moment.

"What is that, jewelry?" asked Tillie. The gloves peeled back a little more and twisted her hands about so that everyone could see that it was actually her skin.

Shit, thought Bridget. *Well, the die is cast now.*

"So," said Tillie finally. "There's more to you than meets the eye. Although, really, there would almost have to be."

Bridget rolled her eyes. "Do you have to be rude on top of everything else?" she asked. Her tartness was probably ill-advised, but restraint hadn't gotten her anywhere good, and the revealing of her palms meant a shift in the dynamic. "I mean, it's not enough to be a pimping black marketeer trafficking in dangerous relics. You've also got to be a snotty bitch?"

Tillie raised her eyebrows in surprise. "You *are* quite the feisty one, aren't you? It must be the magic in you. Honestly, magic people are just coming out of the woodwork suddenly," she mused. "So who are you? What are you? What do you want?"

"I just want to buy some antiques," said Bridget. "It's not too late to make this just an easy, profitable transaction."

"Yes, you just want to buy some antiques. And kill some antiques dealers," said Tillie scornfully. "You already know more than you should, and you've added more to the equation than I like. You're interesting, but I think we need to end this development. Now." She stubbed out her cigarette firmly in a gilt ashtray.

"What, you're just going to kill me?" asked Bridget. It was clear that they *were* just going to kill her and that they were eminently capable of it. Talking bought her time. Where was Wattleman? The door hadn't popped open, and there'd been no chance for him to follow her in. Was he still wandering about the pub looking for her? Had he fallen afoul of something in the cellar? Hell, was he just ogling the women in the parlor? Should she scream or would that alert them?

"It's a pity, it really is," said Tillie. "I spend a lot of effort and money seeking out magic and people with magic. I have people on the street keeping their eyes out for anything unusual, any opportunity, because they know I'll pay for it. And then you just come walking in with your lovely rainbow hands." She shook her head regretfully. "But you're touching on a subject that's very delicate, so I really do think that killing you would be best. Vincent, take care of her, please, and see if you can slice off her hands. There's that taxidermist that comes to visit with Peg, maybe he can do something with them, and we can sell them on."

Vincent nodded, and Bridget felt her clothes begin to draw themselves in all around her, most tightly at her wrists and her throat. She gasped, and then the collar of her blouse was cinching itself in around her windpipe, cutting off her air. Panic exploded in her, but she couldn't struggle—her garments held her too closely. Her chest heaved as she tried frantically to draw breath, but all she could do was make choking noises. Her wrists were agony as the cuffs of her coat pinched tighter and tighter.

The wailing of the air-raid siren in the background suddenly seemed louder through the wooden shields on the windows. Bridget's knees were jelly, but her clothes held her up rigid. As the room wavered in front of her eyes, she could feel her heart punching in her chest, and almost as a counterpoint, she thought she could hear the distant crump of bombs landing on the city.

And then the table with all the bottles flung itself across the room in a horrendous burst of shattering glass and breaking wood, narrowly missing everyone and crashing into a wall. All the people in the room screamed, even Bridget, who managed an explosive gurgling exclamation out of sheer fright. In the shock of the moment, though, she felt the fabric around her relax as one of the flying bottles clipped Vincent and distracted him. She gasped.

"Was that you?" the brother asked Bridget uncertainly.

"I don't think it was her," said the sister, looking around, her eyes narrowed. "She screamed as well, genuine shock."

"And she didn't move a muscle," said Vincent. "I would have felt her flex." As if recalling her, the material abruptly tightened about Bridget again, but this time to restrain, not to throttle.

"It wasn't her," said Wattleman's voice from somewhere near the door. "It was me." Bridget sagged in her clothes, limp with relief.

"What in the bloody hell?" exclaimed Tillie. She had produced a gun from somewhere, and her eyes were darting around looking for something to aim it at. Johnny had Bridget's switchblade in one hand, the blade snapped open.

"You people don't know what you've gotten yourselves into," said Wattleman's voice. It seemed to have moved, was bouncing off the walls from a corner. "You'd be wise to let her go. Now."

No one moved, and Bridget's garments remained rigid around her. Everyone was still, poised, and then they all jumped as one of the sofas was violently flipped onto its back.

"Vince?" asked Johnny. The lean man was looking about intently with the air of a dog trying to catch a scent.

"Don't bother asking *him*," said Wattleman's voice, heavy with contempt. "He'll be no use to you at all. You know why?"

"Why?" asked Johnny carefully.

"Because I'm his worst fucking nightmare," said Wattleman's voice, and his glee was palpable. "I'm merciless, I'm here to kill you all, and I'm stark-bollock naked."

A moment of fascinated horror left the room silent, while outside the siren continued to wail, and the bombs fell in the distance.

Then: "Nice try," said Vincent. He dropped to one knee and flung his arms up. The rug in the center of the room tore itself up from the floor like a net snaring a tiger. Horrified, Bridget caught a glimpse of flesh blurring into existence among the folds of the rug as it hurtled straight up through the air to slam flat against the ceiling. Flat, except for the unmistakable bulge in the middle of a wriggling human being pressed against the wood. "Wanker," said Vincent.

Oh, hell, thought Bridget. *Well, that rescue was nice while it lasted.*

"Whew," said Johnny. He shakily wiped his brow with his sleeve. "Nicely done, Vince. That gave me a turn, I tell you."

"Christ, though, they really *are* coming out of the woodwork," said Tillie.

Bridget realized that, in the excitement, with all the strength and focus that Vincent was bringing to bear on the captured Wattleman, he had forgotten about her and had released his hold on her clothes. The Murcutts were unaware that Bridget was free. They had no reason to think otherwise. As far as they were concerned, she was still pinioned by her garments, so they continued to stare up at the writhing form of Wattleman pinned against the ceiling.

It's up to you now, Bridget thought, *so be quick.* With little movements, she slid the torn remnants of her gloves off and hurriedly ran her fingers around the inside and outside of her collar. She felt the tingle as pearl substance seeped out of her skin, creating an armored ring within the cloth—a gorget around her neck that would not flex. *Let's see him try to crumple that and strangle me,* she thought. Vincent's control over material was remarkable, but the substance she generated was incredibly strong.

Of course, he could probably still do all sorts of unthinkable things—she was uncomfortably aware of her underwear and the potential for an extremely disconcerting attack. Still, this might buy her some time, which could make all the difference.

"He's putting up a fight, isn't he?" said Johnny Murcutt. The flailing be-carpeted figure of Wattleman on the ceiling looked like someone trying to fight his way clear of a rising liquid, except upside down. They could see the palpable strain of an arm forcing itself against the cloth, the shudders as his muscles fought against the inexorable pressure on him.

Bridget hurriedly curled her left hand around her right cuff to bind it into shape, then slid her hand up her sleeve, laying down lustrous strips to protect herself. And then the other arm. She made three strips across her front, at her breasts, the base of her ribs, and low across her abdomen. It took precious moments, but binding up the cloth into a rigid form might hamper Vincent's powers. She took hold of the side seam of her skirt and tore it up halfway, enabling free movement. Finally, she ran careful fingertips over the back of her own right hand, building up glistening, knobby knuckle-dusters.

"So what do you think, Vincent?" Tillie was asking.

"I'll smother him," said the slim man tightly. His arms were still held up, and he was shaking with effort. Sweat was pouring off his face.

"Fine. Good." The carpet pressed itself up tight against the ceiling, squeezing the air out and away. The movements of the humped figure were growing weaker. They could see it twitching, straining against the material, but whatever power Vincent infused through the fabric was enough to bind Wattleman.

Until the hump gathered itself into a ball. The carpet was so tight against Wattleman that they could see the outline of him crouched, his feet braced against the ceiling. And then it extended, the Pawn pushing himself down, his straightened fingers tearing through the rug, against all the strength of Vincent's will. His hands clawed at the tear, widening it, and then he was wriggling through the slit even as the material struggled to close itself about him. Wattleman squirmed, strained, not invisible but undeniable. They all watched transfixed as his naked form pushed itself through the gap and crashed onto the wooden floor. He heaved in great breaths.

"Oh, fuck," said Johnny.

"'Oh, fuck' is right," said Bridget in a tone of deep satisfaction. Startled, they all three turned to her and, to her delight, flinched at the sight of her in her shining armor. "Before, this was strictly professional. But now?" She nodded to Wattleman. "You ready?"

"The fabricomancer is mine," he said flatly.

"You're welcome to him."

And then Wattleman was charging across the room toward the horrified Vincent. He was still visible, so intent on smashing the slim man to pieces that he didn't bother to conceal himself. Vincent clawed his hand through the air, and the curtains tore themselves down from the windows and spun across the room like bolas to wrap themselves around the Pawn's ankles. Everyone—regardless of gender or organizational affiliation—winced as the naked man slammed face-etcetera-down flat on the floor.

Bridget couldn't spare any attention to Wattleman, however, because John Murcutt was addressing himself entirely to the issue of her. His eyes roamed over the strips of armor on her clothes as he stepped closer. He was big and carried himself with the balanced grace of an experienced fighter. He held her switchblade easily, as if well accustomed to it, and she felt a tingle of fear.

Move fast, she told herself.

He darted in abruptly, slashing at her eyes. She raised her left arm, letting the knife skitter off her armored sleeve, and slammed her pearl-encrusted fist at his stomach. He twisted away and danced back, so her weapon-hand just grazed him. His eyes were narrowed—they were getting the measure of each other.

Vicious, she thought. *A street fighter. Nothing like that German's formal training.* This man would be far less predictable, pulling out moves she'd never thought of. Some men on the streets knew tricks no soldier would ever learn. They wouldn't go for the kill you'd expect; they would place greater emphasis on wounding and maiming, bringing death by twelve painful cuts instead of one clean stab.

However, he'd never faced an opponent like her. She stroked her free hand over her right fist once more, building up a thicker gauntlet around her skin, a cestus. She swiftly sculpted a vicious ridge along her knuckles and lashed out with a boxing jab that he dodged but that bought her a little space.

In the background, she caught a glimpse of Wattleman recovering. He rolled over and curled up, ripped the curtains from around his ankles, and sent them fluttering in shreds to the floor. Vincent, looking distinctly panicked at this point, whipped the plaid scarf from around his neck and eeled it through the air; it snapped over the Pawn's face, covering his eyes. Wattleman gave a muffled roar of rage and set about digging his fingers into the cloth.

Tillie Murcutt did not allow herself to be hypnotized by the arresting spectacle of a muscular naked man fighting with a tartan accessory. Instead, she carefully brought her gun around and aimed at Wattleman's head. She fired, and he fell back on the floor, suddenly still.

No! thought Bridget, but Johnny Murcutt burst forward at her again. He grabbed her weapon-hand with his left and with his right he stabbed at her throat. Bridget stepped into the attack, caught the blade in her free hand, and, despite herself, yelped in pain as it slashed across her palm. They struggled for a moment, then she twisted against his grip, breaking it. She planted her feet and shoved him back.

Focus on your own fight! she told herself, *or you're dead!*

Tillie Murcutt stepped forward, cautiously, to investigate the body at her feet. At a gesture from her, Vincent sent his scarf wriggling down from the Pawn's face. She frowned, then gasped as Wattleman's eyes opened, and his hand snapped up to grasp her pistol. She fired madly but had to let go as he tightened his grip and crushed the gun.

"Vincent!" she barked, and the scarf twisted itself into a tight cord around Wattleman's throat. The Pawn thrashed and flailed on the floor, clawing at the taut material turned garrote.

Johnny had fallen back into a fighting stance, ready for Bridget's next move. As their eyes met, she nodded toward the knife in his hand. Despite himself, his eyes flickered from her to the blade, and then he was staring incredulously at the knife in his hand. Rather than blood, it was coated in a thick sleeve of shining white. As a stabbing or cutting implement, it was now as useful as a baguette. Then his eye was caught by something else, and he stared down at his own shirt. There, glistening on his chest was a small, perfect handprint of pearl. He looked back at Bridget, and she raised her eyebrows.

Not as easy as you thought, is it?

His face set in sour determination, he tossed the useless knife to one side and produced her other knife from inside his coat. Abruptly, he vaulted forward. Bridget stepped crisply to the side and brought her hand up, fingers spread wide so the nacre of her skin flashed in the light, and he flinched back. She stepped in smoothly and punched him with her knuckle-dustered hand. He saw it coming and blocked but gave out a cry as her blow smacked into his forearm. They fell back from each other, he panting, she considering.

A little harder and a better angle, and I'd have broken his arm, she thought. His eyes were fixed on her hands now. She'd taught him to fear them. *He'll want to come in close,* she decided, *deny me the room to strike at him, use one hand to stop me from touching him and use his size and strength to force the knife into me.*

Her eyes flickered to the scene behind her enemy. Wattleman had torn the scarf off his throat and was on his feet. The tartan cloth flailed in his hand like a frantic snake as Vincent's power tried to rip it from his grasp. Tillie had produced another gun and was firing at his body and head, which he completely ignored as he advanced inexorably on Vincent.

Then Johnny came forward at Bridget again, his knife held reversed in his hand, his other hand a claw. He was startled when she took two quick steps back and he fixed his eyes on her raised hands. Which was why it was so horrendously effective when, keeping her eyes on his, she stepped forward lightning fast and slammed her foot into the side of his knee. She stepped to the right, crunched down on the knee from the other side, then whipped her foot up into his face with all the merciless precision her savate instructor had instilled in her.

("The English do not use their feet," he had said, shrugging. "They think it is dirty fighting. You know what I call it? Winning.")

Johnny fell to his knees, dropping the knife. He was wobbling, his eyes unfocused, and for a moment it looked as if he would be sick. Bridget glanced over and saw horror in Vincent's eyes as Wattleman bore down on him. The slim man gave a desperate shriek and threw his arms up. The sofa that Wattleman had tossed aside earlier was wrenched from its place, dragged by the cloth covering it, and sent flying at the Pawn. Wattleman set his shoulders, stepped forward, and struck out with his fist.

The sofa exploded.

Timber and stuffing and cloth burst from the dreadful force of that blow. Everyone ducked except for the still-reeling Johnny and the relentless Wattleman, who continued on through the cloud of debris.

And then the other sofa in the room came flying at Wattleman from behind, and before Bridget could cry out a warning, it had punched his legs out from under him. He landed on his back and the sofa halted, then forced itself down onto him. The cloth parts of the furniture tensed and fractured the frame so that it could pin his wrists, denying him leverage, and twisted so that a ridge of wood was forced down onto his throat. He gasped and choked. Cloth unraveled and rewove itself into cords that pushed down with greater force.

Bridget recalled what she had read in Wattleman's file. She knew he could withstand tremendous physical harm and that he could hold his breath for a long time, but he still needed to breathe eventually. There was panic in his eyes, and he looked to her for help.

So she put her hand on the dazed Johnny's face, firmly pressed the heel of her palm against his eye socket, and spread her fingers across his brow and cheek. After a moment of thought, she lifted her hand away to reveal the thick, glossy demi-mask of a handprint that she'd sealed to his skin. She pushed him, and he fell back. His mouth opened, his skin bunching around the rigid pearl-material, and he wailed.

"Stop!" shouted Bridget. All three of them—Tillie, Vincent, the strangled Wattleman—stared at her, aghast. "Let him go."

"Don't, Vincent!" shouted Tillie. "He'll kill us."

"Do you want your brother to stay like this?" demanded Bridget, gesturing to Johnny. "Do you want worse to happen to him? Or to *you?* Because it will! I swear it!" The blond woman stared at her, calculating. Then she raised her pistol and pointed it directly at Bridget's head. "Honestly?" asked Bridget. "Do you think we have time for this? Listen!"

The noise outside from the air raid was so horrendous, they had to shout. Bombs seemed to be going off all around them. Whatever Tillie Murcutt had been about to say was lost, as, with a sound like the end of the world, a tremendous crash came from immediately above them. Everyone flinched, even the man who was being strangled by a settee and the one who had just had half his face locked into a white lustrous mass by a woman half his size.

Bridget didn't have time to think about what was happening before another horrendous crash was *right* above them. Something punched through the ceiling between the combatants and, in the blink of an eye, hurtled down through the floor. There was more noise as it presumably plunged through the floor of the pub below.

A cloud of wood and plaster sprayed into the room from the impact. Those who could clapped their hands over their ears.

Did that—was that just . . . Bridget tried to formulate thoughts. *Was that a bomb?* She could see the same thought occurring to everyone in the room. Then they all came to the same conclusion and crouched down, waiting for fire and shrapnel to erupt through the house.

It didn't.

And it didn't.

And it didn't.

It was impossible to tell how much time passed. The cloud of wood splinters and plaster dust seemed to hang motionless in the air. *Will I die a moment from now? I'm going to die in a moment.*

I might be pregnant.

Johnny Murcutt was curled up whimpering on the floor. Tillie was frozen, her eyes calculating as they met Bridget's. Vincent had turned away and bent down with his hands over his ears; presumably, he had released his grip on the cloth of the couch. Wattleman wrenched the battered furniture off himself, drew in a groaning breath of satisfaction, and bounded across the room to Bridget. She gasped as he picked her up and vaulted toward a window. She felt the impact as his fist shattered the sturdy wooden shield, and then they were out, falling to the street, the city around them lit up in flames.

17

And who the fuck are you, bitch?" The hardness of a pistol pressed against the side of her head.

Through the panic and the fear that sloshed within her, Lyn grimly reflected that her second attempt to enlist an informant was not going nearly as well as the first had.

Buoyed up by her success with Rory Rafferty, Lyn had taken herself for a congratulatory tuna sandwich and cucumber at the nearest Pret a Manger, and while chewing, she'd thought furiously about what to do next.

I can't quite believe it worked. But there was no doubt in her mind. Rafferty had believed, had wanted to believe, and now she had a source in the underworld. But while one source was good, more had to be better. A wider net. More contacts, more information, more opportunity to track down the real murderer. *I can actually do this.*

She'd applied a new iteration of disguise in the bathroom of the Pret. Sunglasses on, hair pulled back in an uncharacteristic (and unforgiving) tight ponytail, startling black lipstick. Prominent characteristics to distract people from her actual face. She regarded the final result dubiously. She didn't know what she resembled, but she consoled herself that it definitely wasn't her usual self. Sufficiently altered, she boarded a bus for the East End. She felt rather nervous going back through the city—the route took her too near the Checquy offices of Apex House and the Rookery for her liking—but she kept her head down and pretended to be focused on doing the cross-word in a copy of the *Times* left on the seat, which seemed like something a fugitive from justice wouldn't bother about.

Her destination was a pub in the West End. It was not a tourist pub; it was situated back several streets from the popular areas in an old building you had to know about in order to find. The Anvil. Owned and run by Terry Kelton.

Lyn had known the name Kelton even before she'd joined the Checquy; it was notorious. The Keltons had been a presence in the district for generations, cheerfully selling disreputable pleasures to consumers and blithely dispensing violence to eliminate competitors. Prostitution and liquor had been the backbone of the family business since the 1770s, but they'd also proven themselves capable of diversi-fication and had expanded into the lucrative trades of smut from the Continent, narcotics from the Levant and the Orient, and exotic dancers from Slough.

In recent years, however, there had been several major busts of Kelton-based drug endeavors. The busts had been so big and so lurid (quite a few of them had taken place in professional dens of iniquity and involved naked people being dragged screaming out of rooms) that (strategically pixelated) videos had made the national news. Several of the clan were sent off to HM Prison Slade out in Cumberland, and there'd been quite a bit of public interest in this dynasty of crimi-nals that catered to the most dubious of recreations. Richard and his colleagues had followed the case with interest.

Those Keltons who had eluded prosecution claimed they'd had nothing to do with any drug trade, that they were solely involved in the legitimate business of erotic adult entertainment and performance art—a claim no one believed, including, apparently, the individual who had been going around frying London criminals.

Lyn had decided on a slightly different strategy for approaching this gang. She would not be dealing with a foot soldier this time but with the head of the firm—Terry Kelton himself. This was partly because he would be able to get her much more information and partly because his was the only name—and his pub's the only address—she'd remembered. The boss, though, would not accept a story about an assassin who'd been secretly in service to one of his captains. Instead, she was going to present herself as a security specialist who was offering her services in these troubled times. And they'd been exceptionally troubled for the Keltons.

The Keltons had been hit hard in the past few weeks, with three deaths by mysterious electrocution. No witnesses. No explanation. Lyn had expected them to be wary of a strange woman showing up in the pub and asking to speak to Terry Kelton, but she hadn't expected to be invited into the back and then have a gun put to the back of her head.

They searched her, roughly and thoroughly. *Stay calm,* she told herself as hands moved briskly along her limbs. *They're paranoid, and rightfully so.* Still, when they lingered on and squeezed her breasts and bum, she had to clench her fists not to react. Her hands with their cheap rings had been examined closely—for what, she was not certain—and there were some contemptuous sniffs. They took her pen and her baton. It was lucky that she hadn't infused electricity into any of her equipment this time because the force with which they handled her and her possessions would have easily unleashed it. She was ordered to open her mouth for an inspection with a penlight. Fingers ran through her hair. There was a whispered conference.

Now that they've established that I'm not carrying a gun or a cattle prod, they'll calm down, she told herself. *I'll be taken to meet Terry Kelton, and we'll follow the script.*

Except that the gun was still pressed hard against her. It had migrated from her head to the small of her back.

Finally, she was hustled down a flight of creaking, stained stairs to the cellar. One man led the way; another followed with the gun. The continued presence of the gun was not promising, and the cellar was far from salubrious. The ceiling was low and arched, and the floors were dirty. It had been a storeroom for decades, if not centuries. She was taken past crates and kegs and a few humming refrigerators. The occasional light bulb swayed above them.

This does not bode well. They came to a heavy door of wood so old it was practically stone. One of the men heaved it open to reveal a large empty room with whitewashed walls and a filthy floor. As a place to conduct an interview regarding security, it was dubious. As a place to conduct a private murder and then lever up flagstones and bury the corpse, it was perfect.

How could you be so stupid? she asked herself. *You managed to fool one uneducated young foot soldier who was racked with grief, so you thought you could manipulate a gang lord?*

"In." A firm nudge from the gun in the small of her back.

You are a bloody fool, Lynette Binns! You are going to die in a cellar and no one will ever know that you were innocent of this whole damn thing. And Emma will never know what happened to her mother.

She stepped in and waited while two elderly folding chairs were fetched from some dank corner. She sat when told to, sighing, and leaned her head back to stare at the ceiling. It was arched, a barrel vault made of small dark bricks that glistened wetly. *How old is this place?* She felt the gun prodding the back of her head, and she sat up straight. She heard the distant creaking of the staircase, and a large man came into the room and sat in front of her. She recognized him from the files she'd read in the Checquy offices and, before that, from the television.

Terry Kelton, the patriarch of the gang, a hard-looking man in his forties. Tall and broad, with jug ears and closely cropped hair. The bent nose and the scarred cheeks showed he was no stranger to violence. The broken capillaries showed he was no stranger to the bottle. A man to be feared.

"And who the fuck are you, bitch?" he asked flatly.

"Kira Schmidt," she said. That was what her fake ID said, the one in the wallet they'd taken.

"Is that German?"

"I suppose if you go back far enough," said Lyn, who'd never given it any thought. "It's by marriage," she improvised. "Divorced, but I kept the name."

Kelton looked over her shoulder at one of the two other men in the room. Lyn flinched as her wallet was tossed from behind her, and Kelton snatched it out of the air. He caught her phone with the same ease.

"Piece of shit," he said. "How old is this?" He wasn't looking for an answer. "No caller history, no stored numbers." He looked at her thoughtfully and put the phone down on the floor next to his chair. Then he took out her wallet. She tensed as he examined her driver's license. "Looks kosher."

It ought to, thought Lyn. It was a real license, technically, since it had been created and provided by the government. She'd left her own license hidden in a sock drawer back at Mandy's.

"What's your middle name?" he asked suddenly, staring at the license.

"Anne," said Lyn tightly. She'd spent hours memorizing all the details of her Checquy-provided alter egos.

"If I went to this address printed on your license, what would I find?"

Probably the biggest surprise of your whole damn life. The address given for Kira Anne Schmidt was one of several properties the Checquy used to establish false backgrounds. Several hundred Checquy cover identities gave that address as their residence. It was maintained by a rota of Checquy housekeepers who were able to deal with any problems that came a-knocking.

"Not much," Lyn said. "It's the place I keep in London, but I travel a lot for my job. You'd find a bed, a toaster, and a suitcase full of clothes."

"No keys," he noted.

"The place has a keypad lock."

"Hmm." He slid the license back into the wallet, took out the money, and thumbed through it quickly and easily. "A hundred and twenty quid in readies." He did not place the cash back in the wallet; he put it in his jacket pocket. "A credit card for Kira A. Schmidt." He added it to the cash. She opened her mouth and then closed it again.

Is he going to just take the money and use the card? A man who ran brothels and worked in the drug trade and whose office policy apparently included taking people prisoner at gunpoint would probably not hesitate to engage in some identity theft and credit card fraud. In which case, a serial-killing supernatural vigilante would be the least of his problems. The Checquy would undoubtedly have put alerts on every account associated with her. She'd kept the card for window dressing in case someone needed extra proof of identity. He looked up at her.

"You've come asking questions at a bad time. People around here are jumpy."

"Yeah, clearly." He didn't like a sassy answer from a woman—she saw it in the way his brows furrowed and his mouth turned down even more. For a second she thought he was going to backhand her.

"And then some tart comes walking in here asking for me. You're not a cop, but you're referring to my lads getting killed. No one has ever seen you around here. You're dressed like no kind of professional, with cheap rings on all your fingers. And there's *this*." He held up her baton. "Tucked away in a special inside pocket in your jacket. A nasty piece, this. Not a cop's issue. This'd be all sorts of illegal. And then there's your hands."

"My hands?"

"Jimmy, who searched you, he knows a woman's hands. He tells me you've got calluses like someone who's done some work with her hands, some boxing, but there's no scars, so you're not a fighter. Not a fistfighter, anyway. So who are you? And what do you have to say about my security?"

"I know you've got problems. Word on the street is that you need a bit of muscle."

"I've *got* muscle. Do you know why this place is called the Anvil? *Don't* shake your head!" The gun ground itself into her hair.

"Why?" she asked tightly. She heard an intake of breath. "I mean, why is it called the Anvil?"

"My great-uncle named it that when he took it over," said Kelton, "'cause every fucker comes along tries to bring the hammer down. The old Bill. Other firms. Back in the Blitz, this area took some heavy pounding from the Luftwaffe. We've seen gangs come and go. Bloody Italians trying to get a foothold. My granddad and his brothers showed them off smartish. Then others. Yardies. Albanians. A mob of bloody Australians most recently, and me and my lads let *them* know how things were gonna be.

"And now someone's going about trying to be hard and new on the street, electrocuting people like I don't know what. Bit of flash, but we don't scare around here." His voice tightened. "They all want to smash us down. To hammer us. But this place is still standing, and *we're* still standing in it, and whatever bullshit you're trying to bring in here, it's not gonna work."

"I'm not bringing any bullshit." Trying her very best to keep her voice level.

"I don't believe you."

"I'm an independent security contractor with experience in body-guarding, counterterrorism, and threat suppression."

"I don't believe you."

"I can offer some highly specialized skills that can help with your problem."

"I. Don't. *Believe.* You."

"Okay," said Lyn. She spoke lightly, calmly, as if this had been merely an unsuccessful job interview and she weren't sitting there with a gun to her head. If she spoke like nothing about the situation bothered her, perhaps she could walk out just as lightly and calmly. "Then there's nothing more to say. If you're not interested in my services, I will just leave."

"Oh, no," he said grimly. "No, no, no. You're a damn sight too familiar with what's been happening. I don't like anything about you."

Don't panic. If you don't panic, maybe he'll be calm. Show him how ridiculous this is. "You think I'm a cop? Your staff here searched me — there's no wire." *Maybe I should imply that I am a cop,* she thought. *Maybe he'd be less likely to kill me if he thought I had a team backing me up.*

But then I'd never get any answers from him.

"You're not a cop. But maybe you're the one doing the killings," he said.

"You think I've been running around London electrocuting various independent businessmen and then walk in here asking to see you armed with *that?*" she said, nodding at her baton in his hands. He stared at her blankly. "I mean, what am I going to electrocute you with? The battery in my watch? Some shocking language?" As soon as the words were out, Lyn regretted them. His lip curled.

"You're a mouthy slut, aren't you?" He whipped his hand out, and the baton extended smoothly and wickedly. "Maybe you want a taste of your own medicine. Would that shut you up?"

Lyn watched, frozen in disbelief, as he brought the baton up. He paused, then brought it whipping down onto her thighs, and she screamed.

"Nope," he said.

The first time he hit her, she flung herself forward off the chair, curled up on the floor, and screamed. He hauled her up off the floor and slung her back in her seat.

"You get off that chair again without my say-so, and I'll use this to break your teeth into your head. You understand?" He pushed the baton against her face, and, whimpering, she nodded. "And then my man there will put a bullet in your head."

He struck her thighs again with the baton, and it felt as if her legs were exploding. He didn't actually break anything, but the pain was horrific. She thought she might vomit. And why was he doing it? It wasn't for interrogation, surely. He didn't ask any questions, just waited until her screams subsided and then struck again.

All the while, the man with the gun was behind her, ready to shoot. When she curled up in her chair, Kelton placed the tip of the baton under her chin and pushed her to sit up straight.

Am I going to allow this to continue? she thought dazedly. *Am I going to let him beat me to death?* She itched to do something, but there was the gun at the back of her head and still the vague possibility that she might be able to salvage this situation. If she couldn't get a contact, then she might obtain some piece of information. She could not believe that he would simply kill her for no reason.

When it finally ended, and she managed to stop screaming and choke back her tears, Lyn sat slumped on the chair, gasping. She looked up at him through her hair and felt true, burning, incandescent loathing.

You are going to be so sorry, she thought. She clenched her teeth in rage. *I'm going to fucking fry you, you monster!* In his eyes, something was seething behind the cruelty. *He's frightened,* she realized blearily. *He's terrified.*

Well, he fucking should be now.

"*Is* it you, then?" Kelton growled.

"What?" she asked weakly.

"Is it you that's going around killing people? That killed my sons and my best pal?"

"No."

"Is it you? I saw their bodies with those burn marks on their skin!"

"No, it's not."

"Is it you?"

"*No!*"

"Who is it, then, you bitch? Who's coming to kill me?" he demanded, screaming into her face. "Who wants me dead?"

"Probably everyone who ever met you, you fucking bastard!" He drew back in shock.

Absolutely no way of salvaging this situation, she realized now. Kelton had apparently come to the same conclusion, because he nodded to the man behind her, and suddenly the metal of the pistol was cold at her temple, just in front of her ear.

He's not bluffing anymore.

Everything in her wanted to use her powers then. The barrel was pressed against her skin, waiting to be turned into a weapon against its user. She could see how it would happen. She could just open up the well within herself, unleash the electricity that coiled there, let it course out and seethe into the material of the gun. And then, to release it from the metal? A simple shift away and back, just lightly tapping the side of her head against the gun, and the man would be engulfed in his own personal ball of lightning.

Except that getting shocked could easily cause him to pull the trigger. Muscles would spasm and contract as the current raced through them. His finger would clench on the trigger, and a bullet would briskly enter her skull, briskly explode through her brain, then briskly continue on into the world to seek its fortune.

And then? Maybe nothing. Maybe her death would snuff out the energy that lived in her body; some sparks might crawl weakly out and then dissipate.

Or perhaps an electrical storm would pour out of her, like the madness in her kitchen. How big would it be? Her heart was pounding so hard, her head felt so full of thoughts, that she could imagine the entire room, the entire building, consumed in all the energy of her life.

Regardless, she would be dead.

Nope. Move.

Still slumped, her hair over her face, she shot her hand up, gripped the pistol, and shoved it up and away from her head. There was the surge in her skin as she poured energy into the gun. Shocked, the man fired instinctively, sending a bullet into the ceiling. The force of the pistol firing was enough to release the electricity, and it flared out, not enough to kill him, not even enough to stun him, but certainly enough to get his undivided attention. The man screamed, wreathed in red flashes, and in his wild spasms, he flung the gun away. Meanwhile, she was moving against Kelton with hard, tightly controlled moves, closing one hand around the baton to yank it away and punching him in the chest with the other, shocking him with the electricity from her rings.

There was still the third man, the one in the corner by the door. Her explosive movements and the bursts of electricity that continued to keep his colleagues shrieking had him aghast. He fumbled in his coat for his gun as Lyn charged at him, adrenaline and rage burning away the throbbing pain in her legs. She held her baton awkwardly, near the wrong end, but it drank up the energy she poured into it. She pressed it against the man's chest; there was a crack, and he was thrown unconscious against the wall.

And back! The man who'd been holding the gun was still behind her. She could almost hear Pawn Fenton scolding her for turning her back on a threat. The electricity around the gunman had faded, and he was down on his knees, scrabbling after the gun. Lyn readjusted her grip on the baton and bore down on him, inexorable. His eyes focused on her just in time to see the baton coming toward him. He wailed and actually covered his face.

A moment passed, and another, and he dared to peek up.

"Flincher." A light tap, a snapping sound, and he was also down and unconscious.

"You..." Kelton's voice behind her was weak and full of hate. She turned to see the man sprawled on the floor against the wall. He did not look well. He was pale and trembling. Also, he had thrown up on himself a bit. His hand was shaking as he tried to reach into his coat.

"Oh no," said Lyn. "None of that."

And she cracked him on the arm with the baton. There was no longer any electricity in it, just a fair amount of almost entirely restrained wrath.

"Argh, you bitch. You bitch!"

"I know, right?" said Lyn. "Can you believe how much it hurts? *I* couldn't."

"I'm gonna—"

"Yeah, just shut your face for a second," said Lyn, and she gave him a little jolt through the baton. He slumped bonelessly, staring incredulously at her, and she moved over cautiously, reached into his coat, and found the pistol he'd been going for. "You must be really worried, to be carrying a gun like this in London. And beating up women for no apparent reason." He made a sound, and she looked around at the men on the floor. "Yes, all right, to be fair, you were right to be worried about me, but you didn't *know* that." She held up the gun. "I'm confiscating this." She tucked it into her jacket pocket. Then she retrieved her money and her credit card.

As an afterthought, she collected the guns from the two unconscious goons. They did not voice any objections, although one of them appeared to have pissed himself. That did not stop her from liberating both their wallets.

"You come to rob my boys? And kill us?"

"I haven't killed them!" she snapped, exasperated. He glared at her.

Just get out, she told herself. There was no point in trying to reason with this vicious, terrified man. She needed to get away.

"You're a monster," he said bitterly. "I fucking knew it when those bodies started showing up. I knew what it was. I remember those damn stories."

"What stories?"

"You think you'll get out?" he continued, ignoring her question. "I've got men, they'll be coming. My lad at the top of the stairs will have heard the shot."

"Yeah, not to mention the sound of screaming," said Lyn. He was silent at that, and, with a chill, she realized why. They'd have been expecting screaming. "You think I can't get through your guys? You've seen what I can do."

"I know what you can do. I know what your kind *can't* do. And I know that you can die like anyone else, you stupid bitch. So...*lads! Help us!*" he yelled out suddenly. "*She's got a gun!*" There was a look of triumph on Kelton's face that disappeared only when she reached out with the baton and shocked him into unconsciousness.

How much time do I have? Kelton had mentioned a man at the top of the stairs. Presumably he had already called for help. *So I need to go now.*

Lyn stepped over the twitching Kelton and moved to the door. She cautiously opened it a crack and winced at the sound of several pairs of feet coming down the stairs. *Maybe there's still time,* she thought. The cellar was full of junk—maybe she could hide. Or perhaps there was another exit. And then a gunshot rang out and a bullet smashed into the plaster by the doorframe. She yelped and slammed the door shut.

Not an option.

Okay, what, then? She scanned the room. There was no other way out, no windows, no grates. No key in the lock. Her eye fell on Kelton. *Maybe take him as hostage? Would they let me walk out with him?* He was currently sitting in a spreading pool of his urine, but perhaps she could wake him up. She didn't like the prospect of trying to get him to walk, though.

And once she got through the front door, what would she do? Hail a cab? The pain in her legs was resurfacing as the adrenaline of kicking three men's arses wore off. She wasn't sure if she could run anywhere if she *did* get out. She looked about briskly. *But at least in here I can control how they come at me.*

Here, then.

All right, take stock. She had the baton, she had three guns and knew how to use them, but a shoot-out was not something she wanted. Not only did it have a good chance of resulting in her getting shot, but it would inevitably draw the police. And the Checquy.

And once they got here, if I was still alive, this tableau with its electrocuted gangsters would hardly help me prove my innocence. I'd be muzzled, shackled, sedated, and sent to Gallows Keep before the day was out.

If they didn't automatically behead me for going rogue.

Or shoot me while I was "trying to escape."

So I need to stop the Kelton crew from coming in with their guns blazing. She could hear noises coming through the door as said crew approached, presumably with said guns getting prepped for any blazing that proved necessary.

Lyn stepped forward and closed her hand around the door handle. She closed her eyes and pumped electricity into the metal. Not enough to kill, at least she hoped not, but enough to shock someone into unconsciousness. It would really depend on the size of the person grabbing the handle. She glanced at the two unconscious goons on the floor, mentally measuring and weighing, and upped the amperage a bit. *That'll buy me a little time.*

And then what? the pessimistic part of her brain asked her. *Think back to Strategy and Tactics class at the Estate. This is essentially the worst position anyone could be in except for that practice scenario they gave us with all the leeches, the sprung floor, and the mayonnaise.*

And then I'll see what happens! she thought back to that part of her brain tartly. She drew away and looked about. The lack of a key in the lock grated on her. No dead bolt, nothing. Given the appearance of the door, she wouldn't have been astounded by an old-fashioned bar and brace. *Although there's no guarantee that such things would have been on this side of the door.* The room felt more like a place of imprisonment than refuge. The only things she had to fortify it were two folding chairs and two unconscious hoodlums.

There was a reason they referred to it as *deadweight.* The two men weren't dead—she checked their pulses guiltily to make sure—but they might as well have been for the difficulty of moving them. All the time, she was painfully aware of the moments passing by. The adrenaline had returned, but she was sweating and gasping for breath by the time the first man was laid against the base of the door with the second man pressed against him like an amorous draft excluder. Hopefully, the door would be more difficult to kick open with a pair of louts braced against it. Plus, the door looked like it had been hewn from the haunch of an Ent—it could probably withstand bullets, possibly a bazooka.

Eventually, though, they'll manage to get the door open, she thought. *Enough to slide through.* She looked at the space they would come through and stood up the folding chairs there as a barricade. More energy flowed from her fingers into the chairs. *Winnow down as many as possible, make their entrance as difficult as possible. Maybe there won't be that many, and the electricity will take them all out.*

But you can't rely on that possibility.

You need to be ready.

She knelt down in the corner behind the door, laid the three guns out on the floor, and, feeling slightly unreal, recalled the procedure to check them. *Safety catch, chamber, clip.*

She was weirdly relieved to find that one of the guns, the one that had been pointed so terrifyingly at her head, already had a bullet in the chamber. To have been coerced down into the cellar with a gun that couldn't actually have shot her would be too galling for words.

Three guns, thirty bullets. Against . . . an unknown number. It was not good, but then nothing about this was good. Lyn weighed her options. Gun in one hand, baton in the other? Two guns? She decided that she wasn't an action star, collapsed the baton against the floor, and tucked it away in her jacket. She'd need both hands for the gun to really make it count.

Kelton's men were getting closer to the other side of the door now, and Lyn remained down on one knee, gun in hand, waiting and ready.

"Lads, I'm in here! Help!" shouted Kelton suddenly from his position against the far wall, and Lyn almost fired off a round. "She's behind the door, she's got guns!"

"Shut the fuck up!" snapped Lyn. Evidently, she'd underestimated how much electricity would be needed for him. She didn't dare turn her attention away from the door to shock him into unconsciousness again—or even just clip him upside the head with an uncharged baton—but she was mightily tempted. The noises of approaching people came closer, and Lyn and Kelton watched the door wide-eyed. There was some muttering of men's voices, a moment's silence; the handle moved *ever* so slightly, and then electricity boiled crimson out of the metal and coursed away through the door.

"Christ!" shouted Kelton. "Oh Christ!" The door handle began shaking, and they could hear shouts: "Knock him off the handle! Shove him away!" Then there was quiet, and Lyn darted forward, charged the handle again, and fell back.

"Don't touch the handle, she's got it rigged!" Kelton yelled.

Lyn shot him a look of loathing.

"Just kick the door in!" Kelton shouted.

I can't wait to see how that works out, Lyn thought darkly. The door looked like it could withstand every kick they could possibly muster up as well as all the kicks of any descendants they might have.

Apparently they came to the same conclusion, because after a few dull thuds of completely ineffectual kicks that failed to even shift the door in its frame, there was a pause and the muffled sound of discussion. One voice seemed quite firm in its indistinct commands, and then there came a bang that actually produced a result. The door itself was fine, but the frame cracked ominously.

Okay, they've found something heavy to use as a battering ram. There was another bang, and the frame splintered a bit.

They're coming in. Lyn took several steps back and brought the pistol up, holding it in two hands as she'd been instructed at the range back on Kirrin Island. *Focus. When they come through, see where you're firing, squeeze the trigger. There is no shooting to wound. Shoot and keep shooting until they go down.*

Hold the gun firmly. Breathe.

Try not to think about the fact that you're about to kill someone.

Breathe.

Breathe.

She waited a beat.

Another beat.

Another.

Well, where the hell are they?

Against her better judgment, she shot a glance over at Kelton. He gave her an equally confused look. She shrugged.

"Lads?" he yelled uncertainly. "What have you done to 'em?" he asked Lyn. *"Lads!"*

"Wait, quiet!" she exclaimed. "Do you hear that?"

There was a choking sound from the other side of the door, hastily cut off. Men's voices were suddenly raised; there were cries and crashes, and over all of it a strange flapping sound came repeatedly.

"What *is* that?" Kelton asked nervously.

"I have no idea."

"Lads!" he shouted. "What's going on?" They both jumped when they heard a gunshot from the other side of the door, followed by two loud flapping sounds. More gunshots, and something slammed against the door. Lyn almost fired her gun.

More cries, and then silence. Lyn took one hand off the gun to wipe the sweat off her brow with her sleeve, then returned it to the grip. Neither she nor Kelton said anything. They were both holding their breath. She could see her pulse pounding in her wrists. The faintest movement caught her eye.

"Look," she whispered to Kelton and jerked the pistol at the top of the door.

A line of pinkish-white material was slowly squeezing itself through the rough crack between the door and the lintel.

"Oh God, what *is* that?" Kelton kept trying to push himself up against the wall, but his muscles were still weak, barely supporting his weight. Periodically, they would spasm, sending him falling back down.

"I don't know," said Lyn tightly.

"Well, shoot it, you stupid cow!"

"They just tried that out there, and it didn't do any good," she said. *Do I want to risk pissing it off?* The material was wriggling out, a single sheet of the stuff. It looked familiar somehow, and Lyn gagged as she realized what it was. "It's *skin*."

It was. The thing broadened, then narrowed, then broadened again—a head, a neck, shoulders. It flopped flatly down on the door for a moment, like rolled-out dough, then bent itself, nauseatingly, to slide up the wall and along the ceiling, rippling as it emerged. The sound of skin pushing itself against the wood and the stone turned her stomach. It was the naked hide of a man, hairless, seemingly faceless. There were white scars peppered and slashed across it and a few holes punched through it.

Bullet holes, she thought faintly. *The men outside hit it, and that didn't stop it.*

Its flattened arms emerged through the gap, and it slowly began hauling itself out from above the door, fingers slapping on the ceiling and clawing their way along. And then it twisted on itself at the neck, the skin creasing as it turned one hundred and eighty degrees, and she realized that they had been watching the thing's back. As the head turned, it inflated a little, and when it brought its compressed face toward them, Kelton and Lyn both screamed.

It was empty. There were no eyes, only ragged circles, and the two people on the floor could see through the holes, see that the thing on the ceiling was just skin, no organs—a clean, empty shell, as if someone had been exquisitely and meticulously flayed and tanned. The skin was so thin that light actually penetrated it, grotesquely illuminating the interior. And yet those empty holes gazed, unmistakably looking at them. It opened its lips slightly, and there was nothing inside. No teeth, no tongue, no *mouth.*

What is this? thought Lyn frantically. *Is this the thing that has been going around killing criminals?* At her side, Kelton was gasping and wheezing. Remembering the fear she'd seen in his eyes earlier, she managed to pity him. *He's certainly got something to be afraid of now.* It sounded as if he were about to have a heart attack. *If it goes after him, I'm going to have to defend the bastard,* she realized. He would be her witness. *And besides, I don't actually want him to get murdered by an empty human pelt.*

She transferred the gun to one hand and reached into her pocket for her baton. She pulled it out and snapped it open, and the half-emerged skin-shell-thing turned its head to peer at her with its horrible empty eyeholes. It looked her up and down—she could *feel* it regarding her—and its lips actually pursed.

Then, as she watched, the face puffed out more, solidified, became rigid, as if it had been laid over a mold. With a shock, Lyn realized that she knew it.

"Oh, bloody hell," she said in horror.

"What? What is it?" Kelton asked brokenly.

"It's my office mate."

It was, unquestionably, the skin of Pawn Liam Seager.

18

Usha was not typically a person to become bored, but it was difficult to be enthusiastic about routine tasks — even highly classified supernatural routine tasks — when everyone else was out having adventures. Pamela and Lady Carmichael had gone off, red-eyed and yawning, to prepare for their ongoing high-security meetings with the rest of the Court.

Meanwhile, Bridget was tracking down supernatural black marketeers with the dubious Wattleman and having a presumably tearful wartime farewell with Gerald Nash.

Usha herself was sitting alone in the Lady's office going through daily reports. Her own work took relatively little time to whip through, especially since there was no one to talk to. Then she read through the day's briefing materials and saw no mentions of any inexplicably charred bodies, although the previous night's bombings had tragically left plenty of explicably charred bodies.

It is still early, though. That damn Nazi could easily have killed a few more people that no one has found yet. If he had any sense, he'd be putting any new charred corpses in bombed-out buildings, she thought sourly. *And taking the extra time to burn their clothes as well.*

And so she sat, at a loose and mildly irritated end, until Pamela called.

"Usha, Lady Carmichael has a task for you," Pamela said. "It requires some tact and a good knowledge of India."

"I have a surfeit of both," Usha said cheerfully, buoyed up by the prospect of something to do. "What does the Lady wish of me?"

It was early afternoon when the Checquy car pulled up at Waterloo station and Usha stepped out. Ignoring people's startled looks at an Indian woman dressed in an exquisite indigo dress of Parisian cut, she swept through the halls and concourses and situated herself at the entrance to a specific platform. The train from Southampton had just arrived, and she scanned all the passengers carefully as they emerged from the steam. The only description she had been given of the man she was to meet was that he was "an old India hand" and would be wearing a disreputable hat. She was not entirely certain why the information had been so scanty. Maybe this was some sort of test?

Or Lady Carmichael is playing with me.

And then a disreputable hat emerged from the clouds surrounding the train. Indeed, the adjective *disreputable* was an understatement. It might have begun life as a well-made bush hat such as she had seen some Englishmen wear in India, but it had evidently suffered immeasurable torments over the years. It was discolored, battered, shapeless, with a multitude of stains. Its crown had clearly endured rumplings, crushings, and sittings-upon. The brim sagged in some places and featured some prominent charring in others, and there was a portion missing that, unless she missed her guess, was the result of a bite.

There could be no more disreputable hat in all the world.

And yet under the hat was an extremely handsome man about her age. Aside from the diabolical chapeau, he was dressed as if he'd just alighted from the posh section of an ocean liner—indeed, he had disembarked from just such a one that morning. Clean-shaven, blond, and tan, with flashing blue eyes, he practically shone with good health.

This is the old India hand with whom the Lady wants me to talk? I could be an older India hand than him, Usha thought. She noticed that the Pawn was missing the fourth and fifth fingers of his left hand and decided to hold off on further judgment.

Their eyes met and she raised her eyebrows.

"Excuse me, sir, are you Mr. Lionel Fadden?" she said cautiously.

"Yes, may I help you?"

"Pawn Fadden, I am Usha Khorana, apprentice to Lady Carmichael. She sends her sincere apologies for not being here to welcome you herself. She was called away and sent me in her place."

"Entirely reasonable," said the man, and he smiled. "Heavy is the head and busy is the schedule, eh?"

"Indeed. You are staying at the Caïssa, I believe?" He nodded. "I am to escort you there."

"Very kind."

"Not too kind," said Usha. "I'm afraid there's also some business to attend to. I understand you have some things you wanted to share directly with the Lady? She asked me to speak with you."

"Jolly good," said Fadden. "We just need to wait for my assistant to catch up. He's a bit slower than I, and I wanted to grab a newspaper, so I trotted on ahead. Ah, there he is! Cyril, over here!" Usha turned to see Pawn Fadden's assistant coming down the platform. In contrast to Fadden's unexpectedly youthful appearance, Cyril was so elderly that he might have been born before the Norman Conquest.

My God, she thought. *Is Fadden feeding on him or something?* She gingerly shook Cyril—Pawn Wilberforce—by the hand and half braced herself for it to snap off at the wrist. He was a pleasant man with twinkling eyes and a long beard, but he seemed horrendously frail.

A porter brought their various trunks and bags to the waiting car and looked startled when Usha intervened to tip him before Fadden or Wilberforce could. And then the car was away, moving through the streets to the Caïssa.

"Poor old London," said Fadden as he looked out the window. "Changed quite a bit since I was last here. And the war hasn't done her any favors." He regarded a bomb-damaged building and made a face. He turned back to Usha. "Khorana—that's a Punjabi name, is it not?"

"It is," said Usha. "My family is based in Lahore."

"Lovely! Spent quite a bit of time in the Punjab back in the fifties and sixties," said Fadden. Usha froze and looked at him, reevaluating her assessment and hastily adding seventy years to his age.

"I—oh. Well, I imagine things have changed a bit since then."

"No doubt the whole country's in a period of change," said Fadden cheerfully.

"Yes indeed," said Usha. "I believe that's one of the things we are to speak about." He nodded. Wilberforce had returned to England to retire to a nice bungalow by the sea, and Fadden was taking long-service leave to see his assistant settled comfortably; Lady Carmichael wanted to get their insights on the situation in India. The war and the distances between the countries necessarily meant delays in reports, and this was an important opportunity to get updates and expert analysis. For the Lady not to have met with these Pawns immediately meant that the Court conference must be very pressing indeed.

The car dropped Fadden and Wilberforce off at the entrance to the Cadgers Club, where a pair of doormen unloaded the luggage. It then drove to the other side of the block so that Usha could sign in to the Mission for the Reclamation of Reduced Females.

It had been agreed that Fadden and Wilberforce would take half an hour to get settled. The arrangements were a trifle unorthodox. Because of the bombings, all the beds had been moved out of the nice, if small, guest rooms upstairs, and all overnight guests were to sleep in the comparative safety of the club's enormous wine cellar. The cellars were not equipped with bathroom facilities, however, and there was a certain amount of to-ing and fro-ing between the floors, especially if, like Fadden and Wilberforce, a guest had a lot of luggage that couldn't be easily transported to the cellar.

Usha decided to go for a wander while the two Pawns unpacked a little and washed up from the journey. There were not many people around at that time of day. Those guests who had stayed overnight had availed themselves of the sadly diminished wartime buffet, which was now being cleared away, and presumably gone off to attend to their business in the city. There were a couple of elderly Pawns reading the papers in the library, and a large streak of green ink appeared to be doing underwater laps in the basement swimming pool.

Eventually Usha returned to the central lobby to find the two men waiting for her. She had reserved a private room for their discussion, and she guided them to it. Tea and biscuits were waiting. Mindful of

Wilberforce's frailness, she took care to see him settled comfortably, although Fadden took it for granted that he'd be fine.

"So the Lady had to cancel, eh?" Fadden said.

"She sends her apologies. She's looking forward to catching up with you soon. But she wanted someone to hear your findings as soon as possible."

"To think, young Sara is the Lady of the Checquy!" Fadden shook his head. "I remember when she was a little girl. Knew her father in India. Good man. A captain. Died too young—jungle fever, damn tragedy. But Sara's tough as nails. She went through a great deal before she was even twelve. Father dead, family fortune vanished overnight. She went from being an heiress to a drudge in an attic." He smiled. "And then it all reappeared tenfold. She came out of it all stronger. I was delighted when she manifested and not at all surprised when she rose to the Court. You'll learn a lot from her, Pawn Khorana."

"I'm not a Pawn," she clarified. "I'm an apprentice."

"My mistake. Well, I expect Sara will learn a great deal from you as well. I always learn a lot from my apprentices."

"You've had a few apprentices over the years?" she asked.

"Oh, yes," he said. "Why, young Wilberforce was once my apprentice." To Usha's stupefaction, he nodded to the elderly man down the table. "Marvelous times, eh, Cyril?" The white-bearded Pawn nodded amiably. "But we're not here to discuss the old days. We've just gotten back, and of course we'll provide a full overview of how things are in the Raj, but there are a few matters that I wanted to bring to the Lady's attention. Things I think would be better addressed sooner rather than later."

"Excellent," Usha said. She unscrewed the cap of her fountain pen, ready to take notes.

"To begin with, there appears to be a supernatural nonhuman entity in India maintaining suspicious connections to London," he said. "I don't know that it's malicious, exactly, but certainly it has connections at a high-enough level that I think further investigation is warranted."

"What's the name of this individual?"

"I don't know."

"This is not a promising beginning," Usha remarked.

"I'm not sure this individual *has* a name. You see, a few months ago I was chatting with this gent, Reggie Groves, in the Bengal Club in Calcutta."

"Is he in the Checquy?" asked Usha.

"No, no," said Fadden. "He's an indigo planter, was down to the city for Christmas. He and I stayed up late playing billiards, and both of us had a few too many burra-pegs, don't you know." Usha nodded. "Anyway, he got to telling some stories about some things he'd seen up-country, quite a few odd things, but one of them was dashed strange.

"He'd been out pigsticking by himself, which was damn silly. If you're going after boar, the first rule is you never go alone. But there you are—he'd done it. And he'd managed to come across some hog snoozing in the sun. He tried to rouse it, you know, gave it a bit of a jab with the lance. Thing jumped up, but rather than running or even turning on him, it just stared at him, and then it *spoke*."

"D'you know," said Groves, "the damnedest thing wasn't that the pig spoke, it was the *way* it spoke. King's English, proper as you like. It sounded like it had been at Rugby and Oxford, had a place in the country. I half expected it to ask me where I'd gone to school."

Reginald Groves was in his thirties and possessed of the muscular leanness that India often baked into Englishmen. It was the combination of the heat, the fanatical devotion to sports and exercise, and the whiskies that did it. He was not the kind of man given to much introspection or brooding—life was there for getting on with, wasn't it?—but as he leaned back, there was a flash of distant thoughtfulness in his eyes that spoke of a man who'd seen something completely outside his understanding of the world.

Both of them were drunk, the kind of intoxication where one becomes calm and contemplative and will speak of things about which one feels very strongly. It was late, and the noises of the city had faded to the faintest of murmurs. The two of them had moved from the billiard table to the long veranda and were sitting in chairs with leg rests, savoring the faint breeze.

"Rum," reflected Fadden.

"Very rum," agreed Groves.

"So what did it say?" Fadden asked finally. "The pig?"

"Asked me what the hell I thought I was doing. I was rather taken aback."

"Naturally."

"I just sort of automatically apologized."

"As one would," put in Fadden helpfully.

"Quite. You know, nursery manners. They're ingrained into one. And I thought I did it quite handsomely. Took off my hat, begged its pardon. But it demanded my name, which I gave, and then it just stalked off into the shrubs."

"Did it say goodbye?"

"No, it didn't." The two of them sat contemplatively for a moment.

"Bit rude," said Fadden finally. "Did you ever see it again?"

"Not hide nor hair. Went out a few times looking, but never with the spear. Rather lost my taste for pigsticking. But two months later, and this is the rummest part, I got a letter from a law firm in London, Billing and Lennard."

"I've heard of them," said Fadden, startled. "That's an important firm."

"Don't I know it! Anyway, got a letter from them, all the proper formal legal bumf, stating that their client, one pig, resident in the Tirhut district, had suffered harm at my hands, and they were dunning me for the costs of medical treatment."

"My word!"

"Two hundred pounds, if you please!"

"That's mighty steep for a doctor. Especially for a pig."

"Quite. And they threatened to bring suit if I didn't pay up!"

"For a *pig*."

"Yes!"

"Amazing," said Fadden. The two men shook their heads, and Fadden finished his drink. "Koi-hai!" he called, summoning a servant.

A man came out of the distant shadows at the end of the veranda, his feet quiet. "Yes, sir?" said the waiter.

"Ah, yes, a chotapeg for me and—Groves? Another for you?"

"Just a small one."

"And a pau-peg for my friend, thank you."

"Yes, sir." He moved away swiftly, and the two men returned to their contemplation of the night.

"So what did you do?" asked Fadden eventually. "About the pig and the letter?"

"Paid, of course! When lawyers get involved, things can get very nasty, and the pig had a point."

"Hmm. You didn't think it was strange that they were able to find you?"

"Well, no, that made a lot of sense. The pig had my name, and it's a small neighborhood. Bound to happen."

"Yes, of course."

"So you believed him?" asked Usha, taking feverish notes.

"Oh, yes," said Fadden. "No doubt about it. A man like that always paid his bills."

"Not about paying! I mean the whole talking-pig-with-a-lawyer thing."

"Absolutely," said Fadden. "I took the opportunity to stop by Groves's plantation a short while later. We had dinner, and I brought up the pig anecdote again. I wanted to make sure it hadn't just been the whisky talking. He was a little embarrassed—he'd clearly said more than he would have liked—but I got him to show me the letter. Completely kosher."

"One of the most prominent firms in London is representing a wild boar in the Bengal Presidency," mused Usha incredulously. "Did you find out anything else about the pig?"

"No. And I had a bit of a look around in the district myself, asked a few questions. Nothing."

"Wouldn't the firm be leaving themselves rather vulnerable? I mean, revealing that one of their clients is a swine?" Usha asked. "It's absurd. At the very least, it would surely expose them to ridicule if it were widely known."

"Absolutely, and the letter addressed that issue. Threatened to bring suit if ever Groves spoke about the matter publicly. I think that explains

his reticence almost as much as the queerness of the whole business."
He smiled. "I've often thought since that the Checquy could cut its
work in half if we just went around threatening to sue people."

"Perhaps the Checquy should contact the firm and ask?"

"No indeed. Not directly. Billing and Lennard are a powerful
firm. Lots of connections. That pig was clearly an important client,
which means either wealth or influence or both. And even the Checquy hesitates when it comes to taking on lawyers. Gorgons and ifrits,
yes, you can't hold us back. But when a damn silk rears its wigged
head, the wise Pawn runs for the hills. Still, this suggests connections
between India and London that we are not aware of. Following it up
in India would be difficult since the only clue we have is an unspecified pig of no certain address."

"Fascinating," said Usha.

"Now, on a different tack, Cyril and I have identified four children and two adults who we judge should be brought to Britain and
enlisted into the Checquy." Usha froze. She felt her cheeks begin to
burn. This was no doubt the sort of conversation that had resulted in
her own acquisition by the Checquy.

*And I doubt these people are going to receive an innocuous personal invita-
tion from Lady Carmichael.*

"That...doesn't seem like very many," she said stiffly.

"I beg your pardon?"

"Given the size of India, that doesn't seem like an awful lot."
Pawns Fadden and Wilberforce exchanged a look, and Usha resisted
the urge to shatter the table.

"Miss Khorana, you are from Lahore, but are you familiar with
how the Checquy operates in India?"

"No," said Usha warily. Her studies had been largely focused on
the British Isles, and her access to the records regarding the subcontinent had been curtailed from the beginning of her apprenticeship.
Ostensibly, this had been to allow her to gain a thorough grounding
in the primary operations of the Checquy first. She'd been told that as
she progressed in her apprenticeship, she would learn more about
operations throughout the empire. In her most suspicious moments,
she'd reflected that India would probably be last on her curriculum,

that she wouldn't see it until the Order was convinced she'd fully accepted and committed to her position with the Checquy.

"I see," said Pawn Fadden. He leaned back and stared at the ceiling, trying to find the right words. "I don't know if you'll be pleased to learn this, but we have nothing like the presence in the Raj that we do here. There is not an office in every city. Our Pawns are scattered about and move a great deal. Something of a roving commission, if you will. Additionally, our situation within the bureaucracy is not as codified, nor does it carry the same authority."

"I see..." She didn't really, but it was a startling piece of information. Suddenly, the Checquy did not seem quite as all-powerful and all-seeing as it had been portrayed to her. Which was very interesting.

"So we don't sweep up every person who shows a bit of ghostly brawn," Fadden said. "We only press those who, if left unchecked, could present a substantial threat to society and the empire."

I'm flattered.

"What about the others? Those who don't present a substantial threat to society?"

"India is a huge land with centuries of tradition," began Fadden expansively before abruptly realizing who he was talking to. "Ahem. My apologies—I'm accustomed to lecturing people who know nothing about India. Sometimes I have to put things in perspective, explain where it is on the map and why it's important." Despite herself, Usha smiled. Fadden continued. "Basically, we've found that most of the time, the land will take care of any nonsubstantial problems that arise. Either the individuals will take care of themselves in society or society will take care of them one way or another."

"I see." *So if my powers had been less "substantial," would the Checquy have left me alone? Would I be free at this very moment?* "Well, I sense that this is a much more complicated situation than we have time for, but I'd be very interested to hear more at a later date."

"It would be my pleasure."

"Now, tell me about these individuals."

He went on to describe six people from different regions in India and explained the nature of their abilities. Perhaps sensing Usha's complicated feelings, he outlined how these people, if left to their own fates, could cause harm. He described how the song of a little girl in Bikaner had permanently blinded thirty-two people and how a father of five in Aizawl, a carpenter, was unknowingly responsible for repeated floods that had caused devastation in the Tlawng and Tuirial River valleys.

Whenever the wind blew from north-northeast and had a temperature above 98 Fahrenheit, a grandmother in Poona dissolved into millions of ravenous locusts. (Interestingly, they were identified as Rocky Mountain locusts—a North American species that was believed to be extinct.) The swarm would last for only a few hours before converging and reforming into a bewildered matron, but the damage was considerable.

A comatose teenage boy in Uttaranchal was currently being held as a guest at a remote tea plantation after it had been found that his presence instantly curdled any milk in a fifteen-mile radius.

As Fadden talked, Usha began to feel distinctly ill at ease. It was clear that something needed to be done about these individuals, but her feelings were a confused mixture of outrage, pity, and pragmatism. She took detailed notes and reviewed the photographs that Wilberforce fumbled out of a satchel.

I am going to have to talk to Lady Carmichael about all of this, she thought unhappily. *She will want to know how I feel about it, and I don't know.* So all she could do was continue to write things down.

After that, inevitably, the discussion turned to the war. Fadden and Wilberforce gave a detailed report on how it was affecting the supernatural in India, and then the conversation became less formal as each of them cataloged the recent shortages and how they were likely to get worse. Usha cautiously mentioned that some of the apprentices were chafing at their inability to contribute to the war effort, and there were knowing and thoughtful noises from the men.

"It's far from the first time," said Fadden. "Every time there's a war, the young people get caught up in the spirit of it. The Crimean. The Klang War. The Latvian War of Independence. The Great War."

"Abyssinia," Pawn Wilberforce said.

"Absolutely, Abyssinia! Damn right, Cyril." The elderly Pawn nodded in acknowledgment. "That madman emperor of theirs takes umbrage because Queen Victoria doesn't reply to a letter, and he imprisons some Europeans. So we send out an army to rescue 'em. Suddenly, all the young Pawns were clamoring to go along and flatten the bloody country for its presumption. I had to drag three little idiots out by their ears after they'd secretly enlisted in the Bombay army so they could go along with old Bob Napier."

"But there's never been Checquy involvement in nonsupernatural war?" asked Usha carefully.

"Not officially, no," said Fadden. "Unofficially? Nothing would surprise me. Go back far enough and for every damn-fool action, there's a damn fool who will do it. Unforgivably stupid."

"But this is different, Lionel," objected Pawn Wilberforce. "This is war on British soil. The apprentices are seeing their own homes bombed and their neighbors killed. It's difficult to just stand by and let that happen, especially when they've spent their whole lives training to protect their countrymen. When they've taken an oath to do so."

Is that what it was for Pamela? wondered Usha. *Spending her whole life protecting people and then being commanded to let them die without lifting a finger? Did watching those explosions build up a rage inside her until she absolutely had to bring the bomber down?*

Once or twice when they were alone, she'd tried to ask her friend about it again. Bridget was too much a child of the Checquy to understand breaking the rules, but Usha had hoped that perhaps Pamela could confess to her. Instead, the Pawn had shaken her head and drawn the conversation back to tracking down the Nazi.

Maybe it's the war in general, she thought bleakly. *It's turned the whole world on its head.*

"Pshaw!" scoffed Fadden. "They know exactly what they're sworn to do and what they're sworn *not* to do. And fighting Nazis is *not* part of their duty."

Well, I guess Pamela couldn't expect any mercy or forgiveness from that side of the room, Usha thought flatly.

"But is it possible that the Nazis have some sort of Checquy equivalent that they could deploy?" she asked innocently. They both stared at her.

"I shouldn't expect so," said Pawn Fadden finally. "Frankly,

Hitler's Reich does not strike me as a body that shows a tremendous amount of restraint. If they had something like the Order, they'd have them out in the field quick-smart. Probably in some ghastly black leather uniform with death's-heads all over it."

"Or else they'd be briskly getting rid of them," said Wilberforce. "They're not at all keen on unusual people."

"So you've never heard of such a thing?" asked Usha.

"A German Checquy?" said Fadden. "No indeed. There were whispers that von Bismarck had a couple of men who could solve problems in an unorthodox way—I remember old Chevalier Fraser used to make knowing references to Otto's *un*-realpolitik. And we've heard about isolated incidents. There's that account of the archbishop of Mainz who was devoured alive by an army of mice."

"And that archbishop of Trier who *was* a mouse," put in Wilberforce.

"What?" said Usha, utterly bewildered.

"Oh, yes, Archbishop Ratbod," mused Fadden. "I never quite understood what was going on there, but the Checquy histories are quite clear on the matter. Definitely a mouse. And apparently quite a canny administrator and an excellent theologian."

"Well, yes, you hear of things happening on the Continent, of course," said Wilberforce. "I recall there was a wave of inexplicable sinkholes in Lisbon back in 1900 that abruptly stopped. I always rather suspected that someone took matters into his or her own supernatural hands to address that issue."

"Hm, yes," said Fadden. "But an actual organization and army like the Checquy? I'd say the closest thing we've ever seen was the bloody Grafters." The mouths of both the Pawns grew tight at the mention of the long-dead Belgian alchemists. "And really, they weren't at all like us."

By the time they were done with their conversation and emerged into the foyer, it was very late in the afternoon. The staff of the Caïssa were drawing blackout curtains to close out an already dark street.

"I always forget how early it gets dark here," Fadden said cheerfully. "Are you heading off home or are you staying the night, Miss Khorana?"

Usha paused. Bridget was out on her mission with Wattleman.

Pamela and Lady Carmichael were not going to be home that evening. There was the sound of happy chatter coming from the direction of the bar and dining room, and sitting in the house with the servants and Mr. Carmichael did not seem nearly as pleasant a prospect as staying here.

"I shall check if they have any beds available," she decided, and they headed over to the receptionist. As it turned out, there were a few free beds down in the cellar, although there was not much privacy, with no separate sections for men and women.

"They've got the beds set up quite nice, though," said the receptionist. "Everyone has a curtained-off little area. It's like boarding school."

"I shall take your word for it," Usha said. "And I'll take a bed too, please."

"Excellent!" said Pawn Fadden. "You'll join us for dinner, I hope?"

"Dinner will also be served in the cellar, if the sirens go off," the receptionist said apologetically.

"Is that also like boarding school?" asked Usha.

"I've no idea," said the receptionist. "I served my apprenticeship in a stone cottage in the Orkneys and then a manor house outside Tring."

"I see," said Usha. "I'd be delighted to join you for dinner," she said to Fadden, "but I need to make a call first."

"Fine, fine. We'll need to freshen up and change for dinner anyway. Shall we meet you in the bar? Past time for a sundowner, eh, Cyril?" They all looked up as the air-raid sirens started sounding. "Ah. I assume drinks will also be served in the cellar?"

"Of course, sir. Just like in boarding school. I expect."

"Do I have time to make a call?" Usha asked her.

"It is entirely up to you, miss."

"I'll meet you in the cellar shortly, then, gentlemen," Usha said.

The foyer had several glass and wood telephone booths with folding doors, and she slid into one to call the Belgrave Square house and advise Leominster of her plans. She explained that she'd be back home first thing in the morning. He informed her that Miss Mangan had not returned to the house.

So she has stayed on the mission with Wattleman, thought Usha. She had been a little worried that Gerald's departure might prove too much for her friend. *Well, that's promising. I expect it's much the best thing for her, throwing herself into work.*

Wattleman's arms were tight and warm around Bridget as they fell from the Moor's Head toward the street. She caught only an impression of the city as they tumbled through the air, but that impression was madness. Gigantic flames from burning buildings were all around them, and the thunder of bombs falling was deafening. The search-lights swept back and forth overhead, and the sound of ack-ack fire blasted continuously.

The impact of their landing punched right through her. She felt Wattleman's legs buckle and he went down on his knees. She spilled out of his arms onto the wet street. He gasped in shock and exertion, too dazed to even remember to become invisible.

"Bloody…*hell*…but that…was painful," he said, wheezing. Bridget could barely hear him over the bombs falling on the city.

"Are you hurt?" she shouted, getting shakily to her feet.

"Hurt, but not damaged."

Bridget looked him over swiftly. There were bruises, including a hideous broad one around his neck where the scarf had strangled him, and he was shaking, but there was no blood, no sign of any broken bones. She was mildly surprised how clinical she was about his naked-ness, but the situation did not allow for drawing-room manners.

"Good," she said, breathless. "*That* was an unmitigated disaster. We have to get out of here."

"Agreed. That coat might get some attention. Take it off," said Wattleman, and Bridget looked down at herself. The broad pearl strips she'd spread across the front were glistening red and orange as the city burned around them.

"And what? Leave it here? It's evidence."

"You just left a man with half his face coated in pearl, and you're worried about evidence?" he asked. They both flinched as a burning building down the street collapsed with an earsplitting crash. "Christ, we're getting hit hard tonight!"

"Yes, so I like having armor on, thanks. Besides, everyone has more important things to stare at than us." She gestured around at the fires. "Oh, shit! Get invisible! We need to go!" She pointed up to the burst-out window of the Moor's Head. The Murcutts and Vincent were staring down at them. The fires glittered on the pearl encrusting half of Johnny's face. As the two Checquy operatives watched, the sister and brother raised their arms and aimed pistols at them.

If Wattleman answered, Bridget didn't hear him, but he stood up in front of her and vanished from view, so she could clearly see the Murcutts opening fire. The muzzles of the pistols flashed again and again, and there were sparks in midair just in front of her as the bullets ricocheted off the Pawn's invisible chest.

Then a warm unseen hand took hers, and they were running through the streets.

Dinner in the cellars actually turned out to be quite pleasant, provided you ignored the fact that the dormitory area was right next to you, just the other side of a thick dark screen hanging from the ceiling.

Fadden and Usha assisted Pawn Wilberforce in negotiating the stairs down, and the maître d' guided them to a table without ever acknowledging that they were in anything other than the club's normal dining room.

Unlike the crypt-like dormitory under Apex House, the Caïssa's bomb shelter was done up nicely. The members of the Checquy had been laying down wine for centuries now, but the most valuable bottles had been removed to the countryside for safekeeping—it had been almost as high a priority as Operation Egg Basket. There were still many racks of wine bottles against the wall, but carpets had been spread over the flagstones, beds had been brought down from the rooms on the club's upper floors, and there was still sufficient space for a well-equipped field kitchen and a large area with several dining tables. Some enterprising soul had moved a few chandeliers down, so it felt as if one were dining in the world's most Gothic bistro.

There were quite a few people dining in the cellar—Usha counted twenty-seven, although she suspected they had come for the company and the shelter rather than the food. The Caïssa employed very good chefs, but they were working with rationed foods and restrictions.

"Not much selection," remarked Fadden. "Why are the lentil cutlets marked with a *V* on the menu?"

"That's for *victory*," said Usha sourly. "They're considered patriotic."

"Why?"

"Because they're terrible. And they help with meat rationing."

"Heavens preserve us," said Fadden. "Well, I'll start with the whitebait."

"You'll be finishing with it," Usha warned. "You only get one course."

"Then I'll have the unpatriotic pork cutlets," said Fadden.

"Very wise," said the waiter. He took the others' orders and sailed away to the kitchen. The three of them talked about how boring all this rationing was, and Usha reminded the two men that they would need to get their ration books now they were back in England. When the food arrived, it was good, the club chefs having done the very best they could.

"Please tell me more about your work in India," Usha suggested.

"Oh, Checquy work, of course," Fadden said. With an effort, he put down his knife and fork. Usha didn't know if it was some aspect of his abilities or a personal habit, but the Pawn had been devouring his dinner with startling speed. Meanwhile, Usha was only a quarter through her course, and Pawn Wilberforce was struggling to make the first incision into his lamb chop. "Well, at the beginning, I was one of our men with John Company."

Usha nodded thoughtfully. "John Company" was an informal name for the British East India Company—the massive trading company that had gradually come to control the majority of the Indian subcontinent. It had been a key element in bringing India into the British Empire. She'd had no idea, however, that Checquy agents had operated within it. It turned out that the company itself had no idea either.

"You're saying you were placed in it secretly?" Usha asked. "As in, they didn't realize you were part of the Checquy?"

"Exactly."

"But why?"

"Because they didn't know about the Checquy."

"How can that be?" asked Usha. "I mean, the company was effectively controlled by the British government."

"There were a lot of forces at play, and it made the situation rather complicated," said Fadden. "Cabals of financiers and civil servants that had been seeded by nabobs back in the old days and that maintained chains of power. Families that had been out there for generations. Paid agents of rajas. Lots of different parties. It made the position of the Checquy deucedly awkward. People were wielding power and authority who weren't necessarily cleared to know about us. People who *couldn't* be trusted to know about us. So a few of us were sent in as spies, bodyguards who were secret even from those we were protecting."

"Fascinating," said Usha, her mind whirling. The British Empire was seeming less and less monolithic in her eyes. "What exactly were you doing?"

"Oh, this and that. Keeping an eye on things," said Fadden vaguely. "Protecting the company from supernatural infiltration or subversion. Jewel in the crown of the empire and all that." Fadden finished his meal and beckoned to a waiter, who shimmered over to take his plate. "Very pleasant grub, lad. Please pass my compliments on to the chef. Now, what's for pudding?"

"There is no pudding, I'm afraid, sir. Because of the air raid and that."

"No pudding? Tch! The sacrifices we make for Britain."

"Was there a great deal of the supernatural in India?" Usha asked, bringing the conversation back to the point.

"Well, we weren't quite so arrogant as to assume that there were no unearthly powers on the subcontinent. I know at least one maharaja's rule was built on the basis of supernatural abilities, and there's a temple in Mysore that's been sealed up for centuries. Legend said it was cursed, but one of my friends, Oakley, was curious, so he oozed in through a back wall. He thought he might find some lost treasure or something. Instead, he found the whole place crawling with snakes made out of living stone. No one knew where they came from or how they had all been corralled in there."

"What happened to Oakley?" asked Usha.

"Oh, he managed to escape, just barely. His arms were paralyzed for the rest of his life, though."

"My God!"

"Hm. It turned out their venom fossilized one's muscles. Rather nasty."

"And they're still there?" asked Usha. "The snakes?"

"Best place for 'em," said Fadden with feeling. "None of us were going in to try and sort them out. It just went to show that some things were best not interfered with. So, we had a presence in India, but always small, always unofficial, and always with an emphasis on observing and letting things come to us rather than us seeking them out. From '58 on, Cyril and I were placed close to the viceroys, creating resources all through the Indian Civil Service."

"Retainers?" asked Usha, using the term for the operatives of the Checquy who did not have any inhuman abilities.

"Unwitting Retainers, I suppose you could call them. Really, they were more like uninformed informants. Much like the networks we have here, they were people who knew whom to contact if reports of anything unnatural came to them. Good Lord, there's young Robling!" exclaimed Fadden suddenly. Usha looked over to see a man in his sixties eating at another table. "I haven't seen him since I recruited him in '97 out of Meerut. Miss Khorana, would you excuse me a moment? I should pop on over and say hello."

"Of course," said Usha. She watched him go over, then turned her attention back to Pawn Wilberforce, who was still struggling manfully with his dinner, which had to have been tepid by that point. It was almost painful to watch him sawing away at the meat—his trembling hands and weak grasp meant that his attempts to cut it were more in the nature of a scraping massage.

"Pawn Wilberforce," she said finally. "I offer this with the profoundest respect, but would you like some assistance with your chop?"

"That's very kind of you, my dear," said Wilberforce. "It *is* a bit awkward, isn't it? I suppose one does need to face facts." He put down the knife and fork with a clatter, but instead of passing the plate along to her, he sat back in his chair with an audible popping of spine and stared intently at his meal.

Usha opened her mouth to say something, but shut it again in surprise as she felt a sudden pressure building around her. It wasn't painful, exactly, but it was uncomfortable, a pulsation against her skin that continued on through her, pressing lightly on her bones and her stomach. She looked around, but no one else appeared to sense it. The waiters moved about the room without any concern, and the conversation at the other tables continued without a single pause.

With a sense of shock, she realized that the sensation was coming to her through her powers—whatever phenomenon Pawn Wilberforce was initiating washed up against her own connection to gravity. It was different from her abilities, though. Gravity remained unaffected, there was no impact on the furnishings or the people, but she could feel a tiny, localized warping occurring, a spot where the natural laws of the universe were being twisted. This aberration in the shape of things, which was grating against all her senses, was focused on the lamb chop. She could almost hear molecules parting as the elderly Pawn stared at his meal and unleashed something terrible.

There was no sound, no flash of light or burst of heat. Instead, the chop and the plate seemed to ripple crazily and then, with a motion that hurt the eyes, the meat divided itself into bite-size pieces. The pulsating sensation stopped, and Usha's senses tentatively unclenched.

"Please forgive an old man his eccentricities." Wilberforce sighed. "I don't like being fussed over. Still, I always feel vaguely ridiculous using my power for something so mundane. It's like dispatching a regiment of cavalry to slice the top off one's hard-boiled egg."

"It's very impressive," Usha said weakly.

"Thank you. I've leveled entire fortresses with it."

"In India?" asked Usha, startled.

"No, once in Nigeria and another time in Sheffield. Well, I say *fortresses*—the one in Sheffield was more of a hive than anything." He picked up his fork and, with only a little difficulty, speared one of the pieces of meat.

"Pawn Wilberforce?"

"Yes, my dear?"

"Forgive me if it's rude to ask, but how old is Pawn Fadden?"

"I don't think it's rude at all," said the elderly man. "Let me see. As I recall, he was born on the same day as the old queen. So"—his lips moved as he calculated—"just about one hundred and twenty years old."

"Is...is he immortal?"

"Well, it's impossible to say until he dies," remarked Wilberforce. "He doesn't age, though. He looks as young as he did when I came on to be his apprentice, and I was fourteen at the time." Usha nodded, looking at the elderly Pawn with interest. "He can certainly be harmed, however. Did you notice his missing fingers?"

"I did."

"I saw him lose those fingers to a sepoy's sword at Cawnpore in '57. He felt it—he's definitely got a normal body in terms of suffering pain and damage, but he doesn't age."

"So you were present for the mutiny?" she asked, startled.

"Ugly business, that," he said, shaking his head. "So sad. Lionel and I got out by the skin of our teeth." His eyes went distant, and he was somewhere else, looking at memories that had stayed with him over the decades. For a moment, Usha could see the boy he had been. "So horrible," he said softly. Then he shook his head again. "And I've seen him grievously injured since. He's not invulnerable."

"How long were you in India?"

"Went over when I was fourteen to be Lionel's apprentice. That would have been '56. Fascinating place—I'm glad I got to see it as it was then. And good adventures too. Real *Boy's Own* stuff."

"I'm still surprised that the Checquy didn't have more of an official presence," remarked Usha. "Fadden's explanation makes sense for India under the East India Company, but from 1858, when the government nationalized the company, surely it was then just part of the empire."

"Well, it was complicated. Are you familiar with the Croatoan?"

"The American Checquy? Not really."

"They came out of us," explained Pawn Wilberforce. "The Checquy had a presence in the British colonies in America pretty much from the beginning. Operatives there built it into quite an effective little setup. Put down some major threats, including some very peculiar mollusks that kept appearing and devouring people. They were a credit to the Order. Then the Americans have their revolution, and suddenly we've got Checquy operatives working in a country that isn't theirs anymore. A few of them came back to Britain, but most elected to remain and protect the populace as the Croatoan. Which meant that suddenly there was a new Checquy-type organization in the world—one that knew all about us. Friendly? Yes. For now. But who knows about the future?"

"I see."

"Yes. We'd inadvertently created a new world power. So there was rather a lot of concern at the possibility that we might do the same in India. The memories of the mutiny were fresh. The powers that be were very worried. And there were other concerns as well. It raised the question of what the Checquy was going to become. Were we going to protect the whole damn world?"

"That's a lot to think about," said Usha faintly.

"Quite," said Wilberforce. "And who knew what unknown powers we might disturb? So we took advantage of the gigantic bureaucracy that already existed in India and used it to identify those cases and individuals that really represented a distinct danger."

They were rejoined by Pawn Fadden, who brought with him three longtime friends. Two of them looked like they were old enough to be his father, and the other one looked like he could be a statue of his father if his father had possessed the resources and the desire to have an effigy carved out of petrified wood and then had the hair and the lips gilded. After Usha and Wilberforce finished their meals, they all settled back over coffee, cheese, cigars, or all of the above, according to personal taste. It was clearly time for rumination—both digestive and philosophical.

"So, Usha, what are your thoughts on the future of India?" Fadden asked suddenly.

Usha glanced up from the scanty cheese platter to find everyone at the table looking at her with interest. She hesitated. This related directly to why her family had sent her to England and why Lady Carmichael's invitation had been so readily accepted.

"Independence is coming," she said carefully. "And soon. Sooner than many think. Even many in power." Some of the men around the table looked shocked at this statement. Others—including Fadden—nodded sagely. "The veneer of unity that the British have spread over the land will be disrupted, if not shattered. I anticipate there will be a partition, which will be hideous and will have long-term implications."

Which is why I was expanding our business presence here and on the Continent, she thought. *And establishing some fallback positions for the family in this country. While Anand does the same in New York and Ashok in Sydney.* She'd had little news of her brothers since the war began, but she scoured briefings and newspapers for word of their cities and was comfortable in assuming they were much safer than she was. *Thank heavens we voted Ashok down in his argument for expanding the family presence in Hong Kong.* It was an invaluable commercial prospect, but the war between China and Japan had everyone nervous, and their father was dubious about the limitations of Japan's ambition.

There was continued discussion. Some of the people at the table seemed unable to grasp the idea that the status quo in India was not universally beloved, regardless of its stability and (for some) profitability. And she, for whose family the status quo had been so profitable, could understand why it might seem impossible to them that change was being sought.

"Gentlemen, thank you for some wonderful conversation and company. I find myself quite exhausted," said Usha. "I think I shall bid you all good night." Her colleagues all wished her sweet dreams, and one of the staff guided her to her curtained cubicle.

As she lay beneath the cool, freshly laundered sheets, the hushed conversations of the other guests murmured in the background. Beyond that, she heard dull, distant, repetitive thuds as the bombs fell on the city.

My God, it sounds hellish out there, thought Usha sleepily. *I pity any poor fools who are abroad in the city tonight.*

This is becoming a habit, thought Bridget. *Two nights in a row of being out during the attacks.* But this time, there were no wardens around to point them toward the nearest shelter. Instead, there were fire crews everywhere, doing their best to halt the inferno as the flames spread across the houses and shops. The sight of Bridget running by herself, her hand held by an invisible companion, barely merited a curious glance from the frantic firemen.

The two ran madly, without any specific destination. Sometimes she was dragging Wattleman along, other times it was him hauling her as they zigzagged down roads and darted down alleys. The city was a nightmare, with screams and sirens and flames everywhere. Smoke filled the streets, setting the two of them coughing as they ran. The crump of bombs falling was still booming in the sky, but Bridget realized that there weren't any bombs landing in their immediate vicinity.

"Where are we going?" she shouted.

"I'm up for suggestions!" Wattleman's voice shouted back. "I've just been trying to put some space between us and them."

"Then stop a moment!" She gasped and hauled back on his hand. "I think we're far enough away." She looked behind her and saw no figures pursuing them. "Should we find a shelter?"

"I'd rather not spend a night in the crowds like this," said Wattleman's voice. "The potential for discovery or, worse, awkwardness would be more than I'd like. Plus, it's bloody freezing."

"Fine," said Bridget. She looked at a street sign. "We're not far from the Caïssa, and it doesn't seem like there are any bombs landing here now. I think they've passed over." The thought of the familiar club filled her with longing. She could picture falling into one of the comfortable guest-room beds and passing out. And if all the beds were taken, she'd be happy to pass out on the floor of the cellars. Anything, really, that facilitated passing out safely was ideal.

"Good idea," said Wattleman's voice. "I could do with a stiff drink." This time, Bridget led the way, at a brisk walking pace, but she didn't let go of the Pawn's hand. Partly because, even though it was Wattleman, it was still comforting to have someone's warm hand in hers, and partly because there was the very real possibility that they would lose each other in the madness.

However, when they finally rounded the corner, they did not see the familiar shape of the Caïssa waiting for them on the square.

Instead, a vast column of pitch-black smoke was rising out of the eviscerated building. The roof was gone, the walls had caved in, and gigantic flames were dancing up into the sky.

19

The empty skin of Pawn Liam Seager regarded Lyn and Kelton from its place on the ceiling. Or it seemed to. It lacked eyes, but the ghastly ragged holes in its face appeared to be looking at them.

This is really, really bad, thought Lyn. *Things were actually better when it was just me and three gangsters, with me getting beaten with my own baton and a gun pointed at my head.* Kelton was whimpering on the floor, and she didn't blame him at all. She rather wanted to join him.

They'd sent Seager after her! *He is supposed to be retired from this work,* she thought bitterly. The Pawn who was feared among his own kind for his mercilessness and his capabilities. The one who was rumored to have killed multiple out-of-control Checquy operatives. *And apparently, I'm to be one of them.* It seemed so unreasonable. *I haven't actually done anything.*

Well, if you ignore the unconscious gangsters that are currently acting as a barricade.

And the crime lord who is weeping in his own piss on the floor.

She and Seager stared at each other for a long moment, or at least, Lyn *thought* they were staring at each other. The lack of eyes made it difficult to be sure.

"Seager, can you hear me?" she asked hesitantly. The skin cocked its head at her but gave no sign that it understood. *I suppose it was too much to hope for.* The skin of his ears was there, but none of the actual hearing apparatus. *So does he actually see me? How is he sensing this? How does he perceive this whole situation when it's just his skin?* She had no doubt that these questions had already been asked and argued over by the scientists of Kirrin Island. Maybe they'd even come up with some answers, but she didn't know them.

"Seager, I'm innocent. I didn't kill those people." She said it clearly, exaggerating her words in case the skin was reading lips, but there was no reaction.

She had to act. She gave a moment's thought to trying to surrender, just lying down on the floor, but there was no telling if Seager would take her prisoner or just briskly kill her and slither out under the door.

But I have to do something, she thought. The bullet holes in his skin showed that the gun was going to be useless, so she reached into her pocket, drew out the baton, and snapped it open. The empty eyeholes of the skin actually narrowed, and she tensed.

She had no idea what Seager was capable of, what his powers let him do. The stories about him had always been vague, more focused on the terrifying results than his actual process. Early on, when she'd heard the rumors about him, she'd tried to sneak a peek at his file, only to find it heavily redacted—not a good sign in an organization in which everybody enjoyed a security clearance higher than the Prince of Wales. The fact that Seager had just taken out an unspecified number of Kelton goons, though, spoke volumes.

Lyn was charging the baton even as she stepped forward. The skin of Seager reached out along the ceiling and hauled itself completely through the gap above the door. The Seager-skin clung to the ceiling for a moment, then dropped and turned to face her. Behind her, Kelton moaned.

Despite herself, Lyn was curious to see if the *whole* skin was going to be there.

As it turned out, Pawn Seager had made some strategic omissions when sending his skin out to fight. He'd included the legs and the feet, but a ragged tear outlined the empty space that was the groin area. There were also jagged strips of the inner thighs missing.

I guess I can't blame him for not wanting to deploy the family jewels unprotected into a combat scenario, she thought. "Seager, I'm trying to find out who is behind those murders. Because it wasn't me. I swear." The skin moved into a crouching position, ready to attack. "Oh, *hell.*"

I don't want to fight you, Seager. If I fight you, then I've made an actual attack against a comrade. There'll be no going back for me after that.

Plus you'll probably kill me.

But only probably.

Well, probably *only probably.*

She took a step back and pumped a little more juice into the baton. It felt like enough to stun a man of Seager's size into unconsciousness. She had no idea what it would do to a disembodied epidermis that was not physically connected to a nervous system. *Don't look into the conspicuous absence of eyes,* she told herself. *Watch its hands and its feet.*

Its hands and feet were weird. Lyn had never thought about how much hands and feet were defined by the bones and meat inside them. These looked like wrinkly dishwashing gloves. To make matters worse, there were neat little holes where the fingernails and toenails should be. And the lack of content to the thing meant that it didn't stand or move like a person. While still, it rippled, crumpled in places, and when it moved, it was almost liquid, bending wherever seemed most convenient. The whole thing was too bizarre.

You don't know what it will do, what it can do. So don't give it the chance to do anything unexpected. Go now!

She was about to lunge forward, and the skin seemed to be gathering itself for something, when there was a massive slamming sound and the door moved forward a little as the frame broke near its handle. The two of them, woman and epidermis, froze and stared at the door. To Lyn's mild gratification, the unconscious men at the base of the door actually seemed to act as quite an effective bulwark. Then the people behind the door really put their weight and that of their battering ram into it.

"Shove at the bottom!" commanded a rough voice. Lyn and the skin watched, transfixed, as slowly, inch by inch, the door pushed the unconscious men aside as it opened.

What should I do now? Pick up a gun? What is Seager going to do? Is our fight canceled on account of gangsters?

There was no way to ask him, and besides, she couldn't drag her eyes away from that door as it moved. When it was open about a foot, someone's head poked partially through the gap—just enough to see into the room with one eye. The eye widened as it took in the spectacle of Lyn's paused standoff with nine-tenths of the outside of Seager.

Well, I could totally have taken that *one out,* thought Lyn through her horror. *Lots of time to line up the shot.* But it would have meant turning her back on Seager.

The head withdrew, and there was the sound of some incredulous conferencing. Lots of questions along the lines of "Whatcha mean, *empty?*"

Then the conferees on the other side of the door appeared to reach a consensus. And there was nothing for Lyn to do. Nowhere to go. There was a massive, concerted grunt, and the door was forced wide open. A gigantic man had kicked it the rest of the way, and now he was standing with a shotgun leveled into the room. Tall, muscular, with long blond hair, he looked like he should have been out sacking a monastery somewhere. He was so astounded by the display in front of him, though, that he appeared to forget that the gun could be fired.

"Benny, kill 'em!" screamed Kelton from his corner. "Kill 'em both!"

Lyn was ninety-nine percent sure that she and Seager's skin exchanged glances. And was it her imagination or did the empty pelt actually shrug a little? The man with the shotgun was still staring open-mouthed at the sheath of a human being that was standing in front of him.

"Benny!" shouted Kelton.

"Oh, yeah, right." He brought the gun up and fired both barrels at them.

As he did so, the Seager-skin moved with unbelievable speed and shoved Lyn out of the way. She fell back, stumbling over her own feet, landed hard on her ass, and instinctively rolled onto her back. The baton fell from her hands, and as the blast of the gun thundered, it was accompanied by a flare of red lightning that climbed through the air to the ceiling and lit up the entire room.

Her heart was pounding. *Have I been shot?* Lyn pressed her hands to her face and her chest. She seemed to be unharmed. She looked up.

"Oh, Liam," she breathed.

The skin was crouched, hunched on the spot where she'd been a moment ago. It must have tried to use that fearsome, swift-as-thought speed to turn its back to the shotgun and curl itself into a ball as the blast came at it, but it hadn't been quite swift enough.

The room was silent as, slowly, the empty skin stood up straight. It uncurled and brought its shoulders back, and Lyn could see that there were new holes peppered through it.

"Oh my God," whispered one of the gangsters.

There was a tiny amount of blood ringing the wounds, but it was seeing the gun smoke drifting through the holes that turned Lyn's stomach. The skin turned its head and nodded at her. She nodded back silently, and it reached out a hand. She picked up her spent baton, then took the proffered hand. It hauled her up to her feet.

Okay, so apparently, we're allies for the moment.

"Right," said Benny finally, sounding only a little unsettled. "We've seen that bullets don't stop it, but they can hurt *her*. So knives for the freak, and guns for the girl."

Despite herself, Lyn had to give him points for pragmatism. It wasn't the kind of thoughtful analysis she'd have expected from a criminal who'd just witnessed an impossibility.

"So get 'em!" shouted Benny. "Five thousand nicker to the one that brings me the head of that skin-thing!" At that, the men rushed into the room. They shoved against one another in their frenzy, one of them tripping over the bodies on the floor. Two of them tried to kick away the turned-over chairs, and the stored electricity lashed out over them. They went down immediately, and their colleagues flinched away from their smoking bodies.

"Yeah, you're all going to get some of that," muttered Lyn. She dropped Seager's hand, charged the baton, and moved forward. There were six men (aside from the two who'd just been unexpectedly tased into unconsciousness by furniture), and four of them—presumably drawn by the prospect of five thousand pounds—produced alarming-looking knives, apparently a standard part of their gooning kit. The other two, however, leveled pistols at her.

Before she could even really start to panic, the Seager-skin was blurring toward them. There were two earsplitting cracks as it whipped its hands through the air. The men howled as the guns were sent flying. One of them stared at his broken fingers in disbelief.

Oh, that's *what that sound was,* thought Lyn, remembering the per-plexing flapping cracks she'd heard coming from the other side of the door. The skin drew down swiftly with a rustling sound, folding and refolding upon itself almost like an accordion, then shot forward again. It held its fist before it, and the combined momentum made for a sickening crack as it struck one of the men on the chin and lifted him clean off the floor in a shocking uppercut.

One of the other men, meanwhile, ignored the plight of his colleague and took the opportunity to slash out at the skin's back with his knife. There were gasps as a long slice opened along where the shoulder blades would have been if they hadn't been somewhere else. Even the goon seemed appalled at the ease with which the skin parted. He was even more appalled when the head turned one hundred and eighty degrees to look at him, then slammed forward with all the force of a hammer.

"See?" screamed Kelton from his corner. "See? Cut it to pieces!" The remaining men closed in around the skin, seemingly forgetting that Lyn existed.

Until she shot one of them in the knee.

After all, flashy as an electrically charged baton might be, she was not going to ignore the fact that there were three loaded guns right by her feet. Plus, with the guns, she didn't have to get too close to her opponents.

The gathered men broke apart hurriedly, and as Lyn tried to aim her pistol at one of them—any one of them—the man named Benny dived forward into an unexpected roll on the floor and came up to kick the gun out of her hand. She bent down to pick up another, but he executed a low, sweeping kick and sent the guns skittering across the floor.

"Right, then," she said flatly and tightened her grip on her baton.

"Watch that rod of hers!" shouted Kelton. "It's a cattle prod or something." Benny raised an eyebrow at her.

"Really?" he asked her.

"Nah," she said dismissively, then lunged at him explosively, her baton thrust out like a saber. The criminal stepped aside stunningly quickly, grabbed her wrist, and twisted it, squeezing so that the pain made her drop the weapon. It landed on the floor and flashed red. Benny danced back, and a knife was suddenly in his hand. The two of them eyed each other carefully.

Meanwhile, in the background, it was chaos. The remaining three men were doing their best to get their knives close to the skin-thing without getting caught by it. Their efforts were stymied by the presence of no fewer than four unconscious colleagues sprawled on the floor in inconvenient locations, another colleague who was lying bleeding and moaning after being shot in the leg, two office chairs that might still offer the possibility of electrocution, and the furious shouts of their urine-soaked boss.

The skin of Pawn Seager, however, moved easily about the room in a way that was terrifyingly alien. It appeared to have been in no way hampered by the gunshot wound, the shotgun wounds, or the vicious knife slice across the shoulders. It stalked the gangsters in a way that was almost cruel in its ease. Where there was an obstacle on the floor, it sprang up and clung flat to the ceiling, holding on with fingers and toes bent backward to hook into invisible crevices so it could look down on them with its empty eyeholes.

Against the unnatural agility of Pawn Seager's skin, the three men were practically helpless, but their fear and their awkwardness made them unpredictable opponents. They scuttled about, ducking their heads and swiping out feverishly with their knives. The skin shot down from the ceiling at one of the men and seemed to pour down onto him as it twisted easily around a desperate thrust of his knife.

The skin moved fluidly and twined itself around the man like a snake. The other two men were circling anxiously, unsure of how to strike without stabbing their colleague, who was screaming as Seager's scalp covered his face. The man flung himself blindly all around the place while Seager's skin tightened like a constrictor. He collapsed, unconscious, and the skin unwound itself to face the other two.

Lyn, meanwhile, was discovering that Benny was a much better fighter than she was. She'd received vigorous, intensive training at the Estate, and it had continued since she'd left, but this was clearly a man who fought for a living and who had been doing so for a long time. He was light on his feet and moved with a powerful certainty that was intimidating. His deft reaction to her attack with the baton had left her disarmed except for her rings.

She swung out at him, her rings fully charged, and he stepped into the attack, striking the inside of her wrist to block her blow—unknowingly avoiding getting shocked. Now he was right by her. He grabbed one of her wrists and she grabbed the wrist of his knife hand. For a second, their eyes locked. He was stronger. There was no question that he'd win in a struggle of muscle against muscle, but she'd been trained by some government-level sneaky fighters.

She dropped and twisted in a maneuver that her judo instructor had warned her could dislocate both her shoulders if she did it wrong.

But she did it right, and Benny found himself being flipped over the shoulder of a woman a good head shorter and a good sixty pounds lighter than him. The breath was smacked out of him, but he was quick enough to roll out of the way of her follow-up punch. Her rings disgorged their energy into the patch of floor where his face had been. Tendrils of electricity flailed red, and she saw his eyes narrow as he took it in. As he got to his feet, she retrieved her baton from the floor.

They stared at each other warily, he red-faced and tense, she sweating and shifting constantly against the throbbing pain in her legs. In the background, one of the two remaining goons was seized by the Seager-skin and gave out a strangled wail as he was hauled up to the ceiling, but the two of them didn't take their calculating eyes off each other.

She knew that time was not on her side. A number of scenarios were possible, and none of them were favorable for her. The Seager-skin might take care of the two men and then come for her, or Benny might manage to take her down, or Checquy backup might arrive, or criminal backup might arrive. Plus, her legs were killing her, and she really needed to go to the toilet.

Her eye was caught by flailing movement behind Benny. The skin was now hanging from the ceiling by its toes and appeared to be smothering the goon it had snagged. Benny caught her distraction and lunged, and she had to dance back. *Stay focused! You need to bring this to a stop now,* she told herself. *So do something different.* She drew back, and, as Seager dropped the goon from the ceiling with a dull thump, she brought the baton down onto the floor. The electricity burst out and danced along the flagstones. It wouldn't actually do any harm—experimentation at the Estate had shown that her energy didn't like stone; it would spread out and dissipate almost immediately, but it would look frightening as hell and hopefully distract her opponent.

Except that he had jumped forward as she began her strike and was already in the air hurtling toward her by the time the electricity was spreading across the floor.

Oh no.

He slammed into her, knocking the breath out of her and sending her flying back against the wall. The baton went skittering out of her hand, and he dived for it. He picked it up carefully by the handle and examined it closely.

"So, is there a button or something?" he asked. "Or do you just need to touch someone with it?"

"It's hard to explain," Lyn said, wheezing. She was trying to reinflate her lungs and stay standing. "But you don't need to worry about it anyway."

"Oh yeah?" He looked at her. "Oh."

"Yeah." She'd taken advantage of his distraction to retrieve one of the pistols and now pointed it at his chest.

"Bloody useless!" Kelton moaned from his corner. The two of them ignored him.

"So you're going to kill me?" asked Benny.

"I'd prefer not to," Lyn said. "Slide that baton over to me, and I'll just knock you out."

"Oh, you'll just knock me out, will you?"

"Uh, yes?"

"Do me a favor!" He snorted sarcastically. "You're the one who's been going around killing people—the nutjob who's been electrocuting them to death."

"Actually, no, that wasn't me," said Lyn. He looked around at the unconscious men littering the room, then looked back at her with the withering scorn of a Siberian husky that has been offered broccoli. "I know it's hard to believe, and that's actually what got me into this situation," she said. "I've never killed anyone in my life."

"You just shot Steve!" He jerked his head at the moaning man crumpled by the door.

"Does he *sound* dead to you?"

"He doesn't sound well!"

"He could have sounded a damn sight worse," snapped Lyn. "Or not be making any sounds at all." She shook her head. "Anyway, I don't have time for this, so I can either shoot you or knock you out with fifty thousand volts. You choose. But I have more control of the volts." He frowned and opened his mouth, then he stiffened and his eyes rolled back in his head.

What's going on? Lyn thought bemusedly.

He went down, crumpling unconscious onto the floor, revealing the Seager-skin standing crouched behind him, its hands closed into fists. It had struck him hard enough to knock him out.

"Ah," said Lyn. "Right." The skin straightened up. She flicked her eyes beyond it. The last goon was slumped against the wall. Evidently the fight had finished and she hadn't even realized it. "Thanks for that." Its eyeholes narrowed, and it stretched out its hand to her.

"What?" she asked. The thing's lips pursed. It pointed at the gun in her hand and snapped its fingers. "That's impressive. I would have thought you needed bones to snap your fingers." The skin held up its other hand, still in a fist. The meaning was clear. "I get it. Either I give you the gun or you give me the fist." She sighed, and her shoulders slumped. "I guess it was always going to come down to this." She raised the gun slowly and turned it so that the handle was pointed toward the hollow skin. She slapped it into the skin's palm, almost petulantly, and electricity exploded out from it.

She kept her hold on the barrel of the gun as the barrage of energy flashed and flared and wrapped itself around the Seager-skin. She had not been sure it would have any effect on the epidermis, divorced as it appeared to be from muscles, organs, a nervous system, and a brain. But it certainly did.

The skin thrashed and, to her horror, crumpled. The empty eyes gaped wider and the ragged edges of the sockets danced. Its mouth opened in a silent scream, its jaw so wide she thought it must tear. The limbs spasmed crazily, as though blasts of air were being pumped through them, and when the electricity eventually spent itself and faded away with a final crackle, the thing fell to the ground.

"I am so sorry, Liam," she told the pile of skin. "I really am."

"You're a fucking monster," said Kelton from his corner.

"Oh, probably," said Lyn wearily. She picked up the baton from where Benny had dropped it and absently charged it up. As she walked over to the gangster, he shrank back. "I'd love to have a good long chat with you," she said. "I think you could tell me a lot of interesting stuff. But I don't have the time now. Maybe later."

"You bitch, you come here again and I'll—*hng! Hgnghngngng! Guh.*"

"Yeah, well, you *would* say that," she said as she pulled the baton back from his neck. She turned her attention to the still-moaning Steve. He cringed when she approached him.

"Get away!"

"Don't be silly," she told him. "If I wanted you dead, I would just shoot you again, somewhere that would kill you a damn sight quicker." She eyed him cautiously. There was quite a bit of blood, but not the sort of spurting or gushing that she'd learned meant really, *really* bad news. "Here, you need to press hard against the wound."

"So I'm not gonna die?"

"Not if you give me your phone and the code to unlock it."

"What?"

"I'll call an ambulance for you," she said. "Once I'm out of here."

"D'ya promise?"

"Yeah," she said. "But first you have to give me some straight answers."

"All right..." he said warily.

"How worried do I need to be about more men appearing with guns? And be truthful, because if there's trouble before I'm out of here, I'll make sure you're the first one to go."

"I believe you," he said. "Well, you've got a bit of time. I think pretty much everyone who was in the bar is here." He gestured at the unconscious men scattered around the room.

"Seems like a lot of troops to have in a pub," she said.

"The boss has been worried 'bout them killings. I'd've said he was paranoid, but..." He shrugged painfully. "Still, when the trouble started, Benny *did* put the call out for everyone to come back in. I'd say you've got only a few minutes before the rest of the lads start pouring in." She looked at him levelly for a second, then nodded.

"All right, give me the phone and your wallet." He tossed it over and told her the code. She unlocked it, just to be sure, and saw that, unsurprisingly, there were no bars. Then she briskly took all the money from his wallet. "I'll be gone in a mo'." She spent the next few minutes acting as quickly as she could. She cast about for some sort of receptacle in which to carry away everyone's guns and noticed that Benny had a compact backpack. Removing it from his unconscious bulk was not the work of a moment, but soon she had a small, incredibly illegal arsenal packed away. She emptied all their wallets of cash, leaving the cards. To her hurried satisfaction, it appeared that it was de rigueur among criminals to carry large amounts of folding money on one's person.

My operating budget is expanding at a rate of knots.

"Look, I 'ate to bother you, but were you gonna be calling that ambulance soon?"

"I'm hurrying," she said in almost exactly the same tone she used when Emma started whining.

"It's just that I *am* bleeding here."

"And whose fault is that?"

He wisely elected not to answer.

"Keep pressure on it. I won't be a minute more." She gingerly pushed the urine-soaked Kelton onto his side to fish out his money clip, which was strained to its limit by a wad of bills that seemed to represent all the wood pulp from the Hundred-Acre Wood. She looked about for her phone and saw that it had been kicked into a corner but was mercifully still intact.

"Okay, I'm done. Steve, is there a way out of this cellar other than the main stairs?"

"Yeah, there's a loading lift and some stairs if you go out and turn right."

"Thank you. Now, once I'm out of here, I'll call the ambulance for you and your degenerate friends. They should be here shortly to save your life."

"Yeah, ta," he said weakly.

"In the meantime, just keep breathing, and, you know, don't go into the light." As she did a final check, making sure she hadn't left anything behind, her eye fell on the puddle of collapsed skin on the floor. "Oh, bugger."

It looked vulnerable and creepy at the same time; it was like finding several dozen hairless newborn puppies in your bathroom sink. Lyn knew immediately that she couldn't possibly leave Seager's epidermis there. If any of the thugs came to consciousness before the skin roused itself—*if* the skin roused itself—there was no telling what they would do to it. And if the authorities arrived and found the skin lying on the floor, it would cause all sorts of trouble. She was going to have to take it with her.

And if he wakes up and attacks me, she thought grimly, *I'll just have to improvise.*

She slung on her backpack and gingerly reached out and touched the skin. *Oh, this is so gross.* It felt, unsurprisingly, exactly like skin. It was cooler than she would have expected, but that made sense, given the fact that it was not connected to a circulatory system. *You don't have time to be creeped out,* she told herself and, gritting her teeth, scooped up the pelt. It weighed about as much as a long leather coat. *Which is kind of what it is,* she thought, and gagged a little.

Just try to ignore the fact that you are slinging a naked man—well, most of a naked man—*over your shoulder.* It flopped about nauseatingly, and she found herself wondering which would be worse, to have its buttocks or the ragged gaping void that was the lack of a crotch touching her shoulder. In the end, she went with buttocks up—the hole was just too disconcerting to have right by her face. She kept her hand on it to prevent it from sliding off. In her other hand was the baton, charged.

Through the door and into the cellar. Five men lay unconscious near the door, the ones Seager had taken down. They were all breathing but appeared to have been beaten fairly rigorously. Livid red lines like whip marks were scored across the cheeks of a couple of them, and, remembering the hideous swiftness of the skin, she could imagine the bewildering battle that had taken place.

Following Steve's instructions, she turned right out the door and hurried through the maze of boxes, kegs, and assorted items. The empty skin flopped on her shoulder. *If I get out of here, what am I going to look like on the street?* she wondered. *People are going to think I'm taking my deflated and mutilated sex doll out for an airing. What am I going to do with it? Dump it in the bin along with the phone?*

Those, however, were problems for the future. First, she needed to find the exit. And, beyond some large humming refrigerators and some dubious-looking crates, there it was: a service lift that looked as if it had been installed during the Industrial Revolution and some concrete steps. Lyn hurried up and banged the door open with her hip.

The daylight was bright in her eyes, and she squinted and looked around. A dead-end back alley, just wide enough for delivery trucks to rumble down and drop off supplies for the pub. Roll-up doors were set into the walls, and the cracked and slimy pavement was dotted here and there with patches of old cobblestones, as if they were erupting back up to the surface. The distant roar of London was muffled by the high walls and the bends of the alley. It was deserted except for a young man who was leaning against a wall and smoking. He jerked upright at the sight of her.

"Pawn Binns!" He gasped.

That tells me everything I need to know. He started to move, but despite the agony of her legs, it was no contest. She was jacked up on adrenaline, while he'd been taking the opportunity to enjoy a sneaky roll-up. She snapped forward, and before he could react, the tip of her baton was a centimeter from his throat.

"Don't. Fucking. Move. Blink twice if you know what I can do with this."

Blink–blink.

"Good. Your name?"

"Pawn Jake Kosloski."

She frowned. The name meant nothing to her. Her eyes raked over him briskly. Just a kid, *maybe* early twenties. Wearing jeans and a T-shirt. Unremarkable. If he hadn't recognized her, she'd have walked right by him.

No point in asking him what his powers are, he'd just lie. But since my

arms and legs haven't fallen off and I haven't had a stroke or been turned to a
pillar of pepper, I'll have to assume I'm in no immediate danger.

"Pawn Kosloski, I have no desire to hurt you, but the past few days
have taught me that we don't always get what we want." He stared at
her in shock, and when he realized what was draped over her shoulder, his eyes widened. "Yeah, that's him. So if you move in a funny
way, if I start to feel funny, if I think you're making a move against
me, then you need to hope that you're lightning-resistant. Got it?"

"Yes."

"Good. Now, we need to hurry. Where's your vehicle?"

"That way."

"Let's move that way, then. You first. I'll have this baton at your
back. And if you think about running, I can chuck this thing. I *will*
nail you with it." It was true; she'd spent hours and hours practicing
throwing the baton. He turned and started walking down the alley.
"Where's the rest of your team?" She presumed that more than one
person had been sent after her.

"The other two are at the truck," he said.

"Two?" A tracking team usually included at least ten people.

"They didn't use an official tracking team," said Kosloski. "You've
gone rogue; they wanted to keep you secret."

I'm that shameful a secret—how nice. "And how did *you* make the cut
for this supersecret team?" she asked, then felt bad. "I mean, I'm sure
you're very good, and you certainly seem very calm and professional,
but you look like you're nine."

"They brought me along to immobilize you for transport once
Pawn Seager captured you."

"Oh," said Lyn warily. "Okay. How were you going to do that?
Do you put people to sleep? Or freeze them or something?"

"No, I temporarily overwrite their personality with my own."

"Stop. *Don't* turn around. What?" She was in a tremendous hurry,
but this sounded like information she needed.

"I download myself into people's brains and take over their bodies."

"You possess them?" asked Lyn weakly.

"The mind in *this* body—in *my* body—isn't controlling them. It's
a separate copy of me in their body."

"You're possessing them."

"I'm not possessing them," he said in a very matter-of-fact tone. "An identical copy of me is occupying them, and only for about twelve thousand heartbeats or so. Then the original personality breaks through, and the copy of me dissipates."

"And you're okay with that? The copy of you in someone else's body is okay with that?"

"It's okay with that because I'm okay with that. And it's a copy of me."

"The copy is okay knowing it's going to last for only twelve thousand heartbeats?" *What is wrong with me? Why am I getting caught up in this conversation?*

"I did a lot of work with therapists at the Estate," he said. "They said that I have now reached the mentality of a nihilist suicide-bombing atheist with an ingrained sense of dedicated service to other people and a keen ability and desire to savor the moment."

"Fucking *meow*," said Lyn weakly. "And what were you going to do with me? What was your plan?"

"Well, I'd have woken up inside you," he began.

"Yuck," said Lyn. "Please rephrase."

"Sorry. I'd have, um, downloaded into you."

"You think that's better?" she asked.

"Okay, I'd have woken up inside your head..." He trailed off questioningly.

"Thank you."

"I'd have put some handcuffs on myself—*yourself*. Then *we'd* have gone to the truck and taken off the cuffs to put on a Faraday straitjacket and gotten in some plastic ankle shackles, and then we'd have been driven to the holding facility and shuffled into a cell and put in additional restraints and then watched TV and eaten peanuts until you resurfaced."

"Why the handcuffs and stuff?" Lyn asked suspiciously. "Why wouldn't you just go to the cell?"

"Sometimes the copy can't maintain control for as long as usual. We found in testing that there were a couple of people at the Estate who broke through it much more quickly."

"And why the peanuts?"

"I'm allergic, but I like them. So if I'm in a body that can eat them, I do."

This is the creepiest thing I've ever heard of, thought Lyn, *even creepier than the giant head louse.* "Can the copy make copies?" she asked.

"No. I can make multiple copies, but they have to come from this body, from the source. And like I said, they last only a few hours."

Well, that's reassuring, she thought. *He won't be taking over the world.*

"Who would want to?" he asked. She gasped. "No, I'm not psychic," he said wearily. "Everyone worries that I might infect the world."

"Okay, okay." She really wanted to ask more about this downloading process, but the possible rousing of the gangsters in the cellar, the potential arrival of new gangsters, and the fact that Seager's skin might wake up at any time and become even more inconvenient than it was now—all of that pushed her to push him with the baton. "Walk, quickly." Perhaps the smart thing to do would be to shock him and leave him in the street, but he was Checquy, and she couldn't leave him vulnerable like that.

They were nearing the end of the alley when the fire door of the building next to them banged open and three men walked out talking about football. They looked at Kosloski and Lyn curiously—a young man with a woman walking directly behind him.

"Calm," said Lyn. "Let's stop for a mo—oh, *fuck you!*" Kosloski lunged directly toward the three men. *Oh no.*

The men looked somewhat nonplussed as the Pawn accosted them, then he seemed to stumble. One of them reached out instinctively to catch him, and Kosloski placed his hand flat on the man's cheek.

"I—oh!" began the man, and he straightened up suddenly and turned his eyes on Lyn. She shivered at that piercing gaze. It recognized her. Kosloski had possessed him.

"Ralph?" said one of the two other men. "You all right?"

"Yeah," said the Kosloski-Ralph without taking his eyes off Lyn. "Here, you help this lad." Kosloski stepped over and placed his hand on the next man's cheek, then the next one.

Oh, crap, thought Lyn. *I'm not going to be able to fight all four of these guys, and I can't outrun them, not with my legs killing me.* There were now two men blocking the alley, staring at her fixedly, while behind them stood Pawn Kosloski and the third man, a large one with a beard. Pawn Kosloski looked at her, shrugged, and started to walk away down the alley, presumably to get backup.

"Wait!" said the third man. Kosloski looked back. "This body is fit. Extremely fit. I think we should change the plan."

"Excuse me?" said Lyn.

"Not you," said the bearded man. "Unless you'd just like to surrender?" He didn't wait for an answer. "I think we three can immobilize and pin her, and you can subdue her."

"I'm still here, you know," said Lyn. All four of them ignored her.

"You're that fit?" said the second man who'd been converted.

"Yep. You?" The second man shifted on his feet and took a couple of deep breaths.

"Not bad," he decided.

"I'm pretty good," said the first convert, stretching his arms across his chest and bouncing on his toes.

"Okay, let's do it," said Pawn Kosloski. "Pack strategy number four?"

"Let's go with number three," said the bearded one. "Who will take point?"

"Fuck it, I'll do it," said the first convert. They began closing in on her. The first convert drew ahead. He cracked his knuckles and bunched his hands into fists.

This may be the end of it, thought Lyn. *In a couple of hours, I could be waking up in Gallows Keep.*

But I'll be damned if I make it easy for them.

She dropped her shoulder and let the dangling skin of Pawn Seager tumble down and puddle at her feet. Then she shrugged her backpack and jacket off onto the ground.

"This is an innocent body, Pawn Binns," said the first convert. "Do you want to hurt a civilian?"

No, thought Lyn. *That's why I didn't pull out a gun. Sneaky bastard, you've probably taken that into account.*

"You brought them into this," she said tightly. "You're free, all

four of you, to just sit down and let me walk away. I'll leave you this."
And she tapped Seager's skin with her toe. "The original can take
him and go back to the truck and get him some medical care. The
other three can find a pub—probably not the Anvil, though—and
have a couple of pints and some pork scratchings. Enjoy your allotted
two hours, maybe leave your hosts with a hangover." They looked at
her. "I'll even pay for the first two rounds."

They didn't answer, just came on at the same inexorable pace.

"You're putting these people in harm's way," she said. "You're
sworn to protect them."

"I don't know that *you're* in a position to get haughty about the
oaths we swear," said the second convert. "And I came to terms with
the implications of my power a long time ago."

"Oh?" said Lyn.

"We're all sacrifices," said Kosloski. "That much you should
understand."

"I'm starting to learn," said Lyn, and she flung her baton suddenly,
not at the man who was closest but off to the side, at the third convert—the big one who'd pushed them to change the plan. It spun
swiftly at him, and, instinctively, he snatched it out of the air. There
was a crimson flare, and he went down, hard. Everyone paused, then
the others came on again like wolves. The original Pawn Kosloski
stayed behind the other two, watching with narrowed eyes.

"And what now?" asked the first convert. "You've used up your
best weapon."

"And you've lost yours. Shall we call it even and go our separate ways?"

There was no answer, and still they came on.

And then the first convert was running at her, and before she knew
it, one hand was gripping her shirt and the other was a fist coming up
at her stomach. But her hand was striking out as well, fingers spread
wide, with the cheap rings on every finger coming into contact with
his chest, and sparks boiled out to drop him, spasming, onto the street.

Before she could regroup, though, the second man grabbed her
from behind and pinned her arms to her sides. She crammed energy
back into the rings and scrabbled to twist her wrists around and press

her fingers into him, but he held her too tight. She slammed her head back and felt the stomach-turning crunch of someone's nose breaking, but he didn't loosen his grasp.

"You just broke a civilian's nose," he said into her ear. "An innocent. And another one is lying on the ground in his own piss because of you." She opened her mouth to reply but then saw movement off to the side.

Kosloski!

His hand was coming to her face, and she twisted madly. She couldn't break out of the grip of the convert, but she threw him off balance, and the two of them went staggering back away from the Pawn. Kosloski was directly in front of her now, and his look of calm determination and that hand with its fingers spread was the most terrifying thing she could remember seeing.

"It doesn't hurt," he said. "The testing at the Estate established that. You just feel my touch, and then the next thing you know, it's a couple of hours later."

"Yeah, and I'm in prison," she growled. He took a step forward, and she lashed out with her foot. He moved back cautiously. "Plus, who knows what you'd do with my body while you're occupying it."

"I would never," he said.

"Yeah, you have such terrific ethics in this regard," she said. "What if one of these bodies were to die while you're using it?"

"Then their family would get a pension, and they'd be buried as heroes," said the Kosloski holding her.

"So your body will get free plastic surgery for that nose I just broke?"

"Yes, of course."

"Well, I suppose that—*hngh!*" She twisted wildly forward and sideways, flung herself to the pavement, and flipped the Kosloski copy over her shoulder. He kept his grip on her, but she flipped with him, pushing herself forward and up into the air and turning with him so that it was he who hit the ground first with her sprawled on her back on top of him. The breath was smacked out of him, and his grip loosened. She squirmed away and slapped her ringed fingers against him, and she felt him go limp as the electricity smashed into him.

Kosloski loomed over her now, the original Kosloski, and his hands were scrabbling frantically to press against her face, but her arms were free, and she clawed his fingers away. He straddled her, and her hands clenched around his wrists, but he was stronger and his spread palms were coming closer and closer, so close that she could feel the heat of his skin.

Her muscles were burning. It took all her strength and focus not to waver and let his hands close that crucial gap to touch her. She couldn't even spare the will to infuse the rings. Was it her imagination or could she feel a pressure through the air from his hands, something pushing against her mind, yearning to come into her? Could she hear his voice in her head? It was getting louder, and she could see how it might drown out all her thoughts.

She slammed her strength into her legs and back, pushing herself up into a bridge, her poor beaten thighs screaming as she threw him off balance. He was still on top of her, but his arms flailed to stop from falling, and she could twist and throw him off. In his shock, he used his arms to break his fall, and she could breathe.

"No!" he screamed. "No!" But she was sitting up, and when she punched him in the jaw, the electricity was there, ready to pour out and shock him into insensibility.

"I am so goddamn tired," Lyn said to the empty skin of Seager as she picked it up and draped it over her shoulder again. "You had better not even *think* of waking up. And when you do wake up, I had better get major points for not just leaving you in this alley with all these Kosloskis." In truth, she'd given it a moment's thought, but there was a difference between leaving some unconscious but normal-looking people for possible discovery and leaving the pelt of a human being. If a civilian found the skin before it woke up, well, that would be bad on all sorts of levels. Plus, she still quite liked Seager.

She grimly surveyed the *tableau inconscient* of men lying about the alleyway. They did not look at all well, but they were all definitely still alive. She winced pityingly at the three men who'd been possessed; they'd had no choice in what they were doing. She felt sufficiently sorry for them to roll them into the recovery position but left the original Kosloski spread-eagled in the middle of the lane.

You and your creepy frickin' powers. The thought of having his greasy little mind engulf hers made her skin crawl.

She hobbled down the alley.

She emerged onto the high street and looked around warily. There were the usual London pedestrians pedestrianing their way about the place, and thanks to the ingrained good manners of the entire populace, nobody stared at her.

God, it's enough to make you wonder why we need a Checquy. We could save the taxpayers a vast amount just by relying on everyone minding their own business.

Parked right by the entrance to the alley was a beat-up moving van so mundane, so devoid of character, so profoundly uninteresting that it could only have been a covert government vehicle. Plus, the fact that it was parked on a double red line in the Congestion Charge Zone of Central London and hadn't been clamped, towed, festooned with tickets, or crushed into a cube (possibly with the occupants still in it) suggested either terrifying government connections or a deal with the devil.

Lyn looked around, then hammered on the back of the van. There was movement within, and a woman opened the door.

"You've got her, then?" she said. "Because the sprog here said that she could taste—oh, *bollocks.*" She was a tall, strong-looking woman who could probably have given Lyn some serious trouble if she weren't now lying unconscious on the floor of the van thanks to a brisk prod with the heavily charged baton.

"Pawn Hatt?" came an uncertain voice from deeper in the van, but Lyn was already clambering up into the vehicle; she stepped over the unconscious Hatt and snapped open the baton.

"Freeze!" shouted Lyn. "If I feel anything even slightly uncanny, I'll—Georgie?"

"Lyn?"

It was indeed her former roommate. They stared at each other incredulously. Georgina was dressed in teenager camouflage: jeans, sneakers, and a T-shirt with a slogan so encrusted with glitter that Lyn couldn't read it. She was also wearing an absolutely flabbergasted expression.

"What are you doing here?" asked Lyn. Despite all the insanity of the past hours, the pain burning in her legs, the horrible need for haste, and the fact that she desperately needed to visit the loo, delighted recognition swept through her.

"They brought me out to track you," said the girl, staring at the body slumped on the floor. "Is—is she dead?"

"No, of course not," said Lyn, slightly hurt. "What do you take me for?"

"Lyn, they said you were—is that Pawn Seager on your shoulder?"

"Well, part of him. God knows where the rest is." Georgina drew aside wordlessly, and Lyn took in the interior of the van. On one side was a long counter with laptops and various communications devices bolted or bungeed down. And at the end were two Plexiglas booths, in one of which was the rest of Pawn Liam Seager. "Oh my God."

There was plenty to catch the eye. Seager's flayed body was standing with its head thrown back. He was wearing only a pair of very short shorts, and his exposed musculature, the fibers of the meat glistening with fluids, was clearly defined, so he gave the peculiar impression of being a censored illustration from a 1980s edition of *Gray's Anatomy*. The only intact patches of skin emerged from the legs of his shorts and spread down his inner thighs. He'd left his eyelids behind too, and they were closed, thankfully. Wherever his skin had departed, a faint, greasy blue light rippled over the exposed meat.

"How does the skin come off?" asked Lyn bemusedly. "Did you see it happen?"

"It's completely gross. It just slides off the top of him," said Georgina.

"But it's a whole single piece," objected Lyn. "It's closed at the feet."

"It tears in places. It sounds absolutely disgusting when it's coming off."

With an effort, Lyn dragged her attention from the still figure and looked back at Georgina. The teenager was inching along the counter in a way that made Lyn immediately suspicious. "Babe, I love you, but stay still and keep your hands where I can see them. I know exactly how good you are." Eyes wide, Georgina stopped and laced her fingers over her stomach. "Thanks. So why are *you* tracking me? They have some Grafters that can act like bloodhounds. You should be at school. Your exams are coming up, aren't they?"

"The way they explained it, they don't want the Grafters to know about Pawns going rogue," said Georgina. "It's still a new relationship between the organizations. That's why they came and got me in a helicopter in the middle of the night, took me to a room in the Apex, and cracked open an ampoule of your sweat for me to reference. Which was a complete waste of time, because I already know your taste."

"Oh my God, you *were* tasting me when we shared a room! I knew it!" Despite herself, she shuddered, and Georgina caught it.

"That is not fair. You *know* how my powers work!" she snapped. "It's like me expecting you not to know what I look like."

"Georgina, don't take that tone with me," Lyn said flatly. "I'm your friend. I am not an authority figure for you to rebel against."

"Yeah, especially now that you've gone rogue—which I can't believe! You're not even a Pawn anymore!"

"I have *not* gone rogue!"

The teenager raised her eyebrows and looked at the unconscious woman on the floor and the presumably unconscious epidermis slung over Lyn's shoulder.

"Look, it's complicated," said Lyn. "But I need you to believe me when I tell you that I didn't kill all those gangsters."

"Then what is going on? Why are you being hunted?"

"Something out there is doing this, and it looks like it's using my powers. As in, *exactly* my powers."

"Do you know how unlikely that is?" asked Georgina. "I mean, the same kinds of powers can crop up in different people, but they're never identical. They showed me the files. These murders even have those double-ring burn marks you do!"

"I know—that's why I went on the run," said Lyn. "And, what, you just followed the taste of me through all of London?"

"No, of course not. I mean, they set me on the trail, but it was pretty faint, and I lost it when you caught the Tube. But then Pawn Seager said you'd probably keep going after criminals and that we should check out the headquarters of the gangs who'd been targeted. When we got here, I tasted you in the building, and Pawn Seager and Pawn Kosloski went to get you. And how on *earth* did you take down Pawn Seager?" she asked. "Like ten minutes ago, he screamed—scared the hell out of me and Pawn Hatt—and went unconscious. Was that you?"

"Yeah, I think so. And then—oh, hell!"

"What? What is it?" asked Georgina warily.

"I forgot, I've got to make a phone call."

"Are you joking?"

Lyn was already unlocking the phone of the man she'd shot and dialing a number she'd been drilled to remember during her time at the Estate. After two rings, a bored voice said, "Office of Qualifications and Examinations Regulation, notifications line."

"This is Pawn Lynette Binns." She waited a moment for a strangled response of incredulity. Instead, there was the distant sound of typing, then a completely unruffled voice.

"Yes, hello, Pawn Binns," said the voice calmly. "I have you down as being on leave?"

"I—yeah? No." *They really are serious about keeping my situation a secret.*

"Oh?" said the voice.

"No, I'm...on assignment," she said, improvising madly and looking over at Georgina, who rolled her eyes. "A discreet assignment for the Court."

"All right," said the voice warily. "What do you need?"

"Send an emergency crew to the Anvil pub in the West End immediately. There are at least a dozen men in the basement in varying states of incapacitation. They witnessed my powers being activated and those of Pawn Liam Seager. At least one of them is in increasingly critical condition from a gunshot." Georgina was staring at her, wide-eyed.

"Don't look at me like that, Georgie, *I* didn't shoot him," said Lyn, covering the phone. "Wait, no, I did. Sorry. I'm losing track. Anyway." She turned her attention back to the person on the phone. "Pawn...something. The one who possesses people?"

"Kosloski," said Georgina quietly.

"Thanks, Georgie. Yes, Pawn Kosloski and the three men he possessed are lying unconscious in the middle of the alley behind the Anvil." Georgina's eyes were now as big as soup plates. "Pawn Seager's epidermis is unconscious here in the team's van. It's suffered some cuts and been shot a couple of times, *not* by me. But I did electrocute it, sorry. I don't know what effect that will have, since it was just skin and not the rest of the body, but—your medical team should probably be aware. Did you get all that?"

"No," said the voice. To her mild satisfaction, it was now sounding somewhat dazed. "But this call is being recorded."

"Great," said Lyn. "Well, then, for the record, I didn't kill any criminals. And if you hurry and help those people in the cellar of the Anvil, then I still won't have. Okay?"

"Oh—okay."

"Grand. Bye!"

"You're *sure* you haven't gone rogue?" asked Georgina icily.

"Look, I need to go," said Lyn. "And I'm afraid you need to stay. Sooo..."

"What? You're not going to just shock me like you did them?"

"Georgie, I don't want to do that," said Lyn. She looked helplessly at her friend. "I don't want to hurt you." She glanced around. "Are there any handcuffs here? Any restraints? There must be."

Georgina sighed. "You can lock me in the other cell," she said. "The one next to Seager. It's where we would have put you."

"Thanks for making this easier than it might have been, babe," said Lyn.

It was hours later when Lyn emerged from the Debden underground station wearing a new broad-brimmed hat and a new coat, skirt, and shoes. The day's clothes were bundled up in a new backpack. After leaving Georgina locked resignedly in the booth, she'd hurried away and embarked on her now-familiar routine of breaking up her trail as much as she could. The money liberated from the various gangsters had enabled several new purchases as well as a couple of cab rides and a new travel card.

Her legs were killing her, and all she wanted was a long hot bath, but she needed to catch the bus to Mandy's house. So she sat at the bus stop and did her very best not to fall asleep. She only realized that she had utterly failed in this endeavor when an extremely polite voice spoke hesitantly to her.

"Excuse me? Excuse me, miss?"

"Hmm? What? What!" She opened her eyes with a start to find, not an oddly courteous SWAT team of Pawns with guns, palms, and vortex-mouths trained on her, but a concerned-looking older gentleman.

"I'm sorry to bother you, but your mobile is ringing and has been for some time."

"Oh, thank you!" She scrabbled in her coat pocket and answered it. "Hello?"

"Kira?"

"What?"

"Uh...is this Kira?" The voice sounded confused but familiar.

That's the name you gave Rory, the greasy criminal nephew in the pawnshop, her brain reminded her. *Do try to keep up.*

"Yes," she said hurriedly. "Hi. Rory?"

"Yeah, look, I wasn't sure if I should call you, but..." He trailed off. "But I'm at a pub with my cousin Max."

"Okay?" The significance of this eluded her.

"We've just come from the garage."

"The garage," she repeated dully.

"It's where the uncles get together," he said. "They called us all in, told us we needed to be going about in pairs until this electro-killer gets taken care of."

"Okay..."

"So, it's me and Max—I'm going to be staying with him—and we were headed to my place to pick up some stuff, and I noticed there was someone following us. I mean, every turn we took, he was there behind us. Every turn." He sounded genuinely frightened. "So we ducked into the first pub we came to." He paused.

"Very sensible," offered Lyn finally, and this seemed to encourage him.

"He didn't come in. I've been looking out the window, and there's someone waiting across the street. He's been standing there for half an hour. I think it's the one who's been doing the killings."

"Text me the address," said Lyn. "I'll be there as soon as I can." She disconnected, sighed, and then dialed. "Hello, Mandy? I'm going to be out a bit late."

20

Bridget and Wattleman stared, transfixed with horror, as flames climbed out of the Caïssa Club. Even in that night of chaos and destruction, it was utter madness. The flames were huge, and they shifted color, with red bleeding into yellow bleeding into purple and back again. Unexpected lights crackled up from the inferno and once, bewilderingly, a sudden burst of darkness—a bolus of unlight that bubbled up through the flames and into the night sky.

A score of smells, acrid and salty and stomach-turningly sweet, seeped around the square, and not all of the smoke was rising into the sky as it should have. A layer of smoke washed itchily around their ankles, and an occasional cascading waterfall of gray smoke poured back down from the clouds above. The heat from the fire had the two Checquy operatives drenched in perspiration. Wattleman's hand squelched in hers. They flinched when a massive blast of sound burst out of the fire and shattered every unbroken window in the square.

"Was that another bomb?" asked Wattleman's voice, sounding dazed. He was still invisible beside her.

"No, there was no explosion," said Bridget. "I think it was from someone in the club. One of us." The full realization of what she was seeing struck her. Until then, it had simply been the shock of seeing a beloved place destroyed, but now all the implications were coming into focus. "They're dying in there. Our people are dying in there."

"Bridget, you summon help." The voice was filled with dreadful resolve. "I'm going in."

"Into *that?*"

"I can walk through fire," said Wattleman tightly. "I can do it." Bridget felt his hand twist out of hers.

"That is not fire, Henry! My God, look at it!" She lunged forward, snatched out blindly, and caught his arm. His skin was slick with sweat and she had to scrabble to keep a grip on him.

"Our people are in there, Bridget!" She felt him try to shake her off, but she held on tighter.

"Our people in there are the thing that will kill you," she said. "Their powers are being unleashed and their control is being lost. Fine, you can withstand fire. But you are not invulnerable, Henry. We don't know what is going on in there, but no one will come out of that alive. Not even you."

For a moment he was visible again, looking back at her, and she saw that there were tears on his face.

"I have to try." His eyes were caught by something behind her, and he vanished. "The firemen are here, but it'll take them time. I have to do what I can." He wrenched himself out of her grasp.

"You cannot go in there," said Bridget, and she made her voice hard. "We can't let anyone in there."

"How can you say that?" his voice demanded.

"We swear to give our lives to protect the populace. The operatives in there are dead. They would not want their deaths to cost additional lives, which is what will happen if you go in!" She had a flickering glimpse of Wattleman naked on his knees, staring at the burning building, clutching his head. He was a man despairing, a man who'd accepted he could do nothing. "Just stay out of the way!" She turned to the fire team that had just careered into the square. The firemen were emerging and looking up in shock at a blaze unlike anything they'd seen before.

"No time for gawping!" shouted one man. "Get the 'oses, and get that fire doused! Make sure it doesn't spread to the other buildings in the square!"

Bridget took off her glittering coat, turned it inside out, and hurried over to where the firemen were bustling about with their hoses. "Excuse me!" she shouted to the man barking orders. "Sir!"

"Stand back, miss. There's no telling what's goin' to 'appen 'ere. Never seen a fire like it. Looks like old 'itler has cooked up a new kind of bomb."

That's a very good explanation, the horribly clinical part of Bridget's mind thought. *I will have to suggest we use that story.* "You mustn't go in there," she said.

"No fear! No one's going in there until the fire's out. Look at it!"

"I know, but you cannot go in even when the fire's out." He looked at her in surprise. "Secret offices for the war effort. The men will be around from the Home Office soon enough to tell you, but you've got to keep your distance."

"Miss, it's a fire," said the leader patiently. "We don't care if it's got Winston Churchill wearing the crown jewels and kissing Betty Grable, we've got to put out the fire."

"Of course. I'll let you get back to your work."

"Hush-hush offices, you say?" She grimaced and nodded. "Damn. Just when it looks like we need everything we can muster up against the Boche. I hope this doesn't hurt the war effort too badly."

Me too, thought Bridget. Behind her outward calm, part of her was screaming.

"Well, I'll keep mum." Another part of the roof fell in, and they both flinched. "If you had people in there, I'm sorry to tell you, miss, but no one'll have survived that."

"I know," Bridget said wearily. She turned and watched as one of the homes of her heart was consumed.

"It looks like a high explosive landed right on the club," said Pamela. She looked up from the document she was reading and wiped her wrist across her eyes.

The Pawn had arrived at the Caïssa while the fire was still raging. It turned out that she had flown there from Bufo Hall, dispatched by Lady Carmichael as soon as word of the bombing reached them. Pamela had coursed above the burning city and alighted unseen, then emerged from the darkness of an alley and immediately took charge of the situation. She had bundled the stunned Bridget and the still-naked and invisible Wattleman into Checquy cars and sent them back to Apex House for brandy and clothing. Now, with the all-clear having gone and the fires put out, she had come to the Apex, and the three of them were in the Lady's office.

"We're still surveying the situation, but the damage goes right down into the cellar where everyone would have been sleeping." The Pawn looked exhausted. The dark patches under her eyes were even more prominent, and her face was drawn. She was still focused, however, efficiently reporting back the information she had been given so far.

"No survivors?" asked Wattleman.

"None found as yet," said Pamela, "and it is not looking promising."

"But they were in the cellar!" exclaimed Bridget. "The shelter. Wouldn't you be safe in the shelter? Isn't that *the point* of a bomb shelter? To shelter from bombs? Otherwise, why are we digging holes in the ground and sleeping under the stairs and tables?" She could hear a mortifying shrillness in her voice.

"They protect you from the blast," Pamela said wearily. "Or shrapnel. But there's no shelter that will save you when a centuries-old building catches fire and collapses into the cellar."

"But how can they *all* be dead?" asked Bridget. "With all those abilities, surely *someone* must have been able to survive."

"Bridget, you know that any gift that would protect from that kind of destruction is very uncommon. And I'm sad to say that even if someone survived the bomb, the subsequent fire, the collapse of the building, and the chaos of the powers unleashed, they would have been, well..." She trailed off, not knowing what words to use.

"How many were lost?" asked Wattleman. "How many of our people?"

"We don't know," said Pamela. "We haven't been able to find the club's sign-in registers, and since we've found no survivors, there are no witnesses of who was there. I've sent word out to the regional offices. All their operatives have to let them know if they're going out of town and where they're staying, but that will take time and will only be useful for active operatives. We don't know about Caïssa staff or London-based operatives or retirees who might have been there." She sighed heavily. "We can't even say for certain how many bodies there are. Just getting in to look is proving very difficult."

"What do you mean?" asked Wattleman. He had resumed his usual unruffled attitude. There was barely a trace of the devastated man who had fallen to his knees in front of the burning Caïssa. The quartermaster's office had sent up some dapper clothes for him, and the only sign that anything might be wrong was the slight sloshing of the brandy in his glass as his hand shook. Bridget looked down at her own brandy and noticed that it too was sloshing.

"You have to understand," said Pamela, "we now have a manifestation site in the middle of London, one unlike anything we've seen before. It's completely incoherent."

"Incoherent?" asked Bridget.

"As you know, the explosion and the fire resulted in at least some of our people unleashing their powers, which may have reacted with one another, like chemicals in a factory explosion. The result is a place that is completely unnatural, like a slice of hell or another planet.

"There are records of similar events," Pamela said wearily. "The sites of major Checquy battles, where mass deaths of our troops have splashed out onto one another—the Grafter invasion, the assault on Brigadoon. There are places that are simply unapproachable even now. But we've never had so many of our people dying in such a small area in the middle of a city.

"We've sent a team in to do a preliminary examination, but the site is still unstable and highly dangerous. One of our people lost his leg below the knee when he accidentally stepped in some remains. His foot and shin just dissolved. Parts of the cellars have collapsed, and there's a chamber that is completely filled with an oily gray liquid that no one has been able to identify. They've found fires that appear to have been ossified, turned to some bone-like substance, but that still burn if they're touched. There's a persistent haze through the cellar that we're extremely wary of. Everyone going in must wear gas masks and protective overalls. A hole just about as wide around as a plump human has been burned or melted into the earth. They dropped a coin down it and couldn't hear it land." Pamela looked around at them.

"It will take months to understand what we are dealing with and decide on next steps. All the while, the public will be walking by curiously every day." She smiled faintly. "I can tell you that the wood from the bar survived completely unscathed."

The door to the office opened, and all three of them stood hurriedly as Lady Carmichael entered. The Lady's back was straight, but her eyes were red, and her lips were pressed together in a way that spoke of emotion. She immediately went to Bridget, held her close, and kissed her on the brow.

"Bridget, Henry, I'm so glad that both of you are safe," she said. She turned to clasp Wattleman's hand. "Everyone, please be seated." She sat on the sofa beside Pamela.

"Lady Carmichael, I didn't expect you to return so soon from the meeting at Bufo Hall," said Pamela uncertainly.

"I received a telephone call from Leominster." The Lady's voice shook a little. "I felt I had to come right away." A fresh dagger of doom went through Bridget's heart.

"Oh Jesus! Is everyone at the house all right?" asked Bridget. "Usha? Mr. Carmichael? The house staff? Is—is it the children? Was there an attack on the countryside?"

"Everyone at the house is fine. And the children are safe. But"— the Lady took a deep breath—"Usha was staying at the Caïssa last night."

"What?" said Pamela, and her face crumpled. "No. No! Oh God, *no!*" The heavy bomb-resistant curtains rustled, but it seemed to Bridget as if all the sound in the room had gone away except for the frantic pounding of her heart and the roar of blood in her ears. She had assumed Usha was at the Carmichael house, safely tucked up in bed, and she could not quite grasp what she had just heard. She looked around, bewildered. Wattleman's drink shattered in his hand. Pamela had stood and was weeping silently, her white-knuckled fists at her sides, as if she were holding back a scream that would destroy everything. Lady Carmichael was still on the couch, her eyes closed.

Bridget buried her face in her hands. Memories of Usha flashed in her mind:

Usha floating elegantly in the center of her bedroom, dancing slowly in midair.

Usha coming down the stairs in a Paris dress, then an impossibly bright sari, then in a set of shooting tweeds with a hat with an incredible swooping brim.

Usha winking at her when Gerald's arrival was announced.

Usha reading the newspaper and intently making notes about the business pages.

Usha raising a withering eyebrow at Wattleman's flirtations.

Usha hurtling down through the sky to take Bridget's hand and save her from death.

Usha standing in the night sky, her hair wafting magnificently about her while the stars burned unbelievably bright.

And then Usha trapped underground, the ceiling falling in on her impossibly slowly while around her, people screamed and burned and tore apart.

There was a low wailing going through the room, and Bridget realized that it was coming from her. And then, despite herself, she threw back her head and let it all come out.

No one tried to stop her from screaming. That was something that Bridget would muse over later. No one held her close and whispered that it would be all right. Everyone in the room accepted that what she was doing was entirely appropriate, entirely natural. Her friend was dead in the middle of a war. Of course she would despair. Of course. When she'd finally wailed herself out and collapsed to her knees on the carpet, gasping for breath, Wattleman wordlessly handed her another brandy, which she threw back. Then she rose to her feet, sat down heavily on the sofa, and leaned back.

"She was my best friend," Pamela said. "I don't think I ever let her know that. All of the things I said to her, about my life, and the Checquy, and our mission, and I never told her the most important thing."

"Some things don't need to be said," the Lady told her gently.

"But some things make all the difference when they're said," Pamela replied. She was staring down at the floor. "I never told her what her friendship meant to me. How grateful I was to know her." She bit her lip so hard that Bridget thought she might draw blood. "She gave me a completely new way of looking at everything." A faint breeze swirled in the room, and Bridget tensed, remembering the last time Pamela had lost her poise. "I would have died in her place if I could have." Wattleman closed his hand on his comrade's shoulder, and she nodded without looking up. The air grew still, and everyone was silent.

They all came back to the world eventually. Lady Carmichael moved to her desk and began looking through the documents that had been recently delivered. Pamela was already making notes on her briefing packet, though she was also drinking a large glass of water, which Bridget knew was a sign that she had a headache coming on. Wattleman started picking up the fragments of his shattered brandy glass.

The clock struck, startling them all. It was well into tomorrow.

"We'll all need to go home and rest," said Lady Carmichael. "And Pamela and I must be back at Bufo Hall in the evening for the Court meeting. However, while we're all here, let's talk about Henry and Bridget's assignment." Bridget looked at her in surprise for a moment. How could Lady Carmichael expect a briefing? Usha was dead. The Caïssa was toxic, malevolent rubble. And she wanted to just go on with business as usual?

Then she sighed, and, like thousands of people throughout the war-torn city and the war-torn country and the war-torn world, she put her grief aside to be addressed later and got on with things.

"Dorothy Hadgraft died yesterday evening," said the Lady.

Who? thought Bridget, confused for a moment. Then she remembered. The one surviving woman from the group known to have purchased from Simony. *That's three deaths on the hands of the Murcutts.*

"We've made progress," said Wattleman. He went on to describe their findings, the death of Simony, and the confrontation with the Murcutts. Periodically, he would pause and look over at Bridget to give her a chance to add her thoughts, or she would interrupt to mention details that she had caught.

"So these Murcutts have a source in the Checquy for magical items, and they have this Vincent person," said Lady Carmichael.

"Plus, presumably, a number of thugs," said Pamela.

"And some prostitutes," said Bridget.

"Yes," said Lady Carmichael. She paused. "The fact that the Murcutts have supernatural assets for use in conflict is what troubles me."

"The Murcutts did not appear to have a significant interest in the items for their capabilities," said Wattleman. "They weren't using them or trying to figure out how to use them as weapons. They were selling them. They seemed to consider Vincent their ace in the hole."

"If they have actual supernatural thugs, I am going to have to make this an official operation." Lady Carmichael sighed. "Which means that others within the Checquy will learn about it." She winced as something else occurred to her. "And since there's the distinct possibility of supernatural combat and fatalities involving civilians, the Prime Minister will have to be notified. Our apparent failure to keep artifacts secure will give him leverage. If the lines are blurred between our bailiwick and the normal world, my position on restricting the use of Checquy assets in the war will be even weaker."

"I don't know if that's necessary, Lady Carmichael," said Bridget.

"Oh?"

"Let's keep this in perspective. They have Vincent, and they know about Pawn Wattleman and me. But I think this problem can still be remedied quickly and discreetly. All we need is an unexpected element to tip the scales."

"I presume that you have something in mind, Bridget," said the Lady dryly.

"Pawn Verrall." All eyes turned to Pamela. "She has substantial powers, she's an experienced fighter, and she already knows about this mission, so there's no need to open it up any further."

"Fine," said the Lady wearily. "There is too much going on in the world. I need this taken care of."

"Are you certain, my Lady?" asked Pamela. "With the Caïssa situation and the work at Bufo Hall—"

"I can delegate the Caïssa work," said the Lady. "I probably should anyway. It will take months and require someone to work on it full-time. And Bufo Hall will not be finished by tomorrow. Will you be all right to do this?" Pamela nodded. "Thank you. In an ideal world,

I would send you out now, but you all need sleep. Henry, you're welcome to come to my house."

"Thank you, my Lady, that's very kind of you, but I think I'll sleep here, in the vaults."

"As you wish. Pamela, before you go home, can you please ask Research to pull together as much information as possible regarding the Murcutts? I'm especially interested in rumors about this Vincent or anyone like him. Also, see what we can learn about this midwife mother of theirs." Pamela nodded as she scribbled down notes.

"Does anyone else have any suggestions or thoughts?" asked the Lady. "Have I missed anything?" They all shook their heads. "Fine. I must go. Consult with one another on how and when you wish to proceed, but be sure to rest first. Keep me posted." They all made to stand as she got up. "Oh, sit down," she said wearily.

There was another silence after the Lady left.

"She was my best friend," Pamela said softly.

She opened her eyes to darkness.

It was completely black. No chink of sunshine or moonlight. No distant glow from a lamp. No thrice-reflected light that might have seeped through the curtains and bounced off the floor and the ceiling to her eyes. Completely, utterly dark.

She listened, straining for the slightest sound, the faintest sign that something else existed, that there were other people in this place. It was impossibly silent.

She lay still, considering. She knew exactly what had happened. The distant thunder of the bombs had grown louder and closer until it seemed as if they must be right on top of her. And then, with an earsplitting roar, the world had collapsed around her, and everything had gone dark.

We were bombed.

I was buried.

She was afraid to move. Afraid to discover that she could not move. Afraid that the slightest shift would bring down onto her the horrendous mass that must be all about her.

Most of all, she was afraid that if she tried to move, she would discover that she had no body. She could feel nothing on her skin, no sheets or wreckage under her back. Nothing on her face. It was as if everything had gone away.

She could not hear her own breath.

Am I dead? Is that what happens? Is your ghost trapped in the place where you died? Is it because of my powers? Perhaps my spirit was transformed and now it will not perish or move on or fade away, even though my body is gone.

Is that what all ghosts are? Checquy-type people who have died?

She wanted to scream but was afraid that she would not stop.

She was also afraid she could not start.

Would she go mad?

She was tiny thoughts in a void.

And then her stomach made a growl. She could not hear the noise, but she felt the rumble inside her body.

I have a body! I am hungry!

I am real.

Tentatively, feeling equal parts hope and fear of what she might discover, her mind did what it did to move her right forefinger against her right thumb.

She felt it. She dug her thumbnail against her fingertip and felt pain.

Real pain!

She opened her mouth to scream in delight and felt the vibration in her throat but heard only the faintest whine, as if the sound were sped up and rushing away. But she was too elated to take much notice.

She carefully brought her arms up and felt about with her hands. There was nothing. No compacted rubble directly above her face or even at arm's length. Nothing to her sides. She touched her chest, and was shocked at how real her skin felt. There was no trace of the borrowed nightgown she had been wearing, not even a torn scrap. Then she brought her arms down to find the surface that she had to be lying on.

Nothing.

She swept her arms behind her wildly, unbelieving, on the brink of starting the scream that would not end.

*There is nothing here but me. I am trapped in some horrendous void.
I am dead.*

Then, like an explosion of revelation, she realized:

*I'm floating in a bubble of my own abilities! When the blast went off and
the building came down, my powers must have activated and created this bubble
to protect me.*

She had no idea where her nightgown was. Perhaps it had been
blown clean off. She had heard of bombs doing strange things—boiling water in nearby ponds, killing people but leaving buildings standing, driving blades of grass through brick walls. Perhaps this was the
same sort of thing.

Or perhaps her power had flung her nightgown away from her. In
seeking automatically to protect her, it had sent out a field, and anything that was not her had been cast away—shrapnel, wreckage, and,
apparently, her own clothes. Presumably the bed and sheets had been
flung away as well.

*Is that why it is so dark? Am I pushing even the light away? Pushing
sound away?*

*And yet there is air here. Perhaps my power is clever enough not to kill me
while protecting me.*

At that thought, she reached out with her powers and realized that
there was a cage of gravity around her. She examined it, frightened of
disturbing it, and saw that it was constructed with more complexity
than she knew how to muster. Bands of force and will crisscrossed,
buttressing so that each one was locked into place by the others. She
looked more closely and saw the kind of inhuman intricacy in its pattern that she had seen when looking at a snowflake through a micro-
scope—perfect, natural, and done without conscious design. In her
case, it must have been the product of pure instinct.

Amazing. She was humbled by the idea that all her training and
experimentation had not produced what she'd managed to do without any thought at all.

*So what do I do now? Should I wait? They will come for us, surely. They
will dig for survivors.*

It was a reassuring thought, but it was met by multiple unreassur-
ing thoughts. She could not be certain, for instance, how much air

was trapped in this bubble with her. She had no idea how big the bubble was, but her powers had never spread out farther than a couple of yards, at most. That did not seem like a great deal of air.

With no light or sound coming to her, how would she know when they had found her? What if they could not break through the shield? Perhaps they had already unearthed it, were hammering away with tools and powers, and she was floating here, completely unaware, waiting for a rescue that had already come and that could not save her from herself.

She wondered what would happen to the bubble if she died from dehydration or suffocation or going mad and gashing her wrists open with her teeth and nails. Would the bubble collapse? Or would it just hold her corpse in darkness forever?

I must act. I must get myself out. I will have to collapse this bubble and use my powers to climb up.

Then she realized that she had no idea which way was up. She was floating without any reference point. She felt her hair carefully and could discern no direction in which it was hanging. It was simply billowing out, as if she were suspended in still water. She had no sense of spinning, but she also had no sense of not spinning.

So what will I do? How do I proceed?

Even if she could propel the bubble she was in, she had no way of knowing whether she was doing so. And what if she began burrowing in the wrong direction, away from the surface? She had a vision of the bubble sinking or tunneling through the earth, bending the laws of physics and carrying her down to the center of the planet. Perhaps it already was. There was no obvious reason it would do so, but nothing about her powers was obliged to make sense.

I cannot wait to be rescued. I must rescue myself.

She hung there in the darkness and pondered. She worked out various possible plans and dismissed them. She examined the cage around her, making mental notes on elements and features and trying to understand what they did. It was beautiful, strong, and self-sustaining, and yet she could see how to collapse it.

Was it her imagination or was the air getting stale?

Do you see what you will do? she asked herself.

I do.

Then do it.

She curled into a crouching position with her hands up in front of her face. It seemed the best position to fall, no matter what direction she fell in. She took a deep breath, reached out with her mind, and yanked on the structure of the bubble.

It fell apart, the pattern immediately unraveling into nothing. And she dropped. She could feel herself falling, but before she could figure out in which direction, the mangled remains of what might have been her bed struck her on her right side. A patter of dirt and pebbles fell on her, and the sound was shocking in its realness. The sudden smells of rock and dust and smoke and blood and spilled wine hammered her. Then there was a horrific grinding above her as the wreckage of the building around her began to collapse.

Now!

She flung out her power to make as close an approximation of the bubble as she could. It was nowhere near as complex, nowhere near as complete, and a damn sight smaller than the original bubble, but it held back all the weight that was pressing down on her. She panted with the effort and could hear herself panting.

That way is down, she told herself firmly. *And that way is up.*

Go up.

She changed the shape of the bubble and the rules inside it. She changed the forces that were wrapped within its fabric. There were cracking and grinding sounds all around her, then a roar as the wreckage and debris were forced aside to make space for the bubble as it rose up in fits and starts.

Into the light.

Bridget was sleeping in her own bed in the Carmichael house when a loud knocking came at the door. She got up, bewildered, thinking that the air-raid siren had gone off, but it was Leominster looking— for the first time ever—emotional. Behind him was a tousled, sleepy Pamela.

"What is it? What's happened?" Bridget asked.

"Miss, it's—it's very good news."

Disbelieving what they'd been told, Pamela and Bridget dressed hurriedly and were driven through the midmorning traffic to Apex House, clutching each other's hands. The lobby and the halls of the building were abuzz with excited chatter. News traveled fast, and coming right on the tail of the tragedy at the Caïssa, this was a jolt of much-needed hope. One of their own had come back. Bridget caught snatches of excited conversation as they hurried to the medical clinic.

"Have you heard?"

"Apparently, there was this unearthly noise, and the ground was shaking..."

"The Lady's Indian apprentice, you know, the gorgeous..."

"Everyone braced, thinking some creature had been woken..."

"My friend said she just rose up out of the earth. The dirt and the rubble just parted."

"Usha Khorana..."

"Not a stitch on, I heard..."

"She's in the clinic right now, being checked."

"Starkers. Wish *I'd* been there..."

"Have you heard?"

"Have you heard?"

"Have you *heard?*"

When they arrived, Usha was seated in a chair, looking regal even in a hospital gown. Several doctors fretted about her, listening to her heart, feeling her brow, peering into her eyes, and checking her for cuts, scrapes, bruises, breaks, or sprains—none of which she appeared to have. She shook the doctors off to rise to her feet and embrace Bridget and Pamela, and all three of them wept a few tears of joy and relief. The doctors hurriedly finished their examinations and admitted that Usha seemed perfectly fine despite having had a building fall on her.

"Thank you, gentlemen," said Usha. "I will let you know if I discover any problems." The doctors, recognizing a dismissal when they heard one, gathered up their various implements, placed them in their little black bags, and took their leave, only to return a moment later to point out sheepishly that the clinic was where they did their work, and perhaps the ladies might like to take *their* leave.

Usha changed into the clothes that Pamela and Bridget had brought from the house. Walking through the halls to the Lady's office, the women were taken aback by the warmth and the smiles they encountered. Usha's hand was shaken and reshaken, and a few ladies came up to kiss her on the cheek. There were scattered moments of applause, and a distant "Hip-hip-*hurrah!*" set Usha blushing.

"You're a hero," said Bridget quietly.

"No, she's just hope," said Pamela. "We've had a lot of bad news. People need to know that good things happen too." She patted Usha's shoulder as if to assure herself that her friend really was alive. Bridget was determined that once they were home, she would give them a couple of minutes without her so Pamela could say what she'd been so distraught about not having said.

That afternoon, Bridget knocked on Usha's bedroom door.

"Who is it?"

"It's Bridget, may I come in?"

"Yes, but I'm getting changed." Her voice sounded oddly solemn through the door. Bridget looked around and then entered. She stopped in surprise. "Do close the door behind you, Bridgey."

"Ye—yes, of course," said Bridget. She pushed the door shut, but did not take her eyes off her friend.

Usha was not getting changed—she was clad in loose-fitting pajamas of soft coral-colored silk—but she *was* in a situation that might require some privacy.

She was floating upside down in the center of the room. Her face was a couple of feet off the floor, and her body was bent back in a sinuous curve. Her legs were in splits, one kicked straight up with her toes pointing at the ceiling and the other curling almost to the back of her head. Her arms were straight out to the side, and her hands bent back at perfect right angles. It was a tableau of vivid supernatural poise and control.

As Bridget watched, she realized that her friend was actually turning slowly in midair. Her eyes were closed, and she was breathing deeply, an unbroken rhythm of calm.

Bridget did not dare make a sound. Usha descended smoothly

until her face hung scant inches above the carpet. She continued to spin gently in midair, and her hair swirled around her, a glossy river of ink.

Abruptly Usha twisted backward in the air, not rising but rotating around her waist, her legs and arms scissoring to bring her upright. She touched the carpet with a toe, then brought both feet to the floor in a semi-crouch with her arms winged behind her like a dancer playing a bird. Then she stood smoothly, her hands coming up with palms pressed together.

She opened her eyes. There was an expression of such utter calm on her face that Bridget found herself envying the other girl with an intensity that was almost painful.

"That was beautiful, Usha."

"Thank you." She smiled. "It's a practice for mind and body. I find that the focus it requires is very calming. It helps me consider a situation in a much more open way."

"Do you have to be floating to do it?" asked Bridget curiously.

"Not at all," said Usha. "It's very old, but I've adapted it to incorporate some techniques Pamela taught me. When things calm down, I'd be happy to teach you a couple of basic moves."

"That would be nice. But right now tea is ready."

In the parlor, the three of them exchanged stories about their experiences of the previous day, except for Pamela, who could not talk about the work of the Court at Bufo Hall. Usha exclaimed over the revelations about the Murcutt family, and Bridget shivered as she heard about Usha's ordeal of being buried alive.

"So, your powers saved you," Bridget said. "But...you don't know how?"

"From what I saw, there are applications—a scope—to my powers that I've never realized. I think that I've been limiting myself. Not to say I didn't have an excellent teacher, of course."

"Thank you," said Pamela wryly, lifting her teacup.

"But I think when this is all through, I'm going to need some time to explore these possibilities."

"That shouldn't be a problem," Pamela said. "We're always encouraged to continue developing our abilities. Sabbatical, part-time duties."

"If we come out of this alive and not in Gallows Keep," Bridget said grimly. In the madness of the Murcutts, the bombing, the fire, and the presumed death of Usha, she had forgotten about the issue of the Nazi. "Pamela, has anything emerged that could help us?"

"No," said the Pawn.

"No leads that we could follow?" asked Usha.

"None," said Pamela. "And the tracking team continues their hunt. They're very good."

"So they're likely to capture him," said Bridget. "And then he'll be questioned, and we'll be incriminated and imprisoned." This prophecy was met with a sober silence.

"Well, look on the bright side," said Pamela. "Gallows Keep would be a very good place to focus on one's work. Not much else to do except stare at the ceiling."

"Don't they keep prisoners drugged?" asked Bridget.

"Sometimes," said Pamela. "In the case of Usha and me, almost definitely. And Bridget, though your powers aren't such that they would need to worry about your bringing down the building, your cunning is certainly something they should be worried about."

"Thank you," said Bridget. "You seem a bit more chipper this afternoon."

"It's remarkable how much one can be cheered up by the return of one's friend from the dead."

"I wasn't dead that long," said Usha. "I mean, did I miss much? Oh! How did things go with Gerald?"

Bridget gave a partial account of the farewell the previous morning, which now felt like several dozen years ago, and of the ring Gerald had given her. She did not tell them everything, of course. What she and Gerald had done in the hotel room was nobody's business but theirs. Her discovery of the broken condom and the possible implications were not something she was prepared to think about just then, let alone share.

Pamela and Usha insisted on seeing the ring. Usha turned it over in her hands and held it up to her eye to check the hallmark.

"Beautiful work," she said. "It would make a lovely engagement ring *or* a lovely gift."

"Yes," said Bridget reluctantly.

"You'll need to ask the Lord and Lady for permission to marry," Pamela reminded her.

"I know. But I don't think I need to worry about that just yet." *I have several dozen other things to worry about. Including the possibility that neither of us will survive to reach that point.*

"But you really love him," said Pamela. It teetered between being a question and statement.

"I do."

"That's lovely," said Pamela. She seemed to be weighing whether or not to say something. "You might want to think about stopping by the Bishops' offices very soon, then," she said carefully. "To update your will to include Gerald." Bridget nodded thoughtfully. Every operative of the Checquy was paid a substantial salary, but the Pawns received especially generous amounts. This was in recognition of their unique abilities and the fact that most of them were removed from their families and thus any possibility of an inheritance. Since they were all raised to be careful with money, there tended to be quite a bit of it left over when they died.

Various traditions had arisen surrounding wills. Of course, the bulk of a Pawn's wealth generally went to the spouse and children (if any), but custom dictated that Pawns also leave some portion of their money to the Checquy and any apprentices they had trained. It was also considered in good taste to leave some money to the families they had left behind; there was a section within the Checquy that specialized in distributing unexpected cash in such a way that it could never be traced back to the long-lost children—through lottery wins, for instance, or bequests from distant (and potentially fictional) relatives, or other, more baroque means. One of Bridget's mentors, Pawn Longmate, would knock on doors in the guise of an Oxbridge don needing to use the bathroom or asking for directions. Extremely charming, he would inevitably be invited in, whereupon he would promptly identify some decrepit and worthless piece of tat—a jug or a table—as a valuable antique. Depending on the size of the inheritance, he would either make an offer for the item on the spot or put the family in contact with an auctioneer or merchant who would make an even more exorbitant one.

They would not need to go through such intricacies to deliver Bridget's money to Gerald, though. As far as he was aware, her father had worked for Carrisford & Crewe and, thanks to Lady Carmichael's tactful talk with his parents, the Nashes understood that she had inherited a respectable amount of money. He'd probably be somewhat taken aback at how much she'd actually saved up, but she would leave him a plausible sum so that it could come in her name.

"That is a good idea, Pamela," said Bridget.

All three of them looked up as one of the maids came in.

"Miss Verrall, there's a courier from the mistress's office."

"That'll be today's summaries," Pamela said. She got up to sign for them, and when she returned, she was flipping through the documents intently. "Well, there's news from our friend."

"Our friend?"

"Our Nazi friend who last we checked was going around incinerating random Londoners."

"Another death?" asked Usha.

"*Two* more deaths," said Pamela grimly. She produced a map from the file and unfolded it on the table. "One in Wapping and one in Wandsworth."

"Have they managed to figure out who *these* victims were?" asked Usha. Pamela nodded.

"Both were criminals. One was a known receiver of stolen goods, and the other was part of a gang who run a protection scheme."

"This is so *odd*," said Bridget. "Why would he be killing criminals? How does he know who they are? And why *those* criminals? They're on opposite sides of the river." She looked at the map. "These murders occurred almost eight miles from each other."

"So he's wandering around a hostile city in wartime without any form of identification," mused Usha. "He's not trying to lie low. He's not trying to escape. What is going through his head?"

"Has the team that's tracking him had any luck?" asked Bridget, worried. The three of them needed some leads, but her stomach turned at the thought of the tracking team's taking him prisoner instead of killing him before he could talk. Given that he could now identify all three of them, it would mean the end of everything.

Is it worse to want this man dead because of what he could do to me rather than because he's a Nazi or because he's killing British citizens?

"They've had no luck. The murders seem almost random, and in the chaos of the attacks, it's not always easy to differentiate a body burned by a supernatural killer from a body burned by, you know, just fire."

"The unburned clothes don't give it away somewhat?" asked Usha skeptically.

Pamela shrugged. "Apparently, odd things happen in fires. And the clothes aren't always unburned. It took them a little while to figure out that the man in Wapping was killed by the same person as the others were. It seems his coat was ignited by the flames from his hair."

"And are the police still looking for the downed German airman whom they don't know to be a supernatural killer?" asked Usha.

Pamela picked up another folder. "It's one of their open cases. There are alerts in the newspapers, so the public is on the lookout when they can spare time from being bombed, working in factories, enlisting, and generally living their lives in a war. But if he's not wearing a uniform or going out in public, and he's not speaking German, then what's to distinguish him?"

"He had a very good haircut," mused Bridget. The two of them looked at her. "It was a very becoming haircut."

"Such things are not unheard of in London," said Pamela.

"I suppose."

"Regardless, I don't know that a very becoming haircut is going to be enough to evoke suspicions that he's a downed Nazi pilot," Pamela said. "Now, we know he speaks English, since he understood the two of you in that house. I don't know if he'd have an accent."

Bridget closed her eyes and rubbed her forehead. *There must be something we're not seeing,* she thought. *Something that will help us find him. Everything leaves a trace.*

Except for that palace from the future that appeared in Hertfordshire. Thank God that thing vanished completely after nine hours. Although it was a tragedy about the three Pawns who were exploring the cellars when it disappeared. She realized that Usha was saying her name. "What?"

"I *said,* what are your plans regarding the Murcutts? Where are your thoughts today?"

"It's been a busy bunch of hours. Anyway, yes, the Murcutts. Pamela, Wattleman, and I are going to track them down, get the answers we need, and remove them as a problem," said Bridget.

"Pamela is going?" said Usha, startled. She looked over at her friend. "They're allowing you to go out in the field?"

"The Murcutts know someone is coming," said Pamela. "We're looking to improve our odds. If I had my way, we'd be sending in a Barghest unit, but we can't make this an official operation."

"That makes sense," said Usha. "But I think I can improve our odds even more."

21

As Lyn walked into the Queen Victoria pub, the temptation to order several stiff drinks was almost overwhelming. After receiving the phone call from Rory, she had gone back to the Underground station and returned to the city. Knackered, but still mindful of the need to break up any trail the Checquy might stumble across, she had taken a route incorporating a train, a bus, and two cabs. And all the while, she was discreetly massaging her aching legs and trying not to fall asleep. A brisk walk through the streets of Walford had woken her up a bit and brought her to Albert Square and the cheerful red-painted pub.

Before she entered, she looked around the square for the suspicious figure Rory had seen following him. But while there were a few people about, there was no one lurking or watching the pub, and the only really eye-catching person was a teenage girl seated on a bench in the garden in the square. She was crying, but not in a creepy or staged sort of way. It was more in the way of a teenage girl whose life has been utterly and completely ruined by a relatively minor event.

Shrugging, Lyn entered the pub, which was doing a good trade. The place was filled with the chatter of regulars drinking, playing the slot machines, and engaging in various local dramas. Her desire for a beer or a cider or a shot of something was pretty damn strong. She didn't generally drink a great deal, and certainly less since she'd learned she could unleash electricity out of her body, but after the day she'd had with Rory in the pawnshop, the events in the cellar of the Anvil, and the confrontation with Pawn Kosloski, an alcoholic beverage felt like something the universe owed her.

But she didn't elbow her way through the crush at the bar and order a drink. There was work to be done, and she had to stay sharp. She looked around for Rory and spotted him and a dubious-looking young man seated at a little table by the front. Their drinks had barely been touched, and they were peering anxiously through the net curtains that covered the lower part of the window. As she headed toward them, Rory saw her and a look of relief came over his face.

"Kira!"

"Are you sure it's her?" said the other man sourly. He was about the same age and size as Rory and was sporting enough hair product to trap a hedgehog and preserve its corpse for eons for future archaeologists to puzzle over.

"It's me," said Lyn flatly.

"He managed to call out to some other woman who came in. Everyone was looking. Completely embarrassing," the young man said.

"I really thought it was her," said Rory weakly.

"This one isn't even blond," said the man in disgust. "The one you thought was her was a blonde."

"I thought it might be a wig. I'm a bit on edge. Anyway, this is her. Kira, this is my cousin Max. Max, this is Kira."

"I don't even know why we're talking to this chick," said Max. "We should have just called the uncles."

"I *told* you, Kira's a professional. She worked with Uncle Lennie and she's looking to get the man who's doing these killings. She's proper hard."

"She doesn't look hard," sniffed Max.

I could be at Mandy's place right now, in the bath with a gin and gin, letting my poor fucking beaten legs recover, thought Lyn. *I should have just ignored Rory's call. Let these two criminals get fried. Plenty more where they came from.*

She maintained her cool and fixed Max with a steely gaze. "I'm hard," she said. She opened her newly commandeered backpack and showed him, lying on top of all her personal detritus and the substantial amount of money she'd confiscated from the thugs at the Anvil, two of the handguns she had confiscated from the thugs at the Anvil. The other gun had apparently migrated to the bottom of the handbag to hang out with the hairbrush, the errant tampon, the loose Polo mints, and the really good change. Still, the appearance of two pistols nestled on a bed of money apparently sent the right message.

"Fuckin' hell!" exclaimed Max. "Yeah, all right. Jesus."

"Now, explain the situation to me. You had your meeting with the uncles, they said you had to hold hands until the problem was solved, and then you thought someone was following you, so you ducked into this pub, and..."

"Well, we couldn't see him very well," began Rory. And then he stopped. Apparently, he felt there was nothing more he needed to add.

My God, who had the nerve to call it organized *crime? These people couldn't organize a drowning at the bottom of the sea.* "I don't understand," said Lyn finally. "Was it foggy or something?"

"No, but it was getting dark, and he wasn't close."

"But he was always *there*," said Max, and for the first time, he sounded more frightened than obnoxious. "We took a path with lots of turns, and he was definitely following us."

"Could you see his face?" asked Lyn patiently.

"No. He was wearing a hood."

"Okay, so, a man in a hoodie."

"Yeah, and a long coat," said Max. "Like a trench coat. Dark gray."

"That does sound pretty weird," said Lyn. *Although it's not impossible that it was just some tedious freak walking around the East End.* "Rory, you said on the phone that you could see this person through the window, that he was hanging about outside. I didn't see anyone like that."

"He was there for about half an hour," said Rory. "Moving about in the garden in the square. We'd see him under a lamppost, and then I couldn't see him anymore."

"All right," she said. "Here's the plan. I'll go out, check for any sign of some guy in a hoodie and a trench coat, and I'll text you if it's clear. You will walk home, and I will follow at a distance, keeping an eye out. When we get to your place, I'll go inside first and check."

"Shouldn't we just get a cab?" asked Max.

"Then we wouldn't be able to lure them out," said Lyn. "Remember, our goal, Max, is to try and kill this person so he stops killing you and your peers."

"Oh, yeah. Cool." It did not appear to occur to him that he would be used as bait.

"It's fuckin' mad, what's been happening. I heard some shit went down today with the Keltons at that pub of theirs," said Rory morosely.

Wow, news travels fast, thought Lyn.

"Bloody smut merchants," said Max. Then, after a pause: "Wouldn't mind having a piece of that pie."

"Maybe there'll be some job openings," said Lyn sourly. "Now, I'm going to have a glass of water and go to the loo, and then we'll head out."

When Lyn left the pub, she stood outside and took a long hard look around the square. Some people were still hanging about (although the weeping teenage girl had vacated the bench), but there was no one in a long coat and a hood. She sent a message—okay—on her phone, and a few moments later, the two men came out of the pub.

"All clear," said Lyn. "Head on home, but not along busy streets. We don't want witnesses. Look for the quiet route. I'll be a bit behind you. *Don't* go out of sight. If you see anything suspicious, stop and call me. If you need to, run. If I yell out, you run. I don't want you getting hit by any crossfire." The two men, who were each a good head taller and a shoulder wider than her, nodded obediently. They turned onto Swenson Lane, a path between two houses, and she followed them, keeping a judicious distance back. It was difficult to judge the right amount of space to leave.

If you're too far, you won't be able to intervene in time, she thought. *But if you're too close, you could tip your hand.*

She was alert, listening for anything out of the ordinary. Her hand was in her coat pocket, holding tight to her baton. She'd given a moment's thought to putting one of the guns in her other pocket, but it would have made everything much more complicated. Looking at the two men walking nervously close to each other, Lyn felt a punch of guilt in her stomach. They were criminals, presumably hard men, but they were afraid, and she'd put them in a situation where they might be killed.

I'll do everything in my power to keep them safe, she resolved. *That'll be my priority. More even than getting this person.*

Maintaining as casual a walk as she could, occasionally pretending to talk on her mobile, she scanned the street. Everyone was a suspect. The shaven-headed man in the tracksuit? The woman in the red coat? Probably not the man in the motorized scooter—but, God, who knew? Maybe one member of the Indian couple? Or both of them! What if it was more than one person? If someone else could have her powers, then maybe many someones else could have her powers. The rules as the Checquy understood them had already been proven wrong. Perhaps they were more wrong than anyone had imagined.

"'Kay, love. Talk to you later," she said to no one on the phone for the benefit of the no one observing and laughed as if something amusing had been said back. *This is ridiculous. I'm now engaging in the same behavior as a high-schooler who wants to look like she has friends.* She snapped the phone closed and put it back into her jeans pocket.

This is all too public, she thought. *The killer has never operated in view of other people. They wouldn't move on a busy street.*

Max and Rory slowed to let her catch up some, then turned off the street onto a path between two buildings. Lyn picked up her pace, and when she saw the path, a little click of realization went off in her head.

This is where they would move.

It was a path that no woman walking alone would ever take, not even at high noon. Everything about it screamed *establishing shot in a police-procedural television show.*

It meandered between buildings and backyards, so one could not see too far ahead or too far behind. It felt old, an organic passageway that could easily have begun as a hunting trail back before there was a London. The height of the buildings and the fences on either side meant that it was much darker than other streets; there was an occasional lamppost with a dull orange light that seemed to defy all known laws of physics by illuminating absolutely nothing, not even the lamp itself. The road had been paved, probably in the middle of the twentieth century by a startled council that realized there was a useful connecting gap between Turpin Road and George Street and they really ought to do something about it. Unwittingly, they had created a prime locale for drug deals, personal assaults, and supernatural vigilantism; it was almost as if they had set out with that express purpose.

The dangerous nature of the route appeared to have occurred to Max and Rory too, because they were walking practically shoulder to shoulder and were casting many alarmed looks back at her as if to reassure themselves that she hadn't evaporated. Indeed, they were so nervous of losing sight of her because of the curves of the path that they slowed to an eventual stop and waited for her.

She caught up to them under one of the useless lampposts with its heavy orange light. She looked around dubiously. Bends in the path ahead and behind meant that a whole gang of criminals could be within a few meters without being seen. Litter was scattered about, and ivy and bushes had expanded over the back fences of houses, so the path was narrow.

"Interesting choice of route," said Lyn tightly.

"You said go for the quiet streets," protested Max.

"I didn't think I needed to warn you against taking Jack the Ripper Alley."

"Is that what this place is called?" asked Rory. Lyn stared at him and felt somewhat less pleased with herself for duping him into believing she was an underworld assassin.

"Quiet!" whispered Lyn sharply. The two men fell silent, and, wide-eyed, everyone looked back into the gloom of the path.

I could swear I heard footsteps. She squinted into the darkness and strained for the faintest hint of someone behind them. She was tense, ready for an attacker to appear out of the shadows. Or even a group of toughs who might have seen her go into the alley and thought they would try their chances.

But there was nothing, only silence, except for the very distant sound of London.

"Right," she said, startling Max and Rory. "We'll walk on out of Crime Alley together, and then I'll fall back again. It would be nice to take some quiet streets where I could still see someone coming up behind us."

"Yeah, all right," said Max, somewhat chastened. "It's not busy once we get off this path."

They walked on together, and Lyn kept looking back for any sign of followers. Once or twice she thought she heard footsteps, but she was so primed for attack that every rustle or faint thud had her heart pounding.

Finally, they emerged onto an actual road with actual lampposts that did their job and cast pools of actual light. Shops lined the street, but they were closed, with roller doors or cages pulled down over their fronts. Above them were offices or perhaps flats. A few lights were on in windows that looked down on the street, but these were muted behind curtains or blinds.

Lyn was opening her mouth to say something when she heard a soft pattering sound behind them in the alley.

Move! She shoved the men away from her and sent them stumbling forward in confusion; she dropped her backpack and threw herself forward and down, then rolled on her shoulder while something hummed over her and smashed onto the footpath. There was a crack and an unmistakable red flare by her head, but Lyn was already coming to her feet, her baton extended in her hand. She threw her energy into it even as she turned to face her attacker.

My God! she thought faintly. *It actually* was *the woman in the red coat!*

The woman in the red coat, whom she had seen back in the square when she first arrived, was blond, about Lyn's age, maybe a couple of years older. Fit. Broad shoulders. Her face was either lightly made up or very expertly made up, but either way, it was a hard face: strong jaw and humorless eyes. She was dressed in loose pants, some sort of hooded top, and the aforementioned long scarlet coat. Lyn's attention was caught momentarily by the lining, which was gray.

Reversible, Lyn thought. *Clever.* The bite of the red was so sharp that it caught the eye and held it. If you were looking for a gray coat, this was so very definitely not it that you dismissed its wearer instantly.

Of even more immediate importance than the coat, however, was the weapon the woman was holding with familiar ease.

She must have concealed it under that long coat, noted Lyn. It was the length of a walking stick, but thicker and made of a dull black metal. A quarter of it was wrapped in leather or rubber, which made it ideal for holding and swinging briskly at things or people against which one held an antipathy. The woman appeared to be readying herself for just such an endeavor.

Other details caught Lyn's eye as she took a few hurried steps back. Plain rings shone on all of the woman's fingers. Her rather smart-looking running shoes appeared to have a couple of strands of wire wrapped around each one lengthwise, from toe to heel.

Lots of metal to charge, Lyn thought. *Lots of ways to kill. This is the person who's been going around murdering criminals.* The woman was ready. Her eyes were flat, fixed on Lyn. *And now this killer wants to kill me.*

And yet, despite the adrenaline that was yowling through Lyn's body, there was also a sense of profound relief. She wasn't insane. It was someone else — *this* someone else — who had been doing the killings. It was a tremendous weight off her mind, one that she hadn't even realized she was carrying.

She was braced for the assailant to come forward, to follow up with another lightning-crack strike, but it wasn't happening. Perhaps Lyn's dive-roll thing and smooth recovery had thrown her. Or perhaps it was the abrupt appearance of the cruel-looking baton in Lyn's hand that was one complicating factor too many, but the woman had paused.

"That's the blond bitch in the pub that you thought was Kira!" Max exclaimed to Rory.

Lyn looked at the woman carefully. Perhaps they *did* look a bit alike. But there was no time to contemplate the implications of that, because the woman's eyes were narrowed, and she was moving forward like a panther, intent, implacable, with the end of that metal rod held in both hands like a sword.

"Get out of here, lads!" Lyn shouted.

"We can help you take her!" answered Rory.

At that moment, red electricity ignited the woman's rod, crawling continuously along the metal.

Uh-oh.

"Fuck, leg it!" exclaimed Rory, having rearranged his priorities with remarkable swiftness. Lyn was distantly aware of the sound of the two men bolting, and part of her rather wished she could join them. Her eyes were glued to the lightning storm that crackled along the woman's weapon. She felt a thrumming in her bones.

How is she doing that? Lyn wondered. *She must just be pouring power into it, but she doesn't need any impact to release it. It's just radiating out.*

She knows more than me.

But she doesn't know everything.

The woman advanced but was frowning slightly now, presumably at Lyn's failure to be completely flabbergasted.

"We don't need to do this," said Lyn. "We could try just talking it out." The woman's lip curled a bit, but she didn't say anything, and she didn't stop her advance. Lyn opened her mouth to say something else, but the woman burst forward, swinging her rod easily at the middle of Lyn's torso.

There was no real muscle behind the blow, although of course, there didn't need to be. Just a single touch, and as far as the woman knew, Lyn would be promptly electrocuted.

The problem was that Lyn didn't know any different. Her own electricity didn't hurt her, but a series of unpleasant tests at the Estate had demonstrated that she wasn't at all immune to regular electricity. Nor had she been immune to the electricity generated by that graphic designer who worked in the Rookery. So who knew what would happen when she got struck by someone else's red lightning? Would she be killed, whereupon the blonde would direct her attention to the rapidly scarpering Max and Rory?

Lyn was not prepared to find out.

Hours of tedious, painful, exhausting, and embarrassing training activated in the hind part of her brain, and she flung herself back, down, and to the side, just barely twisting out of the way of the crackling weapon. The woman stepped forward as Lyn automatically snapped her own weapon behind her, ready to strike, and, presumably despite herself, the woman flinched.

Let's change the tenor of this conversation, thought Lyn grimly, and she took the opportunity to rap her own charged weapon on the street between them. Crimson sparks and streamers poured out and danced along the tarmac, and the blonde jumped back.

"Do you want to talk it out *now?*" Lyn asked as she straightened up. The look of absolute shock on the woman's face was delicious, but it was replaced almost immediately by something so feral that Lyn actually gasped. The blonde roared forward with the rod held up high behind her head in a manner that Lyn recognized from her kendo training.

Fight lines with circles, she thought and spun to the left, giving her baton a nasty extra bit of velocity as she whipped it along. It was all a blur as she tried to keep her footing and move across the woman's path to throw her off balance. She didn't see but felt her baton clip the woman on the hip, and a torrent of electricity flared.

Gotcha! And then she felt a blinding pain in her right forearm as the woman's rod smacked her. It was pouring out its own juice into her, and she was braced to feel the burning, to feel her heart stop. *Fuck, we've killed each other.* But instead, it was a dappling of warmth that faded quickly.

The two of them turned, panting, to face each other. Each one was still crackling with the other's electricity. Lyn held up her arm curiously to watch the other woman's power cascade harmlessly from her hand down her sleeve, burning little holes in the cloth but bringing absolutely no pain. The woman stood stock-still, and Lyn's own lightning stuttered and flashed around her face before dissipating.

Well, now we know, thought Lyn. *We're not going to do any damage to each other this way.* Her arm hurt like a bitch from the impact of the rod, but it didn't appear to be broken. She regarded the other woman, whose face showed no trace of a willingness to compromise. The blonde was still practically humming with hate. *Fine. It'll have to be the old-fashioned way.*

The woman appeared to have come to the same conclusion, because she stepped out of baton-swinging range. Then she pulled on one end of the rod, revealing that most of it was a damn scabbard and she had been carrying a presumably razor-sharp sword around London.

"Holy shit," said Lyn.

Evidently, as far as the blonde was concerned, if eldritch electricity wasn't going to do the job, then cutting Lyn up into pieces was the way to go.

Which meant that Lyn was abruptly out-weaponed. Her decision not to carry one of the guns in her pocket was looking less and less sensible, although what with all the ducking and flinging about of herself that she'd just had to engage in, she was fairly certain that a gun would have spilled out of her pocket and onto the street within the first few moments of the fight. Her backpack was lying several meters away, and she actually gave a moment's thought to dashing to it and fishing out a pistol, but the blonde was already rushing toward her with the sword.

Fucking move!

Her ridiculously thorough training had included facing someone with a sword (it was far from an unusual occurrence in Checquy operations), but it had been predicated on the assumption that she would be able to use her powers. Her baton was strong enough to bear any blow the woman could muster up, but, crucially, it had no cross guard, which meant that if she tried to parry a strike, there was nothing to stop the sword from sliding on down the length of her baton and cutting off her fingers.

Lyn could practically hear Pawn Fenton shouting at her, but she already knew what she needed to do. As the blonde came at her, she stepped into the attack, tapped the sword aside with her baton, and moved in toward the woman. A couple of sparks fizzled when the weapons connected, but both women were too focused on the immediate violence to expend any energy on charging them. The point of the blade passed her, horribly close, and then she was right up against the blonde; she dropped her baton, gripped the woman's wrist with one hand, and tried to punch her in the stomach with the other.

The woman somehow caught her punching hand, and Lyn responded by twisting her opponent's wrist and forcing her to drop the sword. Each gripping the other's left hand, they strained against each other. The blonde's teeth were bared, her lips drawn back with such savage rage that Lyn thought she would try to bite her.

What now? she thought weakly. Her heart was a thudding drum. *Thud!* She was about to try to sweep the woman's legs out from under her when, beneath the screaming of her muscles, she felt a deep heat in her spine. *Thud!* She saw tiny rivulets of red lightning wriggle down over the blonde's face and even tiny flashes through the woman's hair, as if the energy were popping out of her scalp. *Thud!* The heat within Lyn was building. *Thud!* She felt the slickness of sweat dripping into and burning her eyes, and she gasped for breath. *THUD!* But she didn't dare release her hold on the other woman. The blonde — *THUD!* — was breathing rapidly, almost grunting, and Lyn felt a whine rising in her throat that would pour out as a scream.

Push! THUD! Push! THUD! THUD-THUD! THUD-THUD! PUSH! THUD-THUD-THUD! PUUUUUUUSSSSH! THUD-THUD-THUD-THUD-THUD-THUD!

It broke through. Whatever had been building up between the two of them was too big, and it tore up out of them, up out of their skin, and before Lyn's eyes, the blonde's face became a mass of electricity, and then Lyn looked up, dazed, and saw a huge, wavering bolt of lightning climbing up from them into the sky. It struck the clouds, where it bent and forked and forked again and again, spreading out in a lace of constantly shifting red lightning over London.

Lyn was screaming and did not know how to stop. Every inch of her was dancing with energy. Her heartbeat was now repeated deafening cracks as the lightning surged up and spread out again every moment. Her fingers convulsed around the blonde's wrist with every strike, and the blonde's hand convulsed on her skin in the exact same rhythm. Lyn could distantly hear the other woman was screaming as well.

How do we stop? wondered the tiny part of Lyn that was not consumed by the torrent. She could easily imagine this storm devouring them both and she had a sudden image of two pairs of smoking shoes being all that remained. She felt as if her body was going to collapse in on itself.

And then the column of lightning winked out, the lattice of energy above the city unbelievably gone, and the two women released each other's hands and fell back hard onto the street. They were gasping, and if the blonde felt anything like Lyn did, she was as exhausted as she'd ever been in her life.

The night was silent, as if incredulous after the madness that had poured up out of the two women. There were no distant sounds of cars or birds. There wasn't even any wind rustling leaves. The buildings around them were all dark, blacked out by whatever it was that had just happened. And then she heard a police siren in the distance. It was joined by another one, and another.

Lyn sat up weakly and looked around. Her clothes were smoking, although not actually on fire. The pavement glittered, and she realized that every window in the street was shattered. It took all her strength, all her will, but she managed to reach out and snag her baton from where it lay. A few moments of rest, then she rolled herself onto all fours, pushed up with her hands, and got to her feet. There was a little sound behind her. She turned and saw the blonde standing but bent over painfully, like an old woman.

Oh, right, she thought dully. *Her.*

The blonde fumblingly picked up her sword and turned to Lyn. Lyn looked at her and couldn't even muster up the strength to care. *I honestly don't know what I'll do if she makes a move.*

The blonde held the hilt loosely in her fingers, the point resting on the road. She regarded Lyn with exhausted, dead eyes, then she turned and bent down to pick up the scabbard. Without looking back, she started trudging up the street, away from the sirens. The scraping and clanging of the sword tip on the road set Lyn's teeth on edge. The idea of following the blonde was too much to even think about.

"You'd better move yourself as well," Lyn said out loud, and she felt better for saying it. She shuffled over and bent down to retrieve her backpack, and all her muscles shrieked.

"Okay, okay." She set herself to walking down the scariest alley in the world to where she knew she could probably get a kebab and flag down a taxi.

22

Wartime, especially in the Checquy, did not allow for the luxury of sitting around coming to terms with things. Usha had not been blown up by a bomb. She had not been crushed to death by rubble. She had not been consumed by the supernatural death throes of a colleague. She was alive, she was unharmed, and there was work to be done. The only concession was a telephone call placed through to Bufo Hall so that Usha could speak with Lady Carmichael. When Usha returned to the parlor, Pamela and Bridget tactfully ignored the tear marks on Usha's cheeks. Still, she was perfectly calm.

"She's approved my assisting you," said Usha. "I think she was relieved."

"Of course she was!" exclaimed Bridget. "She was horribly distraught when she thought you were dead."

"Not at that," said Usha. "Although, yes, I was very touched at her words. What I meant was, I think she was relieved that I would be joining you in addressing the problem of the Murcutts. I believe if she had her way, she would be accompanying us in our assault on them."

"The worst part of having power is that it's not always wise to use that power," said Pamela softly. Bridget looked at her. For a moment, there had been something strange in the Pawn's voice. Bridget would have thought it was despair, but Pamela was calm, intent, looking through the latest reports in the stream of information that was constantly flowing to the Lady's office and that had been delivered to the house earlier in the day. None of it, however, was the material they needed on the Murcutts.

Bridget reached for the tea. She felt like a well-buttered cat that had been thrown down a bobsleigh run. Over the past several days, she'd been flung about, emotionally battered, intellectually stunned, and had her dignity impinged upon, and she had a strong suspicion that people on the Continent were to blame for the whole thing.

"Well, well, well, three beauties at afternoon tea," said Wattleman from the doorway. Either he had become such a frequent guest that Leominster did not feel the need to announce him or—and this was more likely—he had snuck in through the kitchen.

"Ugh, Henry," said Pamela. "You're too young to sound like such a disgusting old lech." Usha's lip was curled, but Bridget, who had been exposed to far too much of Wattleman over the past couple of days, was beginning to believe that he had been a disgusting old lech in the womb, and possibly in the Fallopian tube. Wattleman ignored the remark, strode over to the sofa, and offered his hand to Usha.

"Miss Khorana, I was terribly glad to learn that we hadn't lost you after all."

"Thank you, Pawn Wattleman," said Usha.

"And am I to understand that you will be joining us on our mission? Excellent, most excellent." He brandished a sheaf of papers. "As I stopped by the office and was directed here, this was pressed upon me by a delightful young lady. Notes on the clan Murcutt."

"What do they say?" asked Bridget, curious to know the backstory on the people who'd nearly killed her the night before.

"Not a tremendous amount that is new," said Wattleman. "But the report does give us some more places to look for them, assuming that they haven't bolted out of town, which I doubt they did, given that one of them has a wife and children, and all of them rely on their London business for their livelihood. There are three houses for us to check. Matilda and John live in the parents' old house, a few miles from the pub. Robert and his family live a couple of streets over, and our auditors found another place nearby that an auntie apparently left to Matilda."

"How is the Moor's Head?" asked Bridget. "Did it blow up in the end?"

"No such luck," Wattleman said. "I walked by this morning and it's still standing, although not open for business. All the doors were locked, including the back door. One of the windows was open, though."

"The windows were all boarded up," objected Bridget.

"One of the windows was open once I wrenched a couple of boards off the wall," amended Wattleman. "I went through the place—no sign of anyone."

"Why didn't you just force open the door if you'd committed to breaking and entering?" asked Usha, frowning.

"I've got some experience in this sort of thing," said Wattleman. "I can push nails back into a wall, but I can't just repair a door that's been broken."

"Was going in not a bit risky?" asked Pamela dubiously. "What if someone had seen—never mind." Wattleman was smirking. "The bottoms of your feet must be like leather by now."

"All right, so three houses, four of us," said Usha. "What's the best way to proceed? My immediate thought is that we just send Pawn Wattleman in secretly. He can climb in a window while invisible and have a look around, and if they're there, he can come and tell us."

"Normally, I'd say that's a fine idea," said Pamela, "but the problem is that they know about Henry and his capabilities, and they'll be on the alert for him. I expect they have this Vincent person staying close to them. He's already proven capable of taking Henry on."

"*And* he can sense things through his powers," said Bridget darkly. "He read the texture of my palms through my gloves. I'm sure he can sense if someone's pushing back curtains or walking on carpet."

"Shall we just go up and knock on doors, then?" asked Pamela.

"Well, it would have to be you doing the knocking, Pamela," said Wattleman. "Miss Khorana might be a bit conspicuous in that area."

"Thank you," said Usha dryly.

"I—yes, sorry. And they know what Bridget and I look like."

"Maybe they wouldn't recognize you with your clothes on," remarked Bridget.

"Can we take that chance, though?" asked Wattleman.

"Plus, these families are very close-knit," said Pamela. "If we go around knocking on doors, word will get around quickly, especially after the events of last night."

"So what shall we do?" asked Usha.

"We should split up and watch the houses, at least for a couple of hours," said Pamela. "If they emerge, we tail them."

"Excellent idea!" said Wattleman. "We sit, we watch, we tail if the opportunity arises. Then, if the end of the day comes and we've had no luck, we meet up back here."

"What if one of us is busy tailing a Murcutt?" asked Bridget.

"Then try to call and leave a message for the others with the switchboard," said Wattleman.

It wasn't a great plan, but lacking additional resources, they couldn't come up with anything better, so everyone nodded, and soon they were dividing up the houses. Privately, Bridget worried that Usha might stand out a little too much. She remembered the reactions they'd gotten on the Underground. Usha wouldn't draw crowds, but she'd catch eyes, and that was not what they wanted. Bridget was bracing herself for an awkward conversation when, thankfully, Usha herself remarked on it, and everyone hastily agreed.

"It's fine," said Usha. "I'll go to Apex House and review the most recent reports." She gave Bridget and Pamela a minuscule *I'll be scanning the reports for any clue that might help us track down the Nazi whom we unleashed upon the populace and who is currently engaged in incinerating them for no apparent reason* look. "Then I'll meet you for supper and we can discuss the situation as it stands."

As it turned out, the other three needed to go to Apex House so they could draw disguises from the quartermaster's section that would let them blend in and hopefully not be recognized. Bridget emerged sporting a blond wig, a cute little purse, and a plain but respectable skirt and blouse, while, much to his own dismay, Wattleman was shorn of his mustache and dressed in laborer's clothes that had apparently not been washed in over a decade of service.

"We'll have to change before supper," he remarked darkly. "I was thinking we might go somewhere nice for a good slap-up meal to celebrate Miss Khorana's turning out to be alive. The Dorchester is very good and supposed to be very well constructed—practically bomb-resistant. But there's no chance of us getting in dressed like this."

"Let's just focus on the mission first," suggested Bridget.

All three of them headed off to their respective assignments with Pamela's admonition that they "observe only, follow if necessary, and absolutely do not engage." If a Murcutt emerged, they should follow, but the absolute priority was to bring back any findings to the others.

"Remember, if necessary, you can always find a telephone box and leave a message with the switchboard," Pamela reminded them.

Bridget found herself assigned to the house that had belonged to the Murcutt parents, and when she arrived, she was a little disappointed. It was hardly the den of a secret criminal enterprise. It was one of a row of houses, respectable but shabby, although the doorstep of each one was gleaming, presumably having been scrubbed that morning by a house-proud housewife. The street was not busy; there were a few children running about on the road, a couple of women carrying shopping, and the occasional man walking about on business.

Bridget was unsure as to exactly where she should take up a perch for surveillance. She could hardly sit on someone else's steps, and while there was a fortuitous bench a few houses down from the Murcutt residence, she felt that spending a few hours on a bench would draw unwelcome eyes. And possibly splinters.

So, the marginally less subtle approach, she decided. She walked across the street from the Murcutt place and two houses down and knocked.

"Yes?" said the old woman who opened the door. She regarded Bridget suspiciously from behind a pair of half-moon glasses and did not appear impressed with her. Apparently, the quartermaster's office had underestimated the respectability of the neighborhood.

"Do you see this money?" Bridget asked, holding up a banknote. The old woman's eyes opened wide, and she allowed as she did. "I will give it to you if you let me sit in your front room for three hours."

"Double it," said the woman, her eyes narrowing. Bridget gave a moment's thought to haggling but decided the additional expense would be worth it, if only to get out of public view.

The woman didn't quite snatch the notes out of Bridget's hand, but she wasn't slow about taking them either. She stood aside, let Bridget enter, and ushered her into a rather dingy parlor. The woman departed, shutting the door behind her, and Bridget took in the place. The decor consisted of a couple of armchairs, a small table with a dried flower arrangement that probably predated Waterloo, and an embroidered sampler on the wall that read

For the ways of man are before the eyes of the Lord, and He pon-
dereth all his goings.

— Proverbs 5:21

You and me both, Lord, thought Bridget. Once she'd dragged one of the armchairs around a bit, she was able to ponder all the goings of the street unseen from behind a pair of net curtains.

If the Lord was also pondering the goings of the street, it was a fair bet that He was almost as bored as she was, because as the hours passed, no one went in or came out of the Murcutt house. The only hint of excitement was when two small boys started fighting with each other in the street, at which point their mothers swooped down and gave them both blows far stronger than the ones they'd been dishing out to each other.

You two should definitely be evacuated, Bridget thought. *For safety from your mothers, if not the bombs.*

She wondered if the deal with the old woman included lavatory access and came to the conclusion that it probably didn't. She was steeling herself for fresh negotiations when the door to the hallway opened and a man came in. Middle-aged, he looked perfectly respectable in his suit, hat, and tidy mustache. The only flaw was his large, brightly patterned orange tie, which gave him a rather spiv-ish look.

He's probably the old woman's son, thought Bridget. *Curious about the cashed-up woman paying to sit in her parlor.*

"Good morning," she began. "I expect you're wondering what I'm doing here."

"Nah."

"What?"

"I know exactly what you're doing here," he said calmly. "Now, don't move a muscle or I'll kill you, then walk away for a pint."

"Excuse me?" Before she could react, he was pointing a gun at her. He didn't move with supernatural speed but with the startling skill of a man who knew how to use a weapon.

"We got word that someone was watching from this house. Gethings, come in," he said over his shoulder without taking his eyes off Bridget. Another man came in behind him, smaller, with cruel eyes. He was much less tidy than the first man and possessed of sufficient beard stubble to find alternative employment as a cheese grater.

"If you try anything, you won't even realize you've been shot until you're dying," said the man with the mustache. "And make no mistake, no one will have heard anything. Even if they hear anything, they won't have heard anything. We own this street. We own the eyes and ears of everybody on it. You understand?"

"'S," said Bridget softly.

"Good." He nodded to the other man. "Gethings, take off one of her gloves."

Oh, shit.

Gethings moved around behind her, never coming between her and the distinct possibility of a bullet. He took her hand firmly, turned it palm up, and skinned the glove partway down. The nacre caught the sunshine through the window, and her palm flared green-blue-purple. "This is the one we're looking for." And suddenly there was the point of a knife at her throat.

My God, these men have fast hands, she thought, but she was already being pushed firmly out of the room. There was a brief pause as the old woman handed over the money Bridget had paid her to the man with the mustache. *Marvelous. I've essentially paid for my own abduction,* Bridget thought grimly. And then she was being hustled out the door and into a large car that had pulled up in front of them. She was pushed onto a seat, the mustache man holding her close to him. All the time, she was horribly aware of the sharp point digging into her throat.

Gethings got in, holding her handbag, and the car started moving. Now that she had time to take it in, the vehicle was far larger than she would have anticipated—large enough for the mustachioed man to kneel on the floor and search her. He looked for, and found, the knife strapped to her calf, then the switchblade on her forearm. Both were confiscated. From there, he briskly ran his hands all over her body, pausing nowhere and finding nothing of interest.

Her wig's wig-ness was established, and it was removed and closely examined before being tossed onto the seat beside her. Bridget noticed that the mustache man (whose name turned out to be Eckersley) seemed quite loath to touch her; he did it with his mouth twisting. He actually wiped his hands on his pants after he'd finished patting her down.

She opened her mouth to say something witty and snide and felt a sharp pain at her neck. There was trickle of warmth on her skin, and she knew she'd been cut. Despite herself, she gasped.

"Just to make it absolutely clear to you what we're about," said the man. "And that you should keep your mouth shut." She nodded silently.

This is no good at all, Bridget thought. It was clear that these men fully expected this little jaunt to end with her death. *You don't abduct someone, let them see your face, and make them bleed if you think they'll be around later to finger you.* If she died, it was going to be completely mortifying. Checquy operatives, even apprentices, were expected to be able to handle themselves. The problem was that they were accustomed to being the hidden, unexpected element. No one was supposed to see them coming, which meant they were not used to being taken by surprise.

Be calm, she told herself. *Break this situation down to its component elements and look for opportunities.*

When she failed to show up at the hotel, the others would come looking for her. *And God help the Murcutts when they do.* The criminal family could have no real idea of what they were unleashing. With the power and the rage that Pamela, Usha, and Wattleman would bring, their homes and business would be rubble and any occupants pellets. But that would be hours from now. She was on her own.

The fact that you are not dead at this very moment means that they want you for something, which is probably why they've got a knife on you now rather than that gun. With a knife, you can be more assured of hurting someone without killing them.

Unless they just don't want your corpse to be found down the street from the Murcutt house. And they don't want to get blood all over the inside of this car.

So either they are going to kill you immediately as soon as they arrive at their destination . . . or they want you for something and then they will kill you.

The man with the knife had already demonstrated his willingness to injure her, but since they knew about her palms, she was not worried about them trying to assault her sexually. Non-Checquy men were generally quite wary of exposing their genitals to potentially malevolent supernatural threats. But she had no doubt that they wouldn't hesitate to kill her if they thought she was trying to pull something.

I think I'll just have to wait and see where they're going.

As it turned out, they were going to the Moor's Head. The car pulled up at the rear, and she was hustled in. *I can't believe they are actually coming back here,* she thought. When she caught the sound of the pub's front-room chatter, she was even more astounded. *They're already open for business? They must have greased a few palms to get that UXB taken care of.* She didn't dare open her mouth to scream for help from the patrons—that knife was still sharp at her throat. She was taken down the back stairs to the cellar.

When they pushed her into the large room, she felt her eyes grow wide. At first glance, the place was mostly unremarkable. It was clearly an old storage room, with the marks of old kegs on the flagstone floor and a musty, urine-y smell that suggested this was a longtime favorite place to store mops and prisoners. It was now empty, except for one startling feature that, once you realized what it was, dominated all your thoughts. Off to one side, lodged in a shattered part of the floor, was the unmistakable shape of an unexploded German bomb.

"Are you out of your goddamn minds?" she asked incredulously. "Do you know what that is?"

"Yeah, but it didn't go off, did it?" Gethings shrugged. "A dud. Bloody Jerries can't do anything proper."

"That doesn't mean it might not go off later!" shouted Bridget.

"You better hope it won't," remarked Eckersley. He tossed her now-disheveled wig in after her, then he and Gethings left and shut the door behind them. She heard a key turning in the lock. She listened carefully, but that was all. No bars slid into place, no padlocks clicked. Just the sound of footsteps moving up the stairs. Bridget turned to regard the bomb. She backed away from it until she was up against the wall, then slid down to sit on the floor.

Did they put me in here with it to kill me? she thought wildly.

Any minute, that bomb might decide to explode, obliterating her, destroying the entire pub, and killing everyone inside. She could not take her eyes off it. Gravity might be dragging down on a crucial component inside that would set the thing off. She strained to hear the *ting* of machinery that would mean her instantaneous death. As a means of disposing of a person, it would be very effective. If the bomb went off, there wouldn't even be fragments of her to identify later. But the fact that the pub appeared to be back in full operation argued against the theory that the Murcutts put her here in order to blow her up.

She gave a moment's thought to trying to coat the thing with pearl, but it would have been pointless. The stuff was strong but nowhere near strong enough to contain a bomb blast, even if she laid down coats upon coats.

And besides, I'd only be covering part of it. The other part is lodged in the floor.

It's hopeless.

After a couple of minutes, Bridget calmed down a bit. One could maintain a horrified panic for only so long if nothing was actually happening. She managed to drag her eyes away from the bomb and looked around the room. It was not promising. There were no windows through which she might try to escape or attract attention and no stuff around that she might use as a weapon except for the bomb itself, and she was not about to attempt to pry the fins off.

It occurred to her to look at the ceiling. Directly over the bomb, from the floor above, some planks had been nailed down. It looked to have been a hasty job, but for all its bodginess, it meant that the hole was quite definitely not a possible escape route.

Then she remembered that she'd been cut and tentatively felt at her neck. Her fingers came away with just a few flakes of dried blood.

She eyed the bomb. Nearly two-thirds of it was driven into the ground, and it had clearly punched through some flagstones. It seemed quite remarkable that it hadn't exploded, but apparently these things happened. Bridget had heard of houses and streets being forced to evacuate because of unexploded bombs while the disposal squad did their work. One report she had read grimly predicted that these UXBs might be turning up for decades, there were so many buried in the rubble. But this one wasn't buried. It was staring her right in the face.

She wouldn't let herself scream, but she let out a long, low groaning wail that emptied her lungs and left her hunched over her knees.

Are you done yet? the sensible part of her brain asked. *Because if you're done, it's time to make some plans.*

Yes, I'm done.

Then let's proceed.

Bridget wasn't sure if it counted as irony, but the Murcutts could not have chosen a better situation in which to imprison her. In any other room, she would simply have sealed them out. She would run her nacreous palms around the door to weld it to the frame with a barrier of pearl, then add strips along and across it to strengthen it. She could then have kicked back and devoted some time to catching up on her sleep and pondering her various other non-Murcutt-related travails while waiting for avenging rescue to arrive in the form of Pamela, Usha, and Wattleman. However, with the bomb squatting over there expectantly in its little crater, there was nothing she wanted more than to vacate the premises—a desire that was not easy to fulfill.

Had they placed her in this situation deliberately? She would not have put that sort of cunning past the sister, who, for all her languid decadence, had struck her as pretty damn canny. *She's the brains of the operation, I'll be bound,* thought Bridget. The brother had seemed more in the vein of what she imagined one's traditional pimp to be like.

Alternatively, perhaps the cellar was just a convenient space in which to secure her—a (nearly) empty room that would keep her off balance and give her nothing with which to escape.

But she was not entirely without resources.

There were many problems with her situation, not least of which was the possibility that a Murcutt or a Murcutt employee might enter at any time and catch her in the middle of her workings. She finally decided to sit right by the door so that she would hear anyone approaching.

Once settled, she unlaced her left shoe, slid it off, fumbled inside, and withdrew a grubby, somewhat crumpled strip of paper half as wide as her forefinger and about as long as her hand. It was the least prepossessing item one could imagine, which was exactly the point. No one was likely to notice it, and if someone did, it would never occur to him to confiscate it.

Bridget laid the paper on the floor, smoothed it out as much as she could, and took off her gloves. What was going to come next would require great delicacy and focus, along with all the skill she possessed. She carefully ran a finger lengthwise down the center of the paper, leaving a fine calligraphic line of pearl. A light touch was vital—if she pressed too hard, too much of the nacre of her skin would come into contact with the paper, and she could easily go over the edge and glue it to the ground. She lifted her finger off and examined the paper carefully. She now had a fingertip-wide strip of rigid pearl with the tiniest of fluttering edges of paper all around it.

She turned it over and carefully repeated the process, and as she finished, let out the breath she hadn't realized she'd been holding. This was the foundation. The pearl stuff would adhere to itself, but she needed a core to begin with, something for the initial layer to grip onto. Checquy masters had spent many hours trying to get her to have the stuff drip out of her hands or even spray across the room, but that wasn't how it worked.

Normally, Bridget did not need to exercise a great deal of finesse with her power. A simple thought, and she could slap down a hand-print in a moment. When intimidating Simony, she'd sloshed the pearl along the table like the trail of a snail. For this, though, she needed to sculpt out the shape she wanted with the finest of touches.

She worked as swiftly as she could, always mindful that her time might be up at any moment. Every stroke of her finger laid down another layer, and the pearl fused together with no seams or flaws. She extended the strip a little and sculpted two small, blunt, flat protrusions at one end. Below them, she used a more liberal hand, building up a rod and thickening it until she had molded a shape that fit perfectly into her closed fist.

Now comes the finicky work. She eyed the strip of pearl above the handle, the part built around that scrap of paper. The task would be a compromise between delicacy and speed, the final shape a compromise between size and concealability, width and taper. Gradually, she gave it the shape she wanted. As she neared the end, she sometimes had to ease out a layer finer than a human hair.

At last she had a dagger, as sharp as she could make it and with a point that, for all its seeming fragility, would not break as it was pushed through cloth and skin and muscle. Despite all the things to worry about, she was very proud of it. Partway through, she'd run two fingers down the edges of the blade, denaturing some of the pearl and sloughing away the excess to give it a merciless sharpness—a move that would have sliced open regular skin down to the bone but in this case just hurt like hell.

With the liquid uniformity of the pearl making it one continuous shape, the dagger didn't look quite real in the dull surroundings of the cellar. It put her in mind of a poniard, the way it tapered from the flat little hilt she'd given it to the merciless point. It was not perfect—there were a couple of wavering irregularities in its length—but it would cut and stab and do harm when called upon without breaking.

Now, how shall we proceed? Bridget had a few ideas for getting herself out of the room. She could mold pearl onto her fist, create a cestus, and set about battering the door down, but the sound would draw people well before the door gave way. Earlier in her training, she'd had some success in sculpting little lock-picking tools onto paper, and there *was* the other slip of paper in her shoe, but then she heard the distant squealing of stairs. She hastily concealed the dagger in the waistband of her skirt and untucked her blouse to cover it.

The door was unlocked and opened to reveal Miss Matilda Murcutt accompanied by the two men who had captured Bridget. The absence of Vincent was interesting—did it mean they felt she wasn't such a threat as to require supernatural force? Or was it just because there wasn't a lot of fabric lying about the cellar?

"Oh, please, don't get up," said Murcutt. "Or we'll kill you."

Despite herself, Bridget was a little intimidated as the woman swept in. She was wearing a magnificent blue silk dress, was again beautifully made up, and her hair was set immaculately. She held a glass of red wine in her hand and looked as if she had just stepped away from one of Lady Carmichael's dinner parties. One of the men put down a chair for her, and she sat easily.

Having been patted down and hustled about and then having done a fair amount of nervous sweating as she made her weapon, Bridget, sitting on the floor, couldn't help but feel like a grubby, recalcitrant child about to be lectured by a society dame. Her untucked shirt didn't help. She didn't get up, though.

"So you survived last night," said Murcutt, unconcerned by Bridget's failure to stand.

"Just," said Bridget coolly.

"And where's your naked friend?"

"He didn't survive it."

Murcutt gave her a long, level stare. "Pity," she said finally. Bridget couldn't tell whether the woman believed her. "We need more fine-looking young men running around without anything on." Her eyes took in Bridget's clothes rumpled state. "You look a mess."

Bridget spread her hands to take in her surroundings. "It's hardly the Ritz." She shrugged.

"Hmm." Murcutt's gaze turned to the disheveled wig lying on the floor. "That is what you were wearing?" She sniffed. "Absolutely preposterous—you do not have the coloring to be a blonde, and it would have made your head look enormous."

Is this how you talk to your prostitutes? wondered Bridget. Tillie Murcutt had a certain undeniable command about her, an authority, but to one who shared a house with Lady Sara Carmichael and Usha Khorana, it was hardly worth noting.

"So, young Miss Caswell with the jeweled palms, who are you?" Murcutt asked, but she clearly didn't expect an answer, which, in any case, wouldn't have been forthcoming. "I've had our men looking out for a woman with gloves acting suspiciously. They've been checking outside the pub, outside my house, and outside my brother's house. I described your naked young man as well, as best I could, but I thought he'd be either invisible or harder to identify." She smirked. "I wasn't looking at his face terribly much."

Ugh, thought Bridget. *You two would deserve each other.*

"But *you?*" continued Murcutt. "Well, you'd have to be covering up your hands, wouldn't you? Here's the thing, though. The fact that they picked you up over by my house means you've got access to information about me. Now, if you'd been following me, I like to think I'd have noticed. And if you'd been asking around, word would have gotten back to me. Especially in my neighborhood, people know enough to be afraid. Which means that you got my address from somewhere else. Police records? Is that what you are? The magic police?"

"I'm not with the police," said Bridget coldly.

"No, maybe not," mused Murcutt. "We keep in close with the local filth. I've got a few of them on the take, and they'd have let me know about the likes of you, especially if you were going to come sniffing around." She wrinkled her nose.

"You know what I think? You're probably somehow connected to the men who used to come around to my mum and try to get her to report any strange babies or unusual happenings. They never actually said *magic,* but she knew what they meant, and she wasn't having a bar of it. Oh, she'd nod along and smile, but if there's one thing the damn government can stay out of, it's the birthing room." Bridget said nothing, and Murcutt's eyes narrowed.

"And then Simony is dead, and you come around looking to buy some magic. And it turns out you've got your own magic, bred in the bone." She smiled, and Bridget tensed, unsure where this was going. Murcutt had proven entirely willing to have her killed last night, but now she was interested in talking.

Is it the wine? Bridget wondered. The woman's speech was unslurred, but she did seem far more open than when they'd met the night before. *Or is it the magic that she's so interested in? Maybe it's both.*

The two women regarded each other.

"They said you were a bit surprised by our new guest," said Murcutt finally. Bridget's brow wrinkled in confusion until the woman nodded over at the bomb.

"Do you seriously think it won't explode?" asked Bridget despite herself.

Murcutt shrugged. "These things don't seem to be much of a problem. If it can fall from thousands of feet up, punch through the roof and a couple of floors, and lodge itself in the ground without blowing up, I don't expect it'll do anything if we leave it alone. They can be quite useful, actually—everyone's so afraid of them. One of our salesmen has taken up residence in a very nice house over in Winchfield Road that's been evacuated because of a UXB in the pavement outside. He says the whole neighborhood is deserted, so he's living like a lord. It's a bloody mansion he's holed up in."

"I'm surprised you haven't turfed him out and taken it yourself," said Bridget sourly. "Since UXBs don't appear to bother you."

"Bad for morale." Murcutt shrugged. "Everyone in the firm knows he's in there. You don't want to be a tyrant to your people—it breeds disloyalty. But he knows who's in charge. Pays his dues. A couple of months back, he brought over a Rothschild '26 from the cellar."

"You do enjoy the high life, don't you?" said Bridget. "Gorgeous clothes, a taste for good liquor. I noticed your bar upstairs."

"And a selection of pleasant company whenever I want it," said Murcutt carelessly. She finished the glass of wine and put it carefully down on the floor next to her.

"Wartime restrictions don't really apply to you."

"I don't let them. Gethings, do you have any of that chocolate?" The man produced a bar and handed it to her. "Ta," she said, unpeeling the wrapper. She turned her attention to Bridget on the floor. "Fancy some? It's the good stuff. Swiss."

"Thank you, no."

"Suit yourself," said Murcutt, breaking off a piece and popping it into her mouth. "I don't know why anyone would deny themselves."

"Self-discipline?" suggested Bridget, and Murcutt snorted.

"I think a lot of what we call *self-discipline* is just following the rules that others make for us," she said. "We don't let ourselves be as free as we could." She regarded Bridget thoughtfully. "You don't strike me as a useless girl who follows all the rules of good society."

"I suppose I'm not exactly what people expect," said Bridget carefully.

"Damn right!" exclaimed Murcutt. "You interest me, and not just because of your magic—although that's pretty bloody interesting. You're like me, you don't fit on the strict little path that everyone thinks women have to follow." She appeared to be weighing a decision, and then she made it. "Gethings, fetch her a chair, would you? And get me another glass of wine."

And so our conversation shifts, thought Bridget. She stood, smoothly but carefully so as not to risk her dagger dropping onto the floor and into the conversation. Once settled, she declined to join Murcutt in a glass of wine but accepted the offer of some water. The two of them regarded each other over the rims of their respective glasses.

"When I was growing up," Murcutt began, "my mum was determined that I should be brought up proper, a lady. Different from her and her mum and her mum's mum. No daughter of Agnes Murcutt was going to be called out at all hours to deliver babies or do abortions on some local girl or on one of the tarts upstairs from the pub who'd gotten herself in trouble. Oh no! I was going to be *respectable*. Do her proud.

"So, while the boys were running wild in the streets, playing with the local kids, I was in the parlor learning how to play the piano and do cross-stitch. While the boys were learning Dad's business and sampling the goods upstairs, I was expected to sit up straight in a pretty dress with starched petticoats, serve tea to the vicar, and make nice conversation in the hopes that he'd marry me."

"Sounds frustrating," said Bridget. To someone who'd been brought up by the Checquy to be a warrior-bureaucrat, it sounded like an enormous waste of a human intellect. Seeing the drive and the passion in Murcutt, she couldn't help but pity the little girl she'd been.

"You have no idea. As far as my mum was concerned, pleasure was something that proper ladies didn't partake in," said Murcutt. "No playing, no toys. No dessert—I'd get fat, and what self-respecting man would want me then?"

"Ridiculous," said Bridget, who'd been trained to be a soldier from the age of two but *had* been allowed desserts.

"I had to be the good girl," Murcutt continued grimly. "And I was. But all the time, I promised myself that when I got the chance, I wouldn't deny myself *anything*. One day, I'd do and learn everything that interested me. I'd taste every delight in the world. Dad died, and Mum was still a holy terror, but then she dropped dead too." She didn't appear overly upset by the loss of her mother. "After that, I was free. I sat down with my brothers and we had a good long chat about the family firm.

"I told them straight up that I was going to live life as I wanted. Eat and drink what I wanted. Read what I wanted. Do what I wanted. Fuck who I wanted."

"And how did your brothers take their sister's abrupt shift from virtuous young lady to gourmand and voluptuary?" asked Bridget warily.

"They were fine with it. Because I have vision." Bridget started a little. "Oh, no, not second sight. I don't *need* second sight. All I need is to see the world without the limitations everyone else sees. All the little rules society treats as sacred. If you can see those for the imaginings they are, then you can do anything.

"I told my brothers we were going to eat the whole world," continued Murcutt dreamily. "Nothing was going to stop us. Not the law. Not some war. Every opportunity, we would snatch it." Bridget found herself nodding along. It was not too dissimilar to the things Usha sometimes said. "And that included magic. And wine." As she spoke, she finished her wine and threw the glass carelessly across the room. Despite herself, Bridget flinched when it shattered on the bomb.

Bloody hell!

"You're absolutely petrified of that thing, aren't you?" Murcutt said with an air of amusement. "I'm a bit surprised that you haven't tried coating it with your shiny pearl paste. Would it hold in an explosion, do you think?"

"No."

"So, it's not absolutely unbreakable, then," mused Murcutt.

"Unbreakable enough," said Bridget. *I think I see where this is going and why she hasn't had me killed right away.* "Human skin and bone will be destroyed before that stuff is."

"Hmm, we've had a bit of a try at getting your handprint off our Johnny's face. Spent a few hours scraping at it. Nothing made a scratch. Not knives, not chisels." Despite herself, Bridget winced. "Not even fire," said Murcutt ruefully. "And we washed it down with everything from carbolic soap to seawater to brandy. Even tried a bit of the Rothschild."

"Not the '26!" exclaimed Bridget in mock horror.

Murcutt gave her a look. "Our Johnny has not had a pleasant night of it."

Good, thought Bridget.

"And when he woke up this morning and it was still there . . . well, you're lucky we didn't have you then."

Bridget wasn't surprised that the Murcutts hadn't had any luck in dislodging the pearl from their Johnny's face. As she had told Wattleman, the Checquy had spent a great deal of time testing the limitations of the pearl and found it was mighty tenacious stuff. The only thing that they'd found that would break it down was a constant flow of well-heated hedgehog urine.

"I don't mind telling you," said Murcutt, "when our Johnny heard we'd picked you up, it took all my persuasion to keep him from coming down here and taking it out of your hide."

"You know, *I* can get it off," said Bridget casually.

"Oh?" said Murcutt, equally casually.

Here we go, thought Bridget. "Mm-hm. It's not easy," she said in as rueful a tone as she could muster. "Much trickier than laying it down."

"So you think you could clean up John's face, then?"

"Yes."

"And how long would that take?"

"Oh, at least several hours," lied Bridget. *Buy yourself as much time as you can. Time for the others to figure out what's happened and come.* "It's very finicky work. Do you know, if my concentration is broken or jarred, I can actually end up laying down more of the stuff instead of dissolving it."

"Really," said Murcutt dryly.

"Absolutely." *So no knives or guns or threats or abuse. Not unless you want your brother's whole head encased.* "But I'd like to talk about what would happen afterwards."

"Afterwards?"

"Well, let's talk about what we each want," said Bridget.

"I want my brother to be able to go out in public and use both his eyes. I expect you want not to be killed or hurt. And you want to be able to leave." There was something about her expression that suggested such an outcome was by no means guaranteed.

"For a start."

"A *start?*" As far as Murcutt was concerned, Bridget's being permitted to leave with body and mind intact already represented an unheard-of concession.

"Let me make a couple of things clear," said Bridget. "I'm not the only one like me. There are others, and they will come. But we don't care about your knocking shop upstairs. We don't care about any other little illegal pies you've got your fingers in." Murcutt's eyes were thoughtful at her words. "But we *do* care very much about where you got those antiques." Murcutt opened her mouth. "Yes, the *magic* antiques. They cannot be out on the streets."

"They're good business," said Murcutt.

"I'm sure they are," said Bridget grimly. "I know how much you were selling them for. But it's unacceptable. I need to know who sold them to you, and I need you to stop selling them and turn over anything you still have. You'll be paid an amount commensurate with what you'd have made for them." She wasn't entirely certain that she had the authority to make this sort of deal or spend the sort of money they might be talking about. But it was the only thing she could think of.

"All this for undoing something *you* did," said Murcutt in a sour tone.

"I didn't start the fight," said Bridget. "And my friend is dead because of you." She sighed. "Miss Murcutt, I think you can understand why it needs to be this way. It looks like you've got at least a lick of sense. Maybe several licks. After all, your man Vincent isn't out on the streets conquering the world by yanking on their vests. You understand why this needs to be kept quiet."

Murcutt nodded. "You'll pay the full value of the pieces?" she said at last. "We're talking hundreds of pounds, you know."

"How many hundreds of pounds?" Bridget asked, hesitating. Murcutt named a figure, and Bridget winced.

"That's for seven pieces, mind," said Murcutt.

"Seven?" said Bridget, aghast at the idea of that many more artifacts lifted from Checquy custody. She couldn't decide if they were woefully overpriced or woefully underpriced. "That's a lot of money." Murcutt nodded. "And you'll give me the source?" countered Bridget.

"Yes," said Murcutt grudgingly.

"Then you'll get your money." This idea had just come to her, but contacts within the Murcutt criminal empire could prove very useful to the Checquy. "Your people and my people might be able to come to some sort of profitable arrangement in the future." The other woman held her gaze with new interest. "And you yourself might be able to learn a great deal from us about the world. About our world." Murcutt's obvious fascination with magic might prove an even more powerful lure than money. "But I'd want some sort of guarantee that I can trust you," Bridget said.

"I will give you my word," said Murcutt.

"Very nice," said Bridget with a hint of sarcasm. Despite herself, she grinned a little. She was finding that she liked this woman. "I suppose the only question is how I could possibly take the word of a family of criminal pimps who have already demonstrated a willingness to kill people and traffic in dangerous goods?"

"My dear, you wound my feelings," said Murcutt, grinning back. "I'm not going to break my word. I see all sorts of interesting possibilities if we can get along."

I don't know if the money will keep me alive, Bridget thought. *But the lure of learning something about magic might.*

23

"It is extremely late," said Mandy when she opened the door. "It's already tomorrow."

"I really am sorry," said Lyn. She was absolutely knackered.

After the lightning battle with the blond woman, she'd staggered away and wandered vaguely through the streets. She'd been so dazed that at one point, she had actually managed to fall into a bush, where she'd stayed for several soothing but scratchy minutes as she pulled body and mind together.

Eventually, she'd found a brightly lit street, bought a kebab, and eaten it in the gutter next to a couple of students who'd been out clubbing and who thankfully didn't feel the need to have a conversation. The three of them had watched police car after police car race by with lights flashing and sirens whooping heading in the direction from which she'd come, but she'd been too exhausted and the students had been too drunk to muster up any comment. It had taken all her strength and intellectual resources to call Mandy and let her know that she would be coming back to the house as soon as she could. The American hadn't sounded pleased on the phone, but Lyn lacked the emotional energy to be concerned.

It was so late that the Underground was no longer running out to Debden station, but Lyn was determined not to leave a trail for the Checquy, so an expensive series of cab rides had ensued. The final driver had actually been obliged to wake her up so that he could drop her off several streets away from the house. She'd walked the remaining distance, and because Mandy had not given her a key, she had had to knock on the door, which set off a Tabernacle Choir–level of dog barking. When the door finally opened, the human and canine residents had looked distinctly unhappy about being awake.

"I've had a few women in your situation stay with me," Mandy said grimly. "And they've dealt in different ways, some of which are not good. Let me smell your breath."

"What?"

"I'm not your mom, but I want to know exactly what I'm letting into my house," said the American woman. "Otherwise you can sleep on the lawn chair out back and find a new place tomorrow." She sniffed Lyn's breath, looked carefully into her eyes, and took her pulse. "You're not drunk and you're not high. So that's something. But you smell like smoke. Like something burning. What the hell have you been up to?"

"I just spent the day walking," said Lyn. "It helps me think."

"Well, I hope you had some useful thoughts because you look like hell," said Mandy. "Go shower and go to bed."

Lyn woke up much earlier than she would have liked, her brain informing her that bacon was cooking somewhere in the house and that she wanted it. She shambled down the stairs and into the kitchen to find Mandy cooking bacon under the very interested gaze of all the dogs, who were sitting expectantly in a semicircle around her like supplicants before the altar of a potentially generous god in a dressing gown. Bruce Springsteen was singing over the radio, and coffee was singing in a French press.

"Morning," said Mandy. "How do you feel?"

"Rested." Lyn yawned. "Ish."

"I would hope so, after a full day's sleep."

"What?"

"You slept all day and all night," said Mandy. "I checked in on you every few hours, but I guess you just needed the shut-eye."

"I was asleep for *thirty hours?*"

"At least," said Mandy. "You got up a couple of times to go to the bathroom, but other than that, you were dead to the world."

"Huh." Lyn could well believe it. She'd been utterly exhausted after that column of lightning had torn itself out of her and the blonde.

"Coffee?" asked Mandy.

"God, yes, please."

"It's in the pot. Then sit. Bacon and eggs in a sec?" Lyn nodded enthusiastically and shuffled over to the pot on the counter. The coffee proved to be so spectacularly foul that she could hardly drink it, but she needed it so badly that she managed to force it down. Mandy came to the table surrounded by an aura of dogs. She called each one by name and tossed it a piece of bacon, all of which were caught in midair.

"Have you seen the news?" asked Mandy.

"I have not," said Lyn through the bacon and eggs. Mandy switched on the television, and the first thing that appeared on the screen was footage of the lightning web from her battle with the blonde. Lyn's body would not allow her to waste any bacon by choking on it, but there was a moment of tension as various natural reactions battled within her nervous system. Lyn hadn't taken in how long she and the blonde were locked in that strange phenomenon. Her mind had been so consumed by the sheer primal experience and the draining torrent of sensation that she'd barely been able to summon up any conscious thought. When she thought back on it, it seemed like an eternity, but she had assumed it had really lasted only a few seconds. As it turned out, it had lasted sufficiently long for hundreds of Londoners to rush to their windows and film several minutes of footage on their phones, which they then posted on the internet.

"Oh, crikey," said Lyn brokenly.

"Amazing, isn't it?" said Mandy. "It's on everywhere." She flicked to another channel, then another. Again and again, crimson electricity coursed across the skies.

Oh, the Checquy are not going to be pleased about this.

"Number-one story in the UK, but it's getting shown everywhere around the world."

They are not going to be pleased at all.

"Did you see it when it happened?" asked Mandy, cheerfully oblivious to Lyn's mounting horror. "It didn't reach quite this far, I don't think. I certainly didn't see anything, though the dogs all went ballistic."

"I did see it," said Lyn weakly. She thought she might faint into the bacon. "It was unbelievable. Did it cause any damage?" She remembered the shattered windows along the street, but suddenly her mind was filled with other possibilities. What if bolts of the electricity had struck back down into the city? What if it had hit people?

"No, nothing like that," said Mandy. "Just a light show. And some scorch marks on the road out in the East End."

Thank God. "What—um, what are they saying caused it?"

"No one has any idea," said Mandy with apparent relish. "I'm quite enjoying watching all the experts scramble over each other. In a minute, I'm sure they'll show another baffled, panicked-looking scientist. I think it's probably climate change, though."

If the Liars haven't been putting out some sort of explanation, then this must be bad, thought Lyn.

The Checquy's Tactical Deception Communications section, known affectionately as "the Liars," covered up supernatural manifestations and ensured that society did not collapse under the weight of stunning revelations that would break all reasonable assumptions about the world. Composed of a skilled team of journalists, psychologists, doctors, spin doctors, spin surgeons, regular surgeons, novelists, historians, hacks, hackers, Grafters, grifters, con artists, performance artists, police specialists, policy specialists, polity specialists, political specialists, veterinarians, veterans, and scientists of every stripe and hue, the section was notorious for veering from periods of tension-laden tedium to bursts of frantic creative activity as they reacted to manifestations, fabricating careful explanations that would be accepted by experts and could withstand most skeptics.

On her second day with the Notifications section, as part of orientation, Lyn and a couple of other new Checquy operatives had been taken on a tour of the Liars' offices. The rooms were situated in the Checquy headquarters for domestic operations, the Hammerstrom Building (informally but universally referred to as "the Rookery") in London. The visiting group had been obliged to stand back in an alcove to avoid being knocked over by the constant hustle of people. Apparently, twenty minutes before they arrived, a railway bridge near Godalming in Surrey had begun liquefying, slowly but not sufficiently slowly to avoid notice.

The visitors had watched in fascination as, in a glassed-off (and mercifully soundproof) room, Liars collaborated and argued over cover stories. In the center of it, on a sort of elevated platform surrounded by multiple screens, a stunning young woman in a sari was overseeing it all, taking in the latest news reports and pulling together teams to formulate explanations, revelations, and, in some cases, diversions.

The Liars' section was known to be the most rigorous placement in the entire Checquy organization. With every shift, an operative could expect to burn as many nervous calories as he or she would in a session of high-impact aerobics done to Brazilian funk. During her visit, Lyn noticed a couple of the Liars simply passed out on daybeds. Huge urns of coffee, tea, Bovril, Irn-Bru, and red cordial stood on a side table.

The rookies were advised that the requirements for Liars to be available for emergency duty were even more stringent than for the

Court or the Barghest commandos. Liars not actively on vacation were required to be on call every hour of every day. Not only did they have to share their schedules with the watch office, but they were also expected to wear trackable wristwatches in case their specific areas of expertise were needed to formulate a plausible story. Indeed, as the new operatives watched, a helicopter was dispatched to pick up a lepidopterist from a dentist appointment.

The pressure and the constant nature of the job was of such a high tenor that it was generally agreed that if you needed to lose weight, this was the section in which to seek a temporary assignment. Checquy brides-to-be were especially infamous for doing a stint there in the weeks leading up to their big day, just to make absolutely sure that they would look their fittest in their wedding dresses.

During her tour, Lyn had been startled to learn that the Blinding—the gigantic nationwide terrorist gas attacks of a couple months earlier—had in fact been the work of a faction of rogue Grafters; that the infamous serial killer of the 1990s known as the Sunday Roaster had actually been a sentient and mobile bonfire; and that the day of any royal wedding was a favored time to conduct Checquy operations, since the potential for witnesses on most streets was massively reduced.

Apparently, though, a vast bloodred electrical extravaganza above London had stymied the creative efforts even of the Liars. No one in the world appeared to know what had caused it—even the freaks and fanatics were hesitating to float their various idiosyncratic theories. To Lyn's relief, absolutely nobody appeared to be claiming that this terrifying, unprecedented atmospheric phenomenon was the result of two women fighting with sticks in Walford, which suggested that no one had actually seen them or, more crucially, filmed them.

"So are you going to go out for another really, really long walk today?" asked Mandy. "Because if so, you can take the dogs. Or at least a couple of them."

"Once again, I am so sorry about coming back so late," began Lyn, but Mandy waved her apology aside.

"I know that you've got a lot going on. I was just a bit worried."

"So you don't want me to leave, then?" asked Lyn. The American shook her head. "Thank you. I think I might stay close to the house today, if that's all right." This would definitely be a day to rest, recharge, and reflect. Mandy nodded her approval. "Although I *will* still go out for a walk after breakfast." There was at least one phone call she really needed to make, and while Mandy didn't strike her as the type to snoop, she didn't want to risk anything being accidentally overheard.

"Good, take the Poms," said Mandy. "If they don't get some fresh air, I have to peel them off the ceiling by noon."

"Hello, Rory? It's Kira."

"Kira!" Lyn actually had to hold the phone a little away from her ear. "Oh my God, it's been two nights, I thought you were dead! Are you all right? Did you kill her?" The tension in the man's voice practically crackled down the phone line.

"I'm afraid I didn't," said Lyn. She leaned back against the park bench. She'd shuffled, whimpering from the pain in her battered legs, to the local dog park and was now half watching Mandy's Pomeranians run around madly like well-groomed glamour stoats.

"You didn't kill her? Christ! So what happened, are you okay?"

"Yeah," said Lyn. "We, um, went at each other pretty hard. I got some good licks in. I don't expect she'll be doing anything for at least a couple of days." *Not if she feels as exhausted I do.* Despite the hours of sleep, she was still as weak as a newborn kitten. She'd had to stop and rest three times during the walk to the dog park, while the two Pomeranians strained at the end of their leashes and became hopelessly entangled.

"Well, she's clearly nuts, running around with a bloody cattle prod."

"Yeah, nuts, but she's definitely dangerous," said Lyn.

"No shit! So, we legged it back to Max's house and locked ourselves in. We only just got there before that lightning thing happened—did you see that?"

"How could I miss it?" asked Lyn.

"Mental, wasn't it?"

"Completely," said Lyn with feeling. "Look, have you been in contact with anyone about this?"

"Yeah, as soon as we got here, Max called his dad and told him all about it."

"Why? Who's Max's dad?"

"Um, he's kind of the head of the whole firm," said Rory in a tone that suggested she should know that.

"Oh, okay," said Lyn, a little taken aback. *That slick little weasel is criminal royalty?* She'd memorized as much as she could of the Checquy dossiers on the gangs, but she'd been much more focused on potential contacts.

"Yeah, so his dad said to stay put, and we've been locked in here ever since."

"Good," said Lyn. "I just wanted to make sure you guys were safe."

"Yeah, we're good."

"Okay, then I think it's time to change our plans up a bit. We know what this murderer looks like now. That gives us an advantage."

"We gave a description to Max's dad, and he's put the word out," said Rory.

"Smart. That way, they're forewarned." *And they'll all be on the lookout for her. Please God, don't let them just start killing random blond women.* "Did you tell Max's dad about me?"

"No," said Rory. "I wasn't sure. Should I? Like, give them your number in case they see her?"

Lyn hesitated. She suddenly had visions of gangsters calling her up and asking awkward questions. Plus, some of them might have the intellectual rigor that Rory lacked and do some poking around. *Still, if I've got a whole bunch of people out on the street looking for her and reporting back to me, it's much more likely I'll find her.*

"Kira?"

"Yeah, sorry. I think it's okay for you to tell them about me and explain that I worked directly with your uncle. But I think it's best if you're my only contact."

"Cool," said Rory.

"If anyone spots her, let me know. And if she shows up near Max's, let me know."

"Right, yeah, okay. Um...do you think she's likely to show up again?"

"I doubt that she'll come after you or Max again," said Lyn, and with a sinking feeling she realized it was true. "She knows you've got a bodyguard who can take her on. And you know what she looks like, so she won't be able to sneak up on you." *I may have blown my one chance at that woman. My one chance to go home.*

"Yeah, that's right!"

"Rory, this woman is good at what she does. Make that clear to Max's dad and the rest of the organization. I'm a trained professional, and I only just got out of this. Don't let anyone else try to take her on."

"Are you sure you don't want to talk to him? You can explain it better than I can."

"I'm sure," said Lyn. "Talk to you soon."

She leaned back and closed her eyes. As far as she could tell, things had gotten worse. Much worse.

The eruption of the red lightning into the sky had done her no favors at all. Given the location, the timing, and the nature of the incident, the Checquy would assume it was her and would be drawing all sorts of dangerous conclusions. The lightning web that had crackled over London represented an exponential increase in power and would force them to reevaluate everything they knew about her. To the Checquy, the threat she represented had just escalated drastically.

They'll think I've been concealing the true scope of my abilities. Or that I'm going critical, like a nuclear reactor melting down. So far, there had been nothing in the news reports about any casualties, but she shuddered to think what would have happened if all that energy hadn't been directed up into the sky.

We could have killed innocent bystanders, she thought, and she felt sick. For the first time since she'd mastered her powers, she was afraid of them. Despite herself, she remembered the terror on her daughter's face when the lightning erupted out of her in the kitchen.

The Checquy will try to kill me on sight, she thought faintly. *I would.*

Nothing she'd done so far would mitigate the Checquy's response. Her mercy toward Pawns Seager and Kosloski and that statuesque woman she'd shocked in the van, and her overture to Georgina— those counted for nothing. Her phone call to the emergency line bought her no latitude. Any uncertainty that the card to her husband might have engendered was now irrelevant. Her insistence that she was not the one behind the gangster killings didn't matter. Her powers made her a threat to the public. To the Checquy, she was no longer a rogue or a vigilante. No longer an apostate.

She was now a manifestation.

The only bright spot was that she now knew that there really was someone with the same powers as her.

Except that she knows how to do things I don't, thought Lyn grimly. She remembered the electricity coursing along the woman's weapon. *How did she do that? Can I do that?* The fact that they looked somewhat alike was…thought-provoking. Were they related? She couldn't guess the woman's age—she looked a few years older than Lyn, but perhaps she'd led a hard life. She might be younger.

The Checquy had told her that powers within families were rare. Whatever caused supernatural abilities to erupt in people didn't appear to be genetic. But there were always exceptions, weren't there?

And what difference does it make? I can't set about researching family connections. I don't know who my family are.

So what do I do? Do I just wait and hope that she goes after a member of the Rafferty gang again and that they call me?

Or what if she never resurfaces? After seeing that there's someone else like her who's willing to kill her, will she go to ground? Escape to a different city or country?

If she does, I'll never be able to prove I'm innocent.

And if I did track her down somehow, how could I defeat her? When our powers reacted, it was insane. Who knows what would happen if we fought again? We could inadvertently kill people. Hell, we could inadvertently destroy buildings.

And I don't know if I would win.

Will I ever get home? she thought hopelessly.

I just don't see a way back.

The rest of the day was spent in a dull daze. She walked the dogs home, then went upstairs to her room and lay on the bed. Despite her exhaustion, she couldn't sleep. All she could do was stare at the ceiling and feel her stomach knotting.

This is hell.

If I stay in London, they'll hunt me down. If I stay in the UK, they'll hunt me down. So, do I run? Do I try to smuggle myself to France or Holland or Belgium? Would they stop looking for me then?

Do I leave Richard and Emma forever?

She took the photo of her husband and her daughter from her wallet and gazed at it, feeling tears seeping out of her eyes. All she could do was clutch at her stomach as she went over the situation again and again in her mind.

Eventually, mercifully, she slept, but when she opened her eyes, it was still daylight, and she couldn't help but moan as everything came back to her. One of the dogs, the elderly golden retriever, nosed its way into the room and leapt creakily up onto the bed to lie down with her. She clutched at it, buried her face in the fur on its neck, and despaired.

It was dark and late when Mandy knocked hesitantly on the half-open door.

"Lyn, did you want some dinner?" she asked gently.

"Please," said Lyn hoarsely. "I'll just wash my face." She had no plans, no idea what she was going to do, but she was desperate for anything that might stop her mind from turning everything over and over.

When she came downstairs, Mandy didn't ask how she was. Presumably the answer was obvious. Lyn accepted the proffered spaghetti Bolognese with dull thanks and nodded absently when Mandy suggested they eat off TV trays in the den. She flinched a little when the late news, inevitably, opened with the story of the lightning over London. Once again, Lyn watched the footage of the discharge spiderwebbing across the sky. She heard the same bewildered analysis, but since no answers were forthcoming, and there was no sign that it was likely to happen again, the news anchor shrugged and moved on to the latest cock-up of the government.

The pasta and wine were good, and with the softness of a golden retriever resting heavily and comfortingly on her feet, Lyn was able, not to forget her despair—never that—but to turn her focus onto other things.

"The ongoing disagreement is showing no sign of stopping," said the newsman heavily, "with the opposition declaring that—" He frowned and put his hand to his ear. "Please hold for one moment."

Lyn looked up from her food, not at the newsman's interruption but at something that wasn't there. She could feel a stirring in her bones. As if they were vibrating just a little. She stared down at her hands, expecting them to be shaking, but they were not.

Is this my powers? she thought. *Have they somehow been changed by that burst the other night? Are they broken?* She was suddenly afraid to put down the fork in her hand in case electricity burst out of it. *It doesn't feel like I'm letting out energy,* she thought. *But what do I even know anymore?* She was horrified to imagine lightning flooding out of her and killing Mandy and the dogs.

"What is *wrong* with them?" asked Mandy. With an effort, Lyn looked over to her and saw that she was staring at the dogs. They had been sprawled around the room on various couches and dog beds, but now all of them were sitting up and staring intently in the same direction—at one of the living-room walls.

"I apologize for the delay," said the newsman on the television. "We are just getting this in. There have been reports of more lightning strikes in locations around London. I think—yes, we're getting some visuals now."

The screen changed to wobbly footage, clearly taken on a phone, showing the view from a window overlooking a night-shrouded park.

"Oh, come on," said a young man's voice—the owner of the phone. "Lars, do you think it will happen again? *Whoa!*" A massive crack overloaded the phone's microphone, and the image shook as a bolt of red lightning flared into the sky, too bright for the camera to really capture but clearly originating at a hidden place within the trees. It did not split, but it lingered for a few seconds longer than lightning should before winking out. "That's f-*bleep*-in' wild!" exclaimed the voice.

"God*damn*," said Mandy, leaning forward. Lyn was silent, transfixed.

"That was footage taken just a few minutes ago at Clapham Common," said the newsman. "The witness who captured it said it was the third lightning strike to occur at that location, each separated by about twenty seconds. We—what? All right we have more footage, this time from Hampstead Heath."

This footage was also taken with a phone, but apparently one of better quality, because it showed the lightning more clearly. It struck once, then, after several seconds, again, and then again, the lightning almost pinkish this time. Once again, it did not fork but endured for a few moments, wavering crazily in the air, before vanishing.

"Oh my Gawd," said the owner of the phone. "Are you seeing this?" She sounded frightened. "What is going *on?*"

The screen cut to the newsroom, with the anchor looking serious as a map of London behind him featured crimson circles.

"We are learning of more such phenomena in green spaces around London, including Hyde Park, Richmond Park, and Wimbledon Common. Fortunately, there have been no injuries and no reports of property damage but the—" The newsman paused again. "Yes, yes, thank you. I've been advised that we have received some startling footage taken from the observation deck of the Shard in Southwark."

The screen cut to a high shot looking out over London. The lights of the city were bright, especially since there was no moon that night.

"Do you see anything?" asked Mandy. She was frowning, peering at the screen. "What are we supposed to be—*Jesus Good Balls!*"

Dotted across the cityscape, some quite close, some so distant that they were just tiny flickers, red bolts of lightning flashed all at once on the screen and then vanished. Then, as if in sync, they reappeared, faded, and reappeared once again.

"It seems," said the newsman solemnly, "that all those lightning strikes occurred almost simultaneously."

What does this mean?

24

Y ou *witch!*"

"Mr. Murcutt," said Bridget calmly. "How nice to see you again." It wasn't, but saying so served to establish her position as unruffled and unafraid. She looked at him with clinical interest and realized exactly how terrified he had to be. He was standing in the middle of the top floor of the Moor's Head, his fists clenched. His clothes—the same as when she'd seen him last—were rumpled and stained, and he was trembling.

The pearl handprint locked to his face was, of course, pristine. It was actually rather lovely, in a horrible sort of way. Still, as it was, he would never be able to go out in public without a mask or something—it occupied too much of his face. She had to steel herself not to gag, knowing that she'd entombed one of his eyes away behind that shining substance. His other eye was bloodshot, filled with rage as it stared at her. The skin around the pearl was an angry mottled red—testament to the various measures the Murcutts had tried in an effort to remove the mark. When he'd opened his mouth to swear at her, the skin had puckered and bunched in a way that looked painful.

"Johnny, Miss Caswell has agreed to remove the brand from your face," Miss Murcutt said pointedly.

"It'll be good as new," agreed Bridget. "Well, as good as it was before." *Christ, I hope he had his eye closed under my hand.* His skin would probably be fine, but she couldn't imagine that having pearl bound to an eye would do it any good.

"You want to let her put her witch hands on me *again?*" asked John incredulously.

"Oh, that's lovely," said Bridget.

"We've come to an arrangement, Johnny," said Tillie serenely. "And each of us understands that a failure to deliver on the arrangement will be very bad."

We didn't actually say that, thought Bridget, but she supposed the unspoken possibilities of disaster had made them both agree. She wasn't entirely certain how much she could trust the Murcutts, but if their deal could be kept to, it might make things much easier. And in the meantime, she'd be buying time for Usha, Pamela, and Wattleman to track her down.

"Will you need anything?" asked Tillie.

"Lots of clean water and some clean cloths," said Bridget. She was thinking of the oily residue that the denaturing produced. It wasn't actually harmful, but it would sting if it got into one's eyes. Also, she wanted to be able to make a show of wiping away the residue as she slowly dissolved the pearl. "Oh, and a cup of tea. And do you think you could maybe get some sandwiches?" She abruptly realized that she was starving.

"Eckersley," said Miss Murcutt simply, and the mustached man hurried out. Bridget took the opportunity to sit in an easy chair and examine the room around her. It was the room that they had fought in (was it only the night before?), but it looked very different, because cloth had been tacked up all over the walls—bedsheets, towels, some gorgeous pieces of expensive silk, as well as rags that had evidently been grabbed hastily. Swatches of material had also been loosely tacked to the ceiling, and they billowed and rippled slightly in the draft. In a narrow gap between a battered bath mat and what looked like a repurposed striped dressing gown, she could see that the hole in the roof had been hastily repaired, with planks hammered down. She presumed that the floor had been similarly repaired, but she could see no sign of it because a mass of carpets had been laid all over, so there was no glimpse of the polished wooden floor. It looked so warm and delightful that she gave a moment's thought to kicking off her shoes and peeling off her socks just to feel the lush softness on her feet.

She wasn't sure, since so many of the pieces overlapped, but she thought there might be some genuinely exquisite tapestries on the walls and floors as well. It all combined to give the air of a patch-work tent.

Of course, this is all for the benefit of Vincent, she realized, *giving him ammunition and warning if any invisible men come creeping about.* She looked around and saw Vincent himself sitting in the same corner he'd occupied last time. They nodded at each other warily. *If things had worked out otherwise, you'd be my colleague. And what will become of you now?*

She had not thought to bargain with Tillie Murcutt on the future of her powered henchman, and she did not expect much could be agreed to on that score, least of all by Vincent. And yet, the Checquy was not likely to look favorably on the prospect of a supernatural thug enforcing his mistress's will in the West End.

That will have to be someone else's problem, she decided. *My immediate problems are, well, much more immediate.*

The other man who had abducted her—Gethings, the grubby one who'd been so eager with the knife—stood by the door. As they entered, they'd also passed a burly man standing guard outside. Gethings had greeted him as "Reg."

Well, I wasn't planning on making a break for it, thought Bridget, *but it's definitely not an option now.* She was aware of her homemade pearl dagger tucked away in the waistband of her skirt. If they were to discover it, what would happen? *Perhaps nothing,* she thought. *They really want John's face cleaned.* Still, it was reassuring to have it, just in case the Murcutts were not as trustworthy as she was.

A meal was brought that turned out to be outstanding. It was all she could do not to bolt it down. Excellent ham and tomatoes on fresh bread with butter. An orange! A couple of hard-boiled eggs. A block of chocolate. Bridget shot a look at Tillie Murcutt, who smiled a lazy cat-in-the-cream smile back.

Say what you like about black marketeers, they do have the best food.

For a moment, it occurred to her that the meal might be poisoned, but she dismissed the idea. They still wanted something from her and would not take that risk. *Plus, even if poison is traditionally a woman's tool, I get the feeling that Tillie Murcutt's weapon of choice is a thug.*

After Bridget had finished her meal and enjoyed her tea (with two lumps of sugar, just because they were there to be had), she turned her attention to her patient.

"Are you ready, then?" Bridget asked Johnny.

"Yes," he said. She saw how afraid he was; there was a horrible tension in his jaw, and all the cords in his neck were standing out.

"Settle yourself on the sofa," she told him. "This will take a while, so you might as well be comfortable." She drew a chair up next to him and took off her gloves. He flinched at the sight of her mother-of-pearl palms. "How did you think this was going to happen?" she asked. "Did you think I was going to lick it off?"

"Will it hurt?"

"I'll be as careful as I can," she said. "Now, just lie back, close your eye, and think of England."

As it turned out, it was almost as tiring to make an easy job look difficult as it was to do an actual difficult job. Matters were helped a little when John flinched violently at her first touch. Despite every inclination she possessed, she actually had to take the time to calm him down, placing her hand gently on his shoulder until he was sufficiently accustomed to her that she could move her other hand onto the pearl demi-mask.

Okay, now, you better make this look good.

Bridget closed her eyes, took a deep breath, and bowed her head. She then proceeded to do absolutely nothing for a good five minutes, during which she grew increasingly bored.

Finally, she could stand it no more and set about denaturing a tiny amount of the pearl. *Easy now,* she told herself. *Not too much to begin with or they'll get inconvenient expectations.* When she'd excavated a tiny divot with a fingertip, she drew back, breathing hard.

"What's wrong?" asked John, opening his eye in panic. "Is it not working?"

"It's working," said Bridget. "But it's not easy." Tillie came over to look.

"All right," she said. "It looks like you can actually deliver." She held up a hand mirror so that her brother could see the tiny amount of progress that had been made. "See, Johnny?" He nodded, and a tear leaked out of his free eye.

"And then back to it," said Bridget, ostentatiously stretching her arms and wiping away the minuscule amount of residue from his face with a towel. She bent her head down and, rather than directing her efforts to the task that was literally at hand, reviewed everything she'd need to do if she ever got back to the office.

I'll need to finish that brief on the internment of the refugee teenage males, she was thinking several minutes later. *Lady Carmichael is not going to be*—*oh, right. It's probably time to make some more progress on this chap's face.* And she dissolved another tiny portion of the pearl.

She fell into a routine, focusing on her breathing, trying to think of ways for her, Pamela, and Usha to track down the Nazi once this mission was completed, and, every once in a while, denaturing a little more pearl.

With every hour that passes, our chances of finding that Nazi get worse and worse. What are we going to do? Meanwhile, the Checquy search team can only be getting closer, since he's leaving murdered criminals all around the town. It's really too bad that he couldn't have decided to kill a couple of Murcutts. That would have cleared our schedule right up.

Even though she was not actually doing anything, it was quite a meditative process, so she only distantly heard the knock on the door and did not look up to see who came in.

"Miss Murcutt?" said a man's diffident voice. "There are a couple of women downstairs asking to see you."

"Are they looking for work?" asked Tillie languidly. She was sitting in an easy chair, a glass of sherry in one hand, reading a book. "What do they look like?"

"Um, well, they're both quite healthy-looking. And one of them is Indian, rather lovely."

Bridget tried not to react. *Oh, here we go.* But she didn't look up from the nothing she was doing.

"But I don't think they're here looking for a job," said the man. "They said they had business with you."

"That sounds interesting. Bring them to the office downstairs, I'll meet them there." She stood up gracefully.

Things are about to happen, so be prepared. The problem was that she didn't know *what* might happen. It was entirely possible that Pamela and Usha (it had to be them) would decide to take a professional, diplomatic approach and explain that they had some questions about the well-being of their colleague Miss Caswell, and they could easily bring the whole damn building down if they weren't satisfied with the answers. If they all kept their heads, in just a few minutes the two of them could be joining Bridget for sandwiches after ratifying her negotiations with Miss Murcutt.

It was equally possible that their arrival was just a distraction and that at any minute Wattleman was going to burst through the ceiling and tear Vincent's head off.

So, if there's a loud noise, you duck and get out of the way.

And if there are more sandwiches, you make sure you get one of the ones with the tomatoes.

Bridget waited, growing increasingly tense, and became so distracted that she forgot herself and liquefied a good-size patch of pearl off John Murcutt's face without meaning to. The door opened and, despite herself, she ducked her head a little.

"As you can see, she's quite well," Tillie Murcutt was saying.

It looks like they took the soft approach.

"Yes," said Pamela coolly. She ignored the wary men around the room and stalked over to the couch where John was lying. Her hand came down firmly on Bridget's shoulder and she gave a comforting squeeze. "I suppose this looks acceptable. Miss Caswell, *are* you quite well?"

"Yes, thank you," said Bridget cautiously.

"Good. Miss Murcutt has explained the deal you two have made. It's not how we would normally do things, but the terms sound quite reasonable, actually."

"Although the amount you have promised for the objects is ridiculous," said Usha. Bridget rolled her eyes at her.

"Market forces," said Bridget dryly. "If Miss Murcutt gets her fair profit, then there won't be any hurt feelings." Usha sniffed.

"The terms have been agreed to," said Pamela, and she sounded a little amused. "And we will adhere to them." She looked down at John Murcutt's face. "I think you could make a bit more progress, though."

"I'll do my best," said Bridget. The message was clear: *It's obvious you've been delaying this, but now you can hurry up so we can go on with other matters.*

"Excellent," said Tillie. "So we're all going to be as courteous as possible, and everyone will end up satisfied."

"Indeed," said Usha.

"Won't you please take a seat?" asked Tillie.

"No," said Usha and Pamela simultaneously, although only Pamela ended it with "Thank you." They exchanged looks.

"Suit yourselves." Tillie shrugged and settled back into her chair. "Can I offer you some sandwiches?"

"No," said Usha and Pamela simultaneously. This time both of them added, "Thank you."

"Yes," said Bridget. Everyone looked at her. "Trust me, they're good," she told her friends.

Tillie smiled. "Gethings, can you have some more sandwiches sent up, please? And ask Hans to come in while you're gone." *She wants to keep us matched in numbers,* mused Bridget. *Or outnumbered, if you count her and her brother. We may be politely discussing sandwiches, but no one's trusting anyone completely just yet.*

"Yes, miss." He went out.

"You have quite a few staff members," remarked Pamela.

"We're always on the lookout for talent," said Tillie. "And the war throws up all sorts of unexpected opportunities."

"Indeed," said Pamela.

There was a knock at the door and Tillie called, "Come!" The door opened, and a dark-haired man came in.

It was the Nazi.

"You!" spat Pamela. The cloths hanging around the room snapped as a wind suddenly swirled through it.

"Die Hexe!" snarled the man in shock. There was suddenly a knife in his grip.

So much for everyone being courteous, thought Bridget. Under her hand, John was sitting up, but she pushed his face down. "I think you and I should just stay out of this," she told him. He started to struggle, but she had taken out her dagger and now put it to his throat. Abruptly, he saw the sense of what she was saying.

"Hans, stop!" Tillie's command cut through the air with such authority that the Nazi paused. She had stood up from the chair, her empty glass held loosely in her hand.

"That man," said Pamela, pointing at him, "has to die." The atmosphere in the room changed again as everyone took in this new demand.

"Now you're trying to change the deal?" said Tillie. "Who is he to you?"

"He's a Nazi," Pamela said. "That should be enough. And his death is nonnegotiable."

"He's one of my people," Tillie said. "I don't just let my people get killed on some bint's say-so." Bridget had the impression that she was stating this as much for the benefit of her own men as to set Pamela straight on the facts.

Bridget could guess how Pamela would reply, but she never got the chance, because the German airman was already rushing toward the Pawn, his knife held low and his face a rictus of hate.

"Hans, no!" shouted Tillie, but this time it made no difference.

Oh, bugger.

Pamela did not hesitate. She moved with the sharp, staccato expertise of a trained boxer, stepping toward him and snapping her arm forward as if throwing a punch, even though he was still several feet away from her. There was a wild rushing sound as all the air in the room was sucked to a point behind her and then roared ahead to slam into the man and send him flying back against the wall. He slid down into a pile on the floor. Bridget couldn't tell whether he was dead or unconscious.

Christ, she thought dazedly. It was nowhere near the full power that she knew Pamela could muster, but it had been stunning. Everyone was gasping, desperately drawing in the air that had expanded itself back through the room. Several of the cloths that had festooned the walls and ceiling had been torn down.

Bridget was awed that, despite all Pamela's rage and hate for the Nazi, she had still shown tight, calculated restraint. If the Pawn had called on all her power, she could easily have killed everyone in the room.

She has so much self-control, she thought weakly. *So much discipline. So what made her bring that plane down?*

The air around them sighed as Pamela moved out of fighting posture to stand regally in the center of the room. Usha moved closer to join her. Everyone was still, staring wide-eyed at the two of them.

Everyone except Vincent. Bridget couldn't tell if Tillie had planned this or if he was acting on his own initiative, but suddenly, every loose scrap of cloth around the room writhed and flung itself toward Pamela and Usha. It was a rainbow chaos, dizzying to see, with streaks of crimson, blue, gray, beige, green, brown, yellow darting sinuously through the air. A strip of calico slapped Bridget's head as it whipped past, and despite herself, she yelped in pain. A bedsheet flapped wildly and actually tore under the strain of being hurled across the room.

Bridget caught a glimpse of Pamela before she and Usha were hidden by the torrent of fabric converging on them. Usha had ducked her head and thrown her hands up to protect her face. The Pawn's fists were clenched at her sides, but there was no sign of any other tension on her part.

And then they were lost to view as pieces of cloth spun wildly around, rippling in and out like a swarm of fish attacking again and again, circling their prey—a wall of movement.

What is Vincent doing? Bridget squinted, trying to work out what she was seeing. Was the material whipping them, flaying them? She had seen Vincent use his abilities before. If he had the strength to imprison and strangle Henry Wattleman, then he could easily do it to Usha and Pamela.

What do I do now? she thought frantically. She looked around. Tillie Murcutt was coming out of a crouch. She, along with everyone else, had instinctively ducked when the air filled with flying strips of material. The two men—Eckersley and Gethings, who had come in right behind the Nazi—were standing back warily. Bridget couldn't blame them—the strips of fabric were snapping through the air like whips.

Vincent had come out of his chair and, standing rigid, he was staring intently at the maelstrom of fabric. His teeth were bared, and she could see perspiration all over his face.

He's not succeeding! she realized, and she looked back to the center of the room. *I think I understand.*

Pamela must have created a ring of air around herself, a column that caught the material and swirled it into an almost solid spinning wall around her and Usha. Every square of cloth, every bolt of fabric was writhing, trying to push its way through. With the roar of the wind and the snapping of the cloth, the noise was hideous. No one dared to go near, or even move, as ragged bits of textile flailed out from the column. As they watched, the trailing end of a cherry-pink strip of cotton was flung out and scythed through a brass lamp, briskly decapitating it.

The cyclone seemed to contract and expand unevenly, and Bridget realized that she was seeing Pamela's and Vincent's abilities struggling against each other. The two powers were so different and the situation so bizarre that it was difficult to tell who was winning.

Oh God, thought Bridget suddenly. *Is Pamela holding back for fear of hurting me? Or is Vincent that good?*

"Stay down," she said directly into John Murcutt's ear. "If you don't move, I swear that I will fix your face. If you move from this couch, I swear I'll leave you worse than you can believe." His eye squinched shut again, and the man jerked his head in a nod. She guided his hand up to the wooden back of the sofa and closed her hand around his wrist and then the wood. She had welded a cuff to lock him to the furniture. "I will come back."

Unless I die doing this.

And then she was moving toward Vincent and leaping at him, gripping her dagger in her hand. Vincent was so intent on the maelstrom in the middle of the room that he saw her only at the last minute, when she was already slashing at his stomach. He flinched, and his clothes rippled and flailed out at her. She felt the beginning of a tug against her arm as her sleeve tightened, but he was too late to stop her dagger from cutting him deeply.

He shouted in pain and clutched at the red line that was seeping and expanding across his now-sliced-open shirt. Bridget drew back the dagger and saw blood beading on its glistening white surface. She shot a look behind her. The column of swirling cloths was collapsing, and so was Pamela. The Pawn's head was bowed, she was gasping for breath, and her clothes were drenched with sweat. Usha was holding up her friend, whom Bridget could see was actually trembling from exertion.

Around the room, everyone else was still frozen, gaping at this development. The Nazi continued to lie slumped against the wall where Pamela had flung him.

Bridget met Tillie Murcutt's eyes, which were narrowed in frantic recalculation. *Yeah, your Nazi is down, and your supernatural weapon is bleeding out on your carpet. So much for our cordial and profitable negotiation.* She was a little surprised that Vincent hadn't thought to yank said carpet out from under Pamela's and Usha's feet. *Or even tried to take control of their clothes.* Still, perhaps with all the material festooning the room, he'd been caught up in the sheer volume of his weaponry. *And after he'd committed himself to using it, he couldn't break off the struggle in case Pamela killed him instantly.*

Speaking of which, you now have to neutralize Vincent. The man was too much of a threat. If he was removed from the equation, they would be in much the stronger position. Did that mean killing him? Bridget had never actually killed anyone, but she knew that she could do it if she needed to. She turned back to him. He had fallen to the floor and was whimpering and clutching at his bleeding stomach. *I really don't think he's going to be able to focus his attention on anything except trying to re-embowel himself,* she decided.

"Bridget!" Usha barked suddenly. "Look out!" An acrid smell exploded in her nostrils, so strong that she started coughing and choking. A strong hand closed on her shoulder and pulled her back violently. She spun and twisted in its grip. She had the impression of a large dark shape in front of her but before she could take in what she was seeing, her empty hand was already slapping hard against a strange, dense surface—not flesh! Not cloth!—and she could feel herself leaving streaks of pearl; she brought her other hand around and stabbed deep and hard with her dagger. The substance gave beneath her blade and then she shoved herself back. The shape was immovable, but she wanted to get some space to take in what she was seeing.

It was roughly humanoid, and large. It resembled nothing so much as a man-shape hewn out of dark gray-black-brown clay. But there were fibers running through it. Its face bore only the faintest trace of features: a lump of nose and indentations where eyes should be. The hands were crude, without fingers and with only a flap of a thumb on each one. The overpowering smell coming off the thing, rich and bitter and rank, was somehow familiar. Bridget was reminded of the whisky one of her masters used to drink on a Sunday evening.

Peat?

Then she noticed the broad, patterned orange tie that was hanging absurdly around its approximation of a neck. The rest of the man's clothes lay ripped apart on the floor.

Eckersley, thought Bridget weakly. *The man with the gun who took me from the parlor. How many supernatural children did old Mother Murcutt deliver and keep secret?*

The Eckersley thing moved after her. It glanced at Usha and Pamela, but Bridget could see it dismiss them, for which she could hardly blame it. Pamela was leaning heavily on Usha and taking in deep breaths of air; she couldn't even keep her head up. Usha was devoting all her attention to keeping her friend from collapsing to the floor. They did not appear to be threats, while Bridget had just removed Vincent from the equation and also just buried her dagger up to the hilt in the peat-man's equivalent of a stomach.

It moved forward after her, and with every movement, it released more of that pungent smell. As it stepped heavily, little puffs of dust rose from it, and then it loomed above her.

Its hand snatched out, much faster than she expected, but she was fast enough to dodge it. And then again, one hand striking after the other, and she twisted back and to the side until it was off balance, and she could duck under its arm to put herself between it and Usha and Pamela.

The situation was not ideal. Pamela and Usha were at one end of the room, with Bridget between them and the hulking mass of this sudden peat-Eckersley. The peat-Eckersley in question stood between her and the door, which Tillie Murcutt was blocking, with Gethings at her side.

And there were various noncombatants scattered about the place: the whimpering Johnny cuffed to his sofa, the Nazi slumped senseless against a wall, and Vincent curled on the ground in his corner, his attention focused on whatever damage she'd managed to inflict on his belly.

We can't stay here, thought Bridget. *If we wait, just holding them off, she'll summon more soldiers. Even if they aren't supernatural, there's only so much we can do.*

But I think we can get out. There's three of us, even if Pamela is almost exhausted. And the Murcutts have only this, admittedly very large, peat-man. If we can get past him, Tillie can't stop us. She stepped back, her dagger ready, and she was about to call to Usha and Pamela when Tillie

Murcutt shouted, "Eckersley, stop!" The peat figure paused. "Gethings, show them what you can do."

Bridget's other onetime escort stepped forward from the door.

She was tense; there was no telling what might happen when unworldly powers were unlimbered.

As she watched, Gethings's eyes went flat and his body split in two lengthwise.

"Oh, what the *hell?*" Bridget shouted.

It wasn't a clean, surgical division. The skin tore itself apart with a wet ripping sound. Dark blue liquid sprayed across the room as the two halves fell away from each other. Instead of viscera trailing out along the floor, the interior of the halves appeared to be filled with long, black, glistening fibers.

Each of the skins twisted and stretched, inverting itself and pushing those fibers up and out to flop down around the limbs in a great mass. They were feathers. The fragments of clothes that remained puddled around the wrists and ankles ripped, and, with a chittering sound, the skin of the arms and feet fell away in a flurry of flakes to reveal two long, leathery gray-black legs. Each leg ended in three toes with long, razor-sharp claws.

From each mass of black feathers, an electric blue neck with an angry pink wattle curled up to a black-beaked head surmounted by a bony half-circle crest. Red-brown eyes stared out.

Two large birds, each about six and a half feet tall, paused, regarding Bridget. Bridget could not take her eyes off those dreadful claws.

They're like goddamn battle... ostriches? she thought. She had never seen anything like them, not even at the zoo. *What I am going to do?* If she got close enough to slash one with her dagger, she would be within range of the clawed feet. *I don't know how to fight a fucking bird, let alone two of them.*

As she agonized, the two birds strutted over to flank Eckersley, whose peat-form seemed entirely reasonable at this point. The Gethings-things looked like they should be slow and lumbering, but as they moved, their latent strength and speed was almost palpable. She swung her head back and forth, painfully aware that she couldn't keep both of them in her line of sight.

The two birds were now directly opposite each other with Bridget in the middle. The peat-man loomed in front of her.

Fine, so the balance has shifted, she thought. *Now's the time for us all to take a breath, acknowledge the situation, and revise our expectations.* "Maybe it's not too late to return to our original deal?" suggested Bridget.

"I think we're past that possibility," said Tillie. "Now, lads, I don't want the Irish girl killed. And both her hands need to remain attached. Or at least one, please." Bridget shot her a look, and the woman shrugged, a little regretfully. Their deal was now dead, and it seemed entirely possible that Bridget, Pamela, and Usha would be joining it.

The peat-thing took a lumbering step toward her, and the streaks of pearl she'd left sealed to its stomach caught her eye. As she watched, it raised a hand and carelessly scraped them off, pulling out divots of itself, which promptly filled up with more peat. The deep cut that she'd gashed into it sealed up wetly without a trace.

I don't like the look of this.

Evidently, neither did Usha. "Bridget, get here!"

Bridget dodged the thing, which was reaching out for her, and scurried back to the other two. One of the birds made some sort of threatening cawing noise behind her. She hopped over the piled-up ring of cloth around her comrades.

"Here, you help Pamela," said Usha. Bridget hurriedly took the Pawn's arm over her shoulder and nearly collapsed herself under the unexpected weight. Pamela was barely standing on her own feet. *Usha must have been using her abilities to help hold her up.*

Usha stepped forward, taking up position between Pamela and Bridget on one side and the advancing forces of two demented killer birds and the shambling peat-figure on the other. Bridget bit her lip— Usha's power was potentially much more devastating than her own, but she'd never actually been in real combat.

But I don't see any other options, Bridget thought. Her knife and her touch would not be enough, not when the peat-Eckersley could just ignore them.

"How are you?" Bridget asked Pamela in a low voice.

"Drained" came the weary reply. She realized that Pamela was utterly exhausted from her struggle with Vincent. *Plus, how much sleep has she had over the past few days?* Taking into account the horrendous exertion of bringing down the Nazi plane, the continuous work, the late-night meetings with the Court, the loss and recovery of her best friend, and the ongoing stress of hunting the Nazi, it was a miracle the Pawn was awake at all.

The peat-man lumbered toward them. At the same time, the two birds approached more swiftly, one on each side of the room. One of them moved purposefully toward Usha so that, when her attention was caught by it, the other could dash past her to Bridget and Pamela.

"Fuck off!" Bridget spat at it and slashed out with her dagger. It was awkward, not just because she was supporting her friend, but because she doubted she could get close enough to stab the gigantic murderous fowl. The bird danced back, its claws clicking on the now mostly bare wooden floor.

The peat-man reached out toward Usha, and Usha reached back. Just her fingertip touched it, but that was all she needed. The thing froze, its head cocked in a humanizing moment of confusion.

And then something began to happen.

A lump of peat came tumbling up and over the thing's shoulder. It was rough, irregular, as if it had torn itself loose from the creature's back. It rolled down the creature's arm to its hand, which Usha's out-stretched finger was still touching.

At the sight of it, the bird-thing that had been menacing Usha stepped back cautiously. Even though it had a beak, Bridget thought she could see an expression of uncertainty on its face. It was afraid to approach her and take advantage of her distraction.

And then more and more peat came loose, like an avalanche. Chunks wrenched themselves out of the thing's shoulders, chest, legs, and stomach, some rushing up the creature's body and some flinging themselves through the air toward Usha's fingertip. But it was not just pieces. The creature's body was almost liquefying in its haste to come apart. Peat came coursing along in frantic rivulets, carving furrows in the creature's substance, all converging.

The peat-man's head collapsed, and the stuff of it was sucked down into its torso. There was no sound as the being crumpled in on itself, growing smaller, inexorably compressing to that point. It was as if it were being drained into a funnel to somewhere else. And then it was lost to sight.

Usha turned to Tillie holding up a perfectly round, smooth sphere the size of a golf ball. Tillie opened her mouth to say something and then closed it. She pursed her lips, and Bridget realized that the woman was looking behind them.

Oh, hell, what now? Bridget was turning to see when the floor was jerked out from under them.

At least, that's what it felt like. Bridget, Usha, and Pamela were sent sprawling. The breath was punched out of Bridget as she landed flat on her back. The carpet they lay on slithered and undulated.

Vincent.

Winded, wheezing, she sat up as best she could and twisted to look at the corner where she'd left him bleeding and clutching his innards. He wasn't dead. He wasn't seated against the wall. Instead, he was standing, sort of. A tangle of strips had torn themselves up from the carpet beneath him to lift him up. She could see that his very clothes were rigid, and he slumped within them, supported by his own will and power.

His blood-soaked shirt was cinched around his midriff, stanching the bleeding from the wound she'd given him. His face was ghastly pale from blood loss, and his eyes were horrible, filled with rage, and fixed on her. He made a sharp, twisting gesture with his hand, and with a gasp Bridget felt her clothes constricting around her. Usha and Pamela made sounds as they felt their garments clamp around them.

"I'll kill you," he snarled at Bridget.

"Vincent, just hold her!" shouted Tillie, but he seemed not to hear her. The birds made a cautious step toward the pinned women, but strips ripped up from the carpet and waved about them threateningly, like tentacles. "Christ, don't kill her!" He didn't acknowledge Tillie's order at all but stared into Bridget's eyes.

The other lads don't stay back when Vincent's at work just because he's supernatural, Bridget thought weakly. *They stay back because he might kill them!*

"I'll crush you to a *pulp!*" he said through gritted teeth. The loathing dripped from his voice, and since she had just cut his belly open, she couldn't blame him. It was the sort of thing that *she* would have taken personally. She felt the breath being squeezed out of her; her muscles twisted and rib bones flexed as her blouse and skirt grew tighter and tighter around her. The material wouldn't let her fall—it held her up painfully. Her dagger fell from her hand as the world started to go dark at the edges.

Usha was facedown on the carpet, unmoving. The ball that had been Eckersley had rolled away from her limp fingers. Half lying on Bridget's legs, where she'd fallen, Pamela was bent at a painful angle by the force that held her, but she was awake, trying to gasp in air. Perhaps it was her abilities, or perhaps it was because Vincent's attention was focused on slowly crushing Bridget and keeping the others pinned, but somehow, Pamela managed to draw in a breath and shout. It boomed through the room.

"Henry! Northeast!"

What the fuck does that mean? Bridget thought, nonplussed even through the pain.

Apparently, what the fuck that meant was instructions, because there was an earsplitting crash, and part of a wall burst in as if struck by a wrecking ball. Dust and plaster exploded everywhere, and Bridget caught a glimpse of Wattleman rushing through the chaos. Even in the dizzying suddenness of it, she had time to notice wearily that he was, inevitably, naked.

Wattleman did not hesitate but headed directly to the—yes, the northeast corner, where Vincent was still half crouched and shielding his face from the detritus of the Pawn's entry. Bridget was distantly aware that her clothes had relaxed around her and that she was drawing in delicious breath, but her eyes were fixed on the naked man bearing down on Vincent like a force of nature. The supernatural gangster started to raise a hand, but Wattleman caught him up, slammed him against the wall, and plowed forward with all his monstrous strength.

It was not clear who in the room was screaming—it was more a case of who was not screaming. Bridget certainly was. Vincent *certainly* was. She caught a glimpse of his mouth open and his eyes gaping as the wall cracked and fell apart under the unstoppable force of

Pawn Henry Wattleman. And then the two men were falling through the hole and out into the world below. She saw the soles of their feet flailing in the air — Vincent's leather shoes were kicking madly while Wattleman's bare feet were already blurring into invisibility.

The room fell into a shocked silence, which meant that they could all hear Vincent's wails followed by a sickening thump.

There were sounds of surprise and distress from the street.

Did — did that just happen? wondered Bridget dazedly. It had taken only a few seconds but had been just as astonishing as the previous evening's transit of the bomb had been. Only with more arse-cheeks.

He couldn't have come in earlier? she thought. Except that they had already learned that Vincent could be a match for Wattleman. Pamela would, of course, have had a plan to ensure that when he struck, it would be most effectively.

Usha was the first of the Checquy women to recover. Bridget had thought she was unconscious, but it seemed that Vincent's powers were just keeping her pinned to the floor. She pushed herself up and rose so lightly that she actually floated in the air for a moment before landing elegantly on her feet. Bridget could have sworn she sensed a ripple of weight and force go out from her friend. Usha put her hand down on Pamela's arm, lifted her easily, and slung her over her shoulder.

Then Bridget felt Usha close her fingers on the back of her shirt, and as the birds suddenly darted forward, her stomach flipped, and they were all three falling up to the ceiling. Usha was already twisting in the air, knowing how to keep herself upright, but Bridget had no idea which way was down, and she flailed madly in Usha's grip as one of the birds launched itself a good three feet into the air, kicking out with those horrible talons and shredding through her swirling skirt. The other bird was also in the air, kicking high, and its talon swiped her arm. She could feel her skin open like cloth under a sword, and she screamed.

"Oh God," Bridget whimpered as she clutched her wounded arm to her chest. Her back hit the ceiling hard enough to crack the plaster. She watched fragments of the ceiling fall up — no, down — no, *up* to the floor, where the two monster birds circled. Usha hadn't landed as gracefully as she usually did, and one of her feet twisted painfully on the ceiling, sending her to her knees. Droplets of Bridget's blood dripped up into the air to splatter on the floor.

"What—what now?" said Bridget. Usha opened her mouth to answer, but then a look of fear flashed onto her face, and the room boomed with a sudden gunshot. A small hole punched into the plaster right by them, and dust puffed out of the ceiling that was now their floor. They turned to look up at a man, someone new to the party. Bridget recognized him as Reg, who'd been standing guard outside the door, which was now open. He was positioned defensively in front of Tillie Murcutt, who was still standing by the door. He had a pistol raised and was carefully sighting at them.

"Don't shoot if there's any risk of hitting the Irish girl," Murcutt said. Reg's eyes narrowed, and his arm was still.

Oh, good, yet another goon. And he appears to have the supernatural power of owning a gun. "Usha!" Bridget shouted in warning, but her friend was already taking action.

Gravity changed again, and the ceiling was suddenly a ramp sloping steeply to the far side of the room. Usha, Pamela, and Bridget started sliding madly, uncontrolled, as if they were going backward down a long broad slide, tumbling over each other, and Usha twisting to keep a hold of the other two. But it wasn't fast enough, because Reg was following them with his gun, firing repeatedly and making holes in the ceiling around them. Tillie was shouting something, but it was lost in the sound of the gunshots. The ramp grew steeper, almost vertical, and they bounced off it and came back down to the ceiling.

Then Usha screamed, and Bridget felt a spray of heat on her face. Usha was bleeding from her shoulder, where she had been shot. She instinctively clutched at her wound, which meant that she let go of Bridget and Pamela.

Suddenly they were both falling up, or down, to the birds, but Usha managed to snag Bridget's collar and haul her back, though she gave a little scream of pain while doing so.

Pamela, however, continued to fall. She flailed frantically in the air and then was suddenly spinning tightly; she landed in a crouch the right way up. She must have used her power to bring herself around. She looked up as the two birds pranced warily toward her. Clearly they were unsure what Pamela might do.

The gunshots had ceased and so, too, for the moment, had that mad slide along the ceiling. *What's happening?* Bridget thought frantically. She looked up to see that Tillie had a gun to Reg's neck.

"Damn it, Reg, I *told* you not to shoot!" she was shouting. "You could have hit her!"

"Miss Tillie, if your brother were here—" the man began.

"Bob is *not* here! And you work for all of us! And I will get us what we want if everyone can calm down."

Looks like there's a disagreement between management and labor, thought Bridget. *So we have a moment.*

She looked down and saw that Pamela was kneeling on the ground, the birds circling around her. Bridget's ears rang from the gunshots, and her pulse hammered in her skull, but she could still hear a faint throbbing sound and caught a glimpse of blurred motion around Pamela. One of the birds approached, almost tentatively, and as its beak touched that blur, Bridget heard a distinct little *tic!* and saw the bird's head get slapped away.

Pamela's spun up another little cyclone around herself. But how long can she keep it up?

Meanwhile, Usha was taking swift, panicked breaths. One hand was still pressed against the bullet wound in her shoulder. The other was clenched in the cloth of Bridget's shirt.

"Let me see, Usha," said Bridget firmly. She'd received some training in battlefield medicine, although none of it had considered exactly this scenario. The injured woman gingerly took her hand away, and Bridget tore the collar of the dress to reveal the wound. Blood was pumping out briskly. She looked at the back of Usha's shoulder and took a breath. "The bullet went through completely. But I need to stop the bleeding." *Or else you'll pass out and we'll fall to the floor.*

"Brace yourself," Bridget said. She lifted her hand and saw, with a faint sense of surprise, that it was dripping with her own blood. In fact, her sleeve was completely soaked in blood, and crimson drops were trickling down her fingertips and falling up to the floor. She abruptly realized that the horrible cut from the bird's talons was killingly painful. The piled-on madness of falling up to the ceiling, getting dropped and caught, and sliding along while being shot at had served to distract her from her wound, but now it was demanding her attention.

I'd better take care of myself too, she thought, light-headed. *But first...* She wiped her hand on her skirt and then pressed down hard with her palm on the front wound on Usha's shoulder to seal a pearl handprint across it. Usha hissed. "And now I have to do the other side."

When it was done, she was not at all certain that her efforts would be enough, but it was all she could think of for the moment. She tore back her sleeve and the wet cloth peeled painfully away from the long cut in her arm. It was a merciless wound, and she couldn't help but whimper as she clenched her hand over the ragged edges of her skin and sealed them together with her power.

Finally, she could take in a breath, and she looked about. There were streaks of blood on the plaster of the ceiling where her arm had dragged along. The two birds were prowling in a wide circle around Pamela, and the Murcutt siblings were staring at the Checquy operatives, the sister with her usual considering gaze and the brother with a look that suggested madness boiling away behind his eye.

"Gethings, kill that bitch on the ground!" Johnny Murcutt shouted suddenly. One of the birds turned its head to Pamela, still crouched weakly on the floor.

"No!" exclaimed Usha and Bridget. Strangely, Tillie Murcutt shouted it too.

"Do it now," he said. "And Reg, shoot the Indian one on the roof!"

"Johnny, shut your damn face!" shouted his sister. She and Reg both had their pistols down at their sides now.

"We'll *make* the other one clean my face! I know how to break a woman." He stared up at Bridget with his single eye.

My God, he's completely cracked, thought Bridget.

"*Do it!*" he shouted. "Kill them! Two hundred quid for each one!"

At his words, Reg started to bring his pistol up again, but Tillie Murcutt grabbed his arm and struggled to pull it down. Apparently she didn't want to shoot her own employee, either because it would change the balance of power or because it would be bad for morale.

Meanwhile, one bird took off running at Pamela with its strange bobbing gait.

"Pamela!" screamed Bridget, helpless on the ceiling. The Pawn brought up a hand, but the bird was moving too fast or she was too weak to maintain the strength of her shield, because it barreled through, knocking her onto her back. The other bird was already moving in, and it struck her in the side with a powerful, razor-sharp kick.

The Pawn screamed and pressed her hand to her side as the bird pranced back a few steps. The two creatures were clearly readying themselves for another attack, but through the exhaustion and pain, Pamela somehow managed to summon her powers again. The air in the room throbbed about them all, weirdly, nauseatingly, as if they were inside another creature. Everyone looked around, then madness erupted as a hundred different gusts of wind struck from all directions. It buffeted all of them back and forth, as if drawn in and out by a dozen giant bellows. The birds were sent staggering back, their claws scrabbling on the floor to stay upright. Tillie was thrown against the wall, and Reg, the man with the gun, had his feet swept out from under him and fell. His head cracked sickeningly against the corner of a table.

Pamela stood, untouched by the chaos she'd unleashed. Her hair and clothes were not blowing about — she was in an island of stillness, but she was swaying. Both hands were pressed hard against the wound in her side.

"Get me down there," Bridget said urgently into Usha's ear. "I have to help her." Usha's black hair was whipping about in the windstorm, but she heard and nodded. "But you stay here."

"What?" asked Usha. "What do you mean?"

"If you're up here, it gives us more flexibility," said Bridget. "We're spread out. Harder to corner." Really, though, her mind was on Usha's wound. Her friend was clearly depleted from the loss of blood.

"Fine. I'll swing you down." The two of them stood, hand in hand, and Bridget felt up become down, but she wasn't falling as much as gliding away from the ceiling. Suddenly she was swinging through the rushing winds to land awkwardly on her feet right by Pamela. The sudden stillness was startling as the Pawn stared at her, eyes wide. She was horribly pale.

"I'm here, Pamela. I'm here," Bridget said. "Just continue doing what you're doing with the air, it's keeping them back."

"I...I..."

"Yes, I know," said Bridget. "Let me see." She gritted her teeth and lifted away Pamela's blood-soaked hand to see the wound. It was a startlingly clean cut, but Bridget's stomach turned at the sight of the gore washing out of her. "Right, this will, um, yes." She gave a moment's thought to sliding her fingers inside and trying to seal off whatever damage had been done there, but she was afraid of making things worse. Her first-aid training had always focused on putting pressure on wounds, so she pressed her palm as flat as she could against Pamela's side. The pumping heat of the blood pouring onto her made her want to scream, but Pamela was already screaming as Bridget held her tight and pressed down mercilessly to release a smooth layer to seal the large gash.

"I'm sorry, I'm sorry, I'm so sorry," Bridget babbled. Pamela had sunk to her knees, moaning, but Bridget couldn't think about that. There was more that she needed to do. She pressed her hands against the pearl she'd laid down, putting extra pressure on the area and casting some more handprints to hold it all tight. She heaved a sigh. Pamela's torso was a mishmash of shining handprints and blood and cloth and strips of pearl, but it was all she could think to do.

For the first time in a while, she looked around. She realized that the wind had died. The birds had collected themselves and gotten to their feet. Tillie Murcutt had picked up Bridget's dagger from the floor, and her brother was still cuffed to the couch, shouting for someone to kill them. Reg lay utterly still where he had come to a rest. His eyes were open and blank. From her vantage point on the ceiling, Usha was crouched, breathing heavily, out of reach, and the large red stain across her dress was appalling.

This is desperate, Bridget thought. *Pamela is dying.* She knelt next to her friend. "Pamela, we need you," she said. "I'm sorry, but we need you." The Pawn was slumped on her knees, and her head actually lolled back; Bridget had to catch her. *Dead?* She laid her gently on the floor and stood up.

This might be it, she thought grimly. The birds were advancing toward them, predatory and inhuman. *I have no earthly idea what I'm going to do.* Her training in boxing, savate, baritsu, and bartitsu had prepared her for a variety of combat scenarios but, astoundingly, none of those martial arts seemed to account for the possibility of engaging in a melee with two large flightless birds.

She was horribly aware of their talons and the ease with which one of them had stabbed Pamela. She could all too easily picture her friend being briskly disemboweled or dismembered. For Bridget, Tillie Murcutt's command that she be left alive to remove the pearl from Johnny's face was all very well, but what would happen afterward?

And there's a distinct difference between leaving me alive and leaving me unharmed, Bridget thought. As far as the present criminal enterprise of Murcutt, Murcutt, Bird, and Bird knew, all she needed to clean up John's face was one working hand and the fear of horrible things being done to her. *I think I'm going to get really fucked up here,* she thought weakly.

"Usha!" she shouted to her friend on the ceiling. "Go! Save yourself! Get out of here—please!" Usha stared at her in astonishment. "Do it!" She couldn't bear the thought of none of them getting out of here. At least Usha might escape. She could punch her way through the ceiling and flee into the attic or fly out the hole that Wattleman had made in the wall and soar away in front of the public. One of them had to get away. "You can bring help!" she suggested, mostly as a spur to get her friend to leave. Help wasn't coming; she knew that.

Usha's face was a portrait of astonishment, and when Bridget saw tears pooling in her eyes, she almost wept herself. "It's fine. It's all right," said Bridget. "*Please* go. Please?"

Usha drew herself up until she was standing upside down on the ceiling. She winced a little as she straightened her shoulders. As far as

Bridget could tell from her inverted expression, there was a look of grim acceptance on her face.

Thank God, she thought. Whatever horrible thing was going to befall her and Pamela, she could bear it if she knew that Usha was free and safe.

I'm going to die.

I might be pregnant.

And then Usha fell from the ceiling.

It wasn't a tumble or an accident. Her will was propelling her, and she turned lightning-fast in the air and landed, crouched, on the back of one of the birds.

The bird made a sound unlike anything anyone had ever heard, a cawing scream, as Usha's power took hold of it and began to compress it the way that peat-man had been sucked into a point of unimaginable attraction. But the bird was not liquid or soil, it was a creature of flesh and bone and feathers and meat, so wet cracks appeared, blood sprayed out, and skin tore.

The other bird was shuddering. Bridget had no idea how Gethings's power worked. Was his mind spread over both birds? Clearly, there was some sort of link between the two, because these were not the tremors of fear. She could actually see the creature's little eyes rolling back in their sockets. It ruffled its feathers chaotically and pranced back and forth as if its legs did not know what to do.

Usha was standing on the floor now, and her face had an expression of merciless intensity that made Bridget's skin rise up into gooseflesh. Usha bore down with her hand on the creature's back, unrelenting, and her will and her powers crushed it. Its head flailed hideously, the neck trembling, and its legs sagged and went limp.

When the first bird gave a final scream, the untouched bird mirrored it, screaming out its own sound, and then went berserk, running and jumping about and pumping its head back and forth. No one dared move — they could only watch. It didn't attack them. It didn't seem to know what was happening or where it was. It crashed into the bar, ricocheted off John's couch, which sent him squealing in terror, then ran headfirst into a wall and fell down, still.

Usha took her hand off the first bird. She hadn't crushed it down to a sphere like the peat-man. She hadn't had to. The smell was atrocious as liquids seeped out of the dead thing.

Jaysus, thought Bridget weakly.

"*Now,* Miss Murcutt, we are going to discuss terms," said Usha, and it sounded like a declaration of war. "Drop the gun." The madam dropped the pistol, which Bridget had forgotten she even had.

I cannot wait to see how this plays out, thought Bridget.

"I would say that the circumstances are not in your favor," said Usha. To punctuate this observation, the uncrushed bird let out a final anguished screech and knocked the bar over onto itself.

"That's probably true," Tillie said dryly. "So . . . is it too late for a constructive renegotiation?"

"Yes," said Bridget.

"No," said Pamela weakly. All eyes turned to the Pawn, who was slowly getting to her feet. "There's still the possibility for this to work out."

"Pamela, you shouldn't move!" exclaimed Usha.

"We're going to get this settled," said Pamela. She was horribly pale. "We will be taking all the artifacts, and you will assist us in securing your source of them. *He*"—and here she nodded at the Nazi on the floor—"will die."

"Previously there was an agreement of payment," Tillie pointed out. Bridget had to acknowledge the woman's courage in the face of profound defeat.

"No payment. But you'll live. And Bridget will cleanse your brother's face." In the background, Johnny whimpered from his couch. Tillie was still, her eyes calculating.

"Fine," she said finally.

"Fine," Pamela said. "But first, Bridget, you will go get help. I am going to sit here with Usha and make sure that our hosts don't do anything abominably stupid." Bridget nodded and got to her feet.

Perhaps this will actually work out all right, she thought, and then her eye caught a flash of movement on the other side of the room.

It was the Nazi. He was rushing forward from the spot against the wall where he'd been flung. A knife flashed in his hand.

"No!" shrieked Bridget. "Oh no!" Pamela turned her head and

threw up her arm, but either the pain of her wounds was too great or she didn't have time to use her power. Nothing stopped the man from plunging his dagger into Pamela's chest.

The Pawn gasped and choked. She brought her hand up weakly to touch the man's hand as it held the dagger in her. For a moment, the man and the woman stared at each other, and what passed between them, Bridget could not understand.

Then she saw him set his jaw, and although he did not move, Pamela stiffened and threw back her head. She was dead, Bridget could see it, dead instantly, but he did not draw his knife out. Instead, bloodred electricity burst out of her wound, boiling out from around the hilt to wrap her in vermilion lightning and burn her corpse.

25

From behind her sunglasses, Lyn looked around carefully at the other occupants of the train carriage. There was a tension among the people of London, an air of wariness—any one of them might be a Checquy operative. Hell, all of them could be. Everyone was on edge, for which she could hardly blame them. The impossible, inexplicable spectacle of countless columns of lightning bursting up to the sky simultaneously had sent shivers of fear up the spine of everyone who saw it, including Lyn herself.

Lyn had spent the next day in Mandy's house again, afraid to go out except for a quick stroll with the labradoodle. She could only presume that, after the multitude of lightning eruptions around London, the Checquy would be out in force throughout the city looking for her. Before, the Court might have tried to keep the fact that she'd gone rogue a secret from the Pawns, but with every news, science, and religious organization talking nonstop about the strange red lightning, they must have had to acknowledge the situation. The rank and file would have drawn connections between Lyn's powers (and her absence) and the spectacle that had the whole nation transfixed.

Presumably, every site from which the lightning had erupted was now crawling with Pawns looking for clues. Any location of strategic importance would be guarded; every location that had anything to do with her personally would be staked out. Every camera in the ring of steel would be looking for her. So she'd stayed in Mandy's living room and read every news item about the lightning that popped up on the internet. Inevitably, none of the stories revealed anything concrete, and she'd been left no wiser about how she should proceed.

Then, that night, just before midnight, numerous lightning columns again blasted from various locations in London up into the sky. Once again they came from parks, churchyards, public gardens, heaths, commons, and playing fields—places away from buildings and streets, with no witnesses on the ground nearby.

Predictably, the world went ballistic.

Before, very few had voiced an opinion about the cause of the lightning. It was so unique and weird that most of the world had held its breath and waited to see what the scientists said. But they hadn't said much, and now the planet's inhabitants stopped keeping their opinions to themselves. People did not need expertise in the subject to have a theory. All they needed was an idea—preferably one that meshed with their already existing beliefs about the world—and the willingness to defend it with all their passion and outrage.

Every aspect of the lightning was seized upon as undeniable proof of a dozen different, conflicting explanations. According to scientists, the fact that the strikes were simultaneous showed that they had to be man-made, while a group of irritatingly photogenic (and thus popular on television) self-described "eco-insightists" who were obviously crazy (and thus even more popular on television) said that the simultaneity was the result of the Earth's natural rhythms and pulsations.

The police said that the multiple locations and the lack of any trace of equipment meant that if the lightning *was* man-made, it was by a highly organized group. The lack of property damage beyond a scorched ring-within-a-ring pattern at each site suggested it was some sort of prank or performance piece.

A group of neo-spiritualists said the multiple locations and the lack of any traces of equipment meant that if the lightning *was* man-made, it was obviously the work of druids. The lack of property damage suggested it was a warning to humanity, presumably because the druids did not have access to e-mail.

The lightning emerged away from buildings so there would be no witnesses, said some. No, it did that because they were the points on Mother Earth that were not sealed by man's concrete, cancerous cities, said others. No, it was because plants were generating the electricity as a result of a mutation from solar radiation, said yet a third group.

It was dragons. No, it was ley lines. No, it was climate change. No, it was terrorists. No, it was foreigners. No, it was the internet. No, it was some bloke I heard talking down the pub.

However, the crimson color of the lightning and the thrumming in her bones that the distant strikes produced left absolutely no doubt in Lyn's mind. It had to be the blond woman. But this knowledge only opened up a thousand more questions. How was she doing this? Had their battle given the blonde some insight into their powers that Lyn had missed? She clearly already had a better understanding of them than Lyn did—causing the lightning to crackle along the length of her sword was a trick that Lyn still could not do. Perhaps during all that fury and madness, as the energy had poured out of the two of them, the other woman had noticed something, some nuance, some sensation, and developed a new technique.

If it was the blonde—and it had to be—why was she doing it? Lyn had scoured the internet for news of more gangland killings but found nothing.

Is this directed toward me? Is she trying to call me out? But if so, what did she expect Lyn to do? All the locations of the lightning strikes had been obsessively mapped out by the media and then re-mapped out by various fanatics around the world. Lyn had looked them over and seen no pattern, no arrow pointing toward a proposed place of confrontation. *Maybe she's trying to drive me away, warn me off.*

Finally, there was the terrifying thought of all the energy it must be taking to create that lightning. Lyn *still* felt tired from her clash with the blonde, and that had been days ago.

If she's able to do this, she must be a hundred times stronger than me.

So what to do?

Lyn had little doubt that the Checquy would track down their quarry eventually. The question was, would it be the blonde or her? The blonde was the source, but they were looking for Lyn. Would it be easier for the Checquy to track her to Mandy's house than to find a woman they didn't know existed? She doubted they would give her a chance to explain before they executed her. And if they found the blonde first, what would happen then? Would they keep hunting Lyn? How would Lyn know if it was over?

Fuck it, thought Lyn finally. *I can't just stay here. Better to be out there looking for something than hiding here hoping for nothing.*

So, on with the wig, on with the shades, on with the makeup, and onto the Tube to the city. She knew that she couldn't go to the sites of the lightning columns, but she would put herself out into the world and see what she could see.

Despite her disguise, though, the old paranoia was back. Every person who looked at her was from the Checquy. She kept waiting for a hand to close on her shoulder, a Taser to shock her to the ground, a hypodermic needle to jab her briskly in the neck, or the Tube carriage and its occupants to fold away into green light as she was sucked into an emerald on someone's ring. But nothing happened—she was just one of many people looking around anxiously, uncertain how the world was going to go crazy today.

As she walked through the streets, she found herself moving away from other people and flinching at every sudden noise. And learning nothing. *This may have been a stupid idea,* she thought. *But I can't go back to approaching hoodlums and asking if they'd like protection.* Given that Pawn Seager had found her by staking out a criminal gang, she assumed that every major criminal enterprise in London was now being covertly observed by supernatural law-enforcement officers, all of whom were probably wondering why they were providing various unknowing criminals with a level of protection usually afforded only to leaders of the nation in times of major crisis.

Lyn had given up any hope of finding answers and was walking down Oxford Street toward the Tube station when she became aware of something. At first, it was lost in the rumble of the buses going by and the hubbub of the people hurrying down the street, but it grew stronger, a familiar sensation in her bones. That same pulsating thrumming that she'd felt when—

Jesus Christ, it's her!

Lyn looked around frantically for the blonde she was sure was coming at her, charging between the shoppers with a drawn samurai sword. *Where is she? Oh my God, oh my God.* Her hand was inside her coat, tight around her baton. *So where are you? Come on!*

Come on!

A beat.

Another beat.

Well?

Deadly assault utterly failed to materialize. The buzzing was still running through her, constant, but it wasn't growing as it had when the blonde had come at her. *Is she just standing somewhere?* Lyn became aware that she was poised in a combat stance in the middle of the footpath, teeth bared, while absolutely nothing happened except that foot traffic was parting around her, giving her the wary space one gave to a person about whom one was not quite sure. *What is going on?*

She straightened up from the battle crouch she'd automatically gone into and gave a mental tip of the hat to Pawn Fenton, whose grueling training sessions had apparently hardwired something resembling fighting instincts into her brain. She looked around uncertainly. That thrumming had to be coming from somewhere. Bewildered, she looked up into the sky for some sort of lightning display, but there was nothing.

Since the prospect of being cut to pieces did not appear to be quite as imminent as it had seemed several fraught moments ago, Lyn took a tremendous risk and closed her eyes.

The pulsation that shivered through her skin, through the *meat* of her, was real. It washed through her constantly, undeniably. It was like she was feeling someone else's heartbeat.

The sensation came from outside her, like a sound or a hot breeze, which meant that she should be able to tell where it was coming from. It was throbbing ahead of her, on her right, not toward the street. She opened her eyes and began walking, hesitantly, until she saw a café with tables set outside. The pulse was definitely coming from there.

Maybe the blonde is here, just chilling, and I can cave her head in with a baton while she's still in the middle of her latte. In which case, as far as all these hundreds of witnesses will be concerned, I'll be the insane woman who just committed vicious bodily assault with a deadly weapon on some innocent coffee drinker.

I think I can live with that.

This opportunity was too important. She wasn't going to try to trail the blonde to a less public place. She couldn't take the chance. The odds of finding her again were astronomical, and besides, she couldn't be certain that the woman wouldn't sense *her* presence. No, it had to be now, before the Checquy tracked her down again. Lyn's hand clenched around the baton in her handbag.

In her mind's eye, she could see the movements she would make.

Lyn walked toward the café, calm, steely in her self-control.

Where was she? Her opposite, her twin, the blond woman with the same power as she. The woman who had seen another like herself and, instead of stopping to learn more, had attacked to kill. That woman was somewhere nearby, and in a few minutes, one of them would be eliminated.

I won't use my power. It wouldn't do any good anyway. So I'll just take her down with the baton. A clip to the head, but not so hard that it kills her; I have to bring her in alive to prove that I'm innocent. I'll immediately surrender to whatever law enforcement shows up. The Checquy will arrive eventually, and I'll be able to show them another person like me.

If she uses her power in public, there will be witnesses. They'll be able to attest that the blonde had electricity. She looked around hopefully for security cameras, but if there were any, they weren't obvious.

And the Liars can earn their paychecks coming up with an explanation.

I could be home this afternoon.

I could be dead in a few minutes.

Focus. Be swift, be controlled, be merciless.

You have to win.

Lyn weaved her way cautiously through the pedestrians, then stopped in confusion. The source of the thrumming was close and sufficiently localized that she was certain it wasn't coming from inside the café. But there was no sign of the blonde at any of the tables outside. A couple of elderly tourists were eating cake at one, a man in a tracksuit was smoking a cigar and texting on his phone at another, and a young man was pouring himself tea from a small pot at a third.

What the buggery hell is going on?

She didn't understand what was happening. Her eye was caught by the young man with the pot of tea. He was in his mid-twenties, clean-shaven, with straight dark hair. Dressed in jeans and a button-down shirt, he was relaxed, now idly stirring his tea and glancing occasionally at passersby. She could have sworn the pulsing was coming from him.

What?

He had noticed her staring at him and raised his eyebrows in a question. She was so flummoxed that she walked hesitantly over to him.

"Um, hi," she said.

"Hello?" he said. She heard a trace of an accent. The thrumming had stopped.

Oh my God, I imagined it all, she thought. He smiled. *This guy who's probably ten years younger than me will think I'm hitting on him.*

"You will think this a strange thing to say," he said. He spoke with a European accent. Dutch? German? "But I think we might be related."

Well, at least he doesn't think I'm hitting on him. Still, it was such an extraordinary, out-of-the-blue statement that she was completely thrown. And then the thrumming returned for a moment, and she felt her eyes drawn to his hands. On the forefinger of each one was a polished silver ring.

"Do you know, I think you might be right," she said breathlessly.

"So extraordinary," he said in a wondering tone. "Would you like to join me for some tea or a coffee?" He gestured to the empty seat at his table.

"I—I would like that very much." She sat, not knowing what to think but keeping her hand closed around the baton in her bag.

"Fantastisch!" he said enthusiastically, seemingly unaware of any uncertainty on her part. He gestured through the window at a waitress, who nodded. She bustled out, took Lyn's order for a coffee, and

bustled back in. The two of them sat quietly for a moment, looking at each other, unsure how to start. Neither of them was ready to commit. It was like two spies meeting up without having been furnished with passwords, both seeking to ensure deniability if it turned out they had accidentally spoken to the wrong person.

"You're from the Continent?" Lyn asked finally. "Your accent..."

"Yes! Some cousins and I came here a couple of days ago. We saw the media stories about the *blitzschlag*—the, uh, the lightning strike, the first one. You know it?" His eyes were fixed on hers.

"Oh, I know it," said Lyn with particular emphasis. "I was actually right there when it happened."

"Yes?" he said, and his smile was one of utter delight.

Lyn found herself smiling in response. "You are interested in lightning?" she asked.

"Oh, yes, it is a family hobby. It was your first time to be by such lightning?" She nodded. "Very intense."

"I was wrung out afterward," she said. He frowned a little, not understanding. "Exhausted."

"Ah, yes. Such an experience takes a lot out of you."

The waitress brought Lyn's coffee and left them.

"It is good?" asked the man. "The coffee?"

"Very good," said Lyn.

"*Und* perhaps, in a bit, I can recommend the sponge cake, it is also very good." He patted his stomach ruefully. "I have eaten perhaps too much of it lately." She smiled a little. If he had eaten too much cake, it did not show.

"So you come to this café often?" she asked.

"I have spent most of the past couple of days here," he said. "They know me now."

"The sponge cake is so good that you keep coming back?" asked Lyn.

"Well, it is, but that is not the reason I come here," said the man. "It is one of the busiest places in London, this street, so I am here hoping to bump into a possible relation."

"Seriously?"

"It worked, didn't it?" She smiled tightly, and he nodded. "Would you like to see a little magic trick?" he asked, with wide eyes. "It is very amusing."

"Sure."

"Do you have a coin?"

She had to scrabble through her handbag to find her wallet, but eventually she scrounged up a fifty-pence piece. He nodded to the table and she put it down. He took up the coin with no flourish and held it up, pinched between his fingers. He turned it this way and that to show that there was nothing else in his grasp. She nodded.

Then she felt it, a slight throbbing sensation. His eyes were on hers, and she nodded again. He brought the coin down slowly, tapped it gently on the table. The faintest red spark flashed for a moment, then was gone. She'd been expecting it, hoping for it, but still, Lyn gasped at the sight.

It's real! she thought wildly. *It's real.*

But what does this mean? Has this guy been working with the blonde? Are there others like me? My God, have they all been murdering criminals around London?

Her hand was still tight around the baton in her handbag. She couldn't forget the fact that the last person she'd met with her powers had tried to cut her to pieces. "That's very good," she said, her mind whirling. She had to respect the cunning of it, the deniability of it. *Just a magic trick.* "I know that trick myself."

"Ah, yes?"

"Do you have a coin?" she asked, like a stage magician using an audience member's watch to prove there'd been no fixing ahead of time.

"As it so happens, I do." He passed over a one-euro coin, and she concentrated. Just the smallest amount was needed, and she focused with all her might to channel a tiny stream into the metal. Still, when it came time to tap the coin on the table, her spark was bigger than his had been. She looked up to see him beaming with such genuine pleasure that it gave her a shock of joy through her heart.

Maybe I can actually relax a little.

"It is so amazing to find a relation one did not know," he said. "I am so, so glad." He put out his hand, and she took it, not realizing that she had taken her hand off her baton to do so. There was a pulsation when their hands met. It was a shadow of what she had felt with the blonde when they fought, and for a moment, she was afraid that the two of them might be about to summon a lightning bolt—she felt how easily it could build into something gigantic—but she closed her will around their point of contact and felt him doing the same.

"It's unbelievable," she said, and her voice shook. His eyes were wet, and so were hers. They let go of each other's hands, and both wiped at their faces.

"I am Jörg," he said. He pronounced it so that it sounded like "York," but she had seen the name written down and knew it was the German version of George.

"Lynette," she said. "Lyn."

"A long-lost cousin," he said. "A miracle. We came here to find you, but I didn't think it would happen." His expression changed. *"Mein Gott,* I should call my uncle! You must meet the others."

"Okay," said Lyn cautiously. She watched as he took out a cheap-looking mobile phone, flipped it open, and made a call. He spoke in German, so swiftly that she could pick out only the occasional word. *Cousine. Gefunden. Lynette.* She smiled to see him so enthusiastic.

"Ja, ich werde sie fragen. Ein Moment." He pressed the phone to his chest. "I am so sorry, I should have thought to ask when would be a convenient time for us all to meet and to have a meal. It is very inconsiderate of me. You have a life, after all."

"Yeah, a few of them," she said without thinking.

"I'm sorry?"

"Nothing," she said. "As it happens, I am free for the rest of the day."

"Oh, good! Perhaps lunch?"

"Lunch would be very nice," she said. He smiled again and spoke into the phone.

After some hurried and extremely excited German, he started listening, and apparently, a great deal was said. He kept nodding and agreeing. *"Ja…ja…ja…ja. Ja, gut. Auf wiedersehen, Onkel."* He hung up.

"Is everything all right?"

"Yes, he was very happy to hear that you and I had found each other. He was just irritated that I had not sought to ask you to bring your relation."

"My relation?"

"Yes, your sibling? Or cousin?" She stared at him, baffled. "Is it a parent?"

"I don't have any family," she told him. She was not prepared to tell him about Richard or Emma, not yet. "Not a blood relation. I was adopted. I don't know my biological family."

"But there is another, yes?" he asked. "There must be. With whom did you make the lightning?"

Oh, hell. She should have seen this from the beginning. "I know who you mean. There is a woman, but I don't know her," Lyn said. "I don't know who she is." Jörg was staring at her, stunned. "I have been hunting her."

"Was?"

"She has been killing people in London. I am trying to stop her."

"And, but, the lightning?"

"I found her. We fought. The lightning just happened."

"Oh, *scheisse.*" He bit his lip, then looked at her in awe. "I bet that was a sight to see."

"Lynette, these are your relations. Well, some of them."

Lyn suddenly felt rather shy. There were about twenty people in the private dining room of the Chinese restaurant, and they were standing and looking at her expectantly. They were of all ages and sizes, men and women. The youngest was a boy in his late teens, the oldest, a silver-haired man. Lyn smiled hesitantly. And then they came forward with warm smiles. She was introduced to Erika and Stefan and Hannah and then she began to lose track of the names. A large man with a military bearing shook her hand firmly; a slim woman in her twenties embraced her and kissed her on both cheeks. With every touch, she felt their powers react to her. Every one of them, she couldn't help noticing, wore at least one ring on each hand.

"*Und* this is Arnwald, my uncle," Jörg said. "Well, really he is my great-uncle. Onkel, this is Lynette."

"Please call me Arndt," said the man.

"Hello," said Lyn nervously. It was clear that this tall, thin man with the magnificent aquiline nose was the leader, if not of the entire family, then at least of everyone present. He had small, dark-rimmed glasses and a high forehead with receding hair. He could easily have looked foreboding, but his eyes were friendly as he took her hand in both of his and held it tightly. She felt the energy within him, and her eyes widened. The man was a storm in himself, but he had a leash on that power, like an ocean told to sit and stay.

Is that what I could become? she thought faintly.

"Lynette, it is so good to meet you," he said. His accent was strong, but he spoke English easily. "I imagine this may be one of the strangest days you have ever had."

Sure, but not by as much as you'd think, she thought. During her cab ride with Jörg, she had given a lot of thought to what she would disclose. She would not make any mention of the Checquy. Specific details of her life—details that might reveal Richard and Emma's location—well, she would gloss over them. Jörg had not pressed her for her last name, which was promising. Of course, he hadn't given his either.

Presumably these people don't all have the same last name, she thought. Jörg had introduced many of them as cousins, but they certainly didn't all look alike. For one thing, they weren't all Caucasian. Two of the men, Emre and Atabey, and one of the women, Elif, were taller than the rest and of slightly darker complexion. At least half Turkish, she guessed. Another cousin was a plump young African woman; she brought Lyn a drink.

"I'm Helga," she said, her eyes dancing.

"Lyn. It's wonderful to meet you." They smiled and clinked glasses together.

And yet, despite the wide variety of people, there were resemblances. As family members were presented to her and as they talked amongst themselves in little groups, Lyn's eye was constantly being caught by familiar facial features—the shape of eyes or the curve of a cheekbone. She realized with a bit of a shock that they reminded her of *herself.* For an adopted child who had never met any blood relations, she found it a startling and thrilling experience to see her own nose on someone else's face.

And as they moved to their seats at the table and gave their orders to the waitstaff, she noticed another resemblance to herself. For all their warmth and welcome—and they *were* welcoming, of that there was no doubt—there was still a caution in these people. The feral child that lived within a part of Lyn's mind and that was always braced for attack recognized it. But another part of her recognized it too— the Pawn of the Checquy, who always had to keep her real self secret from the populace. These people carried the secret of themselves. She could tell that they had been taught never to reveal what they were, and yet they were showing themselves to her. There was a giddiness to it, a release. They had come here to a strange land, discreetly, to find one of their own, and she was so touched by this that she wanted to thank them. She found herself beaming at everyone, and their smiles back warmed a part of her that she hadn't even known was cold.

Still, until she knew exactly what was going on, she had to be cautious. She'd been half braced to walk into the room and find the blonde waiting for her. But the fact that they were meeting in a Chinese restaurant in Pimlico was strangely reassuring. Given all the witnesses, it seemed like the least likely place in which to be murdered or from which to be abducted. And she doubted that even the most dedicated of secret organizations—criminal, government, or otherwise—would bother having everyone fake German accents.

Unless they're the German Checquy.

Or a group of German criminals who have come over to very inefficiently seize control of a small portion of London's criminal underworld.

You have got to calm down.

She was seated next to Arndt, and a troop of waiters had brought in a huge amount of food. The doors were closed, and now everyone in the room was eating with gusto.

"I am guessing that you have some questions?" asked Arndt, chopsticks held expertly in his hand.

"I do," said Lyn. "You probably have some questions as well?"

"Yes, but I think I have more answers, so you can go first."

"So, we are all related?" He nodded. "And this isn't some metaphor, is it? Like, we're brothers and sisters through our powers?"

"Ugh, no, that would be too obnoxious," said Arndt, wrinkling his nose. "No, no, we are all actually related. Presumably, the powers are the result of something genetic. Some of the family have gone into the sciences to try and explain it, but they have not found an answer." Lyn nodded thoughtfully. She wasn't surprised. If the Grafters couldn't identify a gene that gave her her power, then she didn't think a couple of standard-issue scientists could manage it.

"And you're all German?"

"Yes. All German citizens. And we all live in the same area." She waited to see if he would name the area, but he did not.

Apparently we do not yet trust each other completely. She couldn't blame him—they were still feeling each other out. *And besides, I didn't even give them my surname. Or my phone number.* "So I'm guessing that you pay pretty close attention to your relations and their children? Keeping an eye out to see if they develop these powers? Unless everyone in your family can do it?"

"No, not everyone. It is rare. The people in this room represent almost everyone we know to have the ability. There is a grandmother too elderly to travel, and a teenager who could not get out of school to come here. But though we are a very large family, we remain close. And yes, we pay a lot of attention to genealogy."

"Then how did I come to be here?" asked Lyn. "In England? Do I have some ultra-recessive gene or something, like from generations ago? Or did one of your relatives come here on vacation and shag someone and not mention it?"

"There is always the possibility of an unmentioned shagging," said Arndt. "But people in the family who do not have powers are advised that they may be carrying a recessive gene for a very serious disease and so they must be very careful about birth control. It encourages people to have very few children and to be very responsible about who they shag."

"Oh God, it's not Juhász-Koodiaroff-Grassigli syndrome, is it?" asked Lyn.

"No, I have never heard of that," said Arndt. "And while I suppose it is possible that you are the child of a long-lost relation, I doubt it. We have been paying attention to this sort of thing for quite some time. No, we think you are probably the descendant of Lieutenant Hans Brandt, who was shot down over London in 1940 when he was bombing the city as part of the Blitzkrieg."

"I'm descended from a *Nazi?*" Lyn exclaimed incredulously. Everyone in the room paused in their meals and conversations and looked over at her. "I beg your pardon, I'm so sorry," she said, embarrassed.

"No need to apologize," said Arndt. "You are the only one here descended from an actual card-carrying Nazi. Hans was the only member of the family to get involved in the party. Everyone else at the time kept as low a profile as possible. There was the draft, of course, and the younger members were obliged to join the Hitler Youth and the League of German Girls, but our family has always been very wary of organizations and authorities in general."

"Oh."

"You don't need to feel bad about it," Arndt said reassuringly. "You are descended from a variety of people. Hans was the son of a doctor and a poetess. He was the grandson of a brewer. Everyone here is the descendant of merchants, farmers, minor nobility, and at least three warlords. Spring roll?" he asked, holding up a plate.

"Please," said Lyn dazedly. "Wait, did you say *warlords?*"

"Oh yes," he said. "Not recently, don't worry. It was many, many centuries ago. The family maintained a good spoken-word history before we adopted the written word."

"How far back?" she asked breathlessly. From being no one from a lineage of nobody, she was suddenly part of a dynasty.

"The first known of our line was a youth named Melo in the tribe of the Sicambri." He paused. "This was not the famous Melo, brother of Baetorix, by the way."

"Yeah, I was just going to ask about that," lied Lyn.

"It's a common mistake to make," said Arndt, nodding. "We think our Melo may have actually been named for the famous leader, but he was several years younger. Are you familiar with the Sicambri?" Lyn shook her head. "They lived on the east bank of the Rhine River. Julius Caesar encountered them during his push into Gaul around 55

BC. He described them as 'men born for war and raids,' and they were certainly that. They fought against Caesar and for him and then against him again. They loved plunder, taking slaves and cattle, and struck as they wished.

"We know little about Melo, only that his father was a freeman but of little wealth or renown. As he came to manhood, Melo discovered his ability to trap lightning in metal. We've no idea how he came to possess this power, by the way. There is no claim that his mother was a goddess or that he was struck by lightning. The Rhinemaidens are not reported to have slept with him. It simply happened. We can presume, however, that he was more willing to accept the possibility of magic than we might be today." Arndt paused and looked at Lyn consideringly. "I would be very interested to hear *your* story, Lynette. You must have been of very strong will to make the discovery and emerge unscathed."

"Well, I don't know about unscathed," said Lyn. And yet she couldn't imagine how she would have coped without the Checquy to guide and support her.

"I hope we will talk of that later," Arndt said. "But let me tell you more of our ancestor." Lyn felt a little thrill at the idea. "He eventually mastered his abilities and became a powerful warrior. And, armed with that understanding of his power, he did nothing."

"What?" asked Lyn.

"I know, it is not what one would expect, certainly not what a good story calls for, but he did nothing. He made no challenges for leadership. He settled no scores. He concealed his ability from his tribe. Perhaps he was biding his time.

"Then, in 16 BC, the Sicambri joined forces with two neighboring tribes, the Tencteri and the Usipetes. They crossed the Rhine and attacked Gaul. Melo was among them. He had declared himself a man and a warrior grown and insisted on being in the war party."

The librarian part of Lyn's mind perked up and cleared its throat. "Gaul was ruled by the Romans then, right?" she asked.

"Well, not entirely," said Arndt. "There was some village in Brittany that they never managed to conquer. But apart from that, yes, Gaul was occupied by the Romans.

"The historian Tacitus would later write of the battle in his *Annals*. He called it the *clades Lolliana,* or the Lollian disaster. The forces came together. On one side, the ranks of imperial legionnaires from the Italian peninsula with their shields and pila at the ready, and on the other side, screaming, greasy, and possibly naked barbarian hordes from the woods. He tells how the barbarians triumphed and took the standard of the fifth legion back across the river and into their forests as a trophy.

"He does *not* mention the youth among the barbarians who bore weapons that were unimaginable." Arndt smiled. "I expect there were all sorts of reasons why he was not included, even though so many had seen him."

So can I, thought Lyn ruefully. No government wanted anyone's supernatural abilities to be publicized. Apparently that was as true a millennium ago as it was now.

"Melo had waited," said Arndt, "but this was the time to show what he was capable of. The conflict gave rise to stories of a man with a spear that flew as a lightning bolt. A sword that burned men as it cut them down. An ax that hit with all the power of the tempest. A shield that, when struck, would stop the heart of its attacker. He was a storm within the battle, lightning flashing within the chaos. The Gauls who were there—those who survived—likened him to Taranis, the Celtic god of thunder. The surviving Romans muttered anxiously about Jove.

"His comrades loved it. They were a people who respected strength and power, and he had both of those. Plus, of course, he had acquired a substantial amount of booty. He returned across the river a much richer man than when he had crossed it into Gaul.

"By 9 CE, he had been chosen by general acclaim to be the new chief of the Sicambri. As part of an alliance of five tribes, the Sicambri ambushed and destroyed three Roman legions and their auxiliaries in the depths of the Teutoburg Forest. Melo's abilities played a large part in the tribes' triumph, not least because he was accompanied by his son and daughter, who had inherited their father's gift. It was Rome's greatest defeat and meant that they would never again attempt to subjugate the Germanic peoples." He paused and took some contemplative bites of sweet and sour pork.

"And then what happened?" asked Lyn, rapt. "Did Melo and his family go on to conquer the land?" A thought occurred to her. "Oh my God! Do you secretly rule Germany?" *Am I a long-lost secret princess?*

"What? No, of course not. You have to understand, the ability is very rare. And we aren't invulnerable. Melo's son was murdered, despite his powers, with a simple knife to the back. And he had no children—we are all descended from the daughter, Camilla. None of her four children had the ability, but thankfully a granddaughter did, and Camilla was able to pass on everything she knew. Otherwise, they'd have had to start all over again. Still, one granddaughter out of seven grandchildren. You can see why we have not covered the earth.

"Also, status in that society was built on strength and wealth, and our ability represents strength. But that doesn't necessarily equate to grand vision. Melo and, for quite a while, his descendants did not look to the greater implications of their powers. Keeping their neighbors from encroaching on their territory and, in some cases, obtaining chieftainships represented the height of their ambition.

"And they did not always maintain that. The sporadic appearance of the ability meant that power was not reliably passed down as in a monarchy. In some generations, a dozen relations had the power, and in some, only one did. The family expanded, but it also contracted when conflict and disease and times of hardship whittled it down. But it endured, obviously." He looked happily around the room at his family members eating and talking.

"Two of our ancestors helped to sack Rome, and there they encountered some extremely peculiar warriors fighting on the other side. In a wineshop by the Tiber, your I-forget-how-many-greats-grandfather Hathus fought a man and a woman who could do very dangerous things with their own blood. We have garbled stories of long chains of razor-sharp gore hissing around the place and cutting warriors to ribbons.

"Hathus's brother Odoacer lost a foot when he and a group of friends stormed an insula and burst into an apartment to find a Nubian man who summoned silver armor around himself and lashed out with burning lines of white light. Odoacer was the only one to survive, but he did not kill his opponent, who apparently vanished in a cloud of black dust and a blast of strange thudding music." He looked at her over his glasses. "You should be aware that we are not unique. There are others out there with inexplicable abilities."

"I will keep that in mind," said Lyn, straight-faced.

"Anyway, it was the spread of Christianity that prompted a significant change for us. Prior to that, our family's existence was, while not exactly a secret, more of a rumor than an accepted fact. Outsiders hesitated to denounce us because our powers evoked various deities: Taranis. Thor. Jove. Zeus. Donar. Perkūnas. Religions tend to attach significance to lightning—I expect it is the possibility of abrupt and showy destruction from the sky that does it.

"Christianity, however, did not acknowledge the possibility that the divine favored us. Our powers were taken to be a sign of evil. As the eloquent missionaries spread farther afield and their words were heard by more and more people, things became more and more uncomfortable for us. Our tribe, our own relations, began to turn on us. There were mutterings in village streets. Stones were thrown at children. One of the cousins went out hunting and did not come back.

"The family was in one of its smallest iterations at that time— only seventeen descendants of Melo, just two of them with the power. The eldest of the family, a strong-willed grandfather named Ferhonaths, saw that we could be wiped out completely. He made a decision, and overnight, the entire family fled, taking only what could be carried. The few Sicambri who pursued them did not return.

"The fugitives traveled far—at least, far for that time. They reached a pleasant area of hills and rivers populated by tribes who were willing to take in new arrivals, provided that these came with some wealth and a willingness to bend the knee to their leaders.

"The newcomers also came with the firm resolution to keep both their ability and the potential to pass on that ability a deep secret. Privately, they maintained their warrior skills, but they acknowledged that a clean and complete break from their past was necessary. They became herdsmen and farmers, then merchants. Their tight family bonds and singularity of purpose meant that they prospered.

"When Christianity spread into the area, they converted, albeit with a certain sense of irony, given that it was Christianity that had driven them out of their original lands. They married into powerful families that eventually became minor nobility. They kept a clear record of the bloodlines.

"As academia emerged as a viable career, they pursued that as well. The region in which our ancestors settled now boasts a prominent university town, and our family has maintained a strong if discreet presence among the institutions." He smiled. "There are no fewer than six university professors lunching among us today."

"Are you one of them?"

"As it happens, yes. How did you know?"

"Lucky guess," said Lyn. *That, and the palpable pleasure you are taking in giving a lecture.* "And what have you been doing since then?"

"I'm sorry?"

"What do you *do* with your powers? Do you fight monsters?"

"No, we haven't had any monsters," said Arndt. "Not in our region. There are a few records of creatures or individuals that attempted to strike at us or at the community, but they were decidedly unsuccessful, and we have had no problems for several centuries. We have been doing our best to live quiet lives while maintaining our skills and abilities with our power." He coughed. "There is a good deal of training in private gymnasiums and out-of-the-way places where we will not attract attention."

"You're not working with the government in some way?"

"Absolutely *not*," said Arndt with feeling. "We do not get involved in that sort of thing."

"And yet my unspecified-number-of-greats-grandfather fought for the Nazis."

"Yes, Hans was very excited about the rise of the Third Reich. Our family had lost a substantial amount of wealth after the Great War. Hans was a young man with a young man's excitements and frustrations. It chafed him that for all our family's power and our centuries of history, we were living in obscurity in a nation that had been defeated and forcibly impoverished. So he enlisted, much against the family's wishes.

"There was some concern among the uncles and aunts that Hans might reveal his ability to the Reich, or even tell them the story of our family, with its then five lightning-bearers living quietly by the River—" Arndt stopped before saying the name and looked at Lyn thoughtfully. "Well, living in the heart of Germany." It was clear that he was not yet willing to let Lyn know everything. "But Hans did not. A lifetime's worth of lessons and warnings is not easily ignored. He went, and he fought, and he died in the skies over London... or so we thought.

"The rest of the family emerged from the war relatively unscathed. We have grown, as you can see. We are now twenty-two lightning-bearers, as many as there have ever been at one time. We live our lives, we watch over each other, we ensure that tradition and knowledge are maintained. We stand ready to use our powers if ever the occasion calls for it."

"And so you came here, and, after centuries of secrecy, you began unleashing columns of lightning for everyone to see," Lyn said.

"Yes."

"What do they do?" Lyn asked. "The lightning bolts? Because I've been feeling them in my bones. Plus, you've probably seen that they have been freaking out everyone on the planet."

"Well, they have all sorts of applications, of course."

"Oh, yeah, of course," said Lyn, who couldn't think of any beyond terrifying the populace, baffling meteorologists, and possibly bringing down passing aircraft.

"But we were using them as a signal to the ones we were searching for."

"You were signaling?"

"Yes, an attempt to tell you that you were not alone."

"Oh," said Lyn, unexpectedly moved.

"Which brings me to a new topic," said Arndt. "Because you were already not alone. The lightning that you summoned stands proof of that. There is at least one other descendant of Hans Brandt on this island, and Jörg tells me that you do not know who she is."

"No," said Lyn. Arndt looked at her expectantly. "I was adopted as a child," she said heavily. "I don't know anything about my birth family other than they were negligent enough to lose me and never try to find me. I suppose that speaks to their character and standing as much as anything." His face was sober as he took this in. "I grew up to work in law enforcement." This was the closest she would come to acknowledging the existence of the Checquy. "I discovered my powers relatively recently and did my best to learn about them in secret.

"Then, in the course of my work, I became aware of a series of murders, and I saw that they had been committed by someone like me. Two burned rings?"

Arndt winced and nodded. "The *signum manus*," he said. "It has always been a part of our gift."

"I couldn't take what I knew to my superiors," said Lyn. "They would never have believed me. But I felt a responsibility."

"I understand," Arndt said.

"So I took a leave of absence, and I've done my best to track this murderer down. The person was killing criminals, so I used my contacts to try and find him or her. Two men I was protecting were attacked by a blond woman. She carried a sword and had powers like mine. When I showed her what I could do, she attacked me. That's how the lightning came."

"This is all extremely troubling," said Arndt. "The idea of someone using our powers in such a way is very distressing. It is fortunate, I suppose, that we found you and not her. Although . . ." He paused. "I hope you do not take offense, but I think you understand our caution and where it comes from. Do you have any sort of proof of this? That you are the wronged party?"

"Um, I have ID," said Lyn, opening her handbag and digging out the most appropriate of her various false identifications. "Here."

"'Detective Sergeant Lynette Brown of the Metropolitan Police Service,'" Arndt read. "Yes." He examined the card closely, and she could see him considering the situation. Finally, he appeared to come to a decision.

"This is convincing, Lynette. Now, let us think about how we can help you find and subdue this errant cousin of ours without revealing ourselves to your colleagues."

26

The room flashed crimson again and again as the electricity crack-led around Pamela's body. The Nazi jerked his dagger out of the Pawn's chest, and she fell to the floor. Bridget stared in disbelief at her friend, dead. The Nazi was panting, his teeth bared in an expression of feral joy. He was a man who had killed a nightmare that had been haunting him.

There was a shocked silence in the room, broken only by the sound of the Nazi's frenzied breath. No one dared move, until suddenly John Murcutt began to scream, and everyone jumped.

"You fool, you've murdered us!" Johnny shrieked at the startled Nazi. "They'll kill us! They'll kill us all! I'll never get clean!" He flailed about, his one free hand pressed to his chest while his other remained shackled by Bridget's pearl manacle to the back of the sofa.

"Spare us the histrionics, you fool," said Usha grimly. The contempt in her voice was so cold that John actually stopped and stared at her, open-mouthed. "We're not going to kill you. At least not yet. We're not done with you by a damn sight." Bridget let out a breath she hadn't realized she was holding. "So, no, he hasn't murdered you." Usha turned her gaze on the Nazi. "He's murdered himself."

Usha made no movement, but Bridget felt a wave of pressure wash over her. She realized that her hair was floating up gently even though her feet remained firmly on the ground.

"What's happening?" asked Tillie Murcutt, wary. Tendrils of her hair were also drifting about her face, and the material of her dress billowed as she shifted.

"He"—and Usha pointed at the Nazi soldier, who shifted his weight, his dagger tight in his hand—"is going to meet the death that should have come for him days ago." Blood was dripping up out of Usha's wound and drifting in little bubbles about her. Bridget felt a

tremor under her feet. The shreds of the carpet stirred like weeds underwater.

How is she doing this? she thought. It was unlike anything she'd seen her friend do before. Usha had always needed to touch something to affect it. *But she spoke a little about how her powers saved her in the bombing,* she remembered. *How they weren't the way she'd thought.*

What might she do?

"Usha," she said warningly. "Please. Be calm. Remember the mission. We need them."

"Then take them," said Usha through gritted teeth. "Take *them*"— she jerked her head at the Murcutts—"and go. Because after *he* is dead, I am going to bring this hovel down."

The Nazi, who had been taking this all in and backing slowly away, decided at that point to bolt. He turned and sprinted toward the hole in the wall that Wattleman had made when he entered.

"No," said Usha flatly. She flicked her fingers, and with a strangled yell, the man was yanked off his feet and hurtled backward through the air. In his shock, he dropped his dagger, and it bounced on the floor, more electricity flashing out of it with every impact. The struggling man was pulled across the space and came to rest abruptly against Usha's palm. Bridget could hear the breath punched out of him, although Usha had not moved.

"Usha," began Bridget, "we have to—"

"No, this ends here," said Usha. The Nazi was twisting, trying to retaliate, but he suddenly looked as if he were being pulled down by heavy weights at his wrists and ankles. He fell to the floor and Usha knelt gracefully, keeping her hand at the center of his back. "This part of the story ends here."

"But Pamela...her body." Bridget could hardly bear to look at the blackened thing on the floor, the burned body that just a few moments before had been her glorious, brilliant friend.

"*Go.*" The floor trembled underneath them. The Nazi squealed under Usha's gentle, delicate hand. He was straining against the weight of his own flesh.

"I think perhaps you should get my brother," said Tillie Murcutt in Bridget's ear. "It's obviously time for us to leave. Oh Jesus!" This last exclamation was the result of another tremor that swept through the room. Cracks appeared in the walls, and dust shivered up into the air.

"Don't think of trying to escape," warned Bridget, and the two Murcutts flinched as bottles on the bar shattered. Fragments and shards cartwheeled lazily into the air.

"Don't worry," said Tillie dryly. "I think the only safe place will be near you."

"Agreed." Bridget scurried to the sofa where John was whimpering. He flinched away from her and shrieked, and she slapped him. Then she pressed her hand down on the pearl handcuff binding him to the sofa and focused. She could feel it pulping under her touch, but slowly, too horribly slowly. "Pull!" she snapped at him, and with her other hand she yanked at his wrist to try to break through the manacle. "Come *on!*"

Behind her, Usha still knelt by the Nazi, talking to him in a low tone as detritus from the room floated about in the air and the structure of the house groaned and cracked.

The Nazi said something, gasped it out, and Usha bent low to hear him. His cheek was pressed to the floor, but her hand still lay on him lightly.

With a wrench and a cracking sound, the half-dissolved pearl cuff came away from the wooden ridge at the back of the sofa. It was still locked about his wrist with chunks of wood adhered to it, but at least he was free.

"Now, come!" she snapped and dragged him up to his feet.

"Come on, Johnny!" shouted his sister.

With an iron grip on his shoulder, Bridget hustled John across the room. Floating debris bumped off them as they rushed to the door. Tillie was waiting for them. Bridget looked back for a moment, thinking of trying once more to convince Usha to come with them. Her friend was listening to the German as he whispered. She nodded at what he was saying; around her, the floorboards were beginning to warp and curl themselves up.

"Let's go," Bridget said.

Tillie led the way down the hall, her brother and Bridget hurrying behind her. They clattered down the stairs to the floor with all the bedrooms.

"Wait!" exclaimed Bridget. She hauled back on both of them.

"Don't *stop!* We need to get *out!*" shrilled John.

"Yes, we need to get out, but we need to get everyone else out as well." As Bridget spoke, a flicker of movement above her caught her eye. "Look at that!" A crack was tearing itself along the ceiling, and plaster dust leaked down. "Is there a fire alarm or something?"

"No, there's no fire alarm." Tillie snorted. "Here's how you empty a knocking shop." She took a deep breath. "Police raid!" she yelled. "The rozzers are 'ere!"

It was as if she had announced the discovery of a swarm of pubic lice. The hall was suddenly full of men and women in various states of undress, all trying to get away. One man was struggling into his trousers while another was hurriedly wrapping a frilly pink dressing gown around himself. A couple of the women had also prioritized escape over appearances and were bolting wearing nothing but some slippers. One man was wearing a peignoir sexier than anything Bridget owned.

I like those heels he's wearing too, she thought.

It was far from an orderly evacuation; people elbowed and clawed at each other to get away.

"Well, this won't be good for business," said Tillie sourly. Her brother was leaning on her, and she staggered under his weight. It was on the tip of Bridget's tongue to offer to help, but quite aside from the fear with which John regarded her, she liked the fact that this made it harder for the two of them to run away. "Not that I expect much future business anyway. I doubt there will be much of this place left standing."

Bridget nodded. For that matter, she wasn't certain how much of the Murcutts themselves would be left standing. She really had no idea how this all was going to play out, but lurking in the back of her mind was the memory of how Wattleman had disposed of Simony once he'd answered their questions. *And he didn't even have any strong feelings about Simony.* Once he learned the details of Pamela's death, things could get very ugly.

Think about that later, she told herself. "Move," said Bridget brusquely as a new tremor rumbled through the floorboards. They hurried down the hall behind the Murcutts' dissatisfied clients to the other stairs, treading on various dropped personal items and pieces of apparel in the process. They descended the next flight of stairs and ran through the front bar area out to the street to find that there was quite a substantial crowd gathered outside.

Oh, good, thought Bridget dismally. *Lots of witnesses. This just gets better and better.*

A little murmur rose up from some onlookers at the sight of Murcutts *frère et soeur* appearing so discommoded on the street, but the eyes of most of the spectators were focused upward. Even the glistening handprint on the cringing John Murcutt's face and the wood-studded pearl bangle on his wrist failed to grab much attention. Still, he pulled his coat up over his face in an effort to conceal the mask.

Suddenly, the siblings gave out simultaneous exclamations and stumbled awkwardly.

"And what's wrong with *you?*" asked Bridget.

"Something's grabbed me!" snapped Tillie, rubbing at her arm. "It's gripping my arm like a — ow! *Ow!*"

"It's *me,*" said Wattleman's voice quietly, and John moaned. Bridget was beginning to suspect that the gangster's mind was breaking under the pressure of a continuous stream of the profoundly unnatural.

"Henry!" she exclaimed. A wash of relief swept through her.

"Oh, good, the invisible naked chap," said Tillie flatly.

"I don't want the two of you making a break for it and eeling your way away into the crowd," said Wattleman's voice. "You are staying in our custody, and don't think that just because we are in front of lots of people in broad daylight, your arms can't suddenly be fractured for no apparent reason. Understand? *Understand?*"

"Ow, yes!" exclaimed Tillie. Her brother stared dully ahead. Bridget followed his gaze and examined the people in the street. To her relief, they were all fully clothed. It appeared that all the denizens of the Moor's Head who had been engaged in illegal activities had made a break for it. She scanned the faces and didn't see anyone moving intently toward them to render service to the prisoners.

"Where the hell have you been?" Bridget asked Wattleman. "You fell out of that hole ages ago."

"I didn't fall out of the hole, I *made* the hole, and I got knocked out when I hit the ground," said Wattleman's voice testily. "Landed on my bloody head. Actually, my bloody head landed on Vincent's bloody head, which splattered across the cobbles. I only just woke up, lying naked on the street with a group of interested people staring at me."

"No one called an ambulance? Or the police?" asked Bridget incredulously.

"They came flying out of a hole in my place," said Tillie. "People round here know not to interfere with my business."

"Now, what's going on?" asked Wattleman's voice. "What have I missed? Where are Pamela and Khorana?"

"Usha is up there," Bridget said. "She's . . . she's . . ." *She's going to kill the Nazi. But what if he uses his powers on her? What if he burns her like he burned Pamela?* "Christ, I shouldn't have listened to her. I shouldn't have left her. I've got to go back up!" She took a step, but a firm hand closed around her wrist. To her surprise, it was Tillie Murcutt's.

"Your girl was very clear that we had to leave," she said.

"But what if he does something to her?"

"He needed a knife to do his magic," Tillie said, "and she slapped that right out of his hand. When last we saw them, she very definitely had things under control. And you absolutely can't go back in there."

"Why not?" asked Wattleman's voice.

"Usha is going to tear the building apart," Bridget said dully.

"What? Why?"

"Pamela's dead," said Bridget.

"What?" And suddenly the whimpering Murcutt brother was hoisted up on his toes by an invisible force. He kicked, flailed, and made strangled gobbling sounds, and Bridget could see the indentations on his throat where Wattleman was holding him.

"Henry, it wasn't him!"

"Then who?"

"He's dead, or as good as."

"Hmph." There had been a few gasps from the crowd at the

Murcutt brother's situation, but most people's attention was on the upper story of the Murcutts' place.

"Look there!" someone cried out, and the three visible people in Bridget's party and, presumably, the invisible one turned and looked up.

"Oh, heavens," said Bridget. Tillie sighed heavily, while her brother moaned.

Well, bang goes Lady Carmichael's order to keep this whole thing quiet, Bridget thought.

The roof was flexing, bulging out and sinking back in on itself. With every movement, there were loud reports as components of the structure were pushed about in ways they were not intended for. The walls of the upper story were moving too—they rippled, and she could see bricks cracking.

"What is Khorana doing?" asked Wattleman in her ear. "I didn't know she could do that."

"Me neither," muttered Bridget. Usha had mentioned that being bombed gave her some new insights into her abilities, but the building looked like it was *breathing.* The hole that Wattleman had punched in the wall using Vincent as a blunt instrument seemed to gape more widely, but the angle was such that you couldn't see what was happening inside.

And thank God for that, Bridget thought. This pulsation of the building was bad enough, but it could probably be explained somehow. *Something about gas leaks, maybe?* But if the general public had caught sight of her and Usha sliding about on the ceiling while predatory birds dashed around underneath them, it would have been extremely bad.

Almost as bad as having Vincent and Wattleman come flying out of that hole and land on the street. Which reminds me . . .

She looked around for any sign of Vincent, but there was no gap in the crowd where people might be kneeling down attending to an injured man or a body.

"His corpse was over there," said the voice of Wattleman. "By the butcher shop. We flew almost entirely across the street." Bridget shook her head. It must have been a sight—two men bursting out in a spray of masonry and plaster, waving wildly, falling, then hitting the street sickeningly.

"No one is helping him?" she asked.

"Oh, he was beyond help," said Wattleman. "*Obviously* beyond help. It was very messy." She could practically hear his face twisting. "I'm not becoming visible again until I've had a long, hot shower."

"But there's a corpse on the street!"

"As Miss Murcutt said, people around here clearly know not to get involved in her business. And besides, there's a new spectacle to be distracted by."

The number of onlookers seemed to have doubled since Bridget and the Murcutts had come out to the street.

"What Khorana's doing is very impressive," said Wattleman. "I wonder how far she's going to take it. All the way down to the cellar?"

"I suppose if she can, she will," Bridget said. "Perhaps we should move back a bit?"

And then it hit her. "Jesus Christ!"

"What?"

"The bomb!"

"What bomb?" asked Wattleman. "What are you taking about?"

"There's an unexploded bomb in the cellar of the building!"

"Of *that* building? The Moor's Head?"

"You were there when it fell in!" Bridget said.

"But I thought they must have removed it!" exclaimed Wattleman.

"No point," sniffed Tillie.

"Oh, shut up," snapped Bridget. "Still, I can't believe I forgot about it."

"How could you forget about a bomb?" demanded Wattleman incredulously.

"See? They're very easy not to think about," said Tillie. Bridget shot her a look, and she shrugged.

"Henry, we have to get all these people away and..." Bridget looked up anxiously. "Warn Usha?"

"You'll have to guard these two," Wattleman said finally. "I'll go and warn her. If something happens and the bomb goes off, then I'm more likely to withstand it."

"Right." Bridget nodded dubiously. She was not at all certain about her ability to guard the two Murcutts in front of a large number of civilians in a street the Murcutts claimed to own. Judging from the sudden speculative look in Tillie's eyes, she was not at all certain about Bridget's ability either.

"Don't worry, I'll break both their legs before I go in," said Wattleman reassuringly.

"I *beg* your pardon?" squawked Tillie. John just moaned a little, hunched down inside his coat, and drew it a bit farther over his head.

"And it should be easy enough to disperse the crowd," mused Bridget. "We just yell that there's an unexploded bomb in there."

"I like it. It's elegant in its simplicity," said Wattleman.

"And it'll work," she said. She was thinking of the panic when she and Usha had emerged from that house wearing their gas masks.

Before Wattleman could reply or, worse, make good on his offer regarding the Murcutts, there was an exclamation from the crowd and a couple of shrieks, and Bridget's gaze snapped back up to the pub.

"Oh, *fuck*," Bridget, Tillie, and Wattleman said at the same time.

With an earsplitting crash, the roof of the Moor's Head caved in. Parts of the wall cracked and several bricks cascaded down to shatter on the footpath near them. Clouds of dust poured out of the holes in the upstairs wall and out the front door. Because the windows had all been boarded up, the dust shot out into the street in a torrent. There was a groaning sound from deep within the building, as if it were dying.

The crowd, abruptly realizing that what had been an intriguing spectacle was now a building that might very well fall on them, immediately became a mob trying to get away through a roiling mass of dust that engulfed the street. Coughing and choking, people became shapes in the cloud, scrambling over each other. There were screams, and Bridget and the Murcutts were jostled as people fled. Tillie made as if to turn and run, but she was yanked back by Wattleman's invisible grip.

"Are you mad? We can't—can't stay here!" said Tillie, coughing. Her eyes were streaming.

"She has a point," said Wattleman tightly. "It will do us no good, Bridget, if you are killed." He paused. "I suppose we want these two to be alive as well."

"But what about Usha?" choked out Bridget. She pressed the sleeve of her blouse to her nose and mouth and thought wistfully of her gas mask.

"She'll be fine," said Wattleman, wheezing. "After all, she already survived one building collapsing on her because of a bomb."

"She *did?*" asked Tillie. She was gasping and she had followed Bridget's lead in holding a sleeve over her mouth, but her incredulity overcame her discomfort.

"Yes, last night. But she doesn't know how she did it," snapped Bridget. "So there's no guarantee that she'll be able to do it again!" She was wavering, uncertain what to do. They couldn't stay—conditions were becoming unbearable—but she couldn't leave her friend. Not after losing Pamela.

"There she is," said Wattleman. "She's fine."

It was true. Squinting through the billowing clouds of dust, Bridget could make out a silhouette emerging calmly from the door of the Moor's Head. As it came to them, it resolved into Usha, walking gingerly, like someone who has finished hard manual labor. Her hand was pressed against the gunshot wound on her shoulder.

"Oh, thank Christ," said Bridget. For all her weariness and injuries, Usha moved lightly on the ground, and her back was ramrod straight. She was irritatingly serene, and the dust did not appear to be touching her. Her clothes were clean apart from her own bloodstains and the pearl handprints Bridget had made on her shoulder. If Bridget hadn't been so relieved to see her friend, Usha's unruffled mien in the midst of all the chaos she'd wrought would have been incredibly irritating.

"Usha!" she cried. They hugged, and the dust drew back from around Bridget. She breathed in the clean air gratefully. "Are you all right?"

"Apart from absolutely everything, I'm fine," said Usha wearily.

"Right," said Bridget.

"Can you extend that envelope of clean air around the rest of us?" asked Wattleman. "Or even just me?"

"I'm afraid I can't," said Usha. "Bridget, I'm going to need your help. I can't keep this up." Bridget looked at her in puzzlement. "I'm exhausted," she said. "I'm exhausted in my muscles. I'm exhausted in my *powers*."

"Lean on me, then," said Bridget. "And let's get out of here."

The other woman put her arm around Bridget. "Take a breath," warned Usha, and then her weight settled heavily on Bridget's shoulders, and the dust coated them and burned their eyes and throats.

"Can we go now, please?" said Tillie tightly. Her eyes were shut.

"Yes, I don't like the idea of being this close to a collapsing building with a bomb in the cellar," said Wattleman.

"A *bomb?*" repeated Usha.

I can't believe I forgot about that damn thing again. Tillie is right—unless it's exploding or right in front of you, you just don't think about it.

"Long, tedious story, which I'll tell you once we're well away," said Bridget. "But, you know, we should hurry."

The party made its hurried, limping way down one of the side alleys. The dust was thick and almost hid the buildings they passed. There was the distant sound of sirens, and Bridget glimpsed half-visible figures in the clouds as civilians fled. Behind them was the clatter of more bricks falling, followed by thuds and a couple of crashes that echoed off the buildings. Their little group paused, holding their breath, waiting for the sound of the UXB detonating.

But it didn't come.

"Did you actually destroy the whole place?" asked Tillie unhappily.

"I doubt it," said Usha. "Once I saw that the roof was coming down, I got out. I expect I've damaged some walls and floors, but I don't think the whole place will collapse." She didn't seem concerned by the fact that she was talking so freely to a woman who might still be their enemy. Perhaps it was the exhaustion, or perhaps it was because they'd won, sort of.

It doesn't feel like winning, thought Bridget grimly. Every time they paused to take a breath, all she could see in her mind's eye was Pamela transfixed by that blade and then her body going rigid as she died. She wanted to weep, she knew that she should weep, but she was too tired, and there was still too far to go before she could let herself feel anything. She had the sense they were on a death march through the streets of the West End.

And then a thundering boom came behind them and the pavement trembled as the bomb in the cellar finally decided to do its job. They all dropped to the ground, and Bridget felt the invisible weight of Wattleman on her back.

"Get *off* me!" she snapped.

"Wait," he said, and she heard bits of debris pattering down around them. John Murcutt shrieked a little, presumably hit by some fragments. The rain of rubble stopped. They stood up and looked back to see a new column of cloud and smoke rising up from the mass of dust that the building's earlier partial collapse had released.

"That's splendid," said Tillie bitterly. "I don't expect it would have ever gone off if you lot hadn't decided to mess about with things." No one bothered to respond, and they all resumed their exhausted trudging.

"And what now?" said Usha.

"There's a police box just up ahead," said Wattleman. "I noticed it earlier. We'll use it to call the nearest station, and I've got some pass phrases that will set the desk sergeant on to the Apex to get someone sent to us."

He was right—they soon came to a blue kiosk by the stairs to a Tube station. It looked sturdy and secure, a nice little booth just big enough for someone to sit in. Under Wattleman's directions, Bridget opened a little hinged door on the side to reveal a small compartment with a telephone. However, when she picked up the receiver and held it to her ear, there was no sound.

"Nothing. Phone line must be out," she said.

"Typical," sighed Wattleman's voice. "Fine, well, we must press on, then. There's a safe house a few streets over. We can go there." There were some grumbles from captors and captives alike as they continued on down the street.

"How far is this place, Henry?" Bridget asked. "Usha needs a doctor." She was under no illusion that her patch job of her friend's gunshot wound was nearly enough.

"And I need a drink," said Tillie.

"It's not far, Bridget," he said, ignoring Murcutt. "The next street."

It turned out to be a flat in a battered-looking tenement with the key taped to the back of a loose brick. They climbed awkwardly up a set of screamingly warped stairs and unlocked the door to reveal a clean room furnished with four chairs around a wooden table and a small kitchen. A bed with no sheets was visible through a door into another room.

"This place is a hole," said Tillie. "You people have all that power and *this* is your place?"

"I don't live here," said Wattleman's voice testily. "It's a safe house." Tillie raised an eyebrow but settled down in one of the chairs as easily as if it were her own house and they were her guests. Johnny sank down next to her, silent and tense.

"So," said Tillie. "Now that there's some privacy, are you going to kill us like you presumably killed young Simony?"

"That depends," said Wattleman's voice. "First I have to do a few things. Bridget, are you and Usha all right here?"

"Yes, no problem," said Bridget as she helped Usha settle in a chair. "I'll kill them if they do anything funny."

"Grand," said Wattleman's voice. "I have to make a few calls." Footsteps went into the bedroom, and she heard him pick up the telephone. "Hello, operator?" He asked to be put through to Whitehall 19357; there was a pause, and then he asked another operator to put him through to Whitehall 2059691828282. The door closed as Wattleman set about following the intricate telephonic pathway to the office of the Lady of the Checquy.

"So," said Bridget, "Miss Murcutt." She ignored the brother, who had apparently retreated into some despair-based reverie.

"Yes?"

"Cup of tea?"

The woman looked surprised.

"Are you out of your mind?" asked Usha weakly.

"I think it's always best to have a serious conversation over some sort of beverage, and these safe houses never have any good liquor. There's no reason we can't be civilized."

"Her man *shot* me!"

"Yes, but I saw her trying to stop him. And help is on the way,"

Bridget said. "In the meantime, a cup of tea would be the best thing for you. I definitely need one."

"Cup of tea would be very nice," said Tillie warily. She also ignored her brother. Bridget bustled about, and eventually the teapot was on the table.

"I'll be mother," sad Bridget. "There's no milk or sugar," she warned as she poured out the tea into three chipped teacups. "Now, I have some questions." *Which I want to ask before we hand you over to the Checquy.*

"I'm sure you do. Why should I answer them? What's in it for me?"

"Shortly, some very powerful people are going to come and take you into custody," Bridget said flatly. "The custody of these people can be very unpleasant. Unimaginably so. You've seen what we can do. That is nothing compared to what they can do." To her immense satisfaction, Tillie actually paled a little. "Now, Usha and I wield some influence. Our good word can make a difference. If we give it."

"And if I answer your questions, you'll put in a good word for me?"

Not a mention of her brother, Bridget noted. Said brother was currently hunched silently on a chair, staring at the floor and absently rubbing the pearl encrusting part of his face.

"Yes," said Bridget.

Tillie looked at her consideringly, and she took a long sip of tea as she thought. "Ask," she said finally.

"Let's talk about one of your employees."

"Oh?" said Tillie, looking surprised.

"Is something the matter?"

"I was just expecting you to ask about our special antiques again."

"Oh, we'll get to that, never fear," said Bridget. "But first, the matter of your former employee."

"You people have just rendered several of my employees 'former,'" Tillie said tartly. "Along with the place of business that's been in my family for generations."

"I'm talking about the German."

"Oh, Hans. You knew him?" The woman eyed her speculatively.

"No, but we've been looking for him," said Bridget. *Let's see how much she knows.* "Had a description and everything."

"All right," said Tillie. "Well, what do you want to know?"

"You had a Nazi working for you," said Bridget. "An actual German Nazi. How did that come to happen?"

"Matthew seven, seven."

"What?" said Bridget and Usha together.

"You people, honestly," said Tillie, shaking her head. "The Gospel According to Matthew, chapter seven, verse seven: 'Ask, and it shall be given you; seek, and ye shall find; knock, and it shall be opened unto you.'" She leaned forward. "We knew from Mum's stories that there was magic out there, and I saw the possibilities in it. So once we got into this business, we started searching more actively. We already knew Vincent. He lived near us, and Mum had kept an eye on him. Then I went back through Mum's and Gran's records and found a few more notes. That's how we found Gethings. And then we kept an ear out. There's magic in all sorts of places. People see things, and when they've had a few drinks and possibly a nice frolic with a young lady, they talk.

"Plus, we have people out on the streets. The business isn't just booze downstairs and whores upstairs with the occasional magic relic thrown in. We're expanding—we have informants all over. When a man kills another man in a magic way in a back alley and one of our men sees it, we want to know more."

"So the Nazi killed a man?" said Bridget. She tried to remember what the reports had said; as she recalled, one of the Nazi's early victims had indeed been some sort of criminal.

"He killed a man who tried to rob him." Tillie smiled. "Poor bastard probably never realized what he'd brought on himself. One minute you're threatening some shabby-looking cove, the next minute, you're burning in red electricity and gasping your last as you cook in your skin like a jacket potato."

"I think he actually electrocuted them first, then burned them," said Bridget quietly. "That's what happened to Pamela." The memory of watching the light in her friend's eyes go out, the fact that the Pawn had been dead before she burned—knowing that Pamela hadn't suffered too much made the loss of her a little more bearable.

"I never saw it happen myself," said Tillie. "Anyway, our man stayed out of sight but followed the killer to where he was dossing, in some bombed-out house. It was pathetic. Our man made a call and explained the situation, and we sent some strapping lads to bring him in. They had guns. I think Hans saw that he couldn't possibly kill all of them, and the fact that we weren't the police intrigued him. They brought him to the Moor's Head, and we had a chat. I didn't care that he was German, and he didn't care that we were criminals."

"He spoke English?"

"Better than some of our guests," said Tillie. "Of course, an accent straight from Berlin. There was no way he could go into a shop or a pub and not get the rozzers called on him. Really, he wasn't going to last long without our help. So we worked out a deal. He'd kill people for us, and we'd provide him with room, board, wages, and companionship if he wanted it. And he did want it."

Bridget and Usha exchanged a look and Usha raised an eyebrow. Bridget grimaced back in reply.

Yes, yes, you were right, Usha, she thought. *There was sex involved. Congratulations.*

"So he was killing people for you," mused Bridget. "So...oh Jesus. You've been sending him out to kill your rivals."

"Manna from heaven to a firm that was looking to expand in a competitive market. He was very skilled," said Tillie. "I don't know if all the Nazis are trained to fight and kill like he was, but if they are, heaven help England. Even without his powers, he knew his stuff, and with them? Well, he could kill 'em in a moment, couldn't he? Vincent, for all his power, didn't know how to fight. He was more of a bodyguard. And Gethings and Eckersley? I could hardly send them out on the streets to use their powers, could I? No, but Hans was ideal."

"How did he come to be on the streets of London?" asked Bridget. This was the question she was most concerned about. Had Hans told the Murcutts what had brought his plane down? Did they know about *die Hexe,* a woman who could fly and manipulate wind, and did they know that Pamela was that woman?

"Didn't say," said Tillie, so blithely that Bridget believed her. "It was obvious what he was, though. He stood and walked like a soldier.

I reasoned that he'd come down in the Blitz, maybe in that plane that was shot down, and he'd been trying to stay alive ever since." Bridget did her best not to heave an obvious sigh of relief. If the Murcutts had known about Pamela's actions, she wasn't sure what she would have done.

"So you hired a Nazi."

"Only because of his powers," said Tillie with a little indignation. "If he'd been some regular storm trooper, I'd have had him at the bottom of the Thames with a sackful of bricks tied to his ankles."

"How patriotic," remarked Usha through clenched teeth. She was sitting rigidly, her hands clasped around her teacup, although she hadn't taken a sip. She was tense with the effort of keeping herself upright against the pain of her wounds. Tillie looked at her coolly.

"Now, how did you receive the magical items?" Bridget asked.

"A man provided them to us in exchange for guaranteed exclusive access to a young blonde named Eileen and a share of the profits for the sale of the items."

"Who was this man?" asked Bridget, her eyes narrowed. "Do you know his name?"

"Of course I do," Tillie said. "I have the name he gave, and then I have the name of the man who owns the house that I had someone follow him to." They stared at her blankly. "He gave me a false name," she explained. "I wasn't offended. I learned that he also gave a false name at an opium den over in Limehouse." She smiled. "He's a man of many hungers, and he needs funds to feed them."

"But you have his real name?"

"And his address," said Tillie. "But I think I'll keep that information to myself for now. We had a deal before, but circumstances have clearly changed. You don't strike me as the kind of people who would torture information out of me..." She paused and smiled at Bridget's inadvertent flinch.

Bridget wasn't sure if the expression on Usha's face was from the pain of the gunshot wound or the pain of Bridget's terrible poker face.

"Excellent!" said Tillie brightly, catching their looks. "So I'd like to have something to bargain with when it actually comes time to talk to the big fish, whenever they swim up."

"Fine," said Bridget heavily. She sat back. "Miss Murcutt, I'm going to give you some advice. When it comes time to speak to those people, I recommend that you tell them everything about the special antiques, how you got them, and how they were distributed. Come completely clean. After all, as far as you knew, there was no law against that sort of thing."

"And what about Hans?" asked Tillie.

"What about him?"

"We're in a state of war, and I had a Nazi soldier in my employ," she said. "That's high treason to the Crown, a crime that brings the penalty of death by hanging."

"Tell them everything you know," Bridget said. Tillie stared at her. "We're not the police, we don't care about your brothel or your other criminal endeavors. At the moment, there's a team out there looking for a Nazi who can burn people to death with his hands."

"He needed a blade to do it," Tillie corrected her. "Or any bit of metal, really."

"Good to know," said Bridget. "In any case, they'll be very glad to know that he's gone." She looked over at Usha. "He *is* gone, isn't he?"

"Very much so," said her friend flatly. Tillie shuddered a little.

We might actually get through this without escalating the war to a super-natural setting. Or destroying our careers. She looked up as the bedroom door opened.

"Support team is on their way," Wattleman's voice said. "They're bringing a surgeon for Usha, some manacles for the Murcutts, and some clothes for me. And I asked them to let the responders know that the event at the Moor's Head falls within our purview. That Pamela's—" His voice broke. "That Pamela is there." Bridget winced in sympathy. Wattleman and Pamela might have butted heads, but they had known each other since they were children. Even in the Checquy, when you knew your comrades could be lost all too easily, such a loss was painful. He cleared his throat. "They should be here in a few minutes."

"Before then, Bridget, will you help me to the lavatory, please?" asked Usha.

"Oh, of course," Bridget said. Usha leaned on her heavily as they made their way down the hall to the grubby communal bathroom. "Now, how shall we do this?" she asked, once the door was shut.

"I don't need the loo."

"No?"

"No," said Usha. She settled herself gingerly on the lidded toilet and took a breath. "I killed him, Bridget. I killed him by breaking his neck. Then I crushed him down to a paperweight." Her eyes were distant as she gazed at the memory of something dark. "So let that be the end of it."

It's over, thought Bridget. *He's really dead, and it is over.*

But it wasn't worth what it had cost them.

"And Pamela?" asked Bridget quietly. "Did you . . . dispose of her body as well?" The other apprentice shook her head and looked down at her hands.

"I had to leave her behind," said Usha. "I couldn't do that to her. It was bad enough doing it to him."

"It's fine," Bridget assured her. "The Checquy will come for her." She didn't know if they would find her charred body in the remains of the Moor's Head or if it had been utterly destroyed by the explosion, but there would be no questions once Usha and Bridget explained what the Nazi had done. No operative of the Checquy expected an open-casket service, but Pamela would be buried with full honors. Bridget leaned back against the wall and slid down until she was sitting on the floor. The two women sat in silence for a few moments.

"You talked to him," said Bridget. "What did you ask?"

"I asked him if he had told others about us, about Pamela. He said no. And I asked if there were others like him, if the Nazis had more."

"And?"

"He said no."

"Do you believe that?" asked Bridget.

"I think so," Usha said. "He made no sense as a Nazi Checquy soldier. Why would they send a man like him, with his abilities, off in a plane to do a job that a thousand other men could have done?" She sighed. "I think he was a person like us. He knew that he had to keep himself secret but he wanted to fight in any way he could."

"That's such a sad thought," said Bridget. "I like to think that what we are makes us want to be defenders rather than conquerors."

Usha sighed heavily. "You have to see people for who they are," she said. "They're just people. Even us." She sounded immeasurably weary.

"Even them," Bridget said. "I forget sometimes that they're people." Usha looked over at her questioningly. "The Nazis. I just think of them as the bombs that fall from the sky each night. Or maybe a dark cloud washing over the Continent." *Washing over Gerald.* "But they're people too. People like us."

"Do you think Pamela knew what he was?" asked Usha. "And that's why she pulled down that airplane?"

"No," said Bridget. "I don't think we'll ever know why she did it."

"Perhaps the war just got to her."

"Perhaps. But she'd seen so much worse. She'd been brought up for war. You know what she did as a child in Ireland. Our work makes us see terrible things. And all three of us have been in this war for the same amount of time." Bridget bit her lip. "Whatever pushed her to do that, I think it was something terrible, and we'll never know what it was."

They glanced up at a noise from the hall—the Checquy support team had arrived.

Bridget looked at Usha grimly. "Brace yourself to undergo some surgery on the kitchen table."

27

Twenty-one servings of fried ice cream with caramel sauce were brought into the private dining room of the Chinese restaurant as the family of lightning-bearers recovered from some of the best food they'd ever eaten in their lives. Lyn eyed the dessert and decided that if this was going to be her final meal, it would almost be worth it.

"It will have to be just me against her," Lyn said firmly. "I don't want any of you dragged into a fight."

"And you are certain that it must be a fight to the death?" Arndt asked. He looked distressed at the possibility of losing another new-found long-lost cousin.

"I hope not. There's nothing I'd like more than to have a nice, calm conversation with her," said Lyn. "And maybe I can get her to surrender. But this is a woman who has killed multiple people. She's not going to want to turn herself in. So I have to face the possibility that it's going to end badly."

"They *were* all criminals," Arndt pointed out. "The people she killed."

"Regardless," said Lyn. "I hope you'll agree that one shouldn't go around murdering people, even criminals. I work in law enforcement, so I'm a big fan of due process and a fair trial." Arndt nodded. "And when she and I met, and she saw that I had the same powers as she did, she didn't pause—she went right for me. She was enraged. That said, if we find her, I'm willing to give her the chance to be reasonable. But I have to be ready for her not to be reasonable."

"That makes sense," said Arndt reluctantly.

"And I have to be able to produce evidence that she has powers like mine. If I want to go home and go back to my family and my job, then I need proof that it wasn't me committing those murders." At this, Arndt winced.

It hadn't been easy, but Lyn had explained to her relations that others knew about her powers. She hadn't given them even a fraction of the truth—the Checquy was never mentioned by name, and she didn't even suggest that there was a government body that dealt with and was staffed by the supernatural. But she'd said that there were a few people in law enforcement who were aware of her powers and who believed that she was the one responsible for the killings.

To a family with a centuries-old tradition of keeping a low profile, this had been distressing, but she'd assured them that no one suspected there might be more like her. That, in fact, was the problem.

"What are you thinking?" asked Arndt. "How would you like to proceed?"

"I suppose it depends on what help you can provide," Lyn said. "Do you have a way to find her?" Surely, with centuries' worth of teachings, the family had some technique for sniffing out their own? Except that she knew they didn't, because otherwise Jörg wouldn't have been sitting on Oxford Street hoping that a long-lost cousin might come wandering by.

"We have a way to lure her," said Arndt reluctantly. "I think it is safe to assume that she will be hunting you too now?" He looked to Lyn, and she nodded.

The blonde's reaction to meeting her had been unalloyed hate. The only reason that she hadn't tried to kill Lyn after they'd summoned the lightning had been the horrendous exhaustion that had overcome them both. Arndt nodded sagely and told her that it took a great deal of practice to use that skill without its sapping one's strength, although once you had mastered it, you could then use it to call bolts down onto distant targets. The family would usually take camping vacations into remote areas of the Swiss mountains and wait for especially bad weather days to practice.

The lightning summoning that the two of them had inadvertently collaborated on, however, was the key to drawing the blonde in. It turned out that once you had entangled your powers with another's, you would always be more sensitive to the taste of that person's abilities. If he or she was nearby, you would know it.

"Do you know how to radiate your energy out without actually igniting the electricity, as Jörg was doing when he caught your attention?" Arndt asked. Lyn shook her head and thought of that pulsing sensation that had drawn her over to address a perfect stranger. "It is a simple trick—I can teach it to you in a couple of minutes. We will find a place to which we wish to lure her, and then all of us will work with you. We can add our strength to your own, amplifying your signal, so to speak. It will not make your power stronger, simply more pervasive. It will reach farther. Does that make sense?"

"Yes," said Lyn warily.

"The idea is that she will sense the power, recognize it is you, and come. But then what?"

"I'll try to talk to her," said Lyn. "And, if it's possible, get her to turn herself in. I think the people I work with might make allowances for her situation. She's had no support, no explanation of what she is, and she hasn't been killing innocent civilians. It would be complicated, but it might be possible to bring her in—if she agrees to surrender."

"Otherwise?"

"Otherwise, I will try to take her down."

"And do you think you will be able to?"

"I don't know." The blonde had already proven that she was experienced, merciless, and ready to kill. "I don't suppose any of you brought swords with you?"

"Unfortunately not," said Arndt. "We have a number of very good ones back home, but it is not easy to bring such things into other countries."

"I believe you."

"Emre could make you a very nice spear if you would like. He is quick, and he runs a wire down the length of the shaft so you can electrify the blade."

"That is kind of you to offer, but I think I'd be better with what I'm used to," Lyn said. "If we fight and I win, well, I'll need you to be recording it. I'll need evidence of her capabilities."

"And if you take her alive?"

"If I bring her in, then she mustn't be able to speak about you. That's why it has to be just me and her. You'll need to be hidden. If it should all work out for me and I *do* get to go home, I will never reveal your existence to the authorities."

Arndt nodded; he trusted her. "And if you lose?"

"If I lose, I think she'll kill me." Lyn was surprised at how calm she was at the idea. "At that point, it's up to you to act as you see fit."

Arndt looked solemn at this. "We have had rogue members before, but it is very rare," he said. "The most recent was Hans Brandt. Before that, there was a man in the 1820s who killed his wife with his powers. We could not allow him to go to trial, so he was dealt with by the family. It is not our proudest moment."

"I trust you to act appropriately," Lyn said. *It won't matter to me anyway, as I'll be dead.* The prospect of being killed with a sword was not pleasant, but the strain of the past few days had been so terrible that she was willing to accept the possibility. She was eager to face the blonde again. She wanted an end to it.

"And when would you like to do this?" asked Arndt.

"Tonight?" she suggested.

"Certainly."

As they emerged from the cozy warmth of the restaurant, however, their plans changed abruptly. It was bucketing down rain, and a quick examination of the weather forecast revealed that it wasn't expected to stop for a couple of days.

"Well, this isn't good," said Lyn grimly.

"No, this is very good," Arndt said. "It will make witnesses much less likely."

And make it harder for the Checquy to find us, Lyn admitted to herself.

"So I think we should act as soon as possible," Arndt said.

"We should," agreed Lyn. "But first, we need to do a bit of shopping."

The family split up to take a fleet of cabs to run various errands, and Lyn ended up with Arndt, Jörg, Helga, and Elif. She and Arndt discussed the minutiae of the plan. They decided on Regent's Park, as it was relatively central and had good access to the Underground. The family hadn't used it for any previous eruptions of lightning, but Lyn couldn't decide if that made it more or less likely to be staked out by the Checquy. Still, it was convenient, and the heavy sheets of rain made it ideal. Helga had a laptop in her satchel, and they used it to bring up a map of the park to find the ideal spot. They chose an area of open lawn, near the boating lake and away from houses and restaurants.

"Five of us will stand with you," Arndt said. "We must be touching you to share our strength with you. The rest will be stationed around the park watching for anyone approaching. As soon as we know that she is coming to you, we will fall back to those trees by the lake and record the encounter."

"That all sounds good," said Lyn. She was beginning to feel that butterflies-in-the-stomach nervous anticipation. There were so many things to think about: the prospect of having her newfound relations channeling energy into her, the trick Arndt had shown her to cast her energy out into the world as a wave rather than a spark, and the fact that this could lead to her painful death.

Looming over it all was the memory of the blonde, her eyes filled with hate.

She's coming for me, Lyn thought. *Even if she doesn't know it yet.*

The taxi drivers were bewildered by the crowd of passengers who insisted that they wanted to be dropped off in the middle of the park in the pouring rain. Large, hastily purchased umbrellas were opened, but the downpour was so heavy that it was practically deafening, and one or two of the umbrellas threatened to crumple under the deluge. Jörg squinted through the sheets of rain and consulted his mobile phone.

"That way, I think," he said, pointing left.

I'm not sure it will actually make a difference where we go, thought Lyn. The rain was so heavy that there could have been any number of supernatural duels going on within twenty meters of them and she wouldn't have caught a glimpse. As they slogged across the sodden grass, Lyn began to question the wisdom of their plan. A slippery surface and poor visibility was not ideal for a fight, especially if one of the fighters had a sword.

Fuck it, she decided. *She'll be just as disadvantaged as me.* Her only concern was that the rain might prevent the family members from seeing the blonde until it was too late. *Nothing you can do about that, though.* None of them would be radiating energy, so the blonde would have no reason to note their presence.

"This looks good," she said. It was a fairly flat section of lawn with no apparent mud puddles. The trees along the boating pond were dark, indistinct shapes through the rain, but that would help conceal her relatives when they hid. Jörg had helped her pick out a good camera, taking care that it was waterproof. The salesman had rabbited on about its night-vision features, but she hadn't cared how it worked, only that it could capture images effectively in the dark. Jörg was fairly confident that he'd be able to film her and the blonde. She had paid cash.

The family members who were assigned to stand watch went off to their designated spots. Each of them had been given a dull-colored raincoat and umbrella, some sandwiches, a couple of bottles of water, and firm instructions not to desert their posts. Arndt had told them to piss on the grass or in the gutter if they needed to, but they were not to leave their places until directed to do so. Whoever saw the blonde would send a text message to a group chat, then all the sentries would walk to prearranged spots.

"How long do you think it will take for her to come?" asked Lyn, knowing it was a ridiculous question. It depended on so many factors that it was impossible for anyone to say. *Plus, there's no guarantee that she'll come when she senses me. If she senses me.*

All we can do is try. If it doesn't happen today, we'll try again tomorrow. And the next day. All the members of the family had pledged their support for as long as it took.

The cousin named Hannah unfolded a camping stool that she'd been sent to purchase, and Lyn sat down. Her weapon was held loosely in her hands. Her legs were already soaking from the rain, but her relatives held their umbrellas over her while a waterproof blanket was draped around her.

"Are you ready?" asked Arndt.

"Yes."

"And you are certain, Lynette, that this is how you wish to proceed?" he asked. "There would be a place for you with us. We could make it happen."

It was tempting, the idea of a large family waiting to welcome her. She could find a new way to fit into the world. Arndt had hinted that there were many ways for her to use her powers, years of skills that she could learn. It was her birthright. But Emma and Richard were at home waiting for her, and the Checquy would never stop watching them. They would never be able to come to her if she fled to the Continent.

Ridiculous as it might seem, another reason she couldn't go was the oath she'd made to the Checquy. They were her people as well, her comrades, friends, and teachers. She had been proud to be part of a force that fought to protect the innocent and the helpless; she worked with the best people she'd ever known, was privy to a world that made her life more extraordinary. The thought of them despising her, believing her to be a traitor and a rogue operative, was a dagger twisting in her heart.

And besides, there was the blonde. Walking the streets, murdering with their family's power. Full of hate. A sister or a cousin or an aunt. It was Lyn's responsibility to put a stop to it. Not only because she had discovered her. Not only because the woman was blood. Not only because Lyn had taken an oath as a Pawn of the Checquy to protect her countrymen.

It was her responsibility because she made it her responsibility.

"I'm ready," she said flatly. Arndt's hand was firm on her shoulder for a moment, a benediction from a cousin she'd met only a few hours ago, and it gave her strength.

"Begin, then, as I showed you," he said. She took a deep breath and let it out, and as she did so, she called up the energy that was always there waiting. It wanted to pour into the metal touching her skin—the rings on her fingers, the weapon in her hand—but she clenched against that and forced it to stay within her. It was hot inside her skin but not burning. It was exhilarating to feel the power crackling about madly, a storm within her flesh.

Now focus.

She concentrated on herself, on her body, listening beyond the maelstrom of energy for her heartbeat in her chest. She found it and fixed on it, pacing her energy to her pulse until it seemed as if the blood flowing through her body was lightning. She looked down at her hands through hooded eyes and was mildly surprised that her skin wasn't glowing. She felt like a river of hot, crackling light.

"Good," said Arndt from very far away. "We can all feel you radiating out. Continue, and we will join you." She nodded tightly and felt a hand on the side of her head, then another, and another. Five of her relations stood in a ring around her and added their power to her own. A warmth began flooding into her, banishing the chill from the rain and building up the energy inside her so that it became a torrent. "She'll feel that even if she's in Oxford," Arndt said with satisfaction, but Lyn barely heard him. All her attention was on her heartbeat and keeping the energy flowing within her.

Lyn felt as if she were balancing on the top of a column of water that was bursting out of the ground and would never stop. As long as you did not think about anything else and focused entirely upon the task at hand, you would be fine. There was no thought to spare for the idea of the blonde coming for her with a sword and the intent to use it. She couldn't think about Richard and Emma. The Checquy would just have to take care of itself. She was not aware of minutes or hours passing. All she could do was concentrate on the energy that boiled within her. It was all one continuous forever moment.

At one point she risked opening an eye a crack. It felt as though, with all that energy, there had to be a column of lightning reaching up into the sky or a mass of electricity crackling about them, but there was nothing, just the rain and the intent faces of those around her.

She had no idea how long it had been when she felt the flows of energy fading away. The warmth of her cousins' hands was no longer on her head. She slowly came back to the world.

"Don't stop radiating," said Arndt sharply. Lyn looked up at him in a daze but kept the energy circulating inside her. "She's coming."

"Are you sure?" How long had she been sitting there? It was impossible to tell with the rain muting all the light into twilight.

"Erika has sent a message about a woman with an umbrella and a suspicious walking stick," said Arndt. "She's heading directly toward us, about three minutes away. We need to leave you now."

With an effort, Lyn nodded. "If she kills me..." she began.

"We won't permit her to continue what she's doing here," said Arndt. "Unless she surrenders to you, she's not living past this day."

"Good. But if she does kill me, leave my body here."

"You're sure?"

"Yes," said Lyn.

It will eventually go to the Checquy, she thought. *Let them work it out.* She closed her eyes again and felt the rain starting to patter on her head as the family took their umbrellas and hurried away to their hiding place in the trees. Jörg was already ensconced there in the bushes, overseeing the camera set up on a little tripod stand. He was under strict orders not to pan the camera or zoom in, even if the battle went out of shot. If it was to be evidence of Lyn's innocence, there could be no sign that anyone else was involved.

Prepare yourself. She's coming.

Lyn opened her eyes and saw a shape coming toward her through the rain. It was a relief to release the energy inside her and let it pour down into the metal in her hand. She felt her head clearing and became aware of how cold and wet she was. She shifted a little and felt the inevitable aches of someone who hadn't moved for a good long time.

"Don't come any closer!" she called out, and the figure stopped. It was the blonde, dressed in a long coat. As Arndt had said, she was holding an umbrella in one hand and that damn sword-masquerading-as-a-cane thing in the other.

"You," said Lyn. "How did you find me?"

Let her think she tracked me. Don't let her know that she was lured here.

The blonde shrugged, smirking. "And what are you doing out here in the rain?" asked the blonde. She spoke with a Brummie accent.

"Um, I'm meditating," said Lyn hurriedly. She'd given absolutely no thought to an explanation and cast about frantically for why she would be out on a playing field in the rain. "Don't you feel a bond with the storm?"

"No," said the blonde. "Is that how you did the lightning bolts all over the place?" She looked up at the sky warily, as if she were worried that Lyn might abruptly call another bolt out of it.

"I don't know. It always happened when I was asleep." *Don't let her realize that there are others like us out there. And let her think I don't have any real control.*

The woman's eyes narrowed. "You're Jenny's little girl, aren't you? The one who went missing all those years ago?"

"I—maybe?" *Jenny!* Lyn thought. *My mother's name was Jenny? Who is she? And how is she related to this chick?*

Don't let yourself be distracted.

"Well, it doesn't matter," said the blonde. "I don't care about them. I left them all behind to come here and build what I'm building, and I won't let anything stop me. I don't care who you are or what you can do."

"And what are you building, exactly?" asked Lyn. The blonde wasn't a vigilante; she wasn't even a paid assassin. "Your own little kingdom, is it?"

"That's right."

"So you're going around killing criminals? And then what? You'll become the queen of the London underworld?"

"I'm not looking for too much," said the blonde. "The big crime, the serious money, that's all multinationals and cartels. Tech, computer crimes. But this power I've got means that nothing can stop me on the small scale. No little hoodlum, no gang. Once I've taken out the key players from the local gangs and they fear me, they'll all be paying up to me."

Lyn had to hand it to the blonde; she had thought it out. If you were willing to kill people and you had the kind of power they had, then raking out your own patch of London crime made a lot of sense. The power wouldn't let you conquer Europe, but it would certainly let you dominate several dozen people. It was like their ancestor Melo rising to lead the Sicambri but not looking to subjugate all the tribes.

"I don't suppose you'd consider throwing that idea away," said Lyn, "and doing something to help people with your powers?"

The blonde stared at her even more incredulously than she had when Lyn made up the thing about feeling kinship with the storm. Apparently, the suggestion did not even merit an answer. *I had to try.*

"I want what I want," the blonde said. "A few more deaths and they'll be good and terrified, running around without any firm leadership. I'll be in a position to sweep in while they're all off balance. And I won't let anything get in my way. You're the only thing I have to worry about, and that's going to end *now!*" Even as she spoke, the blonde was tossing aside her umbrella and darting forward. She drew her sword, flung the scabbard away, and bore down on Lyn, covering the distance between them in a few steps. Her sword was raised, ready to slice down with all her strength.

"*Ya!*" shouted Lyn, and she tossed back the blanket as she rose to her feet and brought up her weapon to block and catch the blonde's sword. The force of the blonde's strike hammered into her arms, but it was nothing compared to the blinding red flash and the deafening *crack* of electricity erupting into the storm. Tendrils of red lightning radiated out in all directions, scorching the grass and flashing rain into steam.

The blonde stared at Lyn, her eyes wide. It was not the scarred riot baton that had caught her sword. Instead, as if she had produced it from nowhere, Lyn was holding a hand-and-a-half sword, a "bastard sword," as Pawn Fenton had referred to it during the many hours of instruction he'd provided on how to use it.

Didn't see that coming, did you?

Hand-forged, museum-quality, the sword had cost her a multitude of pretty pennies. She and Arndt had purchased it from London's largest stocker of swords for reenactors, live-action role-players, and, most crucially, moneyed and discerning collectors.

The sword was a beautiful thing, so beautiful that it had taken most of the money she'd liberated from the gangsters in the cellar of the Anvil. In fact, it was almost too lovely to trust as a weapon. Lyn had no idea about the origins of the blonde's weapon, but it had proven itself fearsome and effective. She'd been half afraid that the blonde's sword might just slice through her own. But it hadn't.

The curved guards at the hilt of her hand-and-a-half sword caught the blonde's blade easily, just as they'd been designed to do several centuries ago. Now the two women strained against each other, arms trembling.

The blonde snarled. She bore down, using her weight to bring the edge of her sword down to Lyn's face, but Lyn was braced against it. Hours of training with the merciless Pawn Fenton had given her many different tactics to use. She twisted, shoved, and pushed up, sending the blonde staggering back. If she'd had the chance, Lyn would have lunged forward and finished the off-balance woman then and there, but her foot skidded backward on the wet grass, and by the time she'd recovered her footing, the blonde had recovered hers.

It will be about speed, Lyn told herself. Both of them had the electricity power and couldn't hurt each other with it. The blonde's weapon was lighter, but Lyn had trained rigorously with a multitude of weapons, and she was hoping that she'd be faster than the blonde anticipated.

They came together, their feet slipping on the grass, and the blonde struck out at her, almost too fast to see. *Almost.* Lyn had both hands on her sword's hilt and she blocked and cut back at her opponent's head with the speed that had been drilled into her. The blonde deflected it, though, and fought back. A chop at the throat, a cut at an arm, another blurry chop at Lyn's head. Each time, Lyn blocked, but with difficulty. Her enemy was fast and never hesitated. She was fighting to kill, whereas Lyn had only fought to train—at least with a blade. They fell back, both of them panting.

Wherever she learned this, she learned well, thought Lyn grudgingly. A flash of lightning above made them both flinch, each thinking the other had summoned it. It appeared that the storm, which had earlier consisted almost entirely of rain, was ramping up somewhat. *It'll be a good joke on us if we're struck by actual lightning.* Testing conducted gingerly at the Estate had shown that she was not immune to electricity that wasn't her own, and waving metal rods around in the open during a storm seemed almost as bad an idea as fighting a duel against a woman who had experience in killing people.

The blonde came at her again, and Lyn had no more time for thought. It was continuous, ugly fighting without a break. Lyn's wrists and arms burned. They splashed through puddles as the rain grew heavier. The blonde pursued her, pushed her across the field and close to the trees where the family was hiding. She fought back, shouting with every swing of her sword like a tennis player. Even though their powers wouldn't affect each other, there were still crimson sparks and sometimes full bursts of electricity when their weapons smashed together. As they became more and more tired, their strikes became less precise, and their control wavered.

Water flew about as they swung at each other. Both of them were as drenched as if they had gone swimming. One of the cousins had braided Lyn's hair back in some sort of severe German sword-fighting hairstyle, and the blonde's hair had been pulled back, but their exertions meant that their hair was now sodden and flying about the place.

And the weather was taking its toll. The blonde had not removed her raincoat, which meant she was somewhat hampered, while Lyn's lightweight long-sleeved T-shirt allowed free movement but offered next to no protection against the wet and the cold. She could feel her strength ebbing. She was stiff from the hours of sitting in the rain.

Worse, and she was frightened to admit it, the blonde was a better fighter than her. Not much better, but enough.

Then the blonde did her trick with the electricity boiling down the length of the blade. The rain hissed off the crackling weapon menacingly, and despite herself, Lyn shrank back a little. The blonde was suddenly a demon, a witch, a killer queen holding a burning blade.

Please let that have been caught on camera, Lyn thought. *That's my proof that she's like me. That's the moment that will get me home.*

If I live.

The flickering blade distracted her, catching her gaze despite all her training. She didn't see her opponent setting her legs and shoulders for a strike until the blonde's sword was slicing down at her. Lyn flung herself back but not fast enough. The blonde slashed low; Lyn screamed as the tip of the blade cut into her leg, and the electricity seethed off it to flash in her vision.

The blonde was still coming, and Lyn backed up hurriedly. She blinked to clear her eyes, trying to find her footing, to ignore the burning pain in her thigh where the blonde had sliced her. She didn't dare look down to see what damage had been done. The sword had gone deep enough, she knew, that sparks would be sputtering out of her leg along with the blood. She was still standing, though, so it wasn't bad enough to matter.

The blonde advanced without pause. She kept pushing Lyn back, step by step along the slick grass, so she could never get her balance. The other woman was roaring with every attack, and electricity flashed red off every sword strike while thunder crashed above them.

I can't stop her! thought Lyn desperately. There was no opening, no gap in the blonde's relentless attack.

Strike back! You have to strike back! Don't let her keep pushing. If she keeps pushing, she'll win.

Strike!

It was an ugly, awkward move that would have had Pawn Fenton groaning in disgust and Lyn's classmates in her kindergarten-level fight class rolling their eyes. A clumsy stuttering of steps that stopped her retreat but left her completely off balance with a bad stance. A frantic lashing out with her blade that left her vulnerable all along her side.

If either of them had been a worse swordswoman, it wouldn't have worked out the way it did. The blonde would have struck true and killed her in that moment of vulnerability rather than just striking Lyn's left arm and laying it open to the bone. But they'd taken each other's measure and thought they knew what to expect, so Lyn's abrupt and clumsy attack was so grotesque and inconceivably ungainly that the blonde was caught completely off guard. She had been inexorably stalking her weakening prey, and then suddenly the prey had somehow stumbled forward, skidded on a patch of mud, and stabbed her in the shoulder.

The blonde lurched backward, twisting away so that Lyn's blade was pulled out of her flesh.

Push forward! The hilt was slick in her hands now, her legs were screaming, and the slash at her arm was a pulsing blaze of pain, but this was Lyn's only opening, and she had to take it. Quick, brutal strikes. Every time the blonde parried, Lyn followed up whip-fast, never allowing her opponent to recover her stance, never stopping. Exhausting. Relentless. Death by a thousand cuts—a cut to the arm, a strike to the other arm.

All the while, her own arm was screaming, and she felt the horrible heat of her own blood pouring down her fingers.

Push forward!

A terrifying jab at her face made the blonde flinch and then a dreadful thrust under the blonde's sword punched through her shirt and sent her sprawling back onto the grass.

The blonde raised her blade feebly, and Lyn slapped it away with her own, then kicked it out of her hand. The woman struggled to rise, but Lyn planted her foot squarely on her chest. The blonde pressed her hand incredulously to the wound just below her ribs. Electricity sputtered out of the bloody injury. She was gasping. They were both gasping with exertion and exhaustion.

Lyn opened her mouth to ask if the blonde would yield, if she'd surrender, but before she could form the words—

"You...you..." wheezed the blonde. Lyn could see the frustration and rage in her eyes.

She could imagine everything that had happened to bring them to this point. The woman had discovered her powers and hadn't let them break her. Like Melo, she'd bided her time, developed her skills, and made her plans, and then, just when it all seemed within her grasp, Lyn had appeared and taken it all away. All the possibilities, the money, the power—the culmination of what had to be years of work and training—was being snatched out of reach.

"I'll kill you!" the blonde screamed.

"Sorry," said Lyn, and she stabbed forward.

The sensation of the blade sliding into the woman's belly turned Lyn's stomach, and the blonde coughed up blood. A storm of red electricity seethed out of her wound and up Lyn's blade to crackle meaninglessly around her. The woman was screaming, and it was hideous.

I have to finish it, Lyn thought. She pulled the blade out, placed the point of it on the woman's chest, stared into her hate-filled eyes, and bore down into her heart.

Lyn stood slumped, weary to her bones. Weary in her heart. The blonde's eyes were dead and staring; the rain fell onto her face and washed away the blood that she'd choked out at the end, but the rage and loathing were still locked in her expression. Her teeth were bared in a snarl. A few scribbles of electricity still danced over her skin.

It's over, thought Lyn. She felt empty. It was the worst thing she'd ever done, and she was aware, sort of, that it might mean a return to everything that was important to her. But right then, leaning over the body of the woman she'd killed, she couldn't muster up any emotion at all.

The cousins were coming to her through the rain. Hands caught her, wrapped her in a blanket, and lowered her to the wet grass. She heard them saying things but didn't know what they were. All she could see was the blonde screaming up at her, relentless in her hate.

They tended to the cuts on her legs, bandaging around them. Arndt told her that they would take time to heal, but they were not horrifically deep. She nodded dully. The wound to her arm, though, needed immediate medical attention. She screamed a little when they cinched a bandage around it, but then the pain was just one more thing.

"I think that the footage is quite good," Jörg said. "Well, good enough. I waited, of course, until everyone had moved away from you, and then I started filming. It looks like you set the timer and then stepped out into the frame. It is remarkable to look at. You were both moving about so much, there were times where you ran out of shot, but there is a very clear image of her with the electricity lighting up her blade. I wonder how she did that. Do you know?" Lyn shook her head exhaustedly. "Well, that will be something to experiment when I get home." She looked up at him blankly. He wiped the camera down, then he placed it back into its case.

"It will definitely clear your name," he said. "Or at least show that you are not the only one with this power."

"Yeah, good," said Lyn.

"I stopped it after you, uh, you won. But before everyone came out to help. I am not sure how you will explain, though."

"Cut it a little more, please," said Lyn. "Cut out the bit at the end, where I . . ."

Where I kill her.

"If you are certain," said Jörg cautiously.

"I'll tell them I cut it myself, that I didn't want footage of that existing."

She looked around. Arndt and a couple of the cousins were standing over the body of the blonde, their heads bowed. Arndt said something in German, then turned.

"We have not touched her," he assured Lyn. "Or her sword. I understand that everything must be left for your colleagues to find. But a small prayer for a cousin . . ." He trailed off and smiled sadly. "It is not the ending we might have hoped for, but it is better than it could have been. I am glad that you won, Lynette." He cleared his throat uncomfortably. "It did not look like an easy fight."

"No," agreed Lyn.

"We should go now," said Arndt. "You should summon help." He crouched down and kissed her on the brow. "I am glad that we could assist you, at least a little."

"Will I see you again?" she asked weakly.

"There is an e-mail address," he said, and told it to her. It was very simple, easy to remember but nondescript. "Write when you can, once things have settled down. But there is no hurry. Not for days, not for weeks, not for years if you need the time. We will always be glad to hear from you."

The rest of the family bade her farewell. There was a general tenderness but a wariness in some, for which she could not blame them. They had just watched her kill a woman; the corpse lay only a few feet away. Jörg crouched down to place the camera case next to her and shake her hand one final time. And then they were all gone, vanished into the rain.

It's all over, she thought again.

A moment of quiet. The rain had diminished a little, but it still pattered down. The thunder had quieted and the lightning had ceased.

The blonde hadn't asked her any questions, hadn't cared about her. She'd dismissed the fact that Lyn was related to her. She'd seen Lyn as a threat, a rival, not a potential ally. She'd only been interested in what her power could get for her. And she'd been willing to kill people to take it.

It would have been nice if we could have worked things out, Lyn thought. *But I don't think I'll have any nightmares because of this.* It was something that had to be done.

"Okay," Lyn sighed finally. She dug into her coat and pulled out a burner phone that she'd purchased and that Jörg had held on to for her. *Let's see how this works out.* She dialed the number for the notifications line of the Office of Qualifications and Examinations Regulation. "Hi, this is Pawn Lynette Binns." She listened and smiled as she pulled her rings off her fingers, tapped them to release any captured energy, and flipped them away into the grass. "Yes, that's me . . . yes, the Delouser. Could you please put a call through to the watch office?

"I'm ready to come home."

28

Bridget sat, bone-tired and filthy, on the kitchen chair. She felt empty.

She had opened the flat's door to find the Checquy support team taking over the place. Usha was gently led out and down the hallway while a nurse stepped in and vigorously scrubbed Bridget's hands and forearms clean. She was gentle, though, around the sealed-off wound on Bridget's arm. The Murcutts had been hustled into the bedroom at gunpoint and the door shut firmly, two armed guards and, perhaps more frightening, one conspicuously unarmed guard looming over them. Wattleman became visible once they'd swathed him in a bathrobe, and they guided him out to a car, no time to say goodbye, leaving nothing but a residue of blood, sweat, and dirt that had seemingly materialized on the chair once he got up from it.

Checquy surgeons had entered the flat—three men in suits who quickly changed into white gowns. A rubber sheet was laid on the table, and Usha was lifted onto it. An injection was given, and her eyes fluttered shut. Her dusty, bloodstained clothes were cut away, with only a few patches of material left where blood and pearl handprints had glued them to her skin. The surgeons consulted with one another. Glass bottles of blood were produced from an insulated chest, and a nurse held them up to drain down a tube into the patient.

Bridget was directed to dissolve the first handprint, the one on the front of her friend's shoulder, and then told to step out of the way as the surgeons set about their business with their scalpels, their needles and thread, a glowing mouth. And then the second handprint was dissolved, and the wound repaired.

Eventually, Usha lay there cleansed of pearl and dust and blood with neat sutures where she had been shot. The surgeons advised Bridget that her friend would recover, and Usha was wrapped in sheets and carefully carried away on a stretcher by attendants.

Then Bridget had to strip the pearl off her own injured forearm, and a doctor sewed up the ugly jagged wound, dressed it, and shook her bare hand with no hesitation before departing.

"You are to wait here," said one of the nurses. "The guards will remain with you to keep your guests secured."

"Thank you," said Bridget dully.

And so she sat. No one had thought to bring her replacement clothes, so she had washed her hands several times and then her face and tried not to look at the bloodstains on her clothing.

Bridget rested her hands on her stomach and thought about the possibility of a child inside her. It had been only—what? A day? Two?—since she and Gerald had...if they had created something together, what would it be right now? Just a whisper of potentiality.

And if she and Gerald *had* made that potentiality, would it have survived everything she had gone through? The fall through empty space in Wattleman's arms and the jolting landing onto the street, the fear of running through the bombings, the madness of seeing her friends and comrades killed in the Caïssa, the whiplash of despair and relief from losing Usha to finding her alive, the battle with the Murcutts' men, the abrupt switches in gravity, the maelstrom of dust from a collapsing (and then exploding) building—would a whisper be able to withstand all that chaos?

I think yes, she decided, but she didn't know if she hoped it had. She didn't know if she hoped it existed at all.

"Miss Mangan?" She looked up, startled, to see Rebecca Steward at the door. Lady Carmichael's chatelaine had a suitcase in her hand and a wary expression on her face.

"Miss Steward, I'm sorry, I didn't even hear you come in."

"Lady Carmichael is on her way here from Bufo Hall, but once I saw the state of Pawn Wattleman, it occurred to me that you might appreciate a change of clothes." She held up the suitcase. "There's soap, shampoo, a towel, and fresh everything, including shoes."

"You're a goddess," said Bridget gratefully.

"And yet no shrines," said Miss Steward. "You go get cleaned up and use all the water you want."

When Bridget emerged in a smart skirt and blouse, Lady

Carmichael had arrived and was sitting at the table talking quietly with Miss Steward. She stood and embraced Bridget.

"I'm glad you're all right," the Lady said.

"I don't know if I am," said Bridget. "You—have they told you about Pamela?"

"Yes." The Lady's voice was bleak, but her face was calm.

"Why aren't I crying?" Bridget asked. "I care about her desperately, she was my dear friend, and she died horribly. When we thought Usha was dead, I wailed and screamed, but Pamela is gone and all I can do is sit here and not cry."

"Perhaps it's because we thought Usha had died in a stupid, random disaster caused by a war that kills people who have nothing to do with it but Pamela died as a soldier on a mission. She died fighting an enemy. That makes a difference." Lady Carmichael sighed. "Or perhaps it's because we're all exhausted." Bridget looked at the Lady and, for the first time, noticed the dark patches under her eyes and her pallor. She looked almost as weary as Pamela had.

"Sit," said Steward firmly. "Both of you. I'll make tea."

"I never send soldiers out into the field without being aware that I might be sending them to their death and that I will be the cause of it," said Lady Carmichael finally. "I hope they know that they are valued, that I treasure them, and that I never act lightly."

"They do know that," said Bridget. "We do."

"I came to the Checquy later in life. I sometimes wonder if there's some element I've missed, some lesson that everyone else learned as a child and considers obvious, that would make this all seem so much more reasonable," mused the Lady.

"If there's a lesson like that, I missed it too," said Bridget. She wasn't sure if it was appropriate, but she reached out, laid her hand on the Lady's, and held it tightly for a moment. Lady Carmichael looked at her and smiled sadly. Then she took a deep breath.

"Meanwhile, we have two criminals locked up in the next room," the Lady observed. "I suppose we had better deal with that situation. This whole little endeavor has hardly been covert. We're getting reports of two men bursting through the wall of an upper story of a brothel." She paused. "One of them is reported to have been naked. The other one landed headfirst on the street, a maneuver that appears, unsurprisingly, to have been messily fatal. The naked one was breathing but unconscious. Meanwhile, gunshots and screams were heard to come from the top floor. The naked man woke up and was, ahem, 'lost in the crowd.' And then all the occupants of the building rushed out into the street, many of them scantily dressed or in various states of *déshabillé*.

"Then the building partially collapsed. And then it exploded." She looked at Bridget. "There appear to be some gaps in the story. Would you be able to assist me with those?"

"I believe I can, my Lady," said Bridget, and she recounted everything that had happened since they'd last spoken in Lady Carmichael's office. There were some strategic modifications and omissions, of course. Rather than recognizing Pamela as the witch who had torn his aircraft out of the sky, the Nazi had, in Bridget's telling, seized an opportunity to attack intruders.

"I sent you into a much more complicated situation than I anticipated," the Lady said grimly.

"It was more complicated than any of us anticipated," said Bridget gently.

"We still don't know who was providing these Murcutts with the Checquy items?"

"No," Bridget said. "All I've been able to get out of Matilda is that it's a man who has a house in London and is an opium addict."

"I suppose it's something of a lead," Lady Carmichael said.

"Not much of one," said Bridget apologetically.

"We must question the Murcutts. But if they refuse to talk or their information is unreliable, we could try to identify the source in the Checquy. However, I still want to keep the theft of our assets off the books if at all possible. Thank God the Murcutts had actual powered minions — that'll help me justify all this."

"Tillie Murcutt has indicated that she's willing to make a deal," Bridget said.

The Lady pursed her lips thoughtfully for a moment. "Tell me about her."

Bridget gave her impressions and recounted the life story that Miss Murcutt had shared.

"I see. And the brothers?"

"The elder one, Robert, doesn't know anything about the events of today. And Tillie said he's always distanced himself from the supernatural elements of the business. But the brother we have in custody, John—well, he does not appear to be handling things very well," said Bridget. "Quite aside from the fact that he still has my handprint locked across half his face, he's become quite brittle after witnessing all the…activity."

"Hmm."

"I think he would break easily, if, um, that's the route you want to take." The Lady regarded her levelly, and Bridget felt herself flushing. She didn't know if she was suggesting intimidation or torture or what. Everything felt confused now.

"Tillie Murcutt has demonstrated a willingness to be bought, yes?" asked Lady Carmichael.

"Yes. I think it would have worked if that one thug hadn't tried to be clever."

"Let's bring them in," Lady Carmichael said. "I have some experience in doing business."

At that, for the first time, Bridget felt a twinge of pity for Tillie Murcutt.

The siblings were brought in, and when Tillie saw Lady Carmichael, she pulled up short in shock. "Oh my God," she said. "I know who you are. You're famous."

"Well, I'm known," said the Lady placidly.

"You were the little girl in the…"

"Yes."

"And now you own…"

"Yes."

"But really you're with these…"

"Yes."

Tillie kept staring at her in astonishment.

"Would the two of you like to sit down?" Lady Carmichael said.

The siblings sat, the sister still incredulous but managing to look collected in her admittedly dusty coat with the gown underneath.

The brother was hunched over with his coat partially over his head. He chewed at his lips, and his eyes darted back and forth anxiously.

"So, do you own this?" Tillie asked Lady Carmichael. She gestured at Bridget and the guards. "They're your private magic army?"

"No, I'm just a part of it," the Lady said.

"Gosh," said Tillie breathlessly.

"I spoke with my apprentice here." She gestured to Bridget, and Tillie looked at her wide-eyed. "She's advised me that you know the name of the man who provided the artifacts."

"Uh, yes. Yes, I do," said Tillie.

"Excellent. I want that name."

"I...yes, well, I have a few things I want," said Tillie, trying to collect her thoughts.

"Indeed," Lady Carmichael said.

"Of course, your employee will need to remove the, uh, mass from my brother's face. That is a given, so I'd like to begin with the fact that my place of business has been demolished by *your* people."

No mention of the German bomb, I notice, thought Bridget.

"I require the cost of completely reconstructing the building and replacing any and all materials contained within." Bridget's jaw dropped. "I also want compensation for all my lost business during the period that reconstruction takes. It's wartime—builders are at a premium, *if* you can find any. So I'd say two years' profits, minimum. I also need compensation for the loss of my people—a year's salary for each of them."

"This would be for their families?" asked Lady Carmichael.

"I'm their family. I also expect that no mention of any of my family's business will reach the ear of law enforcement. Now, all of this is simply to reimburse me for what I have lost as a result of your activities. I view it as your outstanding existing debt."

"I see," the Lady said. Bridget was still reeling from the outrageousness of the criminal's demands.

"This brings us to the question of a certain name that you want and that I possess. Given that you sent four people with magic powers to get this information, you must want it very badly. Your girl here"—and she nodded to Bridget—"named a price that seemed fair at the time. But it doesn't seem fair now, not when I know who you are and what resources you possess."

"You're thinking of my personal, private monies rather than official funds," warned Lady Carmichael.

Tillie shrugged. "If you want that name badly enough, I know you can afford to throw some cash into the pot." She quoted a figure that made Bridget blanch. Tillie noticed and smiled.

"I see," said Lady Carmichael. "And is there anything else?"

"Yes. I want immunity for me and my brothers from punishment for any crimes, magical or otherwise."

"I'm afraid it's a little late for that," said the Lady. "You've already been found guilty."

"What? But isn't there supposed to be a trial?" asked Tillie, flummoxed.

"Your trial was my apprentice reporting to me," said Lady Carmichael serenely. "She has described your various crimes, and I have found you guilty, which is well within my authority."

"Oh."

"As is exacting immediate punishment."

"Oh."

"I know. It's enough to make one wish for a Star Chamber," Lady Carmichael said without a hint of sympathy. "The punishments reserved for your crimes are quite horrendous." At this, Bridget saw John Murcutt's hands tighten into fists, and she tensed, but nothing happened. "The merest possibility of being spared those punishments should be a sufficiently large incentive for you to offer me complete cooperation." Tillie opened her mouth, but the Lady pressed on. "But I think I can also offer you some things you don't even know you want."

"I...yeah?" Tillie looked wary, as well she might. Bridget herself had no idea what Lady Carmichael was talking about.

The Lady looked to Bridget for a moment. "My apprentice here has spoken eloquently on your behalf, and she has assured me that, oddly, my other apprentice, *whom your man shot,* would also be speaking in your favor if she were not recovering from emergency lifesaving surgery carried out on this very table." Both Murcutts jerked their hands off the table. "I am offering you a place with our organization."

"What?" exclaimed Bridget as Tillie reared back in surprise. Lady Carmichael regarded Bridget levelly, and she could feel a fierce blush rising up in her cheeks. "I beg your pardon, my Lady."

"Granted," said Lady Carmichael easily. Still, Bridget had an unpleasant suspicion that her outburst would result in a patient, gentle, and entirely excruciating lecture later. "Now, where was I?"

"You were offering employment," said Tillie.

"Yes," said Lady Carmichael. "You have some promising qualities. Bridget has recognized your ability to strategize as well as witness the supernatural and emerge unscathed." She paused, presumably taking in the slumped figure of John Murcutt, but she elected to press on. "I'm intrigued by your drive and your skill at recruiting people with unnatural abilities. And of course, there are your connections and understanding of the criminal underworld. You could be extremely valuable."

"Why would we want to work with you?" asked Tillie, her eyes narrowed.

"Oh, make no mistake, you would be working *for* me," said the Lady. "First, we pay very well. But working for us brings additional benefits, and those, I think, would be the real temptation for you."

"Oh?"

"I understand, Miss Murcutt, that you wish to taste every experience you can," said Lady Carmichael. Tillie's eyes widened, and she shot a look at Bridget. Bridget did her best to appear inscrutable, although she suspected her incredulous outburst had rather put paid to that. "You do not resist any pleasure that comes your way." Tillie looked a little abashed. She had strutted her appetites proudly before Bridget, but in the face of Lady Carmichael's assured elegance and power, perhaps they did not seem deliciously decadent but rather sordid and grubby.

"I've seen this before," continued the Lady. "The wealthy can afford to indulge themselves. But if one embraces the life of a voluptuary too much, one becomes jaded. Pleasure becomes perfunctory.

I've seen people slide into degeneracy as they try to recapture the thrill of the new.

"Working for us, however, never gets old. You'll never be known, never have public glory, but if you join us, you'll know things and experience things that your mother never even knew to forbid. Monsters and miracles. The hidden mysteries of the world."

Tillie's eyes were wide, shining. Unconsciously, she licked her lips. "That sounds like something I'd like to do," said the crime boss huskily. She didn't even look to her brother for his thoughts. "Very much." The Lady nodded with a faint smile. "I suppose I won't need this, then." Tillie reached into her coat and drew out, very slowly so that there could be no threat, the pearl poniard Bridget had sculpted and that she had last seen—oh God, she had seen it in Tillie's hand right before Pamela was killed.

Tillie now held it by the point of the blade, pinched between two fingers. Lady Carmichael looked at Bridget and raised an eyebrow.

I really am not covering myself in glory today, Bridget thought sourly. Bad enough that she'd let her weapon—and it really was undeniably hers—be taken from her, but she'd failed to ensure that the prisoner was unarmed before introducing her to the head of the Checquy. In the madness of escaping the Moor's Head, the task had fallen through the cracks, and everyone assumed someone else had taken care of it. Tillie laid the dagger delicately on the table, the handle facing the Lady and Bridget.

"I am extr—" began Lady Carmichael, but John Murcutt suddenly jerked forward, snatched up the dagger, shoved his sister aside, and lunged across the table. Bridget had a blurred impression of a staring bloodshot eye, flesh twisted around her handprint, and teeth bared in rage. He moved so quickly that the guards, who had been lulled by the calm discussion and by his complete lack of participation, were caught totally unprepared.

It wasn't clear whom he was going for, whether he was trying to kill Bridget for what she'd done to him or the Lady for enticing his sister into service, but there was a savage intensity in his attack. Bridget was on her feet without even realizing it, and with her bare hand she caught the blade as it came at her. The edge was razor agony in her hand, and she screamed and then clenched her fingers tighter.

John Murcutt pulled back on the handle and was confronted with a long trailing strand of denatured muck that had previously been the pearl blade. With a roar, he threw it aside and hurled himself forward again, only to be met with a firm, merciless right cross from Miss Steward that sent him staggering back with an extremely broken nose.

"Monsters!" he screamed. "You're fucking monsters!" With blood pouring out of his nose and his red weeping face twisted by Bridget's handprint, he himself looked monstrous. Snarling now, he made to lunge across the table a third time. The guards were just aiming their weapons when a quiet voice spoke:

"Die."

John Murcutt collapsed instantly onto the floor, as limp and still as if he'd been shot in the head.

All eyes in the room swiveled to Lady Carmichael. Her face was blank. She gave no sign of exertion. She simply regarded the corpse on the floor.

I've never seen her use her power before, Bridget thought weakly. It was legend within the Checquy.

Tillie Murcutt's face wore an expression like nothing Bridget had ever seen, incredulous sorrow mixed with horror mixed with morbid fascination. For several long moments, the crime boss gazed at the brother who had just died. Then she set her jaw and turned to Lady Carmichael.

"Am I still being offered the position?" she asked.

29

There was a gentle, respectful rap at the car window, and Bridget rolled it down. She drew back the blackout curtain a crack.

"Yes, Alexandrina?"

"I've got them ready, Bridget." The albino girl was bundled up in a thick, padded coat with a fur-lined hood. Her pale skin was stark in the midst of the black fur.

"What did you decide on?"

"I've set up two relays of prisms. One ends at the tree line. It's far enough back that none of the subjects will wander through it."

"Is that close enough?" asked Bridget.

"I can reposition and rotate the final prism if the Lady wants a better look at any particular person," said Alexandrina confidently. Bridget nodded her approval, and the girl flushed with pleasure. "The second relay curves up from here and goes directly over the site. It will show the circle the subjects have marked out from about forty feet up." Bridget pursed her lips thoughtfully.

"Can you shift it a little bit off center? Like five yards?"

"Yes." The girl hesitated. "May I ask why?"

"Just...in case," said Bridget. Supernatural events tended to have an unhealthy habit of shooting things right up into the sky.

"I'll get right on it," Alexandrina said.

"Thank you. I'll be out in a moment." She rolled up the window and closed the curtain. Lady Carmichael was reading over some documents, a small electric light glowing over her shoulder. "My Lady, I'm just going to check on the situation. We still have a little time." The Lady nodded.

The night was cold, especially after the snug warmth of the Rolls. Alexandrina was standing a few yards away, her back to the car and her arms stretched out in front of her. Her hands twisted as if she were sculpting the air, and Bridget caught a glimpse of the space in front of her wavering in the darkness.

Several soldiers stood nearby dressed in ghillie suits, with foliage and loose strips of fabric giving them a rough, humped appearance. Bridget knew that when they lay down, they would be practically invisible, especially in the darkness. She beckoned to them, and one strode forward with a faint rustling.

"Miss Mangan?"

"Sergeant Morrison, what are our circumstances?" The last time she'd seen him was at the Caïssa Club the night of the lecture, when apprentices had been nervously approaching him. He'd been wearing a suit then. Now he looked like an ambulatory portion of hedge.

"Eleven of our soldiers are in place around the site, ready to move in on the signal. There are only two targets so far." The two targets, middle-aged ladies, had arrived about an hour ago and were bustling around the site.

"The microphones are working?" Two days before, Morrison's team had laboriously concealed microphones around the area, then buried the cables that snaked back to the Checquy camp.

"Oh, aye. They're pickin' up the ladies' chat beautifully. D'ye want to have a listen?" He gestured to one of the headsets on a nearby table.

"Have they said anything interesting?"

"Not really, no," he said. "Just haverin' on about the weather."

"Well, what have they been doing?"

"Oh, they've marked out a circle and made four wee piles of wood at the cardinal points of the compass. I expect they won't be lighting them until the last minute for fear of air-raid wardens driving across the paddocks to shout at them. They'll wait until the others show up."

"They've got another hour yet," said Bridget, looking at her watch. "Our intelligence says they'll be looking to commence the ceremony at midnight. Are the troops all right in this cold?" she asked dubiously.

"Oh, aye. In truth, a ghillie suit's apt to get quite hot, so this is perfect. Plus there's probably a flask of something warming floating about."

And you've probably supplied it, thought Bridget, but without any concern. The soldiers were professional and on a secret mission for the Lady of the Checquy. They wouldn't let themselves drink enough to be hampered.

The entire mission had been an education for Bridget. She'd been brought up as a national secret herself and observed clandestine operations since she was nine years old. Her time in the Lady's office had given her a bird's-eye view of the Checquy's activities around the globe, and she knew a little about secret missions Wattleman and others had undertaken for the Court, but this operation was unusually complex. Different elements of the past few days had different levels of classification. Sometimes she was not sure what she was concealing from whom.

The collapse of the Moor's Head and Pamela's death had to be acknowledged. It was made known to the Order of the Checquy that Pawn Verrall had died in the line of duty while on a mission for the Lady. She had perished while subduing three supernatural criminals, including the fugitive Nazi pilot who had survived the crash of the bomber.

Bridget had stood, stone-faced, in the Cabinet war room as Lady Carmichael and Lord Pease explained to the Prime Minister that there was no indication that the Nazi's powers represented any sort of German Checquy-type operation. Usha had dutifully shared the information she'd extracted from the criminal, and the Lord and Lady passed it along: his powers had ignited during the crash and protected him, and he had lived on the streets until he was drafted into a criminal organization to conduct assassinations.

So the fact of a supernaturally powered Nazi was known and acknowledged, but the circumstances of how he'd come to crash would remain forever between Usha and Bridget.

Miss Murcutt's induction into the Checquy as a Retainer had been the subject of much fascinated gossip in the halls of Apex House, and the Prime Minister was reported to have smirked a little at the thought.

The loss of the artifacts, however, was never to be revealed, not to the greater Order or any government authority. The repercussions would probably have served as a useful warning for staff, but it represented too great a failure on the part of Checquy security to be admitted to.

And the events of this night, if successful, would remain completely off the books, with details known only to the Court, the small troop of soldiers involved, and a couple of staff members, including Bridget.

If all went well, the stolen artifacts would be carefully and quietly reinserted into the archive system. If all went badly, the operation had the potential to be utterly disastrous. Keeping it a secret from the Checquy would be the least of their concerns. The amount of supernatural power being brought together boggled the mind and the bowels.

Bridget looked up. It was one of those incredibly still, clear nights. No moon, so the stars blazed above them. The air almost hurt to breathe, it was so sharp in her throat. She heard the distant sound of waves washing against the cliffs.

It was a perfect night for flying, but Usha was still recovering from her surgery. Lady Carmichael had sent Usha to the Moat House to rest and recuperate. According to Usha's last letter, the country air was very pleasant, her maids were taking very good care of her, and the Carmichael children had managed to get in trouble for smuggling baby piglets up to see her because they would "make her feel happy." In an attempt to be considerate and recognizing that the piglets were rather grubby, the children had washed them in the bath beforehand, in the process using up several bars of an incredibly expensive soap that, thanks to the war, was no longer available. They had also left the tub full of filthy pig water and the floor swimming.

The piglets' mother had, meanwhile, enjoyed a rare nap, but upon awakening she had waddled into the house to seek her abducted progeny, irrevocably soiling several rugs, knocking over a vase of flowers, and driving one of the English maids into hysterics.

Bridget was sorry Usha couldn't be with her to see the culmination of the artifact operation, but she was glad Usha didn't have to be out here on this frigid night.

"Sergeant Morrison," Bridget said now, and he looked at her. "*You* wouldn't happen to have a drop of something warming on your person, would you?" He raised an eyebrow but produced a leather-wrapped flask from within the foliage of his suit and handed it to her.

"Cutty Sark," he said. "Not easy to get hold of in these times."

"Just a wee nip," she assured him. It warmed her down to her toes. "I'm obliged," she said as she handed it back to him, and he made it vanish as if his supernatural ability were hiding flasks rather than appearing in people's perceptions as their mothers. "The situation with the troops sounds excellent. You'll let us know when the targets start to arrive?" He nodded and left to rejoin his men.

"Everything is ready, my Lady," said Bridget once she was back in the car.

"It will be interesting to see who shows up," said Lady Carmichael. "Matilda thinks they will be much of a muchness."

"Matilda," said Bridget and smiled a little. The Lady raised her eyebrows in a question. "Miss Murcutt really strikes me as more of a Tillie."

"That's how I think of her too," said the Lady Carmichael, smiling mischievously. "But she's asked to be called Matilda. I think it reminds her that she's in a new life."

Tillie Murcutt had not gone back to her old activities after the events at the safe house. The Court had convened a few hours after Lady Carmichael made the offer for her to join the Checquy, and they had given their intrigued approval. They briefly discussed whether she could serve the Checquy by rebuilding her establishment and running it afresh. But in the end they agreed unanimously that the Checquy should not be involved in criminal activities, even for intelligence purposes. Bishop Pringle suggested that her death be faked—he could create a corpse that would be a dead ringer, as it were—and she be moved to a new city. It was agreed, however, that her criminal connections in London were too valuable simply to throw away.

At this point, perhaps sensing her own value or possibly because of her innate fearlessness, Tillie stated that she had a few conditions of her own before she was prepared to sign any contract or take any oaths. As far as she was concerned, there was the pressing matter of her other brother, Robert, to be addressed before she would even think about obliging the Checquy with her service, let alone sharing the ins and outs of her supernatural-artifact trade.

There had been some rolling of eyes and heat pits, but everyone had seen that the issue was fairly time-sensitive, especially if Tillie was to retain her access to the criminal world. Any delays might lead to unhelpful questions. Fortunately, the Checquy had experience in pulling together operations quickly.

The next day, in a meeting carefully planned and surveilled by the Checquy, Tillie Murcutt described to Robert a supernatural fight that had broken out between their goons, escalated, wrecked the Moor's Head, and set off the bomb in the basement. She explained that she and John had seen things that no one should ever see and that John had died from injuries he'd sustained in the battle and the collapse of the brothel. It was clear, she said, that that dabbling in the supernatural—seeking out such people and trafficking in such items—was a terrible, dangerous idea.

"It wasn't hard," Tillie told Bridget afterward as she smoked a cigarette in the lounge of Lady Carmichael's house (she had been put in a guest room next to Bridget's). "I was always the one pushing for that line of business. Bob was very skeptical, even when we started selling the items and killing off our rivals."

She had told her brother that she wanted out of the business, that she wanted a quiet life, and she had broken down in extremely convincing sobs. After holding her until she calmed down, he agreed to buy her out—although she had to concede that the value of their empire had fallen significantly with the leveling of the Moor's Head. Giving up her share of the profits from the family business had been a wrench, but the promise of a generous Checquy paycheck had mollified her somewhat.

The plan had worked well, the story reinforced by the state of the pub-turned-brothel-turned-ruin. The building had collapsed completely, the site had been roped off by the authorities, and Checquy workers were sifting through the wreckage. They had removed Pamela's body and taken it away to a Checquy facility. They had also removed the mangled remains of what turned out to be two southern cassowaries.

"Indeed? And what's a cassowary when it's at home?" Tillie asked languidly.

"It's a type of bird from Australia and New Guinea," Bridget said, reading off the notes the scientists had provided. "Large, flightless. They've been known to kill dogs and people."

"And that's what Gethings turned into?" asked Tillie. "Amazing. We always just thought it was some sort of magic bird."

"Did he have any connection to Australia or New Guinea?" asked Bridget.

"Tommy Gethings? No. His family was from around here," Tillie said. "Since always. I think a great-great-great-uncle might have been sent off to Australia for nicking a handkerchief, but he never came back." She looked at Bridget with curiosity. "So why do you think he turned into two of them?"

"Welcome to the world of the inexplicable." Bridget shrugged, and Tillie grinned at her with such spontaneous and genuine delight that she grinned back.

It was so odd to be sitting, calmly and easily, with this woman, forgetting and then remembering with a start that they'd faced each other in bloody battle. They looked up as Lady Carmichael entered the room with Miss Steward, who was carrying a briefcase.

"Miss Murcutt, here are the contracts inducting you as an operative into the Order of the Checquy."

"Let's have at them, then," said Tillie eagerly.

After she'd signed the contracts, and they'd been witnessed by Bridget and Rebecca Steward, Tillie proceeded to sing like a canary. She happily gave them the address and the keys to a storage space under some railway arches in Battersea, where she assured them they would find all the arcane items still in her possession. Then she named the man who had furnished her with the items in exchange for a share of the profits and exclusive access to his favored prostitute.

"James Gregory?" Lady Carmichael gasped.

"Oh, you know him, then?"

"Pawn James Gregory has been with the Checquy since he was two," said Bridget flatly.

"Indeed?"

"Indeed."

Pawn Gregory was now forty-four, a decorated combat veteran who had risen to a sufficiently high rank that his office was three doors down from that of the Lady of the Checquy.

It turned out that he had also developed a taste for opium, alcohol, gambling, and the charms of a young prostitute named Eileen who had fled a life of drudgery in County Mayo and found employment with the Murcutts. All four of those had combined to lead him into a dangerous downward spiral of addiction, expenditure, indiscretion, desperation, and, eventually, theft and treason.

Thank God that Lady Carmichael had the sense not to bring Tillie Murcutt into Apex House until we identified the leak, Bridget thought weakly. Her stomach turned as she imagined Pawn Gregory walking down the hall and bumping into them as they headed to the Lady's office. Confronted with the sudden appearance of Miss Murcutt in the hall, looking decidedly uncontrite, he would probably (and accurately) have assumed the worst. God knows what he would have done.

She had seen him using his powers out on the practice range at Hill Hall—the Lord's country house—during a weekend party. Dressed in his tweeds, leaning on his shooting stick, he was the very picture of a gentleman at his ease until intense golden dots of light were suddenly swimming in the air around him, dipping and zigzagging, flaring and fading in and out like fireflies. Pawn Gregory did not shift, unmoved by the new attendant constellation that wheeled and warped around him. And then, abruptly, all those little motes rushed forward and exploded with unbelievable force. The target dummy and the embankment of soil behind it vanished in a ball of flame. Some songbirds that had been ill-advisedly flying overhead pattered down, completely stunned from the blast. The windows of Hill Hall, which were a good two miles away, were rattled, and, much to Rook Cenci's irritation, her baby daughter was awakened just three minutes after she'd finally gotten her to sleep.

Bridget did not know the upper limits of Pawn Gregory's power. Could he destroy Apex House? He could certainly have killed her, Lady Carmichael, Miss Steward, and Tillie Murcutt on the spot if suddenly confronted with the prospect of being exposed and arrested. Murcutt did not appear to understand what could have happened, but Lady Carmichael certainly looked pale.

But perhaps she's not thinking about the possibility of her own death, thought Bridget, a little ashamed. *She's probably aghast at the fact that a high-ranking Pawn who's spent practically his entire life in the Checquy has broken his oaths, corrupted himself, and sold bits of his comrades to a pimp.*

"Becky, I'll need this confirmed," Lady Carmichael said bleakly. "Call the Apex and find out where Pawn Gregory is at this moment. We need to put eyes on him."

"Yes," said Miss Steward. She stood and went to the telephone.

"Miss Steward," Bridget said suddenly. "Ask for his location as part of a list of others." The Lady and her attendant turned to look at her. "The Murcutt brothel has partially collapsed. Pawn Gregory may be...wary. If word gets to him that the Lady was seeking him out specifically, there's no telling how he might react. Especially if he is as...debauched as Miss Murcutt describes." Miss Murcutt smirked a little at this.

"Good thinking, Bridget," the Lady said.

"I'll put it out that you're setting up a discussion group in the next day or two," said Miss Steward. "That should allay any concerns."

"Thank you, Becky," said Lady Carmichael. "Of course, now I'll have to actually set up some sort of discussion group. As if there weren't enough going on." She looked at her wristwatch and winced. "There is going to be so much to read from Bufo," Bridget heard the Lady mutter to herself.

"My Lady, Pawn Gregory is in his office," Miss Steward reported, her hand over the receiver of the phone.

"Excellent. If he moves, have him followed and watched unobtrusively. Now, as quick as you can, get me Pawn Gaddis on the phone." Peggy Gaddis, a strategist for large-scale operations, had previously performed discreet surveillance for the Court. Once she was within a few yards of her target, she would take up residence in a pore on his face and be in a perfect situation to observe all his activities. One of the advantages of her abilities was that, once they were activated, she no longer needed sleep or sustenance beyond fresh air, which meant that she could stay in position for as long as it took.

"My Lady, I have Pawn Gaddis on the line." The Lady stood and took the receiver from her attendant's outstretched hand. "Hello, Peggy, I'm afraid that I need your assistance, and it must be quiet, very quiet. I cannot give you formal written orders." She paused. "No, nothing like that. Just observation...I knew I could count on you... I can't be certain, but I shouldn't imagine more than a few days at most." She turned away and spoke in low tones, presumably outlining the mission. "No, I shan't require recorded evidence, Peggy. Your sworn oath would be enough. If you've seen nothing within a week, come back in. All right, thank you. Goodbye."

"She'll see," said Tillie. "Everything I've told you is true."

"I'm afraid I believe you," the Lady said, sitting down.

"And then?"

"I want this ended without scandal, without its becoming widely known either within the Checquy or without. If he *is* guilty, then we will need to ensure that Pawn Gregory is eliminated quietly, discreetly, in such a way as to arouse no suspicion." Her mouth twisted as she contemplated the challenges of murdering one of her key executives, then she shook her head.

"More immediately, there is the question of the artifacts that have already been sold. There are still some out in the community. And your first priority, Miss Murcutt, is to work with Bridget to track them down." She stood up to leave.

"What about the naked Mr. Wattleman?" asked Tillie. "I thought this was something he was working on."

"The clothed Pawn Wattleman will be busy retrieving the items from your, ahem, lockup. He will be available for backup as necessary," said Lady Carmichael. "But I would like to see the two of you working together. It will be an invaluable learning experience"—she eyed them thoughtfully—"for the both of you." And with that, she and Miss Steward departed.

"So how did the whole thing work?" Bridget asked Tillie. "Can you take me through it from start to finish?"

"It began when your James Gregory had a bit more to drink than he should have and tried to impress his whore," said Tillie. "So many men do that—I think they forget what the arrangements are. Although not all of them talk about the magic they've seen and show off the little lights they can make. Eileen, of course, knew that I was interested in that sort of thing, and I made a note of it. And then, well, things got worse for him as time went on. Drinking, opium, gambling, paying much more than he should have for exclusivity with Eileen."

"Did you help him along with his downfall?" asked Bridget suspiciously.

"Didn't have to. Any one of those can be a slippery slope, but all together? It wasn't too long before I knew he was pretty desperate, and that's when we slid into our arrangement."

"And so Simony would get the stuff from him?"

"Absolutely not!" exclaimed Tillie, looking shocked. "The first rule in trafficking any sort of dodgy goods is to ensure that you yourself are never made redundant. As the middleman, you must remain essential. Never allow the seller to meet the buyer directly."

"But those women met with Simony," objected Bridget.

"You're getting ahead of yourself," said Tillie. "And Simony was mine—well, mostly." She paused for a second, drawing her thoughts together. "So. Gregory got us the materials somehow. He'd deliver them to me with whatever description he could provide. In exchange, I paid him and gave him time with Eileen in her own room.

"Meanwhile, I put the word out that Simony had occult items to sell. People would come to him, he would come to me, and I provided him with the items—never more than one at a time. And I told him the price. But I never met the customers directly, the customers never met Gregory, and Gregory never met Simony."

"How *did* you find customers? Especially if you never met them directly."

"It wasn't easy," confessed Tillie. "After all, you can't just sidle up to people on the street and ask if they'd like magic beans or bits of human bone for the weekend. It's not like selling silk stockings or petrol vouchers. It took a bit of putting the word out carefully."

"Through your clients?" Bridget asked, her lip curling a bit. "Your...guests upstairs at the Moor's Head?"

"Not just them. And I wouldn't be astounded if we've entertained some others from the Order," said Tillie tartly, "so I shouldn't look down my nose too much if I were you. But no, we have other connections. There's a lot of money and satisfaction in fencing stolen goods. But it means you need a network. If you're going to sell stolen books, you need some friendly faces in Charing Cross Road. For jewelry and stones, I've got people in Hatton Garden. There are places in Mayfair with some hidden wares in their cellars for the discerning gentleman or lady with lots of cash and no questions."

"But how did you find your customers for the, ahem, magic beans?" asked Bridget.

"Funny enough, it all happened through one of my book connections," said Tillie. "Specializes in older stuff. He does a fine business in incunables, whatever they are."

"Incunabula," murmured Bridget.

"Right, them. And he does a nice line in 'occult texts,' as he calls them. Lists of demons. Hammers and spanners of witches and whatnot. Magic spells." She rolled her eyes, then a look of speculation came over her face. "But wait, are those real—spells and whatnot? Do they work? I always thought they had to be bollocks because of knowing Vincent and them. I assumed it was something you had to be born with."

Bridget hesitated. Given Tillie's fascination with the supernatural, she wasn't sure if this was a subject she should be speaking about. *But she'll hear about it eventually anyway,* she thought. *And she is part of the Order now.*

"There are some procedures that seem to work for a very few people," Bridget said carefully. "But it's incredibly dangerous and never ends well. The power has to come from somewhere."

"I see," said Tillie uncertainly. Uncharacteristically, she seemed somewhat cowed by Bridget's seriousness.

"Anyway, back to more immediate issues. You were saying your book man with the incunabula found you customers for the artifacts?"

"One customer."

"What?"

"It was only one that I ever heard of," Tillie said. "My book chap pointed only one person in Simony's direction, a woman. None of my other sources ever had any luck."

"One person?"

"It's a new business, isn't it?" said Tillie in a very reasonable tone. "Just getting started, really. And you'd be amazed how many people *aren't* looking for magic items."

"But Simony said he sold items to fifteen different women. That must mean they all knew this one person, this woman," said Bridget.

"That's what I assumed," agreed Tillie. "Word of mouth, it's the key to a successful business, especially one that can't really advertise."

"So who was this first woman who put the word out?"

"No idea," said Tillie. "Let's go ask my bookseller, since he's the only person who ever met her—aside from Simony, and I'm assuming he's no longer available for questioning?"

"Definitely not," said Bridget.

"Yeah, that's what I thought."

They were driven to a little bookshop in Charing Cross Road. A man in his seventies sat reading behind a desk piled high with books, and he did not look up when they entered, despite the tinkle of the bell at the door. Tillie had to clear her throat pointedly before he would tear his gaze away from his book.

"Miss Murcutt! Good afternoon!" he exclaimed, rising to shake her hand.

"Mr. Jefferson, it's good to see you," said Tillie. She did not bother to introduce Bridget, who was still a little thrown by the idea of questioning someone without having to produce any sort of falsified authority. Instead, she could watch Tillie use her identity like a hammer.

But it turned out that Mr. Jefferson did not know who the woman buyer was. She was certainly not any of the women who had managed to kill themselves with their black-market artifacts. Bridget had brought photos of the three victims, but the bookseller shook his head regretfully.

"I am sorry, my dear," he said, sitting down. "My customer wasn't any of these."

"Who was she, then, Mr. Jefferson?" asked Tillie intently.

"No idea. She knew her subject, certainly, came in with quite a list of books. Definitely not a dilettante. Her list included works in Latin, Greek, Italian, French, German, Cornish, old Norse. I had a couple of the things she wanted and put out feelers for the rest. Several of them I'd never heard of myself, and I've been in this business a while. I'm afraid that I was more interested in the books than the lady."

Under Tillie's and Bridget's questioning, however, Jefferson turned out to know more than he'd realized. With strategic prompts, Bridget helped him remember that the woman—the *lady*, he corrected firmly—was in her forties, well dressed, had brown hair, and spoke with an accent that suggested she came from money.

"Although that might just be my fancy," he confessed, "because she *had* money." She'd purchased some of Jefferson's most expensive stock and hadn't even tried to beat down his prices, which had not fallen in wartime.

The lady's other striking characteristic had been her intense rage regarding the war.

"I just mentioned it in passing," remembered Jefferson. "It's practically replaced the weather as a subject to comment on nowadays, but she absolutely erupted. *Loathed* the Germans, which I thought a touch ironic, since at the time she was buying a pamphlet by Johann Daniel Mylius. Lovely piece it was, all about music magic..." He noticed the women were looking impatient.

"Anyway, the lady was talking very forcefully about the war, and that was when I sensed her interest in the occult was not just academic. She spoke repeatedly of wishing she could do something herself and using her research against *them*. I presumed she meant the Boche.

"It was at that point that I recalled that Miss Murcutt said there were some occult relics available on the market. The lady was very interested when I brought them up, and I gave her the details of that man Simony. Never mentioned you, of course, Miss Murcutt. She paid for her books, thanked me, and left."

"Did you ever see her again?" asked Bridget intently.

"No," he said sourly. "Apparently, whatever she purchased from Mr. Simony meant she no longer needed books."

"But you said she left a list of works she wanted. Was there a name, a telephone number? Or an address?"

"No, she said she'd be back in a few weeks. I had the impression that she wasn't from London, that'd she come up on a research trip." Jefferson shrugged. "I'm sorry, miss, I don't think I can be of much more help."

Later, back at the Carmichael house, Bridget asked Tillie, "Why did you sell the items to regular civilians? It sounds like it would have been much easier just to sell them to other criminals. I would have thought they would be crawling over each other for them."

"We were looking to expand into the territory of other gangs," said Tillie. "We were hardly going to put that sort of power into the hands of competitors."

"But you didn't keep them for yourself? Or arm your own people?"

"I wouldn't trust anyone with that sort of power," sniffed Tillie. "Not unless they were born with it and knew how to use it. And I wouldn't want those things in my house—who knew what they would do? When it's a person with magic powers, you can pay them, buy them off. When it's a hat rack with magic powers, there's not much you can do.

"And besides, none of these items were what you'd call reliable. It wasn't a case of Gregory saying, for instance, 'Here's a tankard, it'll put everyone who drinks from it to sleep.' It was more like: 'This is a brooch, it's magic. Don't hold it in your hand for more than five seconds unless you want magic to happen. Don't use it inside a building. Now, where's my money?' Villains aren't going to go for that sort of uncertainty. They want weapons or tools that work like weapons or tools. Something trustworthy that's going to blow the door off a safe and not eat your arm off. But I know from running tarts that enthusiasts with money will pay hand over fist for what they want, no matter what it is. Even if it's a malevolent hat rack."

"Hypothetical demonic hat racks aside, we've hit a dead end," said Bridget. "We've found no connections among the three women we know about, and we don't know who this mystery lady is, although we are aware that she hates the Nazis. So that's a useful distinguishing feature. Almost as good as brown hair."

"I rather think most of them did," Tillie said. "Hate the Nazis, I mean. Simony mentioned that a couple of his customers said something about putting their purchases to good use for the war effort. When you first came to the pub, I thought that's what you had to be interested in."

You want to do your bit? Bridget remembered wryly that that's what Tillie had said on her first visit to the Moor's Head. It was all very interesting, but it didn't give them any new leads.

Meanwhile, after only a few days of hitchhiking on Pawn Gregory's face, Pawn Gaddis confirmed Tillie's story. And as it turned out, making the Pawn's death appear accidental was startlingly easy. The Lady's most subtle and cunning assassins had simply placed a large supply of dynamite in the cellar of his house outside London, then blown it up when he was in residence. Admittedly, the public was slightly bewildered by the Luftwaffe's decision to bomb an isolated farmhouse, but those within the Checquy simply nodded sagely and remarked how sad it was that poor James's powers had turned on him.

"The drink," some said knowingly.

"Never the same after his wife died," said others.

No one mentioned opium. Or, crucially, in-house assassination.

There was a very large turnout for his funeral, which Bridget, as an aide to the Lady, who was also present, was obliged to attend. It was especially galling coming on the heels of Pamela's funeral, which had drawn fewer attendees. Such a disparity was inevitable, of course—Pamela had been much younger and worked with fewer people—but it was bitter in Bridget's heart to see a traitor honored by so many when her friend had died in service. She could only hope that her fixed facial expression throughout the funeral was taken for somber respect.

Before they blew up Pawn Gregory's house, the Lady's subtle assassins had searched the place and in the shed had found several items that were unquestionably of supernatural provenance, including an antelope spine with a horned skull on both ends, a man's lace-up shoe (the right) that emitted a continuous low hooting, a head-size lozenge of spinel that hovered about a foot off the ground, and nine vials of unidentified fluids of different colors and viscosities. Most of these proved to be missing from the archives, although it could not be established exactly where the liquids had come from.

It was evident that Gregory had been using his authority as a security overseer to steal the items. His rank and roving remit had allowed him near-universal access to Checquy facilities. After his funeral, as the mourners (and Bridget and Lady Carmichael) mingled in a private room at one of London's best hotels, Bridget heard several people recall last seeing him when he'd conducted "surprise spot checks" of different warehouses. Presumably, he had been strolling into archives or transportation hubs and depots, getting all the workers to bustle around nervously, then nicking things as the opportunity arose. They'd found evidence that he'd altered some records, but in some cases, the absence of the items just hadn't yet been discovered.

I wish we knew how he smuggled them out, Bridget thought. Of all the objects to sneakily shove down one's trousers or conceal under one's hat, a malignant supernatural artifact was low on the list of desirables. *And God alone knows how he got that antelope spine out of the warehouse without anyone noticing.* It was longer than she was tall.

In the course of their investigations through his office, his town house, and his country house (before it blew up), they'd found no evidence that anyone else in the Checquy had been involved in the thefts.

Bridget and Tillie continued their investigation but made no significant progress. There were no more clues to follow, and they had resorted to reading through various occult- and mythology-themed journals and magazines for any women contributors who might conceivably be their target.

In the end, though, it was as simple as three letters arriving to the homes of Daisy Foster, Judith Powys, and Dorothy Hadgraft—the three women whose disastrous experiences with their purchased artifacts had started it all. The Checquy had been monitoring their houses (in the case of Judith Powys, the charred remains of her house), and within a day of each other, all three received letters from someone referring to herself as "Sebile." There was no return address, but the text was practically identical. The only difference was that Foster was addressed in the letter as "Circe," Powys as "Hecate," and Hadgraft as "Aradia."

Dearest Sister [Circe or Hecate or Aradia],

The hour is come. All within our circle have obtained the tools that we require for our great undertaking. The most fortuitous time for our work approaches as the seasons flow on and the stars and the moon wheel into a potent alignment.

I hereby invoke your presence, calling you to come to the border of our land and join our gathered sisterhood to strike. We, the quiet ones, shall summon great forces and between us make such a working as will set those who would invade across the water into confusion and retreat.

The rest of the letter was surprisingly prosaic and businesslike, advising of the date, time, and location at which Hecate, Circe, Aradia, and the rest of their sisters were to gather—a point high on the cliffs of Dover, looking across the Channel to France. A list of recommended inns and hotels was provided, and there was an invitation to call Sebile (although no telephone number was given) to coordinate transportation. She would make arrangements for cars to collect them from their lodgings and deliver them back after the ceremony. She would provide the ceremonial vestments, but she warned that the nights were cold and the site could be wet, so warm underwear and Wellington boots would be a good idea.

The Lady's office sprang into action. Lady Carmichael had winced a little but authorized more operatives, including Sergeant Morrison and a coterie of his troops, to be brought in on this highly confidential operation. They identified the location chosen by the "Quiet Circle," as they had taken to referring to the would-be magic-users. They made their preparations to step in and seize the participants and, more crucially, the Checquy artifacts they had obtained. Simony had said (and Tillie confirmed) that fifteen items had been sold, so they were anticipating twelve Quiet Circlers, given that Hecate, Circe, and Aradia were *hors de sorcellerie*. The soldiers would move quickly, before the circle could undertake their ridiculous ritual and hopefully before they could activate their relics and do harm to anyone. Now all there was to do was wait and, in Bridget's case, obsessively check and recheck that everything was ready.

"My Lady, Miss Mangan, they're approaching."

"Thank you, Sergeant," Lady Carmichael said, putting down her documents. "We'll come now." The two of them winced as they emerged into the bitter cold. It took a few moments for their eyes to adjust to the pitch-blackness of the night. The Rolls was just a dark mass behind them.

Bridget automatically looked about and caught some far-off flickers. She recognized them as headlights flashing as approaching cars bounced down the dirt track to the ritual site. The Checquy encampment was sufficiently distant and camouflaged that there was no chance of them being seen by the circle.

"My Lady, if you'll take my arm, I can guide you to the observation point," Sergeant Morrison said. Bridget followed them and managed not to put her foot in any rabbit holes. "And we'll just be going around these screens to where you can see young Alexandrina's work. We've set up these tarps so that the light won't be visible from the site nor catch the eye of any warden or even any Jerry bombers if they fly over."

"Good," Lady Carmichael said. "Good evening, Alexandrina." The albino girl's face was the lightest thing in the darkness, and Bridget could imagine her anxious, eager expression.

They came into a space bounded by dark tarpaulins, and for a moment, Bridget thought fires had been lit in there. Then she realized the glow was the result of Alexandrina's powers. "I've set up two viewing panes, my Lady," Alexandrina said meekly.

"Marvelous work," said the Lady, looking with fascination at the result. It was as if two panes of glass had been hung in thin air, one of them showing a bird's-eye view of the ritual site, the other giving a tall-person's-eye view of it from several yards away. It was the ideal way to observe the situation without getting close. Alexandrina had spent hours placing lenses and prisms to bend the light across the fields to this spot. Bridget looked cautiously at the scenes before them.

The bird's-eye view showed a diamond of four fires burning, one at each point of the compass. Inside, their backs to the fire, was a circle of twelve women. They were all dressed in light green hooded robes so their features could not be seen, and each of them was holding something gently.

They went ahead without Circe, Hecate, and Aradia, she thought. *I wonder if they know what happened to their sisters. Probably.* Despite herself, she felt a stab of respect for them. Whoever these ladies were, they were willing to risk coming to harm for their cause. In their own way, with their unpredictable artifacts, they were just as much soldiers fighting for their homeland as any enlisted man. *If only they weren't directing their skills and their drive to such an absurd endeavor.*

"I'll be going, then, ma'am, to take up my position," Morrison said. Bridget looked at her watch—the ceremony was supposed to start on the stroke of midnight, and the members of the Quiet Circle were to be apprehended at 11:55, so he had twenty minutes to get across the fields and give his men the signal to move in.

"And you understand how this is to play out, Sergeant?" asked the Lady. She looked at him with an intensity that Bridget knew all too well.

"Absolutely, my Lady. It'll go as we discussed."

"Good."

"Oh, before I go, if you ladies will don these headphones, you'll be able to hear everything." Bridget and the Lady put on the heavy headphones; Alexandrina stood by, ready to receive any instructions to reposition the lenses. The microphone placement had been nigh on perfect, because Bridget could clearly hear a woman's voice speaking calmly. She had an upper-class accent and was taking a rather bossy tone.

"—sters, it is imperative that we are all in synchronization, so we will need to commence the ritual on the stroke of midnight. I've brought this clock and set it a little bit early, so we will begin on the twelfth chime." There was a mutter of general agreement from the gathered women as she placed a rather nice ormolu carriage clock on the ground outside the circle. "Very good. Edna—I mean, Diana—will you help me put some more wood on the fires, please?" There was some unintelligible conversation among the women. Then, much to the surprise of the listening Lady and her apprentice, one of the women began singing. It was quite lovely, some piece of music in old English that neither of them could understand.

"Very lovely, Agamede," said the leader approvingly.

"Thank you, Sebile."

Ah, the writer of the letters, thought Bridget. This Sebile had a definite air about her—a combination of coven leader and phys-ed teacher.

Sebile clapped her hands. "Now, sisters, we have seven minutes until we start, so please take this time to review your parts and prepare yourselves." The conversation died away.

Two minutes until our troops move in, thought Bridget. This really had the potential to end badly—no one had any clear idea of how the women would react or what they might be able to do with their relics. The hope was that they would submit to the suddenly appearing shouting soldiers and allow themselves to be taken into custody for trafficking in stolen goods, but if not, it could get very ugly very fast. She realized that her hands were clenched into fists as she stared into Alexandrina's lenses, shifting her gaze back and forth between the views.

She checked her watch anxiously. The tension was terrible. Being able to observe Checquy troops go into action was not a typical situation. One was either in the battle or waiting anxiously in the office for news of it. Now, she was watching the fields, trying to spot which patch of grass or bracken was going to suddenly erupt with a Checquy soldier. She checked her watch again. It was 11:56.

She snuck a look at Lady Carmichael, who did not seem at all concerned. *Is my watch fast? I should have synchronized it with Sergeant Morrison's.* The anticipation was getting terrible. *It must be time. It must.*

"My Lady, what time do you have?" she asked. "Surely the troops should be moving in?" Lady Carmichael was staring, unmoving, at the lenses. "My Lady?"

And then, over the headphones, she heard a clock beginning to chime and felt a stab of panic.

"Has something happened to them? Or did—did they receive the wrong orders? The wrong time?"

At the twelfth stroke, the Quiet Circle would begin their ritual. The thought of those women waving around actual dangerous items in a deluded attempt to cast a spell was too dire for words. Each artifact was bad enough by itself, but who knew how they might react to one another? She remembered the horrific results of the bombing of the Caïssa, the way that people's powers had interacted to create uncontrollable and unimaginable damage.

"We have to give the order!" Bridget exclaimed. "They have to stop this!" She tore off her headphones and was turning to rush from the enclosure when she felt the Lady's hand tight on her wrist. Bewildered, she looked around.

"Do nothing," said Lady Carmichael. Her grip was like iron.

"But…" Bridget trailed off and, almost despite herself, turned back to the lenses as the circle commenced their ridiculous ritual and no one did anything to stop them. She slid the headphones back on.

It began with chanting, almost musical. The women were standing and singing in unison in a language that Bridget did not recognize. Their bodies were perfectly still until, as Bridget watched, horrified, they raised their relics.

Even through the startling clarity of Alexandrina's lenses, it was hard to make out exactly who was holding what. Bridget had made a list of the relics presumed sold based on the best of Tillie's recollections, what Simony had said before Wattleman slit his throat, and her own cautious review of files; she'd been wary of alerting anyone in the Checquy to the problem. She'd identified a couple of relics and their capabilities. It was a disparate collection of objects: a mask, a dinner fork, a Bakelite radio. At least two of them could do significant harm, which made Sergeant Morrison's failure to act all the more unforgivable.

Everyone in the little tarpaulin enclosure flinched away from the lenses as purple fire suddenly flared bright in the hands of one of the women. A dazed part of Bridget's mind noted that it was probably Pawn Santosuosso's other leg bone. She squinted into the lens and saw a stream of flames pouring out of one end of the femur onto the grass.

Bridget could hear a strange warbling drone above the sound of the chanting women and realized it was many birds singing in chorus.

Other relics were being activated. A crimson light pulsed in one woman's hands, and over the headphones came the sound of the waves of the English Channel becoming more intense and crashing heavily into the cliffs. Even at a distance, they could smell something strange wafting from the site — a tang of spices that roiled in Bridget's nostrils and set Alexandrina coughing and choking. Then Bridget felt a peculiar pulsating ache in her ankles as something, some energy or pressure, washed over them from the site of the ritual.

All the while, the women of the circle were chanting, singing, swaying back and forth, and holding up their black-market relics. It was impossible to make out what language they were using, but they were singing feverishly, as if in a frenzy. Their chant became less musical, more staccato, as they shouted a single phrase over and over, building to a crescendo that set Bridget's heart racing. The crashing of the waves against the cliffs was now thunderous, booming like a drum being beaten by a Titan.

The leader raised her relic, and an earsplitting *crack* sounded in the air. Mercifully, it was dulled through the headphones, but they could hear it echoing across the fields, and the tarpaulins hanging around them rippled as the shock wave passed over them.

At that, the chanting stopped abruptly, and the purple flames burning in the lens died away. The red light in the woman's hand winked out. The smell that had writhed in the enclosure around Bridget, Alexandrina, and the Lady vanished as if sucked back to wherever it had come from, and the crisp clean night air was suddenly sharp again in Bridget's nostrils. Over the headphones, she could hear the waters of the Channel calming down to their gentle distant washing.

"And it is done!" announced Sebile in ringing tones. There was a long moment in which absolutely nothing happened. The fires continued to crackle. Bridget heard the women panting, and the one who had been holding Pawn Santosuosso's purloined femur was briskly stamping out the fires that had been ignited by her relic's power.

So now what? wondered Bridget. The Lady still seemed completely unconcerned by the failure of the Checquy troops to strike.

"And you have been heard!" said a woman's voice. Judging from the sound that came over the microphone, she was definitely not part of the circle. Whoever this newcomer was, she spoke with an Irish accent.

"What the *fuck?*" exclaimed Bridget, too startled to realize she'd sworn in front of her leader. She shot a bewildered look at Lady Carmichael, who was staring intently into the lenses.

"Who's that?" said Sebile uncertainly.

"You cried out," said the Irishwoman. "You called forth. I have come."

"Who are you?"

"Whom do you see me as?" asked the woman. Bridget caught a glimpse of her in the lower lens. She was walking toward the circle, out of the darkness. Her back was to the lens, but the firelight glistened off her long red hair. Her bearing was regal, and she appeared to be wearing some sort of dark robe. The women of the circle stared at her in stupefaction.

What the hell is going on? thought Bridget weakly. *Have these daft women actually managed to summon up something?* The woman walked toward the fire, and Alexandrina's lens followed, unprompted. The albino girl was transfixed by the scene before them, and her hands twisted unconsciously, bringing the lens closer to the group. Bridget caught a glimpse of the woman's face as she turned her head to gaze at each member of the circle.

"Mummy?" gasped Sebile suddenly, just as another woman in the circle called out incredulously, "Mama? What are you doing here?"

"What are you talking about?" said another. "It's *my* mother, but she's been dead for…" She trailed off in bewilderment. Another woman had fallen to her knees and tears were pouring down her face. All of them were gazing at the red-haired woman in awe.

"Oh for God's sake," said Bridget in utter disgust. She turned to look at the Lady, who had the good grace to color a little, even if she didn't look away from the lens.

It wasn't some goddess or a member of the fae or a personification of the spirit of the land. It was Sergeant Morrison using his power to deceive the circle. Which meant that when he spoke, Bridget was hearing her own mother's voice. She had just seen her mother's back and her mother's red hair, gotten a glimpse of her mother's face. This was something she had always tried to avoid, and now it had been foisted upon her.

"You see me as the power in your hearts," said Sergeant Morrison, and Bridget felt as if her own heart twisted in her at the thought that this was her mother's voice. "That power has been bent to the purpose that you sought. Now, lay down the items that you used to call me here. They are the price you must pay for my aid and my favor."

Did Lady Carmichael write this script for him? wondered Bridget. Regardless of where he'd come up with the language, it was working, because the circle members were reverently laying their relics on the ground. One or two seemed a little reluctant to give up their artifacts, hesitating before placing them carefully on the grass.

"Now," said Sergeant Morrison, "go forth from this place. The magic you have wrought has begun; changes are emerging in this world. I enjoin you not to pursue this path again. Each of you has been part of a great enchantment, the greatest of the age, but further workings will do you harm and may taint what you have done."

You have got to be joking, thought Bridget. But, as best as she could tell through the lens, the members of the circle were actually accepting these pronouncements. There were awed looks of adoration and pride on their faces as they walked away without speaking. Sergeant Morrison stood in the center of the fires, watching them go. Bridget did her very best not to look at his face. She was not about to have another memory of her birth mother foisted upon her.

I cannot believe this just happened, she thought weakly. But she could see a kind of sense in it. This way, the Checquy recovered its items without having to fight or take any prisoners. Presumably, the ghillie-suited guards would ensure that the women left the area.

And I expect that they'll be followed, identified, and monitored sporadically to make sure they don't try to reenter the world of magic. Although with their source for Checquy relics cut off, it's not likely to be much of a problem. They can be satisfied that they've done their bit, and they'll probably never speak of it.

But it was a fearful risk to have taken, and it had left Sergeant Morrison horribly vulnerable. What if the circle hadn't believed him? What if one of them had lashed out with her relic?

What on earth was she thinking? Bridget stared incredulously at Lady Carmichael. She didn't say anything, of course, not with Alexandrina looking on, but inside, she was seething.

Bridget held her tongue for the next forty-five minutes as the circle vacated the site and drove off to their various inns, lodging houses, and bed-and-breakfasts. The troops then gingerly collected the relics and transported them across the fields to waiting trucks to be driven away to Checquy facilities. The soldiers would remain through the night to excavate the microphone cables and tidy up, making sure there was no trace left of their presence.

Lady Carmichael had nodded once, without any expression, as the women of the circle put down their relics. Then she went back to the car, leaving Bridget to observe the transportation of the items. She hadn't departed, which was just as well, since she was to be Bridget's ride.

"It was all right?" Alexandrina asked Bridget anxiously.

"Hmm?"

"The lenses and the view and everything? Do you think the Lady was pleased?"

"Oh, absolutely," said Bridget. "She's got a lot going on, but I know she thought you did an excellent job."

The albino girl nodded, reassured, and Bridget made a mental note to have her to tea with the Lady in the next couple of days. The operation was theoretically off the books, but with this many people involved, it was inevitable that some details would leak out to the greater Checquy. It would be wise to impress the importance of discretion on the youngest person in the operation.

Although she's only a few months younger than me, Bridget thought wearily, feeling incredibly old. "I'd better go attend the Lady," she said to Alexandrina. "You're all right for a ride home?"

"Yes, I'm traveling with the troops."

"Then I'll see you in London soon," said Bridget, and she shook the girl's hand. "You did good work tonight." She walked across the fields and slid into the warm coziness of the car. Lady Carmichael didn't look up from her papers.

"Everything taken care of?" she asked.

"Yes, ma'am. We can go now," said Bridget. The Lady looked up at her tone, then turned her attention to the driver.

"Cobb, we're fine to leave, thank you."

"Yes, ma'am." The barrier was raised, giving them privacy, and the car moved off. Bridget wrapped a Shetland rug around her poor frozen legs and opened the thermos that the cook at Belgrave Square had packed for them. The tea inside was warm and sweet, and she drank it down.

"I gather you have some questions," Lady Carmichael said.

"I'll confess, I was somewhat taken aback," said Bridget, trying to restrain her anger. "It was very different from the strategy as I had understood it."

"Yes," the Lady agreed. "Can you see the merits of how we proceeded?"

"I suppose," Bridget said. "But it seemed to add a dangerous amount of risk to what was already a very risky endeavor. Sergeant Morrison was left extremely vulnerable. And why on *earth* did you let them undertake that absurd ritual?"

A small part of her mind was aware that her tone was entirely inappropriate, but her frustration was too great. It seemed as if everyone was doing ludicrous things for no reason. Somehow, the events of the night were blending in her mind with the way Pamela had brought down that damned plane—just another senseless act that accomplished nothing and put people in danger. *And it brought her to her death!* thought Bridget with a pang of grief. She wiped at her face. She was full of rage and sorrow and aggravation, and it was spilling out now.

"You know how dangerous those items are," she continued. "Who knows what could have happened with civilians waving them around, chanting? If you had to send in Sergeant Morrison wearing my mother's face, why didn't you send him in before the ritual?"

"Because I wanted the ritual to take place," the Lady said quietly.

"What—*why?*"

"Because I hoped it might work."

"What?"

"Bridget, are you at all familiar with something called Operation Cone of Power?" Bridget frowned and shook her head. It meant nothing to her. "I thought not. It occurred several weeks ago, in August, and was described in one of the dossiers we received, but we get so much information, and there was no sign that it was something we needed to be concerned about." She smiled a little. "It's astounding how skeptical the Checquy can be.

"On the first of August, seventeen people—men and women who would proudly describe themselves as witches and spiritualists—gathered in the woods near Highcliffe-on-Sea, about a hundred and seventy miles from here. It was Lammas Eve, which I gather is an important day in their, um, pagan calendar. They danced naked in the moonlight and performed a ritual intended to affect the mind of

Adolf Hitler and turn him away from the possibility of invading Britain."

"I'm sorry," said Bridget. "These people who were dancing naked in the forest—do they have powers?" The Lady shrugged. "All right, have they ever done anything that would cause the Checquy to take an interest in them? Has there been a demonstrable, tangible result to their rituals?"

"No, not that we can tell."

"Did this ceremony, this Funnel of Power *work?*"

"*Cone* of Power, dear," Lady Carmichael corrected her, "and we've no idea. Although Hitler hasn't tried to invade yet."

"*That's* your rationale for letting the circle undertake their ritual tonight? You think it might actually help the war effort?"

"We—you and I, like the rest of the Checquy—cannot interfere in the war, Bridget. The best we can do is take a few minutes to get out of the way of those who might just possibly make some sort of a difference."

Bridget was speechless. That the Lady was giving even the slightest credence to these people and their efforts was astounding. Their use of actual supernatural items in their ritual was interesting but pointless. Wasn't it? They might have used powerful relics as props, but it was like shaking a gun in the direction of Berlin and praying.

"In August, a German submarine landed on the south coast," said Lady Carmichael, almost conversationally, "at a place called Pepperinge Eye. Armed troops disembarked, enough to take the town. Instead, they were driven off."

"By whom?" asked Bridget warily. "The Home Guard?"

"We don't know. When the Home Guard arrived on the scene, the Germans were hurriedly rowing back to their submarine, and the fields at the site were littered with items from the local history museum."

"Items?"

"Armor. Weaponry. Bagpipes. Military equipment. No one has any idea how they got there or what happened."

"Why didn't I hear about this?" asked Bridget, utterly bewildered. "It would have made a huge splash in the offices!"

"We're not pursuing it," said the Lady. Bridget stared at her. "Bishop Alrich brought it to our attention, and the report was not shared beyond the Court."

"Not *shared?*"

"Lord Pease and I decided that, given the circumstances, it would not be the best use of the Order's resources."

"You're ignoring a manifestation?"

"There is a world of difference between taking action and judiciously not taking action. The latter is the most that we will allow ourselves to do."

"You are permitting supernatural events to take place because they might help the war effort?"

"Legend says that if Britain is ever in the ultimate danger, if someone beats Sir Francis Drake's drum, he will return to defend the country."

"What are you talking about?"

"We are told that King Arthur, his queen, and his knights lie sleeping under the hills of Avalon. They will return to save the kingdom and usher in a new golden age."

"Those are just fairy tales," objected Bridget.

"Perhaps."

"What do you mean, *perhaps*? *Every* country has a king-under-the-mountain legend."

"I always enjoy how adamant the children of the Checquy are about what is possible." Lady Carmichael smiled fondly. "All of us are impossible, but you insist you know what is real. You like to draw these lines. Fine. They are fairy stories. But if they *were* to happen, do you think we would stand in their way? Make no mistake, Bridget. This may not be our nation's darkest hour, but that hour is not far off."

"And so, let's say King Arthur, and Sir Francis, and Fionn mac Cumhaill, and Brân the Blessed, and that Welsh princess with the wyvern were to rise up out of the soil to fight off invaders—supernatural entities attacking normal people. Would I then have to order the Pawns and soldiers of the Checquy to stand forth and defend Nazis from the heroes of this land?"

"I—I don't..."

"This war has a way of blurring the lines of what we can take for granted. The Checquy cannot ignore the doings of normal people. We can't just make our own rules in our own little society, retreat into our private club and secret offices, and let them get on with their lives and the conflict, because, as the tragedy of the Caïssa showed us, what happens out there definitely affects us." She paused and gave a weary sigh. "What do you think will happen if we lose this war?"

"What?"

"We must face the facts. It is entirely possible, Bridget, that the Nazis will triumph. German forces could come across the Channel and conquer us. And if they do, what do you imagine will happen to the Checquy?"

"Well, I, um—" Bridget fumbled. Until now, she had not given the idea much thought. The war itself was so *immediate*—it was bombing raids and food shortages and children being evacuated and Gerald going off to fight. Day-to-day life was so frantic, and that combined with her responsibilities for the Checquy and then the hunt for the downed Nazi kept her from really thinking about the big picture. But of course she should have, and of course the Lady had.

"Our responsibilities are sacrosanct, Bridget. You and I both took oaths, among them a vow not to interfere in the conflicts of parties or nations."

"So the Checquy would... continue our mission in secret?" hazarded Bridget. *Like a secret resistance?*

"Indeed," the Lady said grimly. "Our people on the Channel Islands were ordered not to reveal themselves to the Germans. They continue to protect the residents and even the occupying forces in secret. So that is certainly one option." She was silent, looking to Bridget to follow on.

"And the other option?" said Bridget warily.

"We could, delicately, present ourselves to our conquerors and continue our work within their government."

"*What?*"

"There are precedents."

"You cannot be serious!" exclaimed Bridget. "You would make us servants of the *Nazis?*" She felt breathless, as if she had been punched in the stomach and the head.

"Oliver Cromwell was a dictator who fought in a civil war against the Crown and signed the warrant for the King of England to be executed," said the Lady flatly. "He was a religious fanatic who shut down the theaters, banned Christmas dinners, and had women put in the stocks for doing unnecessary work on Sundays. To say nothing of the untold atrocities he enacted in Ireland. And the Checquy worked with him."

"But—"

"When Ireland became an independent nation, the Order did not allow that development to hamper us in our mission," Lady Carmichael continued. "If the new Irish government had not made accommodations, the Court of the time had contingencies prepared to work around them.

"Our allegiances are not to any government, not truly. We will work within the authority of the land if we can, but our oaths are to a higher cause. We dedicate ourselves to the task of protecting normal people from supernatural malevolence. We do not protect them from themselves or each other." She took a breath.

"That being said, the Order of the Checquy is now too large, and society too complex, for us to operate at the level we do without the support and the authority of a ruling government."

"But these people, the Nazis, they…" Bridget was nauseated. It was incomprehensible, and yet, as the Lady spoke, it all seemed more and more obvious.

"It's much worse than you know, Bridget." The Lady's face was somber, as if she were staring at something unutterably horrible. "There are things occurring on the Continent that are as evil as anything the Checquy has ever encountered in all its centuries, things that make me question if humanity *deserves* to be protected. And yet we must face the possibility that one day a triumphant Adolf Hitler will be driven in a motorcade down the Mall to take up residence in Buckingham Palace, and we must be ready."

"Oh God," breathed Bridget. "You've been preparing for this, haven't you? This is what the Court has been working on during your meetings at Bufo Hall?"

"Yes. And from even before the meetings commenced. We have been planning for quite a while."

"Pamela knew about this," she said, and it wasn't a question.

"Yes."

This is why she did it, thought Bridget. Her face was buried in her hands. *This is why Pamela brought that damn plane down. Because she knew what might happen. She was forced to help plan how to put ourselves in service to the enemy.*

Every day, she and the Lady were laying out strategies to fit the Checquy into the Third Reich.

Oh, Pamela. My poor friend. Bridget wanted to weep. *She must have been despising the work, despising herself. And she went up into the sky and watched the bombers coming to rain fire down on her country, and . . . And then, that night, it was too much, and she cracked.*

A lifetime of discipline, a lifetime of proud service. She fought monsters and traveled the world, saw atrocities and wrangled bureaucrats, and this secret is what broke her.

30

The first thing Lyn saw of the Checquy soldiers was the green lights glowing on their masks where their eyes should be. Initially, they were just shapes approaching her warily through the rain. She could see the vague outlines of weapons pointed at her, and she sighed heavily.

Lyn sat slumped, bone-weary, utterly unconcerned by their professional menace. She found that there was no fear inside her. Instead, despite her exhaustion and her wounds, she felt a deep satisfaction. There was horror as well, of course, and sadness—the woman she'd killed lay a few meters away from her—but she didn't feel any shame. It had been something she needed to do. Now there would be all sorts of new problems and tribulations, but she had finished the task she'd set herself.

Shouted orders came to her as if from a great distance, and she looked up. They were all around her now, dressed in tactical armor. Some pointed guns at her, one had silver flames crackling along his shoulders, and one woman held a coiled whip in each hand. A panther, also dressed in armor, prowled around the ring that closed in on her. There was something, though, that cut through her weariness... "What the hell are you wearing?" she asked.

Over their menacing black armor, each of the soldiers wore a knit sweater. They varied in color and design — there were Scandinavian ones, plain ones, ones with garish Christmas motifs. One soldier wore a sober burgundy cardigan; another had on a sweater-vest with a pattern of different parrots. Even the panther was wearing a sweater — in fact, it was wearing two. Its tail snaked out from the neckhole of a blue sweater that had been hastily repurposed as a pair of panther pants.

I was really enjoying knowing I wasn't insane, she thought wistfully. *So much for that.*

"Never mind the sweaters!" yelled one of the soldiers.

Oh, good. They are *wearing sweaters.*

"Get on the ground, facedown!"

Lyn stared at the yeller, whose blue sweater featured white snowflakes, then shrugged. Clearly he felt that authority could be conveyed through volume. So she did everything they yelled at her to do. She lay facedown on the grass, linked her fingers at the back of her head, and crossed her ankles. They gingerly slid thick plastic gloves onto her hands, then handcuffed and shackled her with strange rubber chains. She lay still and unconcerned as they ran a metal detector over her.

All the while, another team had been screaming similar instructions at the corpse of the blonde cooling a few feet away.

"She's dead, lads," said Lyn. She'd warned them over the phone, but evidently they didn't trust her, for which she supposed she didn't blame them. "You want to be very careful, though. I don't know if any metal on her is still charged."

"Yeah, ta, Lyn," said one of the soldiers absently.

"Don't talk to her!" snapped the yeller.

"Please. What's she going to do, lull us into complacency by warning us of possible dangers?" retorted the soldier.

They lifted Lyn up bodily and carried her across the squelching grass to some waiting vans. She was placed, gently, into the back of one of them and laid down on a mattress. She acknowledged the warnings they gave her, then felt the prick of a needle at her neck. As she drifted off, she was aware that her wet clothes were being cut off her, and then she was rubbed gently with warm towels while her wounds were tended to. Before the doors of the van were closed, she caught a glimpse of soldiers awkwardly carrying a long black rubber bag that, her increasingly foggy mind decided, probably contained the blonde.

When she awoke, she was in a hospital bed. A large window looked out over London, and it was day.

I'm not shackled.

The railings that kept her in bed were plastic, though. There was no metal visible anywhere in the room. There *was*, however, a Georgina visible. She lounged in that boneless teenage way, one leg slung over the arm of her chair. She was reading one of her Japanese comics, the ones that are read backward.

"Hi," Lyn said sleepily. Her voice was scratchy, weaker than she'd expected, but her erstwhile roommate looked up from her book.

"Lynnie!" She stood up and hurried over. "Here, have some water." She offered Lyn a plastic cup. "No, let me hold it." Lyn was fairly certain she could hold her own cup of water, but she submitted to the ministrations.

"What time is it?" she asked finally.

"Early afternoon," said Georgina. "They brought you in yesterday. Sewed up your cuts, scanned you, got everyone with any sort of sensory power to check you over."

"Did you taste me?" asked Lyn suspiciously.

"Yep. You tasted normal."

"Imagine my relief." Lyn sat up with difficulty. She ached horribly, but there were none of the sharp pains she remembered from the sword fight. She looked under the covers and lifted her gown to examine the cuts the blonde had inflicted on her legs, but the wounds had vanished completely.

Thank you, Grafters, she thought. Then she looked sharply at her arm, which was heavily bandaged where the blonde had sliced it open with that terrible blow. She looked questioningly at Georgina.

"They fixed you up there, and you won't have any loss of function, but somebody thought you might want that scar," said Georgina. "Like a battle trophy or something." She shrugged. "It's very macho, but you did get it in a sword fight with a serial killer, so I can see where they were coming from."

"So you heard what happened?"

"*Everyone* heard what happened."

I wonder what they think *happened,* thought Lyn wearily. She wasn't shackled to the bed, which was promising, and she saw no guards, but the fact that everything around was made of plastic indicated a certain lack of trust. *What are they going to do with me?*

Georgina was chattering on. "*I* asked what they thought you would tell your husband about the scar," said the girl, "and they said they wanted to make it your choice."

"Does this mean I am going to see my husband, then?" Lyn asked.

"You'll still have a trial before the Court, but I think that's mainly for appearances, to show that procedure's been followed. Everyone I've talked to is on your side. *I'm* on your side."

"Thanks, G." They smiled at each other. "So when is this trial?"

"At night, obviously, to allow Bishop Alrich to attend," said Georgina. "Tonight, if you're recovered. Otherwise, tomorrow night."

"I'm recovered," said Lyn. She wanted this over and done with, whatever the outcome.

The trial would take place at Apex House, naturally. At dusk, a large man and a large woman came to collect her. They did not give their names. They put her in the back seat of the car that was waiting and crammed themselves in on either side of her. They were driven through the streets of London, and no one spoke. As they drew up to the Apex, she felt a little nauseated. The last time she'd been there, she'd departed out the back, a fugitive. Now she was being deposited at the front as a...what? Prodigal Pawn? Repentant deserter? She didn't dare speculate how the Court would judge her, despite Georgina's optimistic but, let's face it, uninformed reassurances.

For all I know, they'll have me walk myself into my own execution, she brooded. *So why did they stitch up my wounds?*

Maybe I was just a good opportunity for baby Grafters to get some practice.

An older man in purple was waiting for her as the car came to a stop. He opened her door, and once the large woman had levered herself out, he offered his hand to help Lyn out. She was weaker than she had thought and was grateful for the strength of his arm.

"Good evening. I'm Patrick Atchabahian," he said. "I am the principal private secretary to Sir Henry Wattleman, and I will be escorting you to your meeting with the Court."

"Thank you," said Lyn warily.

My meeting, *he says. Not my* trial. *Is he being polite?* She looked around. The large woman had gotten back in the car, which was moving away. "I'm surprised there are no guards."

"To make certain you don't run off?" he said lightly. She smiled weakly, but her unease only increased as he led her through the corridors. It was after regular business hours, but the place seemed more deserted than it should be. Checquy-ing was a twenty-four-hour business, but the halls were empty. They took a lift down to an underground room that appeared to have been designed solely for people to wait in. There were some chairs against the plain white walls, a carpet of dull purple, and that was it. At the other end of the room was a pair of heavy-looking wooden doors.

A number of people, all in different shades of purple, were standing about. Some held briefcases—one man was carrying three briefcases and a handbag—and they all spoke to each other in hushed tones. *The personal staff of the Court,* Lyn thought. The purple livery was the giveaway.

Atchabahian led her past them, and the doors opened at his approach. The Retainers fell silent as they passed, and the doors shut behind them.

The waiting room had been plain, but this room was stark. The heavy concrete walls gave the impression of being very old and very well constructed—able to withstand significant impacts. If you wanted to be paranoid, you could focus on the fact that every surface would be very easy to clean blood off and that there was a drain in the center of the floor.

There were no decorations on the walls, and the only noticeable feature of the room was an oddly semicircular conference table. The flat end was facing her, with a single chair in the center. Seated along the curved side were all the members of the Court of the Checquy.

They did not rise when she entered the room but regarded her silently as she approached. Despite herself, she regarded them back. She noted with faint amusement that they were seated in the positions of their chess titles, the Lord and Lady in the center and the others arrayed accordingly. Of them, she had met only the Lord and Lady previously, and that had been when she took the oath to become a Pawn. Then they had been important busy executives, distracted. Now, the full force of their focus was frightening; they were grim personifications of supernatural authority.

She snuck a glance at each of the Bishops. On one side was a man of Indian descent with an immaculately trimmed beard and a black turban. *Bishop Attariwala,* she thought, which meant that the tall, slender man next to the Lord had to be Alrich, the vampire Bishop. She'd never seen him before but had heard many stories—people in the Checquy were rather proud to have a vampire on their team, but it was pride mixed with fascination, mixed with lust, mixed with fear. Her curiosity piqued by all the anecdotes, she'd looked up his photo on the staff directory to find that there was no photo of him, only a thumbnail reproduction of an oil painting.

"He doesn't register on film or digital photography," one of the girls in the Notifications section had advised her when she'd caught Lyn looking him up. "That was painted in the 1920s." Chillingly, she now saw that the painting continued to be a good likeness. It had captured his flawless white skin and his air of preternatural grace. His features had not changed at all. The only difference was his hair, which was not the rich red of the portrait but a light auburn. Artistic license, she supposed.

Her gaze skittered over the Chevaliers and the Rooks, but Atchabahian was ushering her forward.

For a moment, Lyn was surprised that there were no guards in the room, but then realized why. Not one of the people in the room with her feared anything.

"Good evening, Lynette," said Sir Henry Wattleman. "Please, be seated." He gestured to the empty seat at the flat side of the table. The attendant in purple escorted her to it. "Thank you, Patrick."

"My Lord," said the attendant. "My Lady." He bowed his head to Lady Farrier, and she nodded in acknowledgment. He left the room, closing the doors behind him.

She sat uncomfortably, aware that she was the focus of all their gazes. The Rooks were on either side of her, just visible in her peripheral vision.

"Now, Lynette," said Lady Farrier. "Please, tell us everything."

"I..." she began, but broke off to cough. There was a plastic cup and a jug of water in front of her, and she hastily drank some to clear her throat. "Sorry. Yes, okay." She took a deep breath, wiped her sweaty hands on her skirt, and began. She started with how she had read the police reports and come to the horrified realization of their implications.

Of course, there were some significant omissions in her story—no mention of her newfound German relations, naturally—but no one interrupted her to ask questions. Although she refilled her cup several times, her throat was again dry when she ended with being rendered unconscious in the back of a Checquy van.

"And that's all," she said.

The Court regarded her silently.

"Well," said Bishop Attariwala finally. "That appears to mesh with everything we know and the footage we reviewed." He looked around. "Questions, anyone?"

"Yes," said a petite woman in an exquisitely cut suit. Her face was unremarkable, but her eyes bespoke a keen intelligence.

Rook Myfanwy Thomas, thought Lyn nervously as she turned to look at her. *The biomancer.* The Rook was subject to even more speculative gossip around the organization than the vampire. Her powers were terrifying, and her bureaucratic abilities perhaps even more so. Over the past few months she'd pulled off a series of coups, including the successful incorporation of the Grafters into an organization that had loathed the very memory of them for centuries.

Plus, she'd sparked a brawl at a diplomatic reception, been stabbed at Royal Ascot, and was widely reported to have thrown one of her counterparts out of a window to her death. Under the Rook's gaze, Lyn felt her sudden confidence draining away, and a shiver went up and then down her spine.

Are those her powers? thought Lyn nervously. *Is she using them on me?* The Rook could control other people's bodies, and while officially she could do it only while touching someone, rumor around the cubicles suggested that wasn't necessarily the case.

"Lynette," said the Rook, "you say the first lightning manifestation—the one in the East End—was the result of you and the other woman, your powers interacting?"

"Yes."

"And what about the others? The ones around the city over the following nights?"

"I—they weren't me." As she spoke, Lyn felt a pressure at her wrists and a light touch in her body, as if a finger were being laid gently on her heart. The Rook's eyes were thoughtful, but she said nothing.

"They must have been caused by the other woman, then," said Bishop Alrich. "What was her name again, Rook Thomas?"

"You've identified her?" said Lyn faintly.

"She was Alicia Davies," said Rook Thomas. "Thirty-seven years old. Originally of Birmingham. One of four children." The Rook paused. "Genetic testing confirmed that the two of you shared a grandmother."

"She said I must be Jenny's little girl," said Lyn faintly. The Rook frowned and looked through some papers before nodding.

"She may have been referring to her maternal aunt, Jennifer Perks. No record of a child but..." She shrugged and made a small grimace, acknowledging the circumstances. Then she looked at Lyn sympathetically. "I'm afraid that Jennifer Perks died seventeen years ago. Domestic violence."

"Oh," said Lyn. "I see, I...oh." The Court was respectfully silent for a moment as Lyn took in this revelation.

"We don't know who your father might have been," said Rook Thomas delicately. "We'll be investigating, of course, but since you and Alicia Davies were related through your mothers, that's the lineage we'll be tracing most thoroughly. It's very uncommon for supernatural abilities to be passed down in bloodlines. I expect the Broederschap will be wanting to scrutinize your genetics a bit more closely. And for matters of security, we've already identified seven living people whom we need to keep under observation. If we go back further than your maternal grandparents, then it may be even more." Lyn nodded soberly. Arndt and the family in Germany would have had quite a reaction to this news, but the Rook was already pressing on.

"Alicia Davies's father was gone by the time she was seven." The Rook was reading through a dossier. "We've found that he died shortly after leaving the family. Drove drunk into a wall. Mother never remarried and had no more children. Davies's teachers remember her as clever but undisciplined. She left high school as early as she could, worked as a barmaid, chambermaid, waitress, cleaner. Dabbled in petty crime, which I'm afraid was in keeping with the rest of the family. She served time for theft and for assault. Two husbands, several boyfriends, no children.

"Three years ago, she abruptly moved to London. I expect we can guess why."

I wonder how her powers manifested? Lyn thought. *How did she cope without the Checquy?* She had to respect the blonde—Alicia—for surviving, coming through the experience with her reason intact, and figuring out how she could use that new power to take what she wanted. *I wish the Checquy had found you before you began killing. Maybe you could have been put on a different path. It would have been good to have a cousin, to have someone else with this power.*

"In London, she worked in a variety of pubs around the city, including, as it happens, the one where you clashed with Pawns Seager, Kosloski, and Hatt. We suppose she must have been checking out the criminal community. Meanwhile, she was a regular at various gyms, took classes in kendo, fencing, and unarmed combat."

It was a simple little biography, but it didn't encompass everything.

How could it? In the blonde's face, Lyn had seen a lifetime of resentment, envy, frustration, and rage. A thousand moments, a thousand little stories that had added up to a woman who, when presented with power, hadn't been broken by it. Instead, she had decided that she would kill to take what she wanted. Whatever hungers she'd had curdling away in her, they'd been denied all her life, and Lyn had been the final obstacle. Lyn could still see the hate that had boiled in the other woman's eyes, and she shuddered. With an effort, she dragged herself back to the discussion.

"We have no record of employment for her for the past few months," the Rook was saying. "Presumably she was living on savings."

"Or what she took from the people she killed," Lyn suggested. "These gangsters all seem to carry around large amounts of cash."

"Quite possibly," agreed the Rook.

"She was very resourceful," said one of the men. Lyn thought he must be one of the Chevaliers, the members of the Court responsible for foreign operations. He was a strong-looking man with closely cropped hair and a jaw you could cut yourself on. He held a cigarette, and it appeared to be killing him not to light it. "She mounted quite an effective destabilization program."

"Would she have been successful, Joshua?" asked the Lady.

"I expect so, yes," said the man. "She was capable of violence and strategy, and she had power that could trump many of her opponents' weapons. Once she'd gained control of those gangs and put the thorough fear of her powers into them, I doubt she'd have needed to exercise them very much. In a world without the Checquy, I believe she'd have done very well. And even with the Checquy, there's no guarantee that people would have been too afraid to speak. I suppose word might have gotten to us eventually. Maybe."

"Though not before we'd already have found, tried, and executed the wrong culprit," said the Lady. "The evidence would have been damning. It *was* damning. One of our own, turned rogue. It is among our worst nightmares. In such circumstances, we would have been extremely unlikely to listen to any attempt at an explanation and even less likely to believe it. The potential for harm to the Checquy would have been too great." She pursed her lips and regarded Lyn grimly. "I'm afraid that, for all your actual innocence, you would have been dead and cremated within two hours of being taken into custody. If you hadn't been killed while being apprehended."

The Lady was so matter-of-fact in her pronouncement, so utterly calm, that Lyn felt as if she had been punched in the stomach. She took a few deep breaths and wondered if she was actually going to be sick on the table.

"So…" she said finally.

"So you were quite justified in fleeing," said Sir Henry. "Really, it would have been bloody stupid not to."

"I'm sorry?" said Lyn.

"We are proud of you, Pawn Binns."

Pawn Binns! she thought and felt weak at the knees even though she was sitting. Then she realized what else he had said. *They are proud of me!* She was aware that the Lord was still talking, saying something about courage, promising tenacity, and putting duty above the rules. His speech culminated in that most deadly of phrases: "the finest traditions of the service." But the blood was still roaring in her ears, and her heart was so thunderous inside her chest that she expected lightning to course out of her body.

She was free. She was being welcomed back into an organization that made the world ten thousand more times exciting and rewarding. The Lord was saying that she could go home for some much-deserved leave with her family. It was all too much. The Lord had finished speaking. She looked up foggily at the Court members, all of whom were smiling at her. And yet her gaze was drawn back to the Lady, whose mouth quirked in a little smile.

"Please don't do it again, though," said Lady Farrier.

A nd now, a few days later, Lyn lay with her husband and daughter under a soft, thick white duvet. Warm sunshine flooded in through the window, making her feel like she was floating in light.

The smell of Emma's hair was in her nose, the solid strength of Richard's arms encircled her, and the presence of Skeksis was a warm velvetiness against the soles of her feet. At some early hour, when Emma had snuggled in with them, the dog had grudgingly made his way down to the end of the bed.

Lyn closed her arms around the soft sleepiness of the little girl and shut her eyes. The present was good. She was in her own bed with those she loved best. The Checquy had welcomed her back into its ranks, although she had been aware of a few nervous and awed glances cast her way in the corridors as she'd left her meeting with the Court. She wondered vaguely what nickname this whole thing would earn her. Surely "the Delouser" had been superseded? Regardless, come Monday, she would be happy going to work. She had won.

And tucked away safely in her heart was the knowledge that, out there somewhere in Germany, was the university town Arndt had described, a place of hills and rivers and red roofs, a comfortable home with a family that would always be there for her should she ever want to reach out.

Just the knowledge of that was enough, for now.

Bridget was not pregnant.

Her body had just presented her with undeniable evidence of that fact. Her period had never been particularly predictable, but it had most definitely arrived this morning and brought with it absolute confirmation that the broken condom had not resulted in her and Gerald inadvertently making a baby. She stood in the weak light and considered the situation, still not entirely certain how she felt about it. She realized that she was a little wet around the eyes and rubbed her face against the sleeve of her nightie.

Maybe I'm relieved and *disappointed.*

She had received three letters from Gerald since he left. All of them had been heavily redacted by military censors, even though he hadn't even completed training yet. He was well, the other trainees were good lads, the food was mediocre at best. She had written back to him, all the while agonizing over how she would proceed, what letter she would need to write if she turned out to be carrying his child. Would she tell him? How would he react? Would it change how he felt about her?

All that stress and worry. In the end, it was for nothing, she thought ruefully. *I hope it turns out that way for my other major concern.*

Since the night in Kent when the Quiet Circle had conducted their ritual and Lady Carmichael had revealed the Court's plans in the event of a successful Nazi invasion, Bridget had been attached to the project. She was still an apprentice, but she had taken Pamela's place at the planning meetings at Bufo Hall.

At least until they find a new aide-de-camp for the Lady, she reminded herself as she washed and dressed.

As she went down the stairs of the Moat House, the Carmichaels' country home, Bridget pulled on her white leather gloves and listened to the sound of happy domestic chaos rising up from the hall. Dogs were barking, children were chattering, and crockery appeared to be in a fair amount of danger.

"Bridget!"

"Good morning, Rosalind," said Bridget. She smiled down at the seven-year-old girl, whose pinafore was already stained with jam, milk, dirt, and what appeared, bewilderingly, to be tar.

"Bridget, a courier's already come from Mummy's office," said the girl importantly. "He had packages for you. Tommy and Lil put them in the study."

"Grand," said Bridget. She knew she didn't need to check that the curious children hadn't broached the packages. The one lesson that had been successfully drilled into the small Carmichaels was that anything coming from their mother's office was absolutely sacrosanct. Their adoring mother would not countenance actual corporal punishment, but she would not hesitate to make them regret breaking that rule. "I expect it's more papers for me to read," Bridget said. Every day brought more briefing documents for her to plow through.

"But Mummy is coming down here today," said Rosalind, frowning. "Why didn't she just bring the papers with her?"

"I expect she wants me to read everything before she arrives so that we can talk about it."

Since Bridget had stepped into Pamela's shoes, her daily reading had increased in scale and breadth. She was now expected to be acquainted with the situation of every Checquy outpost across the empire, as she would have to help design contingency plans for them in the event of invasion and occupation. The new axis of power continued to grow.

The Third Reich had already defeated and occupied Poland, Denmark, Norway, Belgium, the Netherlands, Luxembourg, and France. Fascist Italian forces had entered Egypt and established forward camps. The empire of Japan had invaded and occupied French Indochina, and no one expected that Tokyo's ambitions would be so easily satisfied. Not when Southeast Asia and the Pacific lay there to be taken.

In fact, none of the Axis powers gave any sign that they would ever be satiated. And all around the world were the dominions, protectorates, colonies, mandates, and territories of the British Empire, an irresistible temptation to a voracious enemy. Most of them held a Checquy presence. Some of them held a *substantial* Checquy presence. Bridget was painfully aware that scores of Pawns, Retainers, and apprentices around the world—to say nothing of their families— might have their safety, their very destinies determined by how well she did her job. Her dreams were now filled with images of Checquy operatives forced into camps, forbidden to use their powers to rescue themselves or their loved ones.

And the most we can do is hold ourselves back or get out of the way, she thought grimly. Lady Carmichael's policy of periodic benign inaction grated against Bridget's instincts, but it was all she could see to do. Pamela's attack on that bomber had shown Bridget the dangers of the Checquy interfering in the war.

It's so little, she thought. *We're doing so little when we could make all the difference in the world.*

As Bridget entered the breakfast room, she looked enviously at Usha. Her friend was reading the newspaper, blissfully unaware of the secrets that had broken Pamela. Bridget had wanted to bring the other apprentice in on her work. Surely, she had argued to Lady

Carmichael, two apprentices might fill the gap of a Pawn, especially when one of the apprentices had such experience of the world and large-scale organization.

But the Lady had firmly said no, that Usha needed time to rest and recover from her injuries. Her maids, Shirina and Amita, had been fussing over her ever since she arrived. They had clucked over her wounds and set about preparing foods that scorched the mouths of all the British residents of the house. Presumably those dishes also burned out bacteria, germs, ill humors, and negative thoughts, because Usha was recovering swiftly.

"Tea, Miss Bridget?" asked Shirina as Bridget sat down.

"Please," said Bridget. Without a word, Usha passed her the first section of the newspaper. She turned past the front page, which was all personal ads, births, deaths, and marriages, and began scanning the news. The bombing of London continued.

It was all horrible, but she knew there was so much more happening. Her clearance had been changed. She was now privy to new levels of secrets from the government beyond the Checquy. Reports came in from troops around the world and spies in Axis territories; she read messages that had been intercepted from the radio waves and cunningly decoded. She and a few key aides to the Court received that information and applied it to their ongoing work at Bufo Hall. She knew more of the war and the world than some of the highest-ranking people in the government, and it filled her with fear.

There is no guarantee that we will win. We are planning for what happens if evil triumphs.

"Bridget?" said Usha.

"Hmm?"

"Are you all right?"

"Oh, yes," she said and smiled weakly at her friend. "Fine."

"Only you've been staring blankly at the same page of the newspaper for about ten minutes now." Usha put her hand out and held Bridget's wrist. "Were you thinking about Gerald?" she asked gently.

"Oh, a little." *Him and the thousands with him.*

It's his actions and those of all the people like him that will mean the difference. All the people fighting to stop the Nazis. People who have a choice and make it. They decide that there are some things that simply cannot be permitted, so they go out and risk their lives to stop them. She shook her head. *If they lose, then the Nazis will cross the water and conquer this land, and we will have to allow it. We'll have to work for them.*

We save the normal people every day.

I have to trust that they can save us.

ACKNOWLEDGMENTS

My first thanks must go to two magnificent ladies: my agent Mollie Glick and my editor Asya Muchnick. Their work, their support, their patience, and their friendship make this job a lot easier and made this book a lot better.

My editor at HarperCollins Australia, Anna Valdinger, for her knowledge, insight, and humor.

Tracy Roe, queen of copyeditors, who can spot missing text in a quote from a 1940 government pamphlet, can catch the misspelled name of a Germanic tribe, and who tactfully pointed out that the term *pheromone* wasn't coined until 1959.

The staff at Little, Brown, HarperCollins Australia, Head of Zeus, and all my other publishers. Their work makes all the difference.

John Gransbury drew on his experience in the hospitality industry to answer my questions on hotel sheet policy.

Sarah Van Der Wal, a friend I haven't seen since primary school, responded promptly to messaged questions about how to treat gunshot wounds while on the ceiling.

Sandra Hassett told me which parts of the human body would be best for plants to consume.

Ingrid Southworth talked to me about organized crime and helped me realize where my killer would fit in the ecosystem of the underworld. She also confirmed that in the UK, it's a *school disco,* not a *dance.*

David Wilson sat down with me and answered all sorts of questions about flying. Among the invaluable information he shared was a patient explanation of the heights at which various things (people, aircraft) can operate and those at which they can't.

Charles Carey received an infinite number of phone calls and answered an infinite number of questions on an infinite number of topics.

Once again, Erik Davis lent his expertise on weaponry and tactics.

Ross McAlpine became accustomed to receiving texts with various medical questions, ranging from how thick human skin is to what's a good part of one's body in which to get shot.

Charles Reeves for the support and encouragement, and for enduring various fiction-related tirades over the course of many delicious dinners.

Sulari Gentill and I discussed the perspectives and experiences of people in the 1940s. Once we'd finished laughing, I realized I'd gotten some invaluable insights.

Sarah Mangan answered my questions on the history of Ireland.

Rolf Bachmann, Anthony Cutting, and Ransome Mclean listened to my rants when we were supposed to be playing board games.

While Martin Dolan and I were having lunch, he mentioned Operation Cone of Power and opened up a whole new concept for my story.

Kerry Greenwood's *Murder on the Ballarat Train* introduced me to the mechanics of cat-washing.

Hermi Astrolabe Human helped me get an out-of-print history book that was available only in the UK and that proved invaluable for my research. You know someone's a good friend when she'll haul an enormous hardcover in her carry-on from the UK to Australia.

Ali Green cooked the best scrambled eggs I've ever met in my life and then told me how she did it.

While I was writing this book, *The Rook* became a television show, and I had the pleasure of traveling to London to visit the set. The kindness and hospitality of everyone involved in the project made it one of my best experiences ever. I'm especially grateful to writers Sam Holcroft and Al Blyth. Little did they know that I would be bothering them for the rest of their natural lives with questions concerning the minutiae of living in the UK. So far, they've responded to queries on topics as varied as crosswords in the *Times,* playing fields, and the intricacies of parking in London.

Back in 2017, Geoff Binns made a generous winning bid at a charity auction hosted by the Canadian High Commission in Canberra. In doing so, he helped raise funds for OzHarvest and the Tara Costigan Foundation and also won the naming rights for a character in my next book. He decided to name the character after his mother, Lynette "Lyn" Binns, and advised me that she would like to be a hero.

Usha Helweg was a dear friend of my family and was there for us during some difficult times. My memories of her style, her humor, and her kindness played a large part in the creation of Usha Khorana.

As always, there are too many people to thank individually. People I know and people I don't (the internet is so helpful) were generous in their advice and their encouragement, and I'm tremendously grateful.

Finally, and most important, I must thank my parents, Bill and Jeanne O'Malley, for everything.

ABOUT THE AUTHOR

Daniel O'Malley was born and raised in Canberra, Australia. He graduated from Michigan State University and earned a master's degree in medieval history from Ohio State University. He then returned to his childhood home, where he now works full-time as a writer. He is the author of the Checquy novels *The Rook* and *Stiletto,* the first of which won an Aurealis Award.